PRISONERS OF THE STARS

SCIENCE FICTION BY ISAAC ASIMOV

Novels

Pebble in the Sky
The Stars, Like Dust
Foundation
Foundation and Empire
Second Foundation
The Currents of Space
The Caves of Steel
The End of Eternity
The Naked Sun
Fantastic Voyage
The Gods Themselves

Novels originally under the pseudonym "Paul French"

David Starr: Space Ranger
Lucky Starr and the Pirates of the Asteroids
Lucky Starr and the Oceans of Venus
Lucky Starr and the Big Sun of Mercury
Lucky Starr and the Moons of Jupiter
Lucky Starr and the Rings of Saturn

Short Story Collections

I, Robot
The Martian Way and Other Stories
Earth Is Room Enough
Nine Tomorrows
The Rest of the Robots
Asimov's Mysteries
Nightfall and Other Stories
The Early Asimov
Buy Jupiter and Other Stories
The Bicentennial Man and Other Stories

Anthologies

The Hugo Winners
Fifty Short Science Fiction Tales (with Groff Conklin)
Tomorrow's Children
Where Do We Go From Here?
The Hugo Winners, Volume Two
Before the Golden Age
The Hugo Winners, Volume Three
100 Great Science Fiction Short Short Stories (with Martin Harry Greenberg and Joseph D. Olander)

PRISONERS OF THE STARS

THE COLLECTED FICTION OF ISAAC ASIMOV

VOLUME TWO

ISAAC ASIMOV

DOUBLEDAY & COMPANY, INC., GARDEN CITY, NEW YORK
1979

All of the characters in these books are fictitious, and any resemblance to actual persons, living or dead, is purely coincidental.

The Stars, Like Dust

The Martian Way and Other Stories

The Currents of Space

ISBN: 0-385-13270-0
Library of Congress Catalog Card Number 77-25576

Printed in the United States of America

CONTENTS

Introduction

by Isaac Asimov

"The Supreme Court follows the election returns," said Finley Peter Dunne's "Mr. Dooley."

I take that to mean that the Justices in their pursuit of abstract constitutionalism and legal principle cannot help but take note of, and be influenced by, the prevailing changes of mood in the American public.

In the same way, the high and footless imagination of the science fiction writer is inevitably held prisoner by the times and social milieu in which he finds himself. The current assumptions and acceptances are so ingrained that, like the air, one scarcely knows of their presence, yet cannot do without.

In the early decades of the twentieth century, then, how did things seem? What had become so obvious as not to be worth questioning?

1) It was obvious that the Earth had grown small. The source of the Nile had been found and the interiors of the tropical continents posed no particular mysteries. The North Pole and the South Pole had been reached; Antarctica had been outlined. With land and sea at man's mercy, the air was conquered, too, and Lindbergh's solo flight across the Atlantic in 1927 made that finally plain.

And how did this obvious, taken-for-granted fact affect science fiction?

Till the 1920s, science fiction had concerned itself with Earth, which had plenty of room and scope. There were trips in polar regions, adventures with lost tribes in Amazonia, penetrations to Atlantis beneath the sea—and, in the extreme, trips to the Moon.

But Earth had grown small in the 1920s, and so did the old science fiction, therefore. It was necessary to break out of the limited mold, and that came about through the work of Edward Elmer ("Doc") Smith, Ph.D.

He visualized not interplanetary travel, not piddling little jaunts to the Moon and Mars—for the whole Solar system had shrunk along with the Earth. Doc Smith was interested in *interstellar* travel. The

Solar system, one star and its family, was not enough; there were instead the countless billions of stars in the Galaxy and in all the other galaxies.

Smith's first story in this vein was *The Skylark of Space* which appeared as a three-part serial in *Amazing Stories* in 1928. It took science fiction fandom by storm and, overnight, Doc Smith became its idol. For twenty years, Smith wrote his interstellar romances against an ever-expanding background which reached its climax with the publication of *Children of the Lens* as a four-part serial in *Astounding Science Fiction* in 1947.

Naturally, Doc Smith's popularity bred imitators, but the only writer who was in any way comparable was John Wood Campbell, Jr., who, between 1930 and 1932, published a series of galaxy-busting melodramas featuring the team of Wade, Arcot, and Morey.

Placing the Universe in the background, instead of Earth alone, creates problems, of course.

As long as Earth is the scene of adventure, long journeys can be made in a reasonable fraction of a lifetime. One can go by oxcart from village to village and on horseback from province to province, and by ship from continent to continent. The steamship, the locomotive, the automobile, the airplane cut down the time of travel still further until, as the twentieth century wore on, the whole planet was no more than a European province would have been two hundred years ago, as far as reachability was concerned.

But where thousands of miles are involved in intercontinental travel, millions of miles are involved in interplanetary travel and trillions of miles in interstellar travel.

It might seem, of course, that no matter how great the distance, travel time could be cut indefinitely if speed were only increased indefinitely. Suppose someone could travel a trillion miles an hour. Starting from Earth at that speed, Alpha Centauri would be passed in a day, the other end of the Galaxy would be reached in fifty-five years, the Andromeda Galaxy could be reached in a little over fifteen hundred years.

Raise the speed to a quadrillion miles an hour and you could get to the Andromeda Galaxy in a year and a half.

But you can't just *go* at such speeds. You have to *get* to such speeds from a standing start, and to do it you have to undergo acceleration. The problem here is that the human body can only stand so much acceleration and it isn't much. In general, it would take a billion times as long to accelerate to a trillion miles an hour as it would to a thousand miles an hour—and then a billion times as long to decelerate from a trillion miles an hour as from a thousand miles an hour.

In short, for all but the longest journeys, you'll spend most of your time accelerating and decelerating so that it would take much longer to span the Galaxy, *much* longer, than if you could somehow just jump to top speed and back instantly.

Furthermore, acceleration and deceleration can take place only at the expense of energy—huge quantities of it. If you don't have whole suns of energy at your disposal, you have to limit your acceleration and deceleration, attain a lower final velocity, and take longer to get somewhere. You save energy at the expense of time.

Then, too, the faster you go, the greater the resistance of the interstellar medium, the density of which is not *completely* zero. In the end, even if you have the time and the energy, it may prove impossible to gain enough speed to make journeys short enough. You would burn up through friction with the thin wisps of interstellar gas.

Finally, in 1905, the greatest of all possible monkey wrenches was thrown into the works when Albert Einstein showed that it was utterly impossible, under any circumstances, for objects with mass to travel faster than the speed of light. And the speed of light is only about 670 million miles an hour, less than a thousandth of the trillion miles an hour we've been talking about.

Once we take into account the Einstein barrier, it would appear that it would take years of Earth time to reach the very nearest stars, centuries to reach moderately distant ones, millennia to cross the Galaxy, and millions to billions of years to reach other galaxies.

In a way, this quashes interstellar travel except that science fiction writers are unwilling to give in. They bend their ingenuity to circumventing the Einstein barrier. Doc Smith, for instance, spoke of the inertialess drive. He argued that once the property of inertia was removed, it would take no energy to accelerate and then any speed could be attained.

Unfortunately, there are theoretical reasons for supposing that inertia cannot be removed unless mass is removed as well, and that even zero-mass objects, which can accelerate without any energy input, can travel only at the speed of light. They can't go slower, so that no time is wasted on acceleration or deceleration, but they can't go faster, either.

Suppose, though, that we assume the Einstein barrier is only a local phenomenon, a property only of our Universe, and suppose that the Universe is embedded in a far larger matrix that we can call "hyperspace" (which simply means "beyond space"). In hyperspace there need not be any speed limit at all, or if there is, it would be one far higher than the Einstein barrier.

There is no evidence that such a hyperspace exists, but no evidence that it doesn't either. We can speculate, then, that a ship might enter hyperspace, cross any width of it virtually instantaneously, and thus "jump" from one region of ordinary space to a vastly distant other region.

In my books of interstellar travel (for I have followed in the footsteps of Smith and Campbell in setting many of my novels against the vast backdrop of the galaxies), I use the jump through hyperspace routinely, and you will find a description of it on pages 27 and 28 of *The Stars, Like Dust* for instance.

In recent years, oddly enough, some physicists have speculated on the possible existence of so-called "tachyons," particles of imaginary mass that can travel only at speeds greater than light. The thought arises that if a spaceship can be converted into tachyons and then back again into ordinary particles, precisely the same effect will have been achieved as in a jump through hyperspace.

Of course, no one has detected tachyons yet and there are physicists who argue that there are insuperable theoretical objections to their existence, but it is interesting to think that ways around the Einstein barrier might someday be found.

We have seen how far the first assumption of the 1920s has carried us. Is there another? Yes, consider this one—

2) The Earth (of the 1920s) was essentially European. It was the Europeans, and their descendants abroad, who explored, who found "natives," and who took over territory in sublime disregard of them. Almost every spot on Earth was European-inhabited, or European-owned, or European-influenced. And that was the way (it was commonly assumed) that it would have to be, since Europeans, and especially northwestern Europeans, were superior to other groups of

human beings. Certainly no European questioned this and if non-Europeans did, their voices went unheard in the citadels of European power.

And how did this calm assumption affect science fiction?

Smith and Campbell, along with many of those who imitated them, moved outward into the vast spaces beyond the Solar system, taking with them their notions of European supremacy.

Just as Europeans found intelligent life wherever they went on Earth, so did the Earthmen find it wherever they went in the Universe. Just as Europeans found no intelligent life capable of resisting their weapons of war (hence, by logical deduction, no intelligent life superior to themselves), so Earthmen found no form of intelligent life superior—in the long run—to themselves. Earthmen tended to win and—the assumption was—had a right to win.

Even when non-human life forms were allowed to be members of a Galactic Federation, it was always the Terrestrial human beings who, in the end, dominated; who were the heroes.

As the 1930s wore on, however, the easy certainty of European superiority came to be questioned. It had to be, for the rise of Adolf Hitler in Germany, with his unabashed and extreme racism, embarrassed any human being with even a hint of decency in his makeup.

It more than embarrassed me, since I am Jewish and a member of the group that was the prime target and victim of Hitler's criminal paranoia. Consequently when I, as a science fiction writer, wanted to write interstellar romances after the fashion of Smith and Campbell, I could not make the Earthmen-are-superior assumption.

In fact, considering what was going on in Europe, it seemed to me that Earthmen were very likely to be inferior in moral attitudes to extraterrestrials of comparable intelligence and, in fact, would *have* to be if the writer were to try to say something pertinent to the human condition as it was during the years of the late 1930s and early 1940s.

I wrote such a story in 1940 and tried to sell it to *Astounding*, but the editor of *Astounding* was none other than John Campbell and he was still a slave to the assumptions of the 1920s. We argued the story back and forth, with John striving to make Earthmen superior and I resisting; and in the end, when John published the story, he had forced me to incorporate some paragraphs against my will and then unilaterally put in additional ones without my permission.

I was determined not to let that happen again. I did not want to give up the interstellar romance, so I invented the all-human Galaxy when I wrote my Foundation stories. It was not that I believed that Earth would prove the only planet in the Galaxy to be inhabited by intelligent life; in fact, I *don't* believe that. It was merely that, if human beings were the only intelligences in my stories, John would have no reason to try to impose the 1920s on me and I could try to reflect my own views of humanity.

The two novels that are republished in this volume, *The Currents of Space* and *The Stars, Like Dust*, were written after the Foundation stories had been finished. Nevertheless, they are in the Foundation universe.

Each novel takes place during the rise of the First Galactic Empire (whose fall is chronicled in the Foundation stories), and in each case one group of human beings is dominated by another, with the sympathy of the reader enlisted on the side of the underdog.

In neither novel is the natural superiority of one over the other invoked, even as an unspoken assumption. The dominating group is not dominant out of superiority—nor must their domination be broken because they are actually inferior.

It all worked better for me than I could have imagined in those ancient days of four decades ago. The Smith-Campbell romances, which are primarily adventure stories of us-against-the-natives, don't really stand up and now possess only historical interest.

My own interstellar romances, on the other hand, which deal with human-against-human and with political-sociological-psychological factors that don't date easily, seem to stand up. My Foundation books have never gone out of print, either hardback or softback, and sell better now than they did to begin with.

And my other novels, even when allowed to go out of hardback print (though they have remained steadily active in soft covers), can be brought back periodically, as now, for instance, and then do well again.—This is something I attribute to good fortune rather than to foresight, on my part. (And maybe to a little bit of writing talent.)

No writer, of course, is immune to scientific obsolescence, not even one who, like myself, is a trained scientist.

The Currents of Space, for instance, was written nearly thirty years ago, and it includes a theory of supernova formation in which I used the information available to me at that time, plus a certain amount of imagination.

I knew that there were interstellar dust clouds which might differ in chemical composition from place to place. I knew that by the dominant theory of how stars obtained their radiant energy, carbon atoms acted in catalytic fashion in bringing about the fusion of hydrogen to helium.

Why not suppose, then, that stars, passing through carbon-rich areas in space, might find their hydrogen-fusion rate accelerated to the point where they blossom out in a vast explosion?

It all seemed very plausible to me at the time, and I even had the hidden hope that something like that would prove to be the true explanation of supernova formation and that I would receive some credit for the conceptualization.

Alas, in the decades that have passed since, astronomers have become much more confident that they understand the causes of supernova formation. It turns out to depend entirely on mass; on internal mechanisms. The outside environment need not be called upon.

If a star is massive enough, it passes through an evolutionary sequence that ends inevitably in a supernova, and the chemical composition of the interstellar gas about it has nothing to do with it. (By "massive enough," incidentally, we mean at least one and a half times the mass of our Sun so that good old Sol will never go supernova on us. It will change, eventually, in such a way as to make Earth uninhabitable but not in any way so drastic as an enormous overnight explosion.)

Since my own theory of supernova formation is central to the plot and is even expressed in the title, *The Currents of Space*, it might seem that the novel has now become useless.

Fortunately, scientific obsolescence is less offensive than social obsolescence. H. G. Wells's *The War of the Worlds* remains an exciting story even though we know that Mars is, in reality, nothing like the Mars described in the story and even though we know there are no Martians.

Therefore, I have no hesitation in presenting *The Currents of Space* again even though its astronomy is in some respects out of date—though it is only fair to mention the fact that it is.

As for the third book in the collection, *The Martian Way and Other Stories,* that contains a group of four stories written in the early 1950s, in which I show my non-Galactic side. The longest story in the book, "Sucker Bait," does indeed take place on a planet beyond our Solar system, but there is no Galactic Empire. We deal only with Earth and its explorations.

The title story, "The Martian Way," (written during the sad period of McCarthyist terror—as the reader may perhaps detect) deals with interplanetary travel only. And, considering that it was written six years before human beings placed the first artificial satellite into orbit, it does so with considerable realism, I think. To be sure, the first and second stages of rockets are discharged within Earth's atmosphere and wouldn't be available for scavenging in space.

The two shorter stories, "Youth" and "The Deep," do deal with extraterrestrials, demonstrating that I can use them if I have to. In neither case, however, do the 1920-ish notions of Terrestrial superiority arise—and neither did I try to place them in *Astounding.*

One final note, though. These shorter pieces do demonstrate "the reverse approach"; that is, the common habit among science fiction writers of deliberately taking a point of view that is the reverse of the usual.

As an example, in "Sucker Bait," it is brute memory that counts, not keen analytical logic, and in "The Deep," mother love is immoral rather than beautiful.

This is a useful way of doing things since aspects of the human condition can be made clear in more startling fashion if something is deliberately stood on its head.

Science fiction is particularly well adapted to do this sort of thing, since the science fiction writer has total leeway in constructing a society that is different from ours and to do it in such a way as to make the reversal not only possible but, seemingly, natural.

THE STARS, LIKE DUST

One: *THE BEDROOM MURMURED*

The bedroom murmured to itself gently. It was almost below the limits of hearing—an irregular little sound, yet quite unmistakable, and quite deadly.

But it wasn't that which awakened Biron Farrill and dragged him out of a heavy, unrefreshing slumber. He turned his head restlessly from side to side in a futile struggle against the periodic burr-r-r on the end table.

He put out a clumsy hand without opening his eyes and closed contact.

"Hello," he mumbled.

Sound tumbled instantly out of the receiver. It was harsh and loud, but Biron lacked the ambition to reduce the volume.

It said, "May I speak to Biron Farrill?"

Biron said, fuzzily, "Speaking. What d'you want?"

"May I speak to Biron Farrill?" The voice was urgent.

Biron's eyes opened on the thick darkness. He became conscious of the dry unpleasantness of his tongue and the faint odor that remained in the room.

He said, "Speaking. Who is this?"

It went on, disregarding him, gathering tension, a loud voice in the night. "Is anyone there? I would like to speak to Biron Farrill."

Biron raised himself on one elbow and stared at the place where the visiphone sat. He jabbed at the vision control and the small screen was alive with light.

"Here I am," he said. He recognized the smooth, slightly asymmetric features of Sander Jonti. "Call me in the morning, Jonti."

He started to turn the instrument off once more, when Jonti said, "Hello. Hello. Is anyone there? Is this University Hall, Room 526? Hello."

Biron was suddenly aware that the tiny pilot light which would have indicated a live sending circuit was not on. He swore under his breath and pushed the switch. It stayed off. Then Jonti gave up, and the screen went blank, and was merely a small square of featureless light.

Biron turned it off. He hunched his shoulder and tried to burrow into the pillow again. He was annoyed. In the first place, no one had the right to yell at him in the middle of the night. He looked quickly at the gently luminous figures just over the headboard. Three-fifteen. House lights wouldn't go on for nearly four hours.

Besides, he didn't like having to wake to the complete darkness of his room. Four years' custom had not hardened him to the Earthman's habit of building structures of reinforced concrete, squat, thick, and windowless. It was a thousand-year-old tradition dating from the days when the primitive nuclear bomb had not yet been countered by the force-field defense.

But that was past. Atomic warfare had done its worst to Earth. Most of it was hopelessly radioactive and useless. There was nothing left to lose, and yet architecture mirrored the old fears, so that when Biron woke, it was to pure darkness.

Biron rose on his elbow again. That was strange. He waited. It wasn't the fatal murmur of the bedroom he had become aware of. It was something perhaps even less noticeable and certainly infinitely less deadly.

He missed the gentle movement of air that one took so for granted, that trace of continuous renewal. He tried to swallow easily and failed. The atmosphere seemed to become oppressive even as he realized the situation. The ventilating system had stopped working, and now he really had a grievance. He couldn't even use the visiphone to report the matter.

He tried again, to make sure. The milky square of light sprang out and threw a faint, pearly luster on the bed. It was receiving, but it wouldn't send. Well, it didn't matter. Nothing would be done about it before day, anyway.

He yawned and groped for his slippers, rubbing his eyes with the heels of his palms. No ventilation, eh? That would account for the queer smell. He frowned and sniffed sharply two or three times. No use. It was familiar, but he couldn't place it.

He made his way to the bathroom, and reached automatically for the light switch, although he didn't really need it to draw himself a glass of water. It closed, but uselessly. He tried it several times, peevishly. Wasn't *anything* working? He shrugged, drank in the dark, and felt better. He yawned again on his way back to the bedroom where he tried the main switch. All the lights were out.

Biron sat on the bed, placed his large hands on his hard-muscled thighs and considered. Ordinarily, a thing like this would call for a terrific discussion with the service staff. No one expected hotel service in a college dormitory, but, by Space, there were certain minimum standards of efficiency one could demand. Not that it was of vital importance just now. Graduation was coming and he was through. In three days he'd be saying a last good-by to the room and to the University of Earth; to Earth itself, for that matter.

Still, he might report it anyway, without particular comment. He could go out and use the hall phone. They might bring in a self-powered light or even rig up a fan so he could sleep without psychosomatic choking sensations. If not, to Space with them! Two more nights.

In the light of the useless visiphone, he located a pair of shorts. Over them he slipped a one-piece jumper, and decided that that would be enough for the purpose. He retained his slippers. There was no danger of waking anybody even if he clumped down the corridors in spiked shoes, considering the thick, nearly soundproof partitions of this concrete pile, but he saw no point in changing.

He strode toward the door and pulled at the lever. It descended smoothly and he heard the click that meant the door release had been activated. Except that it wasn't. And although his biceps tightened into lumps, nothing was accomplished.

He stepped away. This was ridiculous. Had there been a general power failure? There couldn't have been. The clock was going. The visiphone was still receiving properly.

Wait! It could have been the boys, bless their erratic souls. It was done sometimes. Infantile, of course, but he'd taken part in these foolish practical jokes himself. It wouldn't have been difficult, for instance, for one of his buddies to sneak in during the day and arrange matters. But, no, the ventilation and lights were working when he had gone to sleep.

Very well, then, during the night. The hall was an old, outmoded structure. It wouldn't have taken an engineering genius to hocus the lighting and ventilation circuits. Or to jam the door, either. And now they would wait for morning and see what would happen when good old Biron found he couldn't get out. They would probably let him out toward noon and laugh very hard.

"Ha, ha," said Biron grimly, under his breath. All right, if that's the way it was. But he would have to do something about it; turn the tables some way.

He turned away and his toe kicked something which skidded metallically across the floor. He could barely make out its shadow moving through the dim visiphone light. He reached under the bed, patting the floor in a wide arc. He brought it out and held it close to the light. (They weren't so smart. They should have put the visiphone entirely out of commission, instead of just yanking out the sending circuit.)

He found himself holding a small cylinder with a little hole in the blister on top. He put it close to his nose and sniffed at it. That explained the smell in the room, anyway. It was Hypnite. Of course, the boys would have had to use it to keep him from waking up while they were busy with the circuits.

Biron could reconstruct the proceedings step by step now. The door was jimmied open, a simple thing to do, and the only dangerous part, since he might have wakened then. The door might have been prepared during the day, for that matter, so that it would seem to close and not actually do so. He hadn't tested it. Anyway, once open, a can of Hypnite would be put just inside and the door would be closed again. The anesthetic would leak out slowly, building up to the one-in-ten-thousand concentration necessary to put him definitely under. Then they could enter—masked, of course. Space! A wet handkerchief would keep out the Hypnite for fifteen minutes and that would be all the time needed.

It explained the ventilation system situation. That had to be eliminated to keep the Hypnite from dispersing too quickly. That would have gone first, in fact. The visiphone elimination kept him from getting help; the door jamming kept him from getting out; and the absence of lights induced panic. Nice kids!

Biron snorted. It was socially impossible to be thin-skinned about this. A joke was a joke and all that. Right now, he would have liked to break the door down and have done with it. The well-trained muscles of his torso tensed at the thought, but it would be useless. The door had been built with atom blasts in mind. *Damn* that tradition!

But there had to be some way out. He couldn't let them get away with it. First, he would need a light, a real one, not the immovable and unsatisfactory glow of the visiphone. That was no problem. He had a self-powered flashlight in the clothes closet.

For a moment, as he fingered the closet-door controls, he wondered if they had jammed that too. But it moved open naturally, and slid smoothly into its wall socket. Biron nodded to himself. It made sense. There was no reason, particularly, to jam the closet, and they didn't have too much time, anyway.

And then, with the flashlight in his hand, as he was turning away, the entire structure of his theory collapsed in a horrible instant. He stiffened, his abdomen ridging with tension, and held his breath, listening.

For the first time since awakening, he heard the murmuring of the bedroom. He heard the quiet, irregular chuckling conversation it was holding with itself, and recognized the nature of the sound at once.

It was impossible not to recognize it. The sound was "Earth's death rattle." It was the sound that had been invented one thousand years before.

To be exact, it was the sound of a radiation counter, ticking off the charged particles and the hard gamma waves that came its way, the soft clicking electronic surges melting into a low murmur. It was the sound of a counter, counting the only thing it could count—death!

Softly, on tiptoe, Biron backed away. From a distance of six feet he threw the white beam into the recesses of the closet. The counter was there, in the far corner, but seeing it told him nothing.

It had been there ever since his freshman days. Most freshmen from the Outer Worlds bought a counter during their first week on Earth. They were very conscious of Earth's radioactivity then, and felt the need of protection. Usually they were sold again to the next class, but Biron had never disposed of his. He was thankful for that now.

He turned to the desk, where he kept his wrist watch while sleeping. It was there. His hand was shaking a little as he held it up to the flashlight's beam. The watch strap was an interwoven flexible plastic of an almost liquidly smooth whiteness. And it *was* white. He held it away and tried it at different angles. It *was* white.

That strap had been another freshman purchase. Hard radiation turned it blue, and blue on Earth was the color of death. It was easy to wander into a path of radiating soil during the day if you were lost or careless. The government fenced off as many patches as it could, and of course no one ever approached the huge areas of death that began several miles outside the city. But the strap was insurance.

If it should ever turn a faint blue, you would show up at the hospital for treatment. There was no argument about it. The compound of which it was made was precisely as sensitive to radiation as you were, and appropriate photoelectric instruments could be used to measure the intensity of the blueness so that the seriousness of the case might be determined quickly.

A bright royal blue was the finish. Just as the color would never change back, neither would you. There was no cure, no chance, no hope. You just waited anywhere from a day to a week, and all the hospital could do was to make final arrangements for cremation.

But at least it was still white, and some of the clamor in Biron's thoughts subsided.

There wasn't much radioactivity then. Could it be just another angle of the joke? Biron considered and decided that it couldn't. *Nobody* would do that to anyone else. Not on Earth, anyway, where illegal handling of radioactive material was a capital offense. They took radioactivity seriously here on Earth. They had to, So nobody would do this without overpowering reason.

He stated the thought to himself carefully and explicitly, facing it boldly. The overpowering reason, for instance, of a desire to murder. But why? There could be no motive. In his twenty-three years of life, he had never made a serious enemy. Not *this* serious. Not murder serious.

He clutched at his clipped hair. This was a ridiculous line of thought, but there was no escaping it. He stepped cautiously back to the closet. There had to be something there that was sending out radiation; something that had not been there four hours earlier. He saw it almost at once.

It was a little box not more than six inches in any direction. Biron recognized it and his lower lip trembled slightly. He had never seen one before, but he had heard of them. He lifted the counter and took it into the bedroom. The little murmur fell off, almost ceased. It started again when the thin mica partition, through which the radiation entered, pointed toward the box. There was no question in his mind. It was a radiation bomb.

The present radiations were not in themselves deadly; they were only a fuse. Somewhere inside the box a tiny atomic pile was constructed. Short-lived artificial isotopes heated it slowly, permeating it with the appropriate particles. When the threshold of head and particle density was reached, the pile reacted. Not in an explosion, usually, although the heat of reaction would serve to fuse the box itself into a twist of metal, but in a tremendous burst of deadly radiation that would kill anything living within a radius of six feet to six miles, depending on the bomb's size.

There was no way of telling when the threshold would be reached. Perhaps not for hours, and perhaps the next moment. Biron remained standing helplessly, flashlight held loosely in his damp hands. Half an hour before, the visiphone had awakened him, and he had been at peace then. Now he knew he was going to die.

Biron didn't want to die, but he was penned in hopelessly, and there was no place to hide.

He knew the geography of the room. It was at the end of a corridor, so that there was another room only on one side, and, of course, above and below. He could do nothing about the room above. The room on the same floor was on the bathroom side, and it adjoined via its own bathroom. He doubted that he could make himself heard.

That left the room below.

There were a couple of folding chairs in the room, spare seats to accommodate company. He took one. It made a flat, slapping sound when it hit the floor. He turned it edgewise and the sound became harder and louder.

Between each blow, he waited; wondering if he could rouse the sleeper below and annoy him sufficiently to have him report the disturbance.

Abruptly, he caught a faint noise, and paused, the splintering chair raised above his head. The noise came again, like a faint shout. It was from the direction of the door.

He dropped the chair and yelled in return. He crushed his ear up against the crack where door joined wall, but the fit was good, and the sound even there was dim.

But he could make out his own name being called.

"Farrill! Farrill!" several times over, and something else. Maybe "Are you in there?" or "Are you all right?"

He roared back, "Get the door open." He shouted it three or four times. He was in a feverish sweat of impatience. The bomb might be on the point of letting loose even now.

He thought they heard him. At least, the muffled cry came back, "Watch out. Something, something, blaster." He knew what they meant and backed hurriedly away from the door.

There were a couple of sharp, cracking sounds, and he could actually feel the vibrations sent up in the air of the room. Then there followed a splitting noise and the door was flung inward. Light poured in from the corridor.

Biron dashed out, arms flung wide. "Don't come in," he yelled. "For the love of Earth, don't come in. There's a radiation bomb in there."

He was facing two men. One was Jonti. The other was Esbak, the superintendent. He was only partly dressed.

"A radiation bomb?" he stuttered.

But Jonti said, "What size?" Jonti's blaster was still in his hand, and that alone jarred with the dandyish effect of his ensemble, even at this time of night.

Biron could only gesture with his hands.

"All right," said Jonti. He seemed quite cool about it, as he turned to the superintendent. "You'd better evacuate the rooms in this area, and if you have leadsheets anywhere on the university grounds, have them brought out here to line the corridor. And I wouldn't let anyone in there before morning."

He turned to Biron. "It probably has a twelve- to eighteen-foot radius. How did it get there?"

"I don't know," said Biron. He wiped his forehead with the back of his hand. "If you don't mind, I've got to sit down somewhere." He threw a glance at his wrist, then realized his wrist watch was still in the room. He had a wild impulse to return after it.

There was action now. Students were being hustled out of their rooms.

"Come with me," said Jonti. "I think you had better sit down too."

Biron said, "What brought you out to my room? Not that I'm not thankful, you understand."

"I called you. There was no answer, and I had to see you."

"To see me?" He spoke carefully, trying to control his irregular breathing. "Why?"

"To warn you that your life was in danger."

Biron laughed raggedly. "I found out."

"That was only the first attempt. They'll try again."

"Who are 'they'?"

"Not here, Farrill," said Jonti. "We need privacy for this. You're a marked man, and I may already have endangered myself as well."

Two: *THE NET ACROSS SPACE*

The student lounge was empty; it was dark as well. At four-thirty in the morning it could scarcely have been otherwise. Yet Jonti hesitated a moment as he held the door open, listening for occupants.

"No," he said softly, "leave the lights out. We won't need them to talk."

"I've had enough of the dark for one night," muttered Biron.

"We'll leave the door ajar."

Biron lacked the will to argue. He dropped into the nearest chair and watched the rectangle of light through the closing door narrow down to a thin line. Now that it was all over, he was getting the shakes.

Jonti steadied the door and rested his little swagger stick upon the crack of light on the floor. "Watch it. It will tell us if anyone passes, or if the door moves."

Biron said, "Please, I'm not in a conspiratorial mood. If you don't mind, I'd appreciate your telling me whatever it is you want to tell me. You've saved my life, I know, and tomorrow I'll be properly thankful. Right now, I could do with a short drink and a long rest."

"I can imagine your feelings," Jonti said, "but the too-long rest you might have had has been avoided, momentarily. I would like to make it more than just momentarily. Do you know that I know your father?"

The question was an abrupt one, and Biron raised his eyebrows, a gesture lost in the dark. He said, "He has never mentioned knowing you."

"I would be surprised if he did. He doesn't know me by the name I use here. Have you heard from your father recently, by the way?"

"Why do you ask?"

"Because he is in great danger."

"*What?*"

Jonti's hand found the other's arm in the dimness and gripped it firmly. "Please! Keep your voice as it has been." Biron realized, for the first time that they had been whispering.

Jonti resumed, "I'll be more specific. Your father has been taken into custody. You understand the significance?"

"No, I certainly don't understand. *Who* has taken him into custody, and what are you getting at? Why are you bothering me?" Biron's temples were throbbing. The Hypnite and the near death had made it impossible to fence with the cool dandy sitting so close to him that his whispers were as plain as shouts.

"Surely," came the whisper, "you have some inkling of the work your father is doing?"

"If you know my father, you know he is Rancher of Widemos. That is his work."

Jonti said, "Well, there is no reason you should trust me, other than that I am risking my own life for you. But I already know all you can tell me. As an example, I know that your father has been conspiring against the Tyranni."

"I deny that," said Biron tensely. "Your service to me this night does not give you the right to make such statements about my father."

"You are foolishly evasive, young man, and you are wasting my time. Don't you see that the situation is beyond verbal fencing? I'll say it outright. Your father is in the custody of the Tyranni. He may be dead by now."

"I don't believe you." Biron half rose.

"I am in a position to know."

"Let's break this off, Jonti. I am in no mood for mystery, and I resent this attempt of yours to——"

"Well, to what?" Jonti's voice lost some of its refined edge. "What do I gain by telling you this? May I remind you that this knowledge of mine, which you will not accept, made it plain to me that an attempt might be made to kill you. Judge by what has happened, Farrill."

Biron said, "Start again and tell it straight. I'll listen."

"Very well. I imagine, Farrill, that you know me to be a fellow countryman from the Nebular Kingdoms, although I've been passing myself off as a Vegan."

"I judged that might be a possibility by your accent. It didn't seem important."

"It's important, my friend. I came here because, like your father, I didn't like the Tyranni. They've been oppressing our people for fifty years. That's a long time."

"I'm not a politician."

Again Jonti's voice had an irritated edge to it. "Oh, I'm not one of their agents trying to get you into trouble. I'm telling you the truth. They caught me a year ago as they have caught your father now. But I managed to get away, and came to Earth where I thought I might be safe until I was ready to return. That's all I need tell you about myself."

"It is more than I have asked for, sir." Biron could not force the unfriendliness out of his voice. Jonti affected him unfavorably with his too-precise mannerisms.

"I know that. But it is necessary to tell you so much at least, for it was in this manner that I met your father. He worked with me, or, rather, I with him. He knew me but not in his official capacity as the greatest nobleman on the planet of Nephelos. You understand me?"

Biron nodded uselessly in the darkness and said, "Yes."

"It is not necessary to go into that further. My sources of information have been maintained even here, and I know that he has been imprisoned. It is *knowledge*. If it were merely suspicion, this attempt on your life would have been sufficient proof."

"In what way?"

"If the Tyranni have the father, would they leave the son at large?"

"Are you trying to tell me that the Tyranni set that radiation bomb in my room? That's impossible."

"Why is it impossible? Can't you understand their position? The Tyranni rule fifty worlds; they are outnumbered hundreds to one. In such a position, simple force is insufficient. Devious methods, intrigue, assassination are their specialties. The net they weave across space is a wide one, and close-meshed. I can well believe that it extends across five hundred light-years to Earth."

Biron was still in the grip of his nightmare. In the distance there were the faint sounds of the lead shields being moved into place. In his room the counter must still be murmuring.

He said, "It doesn't make sense. I am going back to Nephelos this week. They would know that. Why should they kill me here? If they'd wait, they'd have me." He was relieved to find the flaw, eager to believe his own logic.

Jonti leaned closer and his spiced breath stirred the hairs on Biron's temple. "Your father is popular. His death—and once imprisoned by the Tyranni, his execution becomes a probability you must face—will be resented even by the cowed slave race the Tyranni are trying to breed. You could rally that resentment as the new Rancher of Widemos, and to execute you as well would double the danger for them. To make martyrs is not their purpose. *But* if you were to die in a faraway world, by accident, it would be convenient for them."

"I don't believe you," said Biron. It had become his only defense.

Jonti rose, adjusting his thin gloves. He said, "You go too far, Farrill. Your role would be more convincing if you pretended to no such complete ignorance. Your father has been shielding you from reality for your own protection, presumably, yet I doubt that you could remain completely uninfluenced by his beliefs. Your hate for the Tyranni cannot help being a reflection of his own. You cannot help being ready to fight them."

Biron shrugged.

Jonti said, "He may even recognize your new adulthood to the point of putting you to use. You are conveniently here on Earth and it is not unlikely you may be combining your education with a definite assignment. An assignment, perhaps, for the failure of which the Tyranni are ready to kill you."

"That's silly melodrama."

"Is it? Let it be so, then. If the truth will not persuade you now, events will later. There will be other attempts on your life, and the next one will succeed. From this moment on, Farrill, you are a dead man."

Biron looked up. "Wait! What's your own private interest in the matter?"

"I am a patriot. I would like to see the Kingdoms free again, with governments of their own choosing."

"No. Your *private* interest. I cannot accept idealism only, because

I won't believe it of you. I am sorry if that offends you." Biron's words pounded doggedly.

Jonti seated himself again. He said, "My lands have been confiscated. Before my exile it was not comfortable to be forced to take orders from those dwarfs. And since then it has become more imperative than ever to become once again the man my grandfather had been before the Tyranni came. Is that enough of a practical reason for wanting a revolution? Your father would have been a leader of that revolution. Failing him, you!"

"I? I am twenty-three and know nothing of all this. You could find better men."

"Undoubtedly I could, but no one else is the son of your father. If your father is killed, you will be Rancher of Widemos, and as such you would be valuable to me if you were only twelve and an idiot besides. I need you for the same reason the Tyranni must be rid of you. And if my necessity is unconvincing to you, surely theirs cannot be. There *was* a radiation bomb in your room. It could only have been meant to kill you. Who else would want to kill you?"

Jonti waited patiently and picked up the other's whisper.

"No one," said Biron. "No one would want to kill me that I know of. Then it's true about my father!"

"It is true. View it as a casualty of war."

"You think that would make it better? They'll put up a monument to him someday, perhaps? One with a radiating inscription that you can see ten thousand miles out in space?" His voice was becoming a bit ragged. "Is that supposed to make me happy?"

Jonti waited, but Biron said nothing more.

Jonti said, "What do you intend doing?"

"I'm going home."

"You still don't understand your position, then."

"I said, I'm going home. What do you want me to do? If he's alive, I'll get him out of there. And if he's dead, I'll—I'll——"

"Quiet!" The older man's voice was coldly annoyed. "You rave like a child. You can't go to Nephelos. Don't you see that you can't? Am I talking to an infant or to a young man of sense?"

Biron muttered, "What do you suggest?"

"Do you know the Director of Rhodia?"

"The friend of the Tyranni? I know the man. I know who he is.

Everyone in the Kingdoms knows who he is. Hinrik V, Director of Rhodia."

"Have you ever met him?"

"No."

"That is what I meant. If you haven't met him, you don't know him. He is an imbecile, Farrill. I mean it literally. But when the Ranchy of Widemos is confiscated by the Tyranni—and it will be, as my lands were—it will be awarded to Hinrik. There the Tyranni will feel them to be safe, and there you must go."

"Why?"

"Because Hinrik, at least, has influence with the Tyranni; as much influence as a lickspittle puppet may have. He may arrange to have you reinstated."

"I don't see why. He's more likely to turn me over to them."

"So he is. But you'll be on your guard against it, and there is a fighting chance you may avoid it. Remember, the title you carry is valuable and important, but it is not all-sufficient. In this business of conspiracy, one must be practical above all. Men will rally about you out of sentiment and respect for your name, but to hold them, you will need money."

Biron considered. "I need time to decide."

"You have no time. Your time ran out when the radiation bomb was planted in your room. Let us take action. I can give you a letter of introduction to Hinrik of Rhodia."

"You know him so well, then?"

"Your suspicion never sleeps very soundly, does it? I once headed a mission to Hinrik's court on behalf of the Autarch of Lingane. His imbecile's mind will probably not remember me, but he will not dare to show he has forgotten. It will serve as introduction and you can improvise from there. I will have the letter for you in the morning. There is a ship leaving for Rhodia at noon. I have tickets for you. I am leaving myself, but by another route. Don't linger. You're all through here, aren't you?"

"There is the diploma presentation."

"A scrap of parchment. Does it matter to you?"

"Not now."

"Do you have money?"

"Enough."

"Very well. Too much would be suspicious." He spoke sharply. "Farrill!"

Biron stirred out of what was nearly a stupor. "What?"

"Get back to the others. Tell no one you are leaving. Let the act speak."

Biron nodded dumbly. Far away in the recesses of his mind there was the thought that his mission remained unaccomplished and that in this way, too, he failed his dying father. He was racked with a futile bitterness. He might have been told more. He might have shared the dangers. He should not have been allowed to act in ignorance.

And now that he knew the truth, or at least more of it, concerning the extent of his father's role in conspiracy, there was an added importance to the document he was to have obtained from Earth's archives. But there was no time any longer. No time to get the document. No time to wonder about it. No time to save his father. No time, perhaps, to live.

He said, "I'll do as you say, Jonti."

Sander Jonti looked briefly out over the university campus as he paused on the steps of the dormitory. Certainly there was no admiration in his glance.

As he stepped down the bricked walk that wound unsubtly through the pseudo-rustic atmosphere affected by all urban campuses since antiquity, he could see the lights of the city's single important street gleam just ahead. Past it, drowned in daytime, but visible now, was the eternal radioactive blue of the horizon, mute witness of prehistoric wars.

Jonti considered the sky for a moment. Over fifty years had passed since the Tyranni had come and put a sudden end to the separate lives of two dozen sprawling, brawling political units in the depths beyond the Nebula. Now, suddenly and prematurely, the peace of strangulation lay upon them.

The storm that had caught them in one vast thunderclap had been something from which they had not yet recovered. It had left only a sort of twitching that futilely agitated a world here and there, now and then. To organize those twitchings, to align them into a single well-timed heave would be a difficult task, and a long one. Well, he had been rusticating here on Earth long enough. It was time to go back.

The others, back home, were probably trying to get in touch with him at his rooms right now.

He lengthened his stride a bit.

He caught the beam as he entered his room. It was a personal beam, for whose security there were as yet no fears and in whose privacy there was no chink. No formal receiver was required; no thing of metal and wires to catch the faint, drifting surges of electrons, with their whispered impulses swimming through hyperspace from a world half a thousand light-years away.

Space itself was polarized in his room, and prepared for reception. Its fabric was smoothed out of randomness. There was no way of detecting that polarization, except by receiving. And in that particular volume of space, only his own mind could act as receiver; since only the electrical characteristics of his own particular nerve-cell system could resonate to the vibrations of the carrier beam that bore the message.

The message was as private as the unique characteristics of his own brain waves, and in all the universe, with its quadrillions of human beings, the odds against a duplication sufficiently close to allow one man to pick up another's personal wave was a twenty-figured number to one.

Jonti's brain tickled to the call as it whined through the endless empty incomprehensibility of hyperspace.

". . . calling . . . calling . . . calling . . . calling . . ."

Sending was not quite so simple a job as receiving. A mechanical contrivance was needed to set up the highly specific carrier wave that would carry back to the contact beyond the Nebula. That was contained in the ornamental button that he carried on his right shoulder. It was automatically activated when he stepped into his volume of space polarization, and after that he had only to think purposefully and with concentration.

"Here I am!" No need for more specific identification.

The dull repetition of the calling signal halted and became words that took form within his mind. "We greet you, sir. Widemos has been executed. The news is, of course, not yet public."

"It does not surprise me. Was anyone else implicated?"

"No, sir. The Rancher made no statements at any time. A brave and loyal man."

"Yes. But it takes more than simply bravery and loyalty, or he would not have been caught. A little more cowardice might have been useful. No matter! I have spoken to his son, the new Rancher, who has already had his brush with death. He will be put to use."

"May one inquire in what manner, sir?"

"It is better to let events answer your question. Certainly I cannot foretell consequences at this early date. Tomorrow he will set off to see Hinrik of Rhodia."

"Hinrik! The young man will run a fearful risk. Is he aware that——"

"I have told him as much as I can," responded Jonti sharply. "We cannot trust him too far until he has proved himself. Under the circumstances as they exist, we can only view him as a man to be risked, like any other man. He is expendable, *quite* expendable. Do not call me here again, as I am leaving Earth."

And, with a gesture of finality, Jonti broke the connection mentally.

Quietly and thoughtfully, he went over the events of the day and the night, weighing each event. Slowly, he smiled. Everything had been arranged perfectly, and the comedy might now play itself out.

Nothing had been left to chance.

Three: *CHANCE AND THE WRIST WATCH*

The first hour of a space-ship's rise from planetary thralldom is the most prosaic. There is the confusion of departure, which is much the same in essence as that which must have accompanied the shoving off of the first hollowed-out tree trunk on some primeval river.

You have your accommodations; your luggage is taken care of; there is the first stiff moment of strangeness and meaningless hustle surrounding you. The shouted last-moment intimacies, the quieting, the muted clang of the air locks, followed by the slow soughing of air as the locks screw inward automatically, like gigantic drills, becoming airtight.

Then the portentous silence and the red signs flicking in every room: "Adjust acceleration suits. . . . Adjust acceleration suits. . . . Adjust acceleration suits."

The stewards scour the corridors, knocking shortly on each door and jerking it open. "Beg pardon. Suits on."

You battle with the suits, cold, tight, uncomfortable, but cradled in a hydraulic system which absorbs the sickening pressures of the take-off.

There is the faraway rumble of the atom-driven motors, on low power for atmospheric maneuvering, followed instantly by the giving back against the slow-yielding oil of the suit cradle. You recede almost indefinitely back, then very slowly forward again as the acceleration decreases. If you survive nausea during this period, you are probably safe from space sickness for duration.

The view-room was not open to the passengers for the first three hours of the flight, and there was a long line waiting when the atmosphere had been left behind and the double doors were ready to separate. There were present not only the usual hundred-per-cent turnout of all Planetaries (those, in other words, who had never been in space before), but a fair proportion of the more experienced travelers as well.

The vision of Earth from space, after all, was one of the tourist "musts."

The view-room was a bubble on the ship's "skin," a bubble of curved two-foot-thick, steel-hard transparent plastic. The retractile iridium-steel lid which protected it against the scouring of the atmosphere and its dust particles had been sucked back. The lights were out and the gallery was full. The faces peering over the bars were clear in the Earth-shine.

For Earth was suspended there below, a gigantic and gleaming orange-and-blue-and-white-patched balloon. The hemisphere showing was almost entirely sunlit; the continents between the clouds, a desert orange, with thin, scattered lines of green. The seas were blue, standing out sharply against the black of space where they met the horizon. And all around in the black, undusted sky were the stars.

They waited patiently, those who watched.

It was not the sunlit hemisphere they wanted. The polar cap, blinding bright, was shifting down into view as the ship maintained the slight, unnoticed sidewise acceleration that was lifting it out of the ecliptic. Slowly the shadow of night encroached upon the globe and the huge World-Island of Eurasia-Africa majestically took the stage, north side "down."

Its diseased, unliving soil hid its horror under a night-induced play of jewels. The radioactivity of the soil was a vast sea of iridescent blue, sparkling in strange festoons that spelled out the manner in which the nuclear bombs had once landed, a full generation before the force-field defense against nuclear explosions had been developed so that no other world could commit suicide in just that fashion again.

The eyes watched until, with the hours, Earth was a bright little half coin in the endless black.

Among the watchers was Biron Farrill. He sat by himself in the front row, arms upon the railing, eyes brooding and thoughtful. This was not the way he had expected to leave Earth. It was the wrong manner, the wrong ship, the wrong destination.

His tanned forearm rubbed against the stubble of his chin and he felt guilty about not having shaved that morning. He'd go back to his room after a while and correct that. Meanwhile, he hesitated to leave. There were people here. In his room he would be alone.

Or was that just the reason he should leave?

He did not like the new feeling he had, that of being hunted; that of being friendless.

All friendship had dropped from him. It had shriveled from the very moment he had been awakened by the phone call less than twenty-four hours earlier.

Even in the dormitory he had become an embarrassment. Old Esbak had pounced upon him when he had returned after his talk with Jonti in the student lounge. Esbak was in turmoil; his voice overshrill.

"Mr. Farrill, I've been looking for you. It has been a most unfortunate incident. I can't understand it. Do you have any explanation?"

"No," he had half shouted, "I don't. When can I get into my room and get my stuff out?"

"In the morning, I am sure. We've just managed to get the equipment up here to test the room. There is no longer any trace of radioactivity above normal background level. It was a very fortunate escape for you. It must have missed you only by minutes."

"Yes, yes, but if you don't mind, I would like to rest."

"Please use my room till morning and then we'll get you relocated for the few days remaining you. Umm, by the way, Mr. Farrill, if you don't mind, there is another matter."

He was being overly polite. Biron could almost hear the egg-shells give slightly beneath his finicky feet.

"What other matter?" asked Biron wearily.

"Do you know of anyone who might have been interested in—er—hazing you?"

"Hazing me like *this?* Of course not."

"What are your plans, then? The school authorities would, of course, be most unhappy to have publicity arise as a result of this incident."

How he kept referring to it as an "incident"! Biron said dryly, "I understand you. But don't worry. I'm not interested in investigations or in the police. I'm leaving Earth soon, and I'd just as soon not have my own plans disrupted. I'm not bringing any charges. After all, I'm still alive."

Esbak had been almost indecently relieved. It was all they wanted from him. No unpleasantness. It was just an incident to be forgotten.

He got into his old room again at seven in the morning. It was quiet and there was no murmuring in the closet. The bomb was no longer there, nor was the counter. They had probably been taken away by Esbak and thrown into the lake. It came under the head of destroying evidence, but that was the school's worry. He threw his belongings into suitcases and then called the desk for assignment to another room. The lights were working again, he noticed, and so, of course, was the visiphone. The one remnant of last night was the twisted door, its lock melted away.

They gave him another room. That established his intention to stay for anyone that might be listening. Then, using the hall phone, he had called an air cab. He did not think anyone saw him. Let the school puzzle out his disappearance however they pleased.

For a moment he had caught sight of Jonti at the space port. They met in the fashion of a glancing blow. Jonti said nothing; gave no sign of recognition, but after he had passed by, there were in Biron's hand a featureless little black globe that was a personal capsule and a ticket for passage to Rhodia.

He spent a moment upon the personal capsule. It was not sealed. He read the message later in his room. It was a simple introduction with minimum wordage.

Biron's thoughts rested for a while upon Sander Jonti, as he watched Earth shrivel with time there in the view-room. He had known the man very superficially until Jonti had whirled so devastatingly into his life, first to save it and then to set it upon a new and untried course. Biron had known his name; he had nodded when they passed; had exchanged polite formalities occasionally, but that was all. He had not liked the man, had not liked his coldness, his overdressed, overmannered personality. But all that had nothing to do with affairs now.

Biron rubbed his crew cut with a restless hand and sighed. He actually found himself hungering for Jonti's presence. The man was at least master of events. He had known what to do; he had known what Biron was to do; he had made Biron do it. And now Biron was alone and feeling very young, very helpless, very friendless, and almost frightened.

Through it all, he studiously avoided thinking of his father. It would not help.

"Mr. Malaine."

The name was repeated two or three times before Biron started at the respectful touch upon his shoulder and looked up.

The robot messenger said again, "Mr. Malaine," and for five seconds Biron stared blankly, until he remembered that that was his temporary name. It had been penciled lightly upon the ticket which Jonti had given him. A stateroom had been reserved in that name.

"Yes, what is it? I am Malaine."

The messenger's voice hissed very faintly as the spool within whirled off its message. "I have been asked to inform you that your stateroom has been changed, and that your baggage has already been shifted. If you will see the purser, you will be given your new key. We trust that this will cause no inconvenience for you."

"What's all this?" Biron whirled in his seat, and several of the thinning group of passengers, still watching, looked up at the explosive sound. "What's the idea?"

Of course, it was no use arguing with a machine that had merely fulfilled its function. The messenger had bowed its metal head respectfully, its gently fixed imitation of a human smile of ingratiation unchanging, and had left.

Biron strode out of the view-room and accosted the ship's officer at the door with somewhat more energy than he had planned.

"Look here. I want to see the captain."

The officer showed no surprise. "Is it important, sir?"

"It sure as Space is. I've just had my stateroom shifted without my permission and I'd like to know the meaning of it."

Even at the time, Biron felt his anger to be out of proportion to the cause, but it represented an accumulation of resentment. He had nearly been killed; he had been forced to leave Earth like a skulking criminal; he was going he knew not where to do he knew not what; and now they were pushing him around aboard ship. It was the end.

Yet, through it all, he had the uncomfortable feeling that Jonti, in his shoes, would have acted differently, perhaps more wisely. Well, he wasn't Jonti.

The officer said, "I will call the purser."

"I want the captain," insisted Biron.

"If you wish, then." And after a short conversation through the small ship's communicator suspended from his lapel, he said urbanely, "You will be called for. Please wait."

Captain Hirm Gordell was a rather short and thickset man, who rose politely and leaned over his desk to shake hands with Biron when the latter entered.

"Mr. Malaine," he said, "I am sorry we had to trouble you."

He had a rectangular face, iron-gray hair, a short, well-kept mustache of slightly darker hue, and a clipped smile.

"So am I," said Biron. "I had a stateroom reservation to which I was entitled and I feel that not even you, sir, had the right to change it without my permission."

"Granted, Mr. Malaine. But, you understand, it was rather an emergency. A last-minute arrival, an important man, insisted on being moved to a stateroom closer the gravitational center of the ship. He had a heart condition and it was important to keep ship's gravity as low as possible for him. We had no choice."

"All right, but why pick on me as the one to be shifted."

"It had to be someone. You are traveling alone; you are a young man who we felt would have no difficulty in taking a slightly higher gravity." His eyes traveled automatically up and down Biron's six-feet-two of hard musculature. "Besides, you will find your new room rather more elaborate than your old one. You have not lost by the exchange. No indeed."

The captain stepped from behind his desk. "May I show you your new quarters personally?"

Biron found it difficult to maintain his resentment. It seemed reasonable, this whole matter, and then again, not reasonable either.

The captain was saying as they left his quarters, "May I have your company at my table for tomorrow night's dinner? Our first Jump is scheduled for that time."

Biron heard himself saying, "Thank you. I will be honored."

Yet he thought the invitation strange. Granted that the captain was merely trying to soothe him, yet surely the method was stronger than necessary.

The captain's table was a long one, taking up an entire wall of the salon. Biron found himself near the center, taking an unsuitable precedence over others. Yet there was his place card before him. The steward had been quite firm; there was no mistake.

Biron was not particularly overmodest. As son of the Rancher of Widemos, there had never been any necessity for the development of any such characteristic. And yet as Biron Malaine, he was quite an ordinary citizen, and these things ought not to happen to ordinary citizens.

For one thing, the captain had been perfectly correct about his new stateroom. It *was* more elaborate. His original room had been what his ticket called for, a single, second class, while the replacement was a double room, first. There was a bathroom adjoining, private, of course, equipped with a stall shower and an air dryer.

It was near "officer's country," and the presence of uniforms was almost overpowering. Lunch had been brought to his room on silver service. A barber made a sudden appearance just before dinner. All this was perhaps to be expected when one traveled on a luxury space liner, first class, but it was too good for Biron Malaine.

It was far too good, for by the time the barber had arrived, Biron had just returned from an afternoon walk that had taken him through the corridors in a purposely devious path. There had been crewmen in his path wherever he had turned—polite, clinging. He shook them free somehow and reached 140 D, his first room, the one he had never slept in.

He stopped to light a cigarette and, in the interval spent thus, the only passenger in sight turned a corridor. Biron touched the signal light briefly and there was no answer.

Well, the old key had not been taken from him yet. An oversight, no doubt. He placed the thin oblong sliver of metal into its orifice and the unique pattern of leaden opacity within the aluminum sheath activated the tiny phototube. The door opened and he took one step inside.

It was all he needed. He left and the door closed automatically behind him. He had learned one thing immediately. His old room was not occupied; neither by an important personage with a weak heart nor by anyone else. The bed and furnishings were too neat; no trunks, no toilet articles were in sight; the very *air* of occupancy was missing.

So the luxury they were surrounding him with served only to prevent his taking further action to get back his original room. They were bribing him to stay quietly out of the old room. Why? Was it the room they were interested in, or was it himself?

And now he sat at the captain's table with the questions unanswered and rose politely with the rest as the captain entered, strode up the steps of the dais on which the long table was set, and took his place.

Why had they moved him?

There was music in the ship, and the walls that separated the salon from the view-room had been retracted. The lights were low and tinged with orange-red. The worst of such space sickness as there might have been after the original acceleration or as the result of first exposure to the minor gravity variations between various parts of the ship had passed by now; the salon was full.

The captain leaned forward slightly and said to Biron, "Good evening, Mr. Malaine. How do you find your new room?"

"Almost too satisfactory, sir. A little rich for my way of life." He said it in a flat monotone, and it seemed to him that a faint dismay passed momentarily over the captain's face.

Over the dessert, the skin of the view-room's glass bubble slid smoothly back into its socket, and the lights dimmed to nearly nothing. Neither sun, earth, nor any planet was in view on that large, dark screen. They were facing the Milky Way, that longwise view of the Galactic Lens, and it made a luminous diagonal track among the hard, bright stars.

Automatically the tide of conversation ebbed. Chairs shifted so that all faced the stars. The dinner guests had become an audience, the music a faint whisper.

The voice over the amplifiers was clear and well balanced in the gathered quiet.

"Ladies, gentlemen! We are ready for our first Jump. Most of you, I suppose, know, at least theoretically, what a Jump is. Many of you, however—more than half, in point of fact—have never experienced one. It is to those last I would like to speak in particular.

"The Jump is exactly what the name implies. In the fabric of space-time itself, it is impossible to travel faster than the speed of light. That is a natural law, first discovered by one of the ancients, the traditional Einstein, perhaps, except that so many things are credited to him. Even at the speed of light, of course, it would take years, in resting time, to reach the stars.

"Therefore one leaves the space-time fabric to enter the little-known realm of hyperspace, where time and distance have no meaning. It is like traveling across a narrow isthmus to pass from one ocean to another, rather than remaining at sea and circling a continent to accomplish the same distance.

"Great amounts of energy are required, of course, to enter this 'space within space' as some call it, and a great deal of ingenious calculation must be made to insure re-entry into ordinary space time at the proper point. The result of the expenditure of this energy and intelligence is that immense distances can be traversed in zero time. It is only the Jump which makes interstellar travel possible.

"The Jump we are about to make will take place in about ten minutes. You will be warned. There is never more than some momentary minor discomfort; therefore, I hope all of you will remain calm. Thank you."

The ship lights went out altogether, and there were only the stars left.

It seemed a long while before a crisp announcement filled the air momentarily: "The Jump will take place in exactly one minute." And then the same voice counted the seconds backwards: "Fifty . . . forty . . . thirty . . . twenty . . . ten . . . five . . . three . . . two . . . one . . ."

It was as though there had been a momentary discontinuity in existence, a bump which joggled only the deep inside of a man's bones. In that immeasurable fraction of a second, one hundred light-years had passed, and the ship, which had been on the outskirts of the solar system, was now in the depths of interstellar space.

Someone near Biron said shakily, "Look at the stars!"

In a moment the whisper had taken life through the large room and hissed itself across the tables: "The stars! See!"

In that same immeasurable fraction of a second the star view had changed radically. The center of the great Galaxy, which stretched thirty thousand light-years from tip to tip, was closer now, and the stars had thickened in number. They spread across the black velvet vacuum in a fine powder, backdropping the occasional brightness of the nearby stars.

Biron, against his will, remembered the beginning of a poem he himself had once written at the sentimental age of nineteen, on the occasion of his first space flight; the one that had first taken him to the Earth he was now leaving. His lips moved silently:

"The stars, like dust, encircle me
In living mists of light;
And all of space I seem to see
In one vast burst of sight."

The lights went on then, and Biron's thoughts were snapped out of space as suddenly as they had entered it. He was in a space liner's salon again, with a dinner dragging to an end, and the hum of conversation rising to a prosaic level again.

He glanced at his wrist watch, half looked away, then, very slowly, brought the wrist watch into focus again. He stared at it for a long minute. It was the wrist watch he had left in his bedroom that night; it had withstood the killing radiation of the bomb, and he had collected it with the rest of his belongings the next morning. How many times had he looked at it since then? How many times had he stared at it, taken mental note of the time and no note at all of the other piece of information it shouted at him?

For the plastic wristband was *white*, not blue. *It was white!*

Slowly the events of that night, *all* of them, fell into place. Strange how one fact could shake all the confusion out of them.

He rose abruptly, murmuring, "Pardon me!" under his breath. It was a breach of etiquette to leave before the captain, but that was a matter of small importance to him then.

He hastened to his room, striding up the ramps rapidly, rather than waiting for the non-gravity elevators. He locked the door behind him and looked quickly through the bathroom and the built-in closets. He had no real hope of catching anyone. What they had had to do, they must have done hours ago.

Carefully, he went through his baggage. They had done a thorough job. With scarcely any sign to show that they had come and gone, they had carefully withdrawn his identification papers, a packet of letters from his father, and even his capsular introduction to Hinrik of Rhodia.

That was why they had moved him. It was neither the old room nor the new that they were interested in; merely the process of moving. For nearly an hour they must have legitimately—*legitimately*, by Space!—concerned themselves with his baggage, and served their own purposes thereby.

Biron sank down upon the double bed and thought furiously, but it didn't help. The trap had been perfect. *Everything* had been planned. Had it not been for the completely unpredictable chance of his leaving his wrist watch in the bedroom that night, he would not even now have realized how close-meshed the Tyranni's net through space was.

There was a soft burr as his door signal sounded.

"Come in," he said.

It was the steward, who said respectfully, "The captain wishes to know if there is anything he can do for you. You seemed ill as you left the table."

"I'm all right," he said.

How they watched him! And in that moment he knew that there was no escape, and that the ship was carrying him politely, but surely, to his death.

Four: *FREE?*

Sander Jonti met the other's eyes coldly. He said, "Gone, you say?"

Rizzett passed a hand over his ruddy face. "*Something* is gone. I don't know its identity. It might have been the document we're after, certainly. All we know about it is that it had been dated somewhere in the fifteenth to twenty-first century of Earth's primitive calendar, and that it is dangerous."

"Is there any definite reason to believe that the missing one is *the* document?"

"Only circumstantial reasoning. It was guarded closely by the Earth government."

"Discount that. An Earthman will treat any document relating to the pre-Galactic past with veneration. It's their ridiculous worship of tradition."

"But this one was stolen and yet they never announced the fact. Why do they guard an empty case?"

"I can imagine their doing that rather than finding themselves forced to admit that a holy relic has been stolen. Yet I cannot believe that young Farrill obtained it after all. I thought you had him under observation."

The other smiled. "He didn't get it."

"How do you know?"

Jonti's agent quietly exploded his land mine. "Because the document has been gone twenty years."

"What?"

"It has not been seen for twenty years."

"Then it can't be the right one. It was less than six months ago that the Rancher learned of its existence."

"Then somebody else beat him to it by nineteen and a half years."

Jonti considered. He said, "It does not matter. It cannot matter."

"Why so?"

"Because I have been here on Earth for months. Before I came, it was easy to believe that there might be information of value on the planet. But consider now. When Earth was the only inhabited planet in the Galaxy, it was a primitive place, militarily speaking. The only weapon they had ever invented worth mentioning was a crude and inefficient nuclear-reaction bomb for which they had not even developed the logical defense." He flung his arm outward in a delicate gesture to where the blue horizon gleamed its sickly radioactivity beyond the thick concrete of the room.

He went on. "All this is placed in sharp focus for me as a temporary resident here. It is ridiculous to assume that it is possible to learn anything from a society at that level of military technology. It is always very fashionable to assume that there are lost arts and lost sciences, and there are always these people who make a cult of primitivism and who make all sorts of ridiculous claims for the prehistoric civilizations on Earth."

Rizzett said, "Yet the Rancher was a wise man. He told us specifically that it was the most dangerous document he knew. You remember what he said. I can quote it. He said, 'The matter is death for the Tyranni, and death for us as well; but it would mean final life for the Galaxy.' "

"The Rancher, like all human beings, can be wrong."

"Consider, sir, that we have no idea as to the nature of the document. It could, for instance, be somebody's laboratory notes which had never been published. It might be something that could relate to a weapon the Earthmen had never recognized as a weapon; something which on the face of it might not be a weapon——"

"Nonsense. You are a military man and should know better. If there is one science into which man has probed continuously and successfully, it is that of military technology. No potential weapon would remain unrealized for ten thousand years. I think, Rizzett, we will return to Lingane."

Rizzett shrugged. He was not convinced.

Nor, a thousandfold, was Jonti. It had been stolen, and that was significant. It had been worth stealing! Anyone in the Galaxy might have it now.

Unwillingly the thought came to him that the Tyranni might have it. The Rancher had been most evasive on the matter. Even Jonti himself had not been trusted sufficiently. The Rancher had said it carried death; it could not be used without having it cut both ways. Jonti's lips clamped shut. The fool and his idiotic hintings! And now the Tyranni had him.

What if a man like Aratap were now in the possession of such a secret as this might be? Aratap! The one man, now that the Rancher was gone, who remained unpredictable; the most dangerous Tyrannian of them all.

Simok Aratap was a small man; a little bandy-legged, narrow-eyed fellow. He had the stumpy, thick-limbed appearance of the average Tyrannian, yet though he faced an exceptionally large and well-muscled specimen of the subject worlds, he was completely self-possessed. He was the confident heir (in the second generation) of those who had left their windy, infertile worlds and sparked across the emptiness to capture and enchain the rich and populous planets of the Nebular Regions.

His father had headed a squadron of small, flitting ships that had struck and vanished, then struck again, and made scrap of the lumbering titanic ships that had opposed them.

The worlds of the Nebula had fought in the old fashion, but the Tyranni had learned a new one. Where the huge, glittering vessels of the opposed navies attempted single combat, they found themselves flailing at emptiness and wasting their stores of energy. Instead, the Tyranni, abandoning power alone, stressed speed and co-operation, so that the opposed Kingdoms toppled one after the other, singly; each waiting (half joyfully at the discomfiture of its neighbors), fallaciously secure behind its steel-shipped ramparts, until its own turn came.

But those wars were fifty years earlier. Now the Nebular Regions were satrapies that required merely the acts of occupation and taxation. Previously there had been worlds to gain, Aratap thought wearily, and now there was little left to do but to contend with single men.

He looked at the young man who faced him. He was *quite* a young man. A tall fellow with very good shoulders indeed; an absorbed, intent face with the hair of his head cut ridiculously short in what was undoubtedly a collegiate affectation. In an unofficial sense, Aratap was sorry for him. He was obviously frightened.

Biron did not recognize the feeling inside him as "fright." If he had been asked to put a name to the emotion, he would have described it as "tension." All his life he had known the Tyranni to be the overlords. His father, strong and vital though he was, unquestioned on his own estate, respectfully heard on others, was quiet and almost humble in the presence of the Tyranni.

They came occasionally to Widemos on polite visits, with questions as to the annual tribute they called taxation. The Rancher of Widemos was responsible for the collection and delivery of these funds on behalf of the planet Nephelos and, perfunctorily, the Tyranni would check his books.

The Rancher himself would assist them out of their small vessels. They would sit at the head of the table at mealtimes, and they would be served first. When they spoke, all other conversation stopped instantly.

As a child, he wondered that such small, ugly men should be so carefully handled, but he learned as he grew up that they were to his father what his father was to a cow hand. He even learned to speak softly to them himself, and to address them as "Excellency."

He had learned so well that now that he faced one of the overlords, one of the Tyranni, he could feel himself shiver with tension.

The ship which he had considered his prison became officially one on the day of landing upon Rhodia. They had signaled at his door and two husky crewmen had entered and stood on either side of him. The captain, who followed, had said in a flat voice, "Biron Farrill, I take you into custody by the power vested in me as captain of this vessel, and hold you for questioning by the Commissioner of the Great King."

The Commissioner was this small Tyrannian who sat before him now, seemingly abstracted and uninterested. The "Great King" was the Khan of the Tyranni, who still lived in the legendary stone palace on the Tyrannian's home planet.

Biron looked furtively about him. He was not physically constrained in any way, but four guards in the slate blue of the Tyrannian Outer Police flanked him, two and two. They were armed. A fifth, with a major's insignia, sat beside the Commissioner's desk.

The Commissioner spoke to him for the first time. "As you may know"—his voice was high-pitched, thin—"the old Rancher of Widemos, your father, has been executed for treason."

His faded eyes were fixed on Biron's. There seemed nothing beyond mildness in them.

Biron remained stolid. It bothered him that he could do nothing.

It would have been so much more satisfying to howl at them, to flail madly at them, but that would not make his father less dead. He thought he knew the reason for this initial statement. It was intended to break him down, to make him give himself away. Well, it wouldn't.

He said evenly, "I am Biron Malaine of Earth. If you are questioning my identity, I would like to communicate with the Terrestrial Consul."

"Ah yes, but we are at a purely informal stage just now. You are Biron Malaine, you say, of Earth. And yet"—Aratap indicated the papers before him—"there are letters here which were written by Widemos to his son. There is a college registration receipt and tickets to commencement exercises made out to a Biron Farrill. They were found in your baggage."

Biron felt desperate but he did not let it show. "My baggage was searched illegally, so that I deny that those can be admitted as evidence."

"We are not in a court of law, Mr. Farrill or Malaine. How do you explain them?"

"If they were found in my baggage, they were placed there by someone else."

The Commissioner passed it by, and Biron felt amazed. His statements sounded so thin, so patently foolish. Yet the Commissioner did not remark upon them, but only tapped the black capsule with his forefinger. "And this introduction to the Director of Rhodia? Also not yours?"

"No, that is mine." Biron had planned that. The introduction did not mention his name. He said, "There is a plot to assassinate the Director——"

He stopped, appalled. It sounded so completely unconvincing when he finally put the beginning of his carefully prepared speech into actual sound. Surely the Commissioner was smiling cynically at him?

But Aratap was not. He merely sighed a little and with quick, practiced gestures removed contact lenses from his eyes and placed them carefully in a glass of saline solution that stood on the desk before him. His naked eyeballs were a little watery.

He said, "And you know of it? Even back on Earth, five hundred light-years away? Our own police here on Rhodia have not heard of it."

"The police are here. The plot is being developed on Earth."

"I see. And are you their agent? Or are you going to warn Hinrik against them?"

"The latter, of course."

"Indeed? And why do you intend to warn him?"

"For the substantial reward which I expect to get."

Aratap smiled. "That, at least, rings true and lends a certain truthful gloss to your previous statements. What are the details of the plot you speak of?"

"That is for the Director only."

A momentary hesitation, then a shrug. "Very well. The Tyranni are not interested and do not concern themselves with local politics. We will arrange an interview between yourself and the Director and that will be our contribution to his safety. My men will hold you until your baggage can be collected, and then you will be free to go. Remove him."

The last was to the armed men, who left with Biron. Aratap replaced his contact lenses, an action which removed instantly that look of vague incompetence their absence had seemed to induce.

He said to the major, who had remained, "We will keep an eye, I think, on this young Farrill."

The officer nodded shortly. "Good! For a moment I thought you might have been taken in. To me, his story was quite incoherent."

"It was. It's just that which makes him maneuverable for the while. All young fools who get their notions of interstellar intrigue from the video spy thrillers are easily handled. He *is*, of course, the son of the ex-Rancher."

And now the major hesitated. "Are you sure? It's a vague and unsatisfactory accusation we have against him."

"You mean that it might be arranged evidence after all? For what purpose?"

"It could mean that he is a decoy, sacrificed to divert our attention from a real Biron Farrill elsewhere."

"No. Improbably theatrical, that. Besides, we have a photocube."

"What? Of the boy?"

"Of the Rancher's son. Would you like to see it?"

"I certainly would."

Aratap lifted the paperweight upon his desk. It was a simple glass cube, three inches on each side, black and opaque. He said, "I meant to confront him with it if it had seemed best. It is a cute process, this one, Major. I don't know if you're acquainted with it. It's been developed recently among the inner worlds. Outwardly, it seems an ordinary photocube, but when it is turned upside down, there's an automatic molecular rearrangement which renders it totally opaque. It is a pleasant conceit."

He turned the cube right side up. The opacity shimmered for a moment, then cleared slowly like a black fog wisping and feathering before the wind. Aratap watched it calmly, hands folded across his chest.

And then it was water-clear, and a young face smiled brightly out of it, accurate and alive, trapped and solidified in mid-breath forever.

"An item," said Aratap, "in the ex-Rancher's possessions. What do you think?"

"It is the young man, without question."

"Yes." The Tyrannian official regarded the photocube thoughtfully. "You know, using this same process, I don't see why six photographs could not be taken in the same cube. It has six faces, and by resting the cube on each of them in turn, a series of new molecular orientations might be induced. Six connected photographs, flowing one into another as you turned, a static phenomenon turned dynamic and taking on new breadth and vision. Major, it would be a new art form." A mounting enthusiasm had crept into his voice.

But the silent major looked faintly scornful, and Aratap left his artistic reflections to say, abruptly, "Then you will watch Farrill?"

"Certainly."

"Watch Hinrik as well."

"*Hinrik?*"

"Of course. It is the whole purpose of freeing the boy. I want some questions answered. Why is Farrill seeing Hinrik? What is the connection between them? The dead Rancher did not play a lone hand. There was—there *must* have been—a well-organized conspiracy behind him. And we have not yet located the workings of that conspiracy."

"But surely Hinrik could not be involved. He lacks the intelligence, even if he had the courage."

"Granted. But it is just because he is half an idiot that he may serve them as a tool. If so, he represents a weakness in our scheme of things. We obviously cannot afford to neglect the possibility."

He gestured absently; the major saluted, turned on his heel, and left.

Aratap sighed, thoughtfully turned the photocube in his hand, and watched the blackness wash back like a tide of ink.

Life was simpler in his father's time. To smash a planet had a cruel grandeur about it; while this careful maneuvering of an ignorant young man was simply cruel.

And yet necessary.

Five: *UNEASY LIES THE HEAD*

The Directorship of Rhodia is not ancient, when compared with Earth, as a habitat for *Homo sapiens*. It is not ancient even when compared with the Centaurian or Sirian worlds. The planets of Arcturus, for instance, had been settled for two hundred years when the first space ships circled the Horsehead Nebula to find the nest of hundreds of oxygen-water planets behind. They clustered thickly and it was a real find, for although planets infest space, few can satisfy the chemical necessities of the human organism.

There are between one and two hundred billion radiant stars in the Galaxy. Among them are some five hundred billion planets. Of these, some have gravities more than 120 per cent that of Earth, or less than 60 per cent, and are therefore unbearable in the long run. Some are too hot, some too cold. Some have poisonous atmospheres. Planetary atmospheres consisting largely or entirely of neon, methane, ammonia, chlorine—even silicon tetrafluoride—have been recorded. Some planets lack water, one with oceans of almost pure sulphur dioxide having been described. Others lack carbon.

Any one of these failings is sufficient, so that not one world in a hundred thousand can be lived on. Yet this still leaves an estimated four million habitable worlds.

The exact number of these which are actually occupied is disputable. According to the *Galactic Almanac*, admittedly dependent on imperfect records, Rhodia was the 1098th world settled by man.

Ironically enough, Tyrann, eventually Rhodia's conqueror, was the 1099th.

The pattern of history in the Trans-Nebular Region was distressingly similar to that elsewhere during the period of development and expansion. Planet republics were set up in rapid succession, each government confined to its own world. With expanding economy, neighboring planets were colonized and integrated with the home society. Small "empires" were established and these inevitably clashed.

Hegemony over sizable regions was established by first one, then another of these governments, depending upon the fluctuations of the fortunes of war and of leadership.

Only Rhodia maintained a lengthy stability, under the able dynasty of the Hinriads. It was perhaps well on the road to establishing finally a universal Trans-Nebular Empire in a stolid century or two, when the Tyranni came and did the job in ten years.

Ironical that it should be the men of Tyrann. Until then, during the seven hundred years of its existence, Tyrann had done little better than maintain a precarious autonomy, thanks largely to the undesirability of its barren landscape, which, because of a planetary water dearth, was largely desert.

But even after the Tyranni came, the Directorship of Rhodia continued. It had even grown. The Hinriads were popular with the people, so their existence served as a means of easy control. The Tyranni did not care who got the cheers as long as they themselves received the taxes.

To be sure, the Directors were no longer the Hinriads of old. The Directorship had always been elective within the family so that the ablest might be chosen. Adoptions into the family had been encouraged for the same purpose.

But now the Tyranni could influence the elections for other reasons, and twenty years earlier, for instance, Hinrik (fifth of that name) had been chosen Director. To the Tyranni, it had seemed a useful choice.

Hinrik had been a handsome man at the time of his election, and he still made an impressive appearance when he addressed the Rhodian Council. His hair had grayed smoothly, and his thick mustache remained, startlingly enough, as black as his daughter's eyes.

At the moment he faced his daughter, and she was furious. She lacked only two inches of his height, and the Director lacked less than an inch of six feet. She was a smoldering girl, dark of hair and of eyes, and, at the moment, loweringly dark of complexion.

She said again, "I can't do it! I *won't* do it!"

Hinrik said, "But, Arta, Arta, this is unreasonable. What am I to do? What *can* I do? In my position, what choice have I?"

"If Mother were alive, *she* would find a way out." And she stamped her foot. Her full name was Artemisia, a royal name that had been borne by at least one female of the Hinriads in every generation.

"Yes, yes, no doubt. Bless my soul! what a way your mother had with her! There are times when you seem all of her and none of me. But surely, Arta, you haven't given him a chance. Have you observed his—ah—better points?"

"Which are those?"

"The ones which . . ." He gestured vaguely, thought awhile and gave it up. He approached her and would have put a consoling hand upon her shoulder, but she squirmed away from him, her scarlet gown shimmering in the air.

"I have spent an evening with him," she said bitterly, "and he tried to kiss me. It was disgusting!"

"But everyone kisses, dear. It's not as though this were your grandmother's time—of respected memory. Kisses are nothing—less than nothing. Young blood, Arta, young blood!"

"Young blood, my foot. The only time that horrible little man has had young blood in him these fifteen years has been immediately after a transfusion. He's four inches shorter than I am, father. How can I be seen in public with a pygmy?"

"He's an important man. Very important!"

"That doesn't add a single inch to his height. He is bowlegged, as they all are, and his breath smells."

"His breath smells?"

Artemisia wrinkled her nose at her father. "That's right; it smells. It has an unpleasant odor. I didn't like it and I let him know it."

Hinrik dropped his jaw wordlessly for a moment, then said in a hoarse half whisper, "You let him know it? You implied that a high official of the Royal Court of Tyrann could have an unpleasant personal characteristic?"

"He did! I have a nose, you know! So when he got too close, I just held it and pushed. A figure of man to admire, that one is. He went flat on his back, with his legs sticking up." She gestured with her fingers in illustration, but it was lost on Hinrik, who, with a moan, hunched his shoulders and put his hands over his face.

He peered miserably from between two fingers. "What will happen now? How can you act so?"

"It didn't do me any good. Do you know what he said? *Do you know what he said?* It was the last straw. It was absolutely the limit. I made up my mind then that I couldn't stand that man if he were ten feet tall."

"But—but—what did he say?"

"He said—straight out of a video, Father—he said, 'Ha! A spirited wench! I like her all the better for that!' and two servants helped him stagger to his feet. But he didn't try to breathe in my face again."

Hinrik doubled into a chair, leaned forward and regarded Artemisia earnestly. "You could go through the motions of marrying him, couldn't you? You needn't be in earnest. Why not merely, for the sake of political expediency——"

"How do you mean, not in earnest, Father? Shall I cross the fingers of my left hand while signing the contract with my right?"

Hinrik looked confused. "No, of course not. What good would that do? How would crossing fingers alter the validity of the contract? Really, Arta, I'm surprised at your stupidity."

Artemisia sighed. "What *do* you mean, then?"

"Mean by what? You see, you've disrupted things. I can't keep my mind on matters properly when you argue with me. What was I saying?"

"I was merely to pretend I was getting married, or something. Remember?"

"Oh yes. I mean, you needn't take it too seriously, you see."

"I can have lovers, I suppose."

Hinrik stiffened and frowned. "Arta! I brought you up to be a modest, self-respecting girl. So did your mother. How can you say such things? It's shameful."

"But isn't that what you mean?"

"*I* can say it. I am a man, a mature man. A girl like you ought not to repeat it."

"Well, I have repeated it and it's out in the open. I don't mind lovers. I'll probably *have* to have them if I'm forced to marry for reasons of state, but there are limits." She placed her hands upon her hips, and the capelike sleeves of her gown slithered away from her tanned and dimpled shoulders. "What will I do between lovers? He'll still be my husband and I just can't bear that particular thought."

"But he's an old man, my dear. Life with him would be short."

"Not short enough, thank you. Five minutes ago he had young blood. Remember?"

Hinrik spread his hands wide and let them drop. "Arta, the man is a *Tyrannian,* and a powerful one. He is in good odor at the Khan's court."

"The Khan might think it's a good odor. He probably would. He probably stinks himself."

Hinrik's mouth was an O of horror. Automatically, he looked over his shoulder. Then he said hoarsely, "Don't ever say anything like that again."

"I will if I feel like it. Besides, the man has had three wives already." She forestalled him. "Not the Khan, the man you want me to marry."

"But they're dead," Hinrik explained earnestly. "Arta, they're not alive. Don't think that. How can you imagine I would let my daughter marry a bigamist? We'll have him produce documents. He married them consecutively, not simultaneously, and they're dead now, entirely dead, all of them."

"It's no wonder."

"Oh, bless my soul, what shall I do?" He made a last effort at dignity. "Arta, it is the price of being a Hinriad and a Director's daughter."

"I didn't ask to be a Hinriad and a Director's daughter."

"That has nothing to do with it. It is just that the history of all the Galaxy, Arta, shows that there are occasions when reasons of state, the safety of planets, the best interests of peoples require that, uh——"

"That some poor girl prostitute herself."

"Oh, this vulgarity! Someday, you'll see—someday you'll say something of the sort in public."

"Well, that's what it is, and I won't do it. I'd rather die. I'd rather do *anything*. And I will."

The Director got to his feet and held out his arms to her. His lips trembled and he said nothing. She ran to him in a sudden agony of tears and clung desperately to him. "I can't, Daddy. I can't. Don't make me."

He patted her awkwardly. "But if you don't, what will happen? If the Tyranni are displeased, they will remove me, imprison me, maybe even exec——" He gagged on the word. "These are very unhappy times, Arta—very unhappy. The Rancher of Widemos was condemned last week and I believe he has been executed. You remember him, Arta? He was at court half a year ago. A big man, with a round head and deep-set eyes. You were frightened of him at first."

"I remember."

"Well, he is probably dead. And who knows? Myself next, perhaps. Your poor, harmless old father next. It is a bad time. He was at our court and that's very suspicious."

She suddenly held herself out at arm's length. "Why should it be suspicious? You weren't involved with him, were you?"

"I? Indeed not. But if we openly insult the Khan of Tyrann by refusing an alliance with one of his favorites, they may choose to think even that."

Hinrik's hand wringing was interrupted by the muted buzz of the extension. He started uneasily.

"I'll take it in my own room. You just rest. You'll feel better after a nap. You'll see, you'll see. It's just that you're a little on edge now."

Artemisia looked after him and frowned. Her face was intensely thoughtful, and for minutes only the gentle tide of her breasts betrayed life.

There was the sound of stumbling feet at the door, and she turned.

"What is it?" The tone was sharper than she had intended.

It was Hinrik, his face sallow with fear. "Major Andros was calling."

"Of the Outer Police?"

Hinrik could only nod.

Artemisia cried, "Surely, he's not——" She paused reluctantly at the threshold of putting the horrible thought into words, but waited in vain for enlightenment.

"There is a young man who wants an audience. I don't know him. Why should he come here? He's from Earth." He was gasping for breath and staggered as he spoke, as though his mind were on a turntable and he had to follow it in its gyrations.

The girl ran to him and seized his elbow. She said sharply, "Sit down, Father. Tell me what has happened." She shook him and some of the panic drained out of his face.

"I don't know exactly," he whispered. "There's a young man coming here with details concerning a plot on my life. On *my* life! And *they* tell me I ought to listen to him."

He smiled foolishly. "I'm loved by the people. No one would want to kill me. Would they? Would they?"

He was watching her eagerly, and relaxed when she said, "Of course no one would want to kill you."

Then he was tense again. "Do you think it might be *they*?"

"Who?"

He leaned over to whisper. "The Tyranni. The Rancher of Widemos was here yesterday, and they killed him." His voice ascended the scale. "And now they're sending someone over to kill me."

Artemisia gripped his shoulder with such force that his mind turned to the present pain.

She said, "Father! Sit quietly! Not a word! Listen to me. No one will kill you. Do you hear me? No one will kill you. It was six months ago that the Rancher was here. Do you remember? Wasn't it six months ago? Think!"

"So long?" whispered the Director. "Yes, yes, it must have been so."

"Now you stay here and rest. You're overwrought. I'll see the young man myself and then I'll bring him to you if it's safe."

"Will you, Arta? Will you? He won't hurt a woman. Surely he wouldn't hurt a woman."

She bent suddenly and kissed his cheek.

"Be careful," he murmured, and closed his eyes wearily.

Six: *THAT WEARS A CROWN*

Biron Farrill waited uneasily in one of the outer buildings on the Palace Grounds. For the first time in his life he experienced the deflating sensation of being a provincial.

Widemos Hall, where he had grown up, had been beautiful in his eyes, and now his memory endowed it with merely barbaric glitter. Its curved lines, its filigree work, its curiously wrought turrets, its elaborate "false windows"— He winced at the thought of them.

But this—this was different.

The Palace Grounds of Rhodia were no mere lump of ostentation built by the petty lords of a cattle kingdom; nor were they the childlike expression of a fading and dying world. They were the culmination, in stone, of the Hinriad dynasty.

The buildings were strong and quiet. Their lines were straight and vertical, lengthening toward the center of each structure, yet avoiding anything as effeminate as a spire effect. They held a bluntness about them, yet lifted into a climax that affected the onlooker without revealing their method of doing so at a casual glance. They were reserved, self-contained, proud.

And as each building was, so was the group as a whole, the huge Palace Central becoming a crescendo. One by one, even the few artificialities remaining in the masculine Rhodian style had dropped away. The very "false windows," so valued as decoration and so useless in a building of artificial light and ventilation, were done away with. And that, somehow, without loss.

It was only line and plane, a geometrical abstraction that led the eye upward to the sky.

The Tyrannian major stopped briefly at his side as he left the inner room.

"You will be received now," he said.

Biron nodded, and after a while a larger man in a uniform of scarlet and tan clicked heels before him. It struck Biron with sudden force that those who had the real power did not need the outward show and could be satisfied with slate blue. He recalled the splendid formality of a Rancher's life and bit his lip at the thought of its futility.

"Biron Malaine?" asked the Rhodian guard, and Biron rose to follow.

There was a little gleaming monorail carriage that was suspended delicately by diamagnetic forces upon a single ruddy shaft of metal. Biron had never seen one before. He paused before entering.

The little carriage, big enough for five or six at the most, swayed with the wind, a graceful teardrop returning the gleam of Rhodia's splendid sun. The single rail was slender, scarcely more than a cable, and ran the length of the carriage's underside without touching. Biron bent and saw blue sky all the length between them. For a moment, as he watched, a lifting gust of wind raised it, so that it hovered a full inch above the rail, as though impatient for flight and tearing at the invisible force field that held it. Then it fluttered back to the rail, closer and still closer, but never touching.

"Get in," said the guard behind him impatiently, and Biron climbed two steps into the carriage.

The steps remained long enough for the guard to follow, then lifted quietly and smoothly into place, forming no break in the carriage's even exterior.

Biron became aware that the outer opacity of the carriage was an illusion. Once within, he found himself sitting in a transparent bubble. At the motion of a small control, the carriage lifted upward. It climbed the heights easily, buffeting the atmosphere which whistled past. For one moment Biron caught the panorama of the Palace Grounds from the apex of the arc.

The structures became a gorgeous whole (could they have been originally conceived other than as an air view?), laced by the shining copper threads, along one or two of which the graceful carriage bubbles skimmed.

He felt himself pressed forward, and the carriage came to a dancing halt. The entire run had lasted less than two minutes.

A door stood open before him. He entered and it closed behind him. There was no one in the room, which was small and bare. For the moment, no one was pushing him, but he felt no comfort because of it. He was under no illusions. Ever since that damned night, others had forced his moves.

Jonti had placed him on the ship. The Tyrannian Commissioner had placed him here. And each move had increased the measure of his desperation.

It was obvious to Biron that the Tyrannian had not been fooled. It had been too easy to get away from him. The Commissioner might have called the Terrestrial Consul. He might have hyper-waved Earth, or taken his retinal patterns. These things were routine; they could not have been omitted accidentally.

He remembered Jonti's analysis of affairs. Some of it might still be valid. The Tyranni would not kill him outright to create another martyr. But Hinrik was their puppet, and he was as capable as they of ordering an execution. And then he would have been killed by one of his own, and the Tyranni would merely be disdainful onlookers.

Biron clenched his fists tightly. He was tall and strong, but he was unarmed. The men who would come for him would have blasters and neuronic whips. He found himself backing against the wall.

He whirled quickly at the small sound of the opening door to his left. The man who entered was armed and uniformed but there was a girl with him. He relaxed a bit. It was only a girl with him. At another time he might have observed the girl closely, since she was worth observation and approval, but at the moment she was only a girl.

They approached together, stopping some six feet away. He kept his eye on the guard's blaster.

The girl said to the guard, "I'll speak to him first, Lieutenant."

There was a little vertical line between her eyes as she turned to him. She said, "Are you the man who has this story of an assassination plot against the Director?"

Biron said, "I was told I would see the Director."

"That is impossible. If you have anything to say, say it to me. If your information is truthful and useful, you will be well treated."

"May I ask you who you are? How do I know you are authorized to speak for the Director?"

The girl seemed annoyed. "I am his daughter. Please answer my questions. Are you from outside the System?"

"I am from Earth." Biron paused, then added, "Your Grace."

The addition pleased her. "Where is that?"

"It is a small planet of the Sirian Sector, Your Grace."

"And what is your name?"

"Biron Malaine, Your Grace."

She stared at him thoughtfully. "From Earth? Can you pilot a space ship?"

Biron almost smiled. She was testing him. She knew very well that space navigation was one of the forbidden sciences in the Tyranni-controlled worlds.

He said, "Yes, Your Grace." He could prove that when the performance test came, *if* they let him live that long. Space navigation was not a forbidden science on Earth, and in four years one could learn much.

She said, "Very well. And your story?"

He made his decision suddenly. To the guard alone, he would not have dared. But this was a girl, and if she were not lying, if she really *were* the Director's daughter, she might be a persuasive factor on his behalf.

He said, "There is no assassination plot, Your Grace."

The girl was startled. She turned impatiently to her companion. "Would you take over, Lieutenant? Get the truth out of him."

Biron took a step forward and met the cold thrust of the guard's blaster. He said urgently, "Wait, Your Grace. Listen to me! It was the only way to see the Director. Don't you understand?"

He raised his voice and sent it after her retreating form. "Will you tell His Excellency, at least, that I am Biron Farrill and claim my Sanctuary Right?"

It was a feeble straw at which to clutch. The old feudal customs had been losing their force with the generations even before the Tyranni came. Now they were archaisms. But there was nothing else. Nothing.

She turned, and her eyebrows were arched. "Are you claiming now to be of the aristocratic order? A moment ago your name was Malaine."

A new voice sounded unexpectedly. "So it was, but it is the second name which is correct. You are Biron Farrill indeed, my good sir. Of course you are. The resemblance is unmistakable."

A small, smiling man stood in the doorway. His eyes, widely spaced and brilliant, were taking in all of Biron with an amused sharpness. He cocked his narrow face upward at Biron's height and said to the girl, "Don't you recognize him, too, Artemisia?"

Artemisia hurried to him, her voice troubled. "Uncle Gil, what are you doing here?"

"Taking care of my interests, Artemisia. Remember that if there were an assassination, I would be the closest of the Hinriads to the possible succession." Gillbret oth Hinriad winked elaborately, then added, "Oh, get the lieutenant out of here. There isn't any danger."

She ignored that and said, "Have you been sounding the communicator again?"

"But yes. Would you deprive me of an amusement? It is pleasant to eavesdrop on them."

"Not if they catch you."

"The danger is part of the game, my dear. The amusing part. After all, the Tyranni do not hesitate to sound the Palace. We can't do much without *their* knowing. Well, turnabout, you know. Aren't you going to introduce me?"

"No, I'm not," she said shortly. "This is none of your business."

"Then I'll introduce you. When I heard his name, I stopped listening and came in." He moved past Artemisia, stepped up to Biron, inspected him with an impersonal smile, and said, "This is Biron Farrill."

"I have said so myself," said Biron. More than half his attention was upon the lieutenant, who still held his blaster in firing position.

"But you have not added that you are the son of the Rancher of Widemos."

"I would have but for your interruption. In any case, you've got the story now. Obviously, I had to get away from the Tyranni, and that without giving them my real name." Biron waited. This was it, he felt. If the next move was not an immediate arrest, there was still a trifling chance.

Artemisia said, "I see. This *is* a matter for the Director. You are sure there is no plot of any sort, then."

"None, Your Grace."

"Good. Uncle Gil, will you remain with Mr. Farrill? Lieutenant, will you come with me?"

Biron felt weak. He would have liked to sit down, but no suggestion to that effect was made by Gillbret, who still inspected him with an almost clinical interest.

"The Rancher's son! Amusing!"

Biron brought his attention downward. He was tired of cautious monosyllables and careful phrases. He said abruptly, "Yes, the Rancher's son. It is a congenital situation. Can I help you in any other way?"

Gillbret showed no offense. His thin face merely creased further as his smile widened. He said, "You might satisfy my curiosity. You really came for Sanctuary? Here?"

"I'd rather discuss that with the Director, sir."

"Oh, get off it, young man. You'll find that very little business can be done with the Director. Why do you suppose you had to deal with his daughter just now? That's an amusing thought, if you'll consider it."

"Do you find everything amusing?"

"Why not? As an attitude toward life, it's an amusing one. It's the only adjective that will fit. Observe the universe, young man. If you can't force amusement out of it, you might as well cut your throat, since there's damned little good in it. I haven't introduced myself, by the way. I'm the Director's cousin."

Biron said coldly, "Congratulations!"

Gillbret shrugged. "You're right. It's not impressive. And I'm likely to remain just that indefinitely since there is no assassination to be expected, after all."

"Unless you whip one up for yourself."

"My dear sir, your sense of humor! You'll have to get used to the fact that nobody takes *me* seriously. My remark was only an expression of cynicism. You don't suppose the Directorship is worth anything these days, do you? Surely you cannot believe that Hinrik was always like this? He was never a great brain, but with every year he becomes more impossible. I forget! You haven't seen him yet. But you will! I hear him coming. When he speaks to you, remember that he is the ruler of the largest of the Trans-Nebular Kingdoms. It will be an amusing thought."

Hinrik bore his dignity with the ease of experience. He acknowledged Biron's painstakingly ceremonious bow with the proper degree of condescension. He said, with a trace of abruptness, "And your business with us, sir?"

Artemisia was standing at her father's side, and Biron noticed, with some surprise, that she was quite pretty. He said, "Your Excellency, I have come on behalf of my father's good name. You must know his execution was unjust."

Hinrik looked away. "I knew your father slightly. He was in Rhodia once or twice." He paused, and his voice quavered a bit. "You are very like him. Very. But he was tried, you know. At least I imagine he was. And according to law. Really, I don't know the details."

"Exactly, Your Excellency. But I would like to learn those details. I am sure that my father was no traitor."

Hinrik broke in hurriedly. "As his son, of course, it is understandable that you should defend your father, but, really, it is difficult to discuss such matters of state now. Highly irregular, in fact. Why don't you see Aratap?"

"I do not know him, Excellency."

"Aratap! The Commissioner! The Tyrannian Commissioner!"

"I have seen him and he sent me here. Surely, you understand that I dare not let the Tyranni——"

But Hinrik had grown stiff. His hand had wandered to his lips, as though to keep them from trembling, and his words were consequently muffled. "Aratap sent you here, you say?"

"I found it necessary to tell him——"

"Don't repeat what you told him. I know," said Hinrik. "I can do nothing for you, Rancher—uh—Mr. Farrill. It is not in my jurisdiction alone. The Executive Council—stop pulling at me, Arta. How can I pay attention to matters when you distract me?—must be consulted. Gillbret! Will you see that Mr. Farrill is taken care of? I will see what can be done. Yes, I will consult the Executive Council. The forms of law, you know. Very important. Very important."

He turned on his heel, mumbling.

Artemisia lingered for a moment and touched Biron's sleeve. "A moment. Was it true, your statement that you could pilot a space ship?"

"Quite true," said Biron. He smiled at her, and after a moment's hesitation, she dimpled briefly in return.

"Gillbret," she said, "I want to speak to you later."

She hurried off. Biron looked after her till Gillbret tweaked at his sleeve.

"I presume you are hungry, perhaps thirsty, would like a wash?" asked Gillbret. "The ordinary amenities of life continue, I take it?"

"Thank you, yes," said Biron. The tension had almost entirely washed out of him. For a moment he was relaxed and felt wonderful. She *was* pretty. *Very* pretty.

But Hinrik was not relaxed. In his own chambers his thoughts whirled at a feverish pace. Try as he might, he could not wriggle out of the inevitable conclusion. It was a trap! Aratap had sent him and it was a trap!

He buried his head in his hands to quiet and deaden the pounding, and then he knew what he *had* to do.

Seven: *MUSICIAN OF THE MIND*

Night settles in time on all habitable planets. Not always, perhaps, at respectable intervals, since recorded periods of rotation vary from fifteen to fifty-two hours. That fact requires the most strenuous psychological adjustment from those traveling from planet to planet.

On many planets such adjustments are made, and the waking-sleeping periods are tailored to fit. On many more the almost universal use of conditioned atmospheres and artificial lighting make the day-night question secondary except in so far as it modifies agriculture. On a few planets (those of the extremes) arbitrary divisions are made which ignore the trivial facts of light and dark.

But always, whatever the social conventions, the coming of night has a deep and abiding psychological significance, dating back to man's prehuman arboreal existence. Night will always be a time of fear and insecurity, and the heart will sink with the sun.

Inside Palace Central there was no sensory mechanism by which one could tell the coming of night, yet Biron felt that coming through some indefinite instinct hidden in the unknown corridors of the human brain. He knew that outdoors the night's blackness was scarcely relieved by the futile sparks of the stars. He knew that, if it were the right time of year, the jagged "hole in space" known as the Horsehead Nebula (so familiar to all the Trans-Nebular Kingdoms) inked out half the stars that might otherwise have been visible.

And he was depressed again.

He had not seen Artemisia since the little talk with the Director, and he found himself resenting that. He had looked forward to dinner; he might have spoken to her. Instead, he had eaten alone, with two guards lounging discontentedly just outside the door. Even Gillbret had left him, presumably to eat a less lonely meal in the company one would expect in a palace of the Hinriads.

So that when Gillbret returned and said, "Artemisia and I have been discussing you," he obtained a prompt and interested reaction.

It merely amused him and he said so. "First I want to show you my laboratory," he had said then. He gestured and the two guards moved off.

"What kind of a laboratory?" asked Biron with a definite loss of interest.

"I build gadgets," was the vague response.

It was not a laboratory to the eye. It was more nearly a library, with an ornate desk in the corner.

Biron looked it over slowly. "And you build gadgets here? What kind of gadgets?"

"Well, special sounding devices to spy out the Tyrannian spy beams in a brand-new way. Nothing *they* can detect. That's how I found out about you, when the first word came through from Aratap. And I have other amusing trinkets. My visisonor, for instance. Do you like music?"

"Some kinds."

"Good. I invented an instrument, only I don't know if you can properly call it music." A shelf of book films slid out and aside at a touch. "This is not really much of a hiding place, but nobody takes *me* seriously, so they don't look. Amusing, don't you think? But I forget, you're the unamused one."

It was a clumsy, boxlike affair, with that singular lack of gloss and polish that marks the homemade object. One side of it was studded with little gleaming knobs. He put it down with that side upward.

"It isn't pretty," Gillbret said, "but who in Time cares? Put the lights out. No, no! No switches or contacts. Just wish the lights were out. Wish hard! Decide you want them out."

And the lights dimmed, with the exception of the faint pearly luster of the ceiling that made them two ghostly faces in the dark. Gillbret laughed lightly at Biron's exclamation.

"Just one of the tricks of my visisonor. It's keyed to the mind like personal capsules are. Do you know what I mean?"

"No, I don't, if you want a plain answer."

"Well," he said, "look at it this way. The electric field of your brain cells sets up an induced one in the instrument. Mathematically, it's fairly simple, but as far as I know, no one has ever jammed all the necessary circuits into a box this size before. Usually, it takes a five-story generating plant to do it. It works the other way too. I can close circuits here and impress them directly upon your brain, so that you'll see and hear without any intervention of eyes and ears. Watch!"

There was nothing to watch, at first. And then something fuzzy scratched faintly at the corner of Biron's eyes. It became a faint blue-violet ball hovering in mid-air. It followed him as he turned away, remained unchanged when he closed his eyes. And a clear, musical tone accompanied it, was part of it, *was* it.

It was growing and expanding and Biron became disturbingly aware that it existed inside his skull. It wasn't really a color, but rather a colored sound, though without noise. It was tactile, yet without feeling.

It spun and took on an iridescence while the musical tone rose in pitch till it hovered above him like falling silk. Then it exploded so that gouts of color splattered at him in touches that burned momentarily and left no pain.

Bubbles of rain-drenched green rose again with a quiet, soft moaning. Biron thrust at them in confusion and became aware that he could not see his hands nor feel them move. There was nothing, only the little bubbles filling his mind to the exclusion of all else.

He cried out soundlessly and the fantasy ceased. Gillbret was standing before him once again in a lighted room, laughing. Biron felt an acute dizziness and wiped shakily at a chilled, moist forehead. He sat down abruptly.

"What happened?" he demanded, in as stiff a tone as he could manage.

Gillbret said, "I don't know. I stayed out of it. You don't understand? It was something your brain had lacked previous experience with. Your brain was sensing directly and it had no method of interpretation for such a phenomenon. So as long as you concentrated on the sensation, your brain could only attempt, futilely, to force the effect into the old, familiar pathways. It attempts separately and simultaneously to interpret it as sight and sound and touch. Were you conscious of an odor, by the way? Sometimes it seemed to me that I smelled the stuff. With dogs I imagine the sensation would be forced almost entirely into odor. I'd like to try it on animals someday.

"On the other hand, if you ignore it, make no attack upon it, it fades away. It's what I do, when I want to observe its effects on others, and it isn't difficult."

He placed a little veined hand upon the instrument, fingering the knobs aimlessly. "Sometimes I think that if one could really study this thing, one could compose symphonies in a new medium; do things one could never do with simple sound or sight. I lack the capacity for it, I'm afraid."

Biron said abruptly, "I'd like to ask you a question."

"By all means."

"Why don't you put your scientific ability to worth-while use instead of——"

"Wasting it on useless toys? I don't know. It may not be entirely useless. This is against the law, you know."

"What is?"

"The visisonor. Also my spy devices. If the Tyranni knew, it could easily mean a death sentence."

"Surely, you're joking."

"Not at all. It is obvious that you were brought up on a cattle ranch. The young people cannot remember what it was like in the old days, I see." Suddenly his head was to one side and his eyes were narrowed to slits. He asked, "Are you opposed to Tyrannian rule? Speak freely. I tell you frankly that *I* am. I tell you also that your father was."

Biron said calmly, "Yes, I am."

"Why?"

"They are strangers, outlanders. What right have they to rule in Nephelos or in Rhodia?"

"Have you always thought that?"

Biron did not answer.

Gillbret sniffed. "In other words, you decided they were strangers and outlanders only after they executed your father, which, after all, was their simple right. Oh, look, don't fire up. Consider it reasonably. Believe me, I'm on your side. But think! Your father was Rancher. What rights did his herdsmen have? If one of them had stolen cattle for his own use or to sell to others, what would have been his punishment? Imprisonment as a thief. If he had plotted the death of your father, for whatever reason, for perhaps a worthy reason in his own eyes, what would have been the result? Execution, undoubtedly. And what right has your father to make laws and visit punishment upon his fellow human beings? *He* was *their* Tyranni.

"Your father, in his own eyes and in mine, was a patriot. But what of that? To the Tyranni, he was a traitor, and they removed him.

Can you ignore the necessity of self-defense? The Hinriads have been a bloody lot in their time. Read your history, young man. All governments kill as part of the nature of things.

"So find a better reason to hate the Tyranni. Don't think it is enough to replace one set of rulers by another; that the simple change brings freedom."

Biron pounded a fist into his cupped palm. "All this objective philosophy is fine. It is very soothing to the man who lives apart. But what if it had been your father who was murdered?"

"Well, wasn't it? My father was Director before Hinrik, and he was killed. Oh, not outright, but subtly. They broke his spirit, as they are breaking Hinrik's now. They wouldn't have *me* as Director when my father died; I was just a little too unpredictable. Hinrik was tall, handsome, and, above all, pliant. Yet not pliant enough, apparently. They hound him continuously, grind him into a pitiful puppet, make sure he cannot even itch without permission. You've seen him. He's deteriorating by the month now. His continual state of fear is pathetically psychopathic. But that—all that—is not why I want to destroy Tyrannian rule."

"No?" said Biron. "You have invented an entirely new reason?"

"An entirely old one, rather. The Tyranni are destroying the right of twenty billion human beings to take part in the development of the race. You've been to school. You've learned the economic cycle. A new planet is settled"—he was ticking the points off on his fingers—"and its first care is to feed itself. It becomes an agricultural world, a herding world. It begins to dig in the ground for crude ore to export, and sends its agricultural surplus abroad to buy luxuries and machinery. That is the second step. Then, as population increases and foreign investments grow, an industrial civilization begins to bud, which is the third step. Eventually, the world becomes mechanized, importing food, exporting machinery, investing in the development of more primitive worlds, and so on. The fourth step.

"Always the mechanized worlds are the most thickly populated, the most powerful, militarily—since war is a function of machines—and they are usually surrounded by a fringe of agricultural, dependent worlds.

"But what has happened to us? We were at the third step, with a growing industry. And now? That growth has been stopped, frozen, forced to recede. It would interfere with Tyrannian control of our industrial necessities. It is a short-term investment on their part, because eventually we'll become unprofitable as we become impoverished. But meanwhile, they skim the cream.

"Besides, if we industrialized ourselves, we might develop weapons of war. So industrialization is stopped; scientific research is forbidden. And eventually the people become so used to that, they lack the realization even that anything is missing. So that you are surprised when I tell you that I could be executed for building a visisonor.

"Of course, someday we will beat the Tyranni. It is fairly inevitable. They can't rule forever. No one can. They'll grow soft and lazy. They will intermarry and lose much of their separate traditions. They will become corrupt. But it may take centuries, because history doesn't hurry. And when those centuries have passed, we will still all be agricultural worlds with no industrial or scientific heritage to speak of, while our neighbors on all sides, those not under Tyrannian control, will be strong and urbanized. The Kingdoms will be semicolonial areas forever. They will *never* catch up, and we will be merely observers in the great drama of human advance."

Biron said, "What you say is not completely unfamiliar."

"Naturally, if you were educated on Earth. Earth occupies a very peculiar position in social development."

"Indeed?"

"Consider! All the Galaxy has been in a continuous state of expansion since the first discovery of interstellar travel. We have always been a growing society, therefore, an immature society. It is obvious that human society reached maturity in only one place and at only one time and that this was on Earth immediately prior to its catastrophe. There we had a society which had temporarily lost all possibility for geographical expansion and was therefore faced with such problems as overpopulation, depletion of resources, and so on; problems that have never faced any other portion of the Galaxy.

"They were *forced* to study the social sciences intensively. We have lost much or all of that and it is a pity. Now here's an amusing thing. When Hinrik was a young man, he was a great Primitivist. He had a library on things Earthly that was unparalleled in the Galaxy. Since he became Director, that's gone by the board along with everything else. But in a way, I've inherited it. Their literature, such scraps as survive, is fascinating. It has a peculiarly introspective flavor to it that we don't have in our extraverted Galactic civilization. It is *most* amusing."

Biron said, "You relieve me. You have been serious for so long that I began to wonder if you had lost your sense of humor."

Gillbret shrugged. "I am relaxing and it is wonderful. First time in months, I think. Do you know what it is to play a part? To split your personality deliberately for twenty-four hours a day? Even when with friends? Even when alone, so that you will never forget inadvertently? To be a dilettante? To be eternally amused? To be of no account? To be so effete and faintly ridiculous that you have convinced all who know you of your own worthlessness? All so that your life may be safe even though it means it has become barely worth living. But, even so, once in a while I can fight them."

He looked up, and his voice was earnest, almost pleading. "You can pilot a ship. I cannot. Isn't that strange? You talk about my scientific ability, yet I cannot pilot a simple one-man space gig. But you can, and it follows then that you must leave Rhodia."

There was no mistaking the pleading, but Biron frowned coldly. "Why?"

Gillbret continued, speaking rapidly: "As I said, Artemisia and I have discussed you and arranged this. When you leave here, proceed directly to her room, where she is waiting for you. I have drawn a diagram for you, so that you won't have to ask your way through the corridors." He was forcing a small sheet of metallene upon Biron. "If anyone does stop you, say that you have been summoned by the Director, and proceed. There will be no trouble if you show no uncertainty——"

"Hold on!" said Biron. He was not going to do it again. Jonti had chevied him to Rhodia and, consequently, succeeded in bringing him before the Tyranni. The Tyrannian Commissioner had then chevied him to Palace Central before he could feel his own secret way there and, consequently, subjected him, nakedly unprepared, to the whims of an unsteady puppet. But that was all! His moves, henceforward, might be severely limited, but, by Space and Time, they would be his own. He felt very stubborn about it.

He said, "I'm here on what is important business to me, sir. I'm not leaving."

"What! Don't be a young idiot." For a moment the old Gillbret was showing through. "Do you think you will accomplish anything here? Do you think you will get out of the Palace alive if you let the morning sun rise? Why, Hinrik will call in the Tyranni and you will be imprisoned within twenty-four hours. He is only waiting this while because it takes him so long to make up his mind to do anything. He is my cousin. I know him, I tell you."

Biron said, "And if so, what is that to you? Why should you be so concerned about me?" He was *not* going to be chevied. He would never again be another man's fleeing marionette.

But Gillbret was standing, staring at him. "I want you to take me with you. I'm concerned about myself. I cannot endure life under the Tyranni any longer. It is only that neither Artemisia nor I can handle a ship or we would have left long ago. It's our lives too."

Biron felt a certain weakening of his resolve. "The Director's daughter? What has she to do with this?"

"I believe that she is the most desperate of us. There is a special death for women. What should be ahead of a Director's daughter who is young, personable, and unmarried, but to become young, personable, and married? And who, in these days, should be the delightful groom? Why, an old, lecherous Tyrannian court functionary who has buried three wives and wishes to revive the fires of his youth in the arms of a girl."

"Surely the Director would never allow such a thing!"

"The Director will allow anything. Nobody waits upon his permission."

Biron thought of Artemisia as he had last seen her. Her hair had been combed back from her forehead and allowed to fall in simple straightness, with a single inward wave at shoulder level. Clear, fair skin, black eyes, red lips! Tall, young, smiling! Probably the description of a hundred million girls throughout the Galaxy. It would be ridiculous to let that sway him.

Yet he said, "Is there a ship ready?"

Gillbret's face wrinkled under the impact of a sudden smile. But, before he could say a word, there came a pounding at the door. It was no gentle interruption of the photobeam, no tender little sound of knuckles on plastic. It was the clang of metal, the overpowering thunder of the weapon of authority.

It was repeated, and Gillbret said, "You'd better open the door."

Biron did so, and two uniforms were in the room. The foremost saluted Gillbret with abrupt efficiency, then turned to Biron: "Biron

Farrill, in the name of the Resident Commissioner of Tyrann and of the Director of Rhodia, I place you under arrest."

"On what charge?" demanded Biron.

"On that of high treason."

A look of infinite loss twisted Gillbret's face momentarily. He looked away. "Hinrik was quick this once; quicker than I had ever expected. An amusing thought!"

He was the old Gillbret, smiling and indifferent, eyebrows a little raised, as though inspecting a distasteful fact with a faint tinge of regret.

"Please follow me," said the guard, and Biron was aware of the neuronic whip resting easily in the other's hand.

Eight: *A LADY'S SKIRTS*

Biron's throat was growing dry. He could have beaten either of the guards in fair fight. He knew that, and he itched for the chance. He might even have made a satisfactory showing against both together. But they had the whips, and he couldn't have lifted an arm without having them demonstrate the fact. Inside his mind he surrendered. There was no other way.

But Gillbret said, "Let him take his cloak, men."

Biron, startled, looked quickly toward the little man and retracted that same surrender. He knew he had no cloak.

The guard whose weapon was out clicked his heels as a gesture of respect. He motioned his whip at Biron. "You heard milord. Get your cloak and snap it up!"

Biron stepped back as slowly as he dared. He retreated to the bookcase and squatted, groping behind the chair for his nonexistent cloak. And as his fingers clawed at the empty space behind the chair, he waited tensely for Gillbret.

The visisonor was just a queer knobbed object to the guards. It would mean nothing to them that Gillbret fingered and stroked the knobs gently. Biron watched the muzzle of the whip intensely and allowed it to fill his mind. Certainly nothing else he saw or heard (*thought* he saw or heard) must enter.

But how much longer?

The armed guard said, "Is your cloak behind that chair? Stand up!" He took an impatient step forward, and then stopped. His eyes narrowed in deep amazement and he looked sharply to his left.

That was it! Biron straightened and threw himself forward and down. He clasped the guard's knees and jerked. The guard was down with a jarring thud, and Biron's large fist closed over the other's hand, grasping for the neuronic whip it contained.

The other guard had his weapon out, but for the moment it was useless. With his free hand, he was brushing wildly at the space before his eyes.

Gillbret's high-pitched laugh sounded. "Anything bothering you, Farrill?"

"Don't see a thing," he grunted, and then, "except this whip I've got now."

"All right, then leave. They can't do anything to stop you. Their minds are full of sights and sounds that don't exist." Gillbret skipped out of the way of the writhing tangle of bodies.

Biron wrenched his arms free and heaved upward. He brought his arm down solidly just below the other's ribs. The guard's face twisted in agony and his body doubled convulsively. Biron rose, whip in hand.

"Careful," cried Gillbret.

But Biron did not turn quickly enough. The second guard was upon him, bearing him down again. It was a blind attack. What it was that the guard thought he was grasping, it was impossible to tell. That he knew nothing of Biron at the moment was certain. His breath rasped in Biron's ear and there was a continuous incoherent gurgle bubbling in his throat.

Biron twisted in an attempt to bring his captured weapon into play and was frighteningly aware of the blank and empty eyes that must be aware of some horror invisible to anyone else.

Biron braced his legs and shifted weight in an effort to break loose, quite uselessly. Three times he felt the guard's whip flung hard against his hip, and flinched at the contact.

And then the guard's gurgle dissolved into words. He yelled, "I'll get you all!" and the very pale, almost invisible shimmer of the ionized air in the path of the whip's energy beam made its appearance. It swept wide through the air, and the path of the beam intersected Biron's foot.

It was as though he had stepped into a bath of boiling lead. Or as if a granite block had toppled upon it. Or as if it had been crunched off by a shark. Actually, nothing had happened to it physically. It was only that the nerve endings that governed the sensation of pain had been universally and maximally stimulated. Boiling lead could have done no more.

Biron's yell tore his throat raw, and he collapsed. It did not even occur to him that the fight was over. Nothing mattered but the ballooning pain.

Yet, though Biron did not know it, the guard's grip had relaxed, and minutes later, when the young man could force his eyes open and blink away the tears, he found the guard backed against the wall, pushing feebly at nothing with both hands and giggling to himself. The first guard was still on his back, arms and legs spread-eagled now. He was conscious, but silent. His eyes were following something in an erratic path, and his body quivered a little. There was froth on his lips.

Biron forced himself to his feet. He limped badly as he made his way to the wall. He used the butt of the whip and the guard slumped. Then back to the first, who made no defense either, his eyes moving silently to the very moment of unconsciousness.

Biron sat down again, nursing his foot. He stripped shoe and stocking from it, and stared in surprise at the unbroken skin. He chafed it and grunted at the burning sensation. He looked up at Gillbret, who had put down his visisonor and was now rubbing one lean cheek with the back of his hand.

"Thank you," said Biron, "for the help of your instrument."

Gillbret shrugged. He said, "There'll be more here soon. Get to Artemisia's room. Please! Quickly!"

Biron realized the sense of that. His foot had subsided to a quiet quiver of pain, but it felt swollen and puffy. He put on a stocking and tucked the shoe under his elbow. He already had one whip, and he relieved the second guard of the other. He stuffed it precariously within his belt.

He turned at the door and asked, with a sense of crawling revulsion, "What did you make them see, sir?"

"I don't know. I can't control it. I just gave them all the power I could and the rest depended on their own complexes. Please don't stand there talking. Do you have the map to Artemisia's room?"

Biron nodded and set off down the corridor. It was quite empty. He could not walk quickly, since trying to do so made his walk a hobble.

He looked at his watch, then remembered that he had somehow never had the time to adjust it to Rhodian local chronometry. It still ran on Standard Interstellar Time as used aboard ship, where one hundred minutes made an hour and a thousand a day. So the figure 876 which gleamed pinkly on the cool metal face of the watch meant nothing now.

Still, it had to be well into the night, or into the planetary sleeping period, at any rate (supposing that the two did not coincide), as otherwise the halls would not be so empty and the bas-reliefs on the wall would not phosphoresce unwatched. He touched one idly as he passed, a coronation scene, and found it to be two-dimensional. Yet it gave the perfect illusion of standing out from the wall.

It was sufficiently unusual for him to stop momentarily in order to examine the effect. Then he remembered and hurried on.

The emptiness of the corridor struck him as another sign of the decadence of Rhodia. He had grown very conscious of all these symbols of decline now that he had become a rebel. As the center of an independent power, the Palace would always have had its sentries and its quiet wardens of the night.

He consulted Gillbret's crude map and turned to the right, moving up a wide, curving ramp. There might have been processions here once, but nothing of that would be left now.

He leaned against the proper door and touched the photosignal. The door moved ajar a bit, then opened wide.

"Come in, young man."

It was Artemisia. Biron slipped inside, and the door closed swiftly and silently. He looked at the girl and said nothing. He was gloomily conscious of the fact that his shirt was torn at the shoulder so that one sleeve flapped loosely, that his clothes were grimy and his face welted. He remembered the shoe he was still carrying, dropped it and wriggled his foot into it.

Then he said, "Mind if I sit down?"

She followed him to the chair, and stood before him, a little annoyed. "What happened? What's wrong with your foot?"

"I hurt it," he said shortly. "Are you ready to leave?"

She brightened. "You'll take us, then?"

But Biron was in no mood to be sweet about it. His foot still twinged and he cradled it. He said, "Look, get me out to a ship. I'm leaving this damn planet. If you want to come along, I'll take you."

She frowned. "You might be more pleasant about it. Were you in a fight?"

"Yes, I was. With your father's guards, who wanted to arrest me for treason. So much for my Sanctuary Right."

"Oh! I'm sorry."

"I'm sorry too. It's no wonder the Tyranni can lord it over fifty worlds with a handful of men. We help them. Men like your father would do anything to keep in power; they would forget the basic duties of a simple gentleman—— Oh, never mind!"

"I said I was sorry, Lord Rancher." She used the title with a cold pride. "Please don't set yourself up as judge of my father. You don't know all the facts."

"I'm not interested in discussing it. We'll have to leave in a hurry, before more of your father's precious guards come. Well, I don't mean to hurt your feelings. It's all right." Biron's surliness canceled out any meaning to his apology, but, damn it, he had never been hit by a neuronic whip before and it *wasn't* fun. And, by Space, they had *owed* him Sanctuary. At least that much.

Artemisia felt angry. Not at her father, of course, but at the stupid young man. He was *so* young. Practically a child, she decided, scarcely older than herself, if that.

The communicator sounded and she said sharply, "Please wait a minute and we'll go."

It was Gillbret's voice, sounding faintly. "Arta? All right at your end?"

"He's here," she whispered back.

"All right. Don't say anything. Just listen. Don't leave your room. Keep him there. There's going to be a search of the Palace, which there's no way of stopping. I'll try to think of something, but, meanwhile, *don't move*." He waited for no reply. Contact was broken.

"So that's that," said Biron. He had heard also. "Shall I stay and get you into trouble, or shall I go out and give myself up? There's no reason to expect Sanctuary anywhere on Rhodia, I suppose."

She faced him in a rage, crying in a choked whisper, "Oh, shut up, you big, ugly fool."

They glared at each other. Biron's feelings were hurt. In a way, he was trying to help her too. There was no reason for her to be insulting.

She said, "I'm sorry," and looked away.

"That's all right," he said coldly, without meaning it. "You're entitled to your opinion."

"You don't have to say the things you do about my father. You don't know what being Director is like. He's working for his people, whatever you may think."

"Oh, sure. He has to sell me to the Tyranni for the sake of the people. That makes sense."

"In a way, it does. He has to show them he's loyal. Otherwise, they might depose him and take over the direct rule of Rhodia. Would that be better?"

"If a nobleman can't find Sanctuary——"

"Oh, you think only of yourself. That's what's wrong with you."

"I don't think it's particularly selfish not to want to die. At least for nothing. I've got some fighting to do before I go. *My* father fought them." He knew he was beginning to sound melodramatic, but she affected him that way.

She said, "And what good did it do your father?"

"None, I suppose. He was killed."

Artemisia felt unhappy. "I keep saying I'm sorry, and this time I really mean it. I'm all upset." Then, in defense, "I'm in trouble, too, you know."

Biron remembered. "I know. All right, let's start all over." He tried to smile. His foot was feeling better anyway.

She said, in an attempt at lightness, "You're not *really* ugly."

Biron felt foolish. "Oh well——"

Then he stopped, and Artemisia's hand flew to her mouth. Abruptly, their heads turned to the door.

There was the sudden, soft sound of many ordered feet on the semi-elastic plastic mosaic that floored the corridor outside. Most passed by, but there was a faint, disciplined heel-clicking just outside the door, and the night signal purred.

Gillbret had to work quickly. First, he had to hide his visisonor. For the first time he wished he had a better hiding place. *Damn* Hinrik for making up his mind so quickly this once, for not waiting till morning. He *had* to get away; he might never have another chance.

Then he called the captain of the guard. He couldn't very well neglect a little matter of two unconscious guards and an escaped prisoner.

The captain of the guard was grim about it. He had the two unconscious men cleared out, and then faced Gillbret.

"My lord, I am not quite clear from your message exactly what happened," he said.

"Just what you see," said Gillbret. "They came to make their arrest, and the young man did not submit. He is gone, Space knows where."

"That is of little moment, my lord," said the captain. "The Palace is honored tonight with the presence of a personage, so it is well guarded despite the hour. He cannot get out and we will draw the net through the interior. But *how* did he escape? My men were armed. He was not."

"He fought like a tiger. From that chair, behind which I hid——"

"I am sorry, my lord, that you did not think to aid my men against an accused traitor."

Gillbret looked scornful. "What an amusing thought, Captain. When your men, with doubled advantage in numbers and weapons, need help from myself, it is time you recruited yourself other men."

"Very well! We will search the Palace, find him, and see if he can repeat the performance."

"I shall accompany you, Captain."

It was the captain's turn to raise his eyebrows. He said, "I would not advise it, my lord. There would be some danger."

It was the kind of remark that one did not make to a Hinriad. Gillbret knew that, but he only smiled and let the wrinkles fill his lean face. "I know that," he said, "but occasionally I find even danger amusing."

It took five minutes for the company of guards to assemble. Gillbret, alone in his room during that time, called Artemisia.

Biron and Artemisia had frozen at the purring of the little signal. It sounded a second time and then there was the cautious rap upon the door, and Gillbret's voice was heard.

"Do let me try, Captain," it said. Then, more loudly, "Artemisia!"

Biron grinned his relief and took a step forward, but the girl put a sudden hand upon his mouth. She called out, "One moment, Uncle Gil," and pointed desperately toward the wall.

Biron could only stare stupidly. The wall was quite blank. Artemisia made a face and stepped quickly past him. Her hand on the wall caused a portion of it to slide noiselessly aside, revealing a dressing room. Her lips motioned a "Get inside!" and her hands were fumbling at the ornamental pin at her right shoulder. The unclasping of that pin broke the tiny force field that held an invisible seam tightly closed down the length of the dress. She stepped out of it.

Biron turned around after stepping across what had been the wall, and its closing endured just long enough for him to see her throwing a white-furred dressing gown across her shoulders. The scarlet dress lay crumpled upon the chair.

He looked about him and wondered if they would search Artemisia's room. He would be quite helpless if a search took place. There was no way out of the dressing room but the way he had entered, and there was nothing in it that could serve as a still more confined hiding place.

Along one wall there hung a row of gowns, and the air shimmered very faintly before it. His hand passed easily through the shimmer, with only a faint tingling where it crossed his wrist, but then it was meant to repel only dust so that the space behind it could be kept aseptically clean.

He might hide behind the skirts. It was what he was doing, really. He had manhandled two guards, with Gillbret's help, to get here, but, now that he was here, he was hiding behind a lady's skirts. A lady's skirts, in fact.

Incongruously, he found himself wishing he had turned a bit sooner before the wall had closed behind him. She had quite a remarkable figure. It was ridiculous of him to have been so childishly nasty awhile back. Of course she was not to blame for the faults of her father.

And now he could only wait, staring at the blank wall; waiting for the sound of feet within the room, for the wall to pull back once more, for the muzzles facing him again, this time without a visisonor to help him.

He waited, holding a neuronic whip in each hand.

Nine: *AND AN OVERLORD'S TROUSERS*

"What's the matter?" Artemisia did not have to feign uneasiness. She spoke to Gillbret, who, with the captain of the guard, was at the door. Half a dozen uniformed men hovered discreetly in the background. Then, quickly, "Has anything happened to Father?"

"No, no," Gillbret reassured her, "nothing has happened that need concern you at all. Were you asleep?"

"Just about," she replied, "and my girls have been about their own affairs for hours. There was no one to answer but myself and you nearly frightened me to death."

She turned to the captain suddenly, with a stiffening attitude. "What is wanted of me, Captain? Quickly, please. This is not the time of day for a proper audience."

Gillbret broke in before the other could more than open his mouth. "A most amusing thing, Arta. The young man, whatsisname—you know—has dashed off, breaking two heads on his way. We're hunting him on even terms now. One platoon of soldiers to one fugitive. And here I am myself, hot on the trail, delighting our good captain with my zeal and courage."

Artemisia managed to look completely bewildered.

Under his breath the captain muttered a monosyllabic imprecation. His lips scarcely moved. He said then, "If you please, my lord, you are not quite plain, and we are delaying matters insufferably. My lady, the man who calls himself the son of the ex-Rancher of Widemos has been arrested for treason. He has managed to escape and is now at large. We must search the Palace for him, room by room."

Artemisia stepped back, frowning. "Including my room?"

"If Your Ladyship permits."

"Ah, but I do not. I would certainly know if there was a strange man in my room. And the suggestion that I might be having dealings with such a man, or any strange man, at this time of night is highly improper. Please observe due respect for my position, Captain."

It worked quite well. The captain could only bow and say, "No such implication was intended, my lady. Your pardon for annoying you at this time of night. Your statement that you have not seen the fugitive is, of course, sufficient. Under the circumstances, it was necessary to assure ourselves of your safety. He is a dangerous man."

"Surely not so dangerous that he cannot be handled by you and your company."

Gillbret's high-pitched voice interposed again. "Captain, come—come. While you exchange courtly sentiments with my niece, our man has had time to rifle the armory. I would suggest that you leave a guard at the Lady Artemisia's door, so that what remains of her sleep will not be further disturbed. Unless, my dear"—and he twinkled his fingers at Artemisia—"you would care to join us."

"I shall satisfy myself," said Artemisia coldly, "in locking my door and retiring, thank you."

"Pick a large one," cried Gillbret. "Take that one. A fine uniform our guards have, Artemisia. You can recognize a guard as far as you can see him by his uniform alone."

"My lord," said the captain impatiently, "there is no time. You delay matters."

At a gesture from him, a guard fell out of the platoon, saluted Artemisia through the closing door, then the captain. The sound of ordered footsteps fell away in both directions.

Artemisia waited, then slid the door quietly open an inch or two. The guard was there, legs apart, back rigid, right hand armed, left hand at his alarm button. He was the guard suggested by Gillbret, a tall one. As tall as Biron of Widemos, though without his breadth of shoulders.

It occurred to her, at that moment, that Biron, though young and, therefore, rather unreasonable in some of his viewpoints, was at least large and well muscled, which was convenient. It had been foolish of her to snap at him. Quite pleasant looking too.

She closed the door, and stepped toward the dressing room.

Biron tensed as the door slid away again. He held his breath and his fingers stiffened.

Artemisia stared at his whips. "Be *careful!*"

He puffed out his breath in relief and stuffed each into a pocket. They were very uncomfortable there, but he had no proper holsters. He said, "That was just in case it was somebody looking for me."

"Come out. And speak in a whisper."

She was still in her night robe, woven out of a smooth fabric with which Biron was unfamiliar, adorned with little tufts of silvery fur, and clinging to the body through some faint static attraction inherent in the material, so that neither buttons, clasps, loops, or seam fields were necessary. Nor, as a consequence, did it do more than merely faintly dim the outlines of Artemisia's figure.

Biron felt his ears reddening, and liked the sensation very much.

Artemisia waited, then made a little whirling gesture with her forefinger and said, "Do you mind?"

Biron looked up at her face. "What? Oh, I'm sorry."

He turned his back to her and remained stiffly attentive to the faint rustling of the change of outer garments. It did not occur to him to wonder why she did not use the dressing room, or why, better still, she had not changed before opening the door. There are depths in feminine psychology, which, without experience, defy analysis.

She was in black when he turned, a two-piece suit which did not reach below the knee. It had that more substantial appearance that went with clothing meant for the outdoors rather than for the ballroom.

Biron said, automatically, "Are we leaving, then?"

She shook her head. "You'll have to do your part first. You'll need other clothes yourself. Get to one side of the door, and I'll have the guard in."

"What guard?"

She smiled briefly. "They left a guard at the door, at Uncle Gil's suggestion."

The door to the corridor ran smoothly along its runners an inch or two. The guard was still there, stiffly immobile.

"Guard," she whispered. "In here, quickly."

There was no reason for a common soldier to hesitate in his obedience to the Director's daughter. He entered the widening door, with a respectful, "At your service, my l——" and then his knees buckled under the weight which came down upon his shoulders, while his words were cut off, without even an interrupting squawk, by the forearm which slammed against his larynx.

Artemisia closed the door hurriedly and watched with sensations that amounted almost to nausea. The life in the Palace of the Hinriads was mild almost to decadence, and she had never before seen a man's face congest with blood and his mouth yawn and puff futilely under the influence of asphyxia. She looked away.

Biron bared his teeth with effort as he tightened the circle of bone and muscle about the other's throat. For a minute the guard's weakening hands ripped futilely at Biron's arm, while his feet groped in aimless kicks. Biron heaved him clear of the floor without relaxing his grip.

And then the guard's hands fell to his sides, his legs hung loosely, and the convulsive and useless heavings of the chest began to subside. Biron lowered him gently to the floor. The guard sprawled out limply, as though he were a sack which had been emptied.

"Is he dead?" asked Artemisia, in a horrified whisper.

"I doubt it," said Biron. "It takes four or five minutes of it to kill a man. But he'll be out of things for a while. Do you have anything to tie him up with?"

She shook her head. For the moment, she felt quite helpless.

Biron said, "You must have some Cellite stockings. They would do fine." He had already stripped the guard of weapons and outer clothing. "And I'd like to wash up too. In fact, I have to."

It was pleasant to step through the detergent mist in Artemisia's bathroom. It left him perhaps a trifle overscented, but the open air would take care of the fragrance, he hoped. At least he was clean, and it had required merely the momentary passage through the fine, suspended droplets that shot past him forcefully in a warm air stream. No special drying chamber was required, since he stepped out dry as well as clean. They didn't have this on Widemos, or on Earth.

The guard's uniform was a bit tight, and Biron did not like the way the somewhat ugly, conical military cap fit over his brachycephalic head. He stared at his reflection with some dissatisfaction. "How do I look?"

"Quite like a soldier," she said.

He said, "You'll have to carry one of these whips. I can't handle three."

She took it between two fingers and dropped it into her bag, which was then suspended from her wide belt by another microforce, so that her hands remained free.

"We had better go now. Don't say a word if we meet anyone, but let me do the talking. Your accent isn't right, and it would be impolite to talk in my presence unless you were directly addressed, anyway. Remember! You're a common soldier."

The guard on the floor was beginning to wriggle a bit and roll his eyes. His wrists and ankles were securely tied in a clump at the small of his back with stockings that had the tensile strength of more than an equal amount of steel. His tongue worked futilely at his gag.

He had been shoved out of the way, so that it was not necessary to step over him to get to the door.

"This way," breathed Artemisia.

At the first turning there was a footstep behind them, and a light hand came down on Biron's shoulder.

Biron stepped to one side quickly and turned, one hand catching the other's arm, while his other snatched at his whip.

But it was Gillbret who said, "Easy, man!"

Biron loosened his grip.

Gillbret rubbed his arm. "I've been waiting for you, but that's no reason to break my bones. Let me stare admiringly at you, Farrill. Your clothes seem to have shrunk on you, but not bad—not bad at all. Nobody would look twice at you in that getup. It's the advantage of a uniform. It's taken for granted that a soldier's uniform holds a soldier and nothing else."

"Uncle Gil," whispered Artemisia urgently, "don't talk so much. Where are the other guards?"

"Everyone objects to a few words," he said pettishly. "The other guards are working their way up the tower. They've decided that our friend is on none of the lower levels, so they've just left some men at the main exits and at the ramps, with the general alarm system in operation as well. We can get past it."

"Won't they miss you, sir?" asked Biron.

"Me? Hah. The captain was glad to see me go, for all his toe scraping. They won't look for me, I assure you."

They were speaking in whispers, but now even those died away. A guard stood at the bottom of the ramp, while two others flanked the large, carved double door that led to the open air.

Gillbret called out, "Any word of the escaped prisoner, men?"

"No, my lord," said the nearest. He clicked his heels together and saluted.

"Well, keep your eyes open," and they walked past them and out, one of the guards at the door carefully neutralizing that section of the alarm as they left.

It was nighttime outside. The sky was clear and starry, the ragged mass of the Dark Nebula blotting out the specks of light near the horizon. Palace Central was a dark mass behind them, and the Palace Field was less than half a mile away.

But after five minutes of walking along the quiet path, Gillbret grew restless.

"There's something wrong," he said.

Artemisia said, "Uncle Gil, you haven't forgotten to arrange to have the ship ready?"

"Of course not," he snapped at her, as nearly as one could snap in a whisper, "but why is the Field Tower lit up? It should be dark."

He pointed up through the trees, to where the tower was a honeycomb of white light. Ordinarily, that would indicate business at the field: ships leaving for space or arriving from it.

Gillbret muttered, "*Nothing* was scheduled for tonight. That was definite."

They saw the answer at a distance, or Gillbret did. He stopped suddenly and spread his arms wide to hold back the others.

"That's all," he said, and giggled almost hysterically. "This time Hinrik has really messed things properly, the idiot. They're here! The Tyranni! Don't you understand? That's Aratap's private armored cruiser."

Biron saw it, gleaming faintly under the lights, standing out among the other undistinguished ships. It was smoother, thinner, more feline than the Rhodian vessels.

Gillbret said, "The captain *said* a 'personage' was being entertained today, and I paid no attention. There's nothing to do now. We can't fight Tyranni."

Biron felt something suddenly snap. "Why not?" he said savagely. "Why can't we fight them? They have no reason to suspect trouble, and we're armed. Let's take the Commissioner's own ship. Let's leave him with his trousers down."

He stepped forward, out of the relative obscurity of the trees and onto the bare field. The others followed. There was no reason to hide. They were two members of the royal family and an escorting soldier.

But it was the Tyranni they were fighting now.

Simok Aratap of Tyrann had been impressed the first time he had ever seen the Palace Grounds at Rhodia years earlier, but it had turned out to be only a shell that had impressed him. The interior was nothing but a musty relic. Two generations earlier Rhodia's legislative chambers had met on these grounds and most of the administrative offices had been quartered there. Palace Central had been the heartbeat of a dozen worlds.

But now the legislative chambers (still existing, for the Khan never interfered with local legalisms) met once a year to ratify the executive orders of the past twelve months. It was quite a formality. The Executive Council was still, nominally, in continuous session, but it consisted of a dozen men who remained on their estates nine weeks in ten. The various executive bureaus were still active, since one could not govern without them, whether the Director or the Khan ruled, but they were now scattered over the planet; made less dependent upon the Director, more conscious of their new masters, the Tyranni.

Which left the Palace as majestic as it had always been in stone and metal, and that only. It housed the Directorial family, a scarcely adequate corps of servants, and an entirely inadequate corps of native guards.

Aratap felt uncomfortable in the shell and was unhappy. It was late, he was tired, his eyes burned so that he longed to remove his contact lenses, and, most of all, he was disappointed.

There was no pattern! He glanced occasionally at his military aide, but the major was listening to the Director with expressionless stolidity. As for Aratap himself, he paid little attention.

"Widemos's son! Indeed?" he would say, in abstraction. Then, later, "And so you arrested him? Quite right!"

But it meant little to him, since events lacked a design. Aratap had a neat and tidy mind which could not bear the thought of individual facts loosely clumped together with no decent arrangement.

Widemos had been a traitor, and Widemos's son had attempted a meeting with the Director of Rhodia. He had attempted it first in secret, and when that had failed, such was the urgency, he had attempted it openly with his ridiculous story of an assassination plot. Surely that must have been the beginning of a pattern.

And now it fell apart. Hinrik was giving up the boy with indecent haste. He could not even wait the night, it seemed. And that did not fit at all. Or else Aratap had not yet learned all the facts.

He focused his attention on the Director again. Hinrik was beginning to repeat himself. Aratap felt a twinge of compassion. The man had been made into such a coward that even the Tyranni themselves grew impatient with him. And yet it was the only way. Only fear could insure absolute loyalty. That and nothing else.

Widemos had not been afraid, and despite the fact that his self-interest had been bound at every point with the maintenance of Tyrannian rule, he had rebelled. Hinrik *was* afraid and that made the difference.

And because Hinrik was afraid, he sat there, lapsing into incoherence as he struggled to obtain some gesture of approval. The major would give none, of course, Aratap knew. The man had no imagination. He sighed and wished he had none either. Politics was a filthy business.

So he said, with some air of animation, "Quite so. I commend your quick decision and your zeal in the service of the Khan. You may be sure he will hear of it."

Hinrik brightened visibly, his relief obvious.

Aratap said, "Have him brought in, then, and let us hear what our cockerel has to say." He suppressed a desire to yawn. He had absolutely no interest in what the "cockerel" had to say.

It was Hinrik's intention at this point to signal for the captain of the guard, but there was no necessity for that, as the captain stood in the doorway, unannounced.

"Excellency," he cried and strode in without waiting for permission.

Hinrik stared hard at his hand, still inches from the signal, as though wondering whether his intention had somehow developed sufficient force to substitute for the act.

He said uncertainly, "What is it, Captain?"

The captain said, "Excellency, the prisoner has escaped."

Aratap felt some of the weariness disappear. What was this? "The details, Captain!" he ordered, and straightened in his chair.

The captain gave them with a blunt economy of words. He concluded, "I ask your permission, Excellency, to proclaim a general alarm. They are yet but minutes away."

"Yes, by all means," stuttered Hinrik, "by all means. A general alarm, indeed. Just the thing. Quickly! Quickly! Commissioner, I cannot understand how it could have happened. Captain, put every man to work. There will be an investigation, Commissioner. If necessary, every man on the guards will be broken. Broken! Broken!"

He repeated the word in near hysteria but the captain remained standing. It was obvious that he had more to say.

Aratap said, "Why do you wait?"

"May I speak to Your Excellency in private?" said the captain abruptly.

Hinrik cast a quick, frightened look at the bland, unperturbed Commissioner. He mustered a feeble indignation. "There are no secrets from the soldiers of the Khan, our friends, our——"

"Say your say, Captain," interposed Aratap gently.

The captain brought his heels together sharply and said, "Since I am ordered to speak, Your Excellency, I regret to inform you that my Lady Artemisia and my Lord Gillbret accompanied the prisoner in his escape."

"He dared to kidnap them?" Hinrik was on his feet. "And my guards allowed it?"

"They were not kidnaped, Excellency. They accompanied him voluntarily."

"How do you know?" Aratap was delighted, and thoroughly awake. It formed a pattern now, after all. A better pattern than he could have anticipated.

The captain said, "We have the testimony of the guard they overpowered, and the guards who, unwittingly, allowed them to leave the building." He hesitated, then added grimly, "When I interviewed my Lady Artemisia at the door of her private chambers, she told me she had been on the point of sleep. It was only later that I realized that when she told me that, her face was elaborately made-up. When I returned, it was too late. I accept the blame for the mismanagement of this affair. After tonight I will request Your Excellency to accept my resignation, but first have I still your permission to sound the general alarm? Without your authority I could not interfere with members of the royal family."

But Hinrik was swaying on his feet and could only stare at him vacantly.

Aratap said, "Captain, you would do better to look to the health of your Director. I would suggest you call his physician."

"The general alarm!" repeated the captain.

"There will be no general alarm," said Aratap. "Do you understand me? No general alarm! No recapture of the prisoner! The incident is closed! Return your men to their quarters and ordinary duties and look to your Director. Come, Major."

The Tyrannian major spoke tensely once they had left the mass of Palace Central behind them.

"Aratap," he said, "I presume you know what you're doing. I kept my mouth shut in there on the basis of that presumption."

"Thank you, Major." Aratap liked the night air of a planet full of green and growing things. Tyrann was more beautiful in its way, but it was a terrible beauty of rocks and mountains. It was dry, dry!

He went on: "You cannot handle Hinrik, Major Andros. In your hands he would wilt and break. He is useful, but requires gentle treatment if he is to remain so."

The major brushed that aside. "I'm not referring to that. Why not the general alarm? Don't you want them?"

"Do you?" Aratap stopped. "Let us sit here for a moment, Andros. A bench on a pathway along a lawn. What more beautiful, and what place is safer from spy beams? Why do you want the young man, Major?"

"Why do I want any traitor and conspirator?"

"Why do you, indeed, if you only catch a few tools while leaving the source of the poison untouched? Whom would you have? A cub, a silly girl, a senile idiot?"

There was the faint splashing of an artificial waterfall nearby. A small one, but decorative. Now that was a real wonder to Aratap. Imagine water, spilling out, running to waste, pouring indefinitely down the rocks and along the ground. He had never educated himself out of a certain indignation over it.

"As it is," said the major, "we have nothing."

"We have a pattern. When the young man first arrived, we connected him with Hinrik, and that bothered us, because Hinrik is—what he is. But it was the best we could do. Now we see it was not Hinrik at all; that Hinrik was a misdirection. It was Hinrik's daughter and cousin he was after, and that makes more sense."

"Why didn't he call us sooner? He waited for the middle of the night."

"Because he is the tool of whoever is the first to reach him, and

Gillbret, I am sure, suggested this night meeting as a sign of great zeal on his part."

"You mean we were called here on purpose? To *witness* their escape?"

"No, not for that reason. Ask yourself. Where do these people intend going?"

The major shrugged. "Rhodia is big."

"Yes, if it were the young Farrill alone who was concerned. But where on Rhodia would two members of the royal family go unrecognized? Particularly the girl."

"They would have to leave the planet, then? Yes, I agree."

"And from where? They can reach the Palace Field in a fifteen-minute walk. Now do you see the purpose of our being here?"

The major said, "*Our ship?*"

"Of course. A Tyrannian ship would seem ideal to them. Otherwise, they would have to choose among freighters. Farrill has been educated on Earth, and, I'm sure, can fly a cruiser."

"Now there's a point. Why do we allow the nobility to send out their sons in all directions? What business has a subject to know more about travel than will suffice him for local trade? We bring up soldiers against us."

"Nevertheless," said Aratap, with polite indifference, "at the moment Farrill has a foreign education, and let us take that into account objectively, without growing angry about it. The fact remains that I am certain they have taken our cruiser."

"I can't believe it."

"You have your wrist caller. Make contact with the ship, if you can."

The major tried, futilely.

Aratap said, "Try the Field Tower."

The major did so, and the small voice came out of the tiny receiver, in minute agitation: "But, Excellency, I don't understand—— There is some mistake. Your pilot took off ten minutes ago."

Aratap was smiling. "You see? Work out the pattern and each little event becomes inevitable. And now do you see the consequences?"

The major did. He slapped his thigh, and laughed briefly. "Of course!" he said.

"Well," said Aratap, "they couldn't know, of course, but they have ruined themselves. Had they been satisfied with the clumsiest Rhodian freighter on the field, they would surely have escaped and—what's the expression?—I would have been caught with my trousers down this night. As it is, my trousers are firmly belted, and nothing can save *them*. And when I pluck them back, in my own good time" —he emphasized the words with satisfaction—"I will have the rest of the conspiracy in my hands as well."

He sighed and found himself beginning to feel sleepy once more. "Well, we have been lucky, and now there is no hurry. Call Central Base, and have them send another ship after us."

Ten: *MAYBE!*

Biron Farrill's training in spationautics back on Earth had been largely academic. There had been the university courses in the various phases of spatial engineering, which, though half a semester was spent on the theory of the hyperatomic motor, offered little when it came to the actual manipulation of ships in space. The best and most skilled pilots learned their art in space and not in schoolrooms.

He had managed to take off without actual accident, though that was more luck than design. The *Remorseless* answered the controls far more quickly than Biron had anticipated. He had manipulated several ships on Earth out into space and back to the planet, but those had been aged and sedate models, maintained for the use of students. They had been gentle, and very, very tired, and had lifted with an effort and spiraled slowly upward through the atmosphere and into space.

The *Remorseless*, on the other hand, had lifted effortlessly, springing upward and whistling through the air, so that Biron had fallen backward out of his chair and all but dislocated his shoulder. Artemisia and Gillbret, who, with the greater caution of the inexperienced, had strapped themselves in, were bruised against the padded webbing. The Tyrannian prisoner had lain pressed against the wall, tearing heavily at his bonds and cursing in a monotone.

Biron had risen shakily to his feet, kicked the Tyrannian into a brooding silence, and made his way along the wall rail, hand over hand against the acceleration, back to his seat. Forward blasts of power quivered the ship and reduced the rate of increasing velocity to a bearable quantity.

They were in the upper reaches of the Rhodian atmosphere by then. The sky was a deep violet and the hull of the ship was hot with air friction, so that warmth could be felt within.

It took hours thereafter to set the ship into an orbit about Rhodia. Biron could find no way of readily calculating the velocity necessary to overcome Rhodia's gravity. He had to work it by hit and miss, varying the velocity with puffs of power forward and backward, watching the massometer, which indicated their distance from the planet's surface by measuring the intensity of the gravitational field. Fortunately, the massometer was already calibrated for Rhodia's mass and radius. Without considerable experimentation, Biron could not have adjusted the calibration himself.

Eventually, the massometer held steady and over a period of two hours showed no appreciable drift. Biron allowed himself to relax, and the others climbed out of their belts.

Artemisia said, "You don't have a very light touch, my Lord Rancher."

"I'm flying, my lady," Biron replied curtly. "If you can do better, you're welcome to try, but only after I myself disembark."

"Quiet, quiet, quiet," said Gillbret. "The ship is too cramped for pettishness, and, in addition, since we *are* to be crushed into an inconvenient familiarity in this leaping prison pen, I suggest we discard the many 'lords' and 'ladies' which will otherwise encrust our conversation to an unbearable degree. I am Gillbret, you are Biron, she is Artemisia. I suggest we memorize those terms of address, or any variation we care to use. And as for piloting the ship, why not use the help of our Tyrannian friend here?"

The Tyrannian glared, and Biron said, "No. There is no way we could trust him. And my own piloting will improve as I get the hang of this ship. I haven't cracked you up yet, have I?"

His shoulder still hurt as a result of the first lurch and, as usual, pain made him peevish.

"Well," said Gillbret, "what *do* we do with him?"

"I don't like to kill him in cold blood," said Biron, "and that won't help us. It would just make the Tyranni doubly excited. Killing one of the master race is really the unforgivable sin."

"But what is the alternative?"

"We'll land him."

"All right. But where?"

"On Rhodia."

"What!"

"It's the one place they won't be looking for us. Besides which, we've got to go down pretty soon, anyway."

"Why?"

"Look, this is the Commissioner's ship, and he's been using it for hopping about the surface of the planet. It isn't provisioned for space voyages. Before we go anywhere, we'll have to take complete inventory aboard ship, and at least make sure that we have enough food and water."

Artemisia was nodding vigorously. "That's right. Good! I wouldn't have thought of that myself. That's very clever, Biron."

Biron made a deprecating gesture, but warmed with pleasure, nevertheless. It was the first time she had used his first name. She could be quite pleasant, when she tried.

Gillbret said, "But he'll radio our whereabouts instantly."

"I don't think so," said Biron. "In the first place, Rhodia has its desolate areas, I imagine. We don't have to drop him into the business section of a city, or into the middle of one of the Tyrannian garrisons. Besides, he may not be so anxious to contact his superiors as you might think. . . . Say, Private, what would happen to a soldier who allowed the Commissioner of the Khan to have his private cruiser stolen from him?"

The prisoner did not answer, but his lip line became pale and thin.

Biron would not have wanted to be in the soldier's place. To be sure, he could scarcely be blamed. There was no reason why he should have suspected trouble resulting from mere politeness to members of the Rhodian royal family. Sticking to the letter of the Tyrannian military code, he had refused to allow them aboard ship without the permission of his commanding officer. If the Director himself had demanded permission to enter, he insisted, he would have to deny it. But, in the meantime, they had closed in upon him, and by the time he realized he should have followed the military code still more closely and had his weapon ready, it was too late. A neuronic whip was practically touching his chest.

Nor had he given in tamely, even then. It had taken a whip blast at his chest to stop him. And, even so, he could face only court-martial and conviction. No one doubted that, least of all the soldier.

They had landed two days later at the outskirts of the city of Southwark. It had been chosen deliberately because it lay far from the main centers of Rhodian population. The Tyrannian soldier had been strapped into a repulsion unit and allowed to flutter downward some fifty miles from the nearest sizable town.

The landing, on an empty beach, was only mildly jerky, and Biron, as the one least likely to be recognized, made the necessary purchases. Such Rhodian currency as Gillbret had had the presence of mind to bring with him had scarcely sufficed for elementary needs, since much of it went for a little biwheel and tow cart, on which he could carry the supplies away piecemeal.

"You might have stretched the money farther," said Artemisia, "if you hadn't wasted so much of it on the Tyrannian mush you bought."

"I think there was nothing else to do," said Biron hotly. "It may be Tyrannian mush to you, but it's a well-balanced food, and will see us through better than anything else I could have gotten."

He was annoyed. It had been stevedore's work, getting all that out of the city and then aboard ship. And it had meant a considerable risk, buying it at one of the Tyrannian-run commissaries in the city. He had expected appreciation.

And there was no alternative anyway. The Tyrannian forces had evolved an entire technique of supply adapted strictly to the fact that they used tiny ships. They couldn't afford the huge storage spaces of other fleets which were stacked with the carcasses of whole animals, neatly hung in rows. They had had to develop a standard food concentrate containing what was necessary in the way of calories and food factors and let it go at that. It took up only one twentieth of the space that an equivalent supply of natural animal food would take, and it could be piled up in the low-temperature storeroom like packaged bricks.

"Well, it tastes awful," said Artemisia.

"Well, you'll get used to it," retorted Biron, mimicking her petulance, so that she flushed and turned away angrily.

What was bothering her, Biron knew, was simply the lack of space and all that accompanied the lack. It wasn't just a question of using a monotonous food stock because in that way more calories could be packed to the cubic inch. It was that there were no separate sleeping rooms, for instance. There were the engine rooms and the control room, which took up most of the ship's space. (After all, Biron thought, this is a warship, not a pleasure yacht.) Then there was the storeroom, and one small cabin, with two tiers of three bunks on either side. The plumbing was located in a little niche just outside the cabin.

It meant crowding; it meant a complete absence of privacy; and it meant that Artemisia would have to adjust herself to the fact that there were no women's clothes aboard, no mirrors, no washing facilities.

Well, she would have to get used to it. Biron felt that he had done enough for her, gone sufficiently out of his way. Why couldn't she be pleasant about it and smile once in a while? She had a nice smile, and he had to admit that she wasn't bad, except for her temper. But oh, that temper!

Well, why waste his time thinking about her?

The water situation was the worst. Tyrann was a desert planet, in the first place, where water was at a premium and men knew its value, so none was included on board ship for washing purposes. Soldiers could wash themselves and their personal effects once they had landed on a planet. During trips a little grime and sweat would not hurt them. Even for drinking purposes, water was barely sufficient for the longer trips. After all, water could be neither concentrated nor dehydrated, but had to be carried in bulk; and the problem was aggravated by the fact that the water content of the food concentrates was quite low.

There were distilling devices to re-use water lost by the body, but Biron, when he realized their function, felt sick and arranged for the disposal of waste products without attempt at water recovery. Chemically, it was a sensible procedure, but one has to be educated into that sort of thing.

The second take-off was, comparatively, a model of smoothness, and Biron spent time playing with the controls afterward. The control board resembled only in the dimmest fashion those of the ships he had handled on Earth. It had been compressed and compacted frightfully. As Biron puzzled out the action of a contact or the purpose of a dial, he wrote out minute directions on paper and pasted them appropriately on the board.

Gillbret entered the pilot room.

Biron looked over his shoulder. "Artemisia's in the cabin, I suppose?"

"There isn't anyplace else she could be and stay inside the ship."

Biron said, "When you see her, tell her I'll make up a bunk here in the pilot room. I'd advise you to do the same, and let her have the cabin to herself." He muttered the addition, "Now there's one childish girl."

"You have your moments, too, Biron," said Gillbret. "You'll have to remember the sort of life she's used to."

"All right. I do remember it, and so what? What sort of life do you think I'm used to? I wasn't born in the mine fields of some asteroidal belt, you know. I was born on the biggest Ranch of Nephelos. But if you're caught in a situation, you've got to make the best of it. Damn it, I can't stretch the hull of the ship. It will hold just so much food and water, and I can't do anything about the fact that there isn't any shower bath. She picks on me as if I personally manufactured this ship." It was a relief to shout at Gillbret. It was a relief to shout at anybody.

But the door opened again, and Artemisia stood there. She said, freezingly, "I would refrain, Mr. Farrill, from shouting, if I were you. You can be distinctly heard all over the ship."

"That," said Biron, "does not bother me. And if the ship bothers *you,* just remember that if your father hadn't tried to kill me off and marry you off, neither one of us would be here."

"Don't talk about my father."

"I'll talk about anyone I please."

Gillbret put his hands over his ears. "*Please!*"

It brought the argument to a momentary halt. Gillbret said, "Shall we discuss the matter of our destination now? It's obvious at this point that the sooner we're somewhere else and out of this ship, the more comfortable we'll be."

"I agree with you there, Gil," said Biron. "Just let's go somewhere where I don't have to listen to her clacking. Talk about women on space ships!"

Artemisia ignored him and addressed Gillbret exclusively. "Why don't we get out of the Nebular area altogether?"

"I don't know about you," said Biron at once, "but I've got to get my Ranch back and do a little something about my father's murder. I'll stay in the Kingdoms."

"I did not mean," said Artemisia, "that we were to leave forever; only till the worst of the search was over. I don't see what you intend doing about your Ranch, anyway. You can't get it back unless the Tyrannian Empire is broken to pieces, and I don't see you doing that."

"You never mind what I intend doing. It's my business."

"Might I make a suggestion?" asked Gillbret mildly.

He took silence for consent, and went on, "Then suppose I tell you where we ought to go, and exactly what we ought to do to help break the Empire to pieces, just as Arta said."

"Oh? How do you propose doing that?" said Biron.

Gillbret smiled. "My dear boy, you're taking a very amusing attitude. Don't you trust me? You look at me as though you think that any enterprise I might be interested in was bound to be a foolish one. I got you out of the Palace."

"I know that. I'm perfectly willing to listen to you."

"Do so, then. I've been waiting for over twenty years for my chance to get away from them. If I had been a private citizen, I could have done it long since; but through the curse of birth, I've been in the public eye. And yet if it hadn't been for the fact that I was born a Hinriad, I would not have attended the coronation of the present Khan of Tyrann, and in that case I would never have stumbled on the secret which will someday destroy that same Khan."

"Go on," said Biron.

"The trip from Rhodia to Tyrann was by Tyrannian warship, of course, as was the trip back. A ship like this, I might say, but rather larger. The trip there was uneventful. The stay on Tyrann had its points of amusement, but, for our purposes now, was likewise uneventful. On the trip back, however, a meteor hit us."

"What?"

Gillbret held up a hand. "I know quite well it's an unlikely accident. The incidence of meteors in space—especially an interstellar space—is low enough to make the chances of collision with a ship completely insignificant, but it does happen, as you know. And it did happen in this case. Of course any meteor that does hit, even when it is the size of a pinhead, as most of them are, can penetrate the hull of any but the most heavily armored ship."

"I know," said Biron. "It's a question of their momentum, which is a product of their mass and velocity. The velocity more than makes up for their lack of mass." He recited it glumly, like a school lesson, and caught himself watching Artemisia furtively.

She had seated herself to listen to Gillbret, and she was so close to him that they were almost touching. It occurred to Biron that her profile was beautiful as she sat there, even if her hair was becoming a little bedraggled. She wasn't wearing her little jacket, and the fluffy whiteness of her blouse was still smooth and unwrinkled after forty-eight hours. He wondered how she managed that.

The trip, he decided, could be quite wonderful if she would only learn to behave herself. The trouble was that no one had ever controlled her properly, that was all. Certainly not her father. She'd become too used to having her own way. If she'd been born a commoner, she would be a very lovely creature.

He was just beginning to slip into a tiny daydream in which *he* controlled her properly and brought her to a state of proper appreciation of himself, when she turned her head and met his eye calmly. Biron looked away and fastened his attention instantly on Gillbret. He had missed a few sentences.

"I haven't the slightest idea why the ship's screen had failed. It was just one of those things to which no one will ever know the answer, but it had failed. Anyway, the meteor struck amidships. It was pebble-sized and piercing the hull slowed it just sufficiently so that it couldn't blaze its way out again through the other side. If it had done that, there would have been little harm to it, since the hull could have been temporarily patched in no time.

"As it was, however, it plunged into the control room, ricocheted off the far wall and slammed back and forth till it came to a halt. It couldn't have taken more than a fraction of a minute to come to a halt, but at an original velocity of a hundred miles a minute, it must have crisscrossed the room a hundred times. Both crewmen were cut to pieces, and I escaped only because I was in the cabin at the time.

"I heard the thin clang of the meteor when it originally penetrated the hull, then the click-clack of its bouncing, and the terrifying short screams of the two crewmen. When I jumped into the control room, there was only the blood everywhere and the torn flesh.

The things that happened next I remember only vaguely, although for years I lived it over step by step in my nightmares.

"The cold sound of escaping air led me to the meteor hole. I slapped a disk of metal over it and air pressure made a decent seal of it. I found the little battered space pebble on the floor. It was warm to the touch, but I hit it with a spanner and split it in two. The exposed interior frosted over instantly. It was still at the temperature of space.

"I tied a cord to the wrist of each corpse and then tied each cord to a towing magnet. I dumped them through the air lock, heard the magnets clank against the hold, and knew that the hard-frozen bodies would follow the ship now wherever it went. You see, once we returned to Rhodia, I knew I would need the evidence of their bodies to show that it had been the meteor that had killed them and not I.

"But how was I to return? I was quite helpless. There was no way *I* could run the ship, and there was nothing I dared try there in the depths of interstellar space. I didn't even know how to use the subetheric communication system, so that I couldn't SOS. I could only let the ship travel on its own course."

"But you couldn't very well do that, could you?" Biron said. He wondered if Gillbret were inventing this, either out of simple romantic imaginings or for some severely practical reason of his own. "What about the Jumps through hyperspace? You must have managed those, or you wouldn't be here."

"A Tyrannian ship," said Gillbret, "once the controls are properly set, will make any number of Jumps quite automatically."

Biron stared his disbelief. Did Gillbret take him for a fool? "You're making that up," he said.

"I am not. It's one of the damned military advances which won their wars for them. They didn't defeat fifty planetary systems, outnumbering Tyrann by hundreds of times in population and resources, just by playing mumblety-peg, you know. Sure they tackled us one at a time, and utilized our traitors very skillfully, but they had a definite military edge as well. Everyone knows that their tactics were superior to ours, and part of that was due to the automatic Jump. It meant a great increase in the maneuverability of their ships and made possible much more elaborate battle plans than any we could set up.

"I'll admit it's one of their best-kept secrets, this technique of theirs. I never learned it until I was trapped alone on the *Bloodsucker*—the Tyranni have the most annoying custom of naming their ships unpleasantly, though I suppose it's good psychology—and watched it happen. I *watched* it make the Jumps without a hand on the controls."

"And you mean to say that this ship can do that too?"

"I don't know. I wouldn't be surprised."

Biron turned to the control board. There were still dozens of contacts he had not determined the slightest use for. Well, later!

He turned to Gillbret again. "And the ship took you home?"

"No, it didn't. When that meteor wove its pattern through the control room, it didn't leave the board untouched. It would have been most amazing if it had. Dials were smashed, the casing battered and dented. There was no way of telling how the previous set of the controls had been altered, but it must have been somehow, because it never took me back to Rhodia.

"Eventually, of course, it began deceleration, and I knew the trip was theoretically over. I couldn't tell where I was, but I managed to maneuver the visiplate so that I could tell there was a planet close enough to show a disk in the ship telescope. It was blind luck, because the disk was increasing in size. The ship was heading for the planet.

"Oh, not directly. That would have been too impossible to hope for. If I had just drifted, the ship would have missed the planet by a million miles, at least, but at that distance I could use ordinary etheric radio. I knew how to do that. It was after this was all over that I began educating myself in electronics. I made up my mind that I would never be quite so helpless again. Being helpless is one of the things that isn't altogether amusing."

Biron prompted, "So you used the radio."

Gillbret went on: "Exactly, and they came and got me."

"Who?"

"The men of the planet. It was inhabited."

"Well, the luck piles up. What planet was it?"

"I don't know."

"You mean they didn't tell you?"

"Amusing, isn't it? They didn't. But it was somewhere among the Nebular Kingdoms!"

"How did you know that?"

"Because they knew the ship I was in was a Tyrannian vessel. They knew that by sight, and almost blasted it before I could convince them I was the only one on board alive."

Biron put his large hands on his knees and kneaded them. "Now hold on and pull back. I don't get this. If they knew it was a Tyrannian vessel and intending blasting it, isn't that the best proof that the world was *not* in the Nebular Kingdoms? that it was anywhere but there?"

"*No*, by the Galaxy." Gillbret's eyes were shining, and his voice climbed in enthusiasm. "It *was* in the Kingdoms. They took me to the surface, and what a world it was! There were men there from all over the Kingdoms. I could tell by the accents. And *they* had no fear of the Tyranni. The place was an arsenal. You couldn't tell from space. It might have been a run-down farming world, but the life of the planet was underground. Somewhere in the Kingdoms, my boy, *somewhere* there is that planet still, and it is *not* afraid of the Tyranni, and it is going to destroy the Tyranni as it would have destroyed the ship I was on then, if the crewmen had been still alive."

Biron felt his heart bound. For a moment he wanted to believe. After all, maybe. Maybe!

Eleven: *AND MAYBE NOT!*

And then again, maybe not!

Biron said, "How did you learn all this about its being an arsenal? How long did you stay? What did you see?"

Gillbret grew impatient. "It wasn't exactly what I saw at all. They didn't conduct me on any tours, or anything like that." He forced himself to relax. "Well, look, this is what happened. By the time they got me off the ship, I was in more or less of a bad state. I had been too frightened to eat much—it's a terrible thing, being marooned in space—and I must have looked worse than I really was.

"I identified myself, more or less, and they took me underground. With the ship, of course. I suppose they were more interested in the ship than in myself. It gave them a chance to study Tyrannian spatio-engineering. They took me to what must have been a hospital."

"But what did you see, Uncle?" asked Artemisia.

Biron interrupted, "Hasn't he ever told *you* this before?"

Artemisia said, "No."

And Gillbret added, "I've never told anyone till now. I was taken to a hospital, as I said. I passed research laboratories in that hospital that must have been better than anything we have on Rhodia. On the way to the hospital I passed factories in which some sort of metalwork was going on. The ships that had captured me were certainly like none I've ever heard about.

"It was all so apparent to me at the time that I have never questioned it in the years since. I think of it as my 'rebellion world,' and I know that someday swarms of ships will leave it to attack the Tyranni, and that the subject worlds will be called upon to rally round the rebel leaders. From year to year I've waited for it to happen. Each new year I've thought to myself: This may be the one. And, each time, I half hoped it wouldn't be, because I was longing to get away first, to join them so that I might be part of the great attack. I didn't want them to start without me."

He laughed shakily. "I suppose it would have amused most people to know what was going on in my mind. In *my* mind. Nobody thought much of me, you know."

Biron said, "All this happened over twenty years ago, and they haven't attacked? There's been no sign of them? No strange ships have been reported? No incidents? And you still think——"

Gillbret fired at him, "Yes, I do. Twenty years isn't too long to organize a rebellion against a planet that rules fifty systems. I was there just at the beginning of the rebellion. I know that too. Slowly, since then, they must have been honeycombing the planet with their underground preparations, developing newer ships and weapons, training more men, organizing the attack.

"It's only in the video thrillers that men spring to arms at a moment's notice; that a new weapon is needed one day, invented the next, mass-produced the third, and used the fourth. These things take time, Biron, and the men of the rebellion world must know they will have to be completely ready before beginning. They won't be able to strike twice.

"And what do you call 'incidents'? Tyrannian ships have disappeared and never been found. Space is big, you might say, and they might simply be lost, but what if they were captured by the rebels? There was the case of the *Tireless* two years back. It reported a strange object close enough to stimulate the massometer, and then was never heard from again. It could have been a meteor, I suppose, but *was it?*

"The search lasted months. They never found it. *I* think the rebels have it. The *Tireless* was a new ship, an experimental model. It would be just what they would want."

Biron said, "Once having landed there, why didn't you stay?"

"Don't you suppose I wanted to? I had no chance. I listened to them when they thought I was unconscious, and I learned a bit more then. They were just starting, out there, at that time. They couldn't afford to be found out then. They knew I was Gillbret oth Hinriad. There was enough identification on the ship, even if I hadn't told them myself, which I had. They knew that if I didn't return to Rhodia there would be a full-scale search that would not readily come to a halt.

"They couldn't risk such a search, so they had to see to it that I was returned to Rhodia. And that's where they took me."

"What!" cried Biron. "But that must have been an even greater risk. How did they do that?"

"I don't know." Gillbret passed his thin fingers through his graying hair, and his eyes seemed to be probing uselessly into the backward stretches of his memory. "They anesthetized me, I suppose. That part all blanks out. Past a certain point there is nothing. I can only remember that I opened my eyes and was back in the *Bloodsucker*; I was in space, just off Rhodia."

"The two dead crewmen were still attached by the tow magnets? They hadn't been removed on the rebellion world?" asked Biron.

"They were still there."

"Was there any evidence at all to indicate that you had been on the rebellion world?"

"None; except for what I remembered."

"How did you know you were off Rhodia?"

"I didn't. I knew I was near a planet; the massometer said so. I used the radio again, and this time it was Rhodian ships that came for me. I told my story to the Tyrannian Commissioner of that day, with appropriate modifications. I made no mention of the rebellion world, of course. And I said the meteor had hit just after the last Jump. I didn't want them to think I knew that a Tyrannian ship could make the Jumps automatically."

"Do you think the rebellion world found out that little fact? Did you tell them?"

"I didn't tell them. I had no chance. I wasn't there long enough. Conscious, that is. But I don't know how long I was unconscious and what they managed to find out for themselves."

Biron stared at the visiplate. Judging from the rigidity of the picture it presented, the ship they were on might have been nailed in space. The *Remorseless* was traveling at the rate of ten thousand miles an hour, but what was that to the immense distances of space. The stars were hard, bright, and motionless. They had a hypnotic quality about them.

He said, "Then where are we going? I take it you still don't know where the rebellion world is?"

"I don't. But I have an idea who would. I am almost sure I know." Gillbret was eager about it.

"Who?"

"The Autarch of Lingane."

"Lingane?" Biron frowned. He had heard the name some time back, it seemed to him, but he had forgotten the connection. "Why he?"

"Lingane was the last Kingdom captured by the Tyranni. It is not, shall we say, as pacified as the rest. Doesn't that make sense?"

"As far as it goes. But how far is that?"

"If you want another reason, there is your father."

"My father?" For a moment Biron forgot that his father was dead. He saw him standing before his mind's eyes, large and alive, but then he remembered and there was that same cold wrench inside him. "How does my father come into this?"

"He was at court six months ago. I gained certain notions as to what he wanted. Some of his talks with my cousin, Hinrik, I overheard."

"Oh, Uncle," said Artemisia impatiently.

"My dear?"

"You had no right to eavesdrop on Father's private discussions."

Gillbret shrugged. "Of course not, but it was amusing, and useful as well."

Biron interrupted, "Now, wait. You say it was six months ago that my father was at Rhodia?" He felt excitement mount.

"Yes."

"Tell me. While there, did he have access to the Director's collection of Primitivism? You told me once that the Director had a large library of matters concerning Earth."

"I imagine so. The library is quite famous and it is usually made available to distinguished visitors, if they're interested. They usually aren't, but your father was. Yes, I remember that very well. He spent nearly a day there."

That checked. It had been half a year ago that his father had first asked his help. Biron said, "You yourself know the library well, I imagine."

"Of course."

"Is there anything in the library that would suggest that there exists a document on Earth of great military value?"

Gillbret was blank of face and, obviously, blank of mind.

Biron said, "Somewhere in the last centuries of prehistoric Earth there must have been such a document. I can only tell you that my father thought it to be the most valuable single item in the Galaxy, and the deadliest. I was to have gotten it for him, but I left Earth too soon, and in any case"—his voice faltered—"he died too soon."

But Gillbret was still blank. "I don't know what you're talking about."

"You don't understand. My father mentioned it to me first six months ago. He must have learned of it in the library on Rhodia. If you've been through it yourself, can't you tell me what it was he must have learned?"

But Gillbret could only shake his head.

Biron said, "Well, continue with your story."

Gillbret said, "They spoke of the Autarch of Lingane, your father and my cousin. Despite your father's cautious phraseology, Biron, it was obvious that the Autarch was the fount and head of the conspiracy.

"And then"—he hesitated—"there was a mission from Lingane and the Autarch himself was at its head. I—I told him of the rebellion world."

"You said awhile ago you told nobody," said Biron.

"Except the Autarch. I *had* to know the truth."

"What did he tell you?"

"Practically nothing. But then, he had to be cautious too. Could he trust me? I might have been working for the Tyranni. How could he know? But he didn't close the door altogether. It's our only lead."

"Is it?" Biron said. "Then we'll go to Lingane. One place, I suppose, is like another."

Mention of his father had depressed him, and, for the moment, nothing mattered much. Let it be Lingane.

Let it be Lingane! That was easy to say. But how does one go about pointing the ship at a tiny speck of light thirty-five light-years away. Two hundred trillion miles. A two with fourteen zeros after it. At ten thousand miles an hour (current cruising speed of the *Remorseless*) it would take well over two million years to get there.

Biron leafed through the *Standard Galactic Ephemeris* with something like despair. Tens of thousands of stars were listed in detail, with their positions crammed into three figures. There were hundreds of pages of these figures, symbolized by the Greek letters ρ (rho), θ (theta), and ϕ (phi).

ρ was the distance from the Galactic Center in parsecs; θ, the angular separation, along the plane of the Galactic Lens from the Standard Galactic Baseline (the line, that is, which connects the Galactic Center and the sun of the planet, Earth); ϕ, the angular separation from the Baseline in the plane perpendicular to that of the Galactic Lens, the two latter measurements being expressed in radians. Given those three figures, one could locate any star accurately in all the vast immensity of space.

That is, on a given date. In addition to the star's position on the standard day for which all the data were calculated, one had to know the star's proper motion, both speed and direction. It was a small correction, comparatively, but necessary. A million miles is virtually nothing compared with stellar distances, but it is a long way with a ship.

There was, of course, the question of the ship's own position. One could calculate the distance from Rhodia by the reading of the massometer, or, more correctly, the distance from Rhodia's sun, since this far out in space the sun's gravitational field drowned out that of any of its planets. The direction they were traveling with reference to the Galactic Baseline was more difficult to determine. Biron had to locate two known stars other than Rhodia's sun. From their apparent positions and the known distance from Rhodia's sun, he could plot their actual position.

It was roughly done but, he felt sure, accurately enough. Knowing his own position and that of Lingane's sun, he had only to adjust the controls for the proper direction and strength of the hyperatomic thrust.

Biron felt lonely and tense. Not frightened! He rejected the word. But tense, definitely. He was deliberately calculating the elements of the Jump for a time six hours later. He wanted plenty of time to check his figures. And perhaps there might be the chance for a nap. He had dragged the bed makings out of the cabin and it was ready for him now.

The other two were, presumably, sleeping in the cabin. He told himself that that was a good thing and that he wanted nobody around bothering him, yet when he heard the small sound of bare feet outside, he looked up with a certain eagerness.

"Hello," he said, "why aren't you sleeping?"

Artemisia stood in the doorway, hesitating. She said, in a small voice, "Do you mind if I come in? Will I be bothering you?"

"It depends on what you do."

"I'll try to do the right things."

She seemed *too* humble, Biron thought suspiciously, and then the reason for it came out.

"I'm awfully frightened," she said. "Aren't you?"

He wanted to say no, not at all, but it didn't come out that way. He smiled sheepishly, and said, "Sort of."

Oddly enough, that comforted her. She knelt down on the floor beside him and looked at the thick volumes opened before him and at the sheets of calculations.

"They had all these books here?"

"You bet. They couldn't pilot a ship without them."

"And you understand all that?"

"Not *all* that. I wish I did. I hope I understand enough. We'll have to Jump to Lingane, you know."

"Is that hard to do?"

"No, not if you know the figures, which are all here, and have the controls, which are all there, *and* if you have experience, which I haven't. For instance, it should be done in several Jumps, but I'm going to try it in one because there'll be less chance of trouble, even though it means a wasteful use of energy."

He shouldn't tell her; there was no point in telling her; it would be cowardly to frighten her; and she'd be hard to handle if she got really frightened, panicky frightened. He kept telling himself all that and it did no good. He wanted to share it with somebody. He wanted part of it off his own mind.

He said, "There are some things I should know that I don't. Things like the mass density between here and Lingane affect the course of the Jump, because that mass density is what controls the curvature of this part of the universe. The *Ephemeris*—that's this big book here—, mentions the curvature corrections that must be made in certain standard Jumps, and from those you're supposed to be able to calculate your own particular corrections. But then if you happen to have a super giant within ten light-years, all bets are off. I'm not even sure if I used the computer correctly."

"But what would happen if you were wrong?"

"We *could* re-enter space too close to Lingane's sun."

She considered that, then said, "You have no idea how much better I feel."

"After what I've just said?"

"Of course. In my bunk I simply felt helpless and lost with so much emptiness in all directions. Now I know that we're going somewhere and that the emptiness is under our control."

Biron was pleased. How different she was. "I don't know about its being under our control."

She stopped him. "It is. I *know* you can handle the ship."

And Biron decided that maybe he could at that.

Artemisia had tucked her long unclad legs under her and sat facing him. She had only her filmy underclothes for cover, but seemed unconscious of the fact, though Biron was definitely not.

She said, "You know, I had an awfully queer sensation in the bunk, almost as if I were floating. That was one of the things that frightened me. Every time I'd turn, I'd give a queer little jump into the air and then flop back slowly as if there were springs in the air holding me back."

"You weren't sleeping in a top bunk, were you?"

"Yes, I was. The bottom ones give me claustrophobia, with another mattress six inches over your head."

Biron laughed. "Then that explains it. The ship's gravitational force is directed toward its base, and falls off as we move away from it. In the top bunk you were probably twenty or thirty pounds lighter than on the floor. Were you ever on a passenger liner? A really big one?"

"Once. When Father and I visited Tyrann last year."

"Well, on the liners they have the gravitation in all parts of the ship directed toward the outer hull, so that the long axis of the ship is always 'up,' no matter where you are. That's why the motors of one of those big babies are always lined up in a cylinder running right along the long axis. No gravity there."

"It must take an awful lot of power to keep an artificial gravity going."

"Enough to power a small town."

"There isn't any danger of our running short of fuel, is there?"

"Don't worry about that. Ships are fueled by the total conversion of mass to energy. Fuel is the last thing we'll run out of. The outer hull will wear away first."

She was facing him. He noted that her face had been cleaned of its make-up and wondered how that had been done; probably with a handkerchief and as little of the drinking water as she could manage. She didn't suffer as a result, for her clear white skin was the more startlingly perfect against the black of her hair and eyes. Her eyes were very warm, thought Biron.

The silence had lasted a little too long. He said hurriedly, "You don't travel very much, do you? I mean, you were on a liner only once?"

She nodded. "Once too often. If we hadn't gone to Tyrann, that filthy chamberlain wouldn't have seen me and—— I don't want to talk about that."

Biron let it go. He said, "Is that usual? I mean, not traveling."

"I'm afraid so. Father is always hopping around on state visits, opening agricultural expositions, dedicating buildings. He usually just makes some speech that Aratap writes for him. As for the rest of us, however, the more we stay in the Palace, the better the Tyranni like it. Poor Gillbret! The one and only time he left Rhodia was to attend the Khan's coronation as Father's representative. They've never let him get into a ship again."

Her eyes were downcast and, absently, she pleated the material of Biron's sleeve where it ended at the wrist. She said, "Biron."

"Yes—Arta?" He stumbled a bit, but it came out.

"Do you think Uncle Gil's story can be true?"

"I don't know."

"Do you suppose it could be his imagination? He's been brooding about the Tyranni for years, and he's never been able to do anything, of course, except to rig up spy beams, which is only childish, and he knows it. He may have built himself a daydream and, over the years, gradually come to believe in it. I *know* him, you see."

"Could be, but let's follow it up a little. We can travel to Lingane, anyway."

They were closer to one another. He could have reached out and touched her, held her in his arms, kissed her.

And he did so.

It was a complete *non sequitur*. Nothing, it seemed to Biron, had led to it. One moment they were discussing Jumps and gravity and Gillbret, and the next she was soft and silky in his arms and soft and silky on his lips.

His first impulse was to say he was sorry, to go through all the silly motions of apology, but when he drew away and would have spoken, she still made no attempt at escape but rested her head in the crook of his left arm. Her eyes remained closed.

So he said nothing at all but kissed her again, slowly and thoroughly. It was the best thing he could have done, and at the time he knew it.

Finally she said, a bit dreamily, "Aren't you hungry? I'll bring you some of the concentrate and warm it for you. Then, if you want to sleep, I can keep an eye on things for you. And—and I'd better put on more of my clothes."

She turned as she was about to go out the door. "The food concentrate tastes very nice after you get used to it. Thank you for getting it."

Somehow *that*, rather than the kisses, was the treaty of peace between them.

When Gillbret entered the control room, hours later, he showed no surprise at finding Biron and Artemisia lost in a foolish kind of conversation. He made no remarks about the fact that Biron's arm was about his niece's waist.

He said, "When are we Jumping, Biron?"

"In half an hour," said Biron.

The half hour passed; the controls were set; conversation languished and died.

At zero time Biron drew a deep breath and yanked a lever the full length of its arc, from left to right.

It was not as it had been on the liner. The *Remorseless* was smaller and the Jump was consequently less smooth. Biron staggered, and for a split second things wavered.

And then they were smooth and solid again.

The stars in the visiplate had changed. Biron rotated the ship, so that the star field lifted, each star moving in a stately arc. One star appeared finally, brilliantly white and more than a point. It was a tiny sphere, a burning speck of sand. Biron caught it, steadied the ship before it was lost again, and turned the telescope upon it, throwing in the spectroscopic attachment.

He turned again to the *Ephemeris*, and checked under the column headed "Spectral Characteristics." Then he got out of the pilot's chair and said, "It's still too far. I'll have to nudge up to it. But, anyway, that's Lingane right ahead."

It was the first Jump he had ever made, and it was successful.

Twelve: *THE AUTARCH COMES*

The Autarch of Lingane pondered the matter, but his cool, well-trained features scarcely creased under the impact of thought.

"And you waited forty-eight hours to tell me," he said.

Rizzett said boldly, "There was no reason to tell you earlier. If we bombarded you with all matters, life would be a burden to you. We tell you now because we still make nothing of it. It is queer, and in our position we can afford nothing queer."

"Repeat this business. Let me hear it again."

The Autarch threw a leg upon the flaring window sill and looked outward thoughtfully. The window itself represented perhaps the greatest single oddity of Linganian architecture. It was moderate in size and set at the end of a five-foot recess that narrowed gently toward it. It was extremely clear, immensely thick, and precisely curved; not so much a window as a lens, funneling the light inward from all directions, so that, looking outward, one eyed a miniature panorama.

From any window in the Autarch's Manor a sweep of vision embracing half the horizon from zenith to nadir could be seen. At the edges there was increasing minuteness and distortion, but that itself lent a certain flavor to what one saw: the tiny flattened motions of the city; the creeping, curved orbits of the crescent-shaped straospherics climbing from the airport. One grew so used to it that unhinging the window to allow the flat tameness of reality to enter would seem unnatural. When the position of the sun made the lenslike windows a focus for impossible heat and light, they were blanked out automatically, rather than opened, rendered opaque by a shift in the polarization characteristics of the glass.

And certainly the theory that a planet's architecture is the reflection of a planet's place in the Galaxy would seem to be borne out by the case of Lingane and its windows.

Like the windows, Lingane was small yet commanded a panoramic view. It was a "planet state" in a Galaxy, which, at the time, had passed beyond that stage of economic and political development. Where most political units were conglomerations of stellar systems, Lingane remained what it had been for centuries—a single inhabited world. This did not prevent it from being wealthy. In fact, it was almost inconceivable that Lingane could be anything else.

It is difficult to tell in advance when a world is so located that many Jump routes may use it as a pivotal intermediate point; or even *must* use it in the interests of optimal economy. A great deal depends on the pattern of development of that region of space. There is the question of the distribution of the naturally habitable planets; the order in which they are colonized and developed; the types of economy they possess.

Lingane discovered its own values early, which was the great turning point of its history. Next to the actual possession of a strategic position, the capacity to appreciate and exploit that position is most important. Lingane had proceeded to occupy small planetoids with neither resources nor capacity for supporting an independent population, choosing them only because they would help maintain Lingane's trade monopoly. They built servicing stations on those rocks. All that ships would need, from hyperatomic replacements to new book reels, could be found there. The stations grew to huge trading posts. From all the Nebular Kingdoms fur, minerals, grain, beef, timber poured in; from the Inner Kingdoms, machinery, appliances, medicinals; finished products of all sorts formed a similar flood.

So that, like its windows, Lingane's minuteness looked out on all the Galaxy. It was a planet alone, but it did well.

The Autarch said, without turning from the window, "Start with the mail ship, Rizzett. Where did it meet this cruiser in the first place?"

"Less than one hundred thousand miles off Lingane. The exact coordinates don't matter. They've been watched ever since. The point is that, even then, the Tyrannian cruiser was in an orbit about the planet."

"As though it had no intention of landing, but, rather, was waiting for something?"

"Yes."

"No way of telling how long they'd been waiting?"

"Impossible, I'm afraid. They were sighted by no one else. We checked thoroughly."

"Very well," said the Autarch. "We'll abandon that for the moment. They stopped the mail ship, which is, of course, interference with the mails and a violation of our Articles of Association with Tyrann."

"I doubt that they were Tyranni. Their unsure actions are more those of outlaws, of prisoners in flight."

"You mean the men on the Tyrannian cruiser? It may be what they want us to believe, of course. At any rate, their only ovcrt action was to ask that a message be delivered directly to me."

"Directly to the Autarch, that is right."

"Nothing else?"

"Nothing else."

"They at no time entered the mail ship?"

"All communications were by visiplate. The mail capsule was shot across two miles of empty space and caught by the ship's net."

"Was it vision communication or sound only?"

"Full vision. That's the point. The speaker was described by several as being a young man of 'aristocratic bearing,' whatever that means."

The Autarch's fist clenched slowly. "Really? And no photo-impression was taken of the face? That was a mistake."

"Unfortunately there was no reason for the mail captain to have anticipated the importance of doing so. If any importance exists! Does all this mean anything to you, sir?"

The Autarch did not answer the question. "And this is the message?"

"Exactly. A tremendous message of one word that we were supposed to bring directly to you; a thing we did not do, of course. It might have been a fission capsule, for instance. Men have been killed that way before."

"Yes, and Autarchs too," said the Autarch. "Just the word 'Gillbret.' One word, 'Gillbret.' "

The Autarch maintained his indifferent calm, but a certain lack of certainty was gathering, and he did not like to experience a lack of certainty. He liked nothing which made him aware of limitations. An Autarch should have no limitations, and on Lingane he had none that natural law did not impose.

There had not always been an Autarch. In its earlier days Lingane had been ruled by dynasties of merchant princes. The families who had first established the subplanetary service stations were the aristocrats of the state. They were not rich in land, hence could not compete in social position with the Ranchers and Grangers of the neighboring worlds. But they were rich in negotiable currency and so could buy and sell those same Ranchers and Grangers; and, by way of high finance, they sometimes did.

And Lingane suffered the usual fate of a planet ruled (or misruled) under such circumstances. The balance of power oscillated from one family to another. The various groups alternated in exile. Intrigues and palace revolutions were chronic, so that if the Directorship of Rhodia was the Sector's prime example of stability and orderly development, Lingane was the example of restlessness and disorder. "As fickle as Lingane," people said.

The outcome was inevitable, if one judges by hindsight. As the neighboring planet states consolidated into group states and became powerful, civil struggles on Lingane became increasingly expensive and dangerous to the planet. The general population was quite willing, finally, to barter anything for general calm. So they exchanged a plutocracy for an autocracy, and lost little liberty in the exchange. The power of several was concentrated in one, but that one, frequently enough, was deliberately friendly to the populace he sought to use as a makeweight against the never-reconciled merchants.

Under the Autarchy, Lingane increased its wealth and strength. Even the Tyranni, attacking thirty years earlier at the height of their power, had been fought to a standstill. They had not been defeated, but they had been stopped. The shock, even of that, had been permanent. Not a planet had been conquered by the Tyranni since the year they had attacked Lingane.

Other planets of the Nebular Kingdoms were outright vassals of the Tyranni. Lingane, however, was an Associated State, theoretically the equal "ally" of Tyrann, with its rights guarded by the Articles of Association.

The Autarch was not fooled by the situation. The chauvinistic of the planet might allow themselves the luxury of considering themselves free, but the Autarch knew that the Tyrannian danger had been held at arm's length this past generation. Only that far. No farther.

And now it might be moving in quickly for the final, long-delayed bear hug. Certainly, he had given it the opportunity it was waiting for. The organization he had built up, ineffectual though it was, was sufficient grounds for punitive action of any type the Tyranni might care to undertake. Legally, Lingane would be in the wrong.

Was the cruiser the first reaching out for the final bear hug?

The Autarch said, "Has a guard been placed on that ship?"

"I said they were watched. Two of our *freighters*"—he smiled one-sidedly, "keep in massometer range."

"Well, what do you make of it?"

"I don't know. The only Gillbret I know whose name by itself would mean anything is Gillbret oth Hinriad of Rhodia. Have you had dealings with him?"

The Autarch said, "I saw him on my last visit to Rhodia."

"You told him nothing, of course."

"Of course."

Rizzett's eyes narrowed. "I thought there might have been a certain lack of caution on your part; that the Tyranni had been the recipients of an equal lack of caution on the part of this Gillbret—the Hinriads are notable weaklings these days—and that this now was a device to trap you into final self-betrayal."

"I doubt it. It comes at a queer time, this business. I have been away from Lingane for a year or more. I arrived last week and I shall leave in a matter of days again. A message such as this reaches me just when I am in a position *to* be reached."

"You don't think it is a coincidence?"

"I don't believe in coincidence. And there is *one* way in which all this would not be coincidence. I will therefore visit that ship. Alone."

"Impossible, sir." Rizzett was startled. He had a small, uneven scar just above his right temple and it suddenly showed red.

"You forbid me?" asked the Autarch dryly.

And he was Autarch, after all, since Rizzett's face fell, and he said, "As you please, sir."

Aboard the *Remorseless*, the wait was proving increasingly unpleasant. For two days they hadn't budged from their orbit.

Gillbret watched the controls with relentless concentration. His voice had an edge to it. "Wouldn't you say they were moving?"

Biron looked up briefly. He was shaving, and handling the Tyranni erosive spray with finicky care.

"No," he said, "they're not moving. Why should they? They're watching us, and they'll keep on watching us."

He concentrated upon the difficult area of the upper lip, and frowned impatiently as he felt the slightly sour taste of the spray upon his tongue. A Tyrannian could handle the spray with a grace that was almost poetic. It was undoubtedly the quickest and closest non-permanent shaving method in existence, in the hands of an expert. In essence, it was an extremely fine air-blown abrasive that scoured off the hairs without harming the skin. Certainly the skin felt like nothing more than the gentle pressure of what might have been an air stream.

However, Biron felt queasy about it. There was the well-known legend, or story, or fact (whatever it was) about the incidence of face cancer being higher among the Tyranni than among other cultural groups, and some attributed this to the Tyranni shave spray. Biron wondered for the first time if it might not be better to have his face completely depilated. It was done in some parts of the Galaxy, as a matter of course. He rejected the thought. Depilation was permanent. The fashion might always shift to mustaches or cheek curls.

Biron was surveying his face in the mirror, wondering how he would look in sideburns down to the angle of the jaw, when Artemisia said from the doorway, "I thought you were going to sleep."

"I did," he said. "Then I woke up." He looked up at her and smiled.

She patted his cheek, then stroked it gently with her fingers. "It's smooth. You look about eighteen."

He carried her hand to his lips. "Don't let that fool you," he said.

She said, "They're still watching?"

"Still watching. Isn't it annoying, these dull interludes that give you time to sit and worry?"

"I don't find this interlude dull."

"You're talking about other aspects of it now, Arta."

She said, "Why don't we cross them up and land on Lingane?"

"We've thought of it. I don't think we're ready for that kind of risk. We can afford to wait till the water supply gets a bit lower."

Gillbret said loudly, "I tell you they *are* moving."

Biron crossed over to the control panel and considered the massometer readings. He looked at Gillbret and said, "You may be right."

He pecked away at the calculator for a moment or two and stared at its dials.

"No, the two ships haven't moved relative to us, Gillbret. What's changed the massometer is that a third ship has joined them. As near as I can tell, it's five thousand miles off, about 46 degree ρ and 192 degrees ϕ from the ship-planet line, if I've got the clockwise and counterclockwise conventions straight. If I haven't, the figures are, respectively, 314 and 168 degrees."

He paused to take another reading. "I think they're approaching. It's a small ship. Do you think you can get in touch with them, Gillbret?"

"I can try," said Gillbret.

"All right. No vision. Let's leave it at sound, till we get some notion of what's coming."

It was amazing to watch Gillbret at the controls of the etheric radio. He was obviously the possessor of a native talent. Contacting an isolated point in space with a tight radio beam remains, after all, a task in which the ship's control-panel information can participate only slightly. He had a notion of the distance of the ship which might be off by a hundred miles plus or minus. He had two angles, either or both of which might easily be wrong by five or six degrees in any direction.

This left a volume of about ten million cubic miles within which the ship might be. The rest was left to the human operator, and a radio beam which was a probing finger not half a mile in cross section at the widest point of its receivable range. It was said that a skilled operator could tell by the feel of the controls how closely the beam missed the target. Scientifically, that theory was nonsense, of course, but it often seemed that no other explanation was possible.

In less than ten minutes the activity gauge of the radio was jumping and the *Remorseless* was both sending and receiving.

In another ten minutes Biron was able to lean back and say, "They're going to send a man aboard."

"Ought we to let them?" asked Artemisia.

"Why not? One man? We're armed."

"But if we let their ship get too close?"

"We're a Tyrannian cruiser, Arta. We've got three to five times their power, even if they were the best warship Lingane had. They're not allowed too much by their precious Articles of Association, and we've got five high-caliber blasters."

Artemisia said, "Do you know how to use the Tyrannian blasters? I didn't know you did."

Biron hated to turn the admiration off, but he said, "Unfortunately, I don't. At least, not yet. But then, the Linganian ship won't know that, you see."

Half an hour later the visiplate showed a visible ship. It was a stubby little craft, fitted with two sets of four fins, as though it were frequently called upon to double for stratospheric flight.

At its first appearance in the telescope, Gillbret shouted in delight. "That's the Autarch's yacht," he cried, and his face wrinkled into a grin. "It's his private yacht. I'm sure of it. I told you that the bare mention of my name was the surest way to get his attention."

There was the period of deceleration and adjustment of velocity on the part of the Linganian ship, until it hung motionless in the plate.

A thin voice came from the receiver. "Ready for boarding?"

"Ready!" clipped Biron. "One person only."

"One person," came the response.

It was like a snake uncoiling. The metal-mesh rope looped outward from the Linganian ship, shooting at them harpoon-fashion. Its thickness expanded in the visiplate, and the magnetized cylinder that ended it approached and grew in size. As it grew closer, it edged toward the rim of the cone of vision, then veered off completely.

The sound of its contact was hollow and reverberant. The magnetized weight was anchored, and the line was a spider thread that did not sag in a normal weighted curve but retained whatever kinks and loops it had possessed at the moment of contact, these moving slowly forward as units under the influence of inertia.

Easily and carefully, the Linganian ship edged away and the line straightened. It hung there then, taut and fine, thinning into space until it was an almost invisible thing, glancing with incredible daintiness in the light of Lingane's sun.

Biron threw in the telescopic attachment, which bloated the ship monstrously in the field of vision, so that one could see the origin of the half-mile length of connecting line and the little figure that was beginning to swing hand over hand along it.

It was not the usual form of boarding. Ordinarily, two ships would maneuver to near-contact, so that extensible air locks could meet and merge under intense magnetic fields. A tunnel through space would connect the ships, and a man could travel from one to the other with no further protection than he needed to wear aboard ship. Naturally, this form of boarding required mutual trust.

By space line, one was dependent upon his space suit. The approaching Linganian was bloated in his, a fat thing of air-extended metal mesh, the joints of which required no small muscular effort to work. Even at the distance at which he was, Biron could see his arms flex with a snap as the joint gave and came to rest in a new groove.

And the mutual velocities of the two ships had to be carefully adjusted. An inadvertent acceleration on the part of either would tear the line loose and send the traveler tumbling through space under the easy grip of the faraway sun and of the initial impulse of the snapping line—with nothing, neither friction nor obstruction, to stop him this side of eternity.

The approaching Linganian moved on confidently and quickly. When he came closer it was easy to see that it was not a simple hand-over-hand procedure. Each time the forward hand flexed, pulling him on, he would let go and float onward some dozen feet before his other hand had reached forward for a new hold.

It was a brachiation through space. The spaceman was a gleaming metal gibbon.

Artemisia said, "What if he misses?"

"He looks too expert to do that," said Biron, "but if he does, he'd still shine in the sun. We'd pick him up again."

The Linganian was close now. He had passed out of the field of the visiplate. In another five seconds there was the clatter of feet on the ship's hull.

Biron yanked the lever that lit the signals which outlined the ship's air lock. A moment later, in answer to an imperative series of raps, the outer door was opened. There was a thump just beyond a blank section of the pilot-room's wall. The outer door closed, the section of wall slid away, and a man stepped through.

His suit frosted over instantly, blanking the thick glass of his helmet and turning him into a mound of white. Cold radiated from him. Biron elevated the heaters and the gush of air that entered was warm and dry. For a moment the frost on the suit held its own, then began to thin and dissolve into a dew.

The Linganian's blunt metal fingers were fumbling at the clasps of the helmet as though he were impatient with his snowy blindness. It lifted off as a unit, the thick, soft insulation inside rumpling his hair as it passed.

Gillbret said, "Your Excellency!" In glad triumph, he said, "Biron, it is the Autarch himself."

But Biron, in a voice that struggled vainly against stupefaction, could only say, "Jonti!"

Thirteen: *THE AUTARCH REMAINS*

The Autarch gently toed the suit to one side and appropriated the larger of the padded chairs.

He said, "I haven't had that sort of exercise in quite a while. But they say it never leaves you once you've learned, and, apparently, it hasn't in my case. Hello, Farrill! My Lord Gillbret, good day. And this, if I remember, is the Director's daughter, the Lady Artemisia!"

He placed a long cigarette carefully between his lips and brought it to life with a single intake of breath. The scented tobacco filled the air with its pleasant odor. "I did not expect to see you quite so soon, Farrill," he said.

"Or at all, perhaps?" said Biron acidly.

"One never knows," agreed the Autarch. "Of course, with a message that read only 'Gillbret'; with the knowledge that Gillbret could not pilot a space ship; with the further knowledge that I had myself sent a young man to Rhodia who *could* pilot a space ship and who was quite capable of stealing a Tyrannian cruiser in his desperation to escape; and with the knowledge that one of the men on the cruiser was reported to be young and of aristocratic bearing, the conclusion was obvious. I am not surprised to see you."

"I think you are," said Biron. "I think you're as surprised as hell to see me. As an assassin, you should be. Do you think I am worse at deduction than you are?"

"I think only highly of you, Farrill."

The Autarch was completely unperturbed, and Biron felt awkward and stupid in his resentment. He turned furiously to the others. "This man is Sander Jonti—the Sander Jonti I've told you of. He may be the Autarch of Lingane besides, or fifty Autarchs. It makes no difference. To me he is Sander Jonti."

Artemisia said, "*He* is the man who——"

Gillbret put a thin and shaking hand to his brow. "Control yourself, Biron. Are you mad?"

"This *is* the man! I am *not* mad!" shouted Biron. He controlled himself with an effort. "All right. There's no point yelling, I suppose. Get off my ship, Jonti. Now that's said quietly enough. Get off my ship."

"My dear Farrill. For what reason?"

Gillbret made incoherent sounds in his throat, but Biron pushed him aside roughly and faced the seated Autarch. "You made one mistake, Jonti. Just one. You couldn't tell in advance that when I got out of my dormitory room back on Earth I would leave my wrist watch inside. You see, my wrist-watch strap happened to be a radiation indicator."

The Autarch blew a smoke ring and smiled pleasantly.

Biron said, "And that strap never turned blue, Jonti. There was no bomb in my room that night. There was only a deliberately planted dud! If you deny it, you are a liar, Jonti, or Autarch, or whatever you please to call yourself.

"What is more, *you* planted that dud. *You* knocked me out with Hypnite and arranged the rest of that night's comedy. It makes quite obvious sense, you know. If I had been left to myself, I would have slept through the night and would never have known that anything was out of the way. So who rang me on the visiphone until he was sure I had awakened? Awakened, that is, to discover the bomb, which had been deliberately placed near a counter so that I couldn't miss it. Who blasted my door in so that I might leave the room before I found out that the bomb was only a dud after all? You must have enjoyed yourself that night, Jonti."

Biron waited for effect, but the Autarch merely nodded in polite interest. Biron felt the fury mount. It was like punching pillows, whipping water, kicking air.

He said harshly, "My father was about to be executed. I would have learned of it soon enough. I would have gone to Nephelos, or not gone. I would have followed my own good sense in the matter, confronted the Tyranni openly or not as I decided. I would have known my chances. I would have been prepared for eventualities.

"But you wanted me to go to Rhodia, to see Hinrik. But, ordinarily, you couldn't expect me to do what *you* wanted. I wasn't likely to go to *you* for advice. Unless, that is, you could stage an appropriate situation. You did!

"I thought I was being bombed and I could think of no reason. You could. You seemed to have saved my life. You seemed to know everything; what I ought to do next, for instance. I was off balance, confused. I followed your advice."

Biron ran out of breath and waited for an answer. There was none. He shouted, "You did not explain that the ship on which I left Earth was a Rhodian ship and that you had seen to it that the captain had been informed of my true identity. You did not explain that you intended me to be in the hands of the Tyranni the instant I landed on Rhodia. Do you deny that?"

There was a long pause. Jonti stubbed out his cigarette.

Gillbret chafed one hand in the other. "Biron, you are being ridiculous. The Autarch wouldn't——"

Then Jonti looked up and said quietly, "But the Autarch would. I admit it all. You are quite right, Biron, and I congratulate you on your penetration. The bomb *was* a dud planted by myself, and I sent you to Rhodia with the intention of having you arrested by the Tyranni."

Biron's face cleared. Some of the futility of life vanished. He said, "Someday, Jonti, I will settle that matter. At the moment, it seems you are Autarch of Lingane with three ships waiting for you out there. That hampers me a bit more than I would like. However, the *Remorseless* is my ship. I am its pilot. Put on your suit and get out. The space line is still in place."

"It is not your ship. You are a pirate rather than a pilot."

"Possession is all the law here. You have five minutes to get into your suit."

"Please. Let's avoid dramatics. We need one another and I have no intention of leaving."

"I don't need *you*. I wouldn't need you if the Tyrannian home fleet were closing in right now and you could blast them out of space for me."

"Farrill," said Jonti, "you are talking and acting like an adolescent. I've let you have your say. May I have mine?"

"No. I see no reason to listen to you."

"Do you see one now?"

Artemisia screamed. Biron made one movement, then stopped. Red with frustration, he remained tense but helpless.

Jonti said, "I do take certain precautions. I am sorry to be so crude as to use a weapon as a threat. But I imagine it will help me force you to hear me."

The weapon he held was a pocket blaster. It was not designed to pain or stun. It killed!

He said, "For years I have been organizing Lingane against the Tyranni. Do you know what that means? It has not been easy. It has been almost impossible. The Inner Kingdoms will offer no help. We've known that from long experience. There is no salvation for the Nebular Kingdoms but what they work out for themselves. But to convince our native leaders of this is no friendly game. Your father was active in the matter and was killed. Not a friendly game at all. Remember that.

"And your father's capture was a crisis to us. It was life and horrible death to us. He was in our inner circles and the Tyranni were obviously not far behind us. They had to be thrown off stride. To do so, I could scarcely temper my dealings with honor and integrity. They fry no eggs.

"I couldn't come to you and say, 'Farrill, we've got to put the Tyranni on a false scent. You're the son of the Rancher and therefore suspicious. Get out there and be friendly with Hinrik of Rhodia so that the Tyranni may look in the wrong direction. Lead them away from Lingane. It may be dangerous; you may lose your life, but the ideals for which your father died come first.'

"Maybe you would have done it, but I couldn't afford to experiment. I maneuvered you into doing it without your knowledge. It was hard, I'll grant you. Still, I had no choice. I thought you might not survive; I tell you that frankly. But you were expendable; and I tell you *that* frankly. As it turned out, you did survive, and I am pleased with that.

"And there was one more thing, a matter of a document——"

Biron said, "What document?"

"You jump quickly. I said your father was working for me. So I know what he knew. You were to obtain that document and you were a good choice, at first. You were on Earth legitimately. You were young and not likely to be suspected. I say, *at first!*

"But then, with your father arrested, you became dangerous. You would be an object of prime suspicion to the Tyranni; and we could not allow the document to fall into your possession, since it would then almost inevitably fall into theirs. We had to get you off Earth before you could complete your mission. You see, it all hangs together."

"Then *you* have it now?" asked Biron.

The Autarch said, "No, I have not. A document which might have been the right one has been missing from Earth for years. If it *is* the right one, I don't know who has it. May I put away the blaster now? It grows heavy."

Biron said, "Put it away."

The Autarch did so. He said, "What has your father told you about the document?"

"Nothing that you don't know, since he worked for you."

The Autarch smiled. "Quite so!" but the smile had little of real amusement in it.

"Are you quite through with your explanation now?"

"Quite through."

"Then," said Biron, "get off the ship."

Gillbret said, "Now wait, Biron. There's more than private pique to be considered here. There's Artemisia and myself, too, you know. We have *something* to say. As far as I'm concerned, what the Autarch says makes sense. I'll remind you that on Rhodia I saved your life, so I think my views are to be considered."

"All right. You saved my life," shouted Biron. He pointed a finger towards the air lock. "Go with him, then. Go on. You get out of here too. You wanted to find the Autarch. There he is! I agreed to pilot you to him, and my responsibility is over. Don't try to tell *me* what to do."

He turned to Artemisia, some of his anger still brimming over. "And what about you? You saved my life too. Everyone went around saving my life. Do you want to go with him too?"

She said calmly, "Don't put words into my mouth, Biron. If I wanted to go with him, I'd say so."

"Don't feel any obligations. You can leave any time."

She looked hurt and he turned away. As usual, some cooler part of himself knew that he was acting childishly. He had been made to look foolish by Jonti and he was helpless in the face of the resentment he felt. And besides, why should they all take so calmly the thesis that it was perfectly right to have Biron Farrill thrown to the Tyranni, like a bone to the dogs, in order to keep them off Jonti's neck. Damn it, what did they think he was?

He thought of the dud bomb, the Rhodian liner, the Tyranni, the wild night on Rhodia, and he could feel the stinging of self-pity inside himself.

The Autarch said, "Well, Farrill?"

And Gillbret said, "Well, Biron?"

Biron turned to Artemisia. "What do *you* think?"

Artemisia said calmly, "I think he has three ships out there still, and is Autarch of Lingane, besides. I don't think you really have a choice."

The Autarch looked at her, and he nodded his admiration. "You are an intelligent girl, my lady. It is good that such a mind should be in such a pleasant exterior." For a measurable moment his eyes lingered.

Biron said, "What's the deal?"

"Lend me the use of your names and your abilities, and I will take you to what my Lord Gillbret called the rebellion world."

Biron said sourly, "You think there *is* one?"

And Gillbret said simultaneously, "Then it *is* yours."

The Autarch smiled. "I think there is a world such as my lord described, but it is not mine."

"It's *not* yours," said Gillbret despondently.

"Does that matter, if I can find it?"

"How?" demanded Biron.

The Autarch said, "It is not so difficult as you might think. If we accept the story as it has been told us, we must believe that there exists a world in rebellion against the Tyranni. We must believe that it is located somewhere in the Nebular Sector and that in twenty years it has remained undiscovered by the Tyranni. If such a situation is to remain possible, there is only one place in the Sector where such a planet can exist."

"And where is that?"

"You do not find the solution obvious? Doesn't it seem inevitable that the world could exist only within the Nebula itself?"

"*Inside* the Nebula!"

Gillbret said, "Great Galaxy, of course."

And, at the moment, the solution did indeed seem obvious and inescapable.

Artemisia said timidly, "Can people live on worlds inside the Nebula?"

"Why not?" said the Autarch. "Don't mistake the Nebula. It is a dark mist in space, but it is not a poison gas. It is an incredibly attenuated mass of sodium, potassium, and calcium atoms that absorb and obscure the light of the stars within it, and, of course, those on the side directly opposite the observer. Otherwise, it is harmless, and, in the direct neighborhood of a star, virtually undetectable.

"I apologize if I seem pedantic, but I have spent the last several months at the University of Earth collecting astronomical data on the Nebula."

"Why there?" said Biron. "It is a matter of little importance, but I met you there and I am curious."

"There's no mystery to it. I left Lingane originally on my own business. The exact nature is of no importance. About six months ago I visited Rhodia. My agent, Widemos—your father, Biron—had been unsuccessful in his negotiations with the Director, whom we had hoped to swing to our side. I tried to improve matters and failed, since Hinrik, with apologies to the lady, is not the type of material for our sort of work."

"Hear, hear," muttered Biron.

The Autarch continued. "But I did meet Gillbret, as he may have told you. So I went to Earth, because Earth is the original home of humanity. It was from Earth that most of the original explorations of the Galaxy set out. It is upon Earth that most of the records exist. The Horsehead Nebula was explored quite thoroughly; at least, it was passed through a number of times. It was never settled, since the difficulties of traveling through a volume of space where stellar observations could not be made were too great. The explorations themselves, however, were all I needed.

"Now listen carefully. The Tyrannian ship upon which my Lord Gillbret was marooned was struck by a meteor after its first Jump. Assuming that the trip from Tyrann to Rhodia was along the usual trade route—and there is no reason to suppose anything else—the point in space at which the ship left its route is established. It would scarcely have traveled more than half a million miles in ordinary space between the first two Jumps. We can consider such a length as a point in space.

"It is possible to make another assumption. In damaging the control panels, it was quite possible that the meteor might have altered the direction of the Jumps, since that would require only an interference with the motion of the ship's gyroscope. This would be difficult but not impossible. To change the *power* of the hyperatomic thrusts, however, would require complete smashing of the engines, which, of course, were not touched by the meteor.

"With unchanged power of thrust, the length of the four remaining Jumps would not be changed, nor, for that matter, would their relative directions. It would be analogous to having a long, crooked wire bent at a single point in an unknown direction through an unknown angle. The final position of the ship would lie somewhere on the surface of an imaginary sphere, the center of which would be that point in space where the meteor struck, and the radius of which would be the vector sum of the remaining Jumps.

"I plotted such a sphere, and that surface intersects a thick extension of the Horsehead Nebula. Some six thousand square degrees of the sphere's surface, one fourth of the total surface, lies in the Nebula. It remains, therefore, only to find a star lying within the Nebula and within one million miles or so of the imaginary surface we are discussing. You will remember that when Gillbret's ship came to rest, it was within reach of a star.

"Now how many stars within the Nebula do you suppose we can find that close to the sphere's surface? Remember there are one hundred billion radiating stars in the Galaxy."

Biron found himself absorbed in the matter almost against his will. "Hundreds, I suppose."

"Five!" replied the Autarch. "Just five. Don't be fooled by the one hundred billion figure. The Galaxy is about seven trillion cubic light-years in volume, so that there are seventy cubic light-years per star on the average. It is a pity that I do not know which of those five have habitable planets. We might reduce the number of possibles to one. Unfortunately, the early explorers had no time for detailed observations. They plotted the positions of the stars, the proper motions, and the spectral types."

"So that in one of those five stellar systems," said Biron, "is located the rebellion world?"

"Only that conclusion would fit the facts we know."

"Assuming Gil's story can be accepted."

"I make that assumption."

"My story is true," interrupted Gillbret intensely. "I swear it."

"I am about to leave," said the Autarch, "to investigate each of the five worlds. My motives in doing so are obvious. As Autarch of Lingane I can take an equal part in their efforts."

"And with two Hinriads and a Widemos on your side, your bid for an equal part, and, presumably, a strong and secure position in the new, free worlds to come, would be so much the better," said Biron.

"Your cynicism doesn't frighten me, Farrill. The answer is obviously yes. If there is to be a successful rebellion, it would, again obviously, be desirable to have your fist on the winning side."

"Otherwise some successful privateer or rebel captain might be rewarded with the Autarchy of Lingane."

"Or the Ranchy of Widemos. Exactly."

"And if the rebellion is not successful?"

"There will be time to judge of that when we find what we look for."

Biron said slowly, "I'll go with you."

"Good! Then suppose we make arrangements for your transfer from this ship."

"Why that?"

"It would be better for you. This ship is a toy."

"It is a Tyrannian warship. We would be wrong in abandoning it."

"As a Tyrannian warship, it would be dangerously conspicuous."

"Not in the Nebula. I'm sorry, Jonti. I'm joining you out of expedience. I can be frank too. I want to find the rebellion world. But there's no friendship between us. I stay at my own controls."

"Biron," said Artemisia gently, "the ship *is* too small for the three of us."

"As it stands, yes, Arta. But it can be fitted with a trailer. Jonti knows that as well as I do. We'd have all the space we needed then, and still be masters at our own controls. And, for that matter, it would effectively disguise the nature of the ship."

The Autarch considered. "If there is to be neither friendship nor trust, Farrill, I must protect myself. You may have your own ship and a trailer to boot, outfitted as you may wish. But I must have some guarantee for your proper behavior. The Lady Artemisia, at least, must come with me."

"*No!*" said Biron.

The Autarch lifted his eyebrows. "No? Let the lady speak."

He turned toward Artemisia, and his nostrils flared slightly. "I dare say you would find the situation very comfortable, my lady."

"You, at least, would *not* find it comfortable, my lord. Be assured of that," she retorted. "I would spare you the discomfort and remain here."

"I think you might reconsider if——" began the Autarch, as two little wrinkles at the bridge of his nose marred the serenity of his expression.

"I think not," interrupted Biron. "The Lady Artemisia has made her choice."

"And you back her choice then, Farrill?" The Autarch was smiling again.

"Entirely! All three of us will remain on the *Remorseless*. There will be no compromise on that."

"You choose your company oddly."

"Do I?"

"I think so." The Autarch seemed idly absorbed in his fingernails. "You seem so annoyed with me because I deceived you and placed your life in danger. It is strange, then, is it not, that you should seem on such friendly terms with the daughter of a man such as Hinrik, who in deception is certainly my master."

"I know Hinrik. Your opinions of him change nothing."

"You know everything about Hinrik?"

"I know enough."

"Do you know that he killed your father?" The Autarch's finger stabbed toward Artemisia. "Do you know that the girl you are so deeply concerned to keep under your protection is the daughter of your father's murderer?"

Fourteen: *THE AUTARCH LEAVES*

The tableau remained unbroken for a moment. The Autarch had lit another cigarette. He was quite relaxed, his face untroubled. Gillbret had folded into the pilot's seat, his face screwed up as though he were going to burst into tears. The limp straps of the pilot's stress-absorbing outfit dangled about him and increased the lugubrious effect.

Biron, paper-white, fists clenched, faced the Autarch. Artemisia, her thin nostrils flaring, kept her eyes not on the Autarch, but on Biron only.

The radio signaled, the soft clickings crashing with the effect of cymbals in the small pilot room.

Gillbret jerked upright, then whirled on the seat.

The Autarch said lazily, "I'm afraid we've been more talkative than I'd anticipated. I told Rizzett to come get me if I had not returned in an hour."

The visual screen was alive now with Rizzett's grizzled head.

And then Gillbret said to the Autarch, "He would like to speak to you." He made room.

The Autarch rose from his chair and advanced so that his own head was within the zone of visual transmission.

He said, "I am perfectly safe, Rizzett."

The other's question was heard clearly: "Who are the crew members on the cruiser, sir?"

And suddenly Biron stood next to the Autarch. "I am Rancher of Widemos," he said proudly.

Rizzett smiled gladly and broadly. A hand appeared on the screen in sharp salute. "Greetings, sir."

The Autarch interrupted. "I will be returning soon with a young lady. Prepare to maneuver for contact air locks." And he broke the visual connection between the two ships.

He turned to Biron. "I assured them it was you on board ship. There was some objection to my coming here alone otherwise. Your father was extremely popular with my men."

"Which is why you can use my name."

The Autarch shrugged.

Biron said, "It is all you can use. Your last statement to your officer was inaccurate."

"In what way?"

"Artemisia oth Hinriad stays with me."

"Still? After what I have told you?"

Biron said sharply, "You have told me nothing. You have made a bare statement, but I am not likely to take your unsupported word for anything. I tell you this without any attempt at tact. I hope you understand me."

"Is your knowledge of Hinrik such that my statement seems inherently implausible to you?"

Biron was staggered. Visibly and apparently, the remark had struck home. He made no answer.

Artemisia said, "I say it's not so. *Do* you have proof?"

"No direct proof, of course. I was not present at any conferences between your father and the Tyranni. But I can present certain known facts and allow you to make your own inferences. First, the old Rancher of Widemos visited Hinrik six months ago. I've said that already. I can add here that he was somewhat overenthusiastic in his efforts, or perhaps he overestimated Hinrik's discretion. At any rate, he talked more than he should have. My Lord Gillbret can verify that."

Gillbret nodded miserably. He turned to Artemisia, who had turned to him with moist and angry eyes. "I'm sorry, Arta, but it's true. I've told you this. It was from Widemos that I heard about the Autarch."

The Autarch said, "And it was fortunate for myself that my lord had developed such long mechanical ears with which to sate his lively curiosity concerning the Director's meetings of state. I was warned of the danger, quite unwittingly, by Gillbret when he first approached me. I left as soon as I could, but the damage, of course, had been done.

"Now, to our knowledge, it was Widemos's only slip, and Hinrik, certainly, has no enviable reputation as a man of any great independence and courage. Your father, Farrill, was arrested within half a year. If not through Hinrik, through this girl's father, then how?"

Biron said, "You did not warn him?"

"In our business we take our chances, Farrill, but he *was* warned. After that he made no contact, however indirect, with any of us, and destroyed whatever proof he had of connection with us. Some among us believed that he should leave the Sector, or, at the very least, go into hiding. He refused to do this.

"I think I can understand why. To alter his way of life would prove the truth of what the Tyranni must have learned, endanger the entire movement. He decided to risk his own life only. He remained in the open.

"For nearly half a year the Tyranni waited for a betraying gesture. They are patient, the Tyranni. None came, so that when they could wait no longer, they found nothing in their net but him."

"It's a lie," cried Artemisia. "It's all a lie. It's a smug, sanctimonious, lying story with no truth in it. If all you said were true, they would be watching you too. You would be in danger yourself. You wouldn't be sitting here, smiling and wasting time."

"My lady, I do not waste my time. I have already tried to do what I could toward discrediting your father as a source of information. I think I have succeeded somewhat. The Tyranni will wonder if they ought to listen further to a man whose daughter and cousin are obvious traitors. And then again, if they are still disposed to believe him, why, I am on the point of vanishing into the Nebula where they will not find me. I should think my actions tend to prove my story rather than otherwise."

Biron drew a deep breath and said, "Let us consider the interview at an end, Jonti. We have agreed to the extent that we will accompany you and that you will grant us needed supplies. That is enough. Granting that all you have just said is true, it is still beside the point. The crimes of the Director of Rhodia are not inherited by his daughter. Artemisia oth Hinriad stays here with me, provided she herself agrees."

"I do," said Artemisia.

"Good. I think that covers everything. I warn you, by the way. You are armed; so am I. Your ships are fighters, perhaps; mine is a Tyrannian cruiser."

"Don't be silly, Farrill. My intentions are quite friendly. You wish to keep the girl here? So be it. May I leave by contact air lock?"

Biron nodded. "We will trust you so far."

The two ships maneuvered ever closer, until the flexible air-lock extensions pouted outward toward one another. Carefully, they edged about, trying for the perfect fit. Gillbret hung upon the radio.

"They'll be trying for contact again in two minutes," he said.

Three times already the magnetic field had been triggered, and each time the extending tubes had stretched toward one another and met off-center, gaping crescents of space between them.

"Two minutes," repeated Biron, and waited tensely.

The second hand moved and the magnetic field clicked into existence a fourth time, the lights dimming as the motors adjusted to the sudden drain of power. Again the air-lock extensions reached out, hovered on the brink of instability, and then, with a noiseless jar, the vibrations of which hummed its way into the pilot room, settled into place properly, clamps automatically locking in position. An airtight seal had been formed.

Biron drew the back of his hand slowly across his forehead and some of the tension oozed out of him.

"There it is," he said.

The Autarch lifted his space suit. There was still a thin film of moisture under it.

"Thanks," he said pleasantly. "An officer of mine will be right back. You will arrange the details of the supplies necessary with him."

The Autarch left.

Biron said, "Take care of Jonti's officer for me for a while, will you, Gil. When he comes in, break the air-lock contact. All you'll have to do is remove the magnetic field. This is the photonic switch you'll flash."

He turned and stepped out of the pilot room. Right now he needed time for himself. Time to think, mostly.

But there was the hurried footstep behind him, and the soft voice. He stopped.

"Biron," said Artemisia, "I want to speak to you."

He faced her. "Later, if you don't mind, Arta."

She was looking up at him intently. "No, now."

Her arms were poised as though she would have liked to embrace him but was not sure of her reception. She said, "You didn't believe what he said about my father?"

"It has no bearing," said Biron.

"Biron," she began, and stopped. It was hard for her to say it. She tried again, "Biron, I know that part of what has been going on between us has been because we've been alone and together and in danger, but——" She stopped again.

Biron said, "If you're trying to say you're a Hinriad, Arta, there's no need. I know it. I won't hold you to anything afterward."

"No. Oh no." She caught his arm and placed her cheek against his hard shoulder. She was speaking rapidly. "That's not it at all. It doesn't matter about Hinriad and Widemos at all. I—I love you, Biron."

Her eyes went up, meeting his. "I think you love me too. I think you would admit it if you could forget that I am a Hinriad. Maybe you will now that I've said it first. You told the Autarch you would not hold my father's deeds against me. Don't hold his rank against me, either."

Her arms were around his neck now. Biron could feel the softness of her breast against him and the warmth of her breath on his lips. Slowly his own hands went upward and gently grasped her forearms. As gently, he disengaged her arms and, still as gently, stepped back from her.

He said, "I am not quits with the Hinriads, my lady."

She was startled. "You told the Autarch that——"

He looked away. "Sorry, Arta. Don't go by what I told the Autarch."

She wanted to cry out that it wasn't true, that her father had not done this thing, that in any case——

But he turned into the cabin and left her standing in the corridor, her eyes filling with hurt and shame.

Fifteen: *THE HOLE IN SPACE*

Tedor Rizzett turned as Biron entered the pilot room again. His hair was gray, but his body was still vigorous and his face was broad, red, and smiling.

He covered the distance between himself and Biron in a stride and seized the young man's hand heartily.

"By the stars," he said, "I'd need no word from you to tell me that you are your father's son. It is the old Rancher alive again."

"I wish it were," said Biron, somberly.

Rizzett's smile faltered. "So do we all. Every one of us. I'm Tedor Rizzett, by the way. I'm a colonel in the regular Linganian forces, but we don't use titles in our own little game. We even say 'sir' to the Autarch. That reminds me!" He looked grave. "We don't have lords and ladies or even Ranchers on Lingane. I hope I won't offend if I forget to throw in the proper title sometimes."

Biron shrugged. "As you said, no titles in our little game. But what about the trailer? I'm to make arrangements with you, I take it."

For a flickering moment he looked across the room. Gillbret was seated, quietly listening. Artemisia had her back to him. Her slim, pale fingers wove an abstracted pattern on the photocontacts of the computer. Rizzett's voice brought him back.

The Linganian had cast an all-inclusive glance about the room. "First time I've ever seen a Tyrannian vessel from the inside. Don't care much for it. Now you've got the emergency air lock due stern, haven't you? It seems to me the power thrusters girdle the midsection."

"That's right."

"Good. Then there won't be any trouble. Some of the old model ships had power thrusters due stern, so that trailers had to be set off at an angle. This makes the gravity adjustment difficult and the maneuverability in atmospheres just about nil."

"How long will it take, Rizzett?"

"Not long. How big would you want it?"

"How big could you get it?"

"Super de luxe? Sure. If the Autarch says so, there's no higher priority. We can get one that's practically a space ship in itself. It would even have auxiliary motors."

"It would have living quarters, I suppose."

"For Miss Hinriad? It would be considerably better than you have here——" He stopped abruptly.

At the mention of her name, Artemisia had drifted past coldly and slowly, moving out of the pilot room. Biron's eyes followed her.

Rizzett said, "I shouldn't have said Miss Hinraid, I suppose."

"No, no. It's nothing. Pay no attention. You were saying?"

"Oh, about the rooms. At least two sizable ones, with a communicating shower. It's got the usual closet room and plumbing arrangements of the big liners. She would be comfortable."

"Good. We'll need food and water."

"Sure. Water tank will hold a two months' supply; a little less if you want to arrange for a swimming pool aboard ship. And you would have frozen whole meats. You're eating Tyrannian concentrate now, aren't you?"

Biron nodded and Rizzett grimaced.

"It tastes like chopped sawdust, doesn't it? What else?"

"A supply of clothes for the lady," said Biron.

Rizzett wrinkled his forehead. "Yes, of course. Well, that will be her job."

"No, sir, it won't. We'll supply you with all necessary measurements and you can supply us with whatever we ask for in whatever the current styles happen to be."

Rizzett laughed shortly and shook his head. "Rancher, she won't like that. She wouldn't be satisfied with any clothes she didn't pick. Not even if they were the identical items she would have picked if she had been given the chance. This isn't a guess, now. I've had experience with the creatures."

Biron said, "I'm sure you're right, Rizzett. But that's the way it will have to be."

"All right, but I've warned you. It will be your argument. What else?"

"Little things. Little things. A supply of detergents. Oh yes, cosmetics, perfume—the things women need. We'll make the arrangements in time. Let's get the trailer started."

And now Gillbret was leaving without speaking. Biron's eyes followed him, too, and he felt his jaw muscles tighten. Hinriads! They were Hinriads! There was nothing he could do about it. They were Hinriads! Gillbret was one and *she* was another.

He said, "And, of course, there'll be clothes for Mr. Hinriad and myself. That won't be very important."

"Right. Mind if I use your radio? I'd better stay on this ship till the adjustments are made."

Biron waited while the initial orders went out. Then Rizzett turned on the seat and said, "I can't get used to seeing you here, moving, talking, alive. You're so like him. The Rancher used to speak about you every once in a while. You went to school on Earth, didn't you?"

"I did. I would have graduated a little over a week ago, if things hadn't been interrupted."

Rizzett looked uncomfortable. "Look, about your being sent to Rhodia the way you were. You mustn't hold it against us. We didn't like it. I mean, this is strictly between us, but some of the boys didn't like it at all. The Autarch didn't consult us, of course. Naturally, he wouldn't. Frankly, it was a risk on his part. Some of us—I'm not mentioning names—even wondered if we shouldn't stop the liner you were on and pull you off. Naturally that would have been the worst thing we could possibly have done. Still, we might have done it, except that in the last analysis, we knew that the Autarch must have known what he was doing."

"It's nice to be able to inspire that kind of confidence."

"We know him. There's no denying it. He's got it here." A finger slowly tapped his forehead. "Nobody knows exactly what makes him take a certain course sometimes. But it always seems the right one. At least he's outsmarted the Tyranni so far and others don't."

"Like my father, for instance."

"I wasn't thinking of him, exactly, but in a sense, you're right. Even the Rancher was caught. But then he was a different kind of man. His way of thinking was straight. He would never allow for crookedness. He would always underestimate the worthlessness of the next man. But then again, that was what we liked best, somehow. He was the same to everyone, you know.

"I'm a commoner for all I'm a colonel. My father was a metalworker, you see. It didn't make any difference to him. And it wasn't that I was a colonel, either. If he met the engineer's 'prentice walking down the corridor, he'd step aside and say a pleasant word or two, and for the rest of the day, the 'prentice would feel like a master engineman. It was the way he had.

"Not that he was soft. If you needed disciplining, you got it, but no more than your share. What you got, you deserved, and you knew it. When he was through, he was through. He didn't keep throwing it at you at odd moments for a week or so. That was the Rancher.

"Now the Autarch, he's different. He's just brains. You can't get next to him, no matter who you are. For instance. He doesn't really have a sense of humor. I can't speak to him the way I'm speaking to you right now. Right now, I'm just talking. I'm relaxed. It's almost free association. With him, you say exactly what's on your mind with no spare words. *And* you use formal phraseology, or he'll tell you you're slovenly. But then, the Autarch's the Autarch, and that's that."

Biron said, "I'll have to agree with you as far as the Autarch's brains are concerned. Did you know that he had deduced my presence aboard this ship before he ever got on?"

"He *did?* We didn't know that. Now, there, that's what I mean. He was going to go aboard the Tyrannian cruiser alone. To us, it seemed suicide. We didn't like it. But we assumed he knew what he was doing, and he did. He could have told us you were probably aboard ship. He must have known it would be great news that the Rancher's son had escaped. But it's typical. He wouldn't."

Artemisia sat on one of the lower bunks in the cabin. She had to bend into an uncomfortable position to avoid having the frame of the second bunk pry into her first thoracic vertebra, but that was a small item to her at the moment.

Almost automatically, she kept passing the palms of her hand down the side of her dress. She felt frayed and dirty, and very tired.

She was tired of dabbing at her hands and face with damp napkins. She was tired of wearing the same clothes for a week. She was tired of hair which seemed dank and stringy by now.

And then she was almost on her feet again, ready to turn about sharply; she wasn't going to see him; she wouldn't look at him.

But it was only Gillbret. She sank down again. "Hello, Uncle Gil."

Gillbret sat down opposite her. For a moment his thin face seemed anxious and then it started wrinkling into a smile. "I think a week of this ship is very unamusing too. I was hoping you could cheer *me* up."

But she said, "Now, Uncle Gil, don't start using psychology on me. If you think you're going to cajole me into feeling a responsibility for you, you're wrong. I'm much more likely to hit you."

"If it will make you feel better——"

"I warn you again. If you hold out your arm for me to hit, I'll do it, and if you say 'Does that make you feel better?' I'll do it again."

"In any case, it's obvious you've quarreled with Biron. What about?"

"I don't see why there's any necessity for discussion. Just leave me alone." Then, after a pause, "He thinks Father did what the Autarch said he did. I hate him for that."

"Your father?"

"No! That stupid, childish, sanctimonious fool!"

"Presumably Biron. Good. You hate him. You couldn't put a knife edge between the kind of hate that has you sitting here like this and something that would seem to my own bachelor mind to be a rather ridiculous excess of love."

"Uncle Gil," she said, "could he really have done it?"

"Biron? Done what?"

"No! Father. Could Father have done it? Could he have informed against the Rancher?"

Gillbret looked thoughtful and very sober. "I don't know." He looked at her out of the corner of his eyes. "You know, he *did* give Biron up to the Tyranni."

"Because he knew it was a trap," she said vehemently. "And it *was*. That horrible Autarch meant it as such. He said so. The Tyranni knew who Biron was and sent him to Father on purpose. Father did the only thing he could do. That should be obvious to anybody."

"Even if we accept that"—and again that sideways look—"he did try to argue you into a rather unamusing kind of marriage. If Hinrik could bring himself to do that——"

She interrupted. "He had no way out there, either."

"My dear, if you're going to excuse every act of subservience to the Tyranni as something he had to do, why, then, how do you know he didn't have to hint something about the Rancher to the Tyranni?"

"Because I'm sure he wouldn't. You don't know Father the way I do. He hates the Tyranni. He *does*. I know it. He wouldn't go out of his way to help them. I admit that he's afraid of them and doesn't dare oppose them openly, but if he could avoid it somehow, he would never help them."

"How do you know he could avoid it?"

But she shook her head violently, so that her hair tumbled about and hid her eyes. It hid the tears a bit too.

Gillbret watched a moment, then spread his hands helplessly and left.

The trailer was joined to the *Remorseless* by a wasp-waist corridor attached to the emergency air lock in the rear of the ship. It was several dozen times larger than the Tyranni vessel in capacity, almost humorously outsized.

The Autarch joined Biron in a last inspection. He said, "Do you find anything lacking?"

Biron said, "No. I think we'll be quite comfortable."

"Good. And by the way, Rizzett tells me the Lady Artemisia is not well, or at least that she looks unwell. If she requires medical attention, it might be wise to send her to my ship."

"She is quite well," said Biron curtly.

"If you say so. Would you be ready to leave in twelve hours?"

"In two hours, if you wish."

Biron passed through the connecting corridor (he had to stoop a little) into the *Remorseless* proper.

He said with a careful evenness of tone, "You've got a private suite back there, Artemisia. I won't bother you. I'll stay here most of the time."

And she replied coldly, "You don't bother me, Rancher. It doesn't matter to me where you are."

And then the ships blasted off, and after a single Jump they found themselves at the edge of the Nebula. They waited for a few hours while the final calculations were made on Jonti's ship. Inside the Nebula it would be almost blind navigation.

Biron stared glumly at the visiplate. There was nothing there! One entire half of the celestial sphere was taken up with blackness, unrelieved by a spark of light. For the first time, Biron realized how warm and friendly the stars were, how they filled space.

"It's like dropping through a hole in space," he muttered to Gillbret.

And then they Jumped again, into the Nebula.

Almost simultaneously Simok Aratap, Commissioner of the Great Khan, at the head of ten armed cruisers, listened to his navigator and said, "That doesn't matter. Follow them anyway."

And not one light-year from the point at which the *Remorseless* entered the Nebula, ten Tyranni vessels did likewise.

Sixteen: *HOUNDS!*

Simok Aratap was a little uncomfortable in his uniform. Tyrannian uniforms were made of moderately coarse materials and fit only indifferently well. It was not soldierlike to complain of such inconveniences. In fact, it was part of the Tyrannian military tradition that a little discomfort on the part of the soldier was good for discipline.

But still Aratap could bring himself to rebel against that tradition to the extent of saying, ruefully, "The tight collar irritates my neck."

Major Andros, whose collar was as tight, and who had been seen in no other than military dress in the memory of man, said, "When alone, it would be quite within regulations to open it. Before any of the officers or men, any deviation from regulation dress would be disturbing influence."

Aratap sniffed. It was the second change induced by the quasi-military nature of the expedition. In addition to being forced into uniform, he had to listen to an increasingly self-assertive military aide. That had begun even before they left Rhodia.

Andros had put it to him baldly.

He had said, "Commissioner, we will need ten ships."

Aratap had looked up, definitely annoyed. At the moment he was getting ready to follow the young Widemos in a single vessel. He laid aside the capsules in which he was preparing his report for the Khan's Colonial Bureau, to be forwarded in the unhappy case that he did not return from the expedition.

"Ten ships, Major?"

"Yes, sir. Less will not do."

"Why not?"

"I intend to maintain a reasonable security. The young man is going somewhere. You say there is a well-developed conspiracy in existence. Presumably, the two fit together."

"And therefore?"

"And therefore we must be prepared for a possibly well-developed conspiracy. One that might be able to handle a single ship."

"Or ten. Or a hundred. Where does security cease?"

"One must make a decision. In cases of military action, it is my responsibility. I suggest ten."

Aratap's contact lenses gleamed unnaturally in the wall light as he raised his eyebrows. The military carried weight. Theoretically, in times of peace, the civilian made the decisions, but here again, military tradition was a difficult thing to set aside.

He said cautiously, "I will consider the matter."

"Thank you. If you do not choose to accept my recommendations, and my suggestions have only been advanced as such, I assure you"—the major's heels clicked sharply, but the ceremonial deference was rather empty, and Aratap knew it—"that would be your privilege. You would leave me, however, no choice but to resign my commission."

It was up to Aratap to retrieve what he could from that position. He said, "It is not my intention to hamper you in any decision you may make on a purely military question, Major. I wonder if you might be as amenable to my decisions in matters of purely political importance."

"What matters are these?"

"There is the problem of Hinrik. You objected yesterday to my suggestion that he accompany us."

The major said dryly, "I consider it unnecessary. With our forces in action, the presence of outlanders would be bad for morale."

Aratap sighed softly, just below the limits of hearing. Yet Andros was a competent man in his way. There would be no use in displaying impatience.

He said, "Again, I agree with you. I merely ask you to consider the political aspects of the situation. As you know, the execution of the old Rancher of Widemos was politically uncomfortable. It stirred up the Kingdoms unnecessarily. However necessary the execution was, it makes it desirable to refrain from having the death of the son attributed to us. As far as the people of Rhodia know, the young Widemos has kidnaped the daughter of the Director, the girl, by the way, being a popular and much publicized member of the Hinriads. It would be quite fitting, quite understandable, to have the Director head the punitive expedition.

"It would be a dramatic move, very gratifying to Rhodian patriotism. Naturally, he would ask for Tyrannian assistance, and receive it, but that can be played down. It would be easy, and necessary, to fix this expedition in the popular mind as a Rhodian one. If the inner workings of the conspiracy are uncovered, it will have been a Rhodian discovery. If the young Widemos is executed, it would be a Rhodian execution, as far as the other Kingdoms are concerned."

The major said, "It would still be a bad precedent to allow Rhodian vessels to accompany a Tyrannian military expedition. They would hamper us in a fight. In that way, the question becomes a military one."

"I did not say, my dear Major, that Henrik would command a ship. Surely you know him better than to think him capable of commanding or even anxious to try. He will stay with us. There will be no other Rhodian aboard ship."

"In that case, I waive my objection, Commissioner," said the major.

The Tyrannian fleet had maintained their position two light-years off Lingane for the better part of a week and the situation was becoming increasingly unstable.

Major Andros advocated an immediate landing on Lingane. "The Autarch of Lingane," he said, "has gone to considerable lengths to have us think him a friend of the Khan, but I do not trust these men who travel abroad. They gain unsettling notions. It is strange that just as he returns, the young Widemos travels to meet him."

"He has not tried to hide either his travels or his return, Major. And we do not know that Widemos goes to meet him. He maintains an orbit about Lingane. Why does he not land?"

"Why does he maintain an orbit? Let us question what he does and not what he does not do."

"I can propose something which will fit the pattern."

"I would be glad to hear it."

Aratap placed a finger inside his collar and tried futilely to stretch it. He said, "Since the young man is waiting, we can presume he is waiting for something or somebody. It would be ridiculous to think that, having gone to Lingane by so direct and rapid a route—a single Jump, in fact—that he is merely waiting out of indecision. I say, then, that he is waiting for a friend or friends to reach him. Thus reinforced, he will proceed elsewhere. The fact that he is not landing on Lingane directly would indicate that he does not consider such an action safe. That would indicate that Lingane in general—the Autarch in particular—is not concerned in the conspiracy, although individual Linganians may be."

"I don't know if we can always trust the obvious solution to be the correct one."

"My dear Major, this is not merely an obvious solution. It is a logical one. It fits a pattern."

"Maybe it does. But just the same, if there are no further developments in twenty-four hours, I will have no choice but to order an advance Linganeward."

Aratap frowned at the door through which the major had left. It was disturbing to have to control at once the restless conquered and the short-sighted conquerors. Twenty-four hours. Something might happen; otherwise he might have to find some way of stopping Andros.

The door signal sounded and Aratap looked up with irritation. Surely it could not be Andros returning. It wasn't. The tall, stooped form of Hinrik of Rhodia was in the doorway, behind him a glimpse of the guard who accompanied him everywhere on the ship. Theoretically, Hinrik had complete freedom of movement. Probably he himself thought he had. At least, he never paid any attention to the guard at his elbow.

Hinrik smiled mistily. "Am I disturbing you, Commissioner?"

"Not at all. Take a seat, Director." Aratap remained standing. Hinrik seemed not to notice that.

Hinrik said, "I have something of importance to discuss with you." He paused, and some of the intentness passed out of his eyes. He added in quite a different tone, "What a large, fine ship this is!"

"Thank you, Director." Aratap smiled tightly. The nine accompanying ships were typically minute in size, but the flagship on which they stood was an outsized model adapted from the designs of the defunct Rhodian navy. It was perhaps the first sign of the gradual softening of the Tyrannian military spirit that more and more of such ships were being added to the navy. The fighting unit was still the tiny two- to three-man cruiser, but increasingly the top brass found reasons for requiring large ships for their own headquarters.

It did not bother Aratap. To some of the older soldiers such increasing softness seemed a degeneration; to himself it seemed increasing civilization. In the end—in centuries, perhaps—it might even happen that the Tyranni would melt away as a single people, fusing with the present conquered societies of the Nebular Kingdoms—and perhaps even that might be a good thing.

Naturally, he never expressed such an opinion aloud.

"I came to tell you something," said Hinrik. He puzzled over it awhile, then added, "I have sent a message home today to my people. I have told them I am well and that the criminal will be shortly seized and my daughter returned to safety."

"Good," said Aratap. It was not news to him. He himself had written the message, though it was not impossible that Hinrik by now had persuaded himself that he was the writer, or even that he actually headed the expedition. Aratap felt a twinge of pity. The man was disintegrating visibly.

Hinrik said, "My people, I believe, are quite disturbed over this daring raid upon the Palace by these well-organized bandits. I think they will be proud of their Director now that I have taken such rapid action in response, eh, Commissioner? They will see that there is still force among the Hinriads." He seemed filled with a feeble triumph.

"I think they will," said Aratap.

"Are we within range of the enemy yet?"

"No, Director, the enemy remains where he was, just off Lingane."

"Still? I remember what I came to tell you." He grew excited, so that the words tumbled out. "It is very important, Commissioner. I have something to tell you. There is treachery on board. I have discovered it. We must take quick action. Treachery—" He was whispering.

Aratap felt impatient. It was necessary to humor the poor idiot of course, but this was becoming a waste of time. At this rate he would become so obviously mad that he would be useless even as a puppet, which would be a pity.

He said, "No treachery, Director. Our men are stanch and true. Someone has been misleading you. You are tired."

"No, no." Hinrik put aside Aratap's arm which, for a moment, had rested upon his shoulder. "Where are we?"

"Why, here!"

"The ship, I mean. I have watched the visiplate. We are near no star. We are in deep space. Did you know that?"

"Why, certainly."

"Lingane is nowhere near. Did you know that?"

"It is two light-years off."

"Ah! Ah! Ah! Commissioner, no one is listening? Are you sure?" He leaned closely, while Aratap allowed his ear to be approached. "Then how do we know the enemy is near Lingane? He is too far to detect. We are being misinformed, and this signifies treachery."

Well, the man might be mad, but the point was a good one. Aratap said, "This is something fit for technical men, Director, and not for men of rank to concern themselves with. I scarcely know myself."

"But as head of the expedition I should know. I am head, am I not?" He looked about carefully. "Actually, I have a feeling that Major Andros does not always carry out my orders. Is he trustworthy? Of course, I rarely give him orders. It would seem strange to order a Tyrannian officer. But then, I must find my daughter. My daughter's name is Artemisia. She has been taken from me, and I am taking all this fleet to get her back. So you see, I must know. I mean, I must know how it is known the enemy is at Lingane. My daughter would be there too. Do you know my daughter? Her name is Artemisia."

His eyes looked up at the Tyranni Commissioner in appeal. Then he covered them with his hand and mumbled something that sounded like "I'm sorry."

Aratap felt his jaw muscles clench. It was difficult to remember that the man before him was a bereaved father and that even the idiot Director of Rhodia might have a father's feelings. He could not let the man suffer.

He said gently, "I will try to explain. You know there is such a thing as a massometer which will detect ships in space."

"Yes, yes."

"It is sensitive to gravitational effects. You know what I mean?"

"Oh yes. Everything has gravity." Hinrik was leaning toward Aratap, his hands gripping one another nervously.

"That's good enough. Now naturally the massometer can only be used when the ship is close, you know. Less than a million miles away or so. Also, it has to be a reasonable distance from any planet, because if it isn't, all you can detect is the planet, which is much bigger."

"And has much more gravity."

"Exactly," said Aratap, and Hinrik looked pleased.

Aratap went on, "We Tyranni have another device. It is a transmitter which radiates through hyperspace in all directions, and what it radiates is a particular type of distortion of the space fabric which is not electromagnetic in character. In other words, it isn't like light or radio or even sub-etheric radio. See?"

Hinrik didn't answer. He looked confused.

Aratap proceeded quickly. "Well, it's different. It doesn't matter how. We can detect that something which is radiated, so that we can always know where any Tyrannian ship is, even if it's halfway across the Galaxy, or on the other side of a star."

Hinrik nodded solemnly.

"Now," said Aratap, "if the young Widemos had escaped in an ordinary ship, it would have been very difficult to locate him. As it is, since he took a Tyrannian cruiser, we know where he is at all times, although he doesn't realize that. That is how we know he is near Lingane, you see. And, what's more, he can't get away, so that we will certainly rescue your daughter."

Hinrik smiled. "That is well done. I congratulate you, Commissioner. A very clever ruse."

Aratap did not delude himself. Hinrik understood very little of what he had said, but that did not matter. It had ended with the assurance of his daughter's rescue, and somewhere in his dim understanding there must be the realization that this, somehow, was made possible by Tyrannian science.

He told himself that he had not gone to this trouble entirely because the Rhodian appealed to his sense of the pathetic. He had to keep the man from breaking down altogether for obvious political reasons. Perhaps the return of his daughter would improve matters. He hoped so.

There was the door signal again and this time it was Major Andros who entered. Hinrik's arm stiffened on the armrest of his chair and his face assumed a hunted expression. He lifted himself and began, "Major Andros——"

But Andros was already speaking quickly, disregarding the Rhodian.

"Commissioner," he said, "the *Remorseless* has changed position."

"Surely he has not landed on Lingane," said Aratap sharply.

"No," said the major. "He has Jumped quite a way from Lingane."

"Ah. Good. He has been joined by another ship, perhaps."

"By many ships, perhaps. We can detect only his, as you are quite aware."

"In any case, we follow again."

"The order has already been given. I would merely like to point out that his Jump has taken him to the edge of the Horsehead Nebula."

"What?"

"No major planetary system exists in the indicated direction. There is only one logical conclusion."

Aratap moistened his lips and left hurriedly for the pilot room, the major with him.

Hinrik remained standing in the middle of the suddenly empty room, looking at the door for a minute or so. Then, with a little shrug of the shoulders, he sat down again. His expression was blank, and for a long while he simply sat.

The navigator said, "The space co-ordinates of the *Remorseless* have been checked, sir. They are definitely inside the Nebula."

"That doesn't matter," said Aratap. "Follow them anyway."

He turned to Major Andros. "So you see the virtues of waiting.

There is a good deal that is obvious now. Wherever else could the conspirators' headquarters be but in the Nebula itself? Where else could we have failed to locate them? A *very* pretty pattern."

And so the squadron entered the Nebula.

For the twentieth time Aratap glanced automatically at the visiplate. Actually, the glances were useless, since the visiplate remained quite black. There was no star in sight.

Andros said, "That's their third stop without landing. I don't understand it. What is their purpose? What are they after? Each stop of theirs is several days long. Yet they do not land."

"It may take them that long," said Aratap, "to calculate their next Jump. Visibility is nonexistent."

"You think so?"

"No. Their Jumps are too good. Each time they land very near a star. They couldn't do as well by massometer data alone, unless they actually knew the locations of the stars in advance."

"Then why don't they land?"

"I think," said Aratap, "they must be looking for habitable planets. Maybe they themselves do not know the location of the center of conspiracy. Or, at least, not entirely." He smiled. "We need only follow."

The navigator clicked heels. "Sir!"

"Yes?" Aratap looked up.

"The enemy has landed on a planet."

Aratap signaled for Major Andros.

"Andros," said Aratap, as the major entered, "have you been told?"

"Yes. I've ordered a descent and pursuit."

"Wait. You may be again premature, as when you wanted to lunge toward Lingane. I think this ship only ought to go."

"Your reasoning?"

"If we need reinforcements, you will be there, in command of the cruisers. If it is indeed a powerful rebel center, they may think only one ship has stumbled upon them. I will get word to you somehow and you can retire to Tyrann."

"Retire!"

"And return with a full fleet."

Andros considered. "Very well. This is our least useful ship in any case. Too large."

The planet filled the visiplate as they spiraled down.

"The surface seems quite barren, sir," said the navigator.

"Have you determined the exact location of the *Remorseless?*"

"Yes, sir."

"Then land as closely as you can without being sighted."

They were entering the atmosphere now. The sky as they flashed along the day half of the planet was tinged with a brightening purple. Aratap watched the nearing surface. The long chase was almost over!

Seventeen: *AND HARES!*

To those who have not actually been in space, the investigation of a stellar system and the search for habitable planets may seem rather exciting, at the least, interesting. To the spaceman, it is the most boring of jobs.

Locating a star, which is a huge glowing mass of hydrogen fusing into helium, is almost too easy. It advertises itself. Even in the blackness of the Nebula, it is only a question of distance. Approach within five billion miles, and it will still advertise itself.

But a planet, a relatively small mass of rock, shining only by reflected light, is another matter. One could pass through a stellar system a hundred thousand times at all sorts of odd angles without ever coming close enough to a planet to see it for what it is, barring the oddest of coincidences.

Rather, one adopts a system. A position is taken up in space at a distance from the star being investigated of some ten thousand times the star's diameter. From Galactic statistics it is known that not one time in fifty thousand is a planet located farther from its primary than that. Furthermore, practically never is a *habitable* planet located farther from its primary than one thousand times its sun's diameter.

This means that from the position in space assumed by the ship, any habitable planet must be located within six degrees of the star.

This represents an area only 1/3600th of the entire sky. That area can be handled in detail with relatively few observations.

The movement of the tele-camera can be so adjusted as to counteract the motion of the ship in its orbit. Under those conditions a time exposure will pin point the constellations in the star's neighborhood; provided, of course, that the blaze of the sun itself is blocked out, which is easily done. Planets, however, will have perceptible proper motions and therefore show up as tiny streaks on the film.

When no streaks appear, there is always the possibility that the planets are behind their primary. The maneuver is therefore repeated from another position in space and, usually, at a point closer to the star.

It is a very dull procedure indeed, and when it has been repeated three times for three different stars, each time with completely negative results, a certain depression of morale is bound to occur.

Gillbret's morale, for instance, had been suffering for quite a while. Longer and longer intervals took place between the moments when he found something "amusing."

They were readying for the Jump to the fourth star on the Autarch's list, and Biron said, "We hit a star each time, anyway. At least Jonti's figures are correct."

Gillbret said, "Statistics show that one out of three stars has a planetary system."

Biron nodded. It was a well-worn statistic. Every child was taught that in elementary Galactography.

Gillbret went on, "That means that the chances of finding three stars at random without a single planet—without one single planet—is two thirds cubed, which is eight twenty-sevenths, or less than one in three."

"So?"

"And we haven't found any. There must be a mistake."

"You saw the plates yourself. And, besides, what price statistics? For all we know, conditions are different inside a Nebula. Maybe the particle fog prevents planets from forming, or maybe the fog is the result of planets that didn't coalesce."

"You don't mean that?" said Gillbret, stricken.

"You're right. I'm just talking to hear myself. I don't know anything about cosmogony. Why the hell are planets formed, anyway?

Never heard of one that wasn't filled with trouble." Biron looked haggard himself. He was still printing and pasting up little stickers on the control panels.

He said, "Anyway, we've got the blasters all worked out, range finders, power control—all that."

It was very difficult not to look at the visiplate. They'd be Jumping again soon, through that ink.

Biron said absently, "You know why they call it the Horsehead Nebula, Gil?"

"The first man to enter it was Horace Hedd. Are you going to tell me that's wrong?"

"It may be. They have a different explanation on Earth."

"Oh?"

"They claim it's called that because it looks like a horse's head."

"What's a horse?"

"It's an animal on Earth."

"It's an amusing thought, but the Nebula doesn't look like any animal to me, Biron."

"It depends on the angle you look at it. Now from Nephelos it looks like a man's arm with three fingers, but I looked at it once from the observatory at the University of Earth. It *does* look a little like a horse's head. Maybe that is how the name started. Maybe there never was any Horace Hedd. Who knows?" Biron felt bored with the matter, already. He was still talking simply to hear himself talk.

There was a pause, a pause that lasted too long, because it gave Gillbret a chance to bring up a subject which Biron did not wish to discuss and could not force himself to stop thinking about.

Gillbret said, "Where's Arta?"

Biron looked at him quickly and said, "Somewhere in the trailer. I don't follow her about."

"The Autarch does. He might as well be living here."

"How lucky for her."

Gillbret's wrinkles became more pronounced and his small features seemed to screw together. "Oh, don't be a fool, Biron. Artemisia is a Hinriad. She can't take what you've been giving her."

Biron said, "Drop it."

"I won't. I've been spoiling to say this. Why are you doing this to her? Because Hinrik might have been responsible for your father's death? Hinrik is my cousin! You haven't changed toward me."

"All right," Biron said, "I haven't changed toward you. I speak to you as I always have. I speak to Artemisia as well."

"As you always have?"

Biron was silent.

Gillbret said, "You're throwing her at the Autarch."

"It's her choice."

"It isn't. It's your choice. Listen, Biron"—Gillbret grew confidential; he put a hand on Biron's knee—"this isn't a thing I like to interfere with, you understand. It's just that she's the only good thing in the Hinriad family just now. Would you be amused if I said I loved her? I have no children of my own."

"I don't question your love."

"Then I advise you for her good. Stop the Autarch, Biron."

"I thought you trusted him, Gil."

"As the Autarch, yes. As an anti-Tyrannian leader, yes. But as a man for a woman, as a man for Artemisia, no."

"Tell her that."

"She wouldn't listen."

"Do you think she would listen if I told her?"

"If you told her properly."

For a moment Biron seemed to hesitate, his tongue dabbing slightly at dry lips. Then he turned away, saying harshly, "I don't want to talk about it."

Gillbret said sadly, "You'll regret this."

Biron said nothing. Why didn't Gillbret leave him alone? It had occurred to him many times that he might regret all this. It wasn't easy. But what could he do? There was no safe way of backing out.

He tried breathing through his mouth to get rid, somehow, of the choking sensation in his chest.

The outlook was different after the next Jump. Biron had set the controls in accordance with the instructions from the Autarch's pilot, and left the manuals to Gillbret. He was going to sleep through this one. And then Gillbret was shaking his shoulder.

"Biron! Biron!"

Biron rolled over in his bunk and out, landing in a crouch, fists balled. "What is it?"

Gillbret stepped back hastily. "Now, take it easy. We've got an F-2 this time."

It sank in. Gillbret drew a deep breath and relaxed. "Don't ever wake me that way, Gillbret. An F-2, you say? I suppose you're referring to the new star."

"I surely am. It looks most amusing, I think."

In a way, it did. Approximately 95 per cent of habitable planets in the Galaxy circled stars of spectral types F or G; diameter from 750 to 1500 thousand miles, surface temperature from five to ten thousand centigrade. Earth's sun was G-0, Rhodia's F-8, Lingane's G-2, as was that of Nephelos. F-2 was a little warm, but not too warm.

The first three stars they had stopped at were of spectral type K, rather small and ruddy. Planets would probably not have been decent even if they had had any.

A good star is a good star! In the first day of photography, five planets were located, the nearest being one hundred and fifty million miles from the primary.

Tedor Rizzett brought the news personally. He visited the *Remorseless* as frequently as the Autarch, lighting the ship with his heartiness. He was whoofing and panting this time from the hand-over-hand exercises along the metal line.

He said, "I don't know how the Autarch does it. He never seems to mind. Comes from being younger, I guess." He added abruptly, "Five planets!"

Gillbret said, "For this star? You're sure?"

"It's definite. Four of them are J-type, though."

"And the fifth?"

"The fifth may be all right. Oxygen in the atmosphere, anyway."

Gillbret set up a thin sort of yell of triumph, but Biron said, "Four are J-type. Oh well, we only need one."

He realized it was a reasonable distribution. The large majority of sizable planets in the Galaxy possessed hydrogenated atmospheres. After all, stars are mostly hydrogen, and they are the source material of planetary building blocks. J-type planets had atmospheres of methane or ammonia, with molecular hydrogen in addition sometimes, and also considerable helium. Such atmospheres were usually deep and extremely dense. The planets themselves were almost invariably thirty thousand miles in diameter and up, with a mean temperature of rarely more than fifty below zero, centigrade. They were quite uninhabitable.

Back on Earth they used to tell him that these planets were called J-type because the J stood for Jupiter, the planet in Earth's solar system which was the best example of the type. Maybe they were right. Certainly, the other planet classification was the E-type and E did stand for Earth. E-types were usually small, comparatively, and their weaker gravity could not retain hydrogen or the hydrogen-containing gases, particularly since they were usually closer to the sun and warmer. Their atmospheres were thin and contained oxygen and nitrogen usually, with, occasionally, an admixture of chlorine, which would be bad.

"Any chlorine?" asked Biron. "How well have they gone over the atmosphere?"

Rizzett shrugged. "We can only judge the upper reaches from out in space. If there were any chlorine, it would concentrate toward ground level. We'll see."

He clapped a hand on Biron's large shoulder. "How about inviting me to a small drink in your room, boy?"

Gillbret looked after them uneasily. With the Autarch courting Artemisia, and his right-hand man becoming a drinking companion of Biron, the *Remorseless* was becoming more Linganian than not. He wondered if Biron knew what he was doing, then thought of the new planet and let the rest go.

Artemisia was in the pilot room when they penetrated the atmosphere. There was a little smile on her face and she seemed quite contented. Biron looked in her direction occasionally. He had said, "Good day, Artemisia," when she came in (she hardly ever did come in; he had been caught by surprise), but she hadn't answered.

She had merely said, "Uncle Gil," very brightly; then, "Is it true we're landing?"

And Gil had rubbed his hands. "It seems so, my dear. We may be getting out of the ship in a few hours, walking on solid surface. How's that for an amusing thought?"

"I hope it's the right planet. If it isn't, it won't be so amusing."

"There's still another star," said Gil, but his brow furrowed and contracted as he said so.

And then Artemisia turned to Biron and said, coolly, "Did you speak, Mr. Farrill?"

Biron, caught by surprise again, started and said, "No, not really."

"I beg your pardon, then. I thought you had."

She passed by him so closely that the plastic flair of her dress brushed his knee and her perfume momentarily surrounded him. His jaw muscles knotted.

Rizzett was still with them. One of the advantages of the trailer was that they could put up a guest overnight. He said, "They're getting details on the atmosphere now. Lots of oxygen, almost 30 per cent, and nitrogen and inert gases. It's quite normal. No chlorine." Then he paused and said, "Hmm."

Gillbret said, "What's the matter?"

"No carbon dioxide. That's not so good."

"Why not?" demanded Artemisia from her vantage point near the visiplate, where she watched the distant surface of the planet blur past at two thousand miles an hour.

Biron said curtly, "No carbon dioxide—no plant life."

"Oh?" She looked at him, and smiled warmly.

Biron, against his will, smiled back, and somehow, with scarcely a visible change in her countenance, she was smiling through him, past him, obviously unaware of his existence; and he was left there, caught in a foolish smile. He let it fade.

It was just as well he avoided her. Certainly, when he was with her, he couldn't keep it up. When he could actually see her, the anesthetic of his will didn't work. It began hurting.

Gillbret was doleful. They were coasting now. In the thick lower reaches of the atmosphere, the *Remorseless*, with its aerodynamically undesirable addition of a trailer, was difficult to handle. Biron fought the bucking controls stubbornly.

He said, "Cheer up, Gil!"

He felt not exactly jubilant himself. Radio signals had brought no response as yet, and if this were *not* the rebellion world, there would be no point in waiting longer. His line of action was set!

Gillbret said, "It doesn't look like the rebellion world. It's rocky and dead, and not much water, either." He turned. "Did they try for carbon dioxide again, Rizzett?"

Rizzett's ruddy face was long. "Yes. Just a trace. About a thousandth of a per cent or so."

Biron said, "You can't tell. They might pick a world like this, just because it would look so hopeless."

"But I saw farms," said Gillbret.

"All right. How much do you suppose we can see of a planet this size by circling it a few times? You know damn well, Gil, that whoever they are, they can't have enough people to fill a whole planet. They may have picked themselves a valley somewhere where the carbon dioxide of the air has been built up, say, by volcanic action, and where there's plenty of nearby water. We could whiz within twenty miles of them and never know it. Naturally, they wouldn't be ready to answer radio calls without considerable investigation."

"You can't build up a concentration of carbon dioxide that easily," muttered Gillbret. But he watched the visiplate intently.

Biron suddenly hoped that it *was* the wrong world. He decided that he could wait no longer. It would have to be settled, *now!*

It was a queer feeling.

The artificial lights had been turned off and sunlight was coming in unhindered at the ports. Actually, it was the less efficient method of lighting the ship, but there was a sudden desirable novelty to it. The ports were open, in fact, and a native atmosphere could be breathed.

Rizzett advised against it on the grounds that lack of carbon dioxide would upset the respiratory regulation of the body, but Biron thought it might be bearable for a short time.

Gillbret had come upon them, heads together. They looked up and leaned away from each other.

Gillbret laughed. Then he looked out of the open port, sighed, and said, "Rocks!"

Biron said mildly, "We're going to set up a radio transmitter at the top of the high ground. We'll get more range that way. At any rate, we ought to be able to contact all of this hemisphere. And if it's negative, we can try the other side of the planet."

"Is that what you and Rizzett were discussing?"

"Exactly. The Autarch and I will do the job. It's his suggestion, which is fortunate, since otherwise I would have had to make the same suggestion myself." He looked fleetingly at Rizzett as he spoke. Rizzett was expressionless.

Biron stood up. "I think it would be best if I unzipped my spacesuit lining and wore that."

Rizzett was in agreement. It was sunny on this planet; there was little water vapor in the air and no clouds, but it was briskly cold.

The Autarch was at the main lock of the *Remorseless*. His overcoat was a thin foamite that weighed a fraction of an ounce, yet did a nearly perfect job of insulation. A small carbon-dioxide cylinder was strapped to his chest, adjusted to a slow leak that would maintain a perceptible CO_2 vapor tension in his immediate vicinity.

He said, "Would you care to search me, Farrill?" He raised his hands and waited, his lean face quietly amused.

"No," said Biron. "Do you want to check *me* for weapons?"

"I wouldn't think of it."

The courtesies were as frigid as the weather.

Biron stepped out into the hard sunlight and tugged at the handle of the two-handled suitcase in which the radio equipment was stowed. The Autarch caught the other.

"Not too heavy," said Biron. He turned, and Artemisia was standing just within the ship, silent.

Her dress was a smooth, unfigured white which folded in a smooth drape that fled before the wind. The semitransparent sleeves whipped back against her arms, turning them to silver.

For a moment Biron melted dangerously. He wanted to return quickly; to run, leap into the ship, grasp her so that his fingers would leave bruises on her shoulders, feel his lips meet hers——

But he nodded briefly instead, and her returning smile, the light flutter of her fingers was for the Autarch.

Five minutes later he turned and there was still that glimmer of white at the open door, and then the rise in the ground cut off the view of the ship. The horizon was free of everything but broken and bare rock now.

Biron thought of what lay ahead, and wondered if he would ever see Artemisia again—and if she would care if he never returned.

Eighteen: *OUT OF THE JAWS OF DEFEAT!*

Artemisia watched them as they became tiny figures, trudging up the bare granite, then dipping below and out of sight. For a moment, just before they disappeared, one of them had turned. She couldn't be sure which one, and, for a moment, her heart hardened.

He had not said a word on parting. Not one word. She turned away from the sun and rock toward the confined metal interior of the ship. She felt alone, terribly alone; she had never felt so alone in her life.

It was that, perhaps, that made her shiver, but it would have been an intolerable confession of weakness to admit that it wasn't simply the cold.

She said peevishly, "Uncle Gil! Why don't you close the ports? It's enough to freeze a person to death." The thermometer dial read plus seven centigrade with the ship's heaters on high.

"My dear Arta," said Gillbret mildly, "if you will persist in your ridiculous habit of wearing nothing but a little fog here and there, you must expect to be cold." But he closed certain contacts, and, with little clicks, the air lock slid shut, the ports sunk inward and molded themselves into the smooth, gleaming hull. As they did so, the thick glass polarized and became nontransparent. The lights of the ship went on and the shadows disappeared.

Artemisia sat down in the heavily padded pilot's seat and fingered the arms aimlessly. *His* hands had often rested there, and the slight warmth that flooded her as she thought that (she told herself) was only the result of the heaters making themselves felt decently, now that the outer winds were excluded.

The long minutes passed, and it became impossible to sit quietly. She might have gone with him! She corrected the rebellious thought instantly as it passed through her mind, and changed the singular "him" to the plural "them."

She said, "Why do they have to set up a radio transmitter anyway, Uncle Gil?"

He looked up from the visiplate, the controls of which he was fingering delicately, and said, "Eh?"

"We've been trying to contact them from out in space," she said, "and we haven't reached anyone. What special good would a transmitter on the planet's surface do?"

Gillbret was troubled. "Why, we must keep trying, my dear. We must find the rebellion world." And, between his teeth, he added to himself, "We must!"

A moment passed, and he said, "I can't find them."

"Find whom?"

"Biron and the Autarch. The ridge cuts me off no matter how I arrange the external mirrors. See?"

She saw nothing but the sunny rock flashing past.

Then Gillbret brought the little gears to rest and said, "Anyway, that's the Autarch's ship."

Artemisia accorded it the briefest of glances. It lay deeper in the valley, perhaps a mile away. It glistened unbearably in the sun. It seemed to her, at the moment, to be the real enemy. *It* was, not the Tyranni. She wished suddenly, sharply, and very strongly that they had never gone to Lingane; that they had remained in space, the three of them only. Those had been funny days, so uncomfortable and yet so warm, somehow. And now she could only try to hurt him. Something *made* her hurt him, though she would have liked——

Gillbret said, "Now what does *he* want?"

Artemisia looked up at him, seeing him through a watery mist, so that she had to blink rapidly to put him into normal focus. "Who?"

"Rizzett. I *think* that's Rizzett. But he's certainly not coming this way."

Artemisia was at the visiplate. "Make it larger," she ordered.

"At this short distance?" objected Gillbret. "You won't see anything. It will be impossible to keep it centered."

"Larger, Uncle Gil."

Muttering, he threw in the telescopic attachment and searched the bloated nubbles of rock that resulted. They jumped faster than the eye could follow at the lightest touch on the controls. For one moment, Rizzett, a large, hazy figure, flashed past, and in that moment his identity was unmistakable. Gillbret backtracked wildly, caught him again, hung on for a moment, and Artemisia said, "He's armed. Did you see that?"

"No."

"He's got a long-range blasting rifle, I tell you!"

She was up, tearing away at the locker.

"Arta! What are you doing?"

She was unzipping the lining from another space suit. "I'm going out there. Rizzett's following them. Don't you understand? The Autarch hasn't gone out to set up a radio. It's a trap for Biron." She was gasping as she forced herself into the thick, coarse lining.

"Stop it! You're imagining things."

But she was staring at Gillbret without seeing him, her face pinched and white. She should have seen it before, the way Rizzett had been coddling that fool. That emotional fool! Rizzett had praised his father, told him what a great man the Rancher of Widemos had been, and Biron had melted immediately. His every action was dictated by the thought of his father. How could a man let himself be so ruled by a monomania?

She said, "I don't know what controls the air lock. Open it."

"Arta, you're not leaving the ship. You don't know where they are."

"I'll find them. Open the air lock."

Gillbret shook his head.

But the space suit she had stripped had borne a holster. She said, "Uncle Gil, I'll use this. I swear I will."

And Gillbret found himself staring at the wicked muzzle of a neuronic whip. He forced a smile. "Don't now!"

"Open the lock!" she gasped.

He did and she was out, running into the wind, slipping across the rocks and up the ridge. The blood pounded in her ears. She had been as bad as he, dangling the Autarch before him for no purpose other than her silly pride. It seemed silly now, and the Autarch's personality sharpened in her mind, a man so studiedly cold as to be bloodless and tasteless. She quivered with repulsion.

She had topped the ridge, and there was nothing ahead of her. Stolidly she walked onward, holding the neuronic whip before her.

Biron and the Autarch had not exchanged a word during their walk, and now they came to a halt where the ground leveled off. The rock was fissured by the action of sun and wind through the millennia. Ahead of them there was an ancient fault, the farther lip of which had crumbled downward, leaving a sheer precipice of a hundred feet.

Biron approached cautiously and looked over it. It slanted outward past the drop, the ground riddled with craggy boulders which, with time and infrequent rains, had scattered out as far as he could see.

"It looks," he said, "like a hopeless world, Jonti."

The Autarch displayed none of Biron's curiosity in his surroundings. He did not approach the drop. He said, "This is the place we found before landing. It's ideal for our purposes."

It's ideal for your purposes, at least, thought Biron. He stepped away from the edge and sat down. He listened to the tiny hiss from his carbon-dioxide cylinder, and waited a moment.

Then he said, very quietly, "What will you tell them when you get back to your ship, Jonti? Or shall I guess?"

The Autarch paused in the act of opening the two-handled suitcase they had carried. He straightened and said, "What are you talking about?"

Biron felt the wind numb his face and rubbed his nose with his gloved hand. Yet he unbuttoned the foamite lining that wrapped him, so that it flapped wide as the gusts hit it.

He said, "I'm talking about your purpose in coming here."

"I would like to set up the radio rather than waste my time discussing the matter, Farrill."

"You won't set up a radio. Why should you? We tried reaching them from space, without a response. There's no reason to expect more of a transmitter on the surface. It's not a question of ionized radio-opaque layers in the upper atmosphere, either, because we tried the sub-ether as well and drew a blank. Nor are we particularly the radio experts in our party. So why did you really come up here, Jonti?"

The Autarch sat down opposite Biron. A hand patted the suitcase idly. "If you are troubled by these doubts, why did *you* come?"

"To discover truth. Your man, Rizzett, told me you were planning this trip, and advised me to join you. I believe that your instructions to him were to tell me that by joining you I might make certain you received no messages that I remained unaware of. It was a reasonable point, except that I don't think you will receive any messages. But I allowed it to persuade me, and I've come with you."

"To discover truth?" said Jonti mockingly.

"Exactly that. I can guess truth already."

"Tell *me* then. Let me discover truth as well."

"You came to kill me. I am here alone with you, and there is a cliff before us over which it would be certain death to fall. There would be no signs of deliberate violence. There would be no blasted limbs or any thought of weapon play. It would make a nice, sad story to take back to your ship. I had slipped and fallen. You might bring back a party to gather me up and give me a decent burial. It would all be very touching and I would be out of your way."

"You believe this, and yet you came?"

"I expect it, so you won't catch me by surprise. We are unarmed and I doubt that you could force me over by muscular power alone."

For a moment Biron's nostrils flared. He half flexed his right arm, slowly and hungrily.

But Jonti laughed. "Shall we concern ourselves with our radio transmitter, then, since your death is now impossible?"

"Not yet. I am not done. I want your admission that you were going to try to kill me."

"Oh? Do you insist that I play my proper role in this impromptu drama you have developed? How do you expect to force me to do so? Do you intend to beat a confession out of me? Now understand, Farrill, you are a young man and I am disposed to make allowances because of that and because of the convenience of your name and rank. However, I must admit you have until now been more trouble than help to me."

"So I have been. By keeping alive, despite you!"

"If you refer to the risks you ran on Rhodia, I have explained it; I will not explain it again."

Biron rose. "Your explanation was not accurate. It has a flaw in it which was obvious from the beginning."

"Really?"

"Really! Stand up and listen to me, or I'll drag you to your feet."

The Autarch's eyes narrowed to slits as he rose. "I would not advise you to attempt violence, youngster."

"Listen." Biron's voice was loud and his cloak still bellied open in the breeze, disregarded. "You said that you sent me to a possible death on Rhodia only to implicate the Director in an anti-Tyrannian plot."

"That remains true."

"That remains a lie. Your prime object was to have me killed. You informed the captain of the Rhodian ship of my identity at the very beginning. You had no real reason for believing that I would ever be allowed to reach Hinrik."

"If I had wanted to kill you, Farrill, I might have planted a real radiation bomb in your room."

"It would have been obviously more convenient to have the Tyranni maneuvered into doing the killing for you."

"I might have killed you in space when I first boarded the *Remorseless*."

"So you might. You came equipped with a blaster and you had it leveled at me at one point. You had expected me on board, but you hadn't told your crew that. When Rizzett called and saw me, it was no longer possible to blast me. You made a mistake then. You told me you *had* told your men I was probably on board, and awhile later Rizzett told me you had not. Don't you brief your men concerning your exact lies as you tell them, Jonti?"

Jonti's face had been white in the cold, but it seemed to whiten further. "I should kill you now for giving me the lie, certainly. But what held back my trigger finger before Rizzett got on the visiplate and saw you?"

"Politics, Jonti. Artemisia oth Hinriad was aboard, and for the moment she was a more important object than myself. I'll give you credit for a quick change of plans. To have killed me in her presence would have ruined a bigger game."

"I had fallen in love so rapidly, then?"

"Love! When the girl concerned is a Hinriad, why not? You lost no time. You tried first to have her transferred to your ship, and when that failed, you told me that Hinrik had betrayed my father." He was silent for a moment, then said, "So I lost her and left you the field undisputed. Now, I presume, she is no longer a factor. She is firmly on your side and you may proceed with your plan to kill me without any fear that by doing it you may lose your chance at the Hinriad succession."

Jonti sighed and said, "Farrill, it is cold, and getting colder. I believe the sun is heading downward. You are unutterably foolish and you weary me. Before we end this farrago of nonsense, will you tell me why I should be in the least interested in killing you anyway? That is, if your obvious paranoia needs any reason."

"There is the same reason that caused you to kill my father."

"*What?*"

"Did you think I believed you for an instant when you said Hinrik had been the traitor? He might have been, were it not for the fact that his reputation as a wretched weakling is so well established. Do you suppose that my father was a complete fool? Could he possibly have mistaken Hinrik for anything but what he was? If he had not known his reputation, would not five minutes in his presence have revealed him completely as a hopeless puppet? Would my father have blabbed foolishly to Hinrik anything that might have been used to support a charge of treason against him? No, Jonti. The man who betrayed my father must have been one who was trusted by him."

Jonti took a step backward and kicked the suitcase aside. He poised himself to withstand a charge and said, "I see your vile implication. My only explanation for it is that you are criminally insane."

Biron was trembling, and not with cold. "My father was popular with your men, Jonti. Too popular. An Autarch cannot allow a competitor in the business of ruling. You saw to it that he did not remain a competitor. And it was your next job to see to it that I did not remain alive either to replace or to avenge him." His voice raised to a shout, which whipped away on the cold air. "Isn't this true?"

"No."

Jonti bent to the suitcase. "I can prove you are wrong!" He flung it open. "Radio equipment. Inspect it. Take a good look at it." He tossed the items to the ground at Biron's feet.

Biron stared at them. "How does that prove anything?"

Jonti rose. "It doesn't. But now take a good look at this."

He had a blaster in his hand, and his knuckles were white with tension. The coolness had left his voice. He said, "I am tired of you. But I won't have to be tired much longer."

Biron said tonelessly, "You hid a blaster in the suitcase with the equipment?"

"Did you think I wouldn't? You honestly came here expecting to be thrown off a cliff and you thought I would try to do it with my hands as though I were a stevedore or a coal miner? I am Autarch of Lingane"—his face worked and his left hand made a flat, cutting gesture before him—"and I am tired of the cant and fatuous idealism of the Ranchers of Widemos." He whispered then, "Move on. Toward the cliff." He stepped forward.

Biron, hands raised, eyes on the blaster, stepped back. "You killed my father, then."

"I killed your father!" said the Autarch. "I tell you this so you may know in the last few moments of your life that the same man who saw to it that your father was blasted to bits in a disintegration chamber will see to it that you will follow him—and keep the Hinriad girl for himself thereafter, along with all that goes with her. Think of that! I will give you an extra minute to think of that! But keep your hands steady, or I will blast you and risk any questions my men may care to ask." It was as though his cold veneer, having cracked, left nothing but a burning passion exposed.

"You tried to kill me before this, as I said."

"I did. Your guesses were in every way correct. Does that help you now? Back!"

"No," said Biron. He brought his hands down and said, "If you're going to shoot, do so."

The Autarch said, "You think I will not dare?"

"I've asked you to shoot."

"And I will." The Autarch aimed deliberately at Biron's head and at a distance of four feet closed contact on his blaster.

Nineteen: *DEFEAT!*

Tedor Rizzett circled the little piece of tableland warily. He was not yet ready to be seen, but to remain hidden was difficult in this world of bare rock. In the patch of tumbled, crystalline boulders he felt safer. He threaded his way through them. Occasionally he paused to pass the soft back of the spongy gloves he wore over his face. The dry cold was deceptive.

He saw them now from between two granite monoliths that met in a V. He rested his blaster in the crotch. The sun was on his back. He felt its feeble warmth soak through, and he was satisfied. If they happened to look in his direction, the sun would be in their eyes and he himself would be that much less visible.

Their voices were sharp in his ear. Radio communication was in operation and he smiled at that. So far, according to plan. His own presence, of course, was not according to plan, but it would be better so. The plan was a rather overconfident one and the victim was not a complete fool, after all. His own blaster might yet be needed to decide the issue.

He waited. Stolidly he watched the Autarch lift his blaster as Biron stood there, unflinching.

Artemisia did not see the blaster lift. She did not see the two figures on the flat rock surface. Five minutes earlier she had seen Rizzett silhouetted for a moment against the sky, and since then she had followed him.

Somehow, he was moving too fast for her. Things dimmed and wavered before her and twice she found herself stretched on the ground. She did not recall falling. The second time, she staggered to her feet with one wrist oozing blood where a sharp edge had scraped her.

Rizzett had gained again and she had to reel after him. When he vanished in the glistening boulder forest, she sobbed in despair. She leaned against a rock, completely weary. Its beautiful flesh-pink tint, the glassy smoothness of its surface, the fact that it stood as an ancient reminder of a primeval volcanic age was lost upon her.

She could only try to fight the sensation of choking that pervaded her.

And then she saw him, dwarfed at the forked-rock formation, his back to her. She held the neuronic whip before her as she ran unevenly over the hard ground. He was sighting along the barrel of his rifle, intent upon the process, taking aim, getting ready.

She wouldn't make it in time.

She would have to distract his attention. She called, "Rizzett!" And again, "Rizzett, don't shoot!"

She stumbled again. The sun was blotting out, but consciousness lingered. It lingered long enough for her to feel the ground jar thuddingly against her, long enough to press her finger upon the whip's contact; and long enough for her to know that she was well out of range, even if her aim was accurate, which it could not be.

She felt arms about her, lifting. She tried to see, but her eyelids would not open.

"Biron?" It was a weak whisper.

The answer was a rough blur of words, but it was Rizzett's voice. She tried to speak further, then abruptly gave up. She had failed!

Everything was blotted out.

The Autarch remained motionless for the space it would take a man to count to ten slowly. Biron faced him as motionlessly, watching the barrel of the blaster that had just been fired point-blank at him. The barrel sank slowly as he watched.

Biron said, "Your blaster seems not to be in firing order. Examine it."

The Autarch's bloodless face turned alternately from Biron to his weapon. He had fired at a distance of four feet. It should have been all over. The congealed astonishment that held him broke suddenly and he disjointed the blaster in a quick movement.

The energy capsule was missing. Where it should have been, there was a useless cavity. The Autarch whimpered with rage as he hurled the lump of dead metal aside. It turned over and over, a black blot against the sun, smashing into the rock with a faint ringing sound.

"Man to man!" said Biron. There was a trembling eagerness in his voice.

The Autarch took a step backward. He said nothing.

Biron took a slow step forward. "There are many ways I could kill you, but not all would be satisfying. If I blasted you, it would mean that a millionth of a second would separate your life from your death. You would have no consciousness of dying. That would be bad. I think that instead there would be considerable satisfaction in using the somewhat slower method of human muscular effort."

His thigh muscles tensed, but the lunge they prepared was never completed. The cry that interrupted was thin and high, packed with panic.

"Rizzett!" it came. "Rizzett, don't shoot!"

Biron whirled in time to see the motion behind the rocks a hundred yards away and the glint of sun on metal. And then the hurled weight of a human body was upon his back. He bent under it, dropping to his knees.

The Autarch had landed fairly, his knees clasped hard about the other's waist, his fist thudding at the nape of Biron's neck. Biron's breath whooshed out in a whistling grunt.

Biron fought off the gathering blackness long enough to throw himself to one side. The Autarch jumped free, gaining clear footing while Biron sprawled on his back.

He had just time to double his legs up against himself as the Autarch lunged down upon him again. The Autarch bounced off. They were up together this time, perspiration turning icy upon their cheeks.

They circled slowly. Biron tossed his carbon-dioxide cylinder to one side. The Autarch likewise unstrapped his, held it suspended a moment by its mesh-metal hose, then stepped in rapidly and swung it. Biron dropped, and both heard and felt it whistle above his head.

He was up again, leaping on the other before the Autarch could regain his balance. One large fist clamped down on the other's wrist, while the other fist exploded in the Autarch's face. He let the Autarch drop and stepped back.

Biron said, "Stand up. I'll wait for you with more of the same. There's no hurry."

The Autarch touched his gloved hand to his face then stared sickly at the blood that smeared off upon it. His mouth twisted and his hand snaked out for the metal cylinder he had dropped. Biron's foot came heavily down upon it, and the Autarch yelled in agony.

Biron said, "You're too close to the edge of the cliff, Jonti. Mustn't reach in that direction. Stand up. I'll throw you the other way now."

But Rizzett's voice rang out: "Wait!"

The Autarch screamed, "Shoot this man, Rizzett! Shoot him now! His arms first, then his legs, and we'll leave him."

Rizzett brought his weapon up slowly against his shoulder.

Biron said, "Who saw to it that your own blaster was unloaded, Jonti?"

"What?" The Autarch stared blankly.

"It was not I who had access to your blaster, Jonti. Who did have? Who is pointing a blaster at you right now, Jonti? Not at me, Jonti, but at *you!*"

The Autarch turned to Rizzett and screamed, "Traitor!"

Rizzett said, in a low voice, "Not I, sir. That man is the traitor who betrayed the loyal Rancher of Widemos to his death."

"That is not I," cried the Autarch. "If he has told you I have, he lies."

"It is you yourself who have told us. I not only emptied your weapon, I also shorted your communicator switch, so that every word you said today was received by myself and by every member of the crew. We all know you for what you are."

"I am your Autarch."

"And also the greatest traitor alive."

For a moment the Autarch said nothing, but looked wildly from one to the other as they watched him with somber, angry faces. Then he wrenched to his feet, pulled together the parted seams of his self-control, and held them tightly by sheer nervous force.

His voice was almost cool as he said, "And if it were all true, what would it matter? You have no choice but to let matters stand as they are. One last intranebular planet remains to be visited. It *must* be the rebellion world, and only I know the co-ordinates."

He retained dignity somehow. One hand hung uselessly from a broken wrist; his upper lip had swollen ludicrously, and blood was caking his cheek, but he radiated the hauteur of one born to rule.

"You'll tell us," said Biron.

"Don't delude yourself that I will under any circumstances. I have told you already that there is an average of seventy cubic light-years per star. If you work by trial and error, without me, the odds are two hundred and fifty quadrillion to one against your coming within a billion miles of any star. *Any* star!"

Something went *click!* in Biron's mind.

He said, "Take him back to the *Remorseless!*"

Rizzett said in a low voice, "The Lady Artemisia——"

And Biron interrupted, "Then it *was* she. Where is she?"

"It's all right. She's safe. She came out without a carbon-dioxide cylinder. Naturally, as the CO_2 washed out of her blood stream, the automatic breathing mechanism of the body slowed. She was trying to run, didn't have the sense to breathe deeply voluntarily, and fainted."

Biron frowned. "Why was she trying to interfere with you, anyway? Making sure her boy friend didn't get hurt?"

Rizzett said, "Yes, she was! Only she thought I was the Autarch's man and was going to shoot *you*. I'll take back this rat now, and, Biron——"

"Yes?"

"Get back as soon as you can. He's still the Autarch, and the crew may need talking to. It's hard to break a lifetime habit of obedience. . . . She's behind that rock. Get to her before she freezes to death, will you? She won't leave."

Her face was almost buried in the hood that covered her head, and her body was formless in the thick, enveloping folds of the space-suit lining, but his steps quickened as he approached her.

He said, "How are you?"

She said, "Better, thank you. I am sorry if I caused any trouble."

They stood looking at each other, and the conversation seemed to have burned itself out in two lines.

Then Biron said, "I know we can't turn time backward, undo things that have been done, unsay things that have been said. But I do want you to understand."

"Why this stress on understanding?" Her eyes flashed. "I have done nothing but understand for weeks now. Will you tell me again about my father?"

"No. I knew your father was innocent. I suspected the Autarch almost from the start, but I had to find out definitely. I could only prove it, Arta, by forcing him to confess. I thought I could get him to confess by trapping him into attempting to kill me, and there was only one way of doing that."

He felt wretched. He went on, "It was a bad thing to do. As bad, almost, as what he did to my father. I don't expect you to forgive me."

She said, "I don't follow you."

He said, "I knew he wanted you, Arta. Politically, you would be a perfect matrimonial object. The name of Hinriad would be more useful for his purposes than that of Widemos. So once he had you, he would need me no longer. I deliberately forced you on him, Arta. I acted as I did, hoping you would turn to him. When you did, he thought he was ready to rid himself of me, and Rizzett and I laid our trap."

"And you loved me all the time?"

Biron said, "Can't you bring yourself to believe that, Arta?"

"And of course you were ready to sacrifice your love to the memory of your father and the honor of your family. How does the old doggerel go? You could not love me half so much, loved you not honor more!"

Biron said, miserably, "Please, Arta! I am not proud of myself but I could think of no other way."

"You might have told me your plan, made me your confederate rather than your tool."

"It was not your fight. If I had failed—and I might have—you would have remained out of it. If the Autarch had killed me and you were no longer on my side, you would be less hurt. You might even have married him, even been happy."

"Since you have won, it might be that I would be hurt at *his* loss."

"But you aren't."

"How do you know?"

Biron said desperately, "At least try to see my motives. Granted that I was foolish—criminally foolish—can't you understand? Can't you try not to hate me?"

She said softly, "I have tried not to love you and, as you see, I have failed."

"Then you forgive me."

"Why? Because I understand? No! If it were a matter of simply understanding, of seeing your motives, I would not forgive you your actions for anything I might have in life. If it were only that and nothing more! But I *will* forgive you, Biron, because I couldn't bear not to. How could I ask you to come back to me unless I forgave you?"

And she was in his arms, her weather-cold lips turning up to his. They were held apart by a double layer of thick garments. His gloved hands could not feel the body they embraced, but his lips were aware of her white, smooth face.

At last he said in concern, "The sun is getting lower. It's going to get colder."

But she said softly, "It's strange, then, that I seem to be getting warmer."

Together they walked back to the ship.

Biron faced them now with an appearance of easy confidence which he did not feel. The Linganian ship was large, and there were fifty in the crew. They sat now facing him. Fifty faces! Fifty Linganian faces bred from birth to unquestioning obedience to their Autarch.

Some had been convinced by Rizzett; others had been convinced by the arranged eavesdropping on the Autarch's statements to Biron earlier that day. But how many others were still uncertain or even definitely hostile?

So far Biron's talking had done little good. He leaned forward, let his voice grow confidential. "And what are you fighting for, men? What are you risking your lives for? A free Galaxy, I think. A Galaxy in which each world can decide what is best in its own way, produce its own wealth for its own good, be slave to none and master of none. Am I right?"

There was a low murmur of what might have been agreement, but it lacked enthusiasm.

Biron went on, "And what is the Autarch fighting for? For himself. He is the Autarch of Lingane. If he won, he would be Autarch of the Nebular Kingdoms. You would replace a Khan by an Autarch. Where would be the benefit of that? Is that worth dying for?"

One in the audience cried out, "He would be one of us, not a filthy Tyranni."

Another shouted, "The Autarch was looking for the rebellion world to offer his services. Was that ambition?"

"Ambition should be made of sterner stuff, eh?" Biron shouted back, ironically. "But he would come to the rebellion world with an organization at his back. He could offer them all of Lingane; he could offer them, he thought, the prestige of an alliance with the Hinriads. In the end, he was pretty sure, the rebellion world would be his to do with what he pleased. Yes, this was ambition.

"And when the safety of the movement ran counter to his own plans, did he hesitate to risk your lives for the sake of his ambition? My father was a danger to him. My father was honest and a friend of liberty. But he was too popular, so he was betrayed. In that betrayal, the Autarch might have brought to ruins the entire cause and all of you with it. Which one of you is safe under a man who will deal with the Tyranni whenever it suits his purpose? Who can be safe serving a cowardly traitor?"

"Better," whispered Rizzett. "Stick to that. Give it to them."

Again the same voice called from the back rows. "The Autarch knows where the rebellion world is. Do *you* know?"

"We will discuss that later. Meanwhile, consider instead that under the Autarch we were all headed for complete ruin; that there is still time to save ourselves by turning from his guidance to a better and nobler way; that it is still possible from the jaws of defeat to snatch——"

"—only defeat, my dear young man," came a soft interrupting voice, and Biron turned in horror.

The fifty crewmen came babbling to their feet, and for a moment it seemed as though they might surge forward, but they had come to council unarmed; Rizzett had seen to that. And now a squad of Tyrannian guardsmen were filing through the various doors, weapons ready.

And Simok Aratap himself, a blaster in each hand, stood behind Biron and Rizzett.

Twenty: *WHERE?*

Simok Aratap weighed carefully the personalities of each of the four who faced him and felt the stirring of a certain excitement within him. This would be the big gamble. The threads of the pattern were weaving toward a close. He was thankful that Major Andros was no longer with him; that the Tyrannian cruisers had gone as well.

He was left with his flagship, his crew and himself. They would be sufficient. He hated unwieldiness.

He spoke mildly, "Let me bring you up to date, my lady and gentlemen. The Autarch's ship has been boarded by a prize crew and is now being escorted back to Tyrann by Major Andros. The Autarch's men will be tried according to law and if convicted will receive the punishment for treason. They are routine conspirators and will be treated routinely. But what shall I do with you?"

Hinrik of Rhodia sat beside him, his face crumpled in utter misery. He said, "Consider that my daughter is a young girl. She was led into this unwittingly. Artemisia, tell them that you were——"

"Your daughter," interposed Aratap, "will probably be released. She is, I believe, the matrimonial object of a highly placed Tyrannian nobleman. Obviously, that will be kept in mind."

Artemisia said, "I'll marry him, if you'll let the rest go."

Biron half rose, but Aratap waved him down. The Tyrannian Commissioner smiled and said, "My lady, please! I can strike bargains, I admit. However, I am not the Khan, but merely one of his servants. Therefore, any bargain I do make will have to be justified thoroughly at home. So what is it exactly that you offer?"

"My agreement to the marriage."

"That is not yours to offer. Your father has already agreed and that is sufficient. Do you have anything else?"

Aratap was waiting for the slow erosion of their wills to resist. The fact that he did not enjoy his role did not prevent him from filling it efficiently. The girl, for instance, might at this moment burst into tears and that would have a salutary effect on the young man. They had obviously been lovers. He wondered if old Pohang would want her under the circumstances, and decided that he probably would. The bargain would still be all in the ancient's favor. For the moment he thought distantly that the girl was very attractive.

And she was maintaining equilibrium. She was not breaking down. Very good, thought Aratap. She was strong willed as well. Pohang would not have joy of his bargain after all.

He said to Hinrik, "Do you wish to plead for your cousin too?"

Hinrik's lips moved soundlessly.

Gillbret cried, "No one pleads for me. I don't want anything of any Tyranni. Go ahead. Order me shot."

"You are hysterical," said Aratap. "You know that I cannot order you shot without trial."

"He is my cousin," whispered Hinrik.

"That will be considered too. You noblemen will someday have to learn that you cannot presume too far on your usefulness to us. I wonder if your cousin has learned that lesson yet."

He was satisfied with Gillbret's reactions. That fellow, at least, sincerely wanted death. The frustration of life was too much for him. Keep him alive, then, and that alone would break him.

He paused thoughtfully before Rizzett. This was one of the Autarch's men. At the thought he felt a faint embarrassment. At the start of the chase, he had dismissed the Autarch as a factor on the basis of what seemed iron logic. Well, it was healthy to miss occasionally. It kept self-confidence balanced at a point safely short of arrogance.

He said, "You're the fool who served a traitor. You would have been better off with us."

Rizzett flushed.

Aratap went on, "If you ever had any military reputation, I am afraid this would destroy it. You are not a nobleman and considerations of state will play no part in your case. Your trial will be public and it will become known that you were a tool of a tool. Too bad."

Rizzett said, "But you are about to suggest a bargain, I suppose?"

"A bargain?"

"Khan's evidence, for instance? You have only a shipload. Wouldn't you want to know the rest of the machinery of revolt?"

Aratap shook his head slightly. "No. We have the Autarch. He will do as a source of information. Even without it, we need only make war on Lingane. There would be little left of revolt thereafter, I'm sure. There will be no bargain of that sort."

And this brought him to the young man. Aratap had left him for last because he was the cleverest of the lot. But he was young, and young people were often not dangerous. They lacked patience.

Biron spoke first, saying, "How did you follow us? Was *he* working with you?"

"The Autarch? Not in this case. I believe the poor fellow was trying to play both sides of the game, with the usual success of the unskillful."

Hinrik interrupted, with an incongruously childish eagerness, "the Tyranni have an invention that follows ships through hyperspace."

Aratap turned sharply. "If your Excellency will refrain from interrupting, I would be obliged," and Hinrik cringed.

It really didn't matter. None of these four would be dangerous hereafter, but he had no desire to decrease by even one any of the uncertainties in the young man's mind.

Biron said, "Now, look, let's have facts, or nothing. You don't have us here because you love us. Why aren't we on the way back to Tyrann with the others? It's that you don't know how to go about killing us. Two of us are Hinriads. I am a Widemos. Rizzett is a well-known officer of the Linganian fleet. And that fifth one you have, your own pet coward and traitor, is still Autarch of Lingane. You can't kill any of us without stinking up the Kingdoms from Tyrann to the edge of the Nebula itself. You've *got* to try to make some sort of bargain with us, because there's nothing else you can do."

Aratap said, "You are not altogether wrong. Let me weave a pattern for you. We followed you, no matter how. You may disregard, I think, the Director's overactive imagination. You paused near three stars without landing on any planet. You came to a fourth and found a planet to land on. There we landed with you, watched, waited. We thought there might be something to wait for and we were right. You quarreled with the Autarch and both of you broadcast without limitation. That had been arranged by you for your own purposes, I know, but it suited our purpose as well. We overheard.

"The Autarch said that only one last intra-nebular planet remained to be visited and that it must be the rebellion world. This is interesting, you see. A rebellion world. You know, my curiosity is aroused. Where would that fifth and last planet be located?"

He let the silence last. He took a seat and watched them dispassionately—first one, then another.

Biron said, "There is no rebellion world."

"You were looking for nothing, then?"

"We were looking for nothing."

"You are being ridiculous."

Biron shrugged wearily. "You are yourself ridiculous if you expect more of an answer."

Aratap said, "Observe that this rebellion world must be the center of the octopus. To find it is my only purpose in keeping you alive. You each have something to gain. My lady, I might free you of your marriage. My Lord Gillbret, we might establish a laboratory for you, let you work undisturbed. Yes, we know more of you than you think." (Aratap turned away hastily. The man's face was working. He might weep and that would be unpleasant.) "Colonel Rizzett, you will be saved the humiliation of court-martial and the certainty of conviction and the ridicule and loss of reputation that would go with it. You, Biron Farrill, would be Rancher of Widemos again. In your case, we might even reverse the conviction of your father."

"And bring him back to life?"

"And restore his honor."

"His honor," said Biron, "rests in the very actions that led to his conviction and death. It is beyond your power to add to or detract from it."

Aratap said, "One of you four will tell me where to find this world you seek. One of you will be sensible. He will gain, whichever one it is, what I have promised. The rest of you will be married, imprisoned, executed—whatever will be worst for you. I warn you, I can be sadistic if I must be."

He waited a moment. "Which one will it be? If you don't speak, the one next to you will. You will have lost everything and I will still have the information I want."

Biron said, "It's no use. You're setting this up so carefully, and yet it won't help you. There is no rebellion world."

"The Autarch says there is."

"Then ask the Autarch your question."

Aratap frowned. The young man was carrying the bluff forward past the point of reason.

He said, "My own inclination is to deal with one of you."

"Yet you have dealt with the Autarch in the past. Do so again. There is nothing you can sell to us that we are willing to buy from you." Biron looked about him. "Right?"

Artemisia crept closer to him and her hand folded slowly about his elbow. Rizzett nodded curtly and Gillbret muttered, "Right!" in a breathless manner.

"You have decided," said Aratap, and put his finger on the correct knob.

The Autarch's right wrist was immobilized in a light metal sheath, which was held magnetically tight to the metal band about his abdomen. The left side of his face was swollen and blue with bruise except for a ragged, force-healed scar that seamed it redly. He stood before them without moving after that first wrench which had freed his good arm from the grip of the armed guard at his side.

"What do you want?"

"I will tell you in a moment," said Aratap. "First, I want you to consider your audience. See whom we have here. There is the young man, for instance, whom you planned death for, yet who lived long enough to cripple you and destroy your plans, although you were an Autarch and he was an exile."

It was difficult to tell whether a flush had entered the Autarch's mangled face. There was no single muscle motion upon it.

Aratap did not look for one. He went on quietly, almost indifferently, "This is Gillbret oth Hinriad, who saved the young man's life and brought him to you. This is the Lady Artemisia, whom, I am told, you courted in your most charming manner and who betrayed you, nevertheless, for love of the youngster. This is Colonel Rizzett, your most trusted military aide, who also ended by betraying you. What do you owe these people, Autarch?"

The Autarch said again, "What do you want?"

"Information. Give it to me and you will be Autarch again. Your earlier dealings with us would be held in your favor at the Khan's court. Otherwise——"

"Otherwise?"

"Otherwise I will get it from these, you see. They will be saved and you will be executed. That is why I ask whether you owe them anything, that you should give them the opportunity of saving their lives by yourself being mistakenly stubborn."

The Autarch's face twisted painfully into a smile. "They cannot save their lives at my expense. They do not know the location of the world you seek. I do."

"I have not said what the information I want is, Autarch."

"There is only one thing you can want." His voice was hoarse—all but unrecognizable. "If my decision is to speak, then my Autarchy will be as before, you say."

"More closely guarded, of course," amended Aratap politely.

Rizzett cried out, "Believe him, and you'll but add treason to treason and be killed for it in the end."

The guard stepped forward, but Biron anticipated him. He flung himself upon Rizzett, struggling backward with him.

"Don't be a fool," he muttered. "There's nothing you can do."

The Autarch said, "I don't care about my Autarchy, or myself, Rizzett." He turned to Aratap. "Will these be killed? That, at least, you must promise." His horridly discolored face twisted savagely. "That one, above all." His finger stabbed toward Biron.

"If that is your price, it is met."

"If I could be his executioner, I would relieve you of all further obligation to me. If my finger could control the execution blast, it would be partial repayment. But if not that, at least I will tell you what he would have you not know. I give you rho, theta, and phi in parsecs and radians: 7352.43, 1.7836, 5.2112. Those three points will determine the position of the world in the Galaxy. You have them now."

"So I have," said Aratap, writing them down.

And Rizzett broke away, crying, "Traitor! Traitor!"

Biron, caught off balance, lost his grip on the Linganian and was thrown to one knee. "Rizzett," he yelled futilely.

Rizzett, face distorted, struggled briefly with the guard. Other guards were swarming in, but Rizzett had the blaster now. With hands and knees he struggled against the Tyrannian soldiers. Hurling himself through the huddle of bodies, Biron joined the fight. He caught Rizzett's throat, choking him, pulling him back.

"Traitor," Rizzett gasped, struggling to maintain aim as the Autarch tried desperately to squirm aside. He fired! And then they disarmed him and threw him on his back.

But the Autarch's right shoulder and half his chest had been blasted away. Grotesquely, the forearm dangled freely from its magnetized sheath. Fingers, wrist, and elbow ended in black ruin. For a long moment it seemed that the Autarch's eyes flickered as his body remained in crazy balance, and then they were glazed and he dropped and was a charred remnant upon the floor.

Artemisia choked and buried her face against Biron's chest. Biron forced himself to look once, firmly and without flinching, at the body of his father's murderer, then turned his eyes away. Hinrik, from a distant corner of the room, mumbled and giggled to himself.

Only Aratap was calm. He said, "Remove the body."

They did so, flaring the floor with a soft heat ray for a few moments to remove the blood. Only a few scattered char marks were left.

They helped Rizzett to his feet. He brushed at himself with both hands, then whirled fiercely toward Biron. "What were *you* doing? I almost missed the bastard."

Biron said wearily, "You fell into Aratap's trap, Rizzett."

"Trap? I killed the bastard, didn't I?"

"That was the trap. You did him a favor."

Rizzett made no answer, and Aratap did not interfere. He listened with a certain pleasure. The young fellow's brains worked smoothly.

Biron said, "If Aratap overheard what he claimed to have overheard, he would have known that only Jonti had the information he wanted. Jonti said that, with emphasis, when he faced us after the fight. It was obvious that Aratap was questioning us only to rattle us, to get us to act brainlessly at the proper time. I was ready for the irrational impulse he counted upon. You were not."

"I had thought," interposed Aratap softly, "that you would have done the job."

"I," said Biron, "would have aimed at you." He turned to Rizzett again. "Don't you see that he didn't want the Autarch alive? The Tyranni are snakes. He wanted the Autarch's information; he didn't want to pay for it; he couldn't risk killing him. You did it for him."

"Correct," said Aratap, "and I have my information."

Somewhere there was the sudden clamor of bells.

Rizzett began, "All right. If I did him a favor, I did myself one at the same time."

"Not quite," said the Commissioner, "since our young friend has not carried the analysis far enough. You see, a new crime has been committed. Where the only crime is treason against Tyrann, your disposal would be a delicate matter politically. But now that the Autarch of Lingane has been murdered, you may be tried, convicted, and executed by Linganian law and Tyrann need play no part in it. This will be convenient for——"

And then he frowned and interrupted himself. He heard the clanging, and stepped to the door. He kicked the release.

"What is happening?"

A soldier saluted. "General alarm, sir. Storage compartments."

"Fire?"

"It is not yet known, sir."

Aratap thought to himself, Great Galaxy! and stepped back into the room. "Where is Gillbret?"

And it was the first anyone knew of the latter's absence.

Aratap said, "We'll find him."

They found him in the engine room, cowering amid the giant structures, and half dragged, half carried him back to the Commissioner's room.

The Commissioner said dryly, "There is no escape on a ship, my lord. It did you no good to sound the general alarm. The time of confusion is even then limited."

He went on, "I think it is enough. We have kept the cruiser you stole, Farrill, my own cruiser, on board ship. It will be used to explore the rebellion world. We will make for the lamented Autarch's reference points as soon as the Jump can be calculated. This will be an adventure of a sort usually missing in this comfortable generation of ours."

There was the sudden thought in his mind of his father in command of a squadron, conquering worlds. He was *glad* Andros was gone. This adventure would be his alone.

They were separated after that. Artemisia was placed with her father, and Rizzett and Biron were marched off in separate directions. Gillbret struggled and screamed.

"I won't be left alone. I won't be in solitary."

Aratap sighed. This man's grandfather had been a great ruler, the history books said. It was degrading to have to watch such a scene. He said, with distaste, "Put my lord with one of the others."

And Gillbret was put with Biron. There was no speech between them till the coming of space-ship "night," when the lights turned a dim purple. It was bright enough to allow them to be watched through the tele-viewing system by the guards, shift and shift about, yet dim enough to allow sleep.

But Gillbret did not sleep.

"Biron," he whispered. "Biron."

And Biron, roused from a dull semi-drowse, said, "What do you want?"

"Biron, I have done it. It is all right, Biron."

Biron said, "Try to sleep, Gil."

But Gillbret went on, "But I've done it, Biron. Aratap may be smart, but I'm smarter. Isn't that amusing? You don't have to worry, Biron. Biron, don't worry. I've fixed it." He was shaking Biron again, feverishly.

Biron sat up. "What's the matter with you?"

"Nothing. Nothing. It's all right. But I fixed it." Gillbret was smiling. It was a sly smile, the smile of a little boy who has done something clever.

"What have you fixed?" Biron was on his feet. He seized the other by the shoulders and dragged him upright as well. "Answer me."

"They found me in the engine room." The words were jerked out. "They thought I was hiding. I wasn't. I sounded the general alarm for the storage room because I had to be alone for just a few minutes—a very few minutes. Biron, I shorted the hyperatomics."

"What?"

"It was easy. It took a minute. And they won't know. I did it cleverly. They won't know until they try to Jump, and then all the fuel will be energy in one chain reaction and the ship and us and Aratap and all knowledge of the rebellion world will be a thin expansion of iron vapor."

Biron was backing away, eyes wide. "You did that?"

"Yes." Gillbret buried his head in his hands and rocked to and fro. "We'll be dead. Biron, I'm not afraid to die, but not alone. Not alone. I had to be with someone. I'm glad I'm with you. I want to be with someone when I die. But it won't hurt; it will be so quick. It won't hurt. It won't—hurt."

Biron said, "Fool! Madman! We might still have won out but for this."

Gillbret didn't hear him. His ears were filled with his own moans. Biron could only dash to the door.

"Guard," he yelled. "*Guard!*" Were there hours or merely minutes left?

Twenty-One: *HERE?*

The soldier came clattering down the corridor. "Get back in there." His voice was sour and sharp.

They stood facing one another. There were no doors to the small bottom-level rooms which doubled as prison cells, but a force field stretched from side to side, top to bottom. Biron could feel it with his hand. There was a tiny resilience to it, like rubber stretched nearly to its extreme, and then it stopped giving, as though the first initial pressure turned it to steel.

It tingled Biron's hand, and he knew that though it would stop matter completely, it would be as transparent as space to the energy beam of a neuronic whip. And there was a whip in the guard's hand.

Biron said, "I've got to see Commissioner Aratap."

"Is that what you're making a noise about?" The guard was not in the best of humors. The night watch was unpopular and he was losing at cards. "I'll mention it after lights-on."

"It won't wait." Biron felt desperate. "It's important."

"It will have to wait. Will you get back, or do you want a bit of the whip?"

"Look," said Biron, "the man with me is Gillbret oth Hinriad. He is sick. He may be dying. If a Hinriad dies on a Tyrannian ship because you will not let me speak to the man in authority, you will not have a good time of it."

"What's wrong with him?"

"I don't know. Will you be quick or are you tired of life?"

The guard mumbled something and was off.

Biron watched him as far as he could see in the dim purple. He strained his ears in an attempt to catch the heightened throbbing of the engines as energy concentration climbed to a pre-Jump peak, but he heard nothing at all.

He strode to Gillbret, seized the man's hair, and pulled his head back gently. Eyes stared into his out of a contorted face. There was no recognition in them, only fear.

"Who are you?"

"It's only me—Biron. How do you feel?"

It took time for the words to penetrate. Gillbret said, blankly, "Biron?" Then, with a quiver of life, "Biron! Are they Jumping? Death won't hurt, Biron."

Biron let the head drop. No point in anger against Gillbret. On the information he had, or thought he had, it was a great gesture. All the more so, since it was breaking him.

But he was writhing in frustration. Why wouldn't they let him speak to Aratap? Why wouldn't they let him out? He found himself at a wall and beat upon it with his fists. If there were a door, he could break it down; if there were bars, he could pull them apart or drag them out of their sockets, by the Galaxy.

But there was a force field, which nothing could damage. He yelled again.

There were footsteps once more. He rushed to the open-yet-not-open door. He could not look out to see who was coming down the corridor. He could only wait.

It was the guard again. "Get back from the field," he barked. "Step back with your hands in front of you." There was an officer with him.

Biron retreated. The other's neuronic whip was on him, unwaveringly. Biron said, "The man with you is not Aratap. I want to speak to the Commissioner."

The officer said, "If Gillbret oth Hinriad is ill, you don't want to see the Commissioner. You want to see a doctor."

The force field was down, with a dim blue spark showing as contact broke. The officer entered, and Biron could see the Medical Group insignia on his uniform.

Biron stepped in front of him. "All right. Now listen to me. This ship mustn't Jump. The Commissioner is the only one who can see to that, and I must see him. Do you understand that? You're an officer. You can have him awakened."

The doctor put out an arm to brush Biron aside, and Biron batted it away. The doctor cried out sharply and called, "Guard, get this man out of here."

The guard stepped forward and Biron dived. They went thumping down together, and Biron clawed up along the guard's body, hand over hand, seizing first the shoulder and then the wrist of the arm that was trying to bring its whip down upon him.

For a moment they remained frozen, straining against one another, and then Biron caught motion at the corner of his eye. The medical officer was rushing past them to sound the alarm.

Biron's hand, the one not holding the other's whip wrist, shot out and seized the officer's ankle. The guard writhed nearly free, and the officer kicked out wildly at him, but, with the veins standing out on his neck and temples, Biron pulled desperately with each hand.

The officer went down, shouting hoarsely. The guard's whip clattered to the floor with a harsh sound.

Biron fell upon it, rolled with it, and came up on his knees and one hand. In his other was the whip.

"Not a sound," he gasped. "Not one sound. Drop anything else you've got."

The guard, staggering to his feet, his tunic ripped, glared hatred and tossed a short, metal-weighted, plastic club away from himself. The doctor was unarmed.

Biron picked up the club. He said, "Sorry. I have nothing to tie and gag you with and no time anyway."

The whip flashed dimly once, twice. First the guard and then the doctor stiffened in agonized immobility and dropped solidly, in one piece, legs and arms bent grotesquely out from their bodies as they lay, in the attitude they had last assumed before the whip struck.

Biron turned to Gillbret, who was watching with dull, soundless vacuity.

"Sorry," said Biron, "but you, too, Gillbret," and the whip flashed a third time.

The vacuous expression was frozen solid as Gillbret lay there on his side.

The force field was still down and Biron stepped out into the corridor. It was empty. This was space-ship "night" and only the watch and the night details would be up.

There would be no time to try to locate Aratap. It would have to be straight for the engine room. He set off. It would be toward the bow, of course.

A man in engineer's work clothes hurried past him.

"When's the next Jump?" called out Biron.

"About half an hour," the engineer returned over his shoulder.

"Engine room straight ahead?"

"And up the ramp." The man turned suddenly. "Who are you?"

Biron did not answer. The whip flared a fourth time. He stepped over the body and went on. Half an hour left.

He heard the noise of men as he sped up the ramp. The light ahead was white, not purple. He hesitated. Then he put the whip into his pocket. They would be busy. There would be no reason for them to suspect him.

He stepped in quickly. The men were pygmies scurrying about the huge matter-energy converters. The room glared with dials, a hundred thousand eyes staring their information out to all who would look. A ship this size, one almost in the class of a large passenger liner, was considerably different from the tiny Tyrannian cruiser he had been used to. There, the engines had been all but automatic. Here they were large enough to power a city, and required considerable supervision.

He was on a railed balcony that circled the engine room. In one corner there was a small room in which two men handled computers with flying fingers.

He hurried in that direction, while engineers passed him without looking at him, and stepped through the door.

The two at the computers looked at him.

"What's up?" one asked. "What are you doing up here? Get back to your post." He had a lieutenant's stripes.

Biron said, "Listen to me. The hyperatomics have been shorted. They've got to be repaired."

"Hold on," said the second man, "I've seen this man. He's one of the prisoners. Hold him, Lancy."

He jumped up and was making his way out the other door. Biron hurdled the desk and the computer, seized the belt of the controlman's tunic and pulled him backward.

"Correct," he said. "I'm one of the prisoners. I'm Biron of Widemos. But what I say is true. The hyperatomics are shorted. Have them inspected, if you don't believe me."

The lieutenant found himself staring at a neuronic whip. He said, carefully, "It can't be done, sir, without orders from Officer of the Day, or from the Commissioner. It would mean changing the Jump calculations and delaying us hours."

"Get the authority, then. Get the Commissioner."

"May I use the communicator?"

"Hurry."

The lieutenant's arm reached out for the flaring mouthpiece of the communicator, and halfway there plummeted down hard upon the row of knobs at one end of his desk. Bells clamored in every corner of the ship.

Biron's club was too late. It came down hard upon the lieutenant's wrist. The lieutenant snatched it away, nursing it and moaning over it, but the warning signals were sounding.

Guards were rocketing in upon the balcony through every entrance. Biron slammed out of the control room, looked in either direction, then hopped the railing.

He plummeted down, landing knees bent, and rolled. He rolled as rapidly as he could to prevent setting himself up as a target. He heard the soft hissing of a needle gun near his ear, and then he was in the shadow of one of the engines.

He stood up in a crouch, huddling beneath its curve. His right leg was a stabbing pain. Gravity was high so near the ship's hull and the drop had been a long one. He had sprained his knee badly. It meant that there would be no more chase. If he won out, it was to be from where he stood.

He called out, "Hold your fire! I am unarmed." First the club and then the whip he had taken from the guard went spinning out toward the center of the engine room. They lay there in stark impotence and plain view.

Biron shouted, "I have come to warn you. The hyperatomics are shorted. A Jump will mean the death of us all. I ask only that you check the motors. You will lose a few hours, perhaps, if I am wrong. You will save your lives, if I am right."

Someone called, "Go down there and get him."

Biron yelled, "Will you sell your lives rather than listen?"

He heard the cautious sound of many feet, and shrank backward. Then there was a sound above. A soldier was sliding down the engine toward him, hugging its faintly warm skin as though it were a bride. Biron waited. He could still use his arms.

And then the voice came from above, unnaturally loud, penetrating every corner of the huge room. It said, "Back to your places. Halt preparations for the Jump. Check the hyperatomics."

It was Aratap, speaking through the public-address system. The order then came, "Bring the young man to me."

Biron allowed himself to be taken. There were two soldiers on each side, holding him as though they expected him to explode. He tried to force himself to walk naturally, but he was limping badly.

Aratap was in semidress. His eyes seemed different: faded, peering, unfocused. It occurred to Biron that the man wore contact lenses.

Aratap said, "You have created quite a stir, Farrill."

"It was necessary to save the ship. Send these guards away. As long as the engines are being investigated, there's nothing more I intend doing."

"They will stay just awhile. At least, until I hear from my engine men."

They waited, silently, as the minutes dragged on, and then there was the flash of red upon the frosted-glass circle above the glowing lettering that read "Engine Room."

Aratap opened contact. "Make your report!"

The words that came were crisp and hurried: "Hyperatomics on the C Bank completely shorted. Repairs under way."

Aratap said, "Have Jump recalculated for plus six hours."

He turned to Biron and said coolly, "You were right."

He gestured. The guards saluted, turned on their heels, and left one by one with a smooth precision.

Aratap said, "The details, please."

"Gillbret oth Hinriad during his stay in the engine room thought the shorting would be a good idea. The man is not responsible for his actions and must not be punished for it."

Aratap nodded. "He has not been considered responsible for years. That portion of the events will remain between you and me only. However, my interest and curiosity are aroused by your reasons for preventing the destruction of the ship. You are surely not afraid to die in a good cause?"

"There is no cause," said Biron. "There is no rebellion world. I have told you so already and I repeat it. Lingane was the center of revolt, and that has been checked. I was interested only in tracking down my father's murderer, the Lady Artemisia only in escaping an unwanted marriage. As for Gillbret, he is mad."

"Yet the Autarch believed in the existence of this mysterious planet. Surely he gave me the co-ordinates of something!"

"His belief is based on a madman's dream. Gillbret dreamed something twenty years ago. Using that as a basis, the Autarch calculated five possible planets as the site of this dream world. It is all nonsense."

The Commissioner said, "And yet something disturbs me."

"What?"

"You are working so hard to persuade me. Surely I will find all this out for myself once I have made the Jump. Consider that it is not impossible that in desperation one of you might endanger the ship and the other save it as a complicated method for convincing me that I need look no further for the rebellion world. I would say to myself: If there were really such a world, young Farrill would have let the ship vaporize, for he is a young man and romantically capable of dying what he would consider a hero's death. Since he has risked his life to prevent that happening, Gillbret is mad, there is no rebellion world, and I will return without searching further. Am I too complicated for you?"

"No. I understand you."

"And since you have saved our lives, you will receive appropriate consideration in the Khan's court. You will have saved your life and your cause. No, young sir, I am not quite so ready to believe the obvious. We will still make the Jump."

"I have no objections," said Biron.

"You are cool," said Aratap. "It is a pity you were not born one of us."

He meant it as a compliment. He went on, "We'll take you back to your cell now, and replace the force field. A simple precaution."

Biron nodded.

The guard that Biron had knocked out was no longer there when they returned to the prison room, but the doctor was. He was bending over the still-unconscious form of Gillbret.

Aratap said, "Is he still under?"

At his voice the doctor jumped up. "The effects of the whip have worn off, Commissioner, but the man is not young and has been under a strain. I don't know if he will recover."

Biron felt horror fill him. He dropped to his knees, disregarding the wrenching pain, and reached out a hand to touch Gillbret's shoulder gently.

"Gil," he whispered. He watched the damp, white face anxiously.

"Out of the way, man." The medical officer was scowling at him. He removed his black doctor's wallet from an inner pocket.

"At least the hypodermics aren't broken," he grumbled. He leaned over Gillbret, the hypodermic, filled with its colorless fluid, poised. It sank deep, and the plunger pressed inward automatically. The doctor tossed it aside and they waited.

Gillbret's eyes flickered, then opened. For a while they stared unseeingly. When he spoke finally, his voice was a whisper. "I can't see, Biron. I can't see."

Biron leaned close again. "It's all right, Gil. Just rest."

"I don't want to." He tried to struggle upright. "Biron, when are they Jumping?"

"Soon, soon!"

"Stay with me, then. I don't want to die alone." His fingers clutched feebly, and then relaxed. His head lolled backward.

The doctor stooped, then straightened. "We were too late. He's dead."

Tears stung at Biron's eyelids. "I'm sorry, Gil," he said, "but you didn't know. You didn't understand." They didn't hear him.

They were hard hours for Biron. Aratap had refused to allow him to attend the ceremonies involved in the burial of a body at space. Somewhere in the ship, he knew, Gillbret's body would be blasted in an atomic furnace and then exhausted into space, where its atoms might mingle forever with the thin wisps of interstellar matter.

Artemisia and Hinrik would be there. Would they understand? Would *she* understand that he had done only what he had to do?

The doctor had injected the cartilaginous extract that would hasten the healing of Biron's torn ligaments, and already the pain in his knee was barely noticeable, but then that was only physical pain, anyway. It could be ignored.

He felt the inner disturbance that meant the ship had Jumped and then the worst time came.

Earlier he had felt his own analysis to be correct. It *had* to be. But what if he were wrong? What if they were now at the very heart of rebellion? The information would go streaking back to Tyrann and the armada would gather. And he himself would die knowing that he might have saved the rebellion, but had risked death to ruin it.

It was during that dark time that he thought of the document again. The document he had once failed to get.

Strange the way the notion of the document came and went. It would be mentioned, and then forgotten. There was a mad, intensive search for the rebellion world and yet no search at all for the mysterious vanished document.

Was the emphasis being misplaced?

It occurred to Biron then that Aratap was willing to come upon the rebellion world with a single ship. What was that confidence he had? Could he dare a planet with a ship?

The Autarch had said the document had vanished years before, but then who had it?

The Tyranni, perhaps. They might have a document the secret of which would allow one ship to destroy a world.

If that were true, what did it matter where the rebellion world was, or if it existed at all.

Time passed and then Aratap entered. Biron rose to his feet.

Aratap said, "We have reached the star in question. There *is* a star there. The co-ordinates given us by the Autarch were correct."

"Well?"

"But there is no need to inspect it for planets. The star, I am told by my astrogators, was a nova less than a million years ago. If it had planets then, they were destroyed. It is a white dwarf now. It can have no planets."

Biron stared. "Then——"

Aratap said, "So you are right. There is no rebellion world."

Twenty-Two: *THERE!*

All of Aratap's philosophy could not completely wipe out the feeling of regret within him. For a while he had not been himself, but his father over again. He, too, these last weeks had been leading a squadron of ships against the enemies of the Khan.

But these were degenerate days, and where there might have been a rebellion world, there was none. There were no enemies of the Khan after all; no worlds to gain. He remained only a Commissioner, still condemned to the soothing of little troubles. No more.

Yet regret was a useless emotion. It accomplished nothing.

He said, "So you are right. There is no rebellion world."

He sat down and motioned Biron into a seat as well. "I want to talk to you."

The young man was staring solemnly at him, and Aratap found himself gently amazed that they had met first less than a month ago. The boy was older now, far more than a month older, and he had lost his fear. Aratap thought to himself, I am growing completely decadent. How many of us are beginning to like individuals among our subjects? How many of us wish them well?

He said, "I am going to release the Director and his daughter. Naturally, it is the politically intelligent thing to do. In fact, it is politically inevitable. I think, though, that I will release them now and send them back on the *Remorseless*. Would you care to pilot them?"

Biron said, "Are you freeing me?"

"Yes."

"Why?"

"You saved my ship, and my life as well."

"I doubt that personal gratitude would influence your actions in matters of state."

Aratap was within a hair of laughing outright. He *did* like the boy. "Then I'll give you another reason. As long as I was tracking a giant conspiracy against the Khan, you were dangerous. When that giant conspiracy failed to materialize, when all I had was a Linganian cabal of which the leader is dead, you were no longer dangerous. In fact, it would be dangerous to try either you or the Linganian captives.

"The trials would be in Linganian courts and therefore not under our full control. They would inevitably involve discussion of the so-called rebellion world. And though there is none, half the subjects of Tyrann would think there might be one after all, that where there was such a deal of drumming, there must be a drum. We would have given them a concept to rally round, a reason for revolt, a hope for the future. The Tyrannian realm would not be free of rebellion this side of a century."

"Then you free us all?"

"It will not be exactly freedom, since none of you is exactly loyal. We will deal with Lingane in our own way, and the next Autarch will find himself bound by closer ties to the Khanate. It will be no longer an Associated State, and trials involving Linganians will not necessarily be tried in Linganian courts hereafter. Those involved in the conspiracy, including those in our hands now, will be exiled to worlds nearer Tyrann, where they will be fairly harmless. You yourself cannot return to Nephelos and need not expect to be restored to your Ranch. You will stay on Rhodia, along with Colonel Rizzett."

"Good enough," said Biron, "but what of the Lady Artemisia's marriage?"

"You wish it stopped?"

"You must know that we would like to marry each other. You said once there might be some way of stopping the Tyrannian affair."

"At the time I said that I was trying to accomplish something. What is the old saying? 'The lies of lovers and diplomats shall be forgiven them.'"

"But there *is* a way, Commissioner. It need only be pointed out to the Khan that when a powerful courtier would marry into an important subject family, it may be motives of ambition that lead him on. A subject revolt may be led by an ambitious Tyrannian as easily as by an ambitious Linganian."

Aratap did laugh this time. "You reason like one of us. But it wouldn't work. Would you want my advice?"

"What would it be?"

"Marry her yourself, quickly. A thing once done would be difficult to undo under the circumstances. We would find another woman for Pohang."

Biron hesitated. Then he put out a hand. "Thank you, sir."

Aratap took it. "I don't like Pohang particularly, anyway. Still, there is one thing further for you to remember. Don't let ambition mislead you. Though you marry the Director's daughter, you will never yourself be Director. You are not the type we want."

Aratap watched the shrinking *Remorseless* in the visiplate and was glad the decision had been made. The young man was free; a message was already on its way to Tyrann through the sub-ether. Major Andros would undoubtedly swell into apoplexy, and there would not be wanting men at court to demand his recall as Commissioner.

If necessary, he would travel to Tyrann. Somehow he would see the Khan and make him listen. Given all the facts, the King of Kings would see plainly that no other course of action was possible, and thereafter he could defy any possible combination of enemies.

The *Remorseless* was only a gleaming dot now, scarcely distinguishable from the stars that were beginning to surround it now that they were emerging from the Nebula.

Rizzett watched the shrinking Tyrannian flagship in the visiplate. He said, "So the man let us go! You know, if the Tyranni were all like him, damned if I wouldn't join their fleet. It upsets me in a way. I have definite notions of what Tyranni are like, and he doesn't fit. Do you suppose he can hear what we say?"

Biron set the automatic controls and swiveled in the pilot's seat. "No. Of course not. He can follow us through hyperspace as he did before, but I don't think he can put a spy beam on us. You remember that when he first captured us all he knew about us was what he overheard on the fourth planet. No more."

Artemisia stepped into the pilot room, her finger on her lips. "Not too loudly," she said. "I think he's sleeping now. It won't be long before we reach Rhodia, will it, Biron?"

"We can do it in one Jump, Arta. Aratap had it calculated for us."

Rizzett said, "I've got to wash my hands."

They watched him leave, and then she was in Biron's arms. He kissed her lightly on forehead and eyes, then found her lips as his arms tensed about her. The kiss came to a lingering and breathless end. She said, "I love you very much," and he said, "I love you more than I can say." The conversation that followed was both as unoriginal as that and as satisfying.

Biron said after a while, "Will he marry us before we land?"

Artemisia frowned a little. "I tried to explain that he's Director and captain of the ship and that there are no Tyranni here. I don't know though. He's quite upset. He's not himself at all, Biron. After he's rested, I'll try again."

Biron laughed softly. "Don't worry. He'll be persuaded."

Rizzett's footsteps were noisy as he returned. He said, "I wish we still had the trailer. There isn't room here to take a deep breath."

Biron said, "We'll be on Rhodia in a matter of hours. We'll be Jumping soon."

"I know." Rizzett scowled. "And we'll stay on Rhodia till we die. Not that I'm complaining overloud; I'm glad I'm alive. But it's a silly end to it all."

"There hasn't been any ending," said Biron softly.

Rizzett looked up. "You mean we can start all over? No, I don't think so. You can, perhaps, but not I. I'm too old and there's nothing left for me. Lingane will be dragged into line and I'll never see it again. That bothers me most of all, I think. I was born there and lived there all my life. I won't be but half a man anywhere else. You're young; you'll forget Nephelos."

"There's more to life than a home planet, Tedor. It's been our great shortcoming in the past centuries that we've been unable to recognize that fact. *All* planets are our home planets."

"Maybe. Maybe. If there *had* been a rebellion world, why, then, it might have been so."

"There *is* a rebellion world, Tedor."

Rizzett said sharply, "I'm in no mood for that, Biron."

"I'm not telling a lie. There *is* such a world and I know its location. I might have known it weeks ago, and so might anyone in our party. The facts were all there. They were knocking at my mind without being able to get in until that moment on the fourth planet when you and I had beat down Jonti. Do you remember him standing there, saying that we would never find the fifth planet without his help? Do you remember his words?"

"Exactly? No."

"I think I do. He said, 'There is an average of seventy cubic light-years per star. If you work by trial and error, without me, the odds are two hundred and fifty quadrillion to one against your coming within a billion miles of any star. *Any* star!' It was at that moment, I think, that the facts got into my mind. I could feel the click."

"Nothing clicks in my mind," said Rizzett. "Suppose you explain a bit."

Artemisia said, "I don't see what you can mean, Biron."

Biron said, "Don't you see that it is exactly those odds which Gillbret is supposed to have defeated? You remember his story. The meteor hit, deflected his ship's course, and at the end of its Jumps, it was actually *within* a stellar system. That could have happened only by a coincidence so incredible as to be not worth any belief."

"Then it *was* a madman's story and there is no rebellion world."

"Unless there is a condition under which the odds against landing within a stellar system are less incredible, and there is such a condition. In fact, there is one set of circumstances, and only one, under which he *must* have reached a system. It would have been inevitable."

"Well?"

"You remember the Autarch's reasoning. The engines of Gillbret's ship were not interfered with, so the power of the hyperatomic thrusts, or, in other words, the lengths of the Jumps, were not changed. Only their direction was changed in such a way that one of five stars in an incredibly vast area of the Nebula was reached. It was an interpretation which, on the very face of it, was improbable."

"But the alternative?"

"Why, that neither power *nor* direction was altered. There is no real reason to suppose the direction of drive to have been interfered with. That was only assumption. What if the ship had simply followed its original course? It had been aimed at a stellar system, therefore it ended in a stellar system. The matter of odds doesn't enter."

"But the stellar system it was aimed at——"

"—was that of Rhodia. So he went to Rhodia. Is that so obvious that it's difficult to grasp?"

Artemisia said, "But then the rebellion world must be at home! That's impossible."

"Why impossible? It is somewhere in the Rhodian System. There are two ways of hiding an object. You can put it where no one can find it, as, for instance, within the Horsehead Nebula. Or else you can put it where no one would ever think of looking, right in front of their eyes in plain view.

"Consider what happened to Gillbret after landing on the rebellion world. He was returned to Rhodia alive. His theory was that this was in order to prevent a Tyrannian search for the ship which might come dangerously close to the world itself. But then why was he kept alive? If the ship had been returned with Gillbret dead, the same purpose would have been accomplished and there would have been no chance of Gillbret's talking, as, eventually, he did.

"Again, that can only be explained by supposing the rebellion world to be within the Rhodian System. Gillbret was a Hinriad, and where else would there be such respect for the life of a Hinriad but in Rhodia?"

Artemisia's hands clenched spasmodically. "But if what you say is true, Biron, then Father is in terrible danger."

"And has been for twenty years," agreed Biron, "but perhaps not in the manner you think. Gillbret once told me how difficult it was to pretend to be a dilettante and a good-for-nothing, to pretend so hard that one had to live the part even with friends and even when alone. Of course, with him, poor fellow, it was largely self-dramatization. He didn't really live the part. His real self came out easily enough with you, Arta. It showed to the Autarch. He even found it necessary to show it to me on fairly short acquaintance.

"But it is possible, I suppose, to really live such a life completely, if your reasons are sufficiently important. A man might live a lie even to his daughter, be willing to see her terribly married rather than risk a lifework that depended on complete Tyrannian trust, be willing to seem half a madman——"

Artemisia found her voice. She said huskily, "You can't mean what you're saying!"

"There is no other meaning possible, Arta. He has been Director over twenty years. In that time Rhodia has been continually strengthened by territory granted it by the Tyranni, because they felt it would be safe with him. For twenty years he has organized rebellion without interference from them, because he was so obviously harmless."

"You're guessing, Biron," said Rizzett, "and this kind of a guess is as dangerous as the ones we've made before."

Biron said, "This is no guess. I told Jonti in that last discussion of ours that he, not the Director, must have been the traitor who murdered my father, because my father would never have been foolish enough to trust the Director with any incriminating information. But the point is—and I knew it at the time—that this was just what my father did. Gillbret learned of Jonti's conspiratorial role through what he overheard in the discussions between my father and the Director. There is no other way in which he could have learned it.

"But a stick points both ways. We thought my father was working for Jonti and trying to enlist the support of the Director. Why is it not equally probable, or even more probable, that he was working for the Director and that his role within Jonti's organization was as an agent of the rebellion world attempting to prevent a premature explosion on Lingane that would ruin two decades of careful planning?

"Why do you suppose it seemed so important to me to save Aratap's ship when Gillbret shorted the motors? It wasn't for myself. I didn't, at the time, think Aratap would free me, no matter what. It wasn't even so much for you, Arta. It was to save the Director. He was the important man among us. Poor Gillbret didn't understand that."

Rizzett shook his head. "I'm sorry. I just can't make myself believe all that."

It was a new voice that spoke. "You may as well. It is true." The Director was standing just outside the door, tall and somber-eyed. It was his voice and yet not quite his voice. It was crisp and sure of itself.

Artemisia ran to him. "Father! Biron says——"

"I heard what Biron said." He was stroking her hair with long, gentle motions of the hand. "And it is true. I would even have let your marriage take place."

She stepped back from him, almost in embarrassment. "You sound so different. You sound almost as if——"

"As if I weren't your father." He said it sadly. "It will not be for long, Arta. When we are back on Rhodia, I will be as you knew me, and you must accept me so."

Rizzett stared at him, his usually ruddy complexion as gray as his hair. Biron was holding his breath.

Hinrik said, "Come here, Biron."

He placed a hand on Biron's shoulder. "There was a time, young man, when I was ready to sacrifice your life. The time may come again in the future. Until a certain day I can protect neither of you. I can be nothing but what I have always seemed. Do you understand that?"

Each nodded.

"Unfortunately," said Hinrik, "damage has been done. Twenty years ago I was not as hardened to my role as I am today. I should have ordered Gillbret killed, but I could not. Because I did not, it is now known that there is a rebellion world and that I am its leader."

"Only we know that," said Biron.

Hinrik smiled bitterly. "You think that because you are young. Do you think Aratap is less intelligent than yourself? The reasoning by which you determined the location and leadership of the rebellion world is based on facts known to him, and he can reason as well as you. It is merely that he is older, more cautious; that he has grave responsibilities. He must be certain.

"Do you think he released you out of sentiment? I believe that you have been freed now for the same reason you were freed once before—simply that you might lead him farther along the path that leads to me."

Biron was pale. "Then I must leave Rhodia?"

"No. That would be fatal. There would seem no reason for you to leave, save the true one. Stay with me and they will remain uncertain. My plans are nearly completed. One more year, perhaps, or less."

"But, Director, there are factors you may not be aware of. There is the matter of the document——"

"For which your father was searching?"

"Yes."

"Your father, my boy, did not know all there was to know. It is not safe to have anyone in possession of all the facts. The old Rancher discovered the existence of the document independently in the references to it in my library. I'll give him credit. He recognized its significance. But if he had consulted me, I would have told him it was no longer on Earth."

"That's exactly it, sir. I am certain the Tyranni have it."

"But of course not. *I* have it. I've had it for twenty years. It was what started the rebellion world, for it was only when I had it that I knew we could hold our winnings once we had won."

"It is a weapon, then?"

"It is the strongest weapon in the universe. It will destroy the Tyranni and us alike, but will save the Nebular Kingdoms. Without it, we could perhaps defeat the Tyranni, but we would only have exchanged one feudal despotism for another, and as the Tyranni are plotted against, we would be plotted against. We and they must both be delivered into the ashcan of outmoded political systems. The time for maturity has come as it once came on the planet Earth, and there will be a new kind of government, a kind that has never yet been tried in the Galaxy. There will be no Khans, no Autarchs, Directors, or Ranchers."

"In the name of Space," roared Rizzett suddenly, "what will there be?"

"People."

"People? How can they govern? There must be some one person to make decisions."

"There is a way. The blueprint I have dealt with a small section of one planet, but it can be adapted to all the Galaxy."

The Director smiled. "Come, children, I may as well marry you. It can do little more harm now."

Biron's hand tightly enclosed Artemisia's and she was smiling at him. They felt the queer inward twinge as the *Remorseless* made its single precalculated Jump.

Biron said, "Before you start, sir, will you tell me something about the blueprint you mention, so that my curiosity will be satisfied and I can keep my mind on Arta?"

Artemisia laughed and said, "You had better do it, Father. I couldn't bear an abstracted groom."

Hinrik smiled. "I know the document by heart. Listen."

And with Rhodia's sun bright on the visiplate, Hinrik began with those words that were older—far older—than any of the planets in the Galaxy save one:

" 'We, the people of the United States, in order to form a more perfect Union, establish justice, insure domestic tranquillity, provide for the common defense, promote the general welfare, and secure the blessings of liberty to ourselves and our posterity, do ordain and establish this Constitution for the United States of America. . . .' "

THE MARTIAN WAY AND OTHER STORIES

THE MARTIAN WAY

1

From the doorway of the short corridor between the only two rooms in the travel-head of the spaceship, Mario Esteban Rioz watched sourly as Ted Long adjusted the video dials painstakingly. Long tried a touch clockwise, then a touch counter. The picture was lousy.

Rioz knew it would stay lousy. They were too far from Earth and at a bad position facing the Sun. But then Long would not be expected to know that. Rioz remained standing in the doorway for an additional moment, head bent to clear the upper lintel, body turned half sidewise to fit the narrow opening. Then he jerked into the galley like a cork popping out of a bottle.

"What are you after?" he asked.

"I thought I'd get Hilder," said Long.

Rioz propped his rump on the corner of a table shelf. He lifted a conical can of milk from the companion shelf just above his head. Its point popped under pressure. He swirled it gently as he waited for it to warm.

"What for?" he said. He upended the cone and sucked noisily.

"Thought I'd listen."

"I think it's a waste of power."

Long looked up, frowning. "It's customary to allow free use of personal video sets."

"Within reason," retorted Rioz.

Their eyes met challengingly. Rioz had the rangy body, the gaunt, cheek-sunken face that was almost the hallmark of the Martian Scavenger, those Spacers who patiently haunted the space routes between Earth and Mars. Pale blue eyes were set keenly in the brown, lined face which, in turn, stood darkly out against the white surrounding syntho-fur that lined the upturned collar of his leathtic space jacket.

Long was altogether paler and softer. He bore some of the marks of the Grounder, although no second-generation Martian could be a Grounder in the sense that Earthmen were. His own collar was thrown back and his dark brown hair freely exposed.

"What do you call within reason?" demanded Long.

Rioz's thin lips grew thinner. He said, "Considering that we're not even going to make expenses this trip, the way it looks, any power drain at all is outside reason."

Long said, "If we're losing money, hadn't you better get back to your post? It's your watch."

Rioz grunted and ran a thumb and forefinger over the stubble on his chin. He got up and trudged to the door, his soft, heavy boots muting the sound of his steps. He paused to look at the thermostat, then turned with a flair of fury.

"I *thought* it was hot. Where do you think you are?"

Long said, "Forty degrees isn't excessive."

"For you it isn't, maybe. But this is space, not a heated office at the iron mines." Rioz swung the thermostat control down to minimum with a quick thumb movement. "Sun's warm enough."

"The galley isn't on Sunside."

"It'll percolate through, damn it."

Rioz stepped through the door and Long stared after him for a long moment, then turned back to the video. He did not turn up the thermostat.

The picture was still flickering badly, but it would have to do. Long folded a chair down out of the wall. He leaned forward waiting through the formal announcement, the momentary pause before the slow dissolution of the curtain, the spotlight picking out the well-known bearded figure which grew as it was brought forward until it filled the screen.

The voice, impressive even through the flutings and croakings induced by the electron storms of twenty millions of miles, began:

"Friends! My fellow citizens of Earth . . ."

2

Rioz's eye caught the flash of the radio signal as he stepped into the pilot room. For one moment, the palms of his hands grew clammy when it seemed to him that it was a radar pip; but that was only his guilt speaking. He should not have left the pilot room while on duty theoretically, though all Scavengers did it. Still, it was the standard nightmare, this business of a strike turning up during just those five minutes when one knocked off for a quick coffee because it seemed certain that space was clear. And the nightmare had been known to happen, too.

Rioz threw in the multi-scanner. It was a waste of power, but while he was thinking about it, he might as well make sure.

Space was clear except for the far-distant echoes from the neighboring ships on the scavenging line.

He hooked up the radio circuit, and the blond, long-nosed head of Richard Swenson, copilot of the next ship on the Marsward side, filled it.

"Hey, Mario," said Swenson.

"Hi. What's new?"

There was a second and a fraction of pause between that and Swenson's next comment, since the speed of electromagnetic radiation is not infinite.

"What a day I've *had*."

"Something happened?" Rioz asked.

"I had a strike."

"Well, good."

"Sure, if I'd roped it in," said Swenson morosely.

"What happened?"

"Damn it, I headed in the wrong direction."

Rioz knew better than to laugh. He said, "How did you do that?"

"It wasn't my fault. The trouble was the shell was moving way out of the ecliptic. Can you imagine the stupidity of a pilot that can't work the release maneuver decently? How was I to know? I got the distance of the shell and let it go at that. I just assumed its orbit was in the usual trajectory family. Wouldn't you? I started along what I thought was a good line of intersection and it was five minutes before I noticed the distance was still going up. The pips were taking their sweet time returning. So then I took the angular projections of the thing, and it was too late to catch up with it."

"Any of the other boys getting it?"

"No. It's 'way out of the ecliptic and'll keep on going forever. That's not what bothers me so much. It was only an inner shell. But I hate to tell you how many tons of propulsion I wasted getting up speed and then getting back to station. You should have heard Canute."

Canute was Richard Swenson's brother and partner.

"Mad, huh?" said Rioz.

"Mad? Like to have killed me! But then we've been out five months now and it's getting kind of sticky. You know."

"I know."

"How are you doing, Mario?"

Rioz made a spitting gesture. "About that much this trip. Two shells in the last two weeks and I had to chase each one for six hours."

"Big ones?"

"Are you kidding? I could have scaled them down to Phobos by hand. This is the worst trip I've ever had."

"How much longer are you staying?"

"For my part, we can quit tomorrow. We've only been out two months and it's got so I'm chewing Long out all the time."

There was a pause over and above the electromagnetic lag.

Swenson said, "What's he like, anyway? Long, I mean."

Rioz looked over his shoulder. He could hear the soft, crackly mutter of the video in the galley. "I can't make him out. He says to me about a week after the start of the trip, 'Mario, why are you a Scavenger?' I just look at him and say, 'To make a living. Why do you suppose?' I mean, what the hell kind of a question is that? Why is anyone a Scavenger?

"Anyway, he says, 'That's not it, Mario.' *He's* telling *me*, you see. He says, 'You're a Scavenger because this is part of the Martian way.' "

Swenson said, "And what did he mean by that?"

Rioz shrugged. "I never asked him. Right now he's sitting in there listening to the ultra-microwave from Earth. He's listening to some Grounder called Hilder."

"Hilder? A Grounder politician, an Assemblyman or something, isn't he?"

"That's right. At least, I think that's right. Long is always doing things like that. He brought about fifteen pounds of books with him, all about Earth. Just plain dead weight, you know."

"Well, he's your partner. And talking about partners, I think I'll get back on the job. If I miss another strike, there'll be murder around here."

He was gone and Rioz leaned back. He watched the even green line that was the pulse scanner. He tried the multi-scanner a moment. Space was still clear.

He felt a little better. A bad spell is always worse if the Scavengers all about you are pulling in shell after shell; if the shells go spiraling down to the Phobos scrap forges with everyone's brand welded on except your own. Then, too, he had managed to work off some of his resentment toward Long.

It was a mistake teaming up with Long. It was always a mistake to team up with a tenderfoot. They thought what you wanted was conversation, especially Long, with his eternal theories about Mars and its great new role in human progress. That was the way he said it—Human Progress: the Martian Way; the New Creative Minority. And all the time what Rioz wanted wasn't talk, but a strike, a few shells to call their own.

At that, he hadn't any choice, really. Long was pretty well known down on Mars and made good pay as a mining engineer. He was a friend of Commissioner Sankov and he'd been out on one or two short scavenging missions before. You can't turn a fellow down flat before a tryout, even though it did look funny. Why should a mining engineer with a comfortable job and good money want to muck around in space?

Rioz never asked Long that question. Scavenger partners are forced too close together to make curiosity desirable, or sometimes even safe. But Long talked so much that he answered the question.

"I had to come out here, Mario," he said. "The future of Mars isn't in the mines; it's in space."

Rioz wondered how it would be to try a trip alone. Everyone said it was impossible. Even discounting lost opportunities when one man had to go off watch to sleep or attend to other things, it was well known that one man alone in space would become intolerably depressed in a relatively short while.

Taking a partner along made a six-month trip possible. A regular crew would be better, but no Scavenger could make money on a ship large enough to carry one. The capital it would take in propulsion alone!

Even two didn't find it exactly fun in space. Usually you had to change partners each trip and you could stay out longer with some than with others. Look at Richard and Canute Swenson. They teamed up every five or six trips because they were brothers. And yet whenever they did, it was a case of constantly mounting tension and antagonism after the first week.

Oh well. Space was clear. Rioz would feel a little better if he went back in the galley and smoothed down some of the bickering with Long. He might as well show he was an old spacehand who took the irritations of space as they came.

He stood up, walked the three steps necessary to reach the short, narrow corridor that tied together the two rooms of the spaceship.

3

Once again Rioz stood in the doorway for a moment, watching. Long was intent on the flickering screen.

Rioz said gruffly, "I'm shoving up the thermostat. It's all right—we can spare the power."

Long nodded. "If you like."

Rioz took a hesitant step forward. Space was clear, so to hell with sitting and looking at a blank, green, pipless line. He said, "What's the Grounder been talking about?"

"History of space travel mostly. Old stuff, but he's doing it well. He's giving the whole works—color cartoons, trick photography, stills from old films, everything."

As if to illustrate Long's remarks, the bearded figure faded out of view, and a cross-sectional view of a spaceship flitted onto the screen. Hilder's voice continued, pointing out features of interest that appeared in schematic color. The communications system of the ship outlined itself in red as he talked about it, the storerooms, the proton micropile drive, the cybernetic circuits . . .

Then Hilder was back on the screen. "But this is only the travel-head of the ship. What moves it? What gets it off the Earth?"

Everyone knew what moved a spaceship, but Hilder's voice was like a drug. He made spaceship propulsion sound like the secret of the ages, like an ultimate revelation. Even Rioz felt a slight tingling of suspense, though he had spent the greater part of his life aboard ship.

Hilder went on. "Scientists call it different names. They call it the Law of Action and Reaction. Sometimes they call it Newton's Third Law. Sometimes they call it Conservation of Momentum. But we don't have to call it any name. We can just use our common sense. When we swim, we push water backward and move forward ourselves. When we walk, we push back against the ground and move forward. When we fly a gyro-flivver, we push air backward and move forward.

"Nothing can move forward unless something else moves backward. It's the old principle of 'You can't get something for nothing.'

"Now imagine a spaceship that weighs a hundred thousand tons lifting off Earth. To do that, something else must be moved downward. Since a spaceship is extremely heavy, a great deal of material must be moved downward. So much material, in fact, that there is no place to keep it all aboard ship. A special compartment must be built behind the ship to hold it."

Again Hilder faded out and the ship returned. It shrank and a truncated cone appeared behind it. In bright yellow, words appeared within it: MATERIAL TO BE THROWN AWAY.

"But now," said Hilder, "the total weight of the ship is much greater. You need still more propulsion and still more."

The ship shrank enormously to add on another larger shell and still another immense one. The ship proper, the travelhead, was a little dot on the screen, a glowing red dot.

Rioz said, "Hell, this is kindergarten stuff."

"Not to the people he's speaking to, Mario," replied Long. "Earth isn't Mars. There must be billions of Earth people who've never even seen a spaceship; don't know the first thing about it."

Hilder was saying, "When the material inside the biggest shell is used up, the shell is detached. It's thrown away, too."

The outermost shell came loose, wobbled about the screen.

"Then the second one goes," said Hilder, "and then, if the trip is a long one, the last is ejected."

The ship was just a red dot now, with three shells shifting and moving, lost in space.

Hilder said, "These shells represent a hundred thousand tons of tungsten, magnesium, aluminum, and steel. They are gone forever from Earth. Mars is ringed by Scavengers, waiting along the routes of space travel, waiting for the cast-off shells, netting and branding them, saving them for Mars. Not one cent of payment reaches Earth for them. They are salvage. They belong to the ship that finds them."

Rioz said, "We risk our investment and our lives. If we don't pick them up, no one gets them. What loss is that to Earth?"

"Look," said Long, "he's been talking about nothing but the drain that Mars, Venus, and the Moon put on Earth. This is just another item of loss."

"They'll get their return. We're mining more iron every year."

"And most of it goes right back into Mars. If you can believe his figures, Earth has invested two hundred billion dollars in Mars and received back about five billion dollars' worth of iron. It's put five hundred billion dollars into the Moon and gotten back a little over twenty-five billion dollars of magnesium, titanium, and assorted light metals. It's put fifty billion dollars into Venus and gotten back nothing. And that's what the taxpayers of Earth are really interested in—tax money out; nothing in."

The screen was filled, as he spoke, with diagrams of the Scavengers on the route to Mars; little, grinning caricatures of ships, reaching out wiry, tenuous arms that groped for the tumbling, empty shells, seizing and snaking them in, branding them MARS PROPERTY in glowing letters, then scaling them down to Phobos.

Then it was Hilder again. "They tell us eventually they will return it all to us. Eventually! Once they are a going concern! We don't know when that will be. A century from now? A thousand years? A million? 'Eventually.' Let's take them at their word. Someday they will give us back all our metals. Someday they will grow their own food, use their own power, live their own lives.

"But one thing they can never return. Not in a hundred million years. *Water!*

"Mars has only a trickle of water because it is too small. Venus has no water at all because it is too hot. The Moon has none because it is too hot and too small. So Earth must supply not only drinking water and washing water for the Spacers, water to run their industries, water for the hydroponic factories they claim to be setting up—but even water to throw away by the millions of tons.

"What is the propulsive force that spaceships use? What is it they throw out behind so that they can accelerate forward? Once it was the gases generated from explosives. That was very expensive. Then the proton micropile was invented—a cheap power source that could heat up any liquid until it was a gas under tremendous pressure. What is the cheapest and most plentiful liquid available? Why, water, of course.

"Each spaceship leaves Earth carrying nearly a million tons—not pounds, *tons*—of water, for the sole purpose of driving it into space so that it may speed up or slow down.

"Our ancestors burned the oil of Earth madly and wilfully. They destroyed its coal recklessly. We despise and condemn them for that, but at least they had this excuse—they thought that when the need arose, substitutes would be found. And they were right. We have our plankton farms and our proton micropiles.

"But there is no substitute for water. None! There never can be. And when our descendants view the desert we will have made of Earth, what excuse will they find for us? When the droughts come and grow——"

Long leaned forward and turned off the set. He said, "That bothers me. The damn fool is deliberately—— What's the matter?"

Rioz had risen uneasily to his feet. "I ought to be watching the pips."

"The hell with the pips." Long got up likewise, followed Rioz through the narrow corridor, and stood just inside the pilot room. "If Hilder carries this through, if he's got the guts to make a real issue out of it—*Wow!*"

He had seen it too. The pip was a Class A, racing after the outgoing signal like a greyhound after a mechanical rabbit.

Rioz was babbling, "Space was clear, I tell you, *clear*. For Mars' sake, Ted, don't just freeze on me. See if you can spot it visually."

Rioz was working speedily and with an efficiency that was the result of nearly twenty years of scavenging. He had the distance in two minutes. Then, remembering Swenson's experience, he measured the angle of declination and the radial velocity as well.

He yelled at Long, "One point seven six radians. You can't miss it, man."

Long held his breath as he adjusted the vernier. "It's only half a radian off the Sun. It'll only be crescent-lit."

He increased magnification as rapidly as he dared, watching for the one "star" that changed position and grew to have a form, revealing itself to be no star.

"I'm starting, anyway," said Rioz. "We can't wait."

"I've got it. I've got it." Magnification was still too small to give it a definite shape, but the dot Long watched was brightening and dimming rhythmically as the shell rotated and caught sunlight on cross sections of different sizes.

"Hold on."

The first of many fine spurts of steam squirted out of the proper vents, leaving long trails of micro-crystals of ice gleaming mistily in the pale beams of the distant Sun. They thinned out for a hundred miles or more. One spurt, then another, then another, as the Scavenger ship moved out of its stable trajectory and took up a course tangential to that of the shell.

"It's moving like a comet at perihelion!" yelled Rioz. "Those damned Grounder pilots knock the shells off that way on purpose. I'd like to——"

He swore his anger in a frustrated frenzy as he kicked steam backward and backward recklessly, till the hydraulic cushioning of his chair had soughed back a full foot and Long had found himself all but unable to maintain his grip on the guard rail.

"Have a heart," he begged.

But Rioz had his eye on the pips. "If you can't take it, man, stay on Mars!" The steam spurts continued to boom distantly.

The radio came to life. Long managed to lean forward through what seemed like molasses and closed contact. It was Swenson, eyes glaring.

Swenson yelled, "Where the hell are you guys going? You'll be in my sector in ten seconds."

Rioz said, "I'm chasing a shell."

"In *my* sector?"

"It started in mine and you're not in position to get it. Shut off that radio, Ted."

The ship thundered through space, a thunder that could be heard only within the hull. And then Rioz cut the engines in stages large enough to make Long flail forward. The sudden silence was more ear-shattering than the noise that had preceded it.

Rioz said, "All right. Let me have the 'scope."

They both watched. The shell was a definite truncated cone now, tumbling with slow solemnity as it passed along among the stars.

"It's a Class A shell, all right," said Rioz with satisfaction. A giant among shells, he thought. It would put them into the black.

Long said, "We've got another pip on the scanner. I think it's Swenson taking after us."

Rioz scarcely gave it a glance. "He won't catch us."

The shell grew larger still, filling the visiplate.

Rioz's hands were on the harpoon lever. He waited, adjusted the angle microscopically twice, played out the length allotment. Then he yanked, tripping the release.

For a moment, nothing happened. Then a metal mesh cable snaked out onto the visiplate, moving toward the shell like a striking cobra. It made contact, but it did not hold. If it had, it would have snapped instantly like a cobweb strand. The shell was turning with a rotational momentum amounting to thousands of tons. What the cable did do was to set up a powerful magnetic field that acted as a brake on the shell.

Another cable and another lashed out. Rioz sent them out in an almost heedless expenditure of energy.

"I'll get this one! By Mars, I'll get this one!"

With some two dozen cables stretching between ship and shell, he desisted. The shell's rotational energy, converted by breaking into heat, had raised its temperature to a point where its radiation could be picked up by the ship's meters.

Long said, "Do you want me to put our brand on?"

"Suits me. But you don't have to if you don't want to. It's my watch."

"I don't mind."

Long clambered into his suit and went out the lock. It was the surest sign of his newness to the game that he could count the number of times he had been out in space in a suit. This was the fifth time.

He went out along the nearest cable, hand over hand, feeling the vibration of the mesh against the metal of his mitten.

He burned their serial number in the smooth metal of the shell. There was nothing to oxidize the steel in the emptiness of space. It simply melted and vaporized, condensing some feet away from the energy beam, turning the surface it touched into a gray, powdery dullness.

Long swung back toward the ship.

Inside again, he took off his helmet, white and thick with frost that collected as soon as he had entered.

The first thing he heard was Swenson's voice coming over the radio in this almost unrecognizable rage: ". . . straight to the Commissioner. Damn it, there are rules to this game!"

Rioz sat back, unbothered. "Look, it hit my sector. I was late spotting it and I chased it into yours. You couldn't have gotten it with Mars for a backstop. That's all there is to it—— You back, Long?"

He cut contact.

The signal button raged at him, but he paid no attention.

"He's going to the Commissioner?" Long asked.

"Not a chance. He just goes on like that because it breaks the monotony. He doesn't mean anything by it. He knows it's our shell. And how do you like that hunk of stuff, Ted?"

"Pretty good."

"Pretty good? It's terrific! Hold on. I'm setting it swinging."

The side jets spat steam and the ship started a slow rotation about the shell. The shell followed it. In thirty minutes, they were a gigantic bolo spinning in emptiness. Long checked the *Ephemeris* for the position of Deimos.

At a precisely calculated moment, the cables released their magnetic field and the shell went streaking off tangentially in a trajectory that would, in a day or so, bring it within pronging distance of the shell stores on the Martian satellite.

Rioz watched it go. He felt good. He turned to Long. "This is one fine day for us."

"What about Hilder's speech?" asked Long.

"What? Who? Oh, that. Listen, if I had to worry about every thing some damned Grounder said, I'd never get any sleep. Forget it."

"I don't think we should forget it."

"You're nuts. Don't bother me about it, will you? Get some sleep instead."

4

Ted Long found the breadth and height of the city's main thoroughfare exhilarating. It had been two months since the Commissioner had declared a moratorium on scavenging and had pulled all ships out of space, but this feeling of a stretched-out vista had not stopped thrilling Long. Even the thought that the moratorium was called pending a decision on the part of Earth to enforce its new insistence on water economy, by deciding upon a ration limit for scavenging, did not cast him entirely down.

The roof of the avenue was painted a luminous light blue, perhaps as an old-fashioned imitation of Earth's sky. Ted wasn't sure. The walls were lit with the store windows that pierced it.

Off in the distance, over the hum of traffic and the sloughing noise of people's feet passing him, he could hear the intermittent blasting as new channels were being bored into Mars' crust. All his life he remembered such blastings. The ground he walked on had been part of solid, unbroken rock when he was born. The city was growing and would keep on growing—if Earth would only let it.

He turned off at a cross street, narrower, not quite as brilliantly lit, shop windows giving way to apartment houses, each with its row of lights along the front façade. Shoppers and traffic gave way to slower-paced individuals and to squawling youngsters who had as yet evaded the maternal summons to the evening meal.

At the last minute, Long remembered the social amenities and stopped off at a corner water store.

He passed over his canteen. "Fill 'er up."

The plump storekeeper unscrewed the cap, cocked an eye into the opening. He shook it a little and let it gurgle. "Not much left," he said cheerfully.

"No," agreed Long.

The storekeeper trickled water in, holding the neck of the canteen close to the hose tip to avoid spillage. The volume gauge whirred. He screwed the cap back on.

Long passed over the coins and took his canteen. It clanked against his hip now with a pleasing heaviness. It would never do to visit a family without a full canteen. Among the boys, it didn't matter. Not as much, anyway.

He entered the hallway of No. 27, climbed a short flight of stairs, and paused with his thumb on the signal.

The sound of voices could be heard quite plainly.

One was a woman's voice, somewhat shrill. "It's all right for you to have your Scavenger friends here, isn't it? I'm supposed to be thankful you manage to get home two months a year. Oh, it's quite enough that you spend a day or two with me. After that, it's the Scavengers again."

"I've been home for a long time now," said a male voice, "and this is business. For Mars' sake, let up, Dora. They'll be here soon."

Long decided to wait a moment before signaling. It might give them a chance to hit a more neutral topic.

"What do I care if they come?" retorted Dora. "Let them hear me. And I'd just as soon the Commissioner kept the moratorium on permanently. You hear me?"

"And what would we live on?" came the male voice hotly. "You tell me that."

"I'll tell you. You can make a decent, honorable living right here on Mars, just like everybody else. I'm the only one in this apartment house that's a Scavenger widow. That's what I am—a widow. I'm worse than a widow, because if I were a widow, I'd at least have a chance to marry someone else—— What did you say?"

"Nothing. Nothing at all."

"Oh, I know what you said. Now listen here, Dick Swenson——"

"I only said," cried Swenson, "that now I know why Scavengers usually don't marry."

"You shouldn't have either. I'm tired of having every person in the neighborhood pity me and smirk and ask when you're coming home. Other people can be mining engineers and administrators and even tunnel borers. At least tunnel borers' wives have a decent home life and their children don't grow up like vagabonds. Peter might as well not have a father——"

A thin boy-soprano voice made its way through the door. It was somewhat more distant, as though it were in another room. "Hey, Mom, what's a vagabond?"

Dora's voice rose a notch. "Peter! You keep your mind on your homework."

Swenson said in a low voice, "It's not right to talk this way in front of the kid. What kind of notions will he get about me?"

"Stay home then and teach him better notions."

Peter's voice called out again. "Hey, Mom, I'm going to be a Scavenger when I grow up."

Footsteps sounded rapidly. There was a momentary hiatus in the sounds, then a piercing, "Mom! Hey, Mom! Leggo my ear! What did I do?" and a snuffling silence.

Long seized the chance. He worked the signal vigorously.

Swenson opened the door, brushing down his hair with both hands.

"Hello, Ted," he said in a subdued voice. Then loudly, "Ted's here, Dora. Where's Mario, Ted?"

Long said, "He'll be here in a while."

Dora came bustling out of the next room, a small, dark woman with a pinched nose, and hair, just beginning to show touches of gray, combed off the forehead.

"Hello, Ted. Have you eaten?"

"Quite well, thanks. I haven't interrupted you, have I?"

"Not at all. We finished ages ago. Would you like some coffee?"

"I think so." Ted unslung his canteen and offered it.

"Oh, goodness, that's all right. We've plenty of water."

"I insist."

"Well, then——"

Back into the kitchen she went. Through the swinging door, Long caught a glimpse of dishes sitting in Secoterg, the "waterless cleaner that soaks up and absorbs grease and dirt in a twinkling. One ounce of water will rinse eight square feet of dish surface clean as clean. Buy Secoterg. Secoterg just cleans it right, makes your dishes shiny bright, does away with water waste——"

The tune started whining through his mind and Long crushed it with speech. He said, "How's Pete?"

"Fine, fine. The kid's in the fourth grade now. You know I don't get to see him much. Well, sir, when I came back last time, he looked at me and said . . ."

It went on for a while and wasn't too bad as bright sayings of bright children as told by dull parents go.

The door signal burped and Mario Rioz came in, frowning and red.

Swenson stepped to him quickly. "Listen, don't say anything about shell-snaring. Dora still remembers the time you fingered a Class A shell out of my territory and she's in one of her moods now."

"Who the hell wants to talk about shells?" Rioz slung off a fur-lined jacket, threw it over the back of the chair, and sat down.

Dora came through the swinging door, viewed the newcomer with a synthetic smile, and said, "Hello, Mario. Coffee for you, too?"

"Yeah," he said, reaching automatically for his canteen.

"Just use some more of my water, Dora," said Long quickly. "He'll owe it to me."

"Yeah," said Rioz.

"What's wrong, Mario?" asked Long.

Rioz said heavily, "Go on. Say you told me so. A year ago when Hilder made that speech, you told me so. Say it."

Long shrugged.

Rioz said, "They've set up the quota. Fifteen minutes ago the news came out."

"Well?"

"Fifty thousand tons of water per trip."

"What?" yelled Swenson, burning. "You can't get off Mars with fifty thousand!"

"That's the figure. It's a deliberate piece of gutting. No more scavenging."

Dora came out with the coffee and set it down all around.

"What's all this about no more scavenging?" She sat down very firmly and Swenson looked helpless.

"It seems," said Long, "that they're rationing us at fifty thousand tons and that means we can't make any more trips."

"Well, what of it?" Dora sipped her coffee and smiled gaily. "If you want my opinion, it's a good thing. It's time all you Scavengers found yourselves a nice, steady job here on Mars. I mean it. It's no life to be running all over space——"

"Please, Dora," said Swenson.

Rioz came close to a snort.

Dora raised her eyebrows. "I'm just giving my opinions."

Long said, "Please feel free to do so. But I would like to say something. Fifty thousand is just a detail. We know that Earth—or at least Hilder's party—wants to make political capital out of a campaign for water economy, so we're in a bad hole. We've got to get water somehow or they'll shut us down altogether, right?"

"Well, sure," said Swenson.

"But the question is how, right?"

"If it's only getting water," said Rioz in a sudden gush of words, "there's only one thing to do and you know it. If the Grounders won't give us water, we'll take it. The water doesn't belong to them just because their fathers and grandfathers were too damned sick-yellow ever to leave their fat planet. Water belongs to people wherever they are. We're people and the water's ours, too. We have a right to it."

"How do you propose taking it?" asked Long.

"Easy! They've got oceans of water on Earth. They can't post a guard over every square mile. We can sink down on the night side of the planet any time we want, fill our shells, then get away. How can they stop us?"

"In half a dozen ways, Mario. How do you spot shells in space up to distances of a hundred thousand miles? One thin metal shell in all that space. How? By radar. Do you think there's no radar on Earth? Do you think that if Earth ever gets the notion we're engaged in waterlegging, it won't be simple for them to set up a radar network to spot ships coming in from space?"

Dora broke in indignantly. "I'll tell you one thing, Mario Rioz. My husband isn't going to be part of any raid to get water to keep up his scavenging with."

"It isn't just scavenging," said Mario. "Next they'll be cutting down on everything else. We've got to stop them now."

"But we don't need their water, anyway," said Dora. "We're not the Moon or Venus. We pipe enough water down from the polar caps for all we need. We have a water tap right in this apartment. There's one in every apartment on this block."

Long said, "Home use is the smallest part of it. The mines use water. And what do we do about the hydroponic tanks?"

"That's right," said Swenson. "What about the hydroponic tanks, Dora? They've got to have water and it's about time we arranged to grow our own fresh food instead of having to live on the condensed crud they ship us from Earth."

"Listen to him," said Dora scornfully. "What do you know about fresh food? You've never eaten any."

"I've eaten more than you think. Do you remember those carrots I picked up once?"

"Well, what was so wonderful about them? If you ask me, good baked protomeal is much better. And healthier, too. It just seems to be the fashion now to be talking fresh vegetables because they're increasing taxes for these hydroponics. Besides, all this will blow over."

Long said, "I don't think so. Not by itself, anyway. Hilder will probably be the next Co-ordinator, and then things may really get bad. If they cut down on food shipments, too——"

"Well, then," shouted Rioz, "what do we do? I still say take it! Take the water!"

"And I say we can't do that, Mario. Don't you see that what

you're suggesting is the Earth way, the Grounder way? You're trying to hold on to the umbilical cord that ties Mars to Earth. Can't you get away from that? Can't you see the Martian way?"

"No, I can't. Suppose you tell me."

"I will, if you'll listen. When we think about the Solar System, what do we think about? Mercury, Venus, Earth, Moon, Mars, Phobos, and Deimos. There you are—seven bodies, that's all. But that doesn't represent 1 per cent of the Solar System. We Martians are right at the edge of the other 99 per cent. Out there, farther from the Sun, there's unbelievable amounts of water!"

The others stared.

Swenson said uncertainly, "You mean the layers of ice on Jupiter and Saturn?"

"Not that specifically, but it *is* water, you'll admit. A thousand-mile-thick layer of water is a lot of water."

"But it's all covered up with layers of ammonia or—or something, isn't it?" asked Swenson. "Besides, we can't land on the major planets."

"I know that," said Long, "but I haven't said that was the answer. The major planets aren't the only objects out there. What about the asteroids and the satellites? Vesta is a two-hundred-mile-diameter asteroid that's hardly more than a chunk of ice. One of the moons of Saturn is mostly ice. How about that?"

Rioz said, "Haven't you ever been in space, Ted?"

"You know I have. Why do you ask?"

"Sure, I know you have, but you still talk like a Grounder. Have you thought of the distances involved? The average asteroid is a hundred twenty million miles from Mars at the closest. That's twice the Venus-Mars hop and you know that hardly any liners do even that in one jump. They usually stop off at Earth or the Moon. After all, how long do you expect anyone to stay in space, man?"

"I don't know. What's your limit?"

"You know the limit. You don't have to ask me. It's six months. That's handbook data. After six months, if you're still in space, you're psychotherapy meat. Right, Dick?"

Swenson nodded.

"And that's just the asteroids," Rioz went on. "From Mars to Jupiter is three hundred thirty million miles, and to Saturn it's seven hundred million. How can anyone handle that kind of distance? Suppose you hit standard velocity or, to make it even, say you get up to a good two hundred kilomiles an hour. It would take you—let's see, allowing time for acceleration and deceleration—about six or seven months to get to Jupiter and nearly a year to get to Saturn. Of course, you could hike the speed to a million miles an hour, theoretically, but where would you get the water to do that?"

"Gee," said a small voice attached to a smutty nose and round eyes. "Saturn!"

Dora whirled in her chair. "Peter, march right back into your room!"

"Aw, Ma."

"Don't 'Aw, Ma' me." She began to get out of the chair, and Peter scuttled away.

Swenson said, "Say, Dora, why don't you keep him company for a while? It's hard to keep his mind on homework if we're all out here talking."

Dora sniffed obstinately and stayed put. "I'll sit right here until I find out what Ted Long is thinking of. I tell you right now I don't like the sound of it."

Swenson said nervously, "Well, never mind Jupiter and Saturn. I'm sure Ted isn't figuring on that. But what about Vesta? We could make it in ten or twelve weeks there and the same back. And two hundred miles in diameter. That's four million cubic miles of ice!"

"So what?" said Rioz. "What do we do on Vesta? Quarry the ice? Set up mining machinery? Say, do you know how long that would take?"

Long said, "I'm talking about Saturn, not Vesta."

Rioz addressed an unseen audience. "I tell him seven hundred million miles and he keeps on talking."

"All right," said Long, "suppose you tell me how you know we can only stay in space six months, Mario?"

"It's common knowledge, damn it."

"Because it's in the *Handbook of Space Flight*. It's data compiled by Earth scientists from experience with Earth pilots and spacemen. You're still thinking Grounder style. You won't think the Martian way."

"A Martian may be a Martian, but he's still a man."

"But how can you be so blind? How many times have you fellows been out for over six months without a break?"

Rioz said, "That's different."

"Because you're Martians? Because you're professional Scavengers?"

"No. Because we're not on a flight. We can put back for Mars any time we want to."

"But you *don't* want to. That's my point. Earthmen have tremendous ships with libraries of films, with a crew of fifteen plus passengers. Still, they can only stay out six months maximum. Martian Scavengers have a two-room ship with only one partner. But we can stick it out more than six months."

Dora said, "I suppose you want to stay in a ship for a year and go to Saturn."

"Why not, Dora?" said Long. "We can do it. Don't you see we can? Earthmen can't. They've got a real world. They've got open sky and fresh food, all the air and water they want. Getting into a ship is a terrible change for them. More than six months is too much for them for that very reason. Martians are different. We've been living on a ship our entire lives.

"That's all Mars is—a ship. It's just a big ship forty-five hundred miles across with one tiny room in it occupied by fifty thousand people. It's closed in like a ship. We breathe packaged air and drink packaged water, which we repurify over and over. We eat the same food rations we eat aboard ship. When we get into a ship, it's the same thing we've known all our lives. We can stand it for a lot more than a year if we have to."

Dora said, "Dick, too?"

"We all can."

"Well, Dick can't. It's all very well for you, Ted Long, and this shell stealer here, this Mario, to talk about jaunting off for a year. You're not married. Dick is. He has a wife and he has a child and that's enough for him. He can just get a regular job right here on Mars. Why, my goodness, suppose you go to Saturn and find there's no water there. How'll you get back? Even if you had water left, you'd be out of food. It's the most ridiculous thing I ever heard of."

"No. Now listen," said Long tightly. "I've thought this thing out. I've talked to Commissioner Sankov and he'll help. But we've got to have ships and men. I can't get them. The men won't listen to me. I'm green. You two are known and respected. You're veterans. If you back me, even if you don't go yourselves, if you'll just help me sell this thing to the rest, get volunteers——"

"First," said Rioz grumpily, "you'll have to do a lot more explaining. Once we get to Saturn, where's the water?"

"That's the beauty of it," said Long. "That's why it's got to be Saturn. The water there is just floating around in space for the taking."

5

When Hamish Sankov had come to Mars, there was no such thing as a native Martian. Now there were two-hundred-odd babies whose grandfathers had been born on Mars—native in the third generation.

When he had come as a boy in his teens, Mars had been scarcely more than a huddle of grounded spaceships connected by sealed underground tunnels. Through the years, he had seen buildings grow and burrow widely, thrusting blunt snouts up into the thin, unbreathable atmosphere. He had seen huge storage depots spring up into which spaceships and their loads could be swallowed whole. He had seen the mines grow from nothing to a huge gouge in the Martian crust, while the population of Mars grew from fifty to fifty thousand.

It made him feel old, these long memories—they and the even dimmer memories induced by the presence of this Earthman before him. His visitor brought up those long-forgotten scraps of thought about a soft-warm world that was as kind and gentle to mankind as the mother's womb.

The Earthman seemed fresh from that womb. Not very tall, not very lean; in fact, distinctly plump. Dark hair with a neat little wave in it, a neat little mustache, and neatly scrubbed skin. His clothing was right in style and as fresh and neatly turned as plastek could be.

Sankov's own clothes were of Martian manufacture, serviceable and clean, but many years behind the times. His face was craggy and lined, his hair was pure white, and his Adam's apple wobbled when he talked.

The Earthman was Myron Digby, member of Earth's General Assembly. Sankov was Martian Commissioner.

Sankov said, "This all hits us hard, Assemblyman."

"It's hit most of us hard, too, Commissioner."

"Uh-huh. Can't honestly say then that I can make it out. Of

course, you understand, I don't make out that I can understand Earth ways, for all that I was born there. Mars is a hard place to live, Assemblyman, and you have to understand that. It takes a lot of shipping space just to bring us food, water, and raw materials so we can live. There's not much room left for books and news films. Even video programs can't reach Mars, except for about a month when Earth is in conjunction, and even then nobody has much time to listen.

"My office gets a weekly summary film from Planetary Press. Generally, I don't have time to pay attention to it. Maybe you'd call us provincial, and you'd be right. When something like this happens, all we can do is kind of helplessly look at each other."

Digby said slowly, "You can't mean that your people on Mars haven't heard of Hilder's anti-Waster campaign."

"No, can't exactly say that. There's a young Scavenger, son of a good friend of mine who died in space"—Sankov scratched the side of his neck doubtfully—"who makes a hobby out of reading up on Earth history and things like that. He catches video broadcasts when he's out in space and he listened to this man Hilder. Near as I can make out, that was the first talk Hilder made about Wasters.

"The young fellow came to me with that. Naturally, I didn't take him very serious. I kept an eye on the Planetary Press films for a while after that, but there wasn't much mention of Hilder and what there was made him out to look pretty funny."

"Yes, Commissioner," said Digby, "it all seemed quite a joke when it started."

Sankov stretched out a pair of long legs to one side of his desk and crossed them at the ankles. "Seems to me it's still pretty much of a joke. What's his argument? We're using up water. Has he tried looking at some figures? I got them all here. Had them brought to me when this committee arrived.

"Seems that Earth has four hundred million cubic miles of water in its oceans and each cubic mile weighs four and a half billion tons. That's a lot of water. Now we use some of that heap in space flight. Most of the thrust is inside Earth's gravitational field, and that means the water thrown out finds its way back to the oceans. Hilder doesn't figure that in. When he says a million tons of water is used up per flight, he's a liar. It's less than a hundred thousand tons.

"Suppose, now, we have fifty thousand flights a year. We don't, of course; not even fifteen hundred. But let's say there are fifty thousand. I figure there's going to be considerable expansion as time goes on. With fifty thousand flights, one cubic mile of water would be lost to space each year. That means that in a million years, Earth would lose *one quarter of 1 per cent* of its total water supply!"

Digby spread his hands, palms upward, and let them drop. "Commissioner, Interplanetary Alloys has used figures like that in their campaign against Hilder, but you can't fight a tremendous, emotion-filled drive with cold mathematics. This man Hilder has invented a name, 'Wasters.' Slowly he has built this name up into a gigantic conspiracy; a gang of brutal, profit-seeking wretches raping Earth for their own immediate benefit.

"He has accused the government of being riddled with them, the Assembly of being dominated by them, the press of being owned by them. None of this, unfortunately, seems ridiculous to the average man. He knows all too well what selfish men can do to Earth's resources. He knows what happened to Earth's oil during the Time of Troubles, for instance, and the way topsoil was ruined.

"When a farmer experiences a drought, he doesn't care that the amount of water lost in space flight isn't a droplet in a fog as far as Earth's over-all water supply is concerned. Hilder has given him something to blame and that's the strongest possible consolation for disaster. He isn't going to give that up for a diet of figures."

Sankov said, "That's where I get puzzled. Maybe it's because I don't know how things work on Earth, but it seems to me that there aren't just droughty farmers there. As near as I could make out from the news summaries, these Hilder people are a minority. Why is it Earth goes along with a few farmers and some crackpots that egg them on?"

"Because, Commissioner, there are such things as worried human beings. The steel industry sees that an era of space flight will stress increasingly the light, nonferrous alloys. The various miners' unions worry about extraterrestrial competition. Any Earthman who can't get aluminum to build a prefab is certain that it is because the aluminum is going to Mars. I know a professor of archaeology who's an anti-Waster because he can't get a government grant to cover his excavations. He's convinced that all government money is going into rocketry research and space medicine and he resents it."

Sankov said, "That doesn't sound like Earth people are much

different from us here on Mars. But what about the General Assembly? Why do they have to go along with Hilder?"

Digby smiled sourly. "Politics isn't pleasant to explain. Hilder introduced this bill to set up a committee to investigate waste in space flight. Maybe three fourths or more of the General Assembly was against such an investigation as an intolerable and useless extension of bureaucracy—which it is. But then how could any legislator be against a mere investigation of waste? It would sound as though he had something to fear or to conceal. It would sound as though he were himself profiting from waste. Hilder is not in the least afraid of making such accusations, and whether true or not, they would be a powerful factor with the voters in the next election. The bill passed.

"And then there came the question of appointing the members of the committee. Those who were against Hilder shied away from membership, which would have meant decisions that would be continually embarrassing. Remaining on the side lines would make that one that much less a target for Hilder. The result is that I am the only member of the committee who is outspokenly anti-Hilder and it may cost me reelection."

Sankov said, "I'd be sorry to hear that, Assemblyman. It looks as though Mars didn't have as many friends as we thought we had. We wouldn't like to lose one. But if Hilder wins out, what's he after, anyway?"

"I should think," said Digby, "that that is obvious. He wants to be the next Global Co-ordinator."

"Think he'll make it?"

"If nothing happens to stop him, he will."

"And then what? Will he drop this Waster campaign then?"

"I can't say. I don't know if he's laid his plans past the Co-ordinacy. Still, if you want my guess, he couldn't abandon the campaign and maintain his popularity. It's gotten out of hand."

Sankov scratched the side of his neck. "All right. In that case, I'll ask you for some advice. What can we folks on Mars do? You know Earth. You know the situation. We don't. Tell us what to do."

Digby rose and stepped to the window. He looked out upon the low domes of other buildings; red, rocky, completely desolate plain in between; a purple sky and a shrunken sun.

He said, without turning, "Do you people really like it on Mars?"

Sankov smiled. "Most of us don't exactly know any other world,

Assemblyman. Seems to me Earth would be something queer and uncomfortable to them."

"But wouldn't Martians get used to it? Earth isn't hard to take after this. Wouldn't your people learn to enjoy the privilege of breathing air under an open sky? You once lived on Earth. You remember what it was like."

"I sort of remember. Still, it doesn't seem to be easy to explain. Earth is just there. It fits people and people fit it. People take Earth the way they find it. Mars is different. It's sort of raw and doesn't fit people. People got to make something out of it. They got to *build* a world, and not take what they find. Mars isn't much yet, but we're building, and when we're finished, we're going to have just what we like. It's sort of a great feeling to know you're building a world. Earth would be kind of unexciting after that."

The Assemblyman said, "Surely the ordinary Martian isn't such a philosopher that he's content to live this terribly hard life for the sake of a future that must be hundreds of generations away."

"No-o, not just like that." Sankov put his right ankle on his left knee and cradled it as he spoke. "Like I said, Martians are a lot like Earthmen, which means they're sort of human beings, and human beings don't go in for philosophy much. Just the same, there's something to living in a growing world, whether you think about it much or not.

"My father used to send me letters when I first came to Mars. He was an accountant and he just sort of stayed an accountant. Earth wasn't much different when he died from what it was when he was born. He didn't see anything happen. Every day was like every other day, and living was just a way of passing time until he died.

"On Mars, it's different. Every day there's something new—the city's bigger, the ventilation system gets another kick, the water lines from the poles get slicked up. Right now, we're planning to set up a news-film association of our own. We're going to call it Mars Press. If you haven't lived when things are growing all about you, you'll never understand how wonderful it feels.

"No, Assemblyman, Mars is hard and tough and Earth is a lot more comfortable, but seems to me if you take our boys to Earth, they'll be unhappy. They probably wouldn't be able to figure out why, most of them, but they'd feel lost; lost and useless. Seems to me lots of them would never make the adjustment."

Digby turned away from the window and the smooth, pink skin of his forehead was creased into a frown. "In that case, Commissioner, I am sorry for you. For all of you."

"Why?"

"Because I don't think there's anything your people on Mars can do. Or the people on the Moon or Venus. It won't happen now; maybe it won't happen for a year or two, or even for five years. But pretty soon you'll all have to come back to Earth, unless——"

Sankov's white eyebrows bent low over his eyes. "Well?"

"Unless you can find another source of water besides the planet Earth."

Sankov shook his head. "Don't seem likely, does it?"

"Not very."

"And except for that, seems to you there's no chance?"

"None at all."

Digby said that and left, and Sankov stared for a long time at nothing before he punched a combination of the local communiline.

After a while, Ted Long looked out at him.

Sankov said, "You were right, son. There's nothing they can do. Even the ones that mean well see no way out. How did you know?"

"Commissioner," said Long, "when you've read all you can about the Time of Troubles, particularly about the twentieth century, nothing political can come as a real surprise."

"Well, maybe. Anyway, son, Assemblyman Digby is sorry for us, quite a piece sorry, you might say, but that's all. He says we'll have to leave Mars—or else get water somewhere else. Only he thinks that we can't get water somewhere else."

"You know we can, don't you, Commissioner?"

"I know we *might*, son. It's a terrible risk."

"If I find enough volunteers, the risk is our business."

"How is it going?"

"Not bad. Some of the boys are on my side right now. I talked Mario Rioz into it, for instance, and you know he's one of the best."

"That's just it—the volunteers will be the best men we have. I hate to allow it."

"If we get back, it will be worth it."

"If! It's a big word, son."

"And a big thing we're trying to do."

"Well, I gave my word that if there was no help on Earth, I'll see that the Phobos water hole lets you have all the water you'll need. Good luck."

6

Half a million miles above Saturn, Mario Rioz was cradled on nothing and sleep was delicious. He came out of it slowly and for a while, alone in his suit, he counted the stars and traced lines from one to another.

At first, as the weeks flew past, it was scavenging all over again, except for the gnawing feeling that every minute meant an additional number of thousands of miles away from all humanity. That made it worse.

They had aimed high to pass out of the ecliptic while moving through the Asteroid Belt. That had used up water and had probably been unnecessary. Although tens of thousands of worldlets look as thick as vermin in two-dimensional projection upon a photographic plate, they are nevertheless scattered so thinly through the quadrillions of cubic miles that make up their conglomerate orbit that only the most ridiculous of coincidences would have brought about a collision.

Still, they passed over the Belt and someone calculated the chances of collision with a fragment of matter large enough to do damage. The value was so low, so impossibly low, that it was perhaps inevitable that the notion of the "space-float" should occur to someone.

The days were long and many, space was empty, only one man was needed at the controls at any one time. The thought was a natural.

First, it was a particularly daring one who ventured out for fifteen minutes or so. Then another who tried half an hour. Eventually, before the asteroids were entirely behind, each ship regularly had its off-watch member suspended in space at the end of a cable.

It was easy enough. The cable, one of those intended for operations at the conclusion of their journey, was magnetically attached at both ends, one to the space suit to start with. Then you clambered out the lock onto the ship's hull and attached the other end there. You paused awhile, clinging to the metal skin by the electromagnets in your boots. Then you neutralized those and made the slightest muscular effort.

Slowly, ever so slowly, you lifted from the ship and even more slowly the ship's larger mass moved an equivalently shorter distance downward. You floated incredibly, weightlessly, in solid, speckled black. When the ship had moved far enough away from you, your gauntleted hand, which kept touch upon the cable, tightened its grip slightly. Too tightly, and you would begin moving back toward the ship and it toward you. Just tightly enough, and friction would halt you. Because your motion was equivalent to that of the ship, it seemed as motionless below you as though it had been painted against an impossible background while the cable between you hung in coils that had no reason to straighten out.

It was a half-ship to your eye. One half was lit by the light of the feeble Sun, which was still too bright to look at directly without the heavy protection of the polarized space-suit visor. The other half was black on black, invisible.

Space closed in and it was like sleep. Your suit was warm, it renewed its air automatically, it had food and drink in special containers from which it could be sucked with a minimal motion of the head, it took care of wastes appropriately. Most of all, more than anything else, there was the delightful euphoria of weightlessness.

You never felt so well in your life. The days stopped being too long, they weren't long enough, and there weren't enough of them.

They had passed Jupiter's orbit at a spot some 30 degrees from its then position. For months, it was the brightest object in the sky, always excepting the glowing white pea that was the Sun. At its brightest, some of the Scavengers insisted they could make out Jupiter as a tiny sphere, one side squashed out of true by the night shadow.

Then over a period of additional months it faded, while another dot of light grew until it was brighter than Jupiter. It was Saturn, first as a dot of brilliance, then as an oval, glowing splotch.

("Why oval?" someone asked, and after a while, someone else said, "The rings, of course," and it was obvious.)

Everyone space-floated at all possible times toward the end, watching Saturn incessantly.

("Hey, you jerk, come on back in, damn it. You're on duty." "Who's on duty? I've got fifteen minutes more by my watch." "You set your watch back. Besides, I gave you twenty minutes yesterday." "You wouldn't give two minutes to your grandmother." "Come on in, damn it, or I'm coming out anyway." "All right, I'm coming. Holy howlers, what a racket over a lousy minute." But no quarrel could possibly be serious, not in space. It felt too good.)

Saturn grew until at last it rivaled and then surpassed the Sun. The rings, set at a broad angle to their trajectory of approach, swept grandly about the planet, only a small portion being eclipsed. Then, as they approached, the span of the rings grew still wider, yet narrower as the angle of approach constantly decreased.

The larger moons showed up in the surrounding sky like serene fireflies.

Mario Rioz was glad he was awake so that he could watch again.

Saturn filled half the sky, streaked with orange, the night shadow cutting it fuzzily nearly one quarter of the way in from the right. Two round little dots in the brightness were shadows of two of the moons. To the left and behind him (he could look over his left shoulder to see, and as he did so, the rest of his body inched slightly to the right to conserve angular momentum) was the white diamond of the Sun.

Most of all he liked to watch the rings. At the left, they emerged from behind Saturn, a tight, bright triple band of orange light. At the right, their beginnings were hidden in the night shadow, but showed up closer and broader. They widened as they came, like the flare of a horn, growing hazier as they approached, until, while the eye followed them, they seemed to fill the sky and lose themselves.

From the position of the Scavenger fleet just inside the outer rim of the outermost ring, the rings broke up and assumed their true identity as a phenomenal cluster of solid fragments rather than the tight, solid band of light they seemed.

Below him, or rather in the direction his feet pointed, some twenty miles away, was one of the ring fragments. It looked like a large, irregular splotch, marring the symmetry of space, three quarters in brightness and the night shadow cutting it like a knife. Other fragments were farther off, sparkling like star dust, dimmer and thicker, until, as you followed them down, they became rings once more.

The fragments were motionless, but that was only because the ships had taken up an orbit about Saturn equivalent to that of the outer edge of the rings.

The day before, Rioz reflected, he had been on that nearest fragment, working along with more than a score of others to mold it into the desired shape. Tomorrow he would be at it again.

Today—today he was space-floating.

"Mario?" The voice that broke upon his earphones was questioning.

Momentarily Rioz was flooded with annoyance. Damn it, he wasn't in the mood for company.

"Speaking," he said.

"I thought I had your ship spotted. How are you?"

"Fine. That you, Ted?"

"That's right," said Long.

"Anything wrong on the fragment?"

"Nothing. I'm out here floating."

"You?"

"It gets me, too, occasionally. Beautiful, isn't it?"

"Nice," agreed Rioz.

"You know, I've read Earth books——"

"Grounder books, you mean." Rioz yawned and found it difficult under the circumstances to use the expression with the proper amount of resentment.

"—and sometimes I read descriptions of people lying on grass," continued Long. "You know that green stuff like thin, long pieces of paper they have all over the ground down there, and they look up at the blue sky with clouds in it. Did you ever see any films of that?"

"Sure. It didn't attract me. It looked cold."

"I suppose it isn't, though. After all, Earth is quite close to the Sun, and they say their atmosphere is thick enough to hold the heat. I must admit that personally I would hate to be caught under open sky with nothing on but clothes. Still, I imagine they like it."

"Grounders are nuts!"

"They talk about the trees, big brown stalks, and the winds, air movements, you know."

"You mean drafts. They can keep that, too."

"It doesn't matter. The point is they describe it beautifully, almost passionately. Many times I've wondered, 'What's it really like? Will I ever feel it or is this something only Earthmen can possibly feel?'

I've felt so often that I was missing something vital. Now I know what it must be like. It's this. Complete peace in the middle of a beauty-drenched universe."

Rioz said, "They wouldn't like it. The Grounders, I mean. They're so used to their own lousy little world they wouldn't appreciate what it's like to float and look down on Saturn." He flipped his body slightly and began swaying back and forth about his center of mass, slowly, soothingly.

Long said, "Yes, I think so too. They're slaves to their planet. Even if they come to Mars, it will only be their children that are free. There'll be starships someday; great, huge things that can carry thousands of people and maintain their self-contained equilibrium for decades, maybe centuries. Mankind will spread through the whole Galaxy. But people will have to live their lives out on shipboard until new methods of interstellar travel are developed, so it will be Martians, not planetbound Earthmen, who will colonize the Universe. That's inevitable. It's got to be. It's the Martian way."

But Rioz made no answer. He had dropped off to sleep again, rocking and swaying gently, half a million miles above Saturn.

7

The work shift of the ring fragment was the tail of the coin. The weightlessness, peace, and privacy of the space-float gave place to something that had neither peace nor privacy. Even the weightlessness, which continued, became more a purgatory than a paradise under the new conditions.

Try to manipulate an ordinarily non-portable heat projector. It could be lifted despite the fact that it was six feet high and wide and almost solid metal, since it weighed only a fraction of an ounce. But its inertia was exactly what it had always been, which meant that if it wasn't moved into position very slowly, it would just keep on going, taking you with it. Then you would have to hike the pseudo-grav field of your suit and come down with a jar.

Keralski had hiked the field a little too high and he came down a little too roughly, with the projector coming down with him at a dangerous angle. His crushed ankle had been the first casualty of the expedition.

Rioz was swearing fluently and nearly continuously. He continued to have the impulse to drag the back of his hand across his forehead in order to wipe away the accumulating sweat. The few times that he had succumbed to the impulse, metal had met silicone with a clash that rang loudly inside his suit, but served no useful purpose. The desiccators within the suit were sucking at maximum and, of course, recovering the water and restoring ion-exchanged liquid, containing a careful proportion of salt, into the appropriate receptacle.

Rioz yelled, "Damn it, Dick, wait till I give the word, will you?"

And Swenson's voice rang in his ears, "Well, how long am I supposed to sit here?"

"Till I say," replied Rioz.

He strengthened pseudo-grav and lifted the projector a bit. He released pseudo-grav, insuring that the projector would stay in place for minutes even if he withdrew support altogether. He kicked the cable out of the way (it stretched beyond the close "horizon" to a power source that was out of sight) and touched the release.

The material of which the fragment was composed bubbled and vanished under its touch. A section of the lip of the tremendous cavity he had already carved into its substance melted away and a roughness in its contour had disappeared.

"Try it now," called Rioz.

Swenson was in the ship that was hovering nearly over Rioz's head.

Swenson called, "All clear?"

"I told you to go ahead."

It was a feeble flicker of steam that issued from one of the ship's forward vents. The ship drifted down toward the ring fragment. Another flicker adjusted a tendency to drift sidewise. It came down straight.

A third flicker to the rear slowed it to a feather rate.

Rioz watched tensely. "Keep her coming. You'll make it. You'll make it."

The rear of the ship entered the hole, nearly filling it. The bellying walls came closer and closer to its rim. There was a grinding vibration as the ship's motion halted.

It was Swenson's turn to curse. "It doesn't fit," he said.

Rioz threw the projector groundward in a passion and went flailing up into space. The projector kicked up a white crystalline dust all about it, and when Rioz came down under pseudo-grav, he did the same.

He said, "You went in on the bias, you dumb Grounder."

"I hit it level, you dirt-eating farmer."

Backward-pointing side jets of the ship were blasting more strongly than before, and Rioz hopped to get out of the way.

The ship scraped up from the pit, then shot into space half a mile before forward jets could bring it to a halt.

Swenson said tensely, "We'll spring half a dozen plates if we do this once again. Get it right, will you?"

"I'll get it right. Don't worry about it. Just you come in right."

Rioz jumped upward and allowed himself to climb three hundred yards to get an over-all look at the cavity. The gouge marks of the ship were plain enough. They were concentrated at one point halfway down the pit. He would get that.

It began to melt outward under the blaze of the projector.

Half an hour later the ship snuggled neatly into its cavity, and Swenson, wearing his space suit, emerged to join Rioz.

Swenson said, "If you want to step in and climb out of the suit, I'll take care of the icing."

"It's all right," said Rioz. "I'd just as soon sit here and watch Saturn."

He sat down at the lip of the pit. There was a six-foot gap between it and the ship. In some places about the circle, it was two feet; in a few places, even merely a matter of inches. You couldn't expect a better fit out of handwork. The final adjustment would be made by steaming ice gently and letting it freeze into the cavity between the lip and the ship.

Saturn moved visibly across the sky, its vast bulk inching below the horizon.

Rioz said, "How many ships are left to put in place?"

Swenson said, "Last I heard, it was eleven. We're in now, so that means only ten. Seven of the ones that are placed are iced in. Two or three are dismantled."

"We're coming along fine."

"There's plenty to do yet. Don't forget the main jets at the other end. And the cables and the power lines. Sometimes I wonder if we'll make it. On the way out, it didn't bother me so much, but just now I was sitting at the controls and I was saying, 'We won't make it. We'll sit out here and starve and die with nothing but Saturn over us.' It makes me feel——"

He didn't explain how it made him feel. He just sat there.

Rioz said, "You think too damn much."

"It's different with you," said Swenson. "I keep thinking of Pete—and Dora."

"What for? She said you could go, didn't she? The Commissioner gave her that talk on patriotism and how you'd be a hero and set for life once you got back, and she said you could go. You didn't sneak out the way Adams did."

"Adams is different. That wife of his should have been shot when she was born. Some women can make hell for a guy, can't they? She didn't want him to go—but she'd probably rather he didn't come back if she can get his settlement pay."

"What's your kick, then? Dora wants you back, doesn't she?"

Swenson sighed. "I never treated her right."

"You turned over your pay, it seems to me. I wouldn't do that for any woman. Money for value received, not a cent more."

"Money isn't it. I get to thinking out here. A woman likes company. A kid needs his father. What am I doing 'way out here?"

"Getting set to go home."

"Ah-h, you don't understand."

8

Ted Long wandered over the ridged surface of the ring fragment with his spirits as icy as the ground he walked on. It had all seemed perfectly logical back on Mars, but that was Mars. He had worked it out carefully in his mind in perfectly reasonable steps. He could still remember exactly how it went.

It didn't take a ton of water to move a ton of ship. It was not mass equals mass, but mass times velocity equals mass times velocity. It didn't matter, in other words, whether you shot out a ton of water at a mile a second or a hundred pounds of water at twenty miles a second. You got the same final velocity out of the ship.

That meant the jet nozzles had to be made narrower and the steam hotter. But then drawbacks appeared. The narrower the nozzle, the more energy was lost in friction and turbulence. The hotter the steam, the more refractory the nozzle had to be and the shorter its life. The limit in that direction was quickly reached.

Then, since a given weight of water could move considerably more than its own weight under the narrow-nozzle conditions, it paid to be big. The bigger the water-storage space, the larger the size of the actual travel-head, even in proportion. So they started to make liners heavier and bigger. But then the larger the shell, the heavier the bracings, the more difficult the weldings, the more exacting the engineering requirements. At the moment, the limit in that direction had been reached also.

And then he had put his finger on what had seemed to him to be the basic flaw—the original unswervable conception that the fuel had to be placed *inside* the ship; the metal had to be built to encircle a million tons of water.

Why? Water did not have to be water. It could be ice, and ice could be shaped. Holes could be melted into it. Travel-heads and jets could be fitted into it. Cables could hold travel-heads and jets stiffly together under the influence of magnetic field-force grips.

Long felt the trembling of the ground he walked on. He was at the head of the fragment. A dozen ships were blasting in and out of sheaths carved in its substance, and the fragment shuddered under the continuing impact.

The ice didn't have to be quarried. It existed in proper chunks in the rings of Saturn. That's all the rings were—pieces of nearly pure ice, circling Saturn. So spectroscopy stated and so it had turned out to be. He was standing on one such piece now, over two miles long, nearly one mile thick. It was almost half a billion tons of water, all in one piece, and he was standing on it.

But now he was face to face with the realities of life. He had never told the men just how quickly he had expected to set up the fragment as a ship, but in his heart, he had imagined it would be two days. It was a week now and he didn't dare to estimate the remaining time. He no longer even had any confidence that the task was a possible one. Would they be able to control jets with enough delicacy through leads slung across two miles of ice to manipulate out of Saturn's dragging gravity?

Drinking water was low, though they could always distill more out of the ice. Still, the food stores were not in a good way either.

He paused, looked up into the sky, eyes straining. *Was* the object growing larger? He ought to measure its distance. Actually, he lacked the spirit to add that trouble to the others. His mind slid back to greater immediacies.

Morale, at least, was high. The men seemed to enjoy being out Saturn-way. They were the first humans to penetrate this far, the first to pass the asteroids, the first to see Jupiter like a glowing pebble to the naked eye, the first to see Saturn—like that.

He didn't think fifty practical, case-hardened, shell-snatching Scavengers would take time to feel that sort of emotion. But they did. And they were proud.

Two men and a half-buried ship slid up the moving horizon as he walked.

He called crisply, "Hello, there!"

Rioz answered, "That you, Ted?"

"You bet. Is that Dick with you?"

"Sure. Come on, sit down. We were just getting ready to ice in and we were looking for an excuse to delay."

"I'm not," said Swenson promptly. "When will we be leaving, Ted?"

"As soon as we get through. That's no answer, is it?"

Swenson said dispiritedly, "I suppose there isn't any other answer."

Long looked up, staring at the irregular bright splotch in the sky.

Rioz followed his glance. "What's the matter?"

For a moment, Long did not reply. The sky was black otherwise and the ring fragments were an orange dust against it. Saturn was more than three fourths below the horizon and the rings were going with it. Half a mile away a ship bounded past the icy rim of the planetoid into the sky, was orange-lit by Saturn-light, and sank down again.

The ground trembled gently.

Rioz said, "Something bothering you about the Shadow?"

They called it that. It was the nearest fragment of the rings, quite close considering that they were at the outer rim of the rings, where the pieces spread themselves relatively thin. It was perhaps twenty miles off, a jagged mountain, its shape clearly visible.

"How does it look to you?" asked Long.

Rioz shrugged. "Okay, I guess. I don't see anything wrong."

"Doesn't it seem to be getting larger?"

"Why should it?"

"Well, doesn't it?" Long insisted.

Rioz and Swenson stared at it thoughtfully.

"It does look bigger," said Swenson.

"You're just putting the notion into our minds," Rioz argued. "If it were getting bigger, it would be coming closer."

"What's impossible about that?"

"These things are on stable orbits."

"They were when we came here," said Long. "There, did you feel that?"

The ground had trembled again.

Long said, "We've been blasting this thing for a week now. First, twenty-five ships landed on it, which changed its momentum right there. Not much, of course. Then we've been melting parts of it away and our ships have been blasting in and out of it—all at one end, too. In a week, we may have changed its orbit just a bit. The two fragments, this one and the Shadow, might be converging."

"It's got plenty of room to miss us in." Rioz watched it thoughtfully. "Besides, if we can't even tell for sure that it's getting bigger, how quickly can it be moving? Relative to us, I mean."

"It doesn't have to be moving quickly. Its momentum is as large as ours, so that, however gently it hits, we'll be nudged completely out of our orbit, maybe in toward Saturn, where we don't want to go. As a matter of fact, ice has a very low tensile strength, so that both planetoids might break up into gravel."

Swenson rose to his feet. "Damn it, if I can tell how a shell is moving a thousand miles away, I can tell what a mountain is doing twenty miles away." He turned toward the ship.

Long didn't stop him.

Rioz said, "There's a nervous guy."

The neighboring planetoid rose to zenith, passed overhead, began sinking. Twenty minutes later, the horizon opposite that portion behind which Saturn had disappeared burst into orange flame as its bulk began lifting again.

Rioz called into his radio, "Hey, Dick, are you dead in there?"

"I'm checking," came the muffled response.

"Is it moving?" asked Long.

"Yes."

"Toward us?"

There was a pause. Swenson's voice was a sick one. "On the nose, Ted. Intersection of orbits will take place in three days."

"You're crazy!" yelled Rioz.

"I checked four times," said Swenson.

Long thought blankly, What do we do now?

9

Some of the men were having trouble with the cables. They had to be laid precisely; their geometry had to be very nearly perfect for the magnetic field to attain maximum strength. In space, or even in air, it wouldn't have mattered. The cables would have lined up automatically once the juice went on.

Here it was different. A gouge had to be plowed along the planetoid's surface and into it the cable had to be laid. If it were not lined up within a few minutes of arc of the calculated direction, a torque would be applied to the entire planetoid, with consequent loss of energy, none of which could be spared. The gouges then had to be redriven, the cables shifted and iced into the new positions.

The men plodded wearily through the routine.

And then the word reached them:

"All hands to the jets!"

Scavengers could not be said to be the type that took kindly to discipline. It was a grumbling, growling, muttering group that set about disassembling the jets of the ships that yet remained intact, carrying them to the tail end of the planetoid, grubbing them into position, and stringing the leads along the surface.

It was almost twenty-four hours before one of them looked into the sky and said, "Holy jeepers!" followed by something less printable.

His neighbor looked and said, "I'll be damned!"

Once they noticed, all did. It became the most astonishing fact in the Universe.

"Look at the Shadow!"

It was spreading across the sky like an infected wound. Men looked at it, found it had doubled its size, wondered why they hadn't noticed that sooner.

Work came to a virtual halt. They besieged Ted Long.

He said, "We can't leave. We don't have the fuel to see us back to Mars and we don't have the equipment to capture another planetoid. So we've got to stay. Now the Shadow is creeping in on us because our blasting has thrown us out of orbit. We've got to change that by continuing the blasting. Since we can't blast the front end any more without endangering the ship we're building, let's try another way."

They went back to work on the jets with a furious energy that received impetus every half hour when the Shadow rose again over the horizon, bigger and more menacing than before.

Long had no assurance that it would work. Even if the jets would respond to the distant controls, even if the supply of water, which depended upon a storage chamber opening directly into the icy body of the planetoid, with built-in heat projectors steaming the propulsive fluid directly into the driving cells, were adequate, there was still no certainty that the body of the planetoid without a magnetic cable sheathing would hold together under the enormously disruptive stresses.

"Ready!" came the signal in Long's receiver.

Long called, "Ready!" and depressed the contact.

The vibration grew about him. The star field in the visiplate trembled.

In the rearview, there was a distant gleaming spume of swiftly moving ice crystals.

"It's blowing!" was the cry.

It kept on blowing. Long dared not stop. For six hours, it blew, hissing, bubbling, steaming into space; the body of the planetoid converted to vapor and hurled away.

The Shadow came closer until men did nothing but stare at the mountain in the sky, surpassing Saturn itself in spectacularity. Its every groove and valley was a plain scar upon its face. But when it passed through the planetoid's orbit, it crossed more than half a mile behind its then position.

The steam jet ceased.

Long bent in his seat and covered his eyes. He hadn't eaten in two days. He could eat now, though. Not another planetoid was close enough to interrupt them, even if it began an approach that very moment.

Back on the planetoid's surface, Swenson said, "All the time I watched that damned rock coming down, I kept saying to myself, 'This can't happen. We can't let it happen.'"

"Hell," said Rioz, "we were all nervous. Did you see Jim Davis? He was green. I was a little jumpy myself."

"That's not it. It wasn't just—dying, you know. I was thinking—I know it's funny, but I can't help it—I was thinking that Dora warned me I'd get myself killed, she'll never let me hear the last of it. Isn't that a crummy sort of attitude at a time like that?"

"Listen," said Rioz, "you wanted to get married, so you got married. Why come to me with your troubles?"

10

The flotilla, welded into a single unit, was returning over its mighty course from Saturn to Mars. Each day it flashed over a length of space that had taken nine days outward.

Ted Long had put the entire crew on emergency. With twenty-five ships embedded in the planetoid taken out of Saturn's rings and unable to move or maneuver independently, the co-ordination of their power sources into unified blasts was a ticklish problem. The jarring that took place on the first day of travel nearly shook them out from under their hair.

That, at least, smoothed itself out as the velocity raced upward under the steady thrust from behind. They passed the one-hundred-thousand-mile-an-hour mark late on the second day, and climbed steadily toward the million-mile mark and beyond.

Long's ship, which formed the needle point of the frozen fleet, was the only one which possessed a five-way view of space. It was an uncomfortable position under the circumstances. Long found himself watching tensely, imagining somehow that the stars would slowly begin to slip backward, to whizz past them, under the influence of the multi-ship's tremendous rate of travel.

They didn't, of course. They remained nailed to the black backdrop, their distance scorning with patient immobility any speed mere man could achieve.

The men complained bitterly after the first few days. It was not only that they were deprived of the space-float. They were burdened by much more than the ordinary pseudo-gravity field of the ships, by the effects of the fierce acceleration under which they were living.

Long himself was weary to death of the relentless pressure against hydraulic cushions.

They took to shutting off the jet thrusts one hour out of every four and Long fretted.

It had been just over a year that he had last seen Mars shrinking in an observation window from this ship, which had then been an independent entity. What had happened since then? Was the colony still there?

In something like a growing panic, Long sent out radio pulses toward Mars daily, with the combined power of twenty-five ships behind it. There was no answer. He expected none. Mars and Saturn were on opposite sides of the Sun now, and until he mounted high enough above the ecliptic to get the Sun well beyond the line connecting himself and Mars, solar interference would prevent any signal from getting through.

High above the outer rim of the Asteroid Belt, they reached maximum velocity. With short spurts of power from first one side jet, then another, the huge vessel reversed itself. The composite jet in the rear began its mighty roaring once again, but now the result was deceleration.

They passed a hundred million miles over the Sun, curving down to intersect the orbit of Mars.

A week out of Mars, answering signals were heard for the first time, fragmentary, ether-torn, and incomprehensible, but they were coming from Mars. Earth and Venus were at angles sufficiently different to leave no doubt of that.

Long relaxed. There were still humans on Mars, at any rate.

Two days out of Mars, the signal was strong and clear and Sankov was at the other end.

Sankov said, "Hello, son. It's three in the morning here. Seems like people have no consideration for an old man. Dragged me right out of bed."

"I'm sorry, sir."

"Don't be. They were following orders. I'm afraid to ask, son. Anyone hurt? Maybe dead?"

"No deaths, sir. Not one."

"And—and the water? Any left?"

Long said, with an effort at nonchalance, "Enough."

"In that case, get home as fast as you can. Don't take any chances, of course."

"There's trouble, then."

"Fair to middling. When will you come down?"

"Two days. Can you hold out that long?"

"I'll hold out."

Forty hours later Mars had grown to a ruddy-orange ball that filled the ports and they were in the final planet-landing spiral.

"Slowly," Long said to himself, "slowly." Under these conditions, even the thin atmosphere of Mars could do dreadful damage if they moved through it too quickly.

Since they came in from well above the ecliptic, their spiral passed from north to south. A polar cap shot whitely below them, then the much smaller one of the summer hemisphere, the large one again, the small one, at longer and longer intervals. The planet approached closer, the landscape began to show features.

"Prepare for landing!" called Long.

11

Sankov did his best to look placid, which was difficult considering how closely the boys had shaved their return. But it had worked out well enough.

Until a few days ago, he had no sure knowledge that they had survived. It seemed more likely—inevitable, almost—that they were nothing but frozen corpses somewhere in the trackless stretches from Mars to Saturn, new planetoids that had once been alive.

The Committee had been dickering with him for weeks before the news had come. They had insisted on his signature to the paper for the sake of appearances. It would look like an agreement, voluntarily and mutually arrived at. But Sankov knew well that, given complete obstinacy on his part, they would act unilaterally and be damned with appearances. It seemed fairly certain that Hilder's election was secure now and they would take the chance of arousing a reaction of sympathy for Mars.

So he dragged out the negotiations, dangling before them always the possibility of surrender.

And then he heard from Long and concluded the deal quickly.

The papers had lain before him and he had made a last statement for the benefit of the reporters who were present.

He said, "Total imports of water from Earth are twenty million tons a year. This is declining as we develop our own piping system. If I sign this paper agreeing to an embargo, our industry will be paralyzed, any possibilities of expansion will halt. It looks to me as if that can't be what's in Earth's mind, can it?"

Their eyes met his and held only a hard glitter. Assemblyman Digby had already been replaced and they were unanimous against him.

The Committee Chairman impatiently pointed out, "You have said all this before."

"I know, but right now I'm kind of getting ready to sign and I want it clear in my head. Is Earth set and determined to bring us to an end here?"

"Of course not. Earth is interested in conserving its irreplaceable water supply, nothing else."

"You have one and a half quintillion tons of water on Earth."

The Committee Chairman said, "We cannot spare water."

And Sankov had signed.

That had been the final note he wanted. Earth had one and a half quintillion tons of water and could spare none of it.

Now, a day and a half later, the Committee and the reporters waited in the spaceport dome. Through thick, curving windows, they could see the bare and empty grounds of Mars Spaceport.

The Committee Chairman asked with annoyance, "How much longer do we have to wait? And, if you don't mind, what are we waiting for?"

Sankov said, "Some of our boys have been out in space, out past the asteroids."

The Committee Chairman removed a pair of spectacles and cleaned them with a snowy-white handkerchief. "And they're returning?"

"They are."

The Chairman shrugged, lifted his eyebrows in the direction of the reporters.

In the smaller room adjoining, a knot of women and children clustered about another window. Sankov stepped back a bit to cast a glance toward them. He would much rather have been with them, been part of their excitement and tension. He, like them, had waited over a year now. He, like them, had thought, over and over again, that the men must be dead.

"You see that?" said Sankov, pointing.

"Hey!" cried a reporter. "It's a ship!"

A confused shouting came from the adjoining room.

It wasn't a ship so much as a bright dot obscured by a drifting white cloud. The cloud grew larger and began to have form. It was a double streak against the sky, the lower ends billowing out and upward again. As it dropped still closer, the bright dot at the upper end took on a crudely cylindrical form.

It was rough and craggy, but where the sunlight hit, brilliant high lights bounced back.

The cylinder dropped toward the ground with the ponderous slowness characteristic of space vessels. It hung suspended on those blasting jets and settled down upon the recoil of tons of matter hurling downward like a tired man dropping into his easy chair.

And as it did so, a silence fell upon all within the dome. The women and children in one room, the politicians and reporters in the other remained frozen, heads craned incredulously upward.

The cylinder's landing flanges, extending far below the two rear jets, touched ground and sank into the pebbly morass. And then the ship was motionless and the jet action ceased.

But the silence continued in the dome. It continued for a long time.

Men came clambering down the sides of the immense vessel, inching down, down the two-mile trek to the ground, with spikes on their shoes and ice axes in their hands. They were gnats against the blinding surface.

One of the reporters croaked, "What is it?"

"That," said Sankov calmly, "happens to be a chunk of matter that spent its time scooting around Saturn as part of its rings. Our boys fitted it out with travel-head and jets and ferried it home. It just turns out the fragments in Saturn's rings are made up out of ice."

He spoke into a continuing deathlike silence. "That thing that looks like a spaceship is just a mountain of hard water. If it were standing like that on Earth, it would be melting into a puddle and maybe it would break under its own weight. Mars is colder and has less gravity, so there's no such danger.

"Of course, once we get this thing really organized, we can have water stations on the moons of Saturn and Jupiter and on the asteroids. We can scale in chunks of Saturn's rings and pick them up and send them on at the various stations. Our Scavengers are good at that sort of thing.

"We'll have all the water we need. That one chunk you see is just under a cubic mile—or about what Earth would send us in two hundred years. The boys used quite a bit of it coming back from Saturn. They made it in five weeks, they tell me, and used up about a hundred million tons! But, Lord, that didn't make any dent at all in that mountain. Are you getting all this, boys?"

He turned to the reporters. There was no doubt they were getting it.

He said, "Then get this, too. Earth is worried about its water supply. It only has one and a half quintillion tons. It can't spare us a single ton out of it. Write down that we folks on Mars are worried about Earth and don't want anything to happen to Earth people. Write down that we'll sell water to Earth. Write down that we'll let them have million-ton lots for a reasonable fee. Write down that in ten years, we figure we can sell it in cubic-mile lots. Write down that Earth can quit worrying because Mars can sell it all the water it needs and wants."

The Committee Chairman was past hearing. He was feeling the future rushing in. Dimly he could see the reporters grinning as they wrote furiously.

Grinning.

He could hear the grin become laughter on Earth as Mars turned the tables so neatly on the anti-Wasters. He could hear the laughter thunder from every continent when word of the fiasco spread. And he could see the abyss, deep and black as space, into which would drop forever the political hopes of John Hilder and of every opponent of space flight left on Earth—his own included, of course.

In the adjoining room, Dora Swenson screamed with joy, and Peter, grown two inches, jumped up and down, calling, "Daddy! Daddy!"

Richard Swenson had just stepped off the extremity of the flange and, face showing clearly through the clear silicone of the headpiece, marched toward the dome.

"Did you ever see a guy look so happy?" asked Ted Long. "Maybe there's something in this marriage business."

"Ah, you've just been out in space too long," Rioz said.

YOUTH

1

There was a spatter of pebbles against the window and the youngster stirred in his sleep. Another, and he was awake.

He sat up stiffly in bed. Seconds passed while he interpreted his strange surroundings. He wasn't in his own home, of course. This was out in the country. It was colder than it should be and there was green at the window.

"Slim!"

The call was a hoarse, urgent whisper, and the youngster bounded to the open window.

Slim wasn't his real name, but the new friend he had met the day before had needed only one look at his slight figure to say, "You're Slim." He added, "I'm Red."

Red wasn't his real name, either, but its appropriateness was obvious. They were friends instantly with the quick, unquestioning friendship of young ones not yet quite in adolescence, before even the first stains of adulthood began to make their appearance.

Slim cried, "Hi, Red!" and waved cheerfully, still blinking the sleep out of himself.

Red kept to his croaking whisper, "Quiet! You want to wake somebody?"

Slim noticed all at once that the sun scarcely topped the low hills in the east, that the shadows were long and soft, and that the grass was wet.

Slim said more softly, "What's the matter?"

Red only waved for him to come out.

Slim dressed quickly, gladly confining his morning wash to the momentary sprinkle of a little lukewarm water. He let the air dry the exposed portions of his body as he ran out, while bare skin grew wet against the dewy grass.

Red said, "You've got to be quiet. If Mom wakes up or Dad or your dad or even any of the hands, then it'll be 'Come on in or you'll catch your death of cold tramping bare in the dew.' "

He mimicked voice and tone faithfully, so that Slim laughed and thought that there had never been so funny a fellow as Red.

Slim said eagerly, "Do you come out here every day like this, Red? Real early? It's like the whole world is just yours, isn't it, Red? No one else around, and all like that." He felt proud at being allowed entrance into this private world.

Red stared at him sidelong. He said carelessly, "I've been up for hours. Didn't you hear it last night?"

"Hear what?"

"Thunder."

"Was there a thunderstorm?" Slim was startled. He never slept through a thunderstorm.

"I guess not. But there was thunder. I heard it, and then I went to the window and it wasn't raining. It was all stars and the sky was just getting sort of almost gray. You know what I mean?"

Slim had never seen it so, but he nodded.

"So I just thought I'd go out," said Red.

They walked along the grassy side of the concrete road that split the panorama right down the middle all the way down to where it vanished among the hills. The road was so old that Red's father couldn't tell Red when it had been built. It didn't have a crack or a rough spot in it.

Red said, "Can you keep a secret?"

"Sure, Red. What kind of a secret?"

"Just a secret. Maybe I'll tell you and maybe I won't. I don't know yet." Red broke a long, supple stem from a fern they passed, methodically stripped it of its leaflets, and swung what was left whip-fashion. For a moment, he was on a wild charger, which reared and champed under his iron control. Then he got tired, tossed the whip aside, and stowed the charger away in a corner of his imagination for future use.

He said, "There'll be a circus around."

Slim said, "That's no secret. I knew that. My dad told me even before we came here——"

"That's not the secret. Fine secret! Ever see a circus?"

"Oh, sure. You bet."

"Like it?"

"Say, there isn't anything I like better."

Red was watching out of the corner of his eyes again. "Ever think you would like to be with a circus? I mean, for good?"

Slim considered. "I guess not. I think I'll be an astronomer like my dad. I think he wants me to be."

"Huh! Astronomer!" said Red.

Slim felt the doors of the new, private world closing on him and astronomy became a thing of dead stars.

He said placatingly, "A circus *would* be more fun."

"You're just saying that."

"No, I'm not. I mean it."

Red grew argumentative. "Suppose you had a chance to join the circus right now. What would you do?"

"I—I——"

"See!" Red affected scornful laughter.

Slim was stung. "I'd join up."

"Go on."

"Try me."

Red whirled at him, strange and intense. "You mean that? You want to go in with me?"

"What do you mean?" Slim stepped back a bit.

"I got something that can get us into the circus. Maybe someday we can even have a circus of our own. We could be the biggest circus fellows in the world. That's if you want to go in with me. Otherwise—— Well, I guess I can do it on my own. I just thought, Let's give good old Slim a chance."

The world was strange and glamorous, and Slim said, "Sure thing, Red. I'm in! What is it, huh, Red? Tell me what it is."

"Figure it out. What's the most important thing in circuses?"

Slim thought desperately. He wanted to give the right answer. Finally he said, "Acrobats?"

"Holy smokes! I wouldn't go five steps to look at acrobats."

"I don't know then."

"Animals, that's what! What's the best side show? Where are the biggest crowds? Even in the main rings the best acts are animal acts."

"Do you think so?"

"Everyone thinks so. You ask anyone. Anyway, I found animals this morning. Two of them."

"And you've got them?"

"Sure. That's the secret. Are you telling?"

"Of course not."

"Okay. I've got them in the barn. Do you want to see them?"

They were almost at the barn; its huge open door black. Too black. They had been heading there all the time. Slim stopped in his tracks.

He tried to make his words casual. "Are they big?"

"Would I fool with them if they were big? They can't hurt you. They're only about so long. I've got them in a cage."

They were in the barn now and Slim saw the large cage suspended from a hook in the roof. It was covered with stiff canvas.

Red said, "We used to have some bird there or something. Anyway, they can't get away from there. Come on, let's go up to the loft."

They clambered up the wooden stairs and Red hooked the cage toward them.

Slim pointed and said, "There's sort of a hole in the canvas."

Red frowned. "How'd that get there?" He lifted the canvas, looked in, and said with relief, "They're still there."

"The canvas looks burned," worried Slim.

"You want to look or don't you?"

Slim nodded slowly. He wasn't sure he wanted to, after all. They might be——

But the canvas had been jerked off and there they were. Two of them, the way Red said. They were small and sort of disgusting-looking. The animals moved quickly as the canvas lifted and were on the side toward the youngsters. Red poked a cautious finger at them.

"Watch out," said Slim in agony.

"They don't hurt you," said Red. "Ever see anything like them?"

"No."

"Can't you see how a circus would jump at a chance to have these?"

"Maybe they're too small for a circus."

Red looked annoyed. He let go the cage which swung back and forth pendulum-fashion. "You're just backing out."

"No, I'm not. It's just——"

"They're not too small, don't worry. Right now, I've only got one worry."

"What's that?"

"Well, I've got to keep them till the circus comes, don't I? I've got to figure out what to feed them meanwhile."

The cage swung and the little trapped creatures clung to its bars, gesturing at the youngsters with queer, quick motions—almost as though they were intelligent.

2

The Astronomer entered the dining room with decorum. He felt very much the guest.

He said, "Where are the youngsters? My son isn't in his room."

The Industrialist smiled. "They've been out for hours. However, breakfast was forced into them by the women some time ago, so there is nothing to worry about. Youth, Doctor, youth!"

"Youth!" The word seemed to depress the Astronomer.

They ate breakfast in silence. The Industrialist said once, "You really think they'll come. The day looks so—*normal*."

The Astronomer said, "They'll come."

That was all.

Afterward the Industrialist said, "You'll pardon me. I can't conceive your playing so elaborate a hoax. You really spoke to them?"

"As I speak to you. At least, in a sense. They can project thoughts."

"I gathered that must be so from your letter. How, I wonder."

"I could not say. I asked them and, of course, they were vague. Or perhaps it was just that I could not understand. It involves a projector for the focusing of thought and, even more than that, conscious attention on the part of both projector and receptor. It was quite a while before I realized they were trying to think at me. Such thought projectors may be part of the science they will give us."

"Perhaps," said the Industrialist. "Yet think of the changes it would bring to society. A thought projector!"

"Why not? Change would be good for us."

"I don't think so."

"It is only in old age that change is unwelcome," said the Astronomer, "and races can be old as well as individuals."

The Industrialist pointed out the window. "You see that road. It was built Beforethewars. I don't know exactly when. It is as good now as the day it was built. We couldn't possibly duplicate it now. The race was young when that was built, eh?"

"Then? Yes! At least they weren't afraid of new things."

"No. I wish they had been. Where is the society of Beforethewars? Destroyed, Doctor! What good were youth and new things? We are better off now. The world is peaceful and jogs along. The race goes nowhere but after all, there is nowhere to go. *They* proved that. The men who built the road. I will speak with your visitors as I agreed, if they come. But I think I will only ask them to go."

"The race is not going nowhere," said the Astronomer earnestly. "It is going toward final destruction. My university has a smaller student body each year. Fewer books are written. Less work is done. An old man sleeps in the sun and his days are peaceful and unchanging, but each day finds him nearer death all the same."

"Well, well," said the Industrialist.

"No, don't dismiss it. Listen. Before I wrote you, I investigated your position in the planetary economy."

"And you found me solvent?" interrupted the Industrialist, smiling.

"Why, yes. Oh, I see, you are joking. And yet—perhaps the joke is not far off. You are less solvent than your father and he was less solvent than his father. Perhaps your son will no longer be solvent. It becomes too troublesome for the planet to support even the industries that still exist, though they are toothpicks to the oak trees of Beforethewars. We will be back to village economy, and then to what? The caves?"

"And the infusion of fresh technological knowledge will be the changing of all that?"

"Not just the new knowledge. Rather the whole effect of change, of a broadening of horizons. Look, sir, I chose you to approach in this matter not only because you were rich and influential with government officials, but because you had an unusual reputation, for these days, of daring to break with tradition. Our people will resist change and you would know how to handle them, how to see to it that—that——"

"That the youth of the race is revived?"

"Yes."

"With its atomic bombs?"

"The atomic bombs," returned the Astronomer, "need not be the end of civilization. These visitors of mine had their atomic bomb, or whatever their equivalent was on their own worlds, and survived it, because they didn't give up. Don't you see? It wasn't the bomb that defeated us, but our own shell shock. This may be the last chance to reverse the process."

"Tell me," said the Industrialist, "what do these friends from space want in return?"

The Astronomer hesitated. He said, "I will be truthful with you. They come from a denser planet. Ours is richer in the lighter atoms."

"They want magnesium? Aluminum?"

"No, sir. Carbon and hydrogen. They want coal and oil."

"Really?"

The Astronomer said quickly, "You are going to ask why creatures who have mastered space travel, and therefore atomic power, would want coal and oil. I can't answer that."

The Industrialist smiled, "But I can. This is the best evidence yet of the truth of your story. Superficially, atomic power would seem to preclude the use of coal and oil. However, quite apart from the energy gained by their combustion, they remain, and always will remain, the basic raw material for all organic chemistry. Plastics, dyes, pharmaceuticals, solvents. Industry could not exist without them, even in an atomic age. Still, if coal and oil are the low price for which they would sell us the troubles and tortures of racial youth, my answer is that the commodity would be dear if offered gratis."

The Astronomer sighed and said, "There are the boys!"

They were visible through the open window, standing together in the grassy field and lost in animated conversation. The Industrialist's son pointed imperiously and the Astronomer's son nodded and made off at a run toward the house.

The Industrialist said, "There is the youth you speak of. Our race has as much of it as it ever had."

"Yes, but we age them quickly and pour them into the mold."

Slim scuttled into the room, the door banging behind him.

The Astronomer said in mild disapproval, "What's this?"

Slim looked up in surprise and came to a halt. "I beg your pardon. I didn't know anyone was here. I am sorry to have interrupted." His enunciation was almost painfully precise.

The Industrialist said, "It's all right, youngster."

But the Astronomer said, "Even if you had been entering an

empty room, son, there would be no cause for slamming a door."

"Nonsense," insisted the Industrialist. "The youngster has done no harm. You simply scold him for being young. You, with your views!"

He said to Slim, "Come here, lad."

Slim advanced slowly.

"How do you like the country, eh?"

"Very much, sir, thank you."

"My son has been showing you about the place, has he?"

"Yes, sir. Red—I mean——"

"No, no. Call him Red. I call him that myself. Now tell me, what are you two up to, eh?"

Slim looked away. "Why—just exploring, sir."

The Industrialist turned to the Astronomer. "There you are, youthful curiosity and adventure lust. The race has not yet lost it."

Slim said, "Sir?"

"Yes, lad."

The youngster took a long time in getting on with it. He said, "Red sent me in for something good to eat, but I don't exactly know what he meant. I didn't like to say so."

"Why, just ask Cook. She'll have something good for young'uns to eat."

"Oh no, sir. I mean for animals."

"For animals?"

"Yes, sir. What do animals eat?"

The Astronomer said, "I am afraid my son is city-bred."

"Well," said the Industrialist, "there's no harm in that. What kind of an animal, lad?"

"A small one, sir."

"Then try grass or leaves, and if they don't want that, nuts or berries would probably do the trick."

"Thank you, sir." Slim ran out again, closing the door gently behind him.

The Astronomer said, "Do you suppose they've trapped an animal alive?" He was obviously perturbed.

"That's common enough. There's no shooting on my estate and it's tame country, full of rodents and small creatures. Red is always coming home with pets of one sort or another. They rarely maintain his interest for long."

He looked at the wall clock. "Your friends should have been here by now, shouldn't they?"

3

The swaying had come to a halt and it was dark. The Explorer was not comfortable in the alien air. It felt as thick as soup and he had to breathe shallowly. Even so——

He reached out in a sudden need for company. The Merchant was warm to the touch. His breathing was rough, he moved in an occasional spasm, and was obviously asleep. The Explorer hesitated and decided not to wake him. It would serve no real purpose.

There would be no rescue, of course. That was the penalty paid for the high profits which unrestrained competition could lead to. The Merchant who opened a new planet could have a ten-year monopoly of its trade, which he might hug to himself or, more likely, rent out to all comers at a stiff price. It followed that planets were searched for in secrecy and preferably away from the usual trade routes. In a case such as theirs then, there was little or no chance that another ship would come within range of their subetherics except for the most improbable of coincidences. Even if they were in their ship, that is, rather than in this—this—*cage*.

The Explorer grasped the thick bars. Even if they blasted those away, as they could, they would be stuck too high in open air for leaping.

It was too bad. They had landed twice before in the scout ship. They had established contact with the natives, who were grotesquely huge, but mild and unaggressive. It was obvious that they had once owned a flourishing technology, but hadn't faced up to the consequences of such a technology. It would have been a wonderful market.

And it was a tremendous world. The Merchant, especially, had been taken aback. He had known the figures that expressed the planet's diameter, but from a distance of two light-seconds, he had stood at the visiplate and muttered, "Unbelievable!"

"Oh, there are larger worlds," the Explorer said. It wouldn't do for an Explorer to be too easily impressed.

"Inhabited?"

"Well, no."

"Why, you could drop your planet into that large ocean and drown it."

The Explorer smiled. It was a gentle dig at his Arcturian homeland, which was smaller than most planets. He said, "Not quite."

The Merchant followed along the line of his thoughts. "And the inhabitants are large in proportion to their world?" He sounded as though the news struck him less favorably now.

"Nearly ten times our height."

"Are you sure they are friendly?"

"That is hard to say. Friendship between alien intelligences is an imponderable. They are not dangerous, I think. We've come across other groups that could not maintain equilibrium after the atomic war stage and you know the results. Introversion. Retreat. Gradual decadence and increasing gentleness."

"Even if they are such monsters?"

"The principle remains."

It was about then that the Explorer felt the heavy throbbing of the engines.

He frowned and said, "We are descending a bit too quickly."

There had been some speculation on the dangers of landing several hours before. The planetary target was a huge one for an oxygen-water world. Though it lacked the size of the uninhabitable hydrogen-ammonia planets and its low density made its surface gravity fairly normal, its gravitational forces fell off, but slowly with distance. In short, its gravitational potential was high and the ship's calculator was a run-of-the-mill model not designed to plot landing trajectories at that potential range. That meant the Pilot would have to use manual controls.

It would have been wiser to install a more high-powered model, but that would have meant a trip to some outpost of civilization; lost time; perhaps a lost secret. The Merchant demanded an immediate landing.

The Merchant felt it necessary to defend his position now. He said angrily to the Explorer, "Don't you think the Pilot knows his job? He landed you safely twice before."

Yes, thought the Explorer, in a scout ship, not in this unmaneuverable freighter. Aloud, he said nothing.

He kept his eye on the visiplate. They were descending too quickly. There was no room for doubt. Much too quickly.

The Merchant said peevishly, "Why do you keep silence?"

"Well then, if you wish me to speak, I would suggest that you strap on your floater and help me prepare the ejector."

The Pilot fought a noble fight. He was no beginner. The atmosphere, abnormally high and thick in the gravitational potential of this world, whipped and burned about the ship, but to the very last, it looked as though he might bring it under control despite that.

He even maintained course, following the extrapolated line to the point on the northern continent toward which they were headed. Under other circumstances, with a shade more luck, the story eventually would have been told and retold as a heroic and masterly reversal of a lost situation. But within sight of victory, tired body and tired nerves clamped a control bar with a shade too much pressure. The ship, which had almost leveled off, dipped down again.

There was no room to retrieve the final error. There was only a mile left to fall. The Pilot remained at his post to the actual landing, his only thought that of breaking the force of the crash, of maintaining the spaceworthiness of the vessel. He did not survive. With the ship bucking madly in a soupy atmosphere, few ejectors could be mobilized and only one of them in time.

When afterward the Explorer lifted out of unconsciousness and rose to his feet, he had the definite feeling that but for himself and the Merchant, there were no survivors. And perhaps that was an overcalculation. His floater had burned out while still sufficiently distant from surface to have the fall stun him. The Merchant might have had less luck, even, than that.

He was surrounded by a world of thick, ropy stalks of grass, and in the distance were trees that reminded him vaguely of similar structures on his native Arcturian world except that their lowest branches were high above what he would consider normal treetops.

He called, his voice sounding basso in the thick air, and the Merchant answered. The Explorer made his way toward him, thrusting violently at the coarse stalks that barred his path.

"Are you hurt?" he asked.

The Merchant grimaced, "I've sprained something. It hurts to walk."

The Explorer probed gently. "I don't think anything is broken. You'll have to walk despite the pain."

"Can't we rest first?"

"It's important to try to find the ship. If it is spaceworthy or if it can be repaired, we may live. Otherwise, we won't."

"Just a few minutes. Let me catch my breath."

The Explorer was glad enough for those few minutes. The Merchant's eyes were already closed. He allowed his to do the same.

He heard the trampling and his eyes snapped open. "Never sleep on a strange planet," he told himself futilely.

The Merchant was awake too and his steady screaming was a rumble of terror.

The Explorer called, "It's only a native of this planet. It won't harm you."

But even as he spoke, the giant had swooped down, and in a moment, they were in its grasp, being lifted closer to its monstrous ugliness.

The Merchant struggled violently and, of course, quite futilely. "Can't you talk to it?" he yelled.

The Explorer could only shake his head. "I can't reach it with the projector. It won't be listening."

"Then blast it. Blast it down."

"We can't do that." The phrase "you fool" had almost been added. The Explorer struggled to keep his self-control. They were swallowing space as the monster moved purposefully away.

"Why not?" cried the Merchant. "You can reach your blaster. I see it in plain sight. Don't be afraid of falling."

"It's simpler than that. If this monster is killed, you'll never trade with this planet. You'll never even leave it. You probably won't live the day out."

"Why? Why?"

"Because this is one of the young of the species. You should know what happens when a trader kills a native young, even accidentally. What's more, if this is the target point, then we are on the estate of a powerful native. This might be one of his brood."

That was how they entered their present prison. They had carefully burned away a portion of the thick, stiff covering and it was obvious that the height from which they were suspended was a killing one.

Now, once again, the prison cage shuddered and lifted in an upward arc. The Merchant rolled to the lower rim and startled awake. The cover lifted and light flooded in. As was the case the time before, there were two specimens of the young. They were not very different in appearance from adults of the species, reflected the Explorer, though, of course, they were considerably smaller.

A handful of reedy green stalks was stuffed between the bar. Its odor was not unpleasant but it carried clods of soil at its ends.

The Merchant drew away and said huskily, "What are they doing?"

The Explorer said, "Trying to feed us, I should judge. At least, this seems to be the native equivalent of grass."

The cover was replaced and they were set swinging again, alone with their fodder.

4

Slim started at the sound of footsteps and brightened when it turned out to be only Red.

He said, "No one's around. I had my eye peeled, you bet."

Red said, "Ssh. Look. You take this stuff and stick it in the cage. I've got to scoot back to the house."

"What is it?" Slim reached reluctantly.

"Ground meat. Holy smokes, haven't you ever seen ground meat? That's what you should've got when I sent you to the house instead of coming back with that stupid grass."

Slim was hurt. "How'd I know they don't eat grass? Besides, ground meat doesn't come loose like that. It comes in cellophane and it isn't that color."

"Sure—in the city. Out here we grind our own and it's always this color till it's cooked."

"You mean it isn't cooked?" Slim drew away quickly.

Red looked disgusted. "Do you think animals eat *cooked* food? Come on, take it. It won't hurt you. I tell you there isn't much time."

"Why? What's doing back at the house?"

"I don't know. Dad and your father are walking around. I think maybe they're looking for me. Maybe the cook told them I took the meat. Anyway, we don't want them coming here after me."

"Didn't you ask the cook before you took this stuff?"

"Who? That crab? Shouldn't wonder if she only let me have a drink of water because Dad makes her. Come on. Take it."

Slim took the large glob of meat though his skin crawled at the touch. He turned toward the barn and Red sped away in the direction from which he had come.

Red slowed when he approached the two adults, took a few deep breaths to bring himself back to normal, and then carefully and nonchalantly sauntered past. (They were walking in the general direction of the barn, he noticed, but not dead on.)

He said, "Hi, Dad. Hello, sir."

The Industrialist said, "Just a moment, Red. I have a question to ask you."

Red turned a carefully blank face to his father. "Yes, Dad?"

"Mother tells me you were out early this morning."

"Not real early, Dad. Just a little before breakfast."

"She said you told her it was because you had been awakened during the night."

Red waited before answering. Should he have told Mom that?

Then he said, "Yes, sir."

"What was it that awakened you?"

Red saw no harm in it. He said, "I don't know, Dad. It sounded like thunder, sort of, and like a collision, sort of."

"Could you tell where it came from?"

"It *sounded* like it was out by the hill." That was truthful, and useful as well, since the direction was almost opposite that in which the barn lay.

The Industrialist looked at his guest. "I suppose it would do no harm to walk toward the hill."

The Astronomer said, "I am ready."

Red watched them walk away, and when he turned, he saw Slim peering cautiously out from among the briers of a hedge.

Red waved at him. "Come on."

Slim stepped out and approached. "Did they say anything about the meat?"

"No. I guess they don't know about that. They went down to the hill."

"What for?"

"Search me. They kept asking about the noise I heard. Listen, did the animals eat the meat?"

"Well," said Slim cautiously, "they were sort of *looking* at it and smelling it or something."

"Okay," Red said, "I guess they'll eat it. Holy smokes, they've got to eat *something.* Let's walk along toward the hill and see what Dad and your father are going to do."

"What about the animals?"

"They'll be all right. A fellow can't spend all his time on them. Did you give them water?"

"Sure. They drank that."

"See. Come on. We'll look at them after lunch. I tell you what. We'll bring them fruit. Anything'll eat fruit."

Together they trotted up the rise, Red, as usual, in the lead.

5

The Astronomer said, "You think the noise was their ship landing?"

"Don't you think it could be?"

"If it were, they may all be dead."

"Perhaps not." The Industrialist frowned.

"If they have landed and are still alive, where are they?"

"Think about that for a while." He was still frowning.

The Astronomer said, "I don't understand you."

"They may not be friendly."

"Oh no. I've spoken with them. They've——"

"You've spoken with them. Call that reconnaissance. What would their next step be? Invasion?"

"But they only have one ship, sir."

"You know that only because they say so. They might have a fleet."

"I've told you about their size. They——"

"Their size would not matter if they have hand weapons that may well be superior to our artillery."

"That is not what I meant."

"I had this partly in mind from the first." The Industrialist went on. "It is for that reason I agreed to see them after I received your letter. Not to agree to an unsettling and impossible trade, but to judge their real purposes. I did not count on their evading the meeting."

He sighed and added, "I suppose it isn't our fault. You are right in one thing, at any rate. The world has been at peace too long. We are losing a healthy sense of suspicion."

The Astronomer's mild voice rose to an unusual pitch and he said,

"I *will* speak. I tell you that there is no reason to suppose they can possibly be hostile. They are small, yes, but that is only important because it is a reflection of the fact that their native worlds are small. Our world has what is for them a normal gravity, but because of our much higher gravitational potential, our atmosphere is too dense to support them comfortably over sustained periods. For a similar reason, the use of the world as a base for interstellar travel, except for trade in certain items, is uneconomical. And there are important differences in chemistry of life due to the basic differences in soils. They couldn't eat our food or we theirs."

"Surely all this can be overcome. They can bring their own food, build domed stations of lowered air pressure, devise specially designed ships."

"They can. And how glibly you can describe feats that are easy to a race in its youth. It is simply that they don't have to do any of that. There are millions of worlds suitable for them in the Galaxy. They don't need this one which isn't."

"How do you know? All this is their information again."

"This I was able to check independently. I am an astronomer, after all."

"That is true. Let me hear what you have to say then while we walk."

"Then, sir, consider that for a long time our astronomers have believed that two general classes of planetary bodies existed. First, the planets which formed at differences far enough from their stellar nuclei to become cool enough to capture hydrogen. These would be large planets rich in hydrogen, ammonia, and methane. We have examples of these in the giant outer planets. The second class would include those planets formed so near the stellar center that the high temperature would make it impossible to capture much hydrogen. These would be smaller planets, comparatively poorer in hydrogen and richer in oxygen. We know that type very well since we live on one. Ours is the only solar system we know in detail, however, and it has been reasonable for us to assume that these were the *only* two planetary classes."

"I take it then that there is another."

"Yes. There is a super-dense class, still smaller, poorer in hydrogen than the inner planets of the solar system. The ratio of occurrence of hydrogen-ammonia planets and these super-dense water-oxygen worlds of theirs over the entire Galaxy—and remember that they have actually conducted a survey of significant sample volumes of the Galaxy, which we, without interstellar travel, cannot do—is about three to one. This leaves them several million super-dense worlds for exploration and colonization."

The Industrialist looked at the blue sky and the green-crowned trees among which they were making their way. He said, "And worlds like ours?"

The Astronomer said softly, "Ours is the first solar system they have found which contains them. Apparently the development of our solar system was unique and did not follow the ordinary rules."

The Industrialist considered that. "What it amounts to is that these creatures from space are asteroid dwellers."

"No, no. The asteroids are something else again. They occur, I was told, in one out of eight stellar systems, but they're completely different from what we've been discussing."

"And how does your being an astronomer change the fact that you are still only quoting their unsupported statements?"

"But they did not restrict themselves to bald items of information. They presented me with a theory of stellar evolution which I had to accept and which is more nearly valid than anything our own astronomy has ever been able to devise, if we except possible lost theories dating from Beforethewars. Mind you, their theory had a rigidly mathematical development and it predicted just such a galaxy as they describe. So you see, they have all the worlds they wish. They are not land-hungry. Certainly not for our land."

"Reason would say so, if what you say is true. But creatures may be intelligent and not reasonable. Our forefathers were presumably intelligent, yet they were certainly not reasonable. Was it reasonable to destroy almost all their tremendous civilization in atomic warfare over causes our historians can no longer accurately determine?" The Industrialist brooded over it. "From the dropping of the first atom bomb over the Eastern Islands of the Sun—I forget the ancient name—there was only one end in sight, and in plain sight. Yet events were allowed to proceed to that end."

He looked up, said briskly, "Well, where are we? I wonder if we are not on a fool's errand after all."

But the Astronomer was a little in advance and his voice came thickly. "No fool's errand, sir. Look there."

6

Red and Slim had trailed their elders with the experience of youth, aided by the absorption and anxiety of their fathers. Their view of the final object of the search was somewhat obscured by the underbrush behind which they remained.

Red said, "Holy smokes. Look at that. It's all shiny silver or something."

But it was Slim who was really excited. He caught at the other. "I know what this is. It's a spaceship. That must be why my father came here. He's one of the biggest astronomers in the world and your father would have to call him if a spaceship landed on his estate."

"What are you talking about? Dad didn't even know that thing was there. He only came here because I told him I heard the thunder from here. Besides, there isn't any such thing as a spaceship."

"Sure, there is. Look at it. See those round things. They're ports. And you can see the rocket tubes."

"How do you know so much?"

Slim was flushed. He said, "I read about them. My father has books about them. Old books. From Beforethewars."

"Huh. Now I know you're making it up. Books from Beforethewars!"

"My father *has* to have them. He teaches at the University. It's his job."

His voice had risen and Red had to pull at him. "You want them to hear us?" he whispered indignantly.

"Well, it is, too, a spaceship."

"Look here, Slim, you mean that's a ship from another world."

"It's *got* to be. Look at my father going round and round it. He wouldn't be so interested if it was anything else."

"Other worlds! Where are there other worlds?"

"Everywhere. How about the planets? They're worlds just like ours, some of them. And other stars probably have planets. There's probably zillions of planets."

Red felt outweighed and outnumbered. He muttered, "You're crazy!"

"All right, then. I'll show you."

"Hey! Where are you going?"

"Down there. I'm going to ask my father. I suppose you'll believe it if *he* tells you. I suppose you'll believe a Professor of Astronomy knows what——"

He had scrambled upright.

Red said, "Hey. You don't want them to see us. We're not supposed to be here. Do you want them to start asking questions and find out about our animals?"

"I don't care. You said I was crazy."

"Snitcher! You promised you wouldn't tell."

"I'm *not* going to tell. But if they find out themselves, it's your fault for starting an argument and saying I was crazy."

"I take it back then," grumbled Red.

"Well, all right. You better."

In a way, Slim was disappointed. He wanted to see the spaceship at closer quarters. Still, he could not break his vow of secrecy even in spirit without at least the excuse of personal insult.

Red said, "It's awfully small for a spaceship."

"Sure, because it's probably a scout ship."

"I'll bet Dad couldn't even get into the old thing."

So much Slim realized to be true. It was a weak point in his argument and he made no answer.

Red rose to his feet; an elaborate attitude of boredom all about him. "Well, I guess we better be going. There's business to do and I can't spend all day here looking at some old spaceship or whatever it is. We've got to take care of the animals if we're going to be circus folks. That's the first rule with circus folks. They've got to take care of the animals. And," he finished virtuously, "that's what I aim to do, anyway."

Slim said, "What for, Red? They've got plenty of meat. Let's watch."

"There's no fun in watching. Besides Dad and your father are going away and I guess it's about lunch time."

Red became argumentative. "Look, Slim, we can't start acting suspicious or they're going to start investigating. Holy smokes, don't you ever read any detective stories? When you're trying to work a big deal without being caught, it's practically the main thing to keep on acting just like always. Then they don't suspect anything. That's the first law——"

"Oh, all right."

Slim rose resentfully. At the moment, the circus appeared to him a rather tawdry and shoddy substitute for the glories of astronomy, and he wondered how he had come to fall in with Red's silly scheme.

Down the slope they went, Slim, as usual, in the rear.

7

The Industrialist said, "It's the workmanship that gets me. I never saw such construction."

"What good is it now?" said the Astronomer bitterly. "There's nothing left. There'll be no second landing. This ship detected life on our planet through accident. Other exploring parties would come no closer than necessary to establish the fact that no superdense worlds existed in our solar system."

"Well, there's no quarreling with a crash landing."

"The ship hardly seems damaged. If only some had survived, the ship might have been repaired."

"If they had survived, there would be no trade in any case. They're too different. Too disturbing. In any case—it's over."

They entered the house and the Industrialist greeted his wife calmly. "Lunch about ready, dear?"

"I'm afraid not. You see——" She looked hesitantly at the Astronomer.

"Is anything wrong?" asked the Industrialist. "Why not tell me? I'm sure our guest won't mind a little family discussion."

"Pray don't pay any attention whatever to me," muttered the Astronomer. He moved miserably to the other end of the living room.

The woman said in low, hurried tones, "Really, dear, Cook's that upset. I've been soothing her for hours and honestly I don't know why Red should have done it."

"Done what?" The Industrialist was more amused than otherwise. It had taken the united efforts of himself and his son months to argue his wife into using the name "Red" rather than the perfectly ridiculous (viewed youngster-fashion) name which was his real one.

She said, "He's taken most of the chopped meat."

"He's eaten it?"

"Well, I hope not. It was raw."

"Then what would he want it for?"

"I haven't the slightest idea. I haven't seen him since breakfast.

Meanwhile Cook's just furious. She caught him vanishing out the kitchen door and there was the bowl of chopped meat just about empty and she was going to use it for lunch. Well, you know Cook. She had to change the lunch menu and that means she won't be worth living with for a week. You'll just have to speak to Red, dear, and make him promise not to do things in the kitchen any more. And it wouldn't hurt to have him apologize to Cook."

"Oh, come. She works for us. If we don't complain about a change in lunch menu, why should she?"

"Because she's the one who has double work made for her, and she's talking about quitting. Good cooks aren't easy to get. Do you remember the one before her?"

It was a strong argument.

The Industrialist looked about vaguely. He said, "I suppose you're right. He isn't here, I suppose. When he comes in, I'll talk to him."

"You'd better start. Here he comes."

Red walked into the house and said cheerfully, "Time for lunch, I guess." He looked from one parent to the other in quick speculation at their fixed stares and said, "Got to clean up first, though," and made for the other door.

The Industrialist said, "One moment, son."

"Sir?"

"Where's your little friend?"

Red said carelessly, "He's around somewhere. We were just sort of walking and I looked around and he wasn't there." This was perfectly true, and Red felt on safe ground. "I told him it was lunch time. I said, 'I suppose it's about lunch time.' I said, 'We got to be getting back to the house.' And he said, 'Yes.' And I just went on, and then when I was about at the creek, I looked around and——"

The Astronomer interrupted the voluble story, looking up from a magazine he had been sightlessly rummaging through. "I wouldn't worry about my youngster. He is quite self-reliant. Don't wait lunch for him."

"Lunch isn't ready in any case, Doctor." The Industrialist turned once more to his son. "And talking about that, son, the reason for it is that something happened to the ingredients. Do you have anything to say?"

"Sir?"

"I hate to feel that I have to explain myself more fully. Why did you take the chopped meat?"

"The chopped meat?"

"The chopped meat." He waited patiently.

Red said, "Well, I was sort of——"

"Hungry?" prompted his father. "For raw meat?"

"No, sir. I just sort of needed it."

"For what exactly?"

Red looked miserable and remained silent.

The Astronomer broke in again. "If you don't mind my putting in a few words—you'll remember that just after breakfast, my son came in to ask what animals ate."

"Oh, you're right. How stupid of me to forget. Look here, Red, did you take it for an animal pet you've got?"

Red recovered indignant breath. He said, "You mean Slim came in here and said I had an animal? He came in here and said that? He said I had an animal?"

"No, he didn't. He simply asked what animals ate. That's all. Now if he promised he wouldn't tell on you, he didn't. It's your own foolishness in trying to take something without permission that gave you away. That happened to be stealing. Now have you an animal? I ask you a direct question."

"Yes, sir." It was a whisper so low as hardly to be heard.

"All right, you'll have to get rid of it. Do you understand?"

Red's mother intervened. "Do you mean to say you're keeping a meat-eating animal, Red? It might bite you and give you blood poison."

"They're only small ones," quavered Red. "They hardly budge if you touch them."

"They? How many do you have?"

"Two."

"Where are they?"

The Industrialist touched her arm. "Don't chivvy the child any further," he said in a low voice. "If he says he'll get rid of them, he will, and that's punishment enough."

He dismissed the matter from his mind.

8

Lunch was half over when Slim dashed into the dining room. For a moment, he stood abashed, and then he said in what was almost hysteria, "I've got to speak to Red. I've got to say something."

Red looked up in fright, but the Astronomer said, "I don't think, son, you're being very polite. You've kept lunch waiting."

"I'm sorry, Father."

"Oh, don't rate the lad," said the Industrialist's wife. "He can speak to Red if he wants to, and there was no damage done to the lunch."

"I've got to speak to Red alone," Slim insisted.

"Now that's enough," said the Astronomer with a kind of gentleness that was obviously manufactured for the benefit of strangers and which had beneath it an easily recognized edge. "Take your seat."

Slim did so, but he ate only when someone looked directly upon him. Even then he was not very successful.

Red caught his eyes. He made soundless words, "Did the animals get loose?"

Slim shook his head slightly. He whispered, "No, it's——"

The Astronomer looked at him hard and Slim faltered to a stop.

With lunch over, Red slipped out of the room, with a microscopic motion at Slim to follow.

They walked in silence to the creek.

Then Red turned fiercely upon his companion. "Look here, what's the idea of telling my dad we were feeding animals?"

Slim said, "I didn't. I asked what you feed animals. That's not the same as saying we were doing it. Besides, it's something else, Red."

But Red had not used up his grievances. "And where did you go, anyway? I thought you were coming to the house. They acted like it was my fault you weren't there."

"But I'm trying to tell you about that, if you'd only shut *up* a second and let me talk. You don't give a fellow a chance."

"Well, go on and tell me if you've got so much to say."

"I'm *trying* to. I went back to the spaceship. The folks weren't there any more and I wanted to see what it was like."

"It isn't a spaceship," said Red sullenly. He had nothing to lose.

"It is, too. I looked inside. You could look through the ports and I looked inside and they were *dead*." He looked sick. "They were dead."

"*Who* were dead?"

Slim screeched, "Animals! Like *our* animals! Only they *aren't* animals. They're people things from other planets."

For a moment, Red might have been turned to stone. It didn't occur to him to disbelieve Slim at this point. Slim looked too genuinely the bearer of just such tidings. He said finally, "Oh, my."

"Well, what are we going to do? Golly, will we get a whopping if they find out!" He was shivering.

"We better turn them loose," said Red.

"They'll tell on us."

"They can't talk our language. Not if they're from another planet."

"Yes, they can. Because I remember my father talking about some stuff like that to my mother when he didn't know I was in the room. He was talking about visitors who could talk with the mind. Telepathery or something. I thought he was making it up."

"Well, holy smokes. I mean—holy smokes." Red looked up. "I tell you. My dad said to get rid of them. Let's sort of bury them somewhere or throw them in the creek."

"He *told* you to do that?"

"He made me say I had animals and then he said, 'Get rid of them.' I got to do what he says. Holy smokes, he's my dad."

Some of the panic left Slim's heart. It was a thoroughly legalistic way out. "Well, let's do it right now then, before they find out. Oh, golly, if they find out, will we be in trouble!"

They broke into a run toward the barn, unspeakable visions in their minds.

9

It was different, looking at them as though they were "people." As animals, they had been interesting; as "people," horrible. Their eyes, which were neutral little objects before, now seemed to watch them with active malevolence.

"They're making noises," said Slim in a whisper.

"I guess they're talking or something," said Red. Funny that those noises which they had heard before had not had significance earlier. He was making no move toward them. Neither was Slim.

The canvas was off but they were just watching. The ground meat, Slim noticed, hadn't been touched.

Slim said, "Aren't you going to do something?"

"Aren't you?"

"You found them."

"It's your turn now."

"No, it isn't. You found them. It's your fault, the whole thing. I was just watching."

"You joined in, Slim. You know you did."

"I don't care. You found them and that's what I'll say when they come here looking for us."

Red said, "All right for you." But the thought of the consequences inspired him anyway, and he reached for the cage door.

Slim said, "Wait!"

Red was glad to. He said, "Now what's biting you?"

"One of them's got something on him that looks like it might be iron or something."

"Where?"

"Right there. I saw it before but I thought it was just part of him. But if he's 'people,' maybe it's a disintegrator gun."

"What's that?"

"I read about it in the books from Beforethewars. Mostly people with spaceships have disintegrator guns. They point them at you and you get disintegratored."

"They didn't point it at us till now," pointed out Red with his heart not quite in it.

"I don't care. I'm not hanging around here and getting disintegratored. I'm getting my father."

"Cowardy-cat. Yellow cowardy-cat."

"I don't care. You can call all the names you want, but if you bother them now, you'll get disintegratored. You wait and see, and it'll be all your fault."

He made for the narrow spiral stairs that led to the main floor of the barn, stopped at its head, then backed away.

Red's mother was moving up, panting a little with the exertion and smiling a tight smile for the benefit of Slim in his capacity as guest.

"Red! You, Red! Are you up there? Now don't try to hide. I know this is where you're keeping them. Cook saw where you ran with the meat."

Red quavered, "Hello, Ma!"

"Now show me those nasty animals. I'm going to see to it that you get rid of them right away."

It was over! And despite the imminent corporal punishment, Red felt something like a load fall from him. At least the decision was out of his hands.

"Right there, Ma. I didn't do anything to them, Ma. I didn't know. They just looked like little animals and I thought you'd let me keep them, Ma. I wouldn't have taken the meat only they wouldn't eat grass or leaves and we couldn't find good nuts or berries and Cook never lets me have anything or I would have asked her and I didn't know it was for lunch and——"

He was speaking on the sheer momentum of terror and did not realize that his mother did not hear him but, with eyes frozen and popping at the cage, was screaming in thin, piercing tones.

10

The Astronomer was saying, "A quiet burial is all we can do. There is no point in any publicity now," when they heard the screams.

She had not entirely recovered by the time she reached them, running and running. It was minutes before her husband could extract sense from her.

She was saying finally, "I tell you they're in the barn. I don't know what they are. No, no——"

She barred the Industrialist's quick movement in that direction. She said, "Don't *you* go. Send one of the hands with a shotgun. I tell you I never saw anything like it. Little horrible beasts with—with—— I can't describe it. To think that Red was touching them and trying to feed them. He was *holding* them, and feeding them meat."

Red began, "I only——"

And Slim said, "It wasn't——"

The Industrialist said quickly, "Now you boys have done enough harm today. March! Into the house! And not a word; not one word! I'm not interested in anything you have to say. After this is all over,

I'll hear you out and as for you, Red, I'll see that you're properly punished."

He turned to his wife, "Now whatever the animals are, we'll have them killed." He added quietly once the youngsters were out of hearing, "Come, come. The children aren't hurt, and after all, they haven't done anything really terrible. They've just found a new pet."

The Astronomer spoke with difficulty. "Pardon me, ma'am, but can you describe these animals?"

She shook her head. She was quite beyond words.

"Can you just tell me if they——"

"I'm sorry," said the Industrialist apologetically, "but I think I had better take care of her. Will you excuse me?"

"A moment. Please. One moment. She said she had never seen such animals before. Surely it is not usual to find animals that are completely unique on an estate such as this."

"I'm sorry. Let's not discuss that now."

"Except that unique animals might have landed during the night."

The Industrialist stepped away from his wife. "What are you implying?"

"I think we had better go to the barn, sir!"

The Industrialist stared a moment, turned, and suddenly and quite uncharacteristically began running. The Astronomer followed and the woman's wail rose unheeded behind them.

11

The Industrialist stared, looked at the Astronomer, turned to stare again.

"Those?"

"Those," said the Astronomer. "I have no doubt we appear as strange and repulsive to them."

"What do they say?"

"Why, that they are uncomfortable and tired and even a little sick, but that they are not seriously damaged, and that the youngsters treated them well."

"Treated them well! Scooping them up, keeping them in a cage, giving them grass and raw meat to eat? Tell me how to speak to them."

"It may take a little time. Think *at* them. Try to listen. It will come to you, but perhaps not right away."

The Industrialist tried. He grimaced with the effort of it, thinking over and over again, The youngsters were ignorant of your identity.

And the thought was suddenly in his mind, We were quite aware of it and because we knew they meant well by us according to their own view of the matter, we did not attempt to attack them.

Attack them? thought the Industrialist, and said it aloud in his concentration.

Why, yes, came the answering thought. We are armed.

One of the revolting little creatures in the cage lifted a metal object and there was a sudden hole in the top of the cage and another in the roof of the barn, each hole rimmed with charred wood.

We hope, the creatures thought, it will not be too difficult to make repairs.

The Industrialist found it impossible to organize himself to the point of directed thought. He turned to the Astronomer. "And with that weapon in their possession, they let themselves be handled and caged? I don't understand it."

But the calm thought came, We would not harm the young of an intelligent species.

12

It was twilight. The Industrialist had entirely missed the evening meal and remained unaware of the fact.

He said, "Do you really think the ship will fly?"

"If they say so," said the Astronomer, "I'm sure it will. They'll be back, I hope, before too long."

"And when they do," said the Industrialist energetically, "I will keep my part of the agreement. What is more I will move sky and earth to have the world accept them. I was entirely wrong, Doctor. Creatures that would refuse to harm children under such provocation as they received are admirable. But you know—I almost hate to say this——"

"Say what?"

"The kids. Yours and mine. I'm almost proud of them. Imagine seizing these creatures, feeding them or trying to, and keeping them hidden. The amazing gall of it. Red told me it was his idea to get a job in a circus on the strength of them. Imagine!"

The Astronomer said, "Youth!"

13

The Merchant said, "Will we be taking off soon?"

"Half an hour," said the Explorer.

It was going to be a lonely trip back. All the remaining seventeen of the crew were dead and their ashes were to be left on a strange planet. Back they would go with a limping ship and the burden of the controls entirely on himself.

The Merchant said, "It was a good business stroke, not harming the young ones. We will get very good terms; *very* good terms."

The Explorer thought, Business!

The Merchant said, "They've lined up to see us off. All of them. You don't think they're too close, do you? It would be bad to burn any of them with the rocket blast at this stage of the game."

"They're safe."

"Horrible-looking things, aren't they?"

"Pleasant enough, inside. Their thoughts are perfectly friendly."

"You wouldn't believe it of them. That immature one, the one that first picked us up——"

"They call him Red."

"That's a queer name for a monster. Makes me laugh. He actually feels *bad* that we're leaving. Only I can't make out exactly why. The nearest I can come to it is something about a lost opportunity with some organization or other that I can't quite interpret."

"A circus," said the Explorer briefly.

"What? Why, the impertinent monstrosity."

"Why not? What would you have done if you had found *him* wandering on *your* native world; found him sleeping on a field on Earth, red tentacles, six legs, pseudopods and all?"

14

Red watched the ship leave. His red tentacles, which gave him his nickname, quivered their regret at lost opportunity to the very last, and the eyes at their tips filled with drifting yellowish crystals that were the equivalent of Earthly tears.

THE DEEP

1

In the end, any particular planet must die. It may be a quick death as its sun explodes. It may be a slow death, as its sun sinks into decay and its oceans lock in ice. In the latter case, at least, intelligent life has a chance of survival.

The direction of survival may be outward into space, to a planet closer to the cooling sun or to a planet of another sun altogether. This particular avenue is closed if the planet is unfortunate enough to be the only significant body rotating about its primary and if, at the time, no other star is within half a thousand light-years.

The direction of survival may be inward, into the crust of the planet. That is always available. A new home can be built underground and the heat of the planet's core can be tapped for energy. Thousands of years may be necessary for the task, but a dying sun cools slowly.

But planetary warmth dies, too, with time. Burrows must be dug deeper and deeper until the planet is dead through and through.

The time was coming.

On the surface of the planet, wisps of neon blew listlessly, barely able to stir the pools of oxygen that collected in the lowlands. Occasionally, during the long day, the crusted sun would flare briefly into a dull red glow and the oxygen pools would bubble a little.

During the long night, a blue-white oxygen frost formed over the pools and on the bare rock, a neon dew formed.

Eight hundred miles below the surface, a last bubble of warmth and life existed.

2

Wenda's relationship to Roi was as close as one could imagine, closer by far than it was decent for her to know.

She had been allowed to enter the ovarium only once in her life and it had been made quite clear to her that it *was* to be only that once.

The Raceologist had said, "You don't quite meet the standards, Wenda, but you are fertile and we'll try you once. It may work out."

She wanted it to work out. She wanted it desperately. Quite early in her life she had known that she was deficient in intelligence, that she would never be more than a Manual. It embarrassed her that she should fail the Race and she longed for even a single chance to help create another being. It became an obsession.

She secreted her egg in an angle of the structure and then returned to watch. The "randoming" process that moved the eggs gently about during mechanical insemination (to insure even gene distribution) did not, by some good fortune, do more than make her own wedged-in egg wobble a bit.

Unobtrusively she maintained her watch during the period of maturation, observed the little one who emerged from the particular egg that was hers, noted his physical markings, watched him grow.

He was a healthy youngster and the Raceologist approved of him.

She had said once, very casually, "Look at that one, the one sitting there. Is he sick?"

"Which one?" The Raceologist was startled. Visibly sick infants at this stage would be a strong reflection upon his own competence. "You mean Roi? Nonsense. I wish all our young were like that one."

At first, she was only pleased with herself, then frightened, finally horrified. She found herself haunting the youngster, taking an interest in his schooling, watching him at play. She was happy when he was near, dull and unhappy otherwise. She had never heard of such a thing, and she was ashamed.

She should have visited the Mentalist, but she knew better. She was not so dull as not to know that this was not a mild aberration to be cured at the twitch of a brain cell. It was a truly psychotic manifestation. She was certain of that. They would confine her if they found out. They would euthanase her, perhaps, as a useless drain on the strictly limited energy available to the race. They might even euthanase the offspring of her egg if they found out who it was.

She fought the abnormality through the years and, to a measure, succeeded. Then she first heard the news that Roi had been chosen for the long trip and was filled with aching misery.

She followed him to one of the empty corridors of the cavern, some miles from the city center. *The* city! There was only one.

This particular cavern had been closed down within Wenda's own memory. The Elders had paced its length, considered its population and the energy necessary to keep it powered, then decided to darken it. The population, not many to be sure, had been moved closer toward the center and the quota for the next session at the ovarium had been cut.

Wenda found Roi's conversational level of thinking shallow, as though most of his mind had drawn inward contemplatively.

Are you afraid? she thought at him.

Because I come out here to think? He hesitated a little, then said, "Yes, I am. It's the Race's last chance. If I fail——"

Are you afraid for yourself?

He looked at her in astonishment and Wenda's thought stream fluttered with shame at her indecency.

She said, "I wish I were going instead."

Roi said, "Do you think you can do a better job?"

"Oh, no. But if *I* were to fail and—and never come back, it would be a smaller loss to the Race."

"The loss is all the same," he said stolidly, "whether it's you or I. The loss is Racial existence."

Racial existence at the moment was in the background of Wenda's mind, if anywhere. She sighed. "The trip is such a long one."

"How long?" he asked with a smile. "Do you know?"

She hesitated. She dared not appear stupid to him.

She said primly, "The common talk is that it is to the First Level."

When Wenda had been little and the heated corridors had extended further out of the city, she had wandered out, exploring as youngsters will. One day, a long distance out, where the chill in the air nipped at her, she came to a hall that slanted upward but was blocked almost instantly by a tremendous plug, wedged tightly from top to bottom and side to side.

On the other side and upward, she had learned a long time later, lay the Seventy-ninth Level; above that the Seventy-eighth and so on.

"We're going past the First Level, Wenda."

"But there's nothing past the First Level."

"You're right. Nothing. All the solid matter of the planet comes to an end."

"But how can there be anything that's nothing? You mean air?"

"No, I mean *nothing*. Vacuum. You know what vacuum is, don't you?"

"Yes. But vacuums have to be pumped and kept airtight."

"That's good for Maintenance. Still, past the First Level is just an indefinite amount of vacuum stretching everywhere."

Wenda thought awhile. She said, "Has anyone ever been there?"

"Of course not. But we have the records."

"Maybe the records are wrong."

"They can't be. Do you know how much space I'm going to cross?"

Wenda's thought stream indicated an overwhelming negative.

Roi said, "You know the speed of light, I suppose."

"Of course," she replied readily. It was a universal constant. Infants knew it. "One thousand nine hundred and fifty-four times the length of the cavern and back in one second."

"Right," said Roi, "but if light were to travel along the distance I'm to cross, it would take it ten years."

Wenda said, "You're making fun of me. You're trying to frighten me."

"Why should it frighten you?" He rose. "But I've been moping here long enough—"

For a moment, one of his six grasping limbs rested lightly in one of hers, with an objective, impassive friendship. An irrational impulse urged Wenda to seize it tightly, prevent him from leaving.

She panicked for a moment in fear that he might probe her mind past the conversational level, that he might sicken and never face her again, that he might even report her for treatment. Then she relaxed. Roi was normal, not sick like herself. He would never dream of penetrating a friend's mind any deeper than the conversational level, whatever the provocation.

He was very handsome in her eyes as he walked away. His grasping limbs were straight and strong, his prehensile, manipulative vibrissae were numerous and delicate and his optic patches were more beautifully opalescent than any she had ever seen.

3

Laura settled down in her seat. How soft and comfortable they made them. How pleasing and unfrightening airplanes were on the inside, how different from the hard, silvery, inhuman luster of the outside.

The bassinet was on the seat beside her. She peeped in past the blanket and the tiny, ruffled cap. Walter was sleeping. His face was the blank, round softness of infancy and his eyelids were two fringed half-moons pulled down over his eyes.

A tuft of light brown hair straggled across his forehead, and with infinite delicacy, Laura drew it back beneath his cap.

It would soon be Walter's feeding time and she hoped he was still too young to be upset by the strangeness of his surroundings. The stewardess was being very kind. She even kept his bottles in a little refrigerator. Imagine, a refrigerator on board an airplane.

The people in the seat across the aisle had been watching her in that peculiar way that meant they would love to talk to her if only they could think of an excuse. The moment came when she lifted Walter out of his bassinet and placed him, a little lump of pink flesh encased in a white cocoon of cotton, upon her lap.

A baby is always legitimate as an opening for conversation between strangers.

The lady across the way said (her words were predictable), "What a *lovely* child. How old is he, my dear?"

Laura said, through the pins in her mouth (she had spread a blanket across her kness and was changing Walter), "He'll be four months old next week."

Walter's eyes were open and he simpered across at the woman, opening his mouth in a wet, gummy grin. (He always enjoyed being changed.)

"Look at him smile, George," said the lady.

Her husband smiled back and twiddled fat fingers.

"Goo," he said.

Walter laughed in a high-pitched, hiccupy way.

"What's his name, dear?" asked the woman.

"He's Walter Michael," Laura said, then added, "After his father."

The floodgates were quite down. Laura learned that the couple were George and Eleanor Ellis, that they were on vacation, that they had three children, two girls and one boy, all grown-up. Both girls had married and one had two children of her own.

Laura listened with a pleased expression on her thin face. Walter (senior, that is) had always said that it was because she was such a good listener that he had first grown interested in her.

Walter was getting restless. Laura freed his arms in order to let some of his feelings evaporate in muscular effort.

"Would you warm the bottle, please?" she asked the stewardess.

Under strict but friendly questioning, Laura explained the number of feedings Walter was currently enjoying, the exact nature of his formula, and whether he suffered from diaper rash.

"I hope his little stomach isn't upset today," she worried. "I mean the plane motion, you know."

"Oh, Lord," said Mrs. Ellis, "he's too young to be bothered by that. Besides, these large planes are wonderful. Unless I look out the window, I wouldn't believe we were in the air. Don't you feel that way, George?"

But Mr. Ellis, a blunt, straightforward man, said, "I'm surprised you take a baby that age on a plane."

Mrs. Ellis turned to frown at him.

Laura held Walter over her shoulder and patted his back gently. The beginnings of a soft wail died down as his little fingers found themselves in his mother's smooth, blond hair and began grubbing into the loose bun that lay at the back of her neck.

She said, "I'm taking him to his father. Walter's never seen his son, yet."

Mr. Ellis looked perplexed and began a comment, but Mrs. Ellis put in quickly, "Your husband is in the service, I suppose?"

"Yes, he is."

(Mr. Ellis opened his mouth in a soundless "Oh" and subsided.)

Laura went on, "He's stationed just outside of Davao and he's going to be meeting me at Nichols Field."

Before the stewardess returned with the bottle, they had discovered that her husband was a master sergeant with the Quartermaster Corps, that he had been in the Army for four years, that they had been married for two, that he was about to be discharged, and that they would spend a long honeymoon there before returning to San Francisco.

Then she had the bottle. She cradled Walter in the crook of her left arm and put the bottle to his face. It slid right past his lips and his gums seized upon the nipple. Little bubbles began to work upward through the milk, while his hands batted ineffectively at the warm glass and his blue eyes stared fixedly at her.

Laura squeezed little Walter ever so slightly and thought how, with all the petty difficulties and annoyances that were involved, it yet remained such a wonderful thing to have a little baby all one's own.

4

Theory, thought Gan, always theory. The folk of the surface, a million or more years ago, could *see* the Universe, could sense it directly. Now, with eight hundred miles of rock above their heads, the Race could only make deductions from the trembling needles of their instruments.

It was only theory that brain cells, in addition to their ordinary electric potentials, radiated another sort of energy altogether. Energy that was not electromagnetic and hence not condemned to the creeping pace of light. Energy that was associated only with the highest functions of the brain and hence characteristic only of intelligent, reasoning creatures.

It was only a jogging needle that detected such an energy field leaking into their cavern, and other needles that pinpointed the origin of the field in such and such a direction ten light-years distant. At least one star must have moved quite close in the time since the surface folk had placed the nearest at five hundred light-years. Or was theory wrong?

"Are you afraid?" Gan burst into the conversational level of thought without warning and impinged sharply on the humming surface of Roi's mind.

Roi said, "It's a great responsibility."

Gan thought, "*Others* speak of responsibility." For generations, Head-Tech after Head-Tech had been working on the Resonizer and the Receiving Station and it was in his time that the final step had to be taken. What did others know of responsibility.

He said, "It is. We talk about Racial extinction glibly enough, but we always assume it will come someday but not now, not in our time. But it will, do you understand? It will. What we are to do today will consume two thirds of our total energy supply. There will not be enough left to try again. There will not be enough for this generation to live out its life. But that will not matter if you follow orders. We have thought of everything. We have spent generations thinking of everything."

"I will do what I am told," said Roi.

"Your thought field will be meshed against those coming from space. All thought fields are characteristic of the individual, and ordinarily the probability of any duplication is very low. But the fields from space number billions by our best estimate. Your field is very likely to be like one of theirs, and in that case, a resonance will be set up as long as our Resonizer is in operation. Do you know the principles involved?"

"Yes, sir."

"Then you know that during resonance, your mind will be on Planet X in the brain of the creature with a thought field identical to yours. That is not the energy-consuming process. In resonance with your mind, we will also place the mass of the Receiving Station. The method of transferring mass in that manner was the last phase of the problem to be solved, and it will take all the energy the Race would ordinarily use in a hundred years."

Gan picked up the black cube that was the Receiving Station and looked at it somberly. Three generations before it had been thought impossible to manufacture one with all the required properties in a space less than twenty cubic yards. They had it now; it was the size of his fist.

Gan said, "The thought field of intelligent brain cells can only follow certain well-defined patterns. All living creatures, on whatever planet they develop, must possess a protein base and an oxygen-water chemistry. If their world is livable for them, it is livable for us."

Theory, thought Gan on a deeper level, always theory.

He went on, "This does not mean that the body you find yourself in, its mind and its emotions, may not be completely alien. So we have arranged for three methods of activating the Receiving Station. If you are strong-limbed, you need only exert five hundred pounds of pressure on any face of the cube. If you are delicate-limbed, you need only press a knob, which you can reach through this single opening in the cube. If you are no-limbed, if your host body is paralyzed or in any other way helpless, you can activate the Station by mental energy alone. Once the Station is activated, we will have two points of reference, not one, and the Race can be transferred to Planet X by ordinary teleportation."

"That," said Roi, "will mean we will use electromagnetic energy."

"And so?"

"It will take us ten years to transfer."

"We will not be aware of duration."

"I realize that, sir, but it will mean the Station will remain on Planet X for ten years. What if it is destroyed in the meantime?"

"We have thought of that, too. We have thought of everything. Once the Station is activated, it will generate a paramass field. It will move in the direction of gravitational attraction, sliding through ordinary matter, until such time as a continuous medium of relatively high density exerts sufficient friction to stop it. It will take twenty feet of rock to do that. Anything of lower density won't affect it. It will remain twenty feet underground for ten years, at which time a counterfield will bring it to the surface. Then one by one, the Race will appear."

"In that case, why not make the activation of the Station automatic? It has so many automatic attributes already——"

"You haven't thought it through, Roi. We have. Not all spots on the surface of Planet X may be suitable. If the inhabitants are powerful and advanced, you may have to find an unobtrusive place for the Station. It won't do for us to appear in a city square. And you will have to be certain that the immediate environment is not dangerous in other ways."

"What other ways, sir?"

"I don't know. The ancient records of the surface record many things we no longer understand. They don't explain because they took those items for granted, but we have been away from the surface for almost a hundred thousand generations and we are puzzled. Our Techs aren't even in agreement on the physical nature of stars, and that is something the records mention and discuss frequently. But what are "storms," "earthquakes," "volcanoes," "tornadoes," "sleet," "landslides," "floods," "lightning," and so on? These are all terms which refer to surface phenomena that are dangerous, but we don't know what they are. We don't know how to guard against them. Through your host's mind, you may be able to learn what is needful and take appropriate action."

"How much time will I have, sir?"

"The Resonizer cannot be kept in continuous operation for longer than twelve hours. I would prefer that you complete your job in two. You will return here automatically as soon as the Station is activated. Are you ready?"

"I'm ready," said Roi.

Gan led the way to the clouded glass cabinet. Roi took his seat, arranged his limbs in the appropriate depressions, his vibrissae dipped in mercury for good contact.

Roi said, "What if I find myself in a body on the point of death?"

Gan said as he adjusted the controls, "The thought field is distorted when a person is near death. No normal thought field such as yours would be in resonance."

Roi said, "And if it is on the point of accidental death?"

Gan said, "We have thought of that, too. We can't guard against it, but the chances of death following so quickly that you have no time to activate the Station mentally are estimated as less than one in twenty trillion, unless the mysterious surface dangers are more deadly than we expect. . . . You have one minute."

For some strange reason, Roi's last thought before translation was of Wenda.

5

Laura awoke with a sudden start. What happened? She felt as though she had been jabbed with a pin.

The afternoon sun was shining in her face and its dazzle made her blink. She lowered the shade and simultaneously bent to look at Walter.

She was a little surprised to find his eyes open. This wasn't one of his waking periods. She looked at her wrist watch. No, it wasn't. And it was a good hour before feeding time, too. She followed the demand-feeding system or the "if-you-want-it-holler-and-you'll-get-it" routine, but ordinarily Walter followed the clock quite conscientiously.

She wrinkled her nose at him. "Hungry, duckie?"

Walter did not respond at all and Laura was disappointed. She would have liked to have him smile. Actually, she wanted him to laugh and throw his pudgy arms about her neck and nuzzle her and say, "Mommie," but she knew he couldn't do any of that. But he *could* smile.

She put a light finger to his chin and tapped it a bit. "Goo-goo-goo-goo." He always smiled when you did that.

But he only blinked at her.

She said, "I hope he isn't sick." She looked at Mrs. Ellis in distress.

Mrs. Ellis put down a magazine. "Is anything wrong, my dear?"

"I don't know. Walter just lies there."

"Poor little thing. He's tired, probably."

"Shouldn't he be sleeping, then?"

"He's in strange surroundings. He's probably wondering what it's all about."

She rose, stepped across the aisle, and leaned across Laura to bring her own face close to Walter's. "You're wondering what's going on, you tiny little snookums. Yes, you are. You're saying, 'Where's my nice little crib and all my nice little funnies on the wall paper?' "

Then she made little squeaking sounds at him.

Walter turned his eyes away from his mother and watched Mrs. Ellis somberly.

Mrs. Ellis straightened suddenly and looked pained. She put a hand to her head for a moment and murmured, "Goodness! The queerest pain."

"Do you think he's hungry?" asked Laura.

"Lord," said Mrs. Ellis, the trouble in her face fading, "they let you know when they're hungry soon enough. There's nothing wrong with him. I've had three children, my dear. I know."

"I think I'll ask the stewardess to warm up another bottle."

"Well, if it will make you feel better . . ."

The stewardess brought the bottle and Laura lifted Walter out of his bassinette. She said, "You have your bottle and then I'll change you and then——"

She adjusted his head in the crook of her elbow, leaned over to peck him quickly on the cheek, then cradled him close to her body as she brought the bottle to his lips——

Walter screamed!

His mouth yawned open, his arms pushed before him with his fingers spread wide, his whole body as stiff and hard as though in tetany, and he screamed. It rang through the whole compartment.

Laura screamed too. She dropped the bottle and it smashed whitely.

Mrs. Ellis jumped up. Half a dozen others did. Mr. Ellis snapped out of a light doze.

"What's the matter?" asked Mrs. Ellis blankly.

"I don't know. I don't know." Laura was shaking Walter frantically, putting him over her shoulder, patting his back. "Baby, baby, don't cry. Baby, what's the matter? Baby——"

The stewardess was dashing down the aisle. Her foot came within an inch of the cube that sat beneath Laura's seat.

Walter was threshing about furiously now, yelling with calliope intensity.

6

Roi's mind flooded with shock. One moment he had been strapped in his chair in contact with the clear mind of Gan; the next (there was no consciousness of separation in time) he was immersed in a medley of strange, barbaric, and broken thought.

He closed his mind completely. It had been open wide to increase the effectiveness of resonance, and the first touch of the alien had been——

Not painful—no. Dizzying, nauseating? No, not that, either. There was no word.

He gathered resilience in the quiet nothingness of mind closure and considered his position. He felt the small touch of the Receiving Station, with which he was in mental liaison. That *had* come with him. Good!

He ignored his host for the moment. He might need him for drastic operations later, so it would be wise to raise no suspicions for the moment.

He explored. He entered a mind at random and took stock first of the sense impressions that permeated it. The creature was sensitive to parts of the electromagnetic spectrum and to vibrations of the air, and, of course, to bodily contact. It possessed localized chemical senses——

That was about all. He looked again in astonishment. Not only was there no direct mass sense, no electro-potential sense, none of the really refined interpreters of the Universe, but there was no mental contact whatever.

The creature's mind was completely isolated.

Then how did they communicate? He looked further. They had a complicated code of controlled air vibrations.

Were they intelligent? Had he chosen a maimed mind? No, they were all like that.

He filtered the group of surrounding minds through his mental tendrils, searching for a Tech, or whatever passed for such among these crippled semi-intelligences. He found a mind which thought of itself as a controller of vehicles. A piece of information flooded Roi. He was on an air-borne vehicle.

Then even without mental contact, they could build a rudimentary mechanical civilization. Or were they animal tools of real intelligences elsewhere on the planet? No . . . Their minds said no.

He plumbed the Tech. What about the immediate environment? Were the bugbears of the ancients to be feared? It was a matter of interpretation. Dangers in the environment existed. Movements of air. Changes of temperature. Water falling in the air, either as liquid or solid. Electrical discharges. There were code vibrations for each phenomenon but that meant nothing. The connection of any of these with the names given to phenomena by the ancestral surface folk was a matter of conjecture.

No matter. Was there danger now? Was there danger here? Was there any cause for fear or uneasiness?

No! The Tech's mind said no.

That was enough. He returned to his host mind and rested a moment, then cautiously expanded . . .

Nothing!

His host mind was blank. At most, there was a vague sense of warmth, and a dull flicker of undirected response to basic stimuli.

Was his host dying after all? Aphasic? Decerebrate?

He moved quickly to the mind nearest, dredging it for information about his host and finding it.

His host was an infant of the species.

An infant? A *normal* infant? And so undeveloped?

He allowed his mind to sink into and coalesce for a moment with what existed in his host. He searched for the motor areas of the brain and found them with difficulty. A cautious stimulus was followed by an erratic motion of his host's extremities. He attempted finer control and failed.

He felt anger. Had they thought of everything after all? Had they thought of intelligences without mental contact? Had they thought of young creatures as completely undeveloped as though they were still in the egg?

It meant, of course, that he could not, in the person of his host, activate the Receiving Station. The muscles and mind were far too weak, far too uncontrolled for any of the three methods outlined by Gan.

He thought intensely. He could scarcely expect to influence much mass through the imperfect focusing of his host's material brain cells, but what about an indirect influence through an adult's brain?

Direct physical influence would be minute; it would amount to the breakdown of the appropriate molecules of adenosine triphosphate and acetylcholine. Thereafter the creature would act on its own.

He hesitated to try this, afraid of failure, then cursed himself for a coward. He entered the closest mind once more. It was a female of the species and it was in the state of temporary inhibition he had noticed in others. It didn't surprise him. Minds as rudimentary as these would need periodic respites.

He considered the mind before him now, fingering mentally the areas that might respond to stimulation. He chose one, stabbed at it, and the conscious areas flooded with life almost simultaneously. Sense impressions poured in and the level of thought rose steeply.

Good!

But not good enough. That was a mere prod, a pinch. It was no order for specific action.

He stirred uncomfortably as emotion cascaded over him. It came from the mind he had just stimulated and was directed, of course, at his host and not at him. Nevertheless, its primitive crudities annoyed him and he closed his mind against the unpleasant warmth of her uncovered feelings.

A second mind centered about his host, and had he been material or had he controlled a satisfactory host, he would have struck out in vexation.

Great caverns, weren't they going to allow him to concentrate on his serious business?

He thrust sharply at the second mind, activating centers of discomfort, and it moved away.

He was pleased. That had been more than a simple, undefined stimulation, and it had worked nicely. He had cleared the mental atmosphere.

He returned to the Tech who controlled the vehicle. He would know the details concerning the surface over which they were passing.

Water? He sorted the data quickly.

Water! And more water!

By the everlasting Levels, the word "ocean" made sense. The old, traditional word "ocean." Who would dream that so much water could exist.

But then, if this was "ocean," then the traditional word "island" had an obvious significance. He thrust his whole mind into the quest for geographical information. The "ocean" was speckled with dots of land but he needed exact——

He was interrupted by a short stab of surprise as his host moved through space and was held against the neighboring female's body.

Roi's mind, engaged as it was, lay open and unguarded. In full intensity, the female's emotions piled in upon him.

Roi winced. In an attempt to remove the distracting animal passions, he clamped down upon the host's brain cells, through which the rawness was funneling.

He did that too quickly, too energetically. His host's mind flooded with a diffuse pain, and instantly almost every mind he could reach reacted to the air vibrations that resulted.

In vexation, he tried to blanket the pain and succeeded only in stimulating it further.

Through the clinging mental mist of his host's pain, he riffled the Techs' minds, striving to prevent contact from slipping out of focus.

His mind went icy. The best chance was almost now! He had perhaps twenty minutes. There would be other chances afterward, but not as good. Yet he dared not attempt to direct the actions of another while his host's mind was in such complete disorganization.

He retired, withdrew into mind closure, maintaining only the most tenuous connection with his host's spinal cells, and waited.

Minutes passed, and little by little he returned to fuller liaison.

He had five minutes left. He chose a subject.

7

The stewardess said, "I think he's beginning to feel a little better, poor little thing."

"He never acted like this before," insisted Laura tearfully. "Never."

"He just had a little colic, I guess," said the stewardess.

"Maybe he's bundled up too much," suggested Mrs. Ellis.

"Maybe," said the stewardess. "It's quite warm."

She unwrapped the blanket and lifted the nightgown to expose a heaving abdomen, pink and bulbous. Walter was still whimpering.

The stewardess said, "Shall I change him for you? He's quite wet."

"Would you please?"

Most of the nearer passengers had returned to their seats. The more distant ceased craning their necks.

Mr. Ellis remained in the aisle with his wife. He said, "Say, look."

Laura and the stewardess were too busy to pay him attention and Mrs. Ellis ignored him out of sheer custom.

Mr. Ellis was used to that. His remark was purely rhetorical, anyway. He bent down and tugged at the box beneath the seat.

Mrs. Ellis looked down impatiently. She said, "Goodness, George, don't be dragging at other people's luggage like that. Sit down. You're in the way."

Mr. Ellis straightened in confusion.

Laura, with eyes still red and weepy, said, "It isn't mine. I didn't even know it was under the seat."

The stewardess, looking up from the whining baby, said, "What is it?"

Mr. Ellis shrugged. "It's a box."

His wife said, "Well, what do you want with it, for heaven's sake?"

Mr. Ellis groped for a reason. What *did* he want with it? He mumbled, "I was just curious."

The stewardess said, "There! The little boy is all nice and dry, and I'll bet in two minutes he'll just be as happy as anything. Hmm? Won't you, little funny-face?"

But little funny-face was still sobbing. He turned his head away sharply as a bottle was once more produced.

The stewardess said, "Let me warm it a bit."

She took it and went back down the aisle.

Mr. Ellis came to a decision. Firmly he lifted the box and balanced it on the arm of his seat. He ignored his wife's frown.

He said, "I'm not doing it any harm. I'm just looking. What's it made of, anyway?"

He rapped it with his knuckles. None of the other passengers seemed interested. They paid no attention to either Mr. Ellis or the box. It was as though something had switched off that particular line of interest among them. Even Mrs. Ellis, in conversation with Laura, kept her back to him.

Mr. Ellis tipped the box up and found the opening. He *knew* it had to have an opening. It was large enough for him to insert a finger, though there was no reason, of course, why he should want to put a finger into a strange box.

Carefully he reached in. There was a black knob, which he longed to touch. He pressed it.

The box shuddered and was suddenly out of his hands and passed through the arm of the chair.

He caught a glimpse of it moving through the floor, and then there was unbroken flooring and nothing more. Slowly he spread out his hands and stared at his palms. Then, dropping to his knees, he felt the floor.

The stewardess, returning with the bottle, said politely, "Have you lost something, sir?"

Mrs. Ellis, looking down, said, "George!"

Mr. Ellis heaved himself upward. He was flushed and flustered. He said, "The box—— It slipped out and went down——"

The stewardess said, "What box, sir?"

Laura said, "May I have the bottle, miss? He's stopped crying."

"Certainly. Here it is."

Walter opened his mouth eagerly, accepting the nipple. Air bubbles moved upward through the milk and there were little swallowing sounds.

Laura looked up radiantly. "He seems fine now. Thank you, Stewardess. Thank you, Mrs. Ellis. For a while there, it almost seemed as though he weren't my little boy."

"He'll be all right," said Mrs. Ellis. "Maybe it was just a bit of airsickness. Sit down, George."

The stewardess said, "Just call me if you need me."

"Thank you," said Laura.

Mr. Ellis said, "The box——" and stopped.

What box? He didn't remember any box.

But one mind aboard the plane could follow the black cube as it dropped in a parabola unimpeded by wind or air resistance, passing through the molecules of gas that lay in its way.

Below it, the atoll was a tiny bull's eye in a huge target. Once, during a time of war, it had boasted an air strip and barracks. The barracks had collapsed, the air strip was a vanishing ragged line, and the atoll was empty.

The cube struck the feathery foliage of a palm and not a frond was disturbed. It passed through the trunk and down to the coral. It sank into the planet itself without the smallest fog of dust kicked up to tell of its entrance.

Twenty feet below the surface of the soil, the cube passed into stasis and remained motionless, mingled intimately with the atoms of the rock, yet remaining distinct.

That was all. It was night, then day. It rained, the wind blew, and the Pacific waves broke whitely on the white coral. Nothing had happened.

Nothing would happen—for ten years.

8

"We have broadcast the news," said Gan, "that you have succeeded. I think you ought to rest now."

Roi said, "Rest? Now? When I'm back with complete minds? Thank you, but no. The enjoyment is too keen."

"Did it bother you so much? Intelligence without mental contact?"

"Yes," said Roi shortly. Gan tactfully refrained from attempting to follow the line of retreating thought.

Instead, he said, "And the surface?"

Roi said, "Entirely horrible. What the ancients called 'Sun' is an unbearable patch of brilliance overhead. It is apparently a source of light and varies periodically; 'day' and 'night,' in other words. There is also unpredictable variation."

" 'Clouds' perhaps," said Gan.

"Why 'clouds'?"

"You know the traditional phrase: 'Clouds hid the Sun.' "

"You think so? Yes, it could be."

"Well, go on."

"Let's see. 'Ocean' and 'island' I've explained. 'Storm' involves wetness in the air, falling in drops. 'Wind' is a movement of air on a huge scale. 'Thunder' is either a spontaneous, static discharge in the air or a great spontaneous noise. 'Sleet' is falling ice."

Gan said, "That's a curious one. Where would ice fall from? How? Why?"

"I haven't the slightest idea. It's all very variable. It will storm at one time and not at another. There are apparently regions on the surface where it is always cold, others where it is always hot, still others where it is both at different times."

"Astonishing. How much of this do you suppose is misinterpretation of alien minds?"

"None. I'm sure of that. It was all quite plain. I had sufficient time to plumb their queer minds. Too much time."

Again his thoughts drifted back into privacy.

Gan said, "This is well. I've been afraid all along of our tendency to romanticize the so-called Golden Age of our surface ancestors. I felt that there would be a strong impulse among our group in favor of a new surface life."

"No," said Roi vehemently.

"Obviously no. I doubt if the hardiest among us would consider even a day of life in an environment such as you describe, with its storms, days, nights, its indecent and unpredictable variations in environment." Gan's thoughts were contented ones. "Tomorrow we begin the process of transfer. Once on the island—— An uninhabited one, you say."

"Entirely uninhabited. It was the only one of that type the vessel passed over. The Tech's information was detailed."

"Good. We will begin operations. It will take generations, Roi, but in the end, we will be in the Deep of a new, warm world, in pleasant caverns where the controlled environment will be conducive to the growth of every culture and refinement."

"And," added Roi, "no contact whatever with the surface creatures."

Gan said, "Why that? Primitive though they are, they could be of help to us once we establish our base. A race that can build aircraft must have some abilities."

"It isn't that. They're a belligerent lot, sir. They would attack with animal ferocity at all occasions and——"

Gan interrupted. "I am disturbed at the psychopenumbra that surrounds your references to the aliens. There's something you are concealing."

Roi said, "I thought at first we could make use of them. If they wouldn't allow us to be friends, at least, we could control them. I made one of them close contact inside the cube and that was difficult. Very difficult. Their minds are basically different."

"In what way?"

"If I could describe it, the difference wouldn't be basic. But I can give you an example. I was in the mind of an infant. They don't have maturation chambers. The infants are in the charge of individuals. The creature who was in charge of my host——"

"Yes."

"She (it was a female) felt a special tie to the young one. There was a sense of ownership, of a relationship that excluded the remainder of their society. I seemed to detect, dimly, something of the emotion that binds a man to an associate or friend, but it was far more intense and unrestrained."

"Well," said Gan, "without mental contact, they probably have no real conception of society and subrelationships may build up. Or was this one pathological?"

"No, no. It's universal. The female in charge was the infant's mother."

"Impossible. Its own mother?"

"Of necessity. The infant had passed the first part of its existence inside its mother. Physically inside. The creature's eggs remain within the body. They are inseminated within the body. They grow within the body and emerge alive."

"Great caverns," Gan said weakly. Distaste was strong within him. "Each creature would know the identity of its own child. Each child would have a particular father——"

"And he would be known, too. My host was being taken five thousand miles, as nearly as I could judge the distance, to be seen by its father."

"Unbelievable!"

"Do you need more to see that there can never be any meeting of minds? The difference is so fundamental, so innate."

The yellowness of regret tinged and roughened Gan's thought train. He said, "It would be too bad. I had thought——"

"What, sir?"

"I had thought that for the first time there would be two intelligences helping one another. I had thought that together we might progress more quickly than either could alone. Even if they were primitive technologically, as they are, technology isn't everything. I had thought we might still be able to learn of them."

"Learn what?" asked Roi brutally. "To know our parents and make friends of our children?"

Gan said, "No. No, you're quite right. The barrier between us must remain forever complete. They will have the surface and we the Deep, and so it will be."

Outside the laboratories Roi met Wenda.

Her thoughts were concentrated pleasure. "I'm glad you're back."

Roi's thoughts were pleasurable too. It was very restful to make clean mental contact with a friend.

SUCKER BAIT

1

The ship *Triple G.* flashed silently out of the nothingness of hyperspace and into the allness of space-time. It emerged into the glitter of the great star cluster of Hercules.

It poised gingerly in space, surrounded by suns and suns and suns, each centering a gravitational field that wrenched at the little bubble of metal. But the ship's computers had done well and it had pinpricked squarely into position. It was within a day's journey—ordinary space-drive journey—of the Lagrange System.

This fact had varying significance to the different men aboard ship. To the crew, it was another day's work and another day's flight pay and then shore rest. The planet for which they were aiming was uninhabited, but shore rest could be a pleasant interlude even on an asteroid. They did not trouble themselves concerning a possible difference of opinion among the passengers.

The crew, in fact, were rather contemptuous of the passengers, and avoided them.

Eggheads!

And so they were, every one of them but one. Scientists, in politer terms—and a heterogeneous lot. Their nearest approach to a common emotion at that moment was a final anxiety for their instruments, a vague desire for a last check.

And perhaps just a small increase of tension and anxiety. It *was* an uninhabited planet. Each had expressed himself as firmly of that belief a number of times. Still, each man's thoughts are his own.

As for the one unusual man on board ship—not a crewman and not really a scientist—his strongest feeling was one of bone-weariness. He stirred to his feet weakly and fought off the last dregs of spacesickness. He was Mark Annuncio, and he had been in bed now for four days, feeding on almost nothing, while the ship wove in and out of the Universe, jumping its light-years of space.

But now he felt less certain of imminent death and he had to answer the summons of the Captain. In his inarticulate way, Mark resented that summons. He was used to having his own way, seeing what he felt like seeing. Who was the Captain to——

The impulse kept returning to tell Dr. Sheffield about this and let it rest there.

But Mark was curious, so he knew he would have to go.

It was his one great vice. Curiosity!

It also happened to be his profession and his mission in life.

2

Captain Follenbee of the *Triple G.* was a hardheaded man. It was how he habitually thought of himself. He had made government-sponsored runs before. For one thing, they were profitable. The Confederacy didn't haggle. It meant a complete overhaul of his ship each time, replacement of defective parts, liberal terms for the crew. It was good business. Damned good business.

This run, of course, was a little different.

It wasn't so much the particular gang of passengers he had taken aboard. (He had expected temperament, tantrums, and unbearable foolishness but it turned out that eggheads were much like normal people.) It wasn't that half his ship had been torn down and rebuilt into what the contract called a "universal central-access laboratory."

Actually, and he hated the thought, it was "Junior"—the planet that lay ahead of them.

The crew didn't know, of course, but he, himself, hard head and all, was beginning to find the matter unpleasant.

But only beginning——

At the moment, he told himself, it was this Mark Annuncio, if that was the name, who was annoying him. He slapped the back of one hand against the palm of the other and thought angrily about it. His large, round face was ruddy with annoyance.

Insolence!

A boy of not more than twenty, with no position that he knew of among the passengers, to make a request like that.

What was behind it? *That* at least ought to be straightened out.

In his present mood, he would like to straighten it out by means of a jacket collar twisted in a fist and a rattle of teeth, but better not —better not——

After all, this was a curious kind of flight for the Confederacy of

Worlds to sponsor, and a twenty-year-old, overcurious rubberneck might be an integral part of the strangeness. What was he on board *for?* There was this Dr. Sheffield, for instance, who seemed to have no job but to play nursemaid for the boy. Now why was that? Who *was* this Annuncio?

He had been space-sick for the entire trip, or was that just a device to keep to his cabin——

There was a light buzzing as the door signal sounded.

It would be the boy.

Easy now, thought the Captain. Easy now.

3

Mark Annuncio entered the Captain's cabin and licked his lips in a futile attempt to get rid of the bitter taste in his mouth. He felt lightheaded and heavyhearted.

At the moment, he would have given up his Service status to be back on Earth.

He thought wishfully of his own familiar quarters; small but private; alone with his own kind. It was just a bed, desk, chair, and closet, but he had all of Central Library on free call. Here there was nothing. He had thought there would be a lot to learn on board ship. He had never been on board ship before. But he hadn't expected days and days of space-sickness.

He was so homesick he could cry, and he hated himself because he knew that his eyes were red and moist and that the Captain would see it. He hated himself because he wasn't large and wide; because he looked like a mouse.

In a word, that was it. He had mouse-brown hair with nothing but silken straightness to it; a narrow, receding chin, a small mouth, and a pointed nose. All he needed were five or six delicate vibrissae on each side of the nose to make the illusion complete. And he was below average in height.

And then he saw the star field in the Captain's observation port and the breath went out of him.

Stars!

Stars as he had never seen them.

Mark had never left the planet Earth before. (Dr. Sheffield told him that was why he was space-sick. Mark didn't believe him. He had read in fifty different books that space-sickness was psychogenic. Even Dr. Sheffield tried to fool him sometimes.)

He had never left Earth before, and he was used to Earth's sky. He was accustomed to viewing two thousand stars spread over half a celestial sphere, with only ten of the first magnitude.

But here they crowded madly. There were ten times the number in Earth's sky in that small square alone. And *bright!*

He fixed the star pattern greedily in his mind. It overwhelmed him. He knew the figures on the Hercules cluster, of course. It contained between one million and ten million stars (no exact census had been taken as yet), but figures are one thing and stars are another.

He wanted to count them. It was a sudden overwhelming desire. He was curious about the number. He wondered if they all had names; if there were astronomic data on all of them. Let's see . . .

He counted them in groups of hundreds. Two—three—he might have used the mental pattern alone, but he liked to watch the actual physical objects when they were so startlingly beautiful—six—seven——

The Captain's hearty voice splattered over him and brought him back to ship's interior.

"Mr. Annuncio. Glad to meet you."

Mark looked up, startled, resentful. Why was his count being interrupted?

He said irritably, "The stars!" and pointed.

The Captain turned to stare. "What about them? What's wrong?"

Mark looked at the Captain's wide back and his overdeveloped posterior. He looked at the gray stubble that covered the Captain's head, at the two large hands with thick fingers that clasped one another in the small of the Captain's back and flapped rhythmically against the shiny plastex of his jacket.

Mark thought, What does *he* care about the stars? Does *he* care about their size and brightness and spectral classes?

His lower lip trembled. The Captain was just one of the noncompos. Everyone on ship was a noncompos. That's what they called them back in the Service. Noncompos. All of them. Couldn't cube fifteen without a computer.

Mark felt very lonely.

He let it go (no use trying to explain) and said, "The stars get so thick here. Like pea soup."

"All appearance, Mr. Annuncio." (The Captain pronounced the *c* in Mark's name like an *s* rather than a *ch* and the sound grated on Mark's ear.) "Average distance between stars in the thickest cluster is over a light-year. Plenty of room, eh? Looks thick, though. Grant you that. If the light were out, they'd shine like a trillion Chisholm points in an oscillating force field."

But he didn't offer to put the lights out and Mark wasn't going to ask him to.

The Captain said, "Sit down, Mr. Annuncio. No use standing, eh? You smoke? Mind if I do? Sorry you couldn't be here this morning. Had an excellent view of Lagrange I and II at six space-hours. Red and green. Like traffic lights, eh? Missed you all trip. Space legs need strengthening, eh?"

He barked out his "eh's" in a high-pitched voice that Mark found devilishly irritating.

Mark said in a low voice, "I'm all right now."

The Captain seemed to find that unsatisfactory. He puffed at his cigar and stared down at Mark with eyebrows hunched down over his eyes. He said slowly, "Glad to see you now, anyway. Get acquainted a little. Shake hands. The *Triple* G.'s been on a good many government-chartered cruises. No trouble. Never had trouble. Wouldn't want trouble. You understand."

Mark didn't. He was tired of trying to. His eyes drifted back hungrily to the stars. The pattern had changed a little.

The Captain caught his eyes for a moment. He was frowning and his shoulders seemed to tremble at the edge of a shrug. He walked to the control panel, and like a gigantic eyelid, metal slithered across the studded observation port.

Mark jumped up in a fury, shrieking, "What's the idea? I'm counting them, you fool."

"*Counting*——" The Captain flushed, but maintained a quality of politeness in his voice. He said, "Sorry! Little matter of business we must discuss."

He stressed the word "business" lightly.

Mark knew what he meant. "There's nothing to discuss. I want to see the ship's log. I called you hours ago to tell you that. You're delaying me."

The Captain said, "Suppose you tell me why you want to see it, eh? Never been asked before. Where's your authority?"

Mark felt astonished. "I can look at anything I want to. I'm in Mnemonic Service."

The Captain puffed strongly at his cigar. (It was a special grade manufactured for use in space and on enclosed space objects. It had an oxidant included so that atmospheric oxygen was not consumed.)

He said cautiously, "That so? Never heard of it. What is it?"

Mark said indignantly, "It's the Mnemonic Service, that's all. It's my job to look at anything I want to and to ask anything I want to. And I've got the right to do it."

"Can't look at the log if I don't want you to."

"You've got no say in it, you—you *noncompos*."

The Captain's coolness evaporated. He threw his cigar down violently and stamped at it, then picked it up and poked it carefully into the ash vent.

"What the Galactic drift is this?" he demanded. "Who are you, anyway? Security agent? What's up? Let's have it straight. Right now."

"I've told you all I have to."

"Nothing to hide," said the Captain, "but I've got rights."

"Nothing to hide?" squeaked Mark. "Then why is this ship called the *Triple G.?*"

"That's its name."

"Go on. No such ship with an Earth registry. I knew that before I got on. I've been waiting to ask you."

The Captain blinked. He said, "Official name is *George G. Grundy*. *Triple G.* is what everyone calls it."

Mark laughed. "All right, then. And after I see the logbook, I want to talk to the crew. I have the right. You ask Dr. Sheffield."

"The crew, too, eh?" The Captain seethed. "Let's talk to Dr. Sheffield, and then let's keep you in quarters till we land. Sprout!"

He snatched at the intercom box.

4

The scientific complement of the *Triple G.* were few in number for the job they had to do, and, as individuals, young. Not as young as Mark Annuncio, perhaps, who was in a class by himself, but even the oldest of them, Emmanuel George Cimon (astrophysicist), was not quite thirty-nine. And with his dark, unthinned hair and large, brilliant eyes, he looked still younger. To be sure, the optic brilliance was partly due to the wearing of contact lenses.

Cimon, who was perhaps overconscious of his relative age, and of the fact that he was the titular head of the expedition (a fact most of the others were inclined to ignore) usually affected an undramatic view of the mission. He ran the dotted tape through his fingers, then let it snake silently back into its spool.

"Run of the mill," he sighed, seating himself in the softest chair in the small passengers' lounge. "Nothing."

He looked at the latest color photographs of the Lagrange binary and was impervious to their beauty. Lagrange I, smaller and hotter than Earth's own sun, was a brilliant green blue, with a pearly green-yellow corona surrounding it like the gold setting of an emerald. It appeared to be the size of a lentil or of a ball bearing out of a Lenser ratchet. A short distance away (as distances go on a photograph) was Lagrange II. It appeared twice the size of Lagrange I, due to its position in space. (Actually, it was only four fifths the diameter of Lagrange I, half its volume, and two thirds its mass.) Its orange red, toward which the film was less sensitive, comparatively, than was the human retina, seemed dimmer than ever against the glory of its sister sun.

Surrounding both, undrowned by the near-by suns, as the result of the differentially polarized lens specifically used for the purpose, was the unbelievable brilliance of the Hercules cluster. It was diamond dust, scattered thickly, yellow, white, blue, and red.

"Nothing," said Cimon.

"Looks good to me," said the other man in the lounge. He was Groot Knoevenaagle (physician; short, plump, and known to man by no name other than Novee).

He went on to ask, "Where's Junior?" then bent over Cimon's shoulder, peering out of slightly myopic eyes.

Cimon looked up and shuddered. "Its name is not Junior. You can't see the planet, Troas, if *that's* what you mean, in this damned wilderness of stars. This picture is *Scientific Earthman* material. It isn't particularly useful."

"Oh, space and back!" Novee was disappointed.

"What difference is it to you, anyway?" demanded Cimon. "Suppose I said one of those dots was Troas. Any one of them. You wouldn't know the difference and what good would it do you?"

"Now wait, Cimon. Don't be so damned superior. It's legitimate sentiment. We'll be living on Junior for a while. For all we know, we'll be dying on it."

"There's no audience, Novee, no orchestra, no mikes, no trumpets, so why be dramatic? We won't be dying on it. If we do, it'll be our own fault, and probably as a result of overeating." He said it with the peculiar emphasis men of small appetite use when speaking to men of hearty appetite, as though a poor digestion were something that came only of rigid virtue and superior intellect.

"A thousand people did die," said Novee softly.

"Sure. About a billion men a day die all over the Galaxy."

"Not this way."

"Not what way?"

With an effort, Novee kept to his usual drawl. "No discussions except at official meetings. That was the decision."

"I'll have nothing to discuss," said Cimon gloomily. "They're just two ordinary stars. Damned if I know why I volunteered. I suppose it was just the chance of seeing an abnormally large Trojan system from close up. It was the thought of looking at a habitable planet with a double sun. I don't know why I should have thought there'd be anything amazing about it."

"Because you thought of a thousand dead men and women," said Novee, then went on hastily, "Listen, tell me something, will you? What's a Trojan planet, anyway?"

The physician bore the other's look of contempt for a moment, then said, "All right. All right. So I don't know. You don't know everything either. What do you know about ultrasonic incisions?"

Cimon said, "Nothing, and I think that's fine. It's my opinion that information outside a professional man's specialty is useless and a waste of psycho-potential. Sheffield's point of view leaves me cold."

"I still want to know. That is if you can explain it."

"I can explain it. As a matter of fact, it was mentioned in the original briefing, if you were listening. Most multiple stars, and that means one third of all stars, have planets of a sort. The trouble is that the planets are never habitable. If they're far enough away from the center of gravity of the stellar system to have a fairly circular orbit, they're cold enough to have helium oceans. If they're close enough to get heat, their orbit is so erratic that at least once in each revolution, they get close enough to one or another of the stars to melt iron.

"Here in the Lagrange System, however, we have an unusual case. The two stars, Lagrange I and Lagrange II, and the planet, Troas (along with its satellite, Ilium), are at the corners of an imaginary equilateral triangle. Got that? Such an arrangement happens to be a stable one, and for the sake of anything you like, don't ask me to tell you why. Just take it as my professional opinion."

Novee muttered under his breath, "I wouldn't dream of doubting it."

Cimon looked displeased and continued, "The system revolves as a unit. Troas is always a hundred million miles from each sun, and the suns are always a hundred million miles from one another."

Novee rubbed his ear and looked dissatisfied. "I know all that. I *was* listening at the briefing. But why is it a *Trojan* planet? Why *Trojan?*"

Cimon's thin lips compressed for a moment as though holding back a nasty word by force. He said, "We have an arrangement like that in the Solar System. The Sun, Jupiter, and a group of small asteroids form a stable equilateral triangle. It so happens that the asteroids had been given such names as Hector, Achilles, Ajax, and other heroes of the Trojan War, hence—— Or do I have to finish?"

"Is that all?" said Novee.

"Yes. Are you through bothering me?"

"Oh, boil your head."

Novee rose to leave the indignant astrophysicist but the door slid open a moment before his hand touched the activator and Boris Vernadsky (geochemist; dark eyebrows, wide mouth, broad face, and with an inveterate tendency to polka-dot shirts and magnetic clip-ons in red plastic) stepped in.

He was oblivious to Novee's flushed face and Cimon's frozen expression of distaste.

He said lightly, "Fellow scientists, if you listen very carefully, you will probably hear an explosion to beat the Milky Way from up yonder in Captain's quarters."

"What happened?" asked Novee.

"The Captain got hold of Annuncio, Sheffield's little pet wizard, and Sheffield went charging updeck, bleeding heavily at each eyeball."

Cimon, having listened so far, turned away, snorting.

Novee said, "Sheffield! The man can't get angry. I've never even heard him raise his voice."

"He did this time. When he found out the kid had left his cabin without telling him and that the Captain was bullyragging him—Wow! Did you know he was up and about, Novee?"

"No, but I'm not surprised. Space-sickness is one of those things. When you have it, you think you're dying. In fact, you can hardly wait. Then, in two minutes it's gone and you feel all right. Weak, but all right. I told Mark this morning we'd be landing next day and I suppose it pulled him through. The thought of a planetary surface in clear prospect does wonders for space-sickness. We *are* landing soon, aren't we, Cimon?"

The astrophysicist made a peculiar sound that could have been interpreted as a grunt of assent. At least, Novee so interpreted it.

"Anyway," said Novee, "what happened?"

Vernadsky said, "Well, Sheffield's been bunking with me since the kid twirled on his toes and went over backward with space-sickness and he's sitting there at the desk with his damn charts and his fist computer chug-chugging away, when the room phone signals and it's the Captain. Well, it turns out he's got the boy with him and he wants to know what the blankety-blank and assorted dot and dash the government means by planting a spy on him. So Sheffield yells back at him that he'll stab him in the groin with a Collamore macroleveling-tube if he's been fooling with the kid and off he goes, leaving the phone activated and the Captain frothing."

"You're making this up," said Novee. "Sheffield wouldn't say anything like that."

"Words to that effect."

Novee turned to Cimon. "You're heading our group. Why don't you do something about this?"

Cimon snarled, "In cases like this, I'm heading the group. My responsibilities always come on suddenly. Let them fight it out. Sheffield talks an excellent fight and the Captain never takes his hands out of the small of his back. Vernadsky's jitterbugging description doesn't mean there'll be physical violence."

"All right, but there's no point in having feuds of any kind in an expedition like ours."

"You mean our mission!" Vernadsky raised both hands in mock awe and rolled his eyes upward. "How I dread the time when we must find ourselves among the rags and bones of the first expedition."

And as though the picture brought to mind by that was not one that bore levity well after all, there was suddenly nothing to say. Even the back of Cimon's head, which was all that showed over the back of the easy chair, seemed a bit the stiffer for the thought.

5

Oswald Mayer Sheffield (psychologist, thin as a string and as tall as a good length of it, and with a voice that could be used either for singing an operatic selection with surprising virtuosity or for making a point of argument, softly but with stinging accuracy) did not show the anger one would have expected from Vernadsky's account.

He was even smiling when he entered the Captain's cabin.

The Captain broke out mauvely as soon as he entered. "Look here, Sheffield——"

"One minute, Captain Follenbee," said Sheffield. "How are you, Mark?"

Mark's eyes fell and his words were muffled. "All right, Dr. Sheffield."

"I wasn't aware you'd gotten out of bed."

There wasn't the shade of reproach in his voice, but Mark grew apologetic. "I was feeling better, Dr. Sheffield, and I feel bad about not working. I haven't done anything in all the time I've been on the ship. So I put in a call to the Captain to ask to see the logbook and he had me come up here."

"All right. I'm sure he won't mind if you go back to your room now."

"Oh, won't I?" began the Captain.

Sheffield's mild eyes rose to meet the Captain. "I'm responsible for him, sir."

And somehow the Captain could think of nothing further to say.

Mark turned obediently and Sheffield watched him leave and waited till the door was well closed behind him.

Then he turned again to the Captain. "What's the bloody idea, Captain?"

The Captain's knees bent a little, then straightened and bent again with a sort of threatening rhythm. The invisible slap of his hands, clasped behind his back, could be heard distinctly. "That's my question. I'm Captain here, Sheffield."

"I know that."

"Know what it means, eh? This ship, in space, is a legally recognized planet. I'm absolute ruler. In space, what I say goes. Central Committee of the Confederacy can't say otherwise. I've got to maintain discipline, and no spy——"

"All right, and now let me tell *you* something, Captain. You're charted by the Bureau of Outer Provinces to carry a government-sponsored research expedition to the Lagrange System, to maintain it there as long as research necessity requires and the safety of the crew and vessel permits, and then to bring us home. You've signed that contract and you've assumed certain obligations, Captain or not. For instance, you can't tamper with our instruments and destroy their research usefulness."

"Who in space is doing that?" The Captain's voice was a blast of indignation.

Sheffield replied calmly, "You are. Hands off Mark Annuncio, Captain. Just as you've got to keep your hands off Cimon's monochrome and Vailleux's microptics, you've got to keep your hands off my Annuncio. And that means each one of your ten, four-striped fingers. Got it?"

The Captain's uniformed chest expanded. "I take no order on board my own ship. Your language is a breach of discipline, *Mister* Sheffield. Any more like that and it's cabin arrest. You *and* your Annuncio. Don't like it, then speak to Board of Review back on Earth. Till then, it's tongue behind teeth."

"Look, Captain, let me explain something. Mark is in the Mnemonic Service——"

"Sure, he said so. Nummonic Service. Nummonic Service. It's plain secret police as far as I'm concerned. Well, not on board *my* ship, eh?"

"Mnemonic Service," said Sheffield patiently. "*Em-en-ee-em-oh-en-eye-see* Service. You don't pronounce the first *em*. It's from a Greek word meaning memory."

The Captain's eyes narrowed. "He remembers things?"

"Correct, Captain. Look, in a way this is my fault. I should have briefed you on this. I would have, too, if the boy hadn't gotten so sick right after the take-off. It drove most other matters out of my mind. Besides, it didn't occur to me that he might be interested in the workings of the ship itself. Space knows why not. He should be interested in everything."

"He should, eh?" The Captain looked at the timepiece on the wall. "Brief me now, eh? But no fancy words. Not many of any other kind, either. Time limited."

"It won't take long, I assure you. Now you're a space-going man, Captain. How many inhabited worlds would you say there were in the Confederation?"

"Eighty thousand," said the Captain promptly.

"Eighty-three thousand two hundred," said Sheffield. "What do you suppose it takes to run a political organization that size?"

Again the Captain did not hesitate. "Computers," he said.

"All right. There's Earth, where half the population works for the government and does nothing but compute and there are computing subcenters on every other world. And even so data gets lost. Every world knows something no other world knows. Almost every man. Look at our little group. Vernadsky doesn't know any biology and I don't know enough chemistry to stay alive. There's not one of us can pilot the simplest space cruiser, except for Fawkes. So we work together, each one supplying the knowledge the others lack.

"Only there's a catch. Not one of us knows exactly which of our own data is meaningful to the other under a given set of circumstances. We can't sit and spout every thing we know. So we guess, and sometimes we don't guess right. Two facts, A and B, can go together beautifully sometimes. So Person A, who knows Fact A, says to Person B, who knows Fact B, 'Why didn't you tell me this ten years ago?' and Person B answers, 'I didn't think it was important,' or, 'I thought everyone knew that.' "

The Captain said, "That's what computers are for."

Sheffield said, "Computers are limited, Captain. They have to be asked questions. What's more, the questions have to be the kind that can be put into a limited number of symbols. What's more, computers are very literal-minded. They answer exactly what you ask and not what you have in mind. Sometimes it never occurs to anyone to ask just the right question or feed the computer just the right symbols, and when that happens, the computer doesn't volunteer information.

"What we need, what all mankind needs, is a computer that is nonmechanical; a computer with imagination. There's one like that, Captain." The psychologist tapped his temple. "In everyone, Captain."

"Maybe," grunted the Captain, "but I'll stick to the usual, eh? Kind you punch a button."

"Are you sure? Machines don't have hunches. Did *you* ever have a hunch?"

"Is this on the point?" The Captain looked at the timepiece again.

Sheffield said, "Somewhere inside the human brain is a record of every datum that has impinged upon it. Very little of it is consciously remembered, but all of it's there, and a small association can bring an individual datum back without a person's knowing where it comes from. So you get a 'hunch' or a 'feeling.' Some people are better at it than others. And some can be trained. Some are almost perfect, like Mark Annuncio and a hundred like him. Someday, I hope, there'll be a billion like him, and we'll *really* have a Mnemonic Service.

"All their lives," Sheffield went on, "they do nothing but read, look, and listen. And train to do that better and more efficiently. It doesn't matter what data they collect. It doesn't have to have obvious sense or obvious significance. It doesn't matter if any man in the Service wants to spend a week going over the records of the space-polo teams of the Canopus Sector for the last century. *Any* datum may be useful someday. That's the fundamental axiom.

"Every once in a while one of the Service may correlate across a gap no machine could possibly manage. The machine would fail because no one machine is likely to possess those two pieces of thoroughly unconnected information, or else, if the machine does have them, no man would be insane enough to ask the right question. One good correlation out of the Service can pay for all the money appropriated for it in ten years or more."

The Captain raised his broad hand. He looked troubled. He said, "Wait a minute. Annuncio said no ship named *Triple G.* was under Earth registry. You mean he knows all registered ships by heart?"

"Probably," said Sheffield. "He may have read through the Merchant-Ship Register. If he did, he knows all the names, tonnages, years of construction, ports of call, numbers of crews, and anything else the register would contain."

"And he was counting stars."

"Why not? It's a datum."

"I'm damned."

"Perhaps, Captain. But the point is that a man like Mark is different from other men. He's got a queer, distorted upbringing and a queer, distorted view of life. This is the first time he's been away from Service grounds since he entered them at the age of five. He's easily upset—and he can be ruined. That mustn't happen, and I'm in charge to see it doesn't. He's my instrument; a more valuable instrument than everything else on this entire ship baled into a neat little ball of plutonium wire. There are only a hundred like him in all the Milky Way."

Captain Follenbee assumed an air of wounded dignity. "All right, then. Logbook. Strictly confidential, eh?"

"Strictly. He talks only to me, and I talk to no one unless a correlation has been made."

The Captain did not look as though that fell under his classification of the word "strictly" but he said, "But no crew." He paused significantly. "You know what I mean."

Sheffield stepped to the door. "Mark knows about that. The crew won't hear about it from him, believe me."

And as he was about to leave, the Captain called out, "Sheffield!"

"Yes?"

"What in space is a noncompos?"

Sheffield suppressed a smile. "Did he call you that?"

"What is it?"

"Just short for *non compos mentis*. Eveyone in the Service uses it for everyone not in the Service. You're one. I'm one. It's Latin for 'not of sound mind.' And you know, Captain—I think they're quite right."

He stepped out the door quickly.

6

Mark Annuncio went through ship's log in some fifteen seconds. He found it incomprehensible, but then most of the material he put into his mind was that. That was no trouble. Nor was the fact that it was dull. The disappointment was that it did not satisfy his curiosity, so he left it with a mixture of relief and displeasure.

He had then gone into the ship's library and worked his way through three dozen books as quickly as he could work the scanner. He had spent three years of his early teens learning how to read by total gestalt and he still recalled proudly that he had set a school record at the final examinations.

Finally he wandered into the laboratory sections of the ship and watched a bit here and a bit there. He asked no questions and he moved on when any of the men cast more than a casual glance at him.

He hated the insufferable way they looked at him, as though he were some sort of queer animal. He hated their air of knowledge, as though there were something of value in spending an entire brain on one tiny subject and remembering only a little of that.

Eventually, of course, he would *have* to ask them questions. It was his job, and even if it weren't, curiosity would drive him. He hoped, though, he could hold off till they had made planetary surface.

He found it pleasant that they were inside a stellar system. Soon he would see a new world with new suns—two of them—and a new moon. Four objects with brand-new information in each; immense storehouses of facts to be collected lovingly and sorted out.

It thrilled him just to think of the amorphous mountain of data waiting for him. He thought of his mind as a tremendous filing system with index, cross index, cross cross index. He thought of it as stretching indefinitely in all directions. Neat. Smooth. Well oiled. Perfect precision.

He thought of the dusty attic that the noncompos called minds and almost laughed. He could see it even talking to Dr. Sheffield, who was a nice fellow for a noncompos. He tried hard and sometimes he almost *understood*. The others, the men on board ship, their minds were lumberyards. Dusty lumberyards with splintery slats of wood tumbled every which way; and only whatever happened to be on top could be reached.

The poor fools! He could be sorry for them if they weren't so sloppy-nasty. If only they *knew* what they were like. If only they *realized*.

Whenever he could, Mark haunted the observation posts and watched the new worlds come closer.

They passed quite close to the satellite Ilium. (Cimon, the astrophysicist, was very meticulous about calling their planetary destination "Troas" and the satellite "Ilium," but everyone else aboard ship called them "Junior" and "Sister" respectively.) On the other side of the two suns, in the opposite Trojan position, were a group of asteroids. Cimon called them "Lagrange Epsilon" but everyone else called them "The Puppies."

Mark thought of all this with vague simultaneity at the moment the thought "Ilium" occurred to him. He was scarcely conscious of it, and let it pass as material of no immediate interest. Still more vague, and still further below his skin of mental consciousness were the dim stirrings of five hundred such homely misnomers of astronomical dignities of nomenclature. He had read about some, picked up others on subetheric programs, heard about still others in ordinary conversation, come across a few in news reports. The material might have been told him directly, or it might have been a carelessly overheard word. Even the substitution of *Triple G.* for *George G. Grundy* had its place in the shadowy file.

Sheffield had often questioned him about what went on in his mind—very gently, very cautiously.

"We want many more like you, Mark, for the Mnemonic Service. We need millions. Billions, eventually, if the race fills up the entire Galaxy, as it will someday. But where do we get them? Relying on inborn talent won't do. We all have that more or less. It's the training that counts, and unless we find out a little about what goes on, we won't know how to train."

And urged by Sheffield, Mark had watched himself, listened to himself, turned his eyes inward and tried to become *aware*. He learned of the filing cases in his head. He watched them marshal past. He observed individual items pop up on call, always tremblingly ready. It was hard to explain, but he did his best.

His own confidence grew with it. The anxieties of his childhood, those first years in Service, grew less. He stopped waking in the middle of the night, perspiration dripping, screaming with fear that he would forget. And his headaches stopped.

He watched Ilium as it appeared in the viewport at closest approach. It was brighter than he could imagine a moon to be. (Figures for albedos of three hundred inhabited planets marched through his mind, neatly arrayed in decreasing order. It scarcely stirred the skin of his mind. He ignored them.)

The brightness he blinked at was concentrated in the vast, irregular patches that Cimon said (he overheard him, in weary response to another's question) had once been sea bottom. A fact popped into Mark's mind. The original report of Hidosheki Makoyama had given the composition of those bright salts as 78.6 per cent sodium chloride, 19.2 per cent magnesium carbonate, 1.4 per cent potassium sulf . . . The thought faded out. It wasn't necessary.

Ilium had an atmosphere. A total of about 100 mm. of mercury. (A little over an eighth of Earth's, ten times Mars', 0.254 that of Coralemon, 0.1376 that of Aurora.) Idly he let the decimals grow to more places. It was a form of exercise, but he grew bored. Instant arithmetic was fifth-grade stuff. Actually, he still had trouble with integrals and wondered if that was because he didn't know what an integral was. A half dozen definitions flashed by, but he had never had enough mathematics to understand the definitions, though he could quote them well enough.

At school, they had always said, "Don't ever get too interested in any one thing or group of things. As soon as you do that, you begin selecting your facts and you must never do that. *Everything, anything* is important. As long as you have the facts on file, it doesn't matter whether you understand them or not."

But the noncompos didn't think so. Arrogant minds with holes in them!

They were approaching Junior itself now. It was bright, too, but in a different way. It had icecaps north and south. (Textbooks of Earth's paleoclimatology drifted past and Mark made no move to stop them.) The icecaps were retreating. In a million years, Junior would have Earth's present climate. It was just about Earth's size and mass and it rotated in a period of thirty-six hours.

It might have been Earth's twin. What differences there were, according to Makoyama's reports, were to Junior's advantage. There was nothing on Junior to threaten mankind as far as was known. Nor would anyone imagine there possibly might be were it not for the fact that humanity's first colony on the planet had been wiped out to the last soul.

What was worse, the destruction had occurred in such a way that a study of all surviving information gave no reasonable clue whatever as to what had happened.

7

Sheffield entered Mark's cabin and joined the boy two hours before landing. He and Mark had originally been assigned a room together. That had been an experiment. Mnemonics didn't like the company of noncompos. Even the best of them. In any case, the experiment had failed. Almost immediately after take-off, Mark's sweating face and pleading eyes made privacy absolutely essential for him.

Sheffield felt responsible. He felt responsible for everything about Mark whether it was actually his fault or not. He and men like himself had taken Mark and children like him and trained them into personal ruin. They had been force-grown. They had been bent and molded. They had been allowed no normal contact with normal children lest they develop normal mental habits. No Mnemonic had contracted a normal marriage, even within the group.

It made for a terrible guilt feeling on Sheffield's part.

Twenty years ago there had been a dozen lads trained at one school under the leadership of U Karaganda, as mad an Asiatic as had ever roused the snickers of a group of interviewing newsmen. Karaganda had committed suicide eventually, under some vague motivation, but other psychologists, Sheffield for one, of greater respectability and undoubtedly of lesser brilliance, had had time to join him and learn from him.

The school continued and others were established. One was even founded on Mars. It had an enrollment of five at the moment. At latest count, there were one hundred three living graduates with full honors (naturally, only a minority of those enrolled actually absorbed the entire course.) Five years ago, the Terrestrial planetary government (not to be confused with the Central Galactic Committee, based on Earth, and ruling the Galactic Confederation) allowed the establishment of the Mnemonic Service as a branch of the Department of the Interior.

It had already paid for itself many times over, but few people knew that. Nor did the Terrestrial government advertise the fact, or any other fact about the Mnemonics. It was a tender subject with them. It was an "experiment." They feared that failure might be politically expensive. The opposition (with difficulty prevented from making a campaign issue out of it as it was) spoke at the planetary conferences of "crackpotism" and "waste of the taxpayers' money." And the latter despite the existence of documentary proof of the precise opposite.

In the machine-centered civilization that filled the Galaxy, it was difficult to learn to appreciate the achievements of naked mind without a long apprenticeship.

Sheffield wondered how long.

But there was no use being depressed in Mark's company. Too much danger of contagion. He said instead, "You're looking fine, sport."

Mark seemed glad to see him. He said thoughtfully, "When we get back to Earth, Dr. Sheffield——"

He stopped, flushed slightly, and said, "I mean supposing we get back, I intend to get as many books and films as I can on folkways. I've hardly read anything on that subject. I was down in the ship's library and they had nothing."

"Why the interest?"

"It's the Captain. Didn't you say he told you that the crew were not to know we were visiting a world on which the first expedition had died?"

"Yes, of course. Well?"

"Because spacemen consider it bad luck to touch on a world like that, especially one that looks harmless? 'Sucker bait,' they call it."

"That's right."

"So the Captain *says*. It's just that I don't see how that can be true. I can think of seventeen habitable planets from which the first expeditions never returned and never established residence. And each one was later colonized and now is a member of the Confederation. Sarmatia is one of them, and it's a pretty big world now."

"There are planets of continuous disaster, too." Sheffield deliberately put that as a declarative statement.

(Never ask informational questions. That was one of the Rules of Karaganda. Mnemonic correlations weren't a matter of the conscious intelligence; they weren't volitional. As soon as a direct question was asked, the resultant correlations were plentiful but only such as any reasonably informed man might make. It was the unconscious mind that bridged the wide, unlikely gaps.)

Mark, as any Mnemonic would, fell into the trap. He said energetically, "No, I've never heard of one. Not where the planet was at all habitable. If the planet is solid ice, or complete desert, that's different. Junior isn't like that."

"No, it isn't," agreed Sheffield.

"Then why should the crew be afraid of it? I kept thinking about that all the time I was in bed. That's when I thought of looking at the log. I'd never actually seen one, so it would be a valuable thing to do in any case. And certainly, I thought, I would find the truth there."

"Uh-huh," said Sheffield.

"And, well—I may have been wrong. In the whole log, the purpose of the expedition was never mentioned. Now that wouldn't be so unless the purpose were secret. It was as if he were even keeping it from the other ship's officers. And the name of the ship *is* given as the *George G. Grundy*."

"It would be, of course," said Sheffield.

"I don't know. I suspected that business about *Triple G.*," said Mark darkly.

Sheffield said, "You seem disappointed that the Captain wasn't lying."

"Not disappointed. Relieved, I think. I thought—I thought——" He stopped, and looked acutely embarrassed, but Sheffield made no effort to rescue him. He was forced to continue. "I thought everyone might be lying to me, not just the Captain. Even *you* might, Dr. Sheffield. I thought you just didn't want me to talk to the crew for some reason."

Sheffield tried to smile and managed to succeed. The occupational disease of the Mnemonic Service was suspicion. They were isolated, these Mnemonics, and they were different. Cause and effect were obvious.

Sheffield said lightly, "I think you'll find in your reading on folkways that these superstitions are not necessarily based on logical analysis. A planet which has become notorious has evil expected of it. The good which happens is disregarded; the bad is cried up, advertised, and exaggerated. The thing snowballs."

He moved away from Mark. He busied himself with an inspection of the hydraulic chairs. They would be landing soon. He felt unnecessarily along the length of the broad webbing of the straps, keeping his back to the youngster. So protected, he said, almost in a whisper, "And, of course, what makes it worse is that Junior is so different."

(Easy now, easy. Don't push. He had tried that trick before this and——)

Mark was saying, "No, it isn't. Not a bit. The other expeditions that failed were different. That's true."

Sheffield kept his back turned. He waited.

Mark said, "The seventeen other expeditions that failed on planets that are now inhabited were all small exploring expeditions. In sixteen of the cases, the cause of death was shipwreck of one sort or another, and in the remaining case, Coma Minor that one was, the failure resulted from a surprise attack by indigenous life forms, not intelligent, of course. I have the details on all of them——"

(Sheffield couldn't forbear holding his breath. Mark *could* give the details on all of them. All the details. It was as easy for him to quote all the records on each expedition, word for word, as it was to say yes or no. And he might well choose to. A Mnemonic had no selectivity. It was one of the things that made ordinary companionship between Mnemonics and ordinary people impossible. Mnemonics were dreadful bores by the nature of things. Even Sheffield, who was trained and inured to listen to it all, and who had no intention of stopping Mark if he were really off on a talk jag, sighed softly.)

"—but what's the use," Mark continued, and Sheffield felt rescued from a horror. "They're just not in the same class with the Junior expedition. That consisted of an actual settlement of 789 men, 207 women, and fifteen children under the age of thirteen. In the course of the next year, 315 women, nine men, and two children were added by immigration. The settlement survived almost two years and the cause of death isn't known, except that from their report, it might be disease.

"Now *that* part is different. But Junior itself has nothing unusual about it, except—of course——"

Mark paused as though the information were too unimportant to bother with and Sheffield almost yelled. He forced himself to say calmly, "*That* difference, of course."

Mark said, "We all know about that. It has two suns and the others only have one."

The psychologist could have cried his disappointment. Nothing! But what was the use? Better luck next time. If you don't have patience with a Mnemonic, you might as well not have a Mnemonic.

He sat down in the hydraulic chair and buckled himself in tightly. Mark did likewise. (Sheffield would have liked to help, but that would have been injudicious.) He looked at his watch. They must be spiraling down even now.

Under his disappointment, Sheffield felt a stronger disturbance. Mark Annuncio had acted wrongly in following up his own hunch that the Captain and everybody else had been lying. Mnemonics had a tendency to believe that because their store of facts was great, it was complete. This, obviously, is a prime error. It is therefore necessary, (thus spake Karaganda) for them to present their correlations to properly constituted authority and never to act upon it themselves.

Well, how significant was this error of Mark's? He was the first Mnemonic to be taken away from Service headquarters; the first to be separated from all of his kind; the first to be isolated among noncompos. What did that do to him? What would it continue to do to him? Would it be bad? If so, how to stop it?

To all of which questions, Dr. Oswald Mayer Sheffield knew no answer.

8

The men at the controls were the lucky ones. They and, of course, Cimon, who, as astrophysicist and director of the expedition, joined them by special dispensation. The others of the crew had their separate duties, while the remaining scientific personnel preferred the relative comfort of their hydraulic seats during the spiral around and down to Junior.

It was while Junior was still far enough away to be seen as a whole that the scene was at its grandest.

North and south, a third of the way to the equator, lay the icecaps, still at the start of their millennial retreat. Since the *Triple G.* was spiraling on a north-south great circle (deliberately chosen for the sake of viewing the polar regions, as Cimon, at the cost of less than maximum safety, insisted), each cap in turn was laid out below them.

Each burned equally with sunlight, the consequence of Junior's untilted axis. And each cap was in sectors, cut like a pie with a rainbowed knife.

The sunward third of each was illuminated by both suns simultaneously into a brilliant white that slowly yellowed westward, and as slowly greened eastward. To the east of the white sector lay another, half as wide, which was reached by the light of Lagrange I only, and the snow there blazed a response of sapphire beauty. To the west, another half sector, exposed to Lagrange II alone, shone in the warm orange red of an Earthly sunset. The three colors graded into one another bandwise, and the similarity to a rainbow was increased thereby.

The final third was dark in contrast, but if one looked carefully enough, it, too, was in parts—unequal parts. The smaller portion was black indeed, but the larger portion had a faint milkiness about it.

Cimon muttered to himself, "Moonlight. Of course," then looked about hastily to see if he had been overheard. He did not like people to observe the actual process by which conclusions were brought to fruition in his mind. Rather they were to be presented to his students and listeners, to all about him in short, in a polished perfection that showed neither birth nor growth.

But there were only spacemen about and they did not hear him. Despite all their space-hardening, they were fixing whatever concentration they could spare from their duties and instruments upon the wonder before them.

The spiral curved, veered away from north-south to north-east-southwest, finally to the east-west, in which a safe landing was most feasible. The dull thunder of atmosphere carried into the pilot room, thin and shrill at first, but gathering body and volume as the minutes passed.

Until now, in the interests of scientific observation (and to the considerable uneasiness of the Captain) the spiral had been tight, deceleration slight, and the planetary circumnavigations numerous. As they bit into Junior's air covering, however, deceleration pitched high and the surface rose to meet them.

The icecaps vanished on either side and there began an equal alternation of land and water. A continent, mountainous on either seacoast and flat in between, like a soup plate with two ice-topped rims, flashed below at lengthening intervals. It spread halfway around Junior and the rest was water.

Most of the ocean at the moment was in the dark sector, and what was not lay in the red-orange light of Lagrange II. In the light of that sun, the waters were a dusky purple with a sprinkling of ruddy specks that thickened north and south. Icebergs!

The land was distributed at the moment between the red-orange half sector and the full white light. Only the eastern seacoast was in the blue green. The eastern mountain range was a startling sight, with its western slopes red and its eastern slopes green.

The ship was slowing rapidly now; the final trip over ocean was done.

Next—landing!

9

The first steps were cautious enough. Slow enough, too. Cimon inspected his photochromes of Junior as taken from space with minute care. Under protest, he passed them among the others of the expedition, and more than a few groaned inwardly at the thought of having placed comfort before a chance to see the original of *that*.

Boris Vernadsky bent over his gas analyzer interminably, a symphony in loud clothes and soft grunts.

"We're about at sea level, I should judge," he said, "going by the value of g."

Then, because he was explaining himself to the rest of the group, he added negligently, "The gravitational constant, that is," which didn't help most of them.

He said, "The atmospheric pressure is just about eight hundred millimeters of mercury, which is about 5 per cent higher than on Earth. And two hundred forty millimeters of that is oxygen as compared to only one hundred fifty on Earth. Not bad."

He seemed to be waiting for approval, but scientists found it best to comment as little as possible on data in another man's specialty.

He went on, "Nitrogen, of course. Dull, isn't it, the way nature repeats itself like a three-year-old who knows three lessons, period. Takes the fun away when it turns out that a water world always has an oxygen-nitrogen atmosphere. Makes the whole thing yawn-worthy."

"What else in the atmosphere?" asked Cimon irritably. "So far all we have is oxygen, nitrogen, and homely philosophy from kindly Uncle Boris."

Vernadsky hooked his arm over his seat and said, amiably enough, "What are you? Director or something?"

Cimon, to whom the directorship meant little more than the annoyance of preparing composite reports for the Bureau, flushed and said grimly, "What else in the atmosphere, Dr. Vernadsky?"

Vernadsky said, without looking at his notes, "Under 1 per cent and over a hundredth of 1 per cent: hydrogen, helium, and carbon dioxide in that order. Under a hundredth of 1 per cent and over a ten thousandth of 1 per cent: methane, argon, and neon in that order. Under a ten thousandth of 1 per cent and over a millionth of a per cent: radon, krypton, and xenon in that order.

"The figures aren't very informative. About all I can get out of them is that Junior is going to be a happy hunting ground for uranium, that it's low in potassium, and that it's no wonder it's such a lovely little double icecap of a world."

He did that deliberately, so that someone could ask him how he knew, and someone, with gratifying wonder, inevitably did.

Vernadsky smiled blandly and said, "Atmospheric radon is ten to a hundred times as high here as on Earth. So is helium. Both radon and helium are produced as by-products of the radioactive breakdown of uranium and thorium. Conclusion: Uranium and thorium minerals are ten to a hundred times as copious in Junior's crust as in Earth's.

"Argon, on the other hand, is over a hundred times as low as on Earth. Chances are Junior has none of the argon it originally started with. A planet of this type has only the argon which forms from the breakdown of K^{40}, one of the potassium isotopes. Low argon; low potassium. Simple, kids."

One of the assembled groups asked, "What about the icecaps?"

Cimon, who knew the answer to that, asked, before Vernadsky could answer the other, "What's the carbon dioxide content exactly?"

"Zero point zero one six em em," said Vernadsky.

Cimon nodded, and vouchsafed nothing more.

"Well?" asked the inquirer impatiently.

"Carbon dioxide is only about half what it is on Earth, and it's the carbon dioxide that gives the hothouse effect. It lets the short waves of sunlight pass through to the planet's surface, but doesn't allow the long waves of planetary heat to radiate off. When carbon dioxide concentration goes up as a result of volcanic action, the planet heats up a bit and you have a carboniferous age, with oceans high and land surface at a minimum. When carbon dioxide goes down as a result of the vegetation refusing to let a good thing alone, fattening up on the good old CO_2 and losing its head about it, temperature drops, ice forms, a vicious cycle of glaciation starts, and *voila*——"

"Anything else in the atmosphere?" asked Cimon.

"Water vapor and dust. I suppose there are a few million air-borne spores of various virulent diseases per cubic centimeter in addition to that." He said it lightly enough, but there was a stir in the room. More than one of the bystanders looked as though he were holding his breath.

Vernadsky shrugged and said, "Don't worry about it for now. My analyzer washes out dust and spores quite thoroughly. But then, that's not my angle. I suggest Rodriguez grow his damn cultures under glass right away. Good thick glass."

10

Mark Annuncio wandered everywhere. His eyes shone as he listened, and he pressed himself forward to hear better. The group suffered him to do so with various degrees of reluctance, in accordance with individual personalities and temperaments. None spoke to him.

Sheffield stayed close to Mark. He scarcely spoke either. He bent all his effort on remaining in the background of Mark's consciousness. He wanted to refrain from giving Mark the feeling of being haunted by himself; give the boy the illusion of freedom instead. He wanted to seem to be there each time by accident only.

It was a most unsuccessful pretense, he felt, but what could he do? He *had* to keep the kid from getting into trouble.

11

Miguel Antonio Rodriguez y Lopez (microbiologist; small, tawny, with intensely black hair, which he wore rather long, and with a reputation, which he did nothing to discourage, of being a Latin in the grand style as far as the ladies were concerned) cultured the dust from Vernadsky's gas-analyzer trap with a combination of precision and respectful delicacy.

"Nothing," he said eventually. "What foolish growths I get look harmless."

It was suggested that Junior's bacteria need not necessarily look harmful; that toxins and metabolic processes could not be analyzed by eye, even by microscopic eye.

This was met with hot contempt, as almost an invasion of professional function. He said, with an eyebrow lifted, "One gets a feeling for these things. When one has seen as much of the microcosm as I have, one can sense danger—or lack of danger."

This was an outright lie, and Rodriguez proved it by carefully transferring samples of the various germ colonies into buffered, isotonic media and injecting hamsters with the concentrated result. They did not seem to mind.

Raw atmosphere was trapped in large jars and several specimens of minor animal life from Earth and other planets were allowed to disport themselves within. None of them seemed to mind either.

12

Nevile Fawkes (botanist; a man who appreciated his own handsomeness by modeling his hair style after that shown on the traditional busts of Alexander the Great, but from whose appearance the presence of a nose far more aquiline than Alexander ever possessed noticeably detracted) was gone for two days, by Junior chronology, in one of the *Triple G.*'s atmospheric coasters. He could navigate one like a dream and was, in fact, the only man outside the crew who could navigate one at all, so he was the natural choice for the task. Fawkes did not seem noticeably overjoyed about that.

He returned, completely unharmed and unable to hide a grin of relief. He submitted to irradiation for the sake of sterilizing the exterior of his flexible air suit (designed to protect men from the deleterious effect of the outer environment, where no pressure differential existed; the strength and jointedness of a true space suit being obviously unnecessary within an atmosphere as thick as Junior's). The coaster was subjected to a more extended irradiation and pinned down under a plastic coverall.

Fawkes flaunted color photographs in great number. The central valley of the continent was fertile almost beyond Earthly dreams. The rivers were mighty, the mountains rugged and snow-covered (with the usual pyrotechnic solar effects). Under Lagrange II alone, the vegetation looked vaguely repellent, seeming rather dark, like dried blood. Under Lagrange I, however, or under the suns together, the brilliant, flourishing green and the glisten of the numerous lakes (particularly north and south along the dead rims of the departing glaciers) brought an ache of homesickness to the hearts of many.

Fawkes said, "Look at these."

He had skimmed low to take a photochrome of a field of huge flowers dripping with scarlet. In the high ultra-violet radiation of Lagrange I, exposure times were of necessity extremely short, and despite the motion of the coaster, each blossom stood out as a sharp blotch of strident color.

"I swear," said Fawkes, "each one of those was six feet across."

They admired the flowers unrestrainedly.

Fawkes then said, "No intelligent life whatever, of course."

Sheffield looked up from the photographs with instant sharpness. Life and intelligence, after all, were by way of being his province. "How do you know?"

"Look for yourself," said the botanist. "There are the photos. No highways, no cities, no artificial waterways, no signs of anything man-made."

"No machine civilization," said Sheffield. "That's all."

"Even ape men would build shelters and use fire," said Fawkes, offended.

"The continent is ten times as large as Africa and you've been over it for two days. There's a lot you could miss."

"Not as much as you'd think," was the warm response. "I followed every sizable river up and down and looked over both seacoasts. Any settlements are bound to be there."

"In allowing seventy-two hours for two eight thousand-mile sea-coasts ten thousand miles apart, plus how many thousand miles of river, that had to be a pretty quick lookover."

Cimon interrupted, "What's this all about? *Homo sapiens* is the only intelligence ever discovered in the Galaxy through a hundred thousand and more explored planets. The chances of Troas possessing intelligence is virtually nil."

"Yes?" said Sheffield. "You could use the same argument to prove there's no intelligence on Earth."

"Makoyama," said Cimon, "in his report mentioned no intelligent life."

"And how much time did he have? It was a case of another quick feel through the haystack with one finger and a report of no needle."

"What the eternal Universe," said Rodriguez waspishly. "We argue like madmen. Call the hypothesis of indigenous intelligence unproven and let it go. We are not through investigating yet, I hope."

13

Copies of those first pictures of Junior's surface were added to what might be termed the open files. After a second trip, Fawkes returned in more somber mood and the meeting was correspondingly more subdued.

New photographs went from hand to hand and were then placed by Cimon himself in the special safe that nothing could open short of Cimon's own hands or an all-destroying nuclear blast.

Fawkes said, "The two largest rivers have a generally north-south course along the eastern edges of the western mountain range. The larger river comes down from the northern icecap, the smaller up from the southern one. Tributaries come in westward from the eastern range, interlacing the entire central plain. Apparently the central plain is tipped, the eastern edge being higher. It's what ought to be expected maybe. The eastern mountain range is the taller, broader, and more continuous of the two. I wasn't able to make actual measurements, but I wouldn't be surprised if they beat the Himalayas. In fact, they're a lot like the Wu Ch'ao range on Hesperus. You have to hit the stratosphere to get over them, and rugged—— Wow!

"Anyway"—he brought himself back to the immediate subject at hand with an effort—"the two main rivers join about a hundred miles south of the equator and pour through a gap in the western range. They make it to the ocean after that in just short of eighty miles.

"Where it hits the ocean is a natural spot for the planetary metropolis. The trade routes into the interior of the continent have to converge there so it would be the inevitable emporium for space trade. Even as far as surface trade is concerned, the continental east coast has to move goods across the ocean. Jumping the eastern range isn't worth the effort. Then, too, there are the islands we saw when we were landing.

"So right there is where I would have looked for the settlement even if we didn't have a record of the latitude and longitude. And those settlers had an eye for the future. It's where they set up shop."

Novee said in a low voice, "They thought they had an eye for the future, anyway. There isn't much left of them, is there?"

Fawkes tried to be philosophic about it. "It's been over a century. What do you expect? There's a lot more left of them than I honestly thought there would be. Their buildings were mostly prefab. They've tumbled and vegetation has forced its way over and through them. The fact that the climate of Junior is glacial is what's preserved it. The trees—or the objects that rather look like trees—are small and obviously very slow-growing.

"Even so, the clearing is gone. From the air, the only way you could tell there had once been a settlement in that spot was that the new growth had a slightly different color and—and, well, *texture*—than the surrounding forests."

He pointed at a particular photograph. "This is just a slag heap. Maybe it was machinery once. I think those are burial mounds."

Novee said, "Any actual remains? Bones?"

Fawkes shook his head.

Novee said, "The last survivors didn't bury themselves, did they?"

Fawkes said, "Animals, I suppose." He walked away, his back to the group. "It was raining when I poked my way through. It went splat, splat on the flat leaves above me and the ground was soggy and spongy underneath. It was dark, gloomy. There was a cold wind. The pictures I took don't get it across. I felt as though there were a thousand ghosts, waiting——"

The mood was contagious.

Cimon said savagely, "Stop that!"

In the background, Mark Annuncio's pointed nose fairly quivered with the intensity of his curiosity. He turned to Sheffield, who was at his side, and whispered, "Ghosts? No authentic case of seeing——"

Sheffield touched Mark's thin shoulder lightly. "Only a way of speaking, Mark. But don't feel badly that he doesn't mean it literally. You're watching the birth of a superstition, and that's something, isn't it?"

14

A semi-sullen Captain Follenbee sought out Cimon the evening after Fawkes' second return and said in his harumphy way, "Never do, Dr. Cimon. My men are unsettled. Very unsettled."

The port shields were open. Lagrange I was six hours gone, and Lagrange II's ruddy light, deepened to crimson in setting, flushed the Captain's face and tinged his short gray hair with red.

Cimon, whose attitude toward the crew in general and the Captain in particular was one of controlled impatience, said, "What is the trouble, Captain?"

"Been here two weeks, Earth time. Still no one leaves without suits. Always irradiate before you come back. Anything wrong with the air?"

"Not as far as we know."

"Why not breathe it then?"

"Captain, that's for me to decide."

The flush on the Captain's face became a real one. He said, "My papers say I don't have to stay if ship's safety is endangered. A frightened and mutinous crew is something I don't want."

"Can't you handle your own men?"

"Within reason."

"Well, what really bothers them? This is a new planet and we're being cautious. Can't they understand that?"

"Two weeks and still cautious. They think we're hiding something. And we are. You know that. Besides, surfacc lcave is necessary. Crew's got to have it. Even if it's just on a bare rock a mile across. Gets them out of the ship. Away from the routine. Can't deny them that."

"Give me till tomorrow," said Cimon contemptuously.

15

The scientists gathered in the observatory the next day.

Cimon said, "Vernadsky tells me the data on air is still negative, and Rodriguez has discovered no air-borne pathogenic organism of any type."

There was a general air of dubiety over the last statement. Novee said, "The settlement died of disease. I'll swear to that."

"Maybe so," said Rodriguez at once, "but can you explain how? It's impossible. I tell you that and I tell you. See here. Almost all Earth-type planets give birth to life and that life is always protein in nature and always either cellular or virus in organization. But that's all. There the resemblance ends.

"You laymen think it's all the same; Earth or any planet. Germs are germs and viruses are viruses. I tell you you don't understand the infinite possibilities for variation in the protein molecule. Even on Earth, every species has its own diseases. Some may spread over several species but there isn't one single pathogenic life form of any type on Earth that can attack all other species.

"You think that a virus or a bacterium developing independently for a billion years on another planet with different amino acids, different enzyme systems, a different scheme of metabolism altogether is just going to happen to find *Homo sapiens* succulent like a lollipop. I tell you it is childishness."

Novee, his physician's soul badly pierced at having been lumped under the phrase, "You laymen," was not disposed to let it go that easily. "*Homo sapiens* brings its own germs with it wherever it goes, Rod. Who's to say the virus of the common cold didn't mutate under some planetary influence into something that was suddenly deadly? Or influenza. Things like that have happened even on Earth. The 2755 para-meas——"

"I know all about the 2755 para-measles epidemic," said Rodriguez, "and the 1918 influenza epidemic, and the Black Death, too. But when has it happened lately? Granted the settlement was a matter of a century and more ago—still that wasn't exactly pre-atomic times, either. They included doctors. They had supplies of antibiotics and for space' sake, they knew the techniques of antibody induction. They're simple enough. And there was the medical relief expedition, too."

Novee patted his round abdomen and said stubbornly, "The symptoms were those of a respiratory infection; dyspnea——"

"I know the list, but I tell you it wasn't a germ disease that got them. It couldn't be."

"What was it, then?"

"That's outside my professional competence. Talking from inside, I tell you it wasn't infection. Even mutant infection. It couldn't be. It *mathematically* couldn't be." He leaned heavily on the adverb.

There was a stir among his listeners as Mark Annuncio shoved his thin body forward into the space immediately before Rodriguez.

For the first time, he spoke at one of these gatherings.

"Mathematically?" he asked eagerly.

Sheffield followed after, his long body all elbows and knees as he made a path. He murmured "Sorry" half a dozen times.

Rodriguez, in an advanced stage of exasperation, thrust out his lower lip and said, "What do *you* want?"

Mark flinched. Less eagerly, he said, "You said you knew it wasn't infection mathematically. I was wondering how—mathematics . . ." He ran down.

Rodriguez said, "I have stated my professional opinion."

He said it formally, stiltedly, then turned away. No man questioned another's professional opinion unless he was of the same specialty. Otherwise the implication, clearly enough, was that the specialist's experience and knowledge was sufficiently dubious to be brought into question by an outsider.

Mark knew this, but then he was of the Mnemonic Service. He tapped Rodriguez's shoulder, while the others standing about listened in stunned fascination, and said, "I know it's your professional opinion, but still I'd like to have it explained."

He didn't mean to sound peremptory. He was just stating a fact.

Rodriguez whirled. "You'd like to have it explained? Who the eternal Universe are *you* to ask me questions?"

Mark was startled at the other's vehemence, but Sheffield had reached him now, and he gained courage. With it, anger. He disregarded Sheffield's quick whisper and said shrilly, "I'm Mark Annuncio of Mnemonic Service and I've asked you a question. I want your statement explained."

"It won't be explained. Sheffield, take this young nut out of here and tuck him into bed, will you? And keep him away from me after this. Damn young jackass." The last was a clearly heard aside.

Sheffield took Mark's wrist but it was wrenched out of his grasp. The young Mnemonic screamed, "You stupid noncompos. You—you moron. You forgettery on two feet. Sieve-mind. Let me go, Dr. Sheffield—— You're no expert. You don't remember anything you've learned, and you haven't learned much in the first place. You're not a specialist; none of you——"

"For space' sake," cried Cimon, "take the young idiot out of here, Sheffield."

Sheffield, his long cheeks burning, stooped and lifted Mark bodily into the air. Holding him close, he made his way out of the room.

Tears squeezed out of Mark's eyes, and just outside the door, he managed to speak with difficulty. "Let me down. I want to hear—I want to hear what they say."

Sheffield said, "Don't go back in. Please, Mark."

"I won't. Don't worry. But——"

He didn't finish the but.

16

Inside the observatory room, Cimon, looking haggard, said, "All right. All right. Let's get back to the point. Come on, now. Quiet! I'm accepting Rodriguez' viewpoint. It's good enough for me and I don't suppose there's anyone else here who questions Rodriguez' professional opinion."

("Better not," muttered Rodriguez, his dark eyes hot with sustained fury.)

Cimon went on. "And since there's nothing to fear as far as infection is concerned, I'm telling Captain Follenbee that the crew may take surface leave without special protection against the atmosphere. Apparently the lack of surface leave is bad for morale. Are there any objections?"

There weren't any.

Cimon said, "I see no reason also why we can't pass on to the next stage of the investigation. I propose that we set up camp at the site of the original settlement. I appoint a committee of five to trek out there. Fawkes, since he can handle the coaster; Novee and Rodriguez to handle the biological data; Vernadsky and myself to take care of the chemistry and physics.

"The rest of you will, naturally, be apprised of all pertinent data in your own specialties, and will be expected to help in suggesting lines of attack, et cetera. Eventually, we may all be out there, but for the while only this small group. And until further notice, communication between ourselves and the main group on ship will be by radio only, since if the trouble, whatever it is, turns out to be localized at settlement site, five men are enough to lose."

Novee said, "The settlement lived on Junior several years before dying out. Over a year, anyway. It could be a long time before we are certain we're safe."

"We," said Cimon, "are not a settlement. We are a group of specialists who are looking for trouble. We'll find it if it's there to find, and when we do find it, we'll beat it. And it won't take us a couple of years, either. Now, are there any objections?"

There were none, and the meeting broke up.

17

Mark Annuncio sat on his bunk, hands clasped about his knee, chin sunken and touching his chest. He was dry-eyed now, but his voice was heady with frustration.

"They're not taking me," he said. "They won't let me go with them."

Sheffield was in the chair opposite the boy, bathed in an agony of perplexity. He said, "They may take you later on."

"No," said Mark fiercely, "they won't. They hate me. Besides, I want to go now. I've never been on another planet before. There's so much to see and find out. They've got no right to hold me back if I want to go."

Sheffield shook his head. Mnemonics were so firmly trained into this belief that they *must* collect facts and that no one or nothing could or ought to stop them. Perhaps when they returned, he might recommend a certain degree of counterindoctrination. After all, Mnemonics had to live in the real world occasionally. More and more with each generation, perhaps, as they grew to play an increasing role in the Galaxy.

He tried an experiment. He said, "It may be dangerous, you know."

"I don't care. I've got to know. I've *got* to find out about this planet. Dr. Sheffield, you go to Dr. Cimon and tell him I'm going along."

"Now, Mark."

"If you don't, I will." He raised his small body from the bed in earnest of leaving that moment.

"Look, you're excited."

Mark's fists clenched. "It's not fair, Dr. Sheffield. I found this planet. It's *my* planet."

Sheffield's conscience hit him badly. What Mark said was true in a way. No one, except Mark, knew that better than Sheffield. And no one, again except Mark, knew the history of Junior better than Sheffield.

It was only in the last twenty years that, faced with the rising tide of population pressure in the older planets and the recession of the Galactic frontier from those same older planets, the Confederation of Worlds began exploring the Galaxy systematically. Before that, human expansion went on hit or miss. Men and women in search of new land and a better life followed rumor as to the existence of habitable planets or sent out amateur groups to find something promising.

A hundred ten years before, one such group found Junior. They didn't report their find officially because they didn't want a crowd of land speculators, promotion men, exploiters and general riffraff following. In the next months, some of the unattached men arranged to have women brought in, so the settlement must have flourished for a while.

It was a year later, when some had died and most or all the rest were sick and dying, that they beamed a cry of help to Pretoria, the nearest inhabited planet. The Pretorian government was in some sort of crisis at the time and relayed the message to the Sector government at Altmark. Pretoria then felt justified in forgetting the matter.

The Altmark government, acting in reflex fashion, sent out a medical ship to Junior. It dropped anti-sera and various other supplies. The ship did not land because the medical officer diagnosed the matter from a distance as influenza and minimized the danger. The medical supplies, his report said, would handle the matter perfectly. It was quite possible that the crew of the ship, fearing contagion, had prevented a landing, but nothing in the official report indicated that.

There was a final report from Junior three months later to the effect that only ten people were left alive and that they were dying. They begged for help. This report was forwarded to Earth itself along with the previous medical report. The Central government, however, was a maze in which reports regularly were forgotten unless someone had sufficient personal interest, and influence, to keep them alive.

No one had much interest in a far-off, unknown planet with ten dying men and women on it.

Filed and forgotten—and for a century, no human foot was felt on Junior.

Then, with the new furor over Galactic exploration, hundreds of ships began darting through the empty vastness, probing here and there. Reports trickled in, then flooded in. Some came from Hidosheki Mikoyama, who passed through the Hercules cluster twice (dying in a crash landing the second time, with his tight and despairing voice coming over the subether in a final message: "Surface coming up fast now; ship walls frictioning into red he——" and no more.)

Last year the accumulation of reports, grown past any reasonable human handling, was fed into the overworked Washington computer on a priority so high that there was only a five-month wait. The operators checked out the data for planetary habitability and lo, Abou ben Junior led all the rest.

Sheffield remembered the wild hoorah over it. The stellar system was enthusiastically proclaimed to the Galaxy and the name Junior was thought up by a bright young man in the Bureau of Outer Provinces who felt the need for personal friendliness between man and world. Junior's virtues were magnified. Its fertility, its climate ("a New England perpetual spring"), and most of all, its vast future, were put across without any feeling of need for discretion. "For the next million years," propagandists declared, "Junior will grow richer. While other planets age, Junior will grow younger as the ice recedes and fresh soil is exposed. Always a new frontier; always untapped resources."

For a million years!

It was the Bureau's masterpiece. It was to be the tremendously successful start of a program of government-sponsored colonization. It was to be the beginning, at long last, of the scientific exploitation of the Galaxy for the good of humanity.

And then came Mark Annuncio, who heard much of all this and was as thrilled at the prospect as any Joe Earthman, but who one day thought of something he had seen while sniffing idly through the "dead matter" files of the Bureau of Outer Provinces. He had seen a medical report about a colony on a planet of a system whose description and position in space tallied with that of the Lagrange group.

Sheffield remembered the day Mark came to him with that news.

He also remembered the face of the Secretary for the Outer Provinces when the news was passed on to *him*. He saw the Secretary's square jaw slowly go slack and a look of infinite trouble come into his eyes.

The government was committed! It was going to ship millions of people to Junior. It was going to grant farmland and subsidize the first seed supplies, farm machinery, factories. Junior was going to be a paradise for numerous voters and a promise of more paradise for a myriad others.

If Junior turned out to be a killer planet for some reason or other, it would mean political suicide for all government figures concerned in the project. That meant some pretty big men, not least the Secretary for the Outer Provinces.

After days of checking and indecision, the Secretary had said to Sheffield, "It looks as though we've got to find out what happened and weave it into the propaganda somehow. Don't you think we could neutralize it that way?"

"If what happened isn't too horrible to neutralize."

"But it can't be, can it? I mean what can it be?" The man was miserably unhappy.

Sheffield shrugged.

The Secretary said, "See here. We can send a ship of specialists to the planet. Volunteers only and good reliable men, of course. We can give it the highest priority rating we can move, and Project Junior carries considerable weight, you know. We'll slow things up here, and hold on till they get back. That might work, don't you think?"

Sheffield wasn't sure, but he got the sudden dream of going on that expedition, of taking Mark with him. He could study a Mnemonic in an off-trail environment, and if Mark *should* be the means of working out the mystery——

From the beginning, a mystery was assumed. After all, people don't die of influenza. And the medical ship hadn't landed; they hadn't *really* observed what was going on. It was fortunate, indeed, that that medical man was now dead thirty-seven years, or he would be slated for court-martial now.

If Mark *should* help solve the matter, the Mnemonic Service would be enormously strengthened. The government had to be grateful.

But now——

Sheffield wondered if Cimon knew the story of how the matter of the first settlement had been brought to light. He was fairly certain that the rest of the crew did not. It was not something the Bureau would willingly speak about.

Nor would it be politic to use the story as a lever to pry concessions out of Cimon. If Mark's correction of Bureau "stupidity" (that would undoubtedly be the opposition's phrasing) were over-publicized, the Bureau would look bad. If they could be grateful, they could be vengeful, too. Retaliation against the Mnemonic Service would not be too petty a thing to expect.

Still——

Sheffield stood up with quick decision. "All right, Mark. I'll get you out to the settlement site. I'll get us both out there. Now you sit down and wait for me. Promise you'll try nothing on your own."

"All right," said Mark. He sat down on his bunk again.

18

"Well now, Dr. Sheffield, what is it?" said Cimon. The astrophysicist sat at his desk, on which papers and film formed rigidly arranged heaps about a small Macfreed integrator, and watched Sheffield step over the threshold.

Sheffield sat carelessly down upon the tautly yanked top sheet of Cimon's bunk. He was aware of Cimon's annoyed glance in that direction and it did not worry him. In fact, he rather enjoyed it.

He said, "I have a quarrel with your choice of men to go to the expedition site. It looks as though you've picked two men for the physical sciences and three for the biological sciences. Right?"

"Yes."

"I suppose you think you've covered the ground like a Danielski ovospore at perihelion."

"Oh, space! Have you anything to suggest?"

"I would like to come along myself."

"Why?"

"You have no one to take care of the mental sciences."

"The *mental* sciences! Good Galaxy! Dr. Sheffield, five men are quite enough to risk. As a matter of fact, Doctor, you and your—uh —ward were assigned to the scientific personnel of this ship by order of the Bureau of Outer Provinces without any prior consultation of myself. I'll be frank. If I had been consulted, I would have advised against you. I don't see the function of mental science in an investigation such as this, which, after all, is purely physical. It is too bad that the Bureau wishes to experiment with Mnemonics on an occasion such as this. We can't afford scenes like that one with Rodriguez."

Sheffield decided that Cimon did not know of Mark's connection with the original decision to send out the expedition.

He sat upright, hands on knees, elbows cocked outward, and let a freezing formality settle over him. "So you wonder about the function of mental science in an investigation such as this, Dr. Cimon. Suppose I told you that the end of the first settlement might possibly be explained on a simple, psychological basis."

"It wouldn't impress me. A psychologist is a man who can explain anything and prove nothing." Cimon smirked like a man who had made an epigram and was proud of it.

Sheffield ignored it. He said, "Let me go into a little detail. In what way is Junior different from every one of the eighty-three thousand inhabited worlds?"

"Our information is as yet incomplete. I cannot say."

"Oh, cobber-vitals. You had the necessary information before you ever came here. Junior has two suns."

"Well, of course." But the astrophysicist allowed a trace of discomfiture to enter his expression.

"Colored suns, mind you. Colored suns. Do you know what that means? It means that a human being, yourself or myself, standing in the full glare of the two suns, would cast two shadows. One blue green, one red orange. The length of each would naturally vary with the time of day. Have you taken the trouble to verify the color distribution in those shadows? The what-do-you-call-'em—reflection spectrum?"

"I presume," said Cimon loftily, "they'd be about the same as the radiation spectra of the suns. What are you getting at?"

"You should check. Wouldn't the air absorb some wave lengths? And the vegetation? What's left? And take Junior's moon, Sister. I've been watching it in the last few nights. It's in colors, too, and the colors change position."

"Well, of course, damn it. It runs through its phases independently with each sun."

"You haven't checked its reflection spectrum, either, have you?"

"We have that somewhere. There are no points of interest about it. Of what interest is it to you, anyway?"

"My dear Dr. Cimon, it is a well-established psychological fact that combinations of red and green colors exert a deleterious effect on mental stability. We have a case here where the red-green chromopsychic picture (to use a technical term) is inescapable and is presented under circumstances which seem most unnatural to the human mind. It is quite possible that chromopsychosis could reach the fatal level by inducing hypertrophy of the trinitarian follicles, with consequent cerebric catatonia."

Cimon looked floored. He said, "I never heard of such a thing."

"Naturally not," said Sheffield (it was his turn to be lofty). "You are not a psychologist. Surely you are not questioning my professional opinion."

"No, of course not. But it's quite plain from the last reports of the expedition that they were dying of something that sounded like a respiratory disease."

"Correct, but Rodriguez denies that and you accepted his professional opinion."

"I didn't say it was a respiratory disease. I said it sounded like one. Where does your red-green chromothingumbob come in?"

Sheffield shook his head. "You laymen have your misconceptions. Granted that there is a physical effect, it still does not imply that there may not be a mental cause. The most convincing point about my theory is that red-green chromopsychosis has been recorded to exhibit itself first as a psychogenic respiratory infection. I take it you are not acquainted with psychogenics."

"No. It's out of my field."

"Well, yes. I should say so. Now my own calculations show me that under the heightened oxygen tension of this world, the psychogenic respiratory infection is both inevitable and particularly severe. For instance, you've observed the moon—Sister, I mean—in the last few nights."

"Yes, I have observed Ilium." Cimon did not forget Sister's official name even now.

"You watched it closely and over lengthy periods? Under magnification?"

"Yes." Cimon was growing uneasy.

"Ah," said Sheffield. "Now the moon colors in the last few nights have been particularly virulent. Surely you must be noticing just a small inflammation of the mucus membrane of the nose, a slight itching in the throat. Nothing painful yet, I imagine. Have you been coughing or sneezing? Is it a little hard to swallow?"

"I believe I——" Cimon swallowed, then drew in his breath sharply. He was testing.

Then he sprang to his feet, fists clenched and mouth working. "Great galaxy, Sheffield, you had no right to keep quiet about this. I can feel it now. What do I do, Sheffield? It's not incurable, is it? Damn it, Sheffield"—his voice went shrill—"why didn't you tell us this before?"

"Because," said Sheffield calmly, "there's not a word of truth in anything I've said. Not one word. There's no harm in colors. Sit down, Dr. Cimon. You're beginning to look foolish."

"You said," said Cimon, thoroughly confused, and in a voice that was beginning to strangle, "that it was your professional opinion that——"

"My professional opinion! Space and little comets, Cimon, what's so magic about a professional opinion? A man can be lying or he can just plain be ignorant, even about the final details of his own specialty. A professional can be wrong because he's ignorant of a neighboring specialty. He may be certain he's right and still be wrong.

"Look at you. You know all about what makes the Universe tick and I'm lost completely except that I know that a star is something that twinkles and a light-year is something that's long. And yet you'll swallow gibberish psychology that a freshman student of mentics would laugh his head off at. Don't you think, Cimon, it's time we worried less about professional opinion and more about over-all coordination?"

The color washed slowly out of Cimon's face. It turned waxy-pale. His lips trembled. He whispered, "You used professional status as a cloak to make a fool of me."

"That's about it," said Sheffield.

"I have never, *never*——" Cimon gasped and tried a new start. "I have never witnessed anything as cowardly and unethical."

"I was trying to make a point."

"Oh, you made it. You made it." Cimon was slowly recovering, his voice approaching normality. "You want me to take that boy of yours with us."

"That's right."

"No. No. Definitely no. It was no before you came in here and it's no a million times over now."

"What's your reason? I mean before I came in."

"He's psychotic. He can't be trusted with normal people."

Sheffield said grimly, "I'll thank you not to use the word, 'psychotic.' You are not competent to use it. If you're so precise in your feeling for professional ethics, remember to stay out of my specialty in my presence. Mark Annuncio is perfectly normal."

"After that scene with Rodriguez? Yes. Oh, yes."

"Mark had the right to ask his question. It was his job to do so and his duty. Rodriguez had no right to be boorish about it."

"I'll have to consider Rodriguez first, if you don't mind."

"Why? Mark Annuncio knows more than Rodriguez. For that matter, he knows more than you or I. Are you trying to bring back an intelligent report or to satisfy a petty vanity?"

"Your statements about what your boy knows do not impress me. I am quite aware he is an efficient parrot. He understands nothing, however. It is my duty to see to it that data is made available to him because the Bureau has ordered that. They did not consult me, but very well. I will co-operate that far. He will receive his data here in the ship."

Sheffield said, "Not adequate, Cimon. He should be on the spot. He may see things our precious specialists will not."

Cimon said freezingly, "Very likely. The answer, Sheffield, is no. There is no argument that can possibly persuade me." The astrophysicist's nose was pinched and white.

"Because I made a fool of you?"

"Because you violated the most fundamental obligation of a professional man. No respectable professional would ever use his specialty to prey on the innocence of a non-associate professional."

"So I made a fool of you."

Cimon turned away. "Please leave. There will be no further communication between us, outside the most necessary business, for the duration of the trip."

"If I go," said Sheffield, "the rest of the boys may get to hear about this."

Cimon started. "You're going to repeat our little affair?" A cold smile rested on his lips, then went its transient and contemptuous way. "You'll broadcast the dastard you were."

"Oh, I doubt they'll take it seriously. Everyone knows psychologists will have their little jokes. Besides, they'll be so busy laughing at you. You know—the very impressive Dr. Cimon scared into a sore throat and howling for mercy after a few mystic words of gibberish."

"Who'd believe you?" cried Cimon.

Sheffield lifted his right hand. Between thumb and forefinger was a small rectangular object, studded with a line of control toggles.

"Pocket recorder," he said. He touched one of the toggles and Cimon's voice was suddenly saying, "Well, now, Dr. Sheffield, what is it?"

It sounded pompous, peremptory, and even a little smug.

"Give me that!" Cimon hurled himself at the lanky psychologist.

Sheffield held him off. "Don't try force, Cimon. I was in amateur wrestling not too long ago. Look, I'll make a deal with you."

Cimon was still writhing toward him, dignity forgotten, panting his fury. Sheffield kept him at arm's length, backing slowly.

Sheffield said, "Let Mark and myself come along and no one will ever see or hear this."

Slowly Cimon simmered down. He gasped, "Will you let me have it, then?"

"After Mark and I are out at the settlement site."

"I'm to trust *you*." He seemed to take pains to make that as offensive as possible.

"Why not? You can certainly trust me to broadcast this if you *don't* agree. I'll play it off for Vernadsky first. He'll love it. You know his corny sense of humor."

Cimon said in a voice so low it could hardly be heard, "You and the boy can come along." Then vigorously, "But remember this, Sheffield. When we get back to Earth, I'll have you before the Central Committee of the G.A.A.S. That's a promise. You'll be deprofessionalized."

Sheffield said, "I'm not afraid of the Galactic Association for the Advancement of Science." He let the syllables resound. "After all, what will you accuse me of? Are you going to play this recording before the Central Committee as evidence? Come, come, let's be friendly about this. You don't want to broadcast your own—uh—mistake before the primmest stuffed shirts in eighty-three thousand worlds."

Smiling gently, he backed out the door.

But when he closed the door between himself and Cimon, his smile vanished. He hadn't liked to do this. Now that he had done it, he wondered if it were worth the enemy he had made.

19

Seven tents had sprung up near the site of the original settlement on Junior. Nevile Fawkes could see them all from the low ridge on which he stood. They had been there seven days now.

He looked up at the sky. The clouds were thick overhead and pregnant with rain. That pleased him. With both suns behind those clouds, the diffused light was gray white. It made things seem almost normal.

The wind was damp and a little raw, as though it were April in Vermont. Fawkes was a New Englander and he appreciated the resemblance. In four or five hours, Lagrange I would set and the clouds would turn ruddy while the landscape would become angrily dim. But Fawkes intended to be back in the tents by then.

So near the equator, yet so cool! Well, that would change with the millennia. As the glaciers retreated, the air would warm up and the soil would dry out. Jungles and deserts would make their appearance. The water level in the oceans would slowly creep higher, wiping out numberless islands. The two large rivers would become an inland sea, changing the configuration of Junior's one large continent; perhaps making several smaller ones out of it.

He wondered if settlement site would be drowned. Probably, he decided. Maybe that would take the curse off it.

He could understand why the Confederation were so damned anxious to solve the mystery of that first settlement. Even if it were a simple matter of disease, there would have to be proof. Otherwise, who would settle the world? The "sucker bait" superstition held for more than merely spacemen.

He, himself—— Well, his first visit to the settlement site hadn't been so bad, though he had been glad to leave the rain and the gloom. Returning was worse. It was difficult to sleep with the thought that a thousand mysterious deaths lay all about, separated from him only by that insubstantial thing, time.

With medical coolness, Novee had dug up the moldering graves of a dozen of the ancient settlers. (Fawkes could not and did not look at the remains.) There had been only crumbling bones, Novee had said, out of which nothing could be made.

"There seem to be abnormalities of bone deposition," he said.

Then on questioning, he admitted that the effects might be entirely owing to a hundred years' exposure to damp soil.

Fawkes had constructed a fantasy that followed him even into his waking hours. It concerned an elusive race of intelligent beings dwelling underground, never being seen but haunting that first settlement a century back with a deadly perseverance.

He pictured a silent bacteriological warfare. He could see them in laboratories beneath the tree roots, culturing their molds and spores, waiting for one that could live on human beings. Perhaps they captured children to experiment upon.

And when they found what they were looking for, spores drifted silently out over the settlement in venomous clouds——

Fawkes knew all this to be fantasy. He had made it up in the wakeful nights out of no evidence but that of his quivering stomach. Yet alone in the forest, he whirled more than once in a sudden horror-filled conviction that bright eyes were staring out of the duskiness of a tree's Lagrange I shadow.

Fawkes' botanist's eye did not miss the vegetation he passed, absorbed as he was. He had deliberately struck out from camp in a new direction, but what he saw was what he had already seen. Junior's forests were neither thick nor tangled. They were scarcely a barrier to travel. The small trees (few were higher than ten feet, although their trunks were nearly as thick as the average Terrestrial tree) grew with considerable room between them.

Fawkes had constructed a rough scheme for arranging the plant life of Junior into some sort of taxonomic order. He was not unaware of the fact that he might be arranging for his own immortality.

There was the scarlet "bayonet tree," for instance. Its huge scarlet flowers attracted insect-like creatures that built small nests within it. Then (at what signal or what impulse Fawkes had not divined) all the flowers on some one given tree would grow a glistening white pistil over night. Each pistil stood two feet high, as though every bloom had been suddenly equipped with a bayonet.

By the next day, the flower had been fertilized and the petals closed shut—about pistil, insects, and all. The explorer, Makoyama, had named it the "bayonet tree," but Fawkes had made so bold as to rename it *Migrania Fawkesii.*

One thing the trees had in common. Their wood was incredibly tough. It would be the task of the biochemist to determine the physical state of the cellulose molecule and that of the biophysicist to determine how water could be transported through the wood's impervious texture. What Fawkes knew from experience was that the blossoms would break if pulled, that the stems would bend only with difficulty and break not at all. His pocketknife was blunted without so much as making a scratch.

The original settlers, in order to clear land, had obviously had to dig out the trees, roots and all.

Compared to Earth, the woods were almost free of animal life. That might be due to the glacial slaughter. Fawkes didn't know.

The insect-like creatures were all two winged. And those wings were feathery little fronds that beat noiselessly. None, apparently, were bloodsuckers.

The only major experience with animals that they had had was the sudden appearance of a large flying creature over the camp. It took high-speed photography to reveal the actual shape of the beast, for the specimen they observed, apparently overcome with curiosity, swooped low over the tents again and again at speeds too great for comfortable, naked-eye observation.

It was four-winged, the forward wings terminating in powerful claws, being membranous and nearly naked, serving the office of gliding planes. The hind pair, covered with a hairlike fuzz, beat rapidly.

Rodriguez suggested the name *Tetrapterus.*

Fawkes paused in his reminiscence to look at a variety of grass he had not seen before. It grew in a dense patch and each stem forked in three toward the top. He brought out his magnifying glass and felt one of the stems gingerly with his finger. Like other grasses on Junior, it——

It was here that he heard the rustle behind him—unmistakable. He listened for a moment, his own heartbeat drowning the sound, then whirled. A small manlike object dodged behind a tree.

Fawkes' breathing nearly stopped. He fumbled for the blaster he wore and his hand seemed to be moving through molasses.

Was his fantasy no fantasy at all? Was Junior inhabited after all?

Numbly Fawkes found himself behind another tree. He couldn't leave it at this. He knew that. He could not report to the rest: "I saw something alive. It might have been the answer to everything. But I was afraid and let it get away."

He would have to make some attempt.

There was a "chalice tree" just behind the tree that hid the creature. It was in bloom, the white and cream flowers lifted turgidly upward, waiting to catch the rain that would soon fall. There was the sharp tinkle of a breaking flower and cream slivers twisted and turned downward.

It wasn't imagination. Something *was* behind the tree.

Fawkes took a deep breath and dashed out, holding his blaster before him, nerving himself to shoot at the slightest sign of danger.

But a voice called out, "Don't. It's only I." A frightened but definitely human face looked out from behind the tree.

It was Mark Annuncio.

Fawkes stopped in mid-stride and stared. Finally, he managed to croak, "What are you doing here?"

Mark said, staring at the blaster in the other's hand, "I was following you."

"Why?"

"To see what you would do. I was interested in what you might find. I thought if you saw me, you would send me away."

Fawkes became conscious of the weapon he was still holding and put it away. It took three tries to get it into the holster.

The first fat drops of rain began to fall. Fawkes said harshly, "Don't say anything about this to the others."

He glared hostilely at the youngster and they walked back to camp separately and in silence.

20

A central hall of prefab had been added to the seven tents now, and the group was together within it, sitting about the long table.

It was a great moment, but a rather subdued one. Vernadsky, who had cooked for himself in his college days, was in charge. He lifted the steaming stew off the short-wave heater and said, "Calories, anyone?"

He ladled the stuff lavishly.

"It smells very good," said Novee doubtfully.

He lifted a piece of meat with his fork. It was purplish and still felt tough despite internal heating. The shredded herbs that surrounded it seemed softer, but looked less edible.

"Well," said Vernadsky, "eat it. Put it in your mouth. I've tasted it and it's good."

He crammed his mouth and chewed. He kept on chewing. "Tough, but good."

Fawkes said gloomily, "It'll probably kill us."

"Nuts," said Vernadsky. "The rats have been living on it for two weeks."

"Two weeks isn't much," said Novee.

Rodriguez said, "Well, one bite won't kill. Say, it *is* good."

And it was. They all agreed eventually. So far, it seemed that whenever Junior's life could be eaten at all, it was good. The grains were almost impossible to grind into flour, but that done, a protein-high bread could be baked. There was some on the table now, dark and heavy. It wasn't bad, either.

Fawkes had studied the herb life on Junior and come to the conclusion that an acre of Junior's surface, properly seeded and watered, could support ten times the number of grazing animals that an acre of Earthly alfalfa could.

Sheffield had been impressed; had spoken of Junior as the granary of a hundred worlds, but Fawkes dismissed his own statements with a shrug.

He said, "Sucker bait."

About a week earlier, the party had been agitated by the sudden refusal of the hamsters and white rats to touch certain new herbs Fawkes had brought in. Mixing small quantities with regular rations had resulted in the death of those that fed on it.

Solution?

Not quite. Vernadsky came in a few hours later and said calmly, "Copper, lead, and mercury."

"What?" said Cimon.

"Those plants. They're high in heavy metals. Probably an evolutionary development to keep from being eaten."

"The first settlers——" began Cimon.

"No. That's impossible. Most of the plants are perfectly all right. Just these, and no person would eat them."

"How do you know?"

"The rats didn't."

"They're just rats."

It was what Vernadsky was waiting for. He said dramatically, "You may hail a modest martyr to science. I tasted the stuff."

"What?" yelled Novee.

"Just a lick. Don't worry. I'm the careful-type martyr. Anyway, the stuff is as bitter as strychnine. What do you expect? If a plant is going to fill itself with lead just to keep the animals off, what good does it do the plant to have the animal find out by dying after he's eaten it? A little bitter stuff in addition acts as a warning. The combination warning and punishment does the trick."

"Besides," said Novee, "it wasn't heavy metal poisoning that killed the settlers. The symptoms aren't right for it."

The rest knew the symptoms well enough. Some in lay terms and some in more technical language. Difficult and painful breathing that grew steadily worse. That's what it amounted to.

Fawkes put down his fork. "Look here, suppose this stuff contains some alkaloid that paralyzes the nerves that control the lung muscles."

"Rats have lung muscles," said Vernadsky. "It doesn't kill them."

"Maybe it's a cumulative thing."

"All right. All right. Any time your breathing gets painful, go back to ship rations and see if you improve. But no fair counting psychosomatics."

Sheffield grunted, "That's my job. Don't worry about it."

Fawkes drew a deep breath, then another. Glumly he put another piece of meat into his mouth.

At one corner of the table, Mark Annuncio, eating more slowly than the rest, thought of Norris Vinograd's monograph on "Taste and Smell." Vinograd had made a taste-smell classification based on enzyme inhibition patterns within the taste buds. Annuncio did not know what that meant exactly but he remembered the symbols, their values, and the descriptive definitions.

While he placed the taste of the stew to three subclassifications, he finished his helping. His jaws ached faintly because of the difficult chewing.

21

Evening was approaching and Lagrange I was low in the sky. It had been a bright day, reasonably warm, and Boris Vernadsky felt pleased. He had made interesting measurements and his brilliantly colored sweater had showed fascinating changes from hour to hour as the suns' positions shifted.

Right now his shadow was a long red thing, with the lowest third of it gray, where the Lagrange II shadow coincided. He held out one arm and it cast two shadows. There was a smeared orange one some fifteen feet away and a denser blue one in the same direction but only five feet away. If he had time, he could work out a beautiful set of shadowgrams.

He was so pleased with the thought that he felt no resentment at seeing Mark Annuncio skirting his trail in the distance.

He put down his nucleometer and waved his hand. "Come here!"

The youngster approached diffidently. "Hello."

"Want something?"

"Just—just watching."

"Oh? Well, go ahead and watch. Do you know what I'm doing?"

Mark shook his head.

"This is a nucleometer," said Vernadsky. "You jab it into the ground like this. It's got a force-field generator at the top so it will penetrate any rock." He leaned on the nucleometer as he spoke, and it went two feet into the stony outcropping. "See?"

Mark's eyes shone, and Vernadsky felt pleased. The chemist said, "Along the sides of the uniped are microscopic atomic furnaces, each of which vaporizes about a million molecules or so in the surrounding rock and decomposes them into atoms. The atoms are then differentiated in terms of nuclear mass and charge and the results may be read off directly on the dials above. Do you follow all that?"

"I'm not sure. But it's a good thing to know."

Vernadsky smiled and said, "Wc cnd up with figures on the different elements in the crust. It's pretty much the same on all oxygen-water planets."

Mark said seriously, "The planet with the most silicon I know of is Lepta, with 32.765 per cent. Earth is only 24.862. That's by weight."

Vernadsky's smile faded. He said dryly, "You have the figures on all the planets, pal?"

"Oh no. I couldn't. I don't think they've all been surveyed. Bischoon and Spenglow's *Handbook of Planetary Crusts* only lists figures for 21,854 planets. I know all those, of course."

Vernadsky, with a definite feeling of deflation, said, "Now Junior has a more even distribution of elements than is usually met up with. Oxygen is low. So far my average is a lousy 42.113. So is silicon, with 22.722. The heavy metals are ten to a hundred times as concentrated as on Earth. That's not just a local phenomenon, either, since Junior's over-all density is 5 per cent higher than Earth's."

Vernadsky wasn't sure why he was telling the kid all this. Partly, he felt, because it was good to find someone who would listen. A man gets lonely and frustrated when there is no one of his own field to talk to.

He went on, beginning to relish the lecture. "On the other hand, the lighter elements are also better distributed. The ocean solids aren't predominantly sodium chloride, as on Earth. Junior's oceans contain a respectable helping of magnesium salts. And take what they call the 'rare lights.' Those are the elements lithium, beryllium, and boron. They're lighter than carbon, all of them, but they are of very rare occurrence on Earth, and in fact, on all planets. Junior, on the other hand, is quite rich in them. The three of them total almost four tenths of a per cent of the crust as compared to about four thousandths on Earth."

Mark plucked at the other's sleeve. "Do you have a list of figures on all the elements? May I see?"

"I suppose so." He took a folded piece of paper out of his hip pocket.

He grinned as Mark took the sheet and said, "Don't publish those figures before I do."

Mark glanced at them once and returned the paper.

"Are you through?" asked Vernadsky in surprise.

"Oh yes," said Mark thoughtfully, "I have it all." He turned on his heel and walked away with no word of parting.

The last glimmer of Lagrange I faded below the horizon.

Vernadsky gazed after Mark and shrugged. He plucked his nucleometer out of the ground, and followed after, walking back toward the tents.

22

Sheffield was moderately pleased. Mark had been doing better than expected. To be sure, he scarcely talked but that was not very serious. At least, he showed interest and didn't sulk. And he threw no tantrums.

Vernadsky was even telling Sheffield that last evening Mark had spoken to him quite normally, without raised voices on either side, about planetary crust analyses. Vernadsky had laughed a bit about it, saying that Mark knew the crust analyses of twenty thousand planets and someday he'd have the boy repeat them all just to see how long it would take.

Mark, himself, had made no mention of the matter. In fact, he had spent the morning sitting in his tent. Sheffield had looked in, seen him on his cot, staring at his feet, and had left him to himself.

What he really needed at the moment, Sheffield felt, was a bright idea for himself. A really bright one.

So far, everything had come to nothing. A whole month of nothing. Rodriguez held fast against any infection. Vernadsky absolutely barred food poisoning. Novee shook his head with vehement negativeness at suggestions of disturbed metabolism. "Where's the evidence?" he kept saying.

What it amounted to was that every physical cause of death was eliminated on the strength of expert opinion. But men, women, and children had died. There must be a reason. Could it be psychological?

He had satirized the matter to Cimon for a purpose before they had come out here, but it was now time and more than time to be serious about it. Could the settlers have been driven to suicide? Why? Humanity had colonized tens of thousands of planets without its having seriously affected mental stability. In fact, the suicide rate, as well as the incidence of psychoses, was higher on Earth than anywhere else in the Galaxy.

Besides, the settlement had called frantically for medical help. They didn't want to die.

Personality disorders? Something peculiar to that one group?

Enough to affect over a thousand people to the death? Unlikely. Besides, how could any evidence be uncovered? The settlement site had been ransacked for any films or records, even the most frivolous. Nothing. A century of dampness left nothing so fragile as purposeful records.

So he was working in a vacuum. He felt helpless. The others, at least, had data; something to chew on. He had nothing.

He found himself at Mark's tent again and looked inside automatically. It was empty. He looked about and spied Mark walking out of the camp and into the woods.

Sheffield cried out after him, "Mark! Wait for me!"

Mark stopped, made as though to go on, thought better of it, and let Sheffield's long legs consume the distance between them.

Sheffield said, "Where are you off to?" (Even after running, it was unnecessary to pant in Junior's rich atmosphere.)

Mark's eyes were sullen. "To the air-coaster."

"Oh?"

"I haven't had a chance to look at it."

"Why, of course you've had a chance," said Sheffield. "You were watching Fawkes like a hawk on the trip over."

Mark scowled. "Everyone was around. I want to see it for myself."

Sheffield felt disturbed. The kid was angry. He'd better tag along and try to find out what was wrong. He said, "Come to think of it, I'd like to see the coaster myself. You don't mind having me along, do you?"

Mark hesitated. Then he said, "We-ell. If you want to." It wasn't exactly a gracious invitation.

Sheffield said, "What are you carrying, Mark?"

"Tree branch. I cut it off with the buzz-field gun. I'm taking it with me just in case anyone wants to stop me." He swung it so that it whistled through the thick air.

"Why should anyone want to stop you, Mark? I'd throw it away. It's hard and heavy. You could hurt someone."

Mark was striding on. "I'm not throwing it away."

Sheffield pondered briefly, then decided against a quarrel at the moment. It would be better to get to the basic reason for this hostility first. "All right," he said.

The air-coaster lay in a clearing, its clear metal surface throwing back green highlights. (Lagrange II had not yet risen.)

Mark looked carefully about.

"There's no one in sight, Mark," said Sheffield.

They climbed aboard. It was a large coaster. It had carried seven men and the necessary supplies in only three trips.

Sheffield looked at its control panel with something quite close to awe. He said, "Imagine a botanist like Fawkes learning to run one of these things. It's so far outside his specialty."

"I can run one," said Mark suddenly.

Sheffield stared at him in surprise. "You can?"

"I watched Dr. Fawkes when we came. I know everything he did. And he has a repair manual for the coaster. I sneaked that out once and read it."

Sheffield said lightly, "Well, that's very nice. We have a spare navigator for an emergency, then."

He turned away from Mark then, so he never saw the tree limb as it came down on his head. He didn't hear Mark's troubled voice saying, "I'm sorry, Dr. Sheffield." He didn't even, properly speaking, feel the concussion that knocked him out.

23

It was the jar of the coaster's landing, Sheffield later thought, that first brought consciousness back. It was a dim, aching sort of thing that had no understanding in it at first.

The sound of Mark's voice was floating up to him. That was his first sensation. Then as he tried to roll over and get a knee beneath him, he could feel his head throbbing.

For a while, Mark's voice was only a collection of sounds that meant nothing to him. Then they began to coalesce into words. Finally, when his eyes fluttered open and light entered stabbingly so that he had to close them again, he could make out sentences. He remained where he was, head hanging, one quivering knee holding him up.

Mark was saying in a breathless, high-pitched voice, ". . . a thousand people all dead. Just graves. And nobody knows why."

There was a rumble Sheffield couldn't make out. A hoarse, deep voice.

Then Mark again, "It's true. Why do you suppose all the scientists are aboard?"

Sheffield lifted achingly to his feet and rested against one wall. He put his hand to his head and it came away bloody. His hair was caked and matted with it. Groaning, he staggered toward the coaster's cabin door. He fumbled for the hook and yanked it inward.

The landing ramp had been lowered. For a moment, he stood there, swaying, afraid to trust his legs.

He had to take in everything by installments. Both suns were high in the sky and a thousand feet away the giant steel cylinder of the *Triple G.* reared its nose high above the runty trees that ringed it.

Mark was at the foot of the ramp, semi-circled by members of the crew. The crewmen were stripped to the waist and browned nearly black in the ultraviolet of Lagrange I. (Thanks only to the thick atmosphere and the heavy ozone coating in the upper reaches for keeping UV down to a livable range.)

The crewman directly before Mark was leaning on a baseball bat. Another tossed a ball in the air and caught it. Many of the rest were wearing gloves.

Funny, thought Sheffield erratically, Mark landed right in the middle of a ball park.

Mark looked up and saw him. He screamed excitedly, "All right, ask him. Go ahead, ask him. Dr. Sheffield, wasn't there an expedition to this planet once and they all died mysteriously?"

Sheffield tried to say, "Mark, what are you doing?" He couldn't. When he opened his mouth, only a moan came out.

The crewman with the bat said, "Is this little gumboil telling the truth, mister?"

Sheffield held on to the railing with two perspiring hands. The crewman's face seemed to waver. The face had thick lips on it and small eyes buried under bristly eyebrows. It wavered very badly.

Then the ramp came up and whirled about his head. There was ground gripped in his hands suddenly and a cold ache on his cheekbone. He gave up the fight and let go of consciousness again.

24

He came awake less painfully the second time. He was in bed now and two misty faces leaned over him. A long, thin object passed across his line of vision and a voice, just heard above the humming in his ears, said, "He'll come to now, Cimon."

Sheffield closed his eyes. Somehow he seemed to be aware of the fact that his skull was thoroughly bandaged.

He lay quietly for a minute, breathing deeply. When he opened his eyes again, the faces above him were clear. There was Novee's round face, a small, professionally serious line between his eyes that cleared away when Sheffield said, "Hello, Novee."

The other man was Cimon, jaws set and angry, yet with a look of something like satisfaction in his eyes.

Sheffield said, "Where are we?"

Cimon said coldly, "In space, Dr. Sheffield. Two days out in space."

"Two days out——" Sheffield's eyes widened.

Novee interposed. "You've had a bad concussion, nearly a fracture, Sheffield. Take it easy."

"Well, what hap—— Where's Mark? *Where's Mark?*"

"Easy. Easy now." Novee put a hand on each of Sheffield's shoulders and pressed him down.

Cimon said, "Your boy is in the brig. In case you want to know why, he deliberately caused mutiny on board ship, thus endangering the safety of five men. We were almost marooned at our temporary camp because the crew wanted to leave immediately. He persuaded them, the Captain did, to pick us up."

Sheffield remembered now, very vaguely. There was just that fuzzy memory of Mark and a man with a bat. Mark saying ". . . a thousand people all dead. . . ."

The psychologist hitched himself up on one elbow with a tremendous effort. "Listen, Cimon, I don't know why Mark did it, but let me talk to him. I'll find out."

Cimon said, "No need of that. It will all come out at the trial."

Sheffield tried to brush Novee's restraining arm to one side. "But why make it formal? Why involve the Bureau? We can settle this among ourselves."

"That's exactly what we intend to do. The Captain is empowered by the laws of space to preside over trials involving crimes and misdemeanors in deep space."

"The Captain. A trial here? On board ship? Cimon, don't let him do it. It will be murder."

"Not at all. It will be a fair and proper trial. I'm in full agreement with the Captain. Discipline demands a trial."

Novee said uneasily, "Look, Cimon, I wish you wouldn't. He's in no shape to take this."

"Too bad," said Cimon.

Sheffield said, "But you don't understand. I'm responsible for the boy."

"On the contrary, I do understand," said Cimon. "It's why we've been waiting for you to regain consciousness. You're standing trial with him."

"What!"

"You are generally responsible for his actions. Specifically, you were with him when he stole the air-coaster. The crew saw you at the coaster's cabin door while Mark was inciting mutiny."

"But he cracked my skull in order to take the coaster. Can't you see that's the act of a seriously disturbed mind? He can't be held responsible."

"We'll let the Captain decide, Sheffield. You stay with him, Novee." He turned to go.

Sheffield called on what strength he could muster. "Cimon," he shouted, "you're doing this to get back at me for the lesson in psychology I taught you. You're a narrow—petty——"

He fell back on his pillow, breathless.

Cimon, from the door, said, "And by the way, Sheffield, the penalty for inciting mutiny on board ship is death!"

25

Well, it was a *kind* of trial, Sheffield thought grimly. Nobody was following accurate legal procedure, but then, the psychologist felt certain, no one knew the accurate legal procedure, least of all the Captain.

They were using the large assembly room where, on ordinary cruises, the crew got together to watch subetheric broadcasts. At this time, the crew were rigidly excluded, though all the scientific personnel were present.

Captain Follenbee sat behind a desk just underneath the subetheric reception cube. Sheffield and Mark Annuncio sat by themselves at his left, faces toward him.

The Captain was not at ease. He alternated between informal

exchanges with the various "witnesses" and sudden super-judicial blasts against whispering among the spectators.

Sheffield and Mark, having met one another in the "courtroom" for the first time since the flight of the air-coaster, shook hands solemnly on the former's initiative. Mark had hung back at first, looking up briefly at the crisscross of tape still present on the shaven patch on Sheffield's skull.

"I'm sorry, Dr. Sheffield. I'm very sorry."

"It's all right, Mark. How have they been treating you?"

"All right, I guess."

The Captain's voice boomed out, "No talking among the accused."

Sheffield retorted in a conversational tone, "Listen, Captain, we haven't had lawyers. We haven't had time to prepare a case."

"No lawyers necessary," said the Captain. "This isn't a court trial on Earth. Captain's investigation. Different thing. Just interested in facts, not legal fireworks. Proceedings can be reviewed back on Earth."

"And we can be dead by then," said Sheffield hotly.

"Let's get on with it," said the Captain, banging his desk with an aluminum T-wedge.

Cimon sat in the front row of the audience, smiling thinly. It was he whom Sheffield watched most uneasily.

The smile never varied as witnesses were called upon to state that they had been informed that the crew were on no account to be told of the true nature of the trip; that Sheffield and Mark had been present when told. A mycologist testified to a conversation he had had with Sheffield which indicated the latter to be well aware of the prohibition.

It was brought out that Mark had been sick for most of the trip out to Junior, that he had behaved erratically after they had landed on Junior.

"How do you explain all that?" asked the Captain.

From the audience, Cimon's calm voice suddenly sounded. "He was frightened. He was willing to do anything that would get him off the planet."

Sheffield sprang to his feet. "His remarks are out of order. He's not a witness."

The Captain banged his T-wedge and said, "Sit down!"

The trial went on. A crew member was called in to testify that Mark had informed them of the first expedition and that Sheffield had stood by while that was done.

Sheffield cried, "I want to cross-examine!"

The Captain said, "You'll get your chance later."

The crewman was shooed out.

Sheffield studied the audience. It seemed obvious that their sympathy was not entirely with the Captain. He was psychologist enough to be able to wonder, even at this point, how many of them were secretly relieved at having left Junior and actually grateful to Mark for having precipitated the matter as he did. Then, too, the obvious kangaroo nature of the court didn't sit well with them. Vernadsky was frowning darkly while Novee stared at Cimon with obvious distaste.

It was Cimon who worried Sheffield. He, the psychologist felt, must have argued the Captain into this and it was he who might insist on the extreme penalty. Sheffield was bitterly regretful of having punctured the man's pathological vanity.

But what really puzzled Sheffield above all was Mark's attitude. He was showing no signs of space-sickness or of unease of any kind. He listened to everything closely but seemed moved by nothing. He acted as though nothing mundane concerned him at the moment; as though certain information he himself held made everything else of no account.

The Captain banged his T-wedge and said, "I guess we have it all. Facts all clear. No argument. We can finish this."

Sheffield jumped up again. "Hold on. Aren't we getting our turn?"

"Quiet," ordered the Captain.

"*You* keep quiet." Sheffield turned to the audience. "Listen, we haven't had a chance to defend ourselves. We haven't even had the right to cross-examine. Is that just?"

There was a murmur that buzzed up above the sound of the T-wedge.

Cimon said coldly, "What's there to defend?"

"Maybe nothing," shouted back Sheffield, "in which case what have you to lose by hearing us? Or are you afraid we have considerable to defend?"

Individual calls from the audience were sounding now. "Let him talk!"

Cimon shrugged. "Go ahead."

The Captain said sullenly, "What do you want to do?"

Sheffield said, "Act as my own lawyer and call Mark Annuncio as witness."

Mark stood up calmly enough. Sheffield turned his chair to face the audience and motioned him down again.

Sheffield decided there was no use in trying to imitate the courtroom dramas he had watched on the subether. Pompous questions on name and condition of past life would get nowhere. Better to be direct.

So he said, "Mark, did you know what would happen when you told the crew about the first expedition?"

"Yes, Dr. Sheffield."

"Why did you do it then?"

"Because it was important that we all get away from Junior without losing a minute. Telling the crew the truth was the fastest way of getting us off the planet."

Sheffield could feel the bad impression that answer made on the audience, but he could only follow his instinct. That, and his psychologist's decision that only special knowledge could make Mark or any Mnemonic so calm in the face of adversity. After all, special knowledge was their business.

He said, "Why was it important to leave Junior, Mark?"

Mark didn't flinch. He looked straight at the watching scientists. "Because I know what killed the first expedition, and it was only a question of time before it killed us. In fact, it may be too late already. We may be dying now. We may, every one of us, be dead men."

Sheffield let the murmur from the audience well up and subside. Even the Captain seemed shocked into T-wedge immobility while Cimon's smile grew quite faint.

For the moment, Sheffield was less concerned with Mark's "knowledge," whatever it was, than that he had acted independently on the basis of it. It had happened before. Mark had searched the ship's log on the basis of a theory of his own. Sheffield felt pure chagrin at not having probed that tendency to the uttermost then and there.

So his next question, asked in a grim enough voice, was, "Why didn't you consult me about this, Mark?"

Mark faltered a trifle. "You wouldn't have believed me. It's why I had to hit you to keep you from stopping me. None of them would have believed me. They all hated me."

"What makes you think they hated you?"

"Well, you remember about Dr. Rodriguez."

"That was quite a while ago. The others had no arguments with you."

"I could tell the way Dr. Cimon looked at me. And Dr. Fawkes wanted to shoot me with a blaster."

"What?" Sheffield whirled, forgetting in his own turn any formality due the trial. "Say, Fawkes, did you try to shoot him?"

Fawkes stood up, face crimson, as all turned to look at him. He said, "I was out in the woods and he came sneaking up on me. I thought it was an animal and took precautions. When I saw it was he, I put the blaster away."

Sheffield turned back to Mark. "Is that right?"

Mark turned sullen again. "Well—I asked Dr. Vernadsky to see some data he had collected and he told me not to publish it before he did. He tried to make out that I was dishonest."

"For the love of Earth, I was only joking," came a yell from the audience.

Sheffield said hurriedly, "Very well, Mark, you didn't trust us and you felt you had to take action on your own. Now, Mark, let's get to the point. What did you think killed the first settlers?"

Mark said, "It might have killed the explorer, Makoyama, too, for all I know except that he died in a crash two months and three days after reporting on Junior, so we'll never know."

"All right, but what is it you're talking about?"

A hush fell over everyone.

Mark looked about and said, "The dust."

There was general laughter, and Mark's cheeks flamed.

Sheffield said, "What do you mean?"

"The dust! The dust in the air. It has beryllium in it. Ask Dr. Vernadsky."

Vernadsky stood up and pushed his way forward. "What's this?"

"Sure," said Mark. "It was in the data you showed me. Beryllium was very high in the crust, so it must be in the dust in the air as well."

Sheffield said, "What if beryllium is there? Let me ask the questions, Vernadsky. Please."

"Beryllium poisoning, that's what. If you breathe beryllium dust, non-healing granulomata, whatever they are, form in the lungs. Anyway, it gets hard to breathe and eventually you die."

A new voice, quite agitated, joined the melee. "What are you talking about? You're no physician." It was Novee.

"I know that," said Mark earnestly, "but I once read a very old book about poisons. It was so old it was printed on actual sheets of paper. The library had some and I went through them because it was such a novelty, you know."

"All right," said Novee. "What did you read? Can you tell me?"

Mark's chin lifted. "I can quote it. Word for word. 'A surprising variety of enzymatic reactions in the body are activated by any of a number of divalent metallic ions of similar ionic radius. Among these are magnesium, manganous, zinc, ferrous, cobaltous, and nickelous ions, as well as others. Against all of these, the beryllium ion, which has a similar charge and size, acts as an inhibitor. Beryllium therefore serves to derange a number of enzyme-catalyzed reactions. Since the lungs have, apparently, no way of excreting beryllium, diverse metabolic derangements causing serious illness and death can result from inhaling dust containing certain beryllium salts. Cases exist in which one known exposure has resulted in death. The onset of symptoms is insidious, being delayed sometimes for as long as three years after exposure. Prognosis is not good.' "

The Captain leaned forward in agitation. "What's all this, Novee? Is what he's saying making sense?"

Novee said, "I don't know if he's right or not, but there's nothing absurd in what he's saying."

Sheffield said sharply, "You mean you don't know if beryllium is poisonous or not."

"No, I don't," said Novee. "I've never read anything about it. No case has ever come up."

"Isn't beryllium used for anything?" Sheffield turned to Vernadsky. "Is it?"

Vernadsky said in vast surprise, "No, it isn't. Damn it, I can't think of a single use. I tell you what, though. In the early days of atomic power, it was used in the primitive uranium piles as a neutron decelerator, along with other things like paraffin and graphite. I'm almost sure of that."

"It isn't used now, though?" asked Sheffield.

"No."

An electronics man said quite suddenly, "I think beryllium-zinc coatings were used in the first fluorescent lights. I seem to recall a mention of that."

"No more, though?" asked Sheffield.

"No."

Sheffield said, "Well then, listen, all of you. In the first place, anything Mark quotes is accurate. That's what the book said. It's my opinion that beryllium is poisonous. In ordinary life, it doesn't matter because the beryllium content of the soil is so low. When man concentrates beryllium to use in nuclear piles or in fluorescent lights or even in alloys, he comes across the toxicity and looks for substitutes.

"He finds substitutes, forgets about beryllium, and eventually forgets about its toxicity. And then we come across an unusual beryllium-rich planet like Junior and we can't figure out what hits us."

Cimon didn't seem to be listening. He said in a low voice, "What does that mean, 'Prognosis is not good.'"

Novee said abstractedly, "It means that if you've got beryllium poisoning, you won't recover."

Cimon fell back in his chair, chewing his lip.

Novee said to Mark, "I suppose the symptoms of beryllium poisoning——"

Mark said at once, "I can give you the full list. I don't understand the words but——"

"Was one of them 'dyspnea'?"

"Yes."

Novee sighed and said, "I say that we get back to Earth as quickly as possible and get under medical investigation."

Cimon said weakly, "But if we won't recover, what use is it?"

Novee said, "Medical science has advanced since the days of books printed on paper. Besides, we may not have received the toxic dose. The first settlers survived for over a year of continuous exposure. We've had only a month, thanks to Mark Annuncio's quick and drastic action."

Fawkes, miserably unhappy, yelled, "For space' sake, Captain, get out of here and get this ship back to Earth."

It amounted to the end of the trial. Sheffield and Mark walked out among the first.

Cimon was the last to stir out of his chair, and when he did, it was with the listless gait of a man already dead in all but fact.

26

The Lagrange System was only a star lost in the receding cluster. Sheffield looked at that large patch of light and said, "So beautiful a planet." He sighed. "Well, let's hope we live. In any case, the government will watch out for beryllium-high planets in the future. There'll be no catching mankind with that particular variety of sucker bait any more."

Mark did not respond to that idealism. The trial was over; the excitement was gone. There were tears in his eyes. He could only think that he might die; and that if he did, there were so many things, so many, many things in the Universe that he would never learn.

THE CURRENTS OF SPACE

Prolog: *A YEAR BEFORE*

The man from Earth came to a decision. It had been slow in coming and developing, but it was here.

It had been weeks since he had felt the comforting deck of his ship and the cool, dark blanket of space about it. Originally, he had intended a quick report to the local office of the Interstellar Spatio-analytic Bureau and a quicker retreat to space. Instead, he had been held here.

It was almost like a prison.

He drained his tea and looked at the man across the table. He said, "I'm not staying any longer."

The other man came to a decision. It had been slow in coming and developing, but it was here. He would need time, much more time. The response to the first letters had been nil. They might have fallen into a star for all they had accomplished.

That had been no more than he had expected, or, rather, no less. But it was only the first move.

It was certain that, while future moves developed, he could not allow the man from Earth to squirm out of reach. He fingered the smooth black rod in his pocket.

He said, "You don't appreciate the delicacy of the problem."

The Earthman said, "What's delicate about the destruction of a planet? I want you to broadcast the details to all of Sark; to everyone on the planet."

"We can't do that. You know it would mean panic."

"You said at first you would do it."

"I've thought it over and it just isn't practical."

The Earthman turned to a second grievance. "The representative of the I.S.B. hasn't arrived."

"I know it. They are busy organizing proper procedures for this crisis. Another day or two."

"Another day or two! It's always another day or two! Are they so busy they can't spare me a moment? They haven't even seen my calculations."

"I have offered to bring your calculations to them. You don't want me to."

"And I still don't. They can come to me or I can go to them." He added violently, "I don't think you believe me. You don't believe Florina will be destroyed."

"I believe you."

"You don't. I know you don't. I see you don't. You're humoring me. You can't understand my data. You're not a Spatio-analyst. I don't even think you're who you say you are. Who are you?"

"You're getting excited."

"Yes, I am. Is that surprising? Or are you just thinking, Poor devil, Space has him. You think I'm crazy."

"Nonsense."

"Sure you do. That's why I want to see the I.S.B. They'll know if I'm crazy or not. They'll know."

The other man remembered his decision. He said, "Now you're not feeling well. I'm going to help you."

"No, you're not," shouted the Earthman hysterically, "because I'm going to walk out. If you want to stop me, kill me, except that you won't dare. The blood of a whole world of people will be on your hands if you do."

The other man began shouting, too, to make himself heard. "I won't kill you. Listen to me, I won't kill you. There's no need to kill you."

The Earthman said, "You'll tie me up. You'll keep me here. Is that what you're thinking? And what will you do when the I.S.B. starts looking for me? I'm supposed to send in regular reports, you know."

"The Bureau knows you're safely with me."

"Do they? I wonder if they know I've reached the planet at all? I wonder if they received my original message?" The Earthman was giddy. His limbs felt stiff.

The other man stood up. It was obvious to him that his decision had come none too soon. He walked slowly about thc long table, toward the Earthman.

He said soothingly, "It will be for your own good." He took the black rod from his pocket.

The Earthman croaked, "That's a psychic probe." His words were slurred, and when he tried to rise, his arms and legs barely quivered.

He said, between teeth that were clenching in rigor, "Drugged!"

"Drugged!" agreed the other man. "Now look, I won't hurt you. It's difficult for you to understand the true delicacy of the matter while you're so excited and anxious about it. I'll just remove the anxiety. Only the anxiety."

The Earthman could no longer talk. He could only sit there. He could only think numbly, Great Space, I've been drugged. He wanted to shout and scream and run, but he couldn't.

The other had reached the Earthman now. He stood there, looking down at him. The Earthman looked up. His eyeballs could still move.

The psychic probe was a self-contained unit. Its wires needed only to be fixed to the appropriate places on the skull. The Earthman watched in panic until his eye muscles froze. He did not feel the fine sting as the sharp, thin leads probed through skin and flesh to make contact with the sutures of his skull bones.

He yelled and yelled in the silence of his mind. He cried, No, you don't understand. It's a planet full of people. Don't you see that you can't take chances with hundreds of millions of living people?

The other man's words were dim and receding, heard from the other end of a long, windy tunnel. "It won't hurt you. In another hour you'll feel well, really well. You'll be laughing at all this with me."

The Earthman felt the thin vibration against his skull and then that faded too.

Darkness thickened and collapsed about him. Some of it never lifted again. It took a year for even parts of it to lift.

One: *THE FOUNDLING*

Rik put down his feeder and jumped to his feet. He was trembling so hard he had to lean against the bare milk-white wall.

He shouted, "I remember!"

They looked at him and the gritty mumble of men at lunch died somewhat. Eyes met his out of faces indifferently clean and indifferently shaven, glistening and white in the imperfect wall illumination. The eyes reflected no great interest, merely the reflex attention enforced by any sudden and unexpected cry.

Rik cried again, "I remember my job. I had a job!"

Someone called, "Shoddop!" and someone else yelled, "Siddown!"

The faces turned away, the mumble rose again. Rik stared blankly along the table. He heard the remark, "Crazy Rik," and a shrug of shoulders. He saw a finger spiral at a man's temple. It all meant nothing to him. None of it reached his mind.

Slowly he sat down. Again he clutched his feeder, a spoonlike affair, with sharp edges and little tines projecting from the front curve of the bowl, which could therefore with equal clumsiness cut, scoop and impale. It was enough for a millworker. He turned it over and stared without seeing at his number on the back of the handle. He didn't have to see it. He knew it by heart. All the others had registration numbers, just as he had, but the others had names also. He didn't. They called him Rik because it meant something like "moron" in the slang of the kyrt mills. And often enough they called him "Crazy Rik."

But perhaps he would be remembering more and more now. This was the first time since he had come to the mill that he had remembered anything at all from before the beginning. If he thought hard! If he thought with all his mind!

All at once he wasn't hungry; he wasn't the least hungry. With a sudden gesture, he thrust his feeder into the jellied briquet of meat and vegetables before him, pushed the food away, and buried his eyes in the heels of his palms. His fingers thrust and clutched at his hair and painstakingly he tried to follow his mind into the pitch from which it had extracted a single item—one muddy, undecipherable item.

Then he burst into tears, just as the clanging bell announced the end of his lunch shift.

Valona March fell in beside him when he left the mill that evening. He was scarcely conscious of her at first, at least as an individual. It was only that he heard his footsteps matched. He stopped and looked at her. Her hair was something between blond and brown. She wore it in two thick plaits that she clamped together with little magnetized green-stoned pins. They were very cheap pins and had a faded look about them. She wore the simple cotton dress which was all that was needed in that mild climate, just as Rik himself needed only an open, sleeveless shirt and cotton slacks.

She said, "I heard something went wrong lunchtime."

She spoke in the sharp, peasant accents one would expect. Rik's own language was full of flat vowels and had a nasal touch. They laughed at him because of it and imitated his way of speaking, but Valona would tell him that that was only their own ignorance.

Rik mumbled, "Nothing's wrong, Lona."

She persisted. "I heard you said you remembered something. Is that right, Rik?"

She called him Rik too. There wasn't anything else to call him. He couldn't remember his real name. He had tried desperately enough. Valona had tried with him. One day she had obtained a torn city directory somehow and had read all the first names to him. None had seemed more familiar than any other.

He looked her full in the face and said, "I'll have to quit the mill."

Valona frowned. Her round, broad face with its flat, high cheekbones was troubled. "I don't think you can. It wouldn't be right."

"I've got to find out more about myself."

Valona licked her lips. "I don't think you should."

Rik turned away. He knew her concern to be sincere. She had obtained the mill job for him in the first place. He had had no experience with mill machinery. Or perhaps he had, but just didn't remember. In any case, Lona had insisted that he was too small for manual labor and they had agreed to give him technical training without charge. Before that, in the nightmarish days when he could scarcely make sounds and when he didn't know what food was for, she had watched him and fed him. She had kept him alive.

He said, "I've got to."

"Is it the headaches again, Rik?"

"No. I really remember something. I remember what my job was before—— *Before!*"

He wasn't sure he wanted to tell her. He looked away. The warm, pleasant sun was at least two hours above the horizon. The monotonous rows of workers' cubicles that stretched out and round the mills were tiresome to look at, but Rik knew that as soon as they topped the rise the field would lie before them in all the beauty of crimson and gold.

He liked to look at the fields. From the very first the sight had soothed and pleased him. Even before he knew that the colors were crimson and gold, before he knew that there were such things as colors, before he could express his pleasure in anything more than a soft gurgle, the headaches would flicker away faster in the fields. In those days Valona would borrow a diamagnetic scooter and take him out of the village every idle-day. They would skim along, a foot above the road, gliding on the cushioned smoothness of the counter-gravity field, until they were miles and miles away from any human habitation and there would be left only the wind against his face, fragrant with the kyrt blossoms.

They would sit beside the road then, surrounded by color and scent, and between them share a food briquet, while the sun glowed down upon them until it was time to return again.

Rik was stirred by the memory. He said, "Let's go to the fields, Lona."

"It's late."

"Please. Just outside town."

She fumbled at the thin money pouch she kept between herself and the soft blue leather belt she wore, the only luxury of dress she allowed herself.

Rik caught her arm. "Let's walk."

They left the highway for the winding, dustless, packed-sand roads half an hour later. There was a heavy silence between them and Valona felt a familiar fear clutching at her. She had no words to express her feelings for him, so she had never tried.

What if he should leave her? He was a little fellow, no taller than herself and weighing somewhat less, in fact. He was still like a helpless child in many ways. But before they had turned his mind off he must have been an educated man. A very important educated man.

Valona had never had any education besides reading and writing and enough trade-school technology to be able to handle mill machinery, but she knew enough to know that all people were not so limited. There was the Townman, of course, whose great knowledge was so helpful to all of them. Occasionally Squires came on inspection tours. She had never seen them close up but once, on a holiday, she had visited the city and seen a group of incredibly gorgeous creatures at a distance. Occasionally the millworkers were allowed to listen to what educated people sounded like. They spoke differently, more fluently, with longer words and softer tones. Rik talked like that more and more as his memory improved.

She had been frightened at his first words. They came so suddenly after long whimpering over a headache. They were pronounced queerly. When she tried to correct him he wouldn't change.

Even then she had been afraid that he might remember too much and then leave her. She was only Valona March. They called her Big Lona. She had never married. She never would. A large, big-footed girl with work-reddened hands like herself could never marry. She had never been able to do more than look at the boys with dumb resentment when they ignored her at the idle-day dinner festivals. She was too big to giggle and smirk at them.

She would never have a baby to cuddle and hold. The other girls did, one after the other, and she could only crowd about for a quick glimpse of something red and hairless with screwed-up eyes, fists impotently clenched, gummy mouth——

"It's your turn next, Lona."

"When will you have a baby, Lona?"

She could only turn away.

But when Rik had come, he was like a baby. He had to be fed and taken care of, brought out into the sun, soothed to sleep when the headaches racked him.

The children would run after her, laughing. They would yell, "Lona's got a boy friend. Big Lona's got a crazy boy friend. Lona's boy friend is a rik."

Later on, when Rik could walk by himself (she had been as proud the day he took his first step as though he were really only one year old, instead of more like thirty-one) and stepped out, unescorted, into the village streets, they had run about him in rings, yelling their laughter and foolish ridicule in order to see a grown man cover his eyes in fear, and cringe, with nothing but whimpers to answer them. Dozens of times she had come charging out of the house, shouting at them, waving her large fists.

Even grown men feared those fists. She had felled her section head with a single wild blow the first day she had brought Rik to work at the mill because of a sniggering indecency concerning them which she overheard. The mill council fined her a week's pay for that incident, and might have sent her to the City for further trial at the Squire's court, but for the Townman's intervention and the plea that there had been provocation.

So she wanted to stop Rik's remembering. She knew she had nothing to offer him; it was selfish of her to want him to stay mind-blank and helpless forever. It was just that no one had ever before depended upon her so utterly. It was just that she dreaded a return to loneliness.

She said, "Are you sure you remember, Rik?"

"Yes."

They stopped there in the fields, with the sun adding its reddening blaze to all that surrounded them. The mild, scented evening breeze would soon spring up, and the checkerboard irrigation canals were already beginning to purple.

He said, "I can trust my memories as they come back, Lona. You know I can. You didn't teach me to speak, for instance. I remembered the words myself. Didn't I? Didn't I?"

She said reluctantly, "Yes."

"I even remember the times you took me out into the fields before I could speak. I keep remembering new things all the time. Yesterday I remembered that once you caught a kyrt fly for me. You held it closed in your hands and made me put my eye to the space between your thumbs so that I could see it flash purple and orange in the darkness. I laughed and tried to force my hand between yours to get it, so that it flew away and left me crying after all. I didn't know it was a kyrt fly then, or anything about it, but it's all very clear to me now. You never told me about that, did you, Lona?"

She shook her head.

"But it did happen, didn't it? I remember the truth, don't I?"

"Yes, Rik."

"And now I remember something about myself from before. There must have been a *before*, Lona."

There must have been. She felt the weight on her heart when she thought that. It was a different before, nothing like the now they lived in. It had been on a different world. She knew that because one word he had never remembered was kyrt. She had to teach him the word for the most important object on all the world of Florina.

"What is it you remember?" she asked.

At this, Rik's excitement seemed suddenly to die. He hung back. "It doesn't make much sense, Lona. It's just that I had a job once, and I know what it was. At least, in a way."

"What was it?"

"I analyzed Nothing."

She turned sharply upon him, peering into his eyes. For a moment she put the flat of her hand upon his forehead, until he moved away irritably. She said, "You don't have a headache again, Rik, have you? You haven't had one in weeks."

"I'm all right. Don't you go bothering me."

Her eyes fell, and he added at once, "I don't mean that you bother me, Lona. It's just that I feel fine and I don't want you to worry."

She brightened. "What does 'analyzed' mean?" He knew words she didn't. She felt very humble at the thought of how educated he must once have been.

He thought a moment. "It means—it means 'to take apart.' You know, like we would take apart a sorter to find out why the scanning beam was out of alignment."

"Oh. But, Rik, how can anyone have a job not analyzing anything? That's not a job."

"I didn't say I didn't analyze anything. I said I analyzed Nothing. With a capital N."

"Isn't that the same thing?" It was coming, she thought. She was beginning to sound stupid to him. Soon he would throw her off in disgust.

"No, of course not." He took a deep breath. "I'm afraid I can't explain though. That's all I remember about that. But it must have been an important job. That's the way it feels. I *couldn't* have been a criminal."

Valona winced. She should never have told him that. She had told herself it was only for his own protection that she warned him, but now she felt that it had really been to keep him bound tighter to herself.

It was when he had first begun to speak. It was so sudden it had frightened her. She hadn't even dared speak to the Townman about it. The next idle-day she had withdrawn five credits from her life-hoard—there would never be a man to claim it as dowry, so that it didn't matter—and taken Rik to a City doctor. She had the name and address on a scrap of paper, but even so it took two frightening hours to find her way to the proper building through the huge pillars that held the Upper City up to the sun.

She had insisted on watching and the doctor had done all sorts of fearful things with strange instruments. When he put Rik's head between two metal objects and then made it glow like a kyrt fly in the night, she had jumped to her feet and tried to make him stop. He called two men who dragged her out, struggling wildly.

Half an hour afterward the doctor came out to her, tall and frowning. She felt uncomfortable with him because he was a Squire, even though he kept an office down in the Lower City, but his eyes were mild, even kind. He was wiping his hands on a little towel, which he tossed into a wastecan, even though it looked perfectly clean to her.

He said, "When did you meet this man?"

She had told him the circumstances cautiously, reducing it to the very barest essentials and leaving out all mention of the Townman and the patrollers.

"Then you know nothing about him?"

She shook her head. "Nothing before that."

He said, "This man has been treated with a psychic probe. Do you know what that is?"

At first she had shaken her head again, but then she said in a dry whisper, "Is it what they do to crazy people, Doctor?"

"And to criminals. It is done to change their minds for their own good. It makes their minds healthy, or it changes the parts that make them want to steal and kill. Do you understand?"

She did. She grew brick-red and said, "Rik never stole anything or hurt anybody."

"You call him Rik?" He seemed amused. "Now look here, how do you know what he did before you met him? It's hard to tell from the condition of his mind now. The probing was thorough and brutal. I can't say how much of his mind has been permanently removed and how much has been temporarily lost through shock. What I mean is that some of it will come back, like his speaking, as time goes on, but not all of it. He should be kept under observation."

"No, no. He's got to stay with me. I've been taking good care of him, Doctor."

He frowned, and then his voice grew milder. "Well, I'm thinking of you, my girl. Not all the bad may be out of his mind. You wouldn't want him to hurt you someday."

At that moment a nurse led out Rik. She was making little sounds to quiet him, as one would an infant. Rik put a hand to his head and stared vacantly, until his eyes focused on Valona; then he held out his hands and cried, feebly, "Lona——"

She sprang to him and put his head on her shoulder, holding him tightly. She said to the doctor, "He wouldn't hurt me, no matter what."

The doctor said thoughtfully, "His case will have to be reported, of course. I don't know how he escaped from the authorities in the condition he must have been in."

"Does that mean they'll take him away, Doctor?"

"I'm afraid so."

"Please, Doctor, don't do that." She wrenched at the handkerchief, in which were the five gleaming pieces of credit-alloy. She said, "You can have it all, Doctor. I'll take good care of him. He won't hurt anyone."

The doctor looked at the pieces in his hand. "You're a millworker, aren't you?"

She nodded.

"How much do they pay you a week?"

"Two point eight credits."

He tossed the coins gently, brought them together in his closed palm with a tinkle of metal, then held them out to her. "Take it, girl. There's no charge."

She accepted them with wonder. "You're not going to tell anyone, Doctor?"

But he said, "I'm afraid I have to. It's the law."

She had driven blindly, heavily, back to the village, clutching Rik to her desperately.

The next week on the hypervideo newscast there had been the

news of a doctor dying in a gyro-crash during a short failure in one of the local transit power-beams. The name was familiar and in her room that night she compared it with that on the scrap of paper. It was the same.

She was sad, because he had been a good man. She had received his name once long before from another worker as a Squire doctor who was good to the mill hands and had saved it for emergencies. And when the emergency had come he had been good to her too. Yet her joy drowned the sorrow. He had not had the time to report Rik. At least, no one ever came to the village to inquire.

Later, when Rik's understanding had grown, she had told him what the doctor had said so that he would stay in the village and be safe.

Rik was shaking her and she left her reveries.

He said, "Don't you hear me? I couldn't be a criminal if I had an important job."

"Couldn't you have done wrong?" she began hesitantly. "Even if you were a big man, you might have. Even Squires——"

"I'm sure I haven't. But don't you see that I've got to find out so that others can be sure? There's no other way. I've got to leave the mill and the village and find out more about myself."

She felt the panic rise. "Rik! That would be dangerous. Why should you? Even if you analyzed Nothing, why is it so important to find out more about it?"

"Because of the other thing I remember."

"What other thing?"

He whispered, "I don't want to tell you."

"You ought to tell somebody. You might forget again."

He seized her arm. "That's right. You won't tell anyone else, will you, Lona? You'll just be my spare memory in case I forget."

"Sure, Rik."

Rik looked about him. The world was very beautiful. Valona had once told him that there was a huge shining sign in the Upper City, miles above it even, that said: "Of all the Planets in the Galaxy, Florina is the Most Beautiful."

And as he looked about him he could believe it.

He said, "It is a terrible thing to remember, but I always remember correctly, when I do remember. It came this afternoon."

"Yes?"

He was staring at her in horror. "Everybody in the world is going to die. Everybody on Florina."

Two: *THE TOWNMAN*

Myrlyn Terens was in the act of removing a book-film from its place on the shelf when the door-signal sounded. The rather pudgy outlines of his face had been set in lines of thought, but now these vanished and changed into the more usual expression of bland caution. He brushed one hand over his thinning, ruddy hair and shouted, "One minute."

He replaced the film and pressed the contact that allowed the covering section to spring back into place and become indistinguishable from the rest of the wall. To the simple millworkers and farmhands he dealt with, it was a matter of vague pride that one of their own number, by birth at any rate, should own films. It lightened, by tenuous reflection, the unrelieved dusk of their own minds. And yet it would not do to display the films openly.

The sight of them would have spoiled things. It would have frozen their none too articulate tongues. They might boast of their Townman's books, but the actual presence of them before their eyes would have made Terens seem too much the Squire.

There were, of course, the Squires as well. It was unlikely in the extreme that any of them would visit him socially at his house, but should one of them enter, a row of films in sight would be injudicious. He was a Townman and custom gave him certain privileges but it would never do to flaunt them.

He shouted again, "I'm coming!"

This time he stepped to the door, closing the upper seam of his tunic as he went. Even his clothing was somewhat Squirelike. Sometimes he almost forgot he had been born on Florina.

Valona March was on the doorstep. She bent her knees and ducked her head in respectful greeting.

Terens threw the door wide. "Come in, Valona. Sit down. Surely it's past curfew. I hope the patrollers didn't see you."

"I don't think so, Townman."

"Well, let's hope that's so. You've got a bad record, you know."

"Yes, Townman. I am very grateful for what you have done for me in the past."

"Never mind. Here, sit down. Would you like something to eat or drink?"

She seated herself, straight-backed, at the edge of a chair and shook her head. "No, thank you, Townman. I have eaten."

It was good form among the villagers to offer refreshment. It was bad form to accept. Terens knew that. He didn't press her.

He said, "Now what's the trouble, Valona? Rik again?"

Valona nodded, but seemed at a loss for further explanation.

Terens said, "Is he in trouble at the mill?"

"No, Townman."

"Headaches again?"

"No, Townman."

Terens waited, his light eyes narrowing and growing sharp. "Well, Valona, you don't expect me to guess your trouble, do you? Come, speak out or I can't help you. You do want help, I suppose."

She said, "Yes, Townman," then burst out, "How shall I tell you, Townman? It sounds almost crazy."

Terens had an impulse to pat her shoulder, but he knew she would shrink from the touch. She sat, as usual, with her large hands buried as far as might be in her dress. He noticed that her blunt, strong fingers were intertwined and slowly twisting.

He said, "Whatever it is, I will listen."

"Do you remember, Townman, when I came to tell you about the City doctor and what he said?"

"Yes, I do, Valona. And I remember I told you particularly that you were never to do anything like that again without consulting me. Do *you* remember that?"

She opened her eyes wide. She needed no spurt to recollect his anger. "I would never do such a thing again, Townman. It's just that I want to remind you that you said you would do everything to help me keep Rik."

"And so I will. Well, then, have the patrollers been asking about him?"

"No. Oh, Townman, do you think they might?"

"I'm sure they won't." He was losing patience. "Now, come, Valona, tell me what is wrong."

Her eyes clouded. "Townman, he says he will leave me. I want you to stop him."

"Why does he want to leave you?"

"He says he is remembering things."

Interest leaped into Terens' face. He leaned forward and almost he reached out to grip her hand. "Remembering things? What things?"

Terens remembered the day Rik had first been found. He had seen the youngsters clustered near one of the irrigation ditches just outside the village. They had raised their shrill voices to call him.

"Townman! Townman!"

He had broken into a run. "What's the matter, Rasie?" He had made it his business to learn the youngsters' names when he came to town. That went well with the mothers and made the first month or two easier.

Rasie was looking sick. He said, "Looky here, Townman."

He was pointing at something white and squirming, and it was Rik. The other boys were yelling at once in confused explanation. Terens managed to understand that they were playing some game that involved running, hiding and pursuing. They were intent on telling him the name of the game, its progress, the point at which they had been interrupted, with a slight subsidiary argument as to exactly which individual or side was "winning." All that didn't matter, of course.

Rasie, the twelve-year-old black-haired one, had heard the whimpering and had approached cautiously. He had expected an animal, perhaps a field rat that would make good chasing. He had found Rik.

All the boys were caught between an obvious sickness and an equally obvious fascination at the strange sight. It was a grown human being, nearly naked, chin wet with drool, whimpering and crying feebly, arms and legs moving about aimlessly. Faded blue eyes shifted in random fashion out of a face that was covered with a brown stubble. For a moment the eyes caught those of Terens and seemed to focus. Slowly the man's thumb came up and inserted itself into his mouth.

One of the children laughed. "Looka him, Townman. He's finger-sucking."

The sudden shout jarred the prone figure. His face reddened and screwed up. A weak whining, unaccompanied by tears, sounded but his thumb remained where it was. It showed wet and pink in contrast to the rest of the dirt-smeared hand.

Terens broke his own numbness at the sight. He said, "All right, look, fellows, you shouldn't be running around here in the kyrt field. You're damaging the crop and you know what that will mean if the farm hands catch you. Get going, and keep quiet about this. And listen, Rasie, you run to Mr. Jencus and get him to come here."

Ull Jencus was the nearest thing to a doctor the town had. He had passed some time as apprentice in the offices of a real doctor in the city and on the strength of it he had been relieved of duty on the farms or in the mills. It didn't work out too badly. He could take temperatures, administer pills, give injections and, most important, he could tell when some disorder was sufficiently serious to warrant a trip to the city hospital. Without such semiprofessional backing, those unfortunates stricken with spinal meningitis or acute appendicitis might suffer intensively but usually not for long. As it was, the foremen muttered and accused Jencus in everything but words of being an accessory after the fact to a conspiracy of malingering.

Jencus helped Terens lift the man into the scooter cart and, as unobtrusively as they might, carried him into town.

Together they washed off the accumulated and hardened grime and filth. There was nothing to be done about the hair. Jencus shaved the entire body and did what he could by way of physical examination.

Jencus said, "No infection I c'n tell of, Townman. He's been fed. Ribs don't stick out too much. *I* don't know what to make of it. How'd he get out there, d'you suppose, Townman?"

He asked the question with a pessimistic tone as though no one could expect Terens to have the answer to anything. Terens accepted that philosophically. When a village has lost the Townman it has grown accustomed to over a period of nearly fifty years, a newcomer of tender age must expect a transition period of suspicion and distrust. There was nothing personal in it.

Terens said, "I'm afraid I don't know."

"Can't walk, y'know. Can't walk a step. He'd have to be *put* there. Near's I c'n make out, he might's well be a baby. Everything else seems t'be gone."

"Is there a disease that has this effect?"

"Not's I know of. Mind trouble might do it, but I don't know nothing 'tall about that. Mind trouble I'd send to the City. Y'ever see this one, Townman?"

Terens smiled and said gently, "I've just been here a month."

Jencus sighed and reached for his handkerchief. "Yes. Old Townman, he was a fine man. Kept us well, he did. *I* been here 'most sixty years, and never saw this fella before. Must be from 'nother town."

Jencus was a plump man. He had the look of having been born plump, and if to this natural tendency is added the effect of a largely sedentary life, it is not surprising that he tended to punctuate even short speeches by a puff and a rather futile swipe at his gleaming forehead with his large red handkerchief.

He said, "Don't 'xactly know what t'say t'the patrollers."

The patrollers came all right. It was impossible to avoid that. The boys told their parents; their parents told one another. Town life was quiet enough. Even this would be unusual enough to be worth the telling in every possible combination of informer and informee. And in all the telling, the patrollers could not help but hear.

The patrollers, so called, were members of the Florinian Patrol. They were not natives of Florina and, on the other hand, they were not countrymen of the Squires from the planet Sark. They were simply mercenaries who could be counted on to keep order for the sake of the pay they got and never to be led into the misguidance of sympathy for Florinians through any ties of blood or birth.

There were two of them and one of the foremen from the mill came with them, in the fullness of his own midget authority.

The patrollers were bored and indifferent. A mindless idiot might be part of the day's work but it was scarcely an exciting part. One said to the foreman, "Well, how long does it take you to make an identification? Who is this man?"

The foreman shook his head energetically. "I never saw him, Officer. He's no one around here!"

The patroller turned to Jencus. "Any papers on him?"

"No, sir. He just had a rag 'bout him. Burned it t'prevent infection."

"What's wrong with him?"

"No mind, near's I c'n make out."

At this point Terens took the patrollers aside. Because they were bored they were amenable. The patroller who had been asking the questions put up his notebook and said, "All right, it isn't even worth making a record of. It has nothing to do with us. Get rid of it somehow."

Then they left.

The foreman remained. He was a freckled man, red of hair, with a large and bristly mustache. He had been a foreman of rigid principles for five years and that meant his responsibility for the fulfillment of quota in his mill rested heavily upon him.

"Look here," he said fiercely. "What's to be done about this? The damn folk are so busy talking, they ain't working."

"Send him t'City hospital, near's I c'n make out," said Jencus, wielding his handkerchief industriously. "Noth'n' I c'n do."

"To the City!" The foreman was aghast. "Who's going to pay? Who'll stand the fees? He ain't none of us, is he?"

"Not's far's I know," admitted Jencus.

"Then why should *we* pay? Find out who he belongs to. Let *his* town pay."

"How we going t'find out? Tell me that."

The foreman considered. His tongue licked out and played with the coarse reddish foliage of his upper lip. He said, "Then we'll just have to get rid of him. Like the patroller said."

Terens interrupted. "Look here. What do you mean by that?"

The foreman said, "He might as well be dead. It would be a mercy."

Terens said, "You can't kill a living person."

"Suppose *you* tell me what to do then."

"Can't one of the townpeople take care of him?"

"Who'd want to? Would you?"

Terens ignored the openly insolent attitude. "I've got other work to do."

"So have all the folk. I can't have anyone neglecting mill work to take care of this crazy thing."

Terens sighed, and said without rancor, "Now, Foreman, let's be reasonable. If you *don't* make quota this quarter I might suppose it's because one of your workers is taking care of this poor fellow, and I'll speak up for you to the Squires. Otherwise I'll just say that I don't know of any reason you couldn't make quota, in case you don't make it."

The foreman glowered. The Townman had only been here a month, and already he was interfering with men who had lived in town all their lives. Still, he had a card marked with Squire's marks. It wouldn't do to stand too openly against him too long.

He said, "But who'd take him?" A horrible suspicion smote him. "*I* can't. I got three kids of my own and my wife ain't well."

"I didn't suggest that you should."

Terens looked out the window. Now that the patrollers had left, the squirming, whispering crowd had gathered closer about the Townman's house. Most were youngsters, too young to be working, others were farm hands from the nearer farms. A few were mill-workers, away from their shifts.

Terens saw the big girl at the very edge of the crowd. He had noticed her often in the past month. Strong, competent, and hard-working. Good natural intelligence hidden under that unhappy expression. If she were a man she might have been chosen for Townman's training. But she was a woman; parents dead, and plain enough she was to preclude romantic side interests. A lone woman, in other words, and likely to remain so.

He said, "What about her?"

The foreman looked, then roared, "Damn it. She ought to be at work."

"All right," soothed Terens. "What's her name?"

"That's Valona March."

"That's right. I remember now. Call her in."

From that moment Terens had made himself an unofficial guardian of the pair. He had done what he could to obtain additional food rations for her, extra clothing coupons and whatever else was required to allow two adults (one unregistered) to live on the income of one. He had been instrumental in helping her obtain training for Rik at the kyrt mills. He had intervened to prevent greater punishment on the occasion of Valona's quarrel with a section head. The death of the City doctor had made it unnecessary for him to attempt further action there than he had taken, but he had been ready.

It was natural for Valona to come to him in all her troubles, and he was waiting now for her to answer his question.

Valona was still hesitating. Finally she said, "He says everyone in the world will die."

Terens looked startled. "Does he say how?"

"He says he doesn't know how. He just says he remembers that from before he was like, you know, like he is. And he says he remembers he had an important job, but I don't understand what it is."

"How does he describe it?"

"He says he an—analyzes Nothing with a capital N."

Valona waited for comment, then hastened to explain, "Analyze means taking something apart like——"

"I know what it means, girl." Terens remained lost.

Valona watched him anxiously. "Do *you* know what he means, Townman?"

"Perhaps, Valona."

"But, Townman, how can anyone do anything to Nothing?"

Terens got to his feet. He smiled briefly. "Why, Valona, don't you know that everything in all the Galaxy is mostly Nothing?"

No light of understanding dawned on Valona, but she accepted that. The Townman was a very educated man. With an unexpected twinge of pride, she was suddenly certain that her Rik was even more educated.

"Come." Terens was holding his hand out to her.

She said, "Where are we going?"

"Well, where's Rik?"

"Home," she said. "Sleeping."

"Good. I'll take you there. Do you want the patrollers to find you on the street alone?"

The village seemed empty of life in the nighttime. The lights along the single street that split the area of workers' cabins in two gleamed without glare. There was a hint of rain in the air, but only of that light warm rain that fell almost every night. There was no need to take special precautions against it.

Valona had never been out so late on a working evening and it was frightening. She tried to shrink away from the sound of her own footsteps, while listening for the possible distant step of the patrollers.

Terens said, "Stop trying to tiptoe, Valona. I'm with you."

His voice boomed in the quiet and Valona jumped. She hurried forward in response to his urging.

Valona's hut was as dark as the rest and they stepped in gingerly. Terens had been born and brought up in just such a hut and though he had since lived on Sark and now occupied a house with three rooms and plumbing, there was still something of a nostalgia about the barrenness of its interior. One room was all that was required, a bed, a chest of drawers, two chairs, a smooth poured-cement floor, a closet in one corner.

There was no need for kitchen facilities, since all meals were eaten at the mill, nor for a bathroom, since a line of community outhouses and shower cells ran along the space behind the houses. In the mild, unvarying climate, windows were not adapted for protection against cold and rain. All four walls were pierced by screened openings and eaves above were sufficient ward against the nightly windless sprinkles.

In the flare of a little pocket light which he held cupped in one palm Terens noted that one corner of the room was marked off by a battered screen. He remembered getting it for Valona rather recently when Rik had become too little of a child or too much of a man. He could hear the regular breathing of sleep behind it.

He nodded his head in that direction. "Wake him, Valona."

Valona tapped on the screen. "Rik! Rik, baby!"

There was a little cry.

"It's only Lona," said Valona. They rounded the screen and Terens played his little light upon their own faces, then upon Rik.

Rik threw an arm up against the glare. "What's the matter?"

Terens sat down on the edge of the bed. Rik slept in the standard cottage bed, he noted. He had obtained for Valona an old, rather rickety cot at the very first, but she had reserved that for herself.

"Rik," he said, "Valona says you're beginning to remember things."

"Yes, Townman." Rik was always very humble before the Townman, who was the most important man he had ever seen. Even the mill superintendent was polite to the Townman. Rik repeated the scraps his mind had gathered during the day.

Terens said, "Have you remembered anything else since you told this to Valona?"

"Nothing else, Townman."

Terens kneaded the fingers of one hand with those of the other. "All right, Rik. Go back to sleep."

Valona followed him out the house. She was trying hard to keep her face from twisting and the back of one rough hand slid across her eyes. "Will he have to leave me, Townman?"

Terens took her hands and said gravely, "You must be a grown woman, Valona. He will have to come with me for just a short while but I'll bring him back."

"And after that?"

"I don't know. You must understand, Valona. Right now it is the most important thing in all the world that we find out more about Rik's memories."

Valona said suddenly, "You mean everybody on Florina might die, the way he says?"

Terens' grip tightened. "Don't ever say that to anyone, Valona, or the patrollers may take Rik away forever. I mean that."

He turned away and walked slowly and thoughtfully back to his house without really noticing that his hands were trembling. He tried futilely to sleep and after an hour of that he adjusted the narco-field. It was one of the few pieces of Sark he had brought with him when he first returned to Florina to become Townman. It fitted about his skull like a thin black felt cap. He adjusted the controls to five hours and closed contact.

He had time to adjust himself comfortably in bed before the delayed response shorted the conscious centers of his cerebrum and blanketed him into instantaneous, dreamless sleep.

Three: *THE LIBRARIAN*

They left the diamagnetic scooter in a scooter-cubby outside the City limits. Scooters were rare in the City and Terens had no wish to attract unnecessary attention. He thought for a savage moment of those of the Upper City with their diamagnetic ground-cars and anti-grav gyros. But that was the Upper City. It was different.

Rik waited for Terens to lock the cubby and fingerprint-seal it. He was dressed in a new one-piece suit and felt a little uncomfortable. Somewhat reluctantly he followed the Townman under the first of the tall bridge-like structures that supported the Upper City.

On Florina, all other cities had names, but this one was simply the "City." The workers and peasants who lived in it and around it were considered lucky by the rest of the planet. In the City there were better doctors and hospitals, more factories and more liquor stores, even a few dribbles of very mild luxury. The inhabitants themselves were somewhat less enthusiastic. They lived in the shadow of the Upper City.

The Upper City was exactly what the name implied, for the City was double, divided rigidly by a horizontal layer of fifty square miles of cementalloy resting upon some twenty thousand steel-girdered pillars. Below in the shadow were the "natives." Above, in the sun, were the Squires. It was difficult to believe in the Upper City that the planet of its location was Florina. The population was almost exclusively Sarkite in nature, together with a sprinkling of patrollers. They were the upper class in all literalness.

Terens knew his way. He walked quickly, avoiding the stares of passers-by, who surveyed his Townman clothing with a mixture of envy and resentment. Rik's shorter legs made his gait less dignified as he tried to keep up. He did not remember very much from his only other visit to the City. It seemed so different now. Then it had been cloudy. Now the sun was out, pouring through the spaced openings in the cementalloy above to form strips of light that made the intervening space all the darker. They plunged through the bright strips in a rhythmic, almost hypnotic fashion.

Oldsters sat on wheeled chairs in the strips, absorbing the warmth and moving as the strip moved. Sometimes they fell asleep and would remain behind in the shade, nodding in their chairs until the squeaking of the wheels when they shifted position woke them. Occasionally mothers nearly blocked the strips with their carriaged offspring.

Terens said, "Now, Rik, stand up straight. We're going up."

He was standing before a structure that filled the space between four square-placed pillars, and from ground to Upper City.

Rik said, "I'm scared."

Rik could guess what the structure was. It was an elevator that lifted to the upper level.

These were necessary, of course. Production was below, but consumption was above. Basic chemicals and raw food staples were shipped into Lower City, but finished plastic ware and fine meals were matters for Upper City. Excess population spawned below; maids, gardeners, chauffeurs, construction laborers were used above.

Terens ignored Rik's expression of fright. He was amazed that his own heart beat so violently. Not fright, of course. Rather a fierce satisfaction that he was going up. He would step all over that sacred cementalloy, stamp on it, scuff his dirt upon it. He could do that as a Townman. Of course he was still only a Florinian native to the Squires, but he was a Townman and he could step on the cementalloy whenever he pleased.

Galaxy, he hated them!

He stopped himself, drew a firm breath and signaled for the elevator. There was no use thinking hate. He had been on Sark for many years; on Sark itself, the center and breeding place of the Squires. He had learned to bear in silence. He ought not forget what he had learned now. Of all times, not now.

He heard the whir of the elevator settling at the lower level, and the entire wall facing him dropped into its slot.

The native who operated the elevator looked disgusted. "Just two of you."

"Just two," said Terens, stepping in. Rik followed.

The operator made no move to restore the fallen wall to its original position. He said, "Seems to me you guys could wait for the two o'clock load and move with it. I ain't supposed to run this thing up and down for no two guys." He spat carefully, making sure that the sputum hit lower-level concrete and not the floor of his elevator.

He went on, "Where's your employment tickets?"

Terens said, "I'm a Townman. Can't you see it by my clothes?"

"Clothes don't mean nothing. Listen, you think I'm risking my job because you maybe picked up some uniform somewheres? Where's your card?"

Terens, without another word, presented the standard document-folder all natives had to carry at all times: registration number, employment certificate, tax receipts. It was open to the crimson of his Townman's license. The operator scanned it briefly.

"Well, maybe you picked that up, too, but that's not my business. You got it and I pass you, though Townman's just a fancy name for a native to my way of figgering. What about the other guy?"

"He's in my charge," said Terens. "He can come with me, or shall we call a patroller and check into the rules?"

It was the last thing Terens wanted but he suggested it with suitable arrogance.

"Awrright! Y'don't have to get sore." The elevator wall moved up, and with a lurch the elevator climbed. The operator mumbled direfully under his breath.

Terens smiled tightly. It was almost inevitable. Those who worked directly for the Squires were only too glad to identify themselves with the rulers and make up for their real inferiority by a tighter adherence to the rules of segregation, a harsh and haughty attitude toward their fellows. They were the "uppermen" for whom the other Florinians reserved their particular hate, unalloyed by the carefully taught awe they felt for the Squires.

The vertical distance traveled was thirty feet, but the door opened again to a new world. Like the native cities of Sark, Upper City was laid out with a particular eye to color. Individual structures, whether dwelling places or public buildings, were inset in an intricate multicolored mosaic which, close at hand, was a meaningless jumble, but at a distance of a hundred yards took on a soft clustering of hues that melted and changed with the angle of view.

"Come on, Rik," said Terens.

Rik was staring wide-eyed. Nothing alive and growing! Just stone and color in huge masses. He had never known houses could be so huge. Something stirred momentarily in his mind. For a second the hugeness was not so strange . . . And then the memory closed down again.

A ground-car flashed by.

"Are those Squires?" Rik whispered.

There had been time for only a glance. Hair close-cropped, wide, flaring sleeves of glossy, solid colors ranging from blue to violet, knickers of a velvety appearance and long, sheer hose that gleamed as if it were woven of thin copper wire. They wasted no glance at Rik and Terens.

"Young ones," said Terens. He had not seen them at such close quarters since he left Sark. On Sark they were bad enough but at least they had been in place. Angels did not fit here, thirty feet over Hell. Again he squirmed to suppress a useless tremble of hatred.

A two-man flatcar hissed up behind them. It was a new model that had built-in air controls. At the moment it was skimming smoothly two inches above surface, its gleaming flat bottom curled upward at all edges to cut air resistance. Still, the slicing of air against its lower surface sufficed to produce the characteristic hiss which meant "patrollers."

They were large, as all patrollers were; broad-faced, flat-cheeked, long, straight black hair, light brown in complexion. To the natives, all patrollers looked alike. The glossy black of their uniforms, enhanced as they were by the startling silver of strategically placed buckles and ornamental buttons, depressed the importance of the face and encouraged the impression of likeness still more.

One patroller was at the controls. The other leaped out lightly over the shallow rim of the car.

He said, "Folder!" stared mechanically and momentarily at it and flipped it back at Terens. "Your business here."

"I intend consulting the library, Officer. It is my privilege."

The patroller turned to Rik. "What about you?"

"I—" began Rik.

"He is my assistant," interposed Terens.

"He has no Townman privileges," said the patroller.

"I'll be responsible for him."

The patroller shrugged. "It's your lookout. Townmen have privileges, but they're not Squires. Remember that, boy."

"Yes, Officer. By the way, could you direct me to the library?"

The patroller directed him, using the thin, deadly barrel of a needle-gun to indicate direction. From their present angle, the library was a blotch of brilliant vermilion deepening into crimson toward the upper stories. As they approached, the crimson crept downward.

Rik said with sudden vehemence, "I think it's ugly."

Terens gave him a quick, surprised glance. He had been accustomed to all this on Sark, but he, too, found the garishness of Upper City somewhat vulgar. But then, Upper City was more Sark than Sark itself. On Sark, not all men were aristocrats. There were even poor Sarkites, some scarcely better off than the average Florinian. Here only the top of the pyramid existed, and the library showed that.

It was larger than all but a few on Sark itself, far larger than Upper City required, which showed the advantage of cheap labor. Terens paused on the curved ramp that led to the main entrance. The color scheme on the ramp gave the illusion of steps, somewhat disconcerting to Rik, who stumbled, but giving the library the proper air of archaism that traditionally accompanied academic structures.

The main hall was large, cold, and all but empty. The librarian behind the single desk it contained looked like a small, somewhat wrinkled pea in a bloated pod. She looked up and half rose.

Terens said quickly, "I'm a Townman. Special privileges. I am responsible for this native." He had his papers ready and marched them before him.

The librarian seated herself and looked stern. She plucked a metal sliver from a slot and thrust it at Terens. The Townman placed his right thumb firmly upon it. The librarian took the sliver and put it in another slot where a dim violet light shone briefly.

She said, "Room 242."

"Thank you."

The cubicles on the second floor had that icy lack of personality that any link in an endless chain would have. Some were filled, their glassite doors frosted and opaque. Most were not.

"Two forty-two," said Rik. His voice was squeaky.

"What's the matter, Rik?"

"I don't know. I feel very excited."

"Ever been in a library before?"

"I don't know."

Terens put his thumb on the round aluminum disk which, five minutes before, had been sensitized to his thumbprint. The clear glass door swung open and, as they stepped within, it closed silently and, as though a blind had been drawn, became opaque.

The room was six feet in each direction, without window or adornment. It was lit by the diffuse ceiling glow and ventilated by a forced-air draft. The only contents were a desk that stretched from wall to wall and an upholstered backless bench between it and the door. On the desk were three "readers." Their frosted-glass fronts slanted backward at an angle of thirty degrees. Before each were the various control-dials.

"Do you know what this is?" Terens sat down and placed his soft, plump hand upon one of the readers.

Rik sat down too.

"Books?" he asked eagerly.

"Well." Terens seemed uncertain. "This is a library, so your guess doesn't mean much. Do you know how to work the reader?"

"No. I don't think so, Townman."

"You're sure? Think about it a little."

Rik tried valiantly. "I'm sorry, Townman."

"Then I'll show you. Look! First, you see, there's this knob, labeled 'Catalog' with the alphabet printed about it. Since we want the encyclopedia first, we'll turn the knob to E and press downward."

He did so and several things happened at once. The frosted glass flared into life and printing appeared upon it. It stood out black on yellow as the ceiling light dimmed. Three smooth panels moved out like so many tongues, one before each reader, and each was centered by a tight light-beam.

Terens snapped a toggle switch and the panels moved back into their recesses.

He said, "We won't be taking notes."

Then he went on, "Now we can go down the list of E's by turning this knob."

The long line of alphabetized materials, titles, authors, catalog numbers flipped upward, then stopped at the packed column listing the numerous volumes of the encyclopedia.

Rik said suddenly, "You press the numbers and letters after the book you want on these little buttons and it shows on the screen."

Terens turned on him. "How do you know? Do you remember that?"

"Maybe I do. I'm not sure. It just seems the right thing."

"Well, call it an intelligent guess."

He punched a letter-number combination. The light on the glass faded, then brightened again. It said: "Encyclopedia of Sark, Volume 54, Sol–Spec."

Terens said, "Now look, Rik, I don't want to put any ideas in your head, so I won't tell you what's in my mind. I just want you to look through this volume and stop at anything that seems familiar. Do you understand?"

"Yes."

"Good. Now take your time."

The minutes passed. Suddenly Rik gasped and sent the dials spinning backward.

When he stopped, Terens read the heading and looked pleased. "You remember now? This isn't a guess? You remember?"

Rik nodded vigorously. "It came to me, Townman. Very suddenly."

It was the article on Spatio-analysis.

"I know what it says," Rik said. "You'll see, you'll see." He was having difficulty breathing normally and Terens, for his part, was almost equally excited.

"See," said Rik, "they always have this part."

He read aloud haltingly, but in manner far more proficient than could be accounted for by the sketchy lessons in reading he had received from Valona. The article said:

" 'It is not surprising that the Spatio-analyst is by temperament an introverted and, often enough, maladjusted individual. To devote the greater part of one's adult life to the lonely recording of the terrible emptiness between the stars is more than can be asked of someone entirely normal. It is perhaps with some realization of this that the Spatio-analytic Institute has adopted as its official slogan the somewhat wry statement, "We Analyze Nothing." ' "

Rik finished with what was almost a shriek.

Terens said, "Do you understand what you've read?"

The smaller man looked up with blazing eyes. "It said, 'We Analyze Nothing.' That's what I remembered. I was one of them."

"You were a Spatio-analyst?"

"Yes," cried Rik. Then, in a lower voice, "My head hurts."

"Because you're remembering?"

"I suppose so." He looked up, forehead furrowed. "I've got to remember more. There's danger. Tremendous danger! I don't know what to do."

"The library's at our disposal, Rik." Terens was watching carefully, weighing his words. "Use the catalog yourself and look up some texts on Spatio-analysis. See where that leads you."

Rik flung himself upon the reader. He was shaking visibly. Terens moved aside to give him room.

"How about Wrijt's *Treatise of Spatio-analytic Instrumentation?*" asked Rik. "Doesn't that sound right?"

"It's all up to you, Rik."

Rik punched the catalog number and the screen burned brightly and steadily. It said, "Please Consult Librarian for Book in Question."

Terens reached out a quick hand and neutralized the screen. "Better try another book, Rik."

"But . . ." Rik hesitated, then followed orders. Another search through the catalog and then he chose Enning's *Composition of Space.*

The screen filled itself once more with a request to consult the librarian. Terens said, "Damn!" and deadened the screen again.

Rik said, "What's the matter?"

Terens said, "Nothing. Nothing. Now don't get panicky, Rik. I just don't quite see——"

There was a little speaker behind the grillwork on the side of the reading mechanism. The librarian's thin, dry voice emerged therefrom and froze them both.

"Room 242! Is there anyone in Room 242?"

Terens answered harshly, "What do you want?"

The voice said, "What book is it you want?"

"None at all. Thank you. We are only testing the reader."

There was a pause as though some invisible consultation was proceeding. Then the voice said with an even sharper edge to it, "The record indicates a reading request for Wrijt's *Treatise of Spatio-*

analytical Instrumentation, and Enning's *Composition of Space*. Is that correct?"

"We were punching catalog numbers at random," said Terens.

"May I ask your reason for desiring those books?" The voice was inexorable.

"I tell you we don't want them. . . . Now stop it." The last was an angry aside to Rik, who had begun whimpering.

A pause again. Then the voice said, "If you will come down to the desk you may have access to the books. They are on a reserved listing and you will have to fill out a form."

Terens held out a hand to Rik. "Let's go."

"Maybe we've broken a rule," quavered Rik.

"Nonsense, Rik. We're leaving."

"We won't fill out the form?"

"No, we'll get the books some other time."

Terens was hurrying, forcing Rik along with him. He strode down the main lobby. The librarian looked up.

"Here now," she cried, rising and circling the desk. "One moment. One moment!"

They weren't stopping for her.

That is, until a patroller stepped in front of them. "You're in an awful hurry, laddies."

The librarian, somewhat breathless, caught up to them. "You're 242, aren't you?"

"Look here," said Terens firmly, "why are we being stopped?"

"Didn't you inquire after certain books? We'd like to get them for you."

"It's too late. Another time. Don't you understand that I don't want the books? I'll be back tomorrow."

"The library," said the woman primly, "at all times endeavors to give satisfaction. The books will be made available to you in one moment." Two spots of red burned high upon her cheekbones. She turned away, hurrying through a small door that opened at her approach.

Terens said, "Officer, if you don't mind——"

But the patroller held out his moderately long, weighted neuronic whip. It could serve as an excellent club, or as a longer-range weapon of paralyzing potentialities. He said, "Now, laddy, why don't you sit down quietly and wait for the lady to come back? It would be the polite thing to do."

The patroller was no longer young, no longer slim. He looked close to retirement age and he was probably serving out his time in quiet vegetation as library guard, but he was armed and the joviality on his swarthy face had an insincere look about it.

Terens' forehead was wet and he could feel the perspiration collecting at the base of his spine. Somehow he had underestimated the situation. He had been sure of his own analysis of the matter, of everything. Yet here he was. He shouldn't have been so reckless. It was his damned desire to invade Upper City, to stalk through the library corridors as though he were a Sarkite. . . .

For a desperate moment he wanted to assault the patroller and then, unexpectedly, he didn't have to.

It was just a flash of movement at first. The patroller started to turn a little too late. The slower reactions of age betrayed him. The neuronic whip was wrenched from his grasp and before he could do more than emit the beginning of a hoarse cry it was laid along his temple. He collapsed.

Rik shrieked with delight, and Terens cried, "Valona! By all the devils of Sark, *Valona!*"

Four: *THE REBEL*

Terens recovered almost at once. He said, "Out. Quickly!" and began walking.

For a moment he had the impulse to drag the patroller's unconscious body into the shadows behind the pillars that lined the main hall, but there was obviously no time.

They emerged onto the ramp, with the afternoon sun making the world bright and warm about them. The colors of Upper City had shifted to an orange motif.

Valona said anxiously, "Come on!" but Terens caught her elbow.

He was smiling, but his voice was hard and low. He said, "Don't run. Walk naturally and follow me. Hold on to Rik. Don't let him run."

A few steps. They seemed to be moving through glue. Were there sounds behind them from the library? Imagination? Terens did not dare look.

"In here," he said. The sign above the driveway he indicated flickered a bit in the light of afternoon. It didn't compete very well with Florina's sun. It said: Ambulance Entrance.

Up the drive, through a side entrance, and between incredibly white walls. They were blobs of foreign material against the aseptic glassiness of the corridor.

A woman in uniform was looking at them from a distance. She hesitated, frowned, began to approach. Terens did not wait for her. He turned sharply, followed a branch of the corridor, then another one. They passed others in uniform and Terens could imagine the uncertainty they aroused. It was quite unprecedented to have natives wandering about unguarded in the upper levels of a hospital. What did one do?

Eventually, of course, they would be stopped.

So Terens felt his heartbeat step up when he saw the unobtrusive door that said: To Native Levels. The elevator was at their level. He herded Rik and Valona within and the soft lurch as the elevator dropped was the most delightful sensation of the day.

There were three kinds of buildings in the City. Most were Lower Buildings, built entirely on the lower level. Workers' houses, ranging up to three stories in height. Factories, bakeries, disposal plants. Others were Upper Buildings: Sarkite homes, theaters, the library, sports arenas. But some few were Doubles, with levels and entrances both below and above; the patroller stations, for instance, and the hospitals.

One could therefore use a hospital to go from Upper City to Lower City and avoid in that manner the use of the large freight elevators with their slow movements and overattentive operators. For a native to do so was thoroughly illegal, of course, but the added crime was a pinprick to those already guilty of assaulting patrollers.

They stepped out upon the lower level. The stark aseptic walls were there still, but they had a faintly haggard appearance as though they were less often scrubbed. The upholstered benches that lined the corridors on the upper level were gone. Most of all there was the uneasy babble of a waiting room filled with wary men and frightened women. A single attendant was attempting to make sense out of the mess, and succeeding poorly.

She was snapping at a stubbled oldster who pleated and unpleated the wrinkled knee of his raveling trousers and who answered all questions in an apologetic monotone.

"Exactly what is your complaint? . . . How long have you had these pains? . . . Ever been to the hospital before? . . . Now look, you people can't expect to bother us over every little thing. You sit down and the doctor will look at you and give you more medicine."

She cried shrilly, "Next!" then muttered something to herself as she looked at the large timepiece on the wall.

Terens, Valona and Rik were edging cautiously through the crowd. Valona, as though the presence of fellow Florinians had freed her tongue of paralysis, was whispering intensely.

"I had to come, Townman. I was so worried about Rik. I thought you wouldn't bring him back and——"

"How did you get to Upper City, anyway?" demanded Terens over his shoulder, as he shoved unresisting natives to either side.

"I followed you and saw you go up the freight elevator. When it came down I said I was with you and he took me up."

"Just like that."

"I shook him a little."

"Imps of Sark," groaned Terens.

"I had to," explained Valona miserably. "Then I saw the patrollers pointing out a building to you. I waited till they were gone and went there too. Only I didn't dare go inside. I didn't know what to do so I sort of hid until I saw you coming out with the patroller stopping——"

"You people there!" It was the sharp, impatient voice of the receptionist. She was standing now, and the hard rapping of her metal stylus on the cementalloy desk top dominated the gathering and reduced them to a hard-breathing silence.

"Those people trying to leave. Come here. You cannot leave without being examined. There'll be no evading workdays with pretended sick calls. Come back here!"

But the three were out in the half shadow of Lower City. There were the smells and noise of what the Sarkites called the Native Quarter about them and the upper level was once more only a roof above them. But however relieved Valona and Rik might feel at being away from the oppressive richness of Sarkite surroundings, Terens felt no lifting of anxiety. They had gone too far and henceforth there might be no safety anywhere.

That thought was still passing through his turbulent mind when Rik called, "Look!"

Terens felt salt in his throat.

It was perhaps the most frightening sight the natives of the Lower

City could see. It was like a giant bird floating down through one of the openings in the Upper City. It shut off the sun and deepened the ominous gloom of that portion of the City. But it wasn't a bird. It was one of the armed ground-cars of the patrollers.

Natives yelled and began running. They might have no specific reason to fear, but they scattered anyway. One man, nearly in the path of the car, stepped aside reluctantly. He had been hurrying on his way, intent on some business of his own, when the shadow caught him. He looked about him, a rock of calm in the wildness. He was of medium height, but almost grotesquely broad across the shoulders. One of his shirt sleeves was slit down its length, revealing an arm like another man's thigh.

Terens was hesitating, and Rik and Valona could do nothing without him. The Townman's inner uncertainty had mounted to a fever. If they ran, where could they go? If they remained where they were, what could they do? There was a chance that the patrollers were after others altogether, but with a patroller unconscious on the library floor through their act, the chances of that were negligible.

The broad man was approaching at a heavy half trot. For a moment he paused in passing them, as though with uncertainty. He said in a conversational voice, "Khorov's bakery is second left, beyond the laundry."

He veered back.

Terens said, "Come on."

He was sweating freely as he ran. Through the uproar, he heard the barking orders that came naturally to patroller throats. He threw one look over his shoulder. A half dozen of them were piling out of the ground-car, fanning out. They would have no trouble, he knew. In his damned Townman's uniform, he was as conspicuous as one of the pillars supporting the Upper City.

Two of the patrollers were running in the right direction. He didn't know whether or not they had seen him, but that didn't matter. Both collided with the broad man who had just spoken to Terens. All three were close enough for Terens to hear the broad man's hoarse bellow and the patrollers' sharp cursing. Terens herded Valona and Rik around the corner.

Khorov's bakery was named as such by an almost defaced "worm" of crawling illuminated plastic, broken in half a dozen places, and was made unmistakable by the wonderful odor that filtered through its open door. There was nothing to do but enter, and they did.

An old man looked out from the inner room within which they could see the flour-obscured gleam of the radar furnaces. He had no chance to ask their business.

Terens began, "A broad man——" He was holding his arms apart in illustration, and the cries of "Patrollers! Patrollers!" began to be heard outside.

The old man said hoarsely, "This way! Quickly!"

Terens held back. "In there?"

The old man said, "This one is a dummy."

First Rik, then Valona, then Terens crawled through the furnace door. There was a faint click and the back wall of the furnace moved slightly and hung freely from hinges above. They pushed through it and into a small room, dimly lit, beyond.

They waited. Ventilation was bad, and the smell of baking increased hunger without satisfying it. Valona kept smiling at Rik, patting his hand mechanically from time to time. Rik stared back at her blankly. Once in a while he put a hand to his flushed face.

Valona began, "Townman——"

He snapped back in a tight whisper, "Not now, Lona. Please!"

He passed the back of his hand across his forehead, then stared at the dampness on his knuckles.

There was a click, magnified by the close confinement of their hiding place. Terens stiffened. Without quite realizing it, he raised clenched fists.

It was the broad man, poking his immense shoulders through the opening. They scarcely fit.

He looked at Terens and was amused. "Come on, man. We're not going to be fighting."

Terens looked at his fists, and let them drop.

The broad man was in markedly poorer condition now than when they had first seen him. His shirt was all but removed from his back and a fresh weal, turning red and purple, marked one cheekbone. His eyes were little and the eyelids crowded them above and below.

He said, "They've stopped looking. If you're hungry, the fare here isn't fancy, but there's enough of it. What do you say?"

It was night in the City. There were lights in the Upper City that lit the sky for miles, but in the Lower City the darkness was clammy.

The shades were drawn tightly across the front of the bakery to hide the illegal, past-curfew lights away from it.

Rik felt better with warm food inside him. His headache began to recede. He fixed his eyes on the broad man's cheek.

Timidly he asked, "Did they hurt you, mister?"

"A little," said the broad one. "It doesn't matter. It happens every day in my business." He laughed, showing large teeth. "They had to admit I hadn't done anything but I was in their way while they were chasing someone else. The easiest way of getting a native out of the way——" His hand rose and fell, holding an invisible weapon, butt-first.

Rik flinched away and Valona reached out an anxious, protective arm.

The broad man leaned back, sucking at his teeth to get out particles of food. He said, "I'm Matt Khorov, but they just call me the Baker. Who are you people?"

Terens shrugged. "Well . . ."

The Baker said, "I see your point. What I don't know won't hurt anyone. Maybe. Maybe. At that, though, you might trust me. I saved you from the patrollers, didn't I?"

"Yes. Thank you." Terens couldn't squeeze cordiality into his voice. He said, "How did you know they were after us? There were quite a few people running."

The other smiled. "None of them had the faces you three were wearing. Yours could have been ground up and used for chalk."

Terens tried to smile in return. He didn't succeed well. "I'm not sure I know why you risked your life. Thank you, anyway. It isn't much, just saying 'Thank you,' but there's nothing else I can do right now."

"You don't have to do anything." The Baker's vast shoulders leaned back against the wall. "I do this as often as I can. It's nothing personal. If the patrollers are after someone I do my best for him. I hate the patrollers."

Valona gasped. "Don't you get into trouble?"

"Sure. Look at this." He put a finger gently on his bruised cheek. "But you don't think I ought to let it stop me, I hope. That's why I built the dummy oven. So the patrollers wouldn't catch me and make things too hard for me."

Valona's eyes were wide with mingled fright and fascination.

The Baker said, "Why not? You know how many Squires there

are on Florina? Ten thousand. You know how many patrollers? Maybe twenty thousand. And there are five hundred million of us natives. If we all lined up against them . . ." He snapped his fingers.

Terens said, "We'd be lining up against needle-guns and blaster-cannon, Baker."

The Baker retorted, "Yeah. We'd have to get some of our own. You Townmen have been living too close to the Squires. You're scared of them."

Valona's world was being turned upside down today. This man fought with patrollers and spoke with careless self-confidence to the Townman. When Rik plucked at her sleeve she disengaged his fingers gently and told him to sleep. She scarcely looked at him. She wanted to hear what this man said.

The broad man was saying, "Even with needle-guns and blaster-cannon, the only way the Squires hold Florina is with the help of a hundred thousand Townmen."

Terens looked offended, but the Baker went on, "For instance, look at you. Very nice clothes. Neat. Pretty. You've got a nice little shack, too, I'll bet, with book-films, a private hopper and no curfew. You can even go to Upper City if you want to. The Squires wouldn't do that for you for nothing."

Terens felt in no position to lose his temper. He said, "All right. What do you want the Townmen to do? Pick fights with the patrollers? What good would it do? I admit I keep my town quiet and up to quota, but I keep them out of trouble. I try to help them, as much as the law will allow. Isn't that something? Someday——"

"Aah, someday. Who can wait for someday? When you and I are dead, what difference will it make who runs Florina? To us, I mean."

Terens said, "In the first place, I hate the Squires more than you do. Still——" He stopped, reddening.

The Baker laughed. "Go ahead. Say it again. I won't turn you in for hating the Squires. What did you do to get the patrollers after you?"

Terens was silent.

The Baker said, "I can make a guess. When the patrollers fell over me they were plenty sore. Sore in person, I mean, and not just because some Squire told them to be sore. I know them and I can tell.

So I figure that there's only one thing that could have happened. You must've knocked down a patroller. Or killed him, maybe."

Terens was still silent.

The Baker lost none of his agreeable tone. "It's all right to keep quiet but there's such a thing as being too cautious, Townman. You're going to need help. They know who you are."

"No, they don't," said Terens hastily.

"They must have looked at your cards in the Upper City."

"Who said I was in the Upper City?"

"A guess. I'll bet you were."

"They looked at my card, but not long enough to read my name."

"Long enough to know you're a Townman. All they have to do is find a Townman missing from his town or one who can't account for his movements today. The wires all over Florina are probably scorching right now. I think you're in trouble."

"Maybe."

"You know there's no maybe. Want help?"

They were talking in whispers. Rik had curled up in the corner and gone to sleep. Valona's eyes were moving from speaker to speaker.

Terens shook his head. "No, thanks. I—I'll get out of this."

The Baker's ready laughter came. "It will be interesting to see how. Don't look down on me because I haven't got an education. I've got other things. Look, you spend the night thinking about it. Maybe you'll decide you can use help."

Valona's eyes were open in the darkness. Her bed was only a blanket thrown on the floor, but it was nearly as good as the beds she was used to. Rik slept deeply on another blanket in an opposite corner. He always slept deeply on days of excitement after his headaches passed.

The Townman had refused a bed and the Baker had laughed (he laughed at everything, it seemed), turned out the light and told him he was welcome to sit up in the darkness.

Valona's eyes remained open. Sleep was far away. Would she ever sleep again? She had knocked down a patroller!

Unaccountably, she was thinking of her father and mother.

They were very misty in her mind. She had almost made herself forget them in the years that had stretched between them and herself. But now she remembered the sound of whispered conversations during the night, when they thought her asleep. She remembered people who came in the dark.

The patrollers had awakened her one night and asked her questions she could not understand but tried to answer. She never saw her parents again after that. They had gone away, she was told, and the next day they had put her to work when other children her age still had two years of play time. People looked after her as she passed and other children weren't allowed to play with her, even when work time was over. She learned to keep to herself. She learned not to speak. So they called her "Big Lona" and laughed at her and said she was a half-wit.

Why did the conversation tonight remind her of her parents?

"Valona."

The voice was so close that its light breath stirred her hair and so low she scarcely heard it. She tensed, partly in fear, partly in embarrassment. There was only a sheet over her bare body.

It was the Townman. He said, "Don't say anything. Just listen. I am leaving. The door isn't locked. I'll be back, though. Do you hear me? Do you understand?"

She reached in the darkness, caught his hand, pressed it with her fingers. He was satisfied.

"And watch Rik. Don't let him out of your sight. And Valona." There was a long pause. Then he went on, "Don't trust this Baker too much. I don't know about him. Do you understand?"

There was a faint noise of motion, an even fainter distant creak, and he was gone. She raised herself to one elbow and, except for Rik's breathing and her own, there was only silence.

She put her eyelids together in the darkness, squeezing them, trying to think. Why did the Townman, who knew everything, say this about the Baker, who hated patrollers and had saved them? Why?

She could think of only one thing. He had been there. Just when things looked as black as they could be, the Baker had come and had acted quickly. It was almost as though it had been arranged or as if the Baker had been waiting for it all to happen.

She shook her head. It seemed strange. If it weren't for what the Townman had said, she would never think this.

The silence was broken into quivering pieces by a loud and unconcerned remark. "Hello? Still here?"

She froze as a beam of light caught her full. Slowly she relaxed and bunched the sheet about her neck. The beam fell away.

She did not have to wonder about the identity of the new speaker. His squat broad form bulked in the half-light that leaked backward from the flash.

The Baker said, "You know, I thought you'd go with him."

Valona said weakly, "Who, sir?"

"The Townman. You know he left, girl. Don't waste time pretending."

"He'll be back, sir."

"Did he say he would be back? If he did, he's wrong. The patrollers will get him. He's not a very smart man, the Townman, or he'd know when a door is left open for a purpose. Are you planning to leave too?"

Valona said, "I'll wait for the Townman."

"Suit yourself. It will be a long wait. Go when you please."

His light-beam suddenly left her altogether and traveled along the floor, picking out Rik's pale, thin face. Rik's eyelids crushed together automatically, at the impact of the light, but he slept on.

The Baker's voice grew thoughtful. "But I'd just as soon you left that one behind. You understand that, I suppose. If you decide to leave, the door is open, but it isn't open for *him*."

"He's just a poor, sick fellow——" Valona began in a high, frightened voice.

"Yes? Well, I collect poor sick fellows and that one stays here. Remember!"

The light-beam did not move from Rik's sleeping face.

Five: *THE SCIENTIST*

Dr. Selim Junz had been impatient for a year, but one does not become accustomed to impatience with time. Rather the reverse. Nevertheless the year had taught him that the Sarkite Civil Service could not be hurried; all the more so since the civil servants themselves were largely transplanted Florinians and therefore dreadfully careful of their own dignity.

He had once asked old Abel, the Trantorian Ambassador, who had lived on Sark so long that the soles of his boots had grown roots, why the Sarkites allowed their government departments to be run by the very people they despised so heartily.

Abel had wrinkled his eyes over a goblet of green wine.

"Policy, Junz," he said. "Policy. A matter of practical genetics, carried out with Sarkite logic. They're a small, no-account world, these Sarkites, in themselves, and are only important so long as they control that everlasting gold mine, Florina. So each year they skim Florina's fields and villages, bringing the cream of its youth to Sark for training. The mediocre ones they set to filing their papers and filling their blanks and signing their forms and the really clever ones they send back to Florina to act as native governors for the towns. Townmen they call them."

Dr. Junz was a Spatio-analyst, primarily. He did not quite see the point of all this. He said so.

Abel pointed a blunt old forefinger at him and the green light shining through the contents of his goblet touched the ridged fingernail and subdued its yellow-grayness.

He said, "You will never make an administrator. Ask me for no recommendations. Look, the most intelligent elements of Florina are won over to the Sarkite cause wholeheartedly, since while they serve Sark they are well taken care of, whereas if they turn their backs on Sark the best they can hope for is a return to a Florinian existence, which is not good, friend, not good."

He swallowed the wine at a draught and went on. "Further, neither the Townmen nor Sark's clerical assistants may breed without losing their positions. Even with female Florinians, that is. Interbreeding with Sarkites is, of course, out of the question. In this way the best of the Florinian genes are being continually withdrawn from circulation, so that gradually Florina will be composed only of hewers of wood and drawers of water."

"They'll run out of clerks at that rate, won't they?"

"A matter for the future."

So Dr. Junz sat now in one of the outer anterooms of the Department for Florinian Affairs and waited impatiently to be allowed past the slow barriers, while Florinian underlings scurried endlessly through a bureaucratic maze.

An elderly Florinian, shriveled in service, stood before him.

"Dr. Junz?"

"Yes."

"Come with me."

A flashing number on a screen would have been as efficient in summoning him and a fluro-channel through the air as efficient in guiding him, but where manpower is cheap, nothing need be substituted. Dr. Junz thought "manpower" advisedly. He had never seen women in any government department on Sark. Florinian women were left on their planet, except for some house servants who were likewise forbidden to breed, and Sarkite women were, as Abel said, out of the question.

He was gestured to a seat before the desk of the Clerk to the Undersecretary. He knew the man's title from the channeled glow etched upon the desk. No Florinian could, of course, be more than a clerk, regardless of how much of the actual threads of office ran through his white fingers. The Undersecretary and the Secretary of Florinian Affairs would themselves be Sarkites, but though Dr. Junz might meet them socially, he knew he would never meet them here in the department.

He sat, still impatiently, but at least nearer the goal. The Clerk was glancing carefully through the file, turning each minutely coded sheet as though it held the secrets of the universe. The man was quite young, a recent graduate perhaps, and like all Florinians, very fair of skin and light of hair.

Dr. Junz felt an atavistic thrill. He himself came from the world of Libair, and like all Libairians, he was highly pigmented and his skin was a deep, rich brown. There were few worlds in the Galaxy in which the skin color was so extreme as on either Libair or Florina. Generally, intermediate shades were the rule.

Some of the radical young anthropologists were playing with the notion that men of worlds like Libair, for instance, had arisen by independent but convergent evolution. The older men denounced bitterly any notion of an evolution that converged different species to the point where interbreeding was possible, as it certainly was among all the worlds in the Galaxy. They insisted that on the original planet, whatever it was, mankind had already been split into subgroups of varying pigmentation.

This merely placed the problem farther back in time and answered nothing so that Dr. Junz found neither explanation satisfying. Yet even now he found himself thinking of the problem at times. Legends of a past of conflict had lingered, for some reason, on the dark worlds. Libairian myths, for instance, spoke of times of war between men of different pigmentation and the founding of Libair itself was held due to a party of browns fleeing from a defeat in battle.

When Dr. Junz left Libair for the Arcturian Institute of Spatial Technology and later entered his profession, the early fairy tales were forgotten. Only once since then had he really wondered. He had happened upon one of the ancient worlds of the Centaurian Sector in the course of business; one of those worlds whose history could be counted in millennia and whose language was so archaic that its dialect might almost be that lost and mythical language, English. They had a special word for a man with dark skin.

Now why should there be a special word for a man with dark skin? There was no special word for a man with blue eyes, or large ears, or curly hair. There was no——

The Clerk's precise voice broke his reverie. "You have been at this office before, according to the record."

Dr. Junz said with some asperity, "I have indeed, sir."

"But not recently."

"No, not recently."

"You are still in search of a Spatio-analyst who disappeared"—the Clerk flipped sheets—"some eleven months and thirteen days ago."

"That's right."

"In all that time," said the Clerk in his dry, crumbly voice out of which all the juice seemed carefully pressed, "there has been no sign of the man and no evidence to the effect that he ever was anywhere in Sarkite territory."

"He was last reported," said the scientist, "in space near Sark."

The Clerk looked up and his pale blue eyes focused for a moment on Dr. Junz, then dropped quickly. "This may be so, but it is not evidence of his presence *on* Sark."

Not evidence! Dr. Junz's lips pressed tightly together. It was what the Interstellar Spatio-analytic Bureau had been telling him with increasing bluntness for months.

No evidence, Dr. Junz. We feel that your time might be better employed, Dr. Junz. The Bureau will see to it that the search is maintained, Dr. Junz.

What they really meant was, Stop wasting our dough, Junz!

It had begun, as the Clerk had carefully stated, eleven months and thirteen days ago by Interstellar Standard Time (the Clerk would, of course, not be guilty of using local time on a matter of this nature).

Two days before that he had landed on Sark on what was to be a routine inspection of the Bureau's offices on that planet, but which turned out to be—well, which turned out to be what it was.

He had been met by the local representative of the I.S.B., a wispy young man who was marked in Dr. Junz's thoughts chiefly by the fact that he chewed, incessantly, some elastic product of Sark's chemical industry.

It was when the inspection was almost over and done with that the local agent had recalled something, parked his lasto-plug in the space behind his molars and said, "Message from one of the field men, Dr. Junz. Probably not important. You know *them*."

It was the usual expression of dismissal: You know *them*. Dr. Junz looked up with a momentary flash of indignation. He was about to say that fifteen years ago he himself had been a "field man," then he remembered that after three months he had been able to endure it no longer. But it was that bit of anger that made him read the message with an earnest attention.

It went: *Please keep direct coded line open to I.S.B. Central HQ for detailed message involving matter of utmost importance. All Galaxy affected. Am landing by minimum trajectory.*

The agent was amused. His jaws had gone back to their rhythmic champing and he said, "Imagine, sir. 'All Galaxy affected.' That's pretty good, even for a field man. I called him after I got this to see if I could make any sense out of him, but that flopped. He just kept saying that the life of every human being on Florina was in danger. You know, half a billion lives at stake. He sounded very psychopathic. So, frankly, I don't want to try to handle him alone when he lands. What do you suggest?"

Dr. Junz had said, "Do you have a transcript of your talk?"

"Yes, sir." There was a few minutes searching. A sliver of film was finally found.

Dr. Junz ran it through the reader. He frowned. "This is a copy, isn't it?"

"I sent the original to the Bureau of Extra-Planetary Transportation here on Sark. I thought it would be best if they met him on the landing field with an ambulance. He's probably in a bad way."

Dr. Junz felt the impulse to agree with the young man. When the lonely analysts of the depths of space finally broke over their jobs, their psychopathies were likely to be violent.

Then he said, "But wait. You sound as though he hasn't landed yet."

The agent looked surprised. "I suppose he has, but nobody's called me about it."

"Well, call Transportation and get the details. Psychopathic or not, the details must be on our records."

The Spatio-analyst had stopped in again the next day on a last-minute check before he left the planet. He had other matters to attend to on other worlds, and he was in a moderate hurry. Almost at the doorway, he said, over his shoulder, "How's our field man doing?"

The agent said, "Oh, say—I meant to tell you. Transportation hasn't heard from him. I sent out the energy pattern of his hyper-atomic motors and they say his ship is nowhere in near space. The guy must have changed his mind about landing."

Dr. Junz decided to delay his departure for twenty-four hours. The next day he was at the Bureau of Extra-Planetary Transportation in Sark City, capital of the planet. He met the Florinian bureaucracy for the first time and they shook their heads at him. They had received the message concerning the prospective landing of an analyst of the I.S.B. Oh yes, but no ship had landed.

But it was important, Dr. Junz insisted. The man was very sick. Had they not received a copy of the transcript of his talk with the local I.S.B. agent? They opened their eyes wide at him. Transcript? No one could be found who remembered receiving that. They were sorry if the man were sick, but no I.S.B. ship had landed, and no I.S.B. ship was anywhere in near space.

Dr. Junz went back to his hotel room and thought many thoughts. The new deadline for his leaving passed. He called the desk and arranged to be moved to another suite more adapted to an extended occupancy. Then he arranged an appointment with Ludigan Abel, the Trantorian Ambassador.

He spent the next day reading books on Sarkite history, and when it was time for the appointment with Abel, his heart had become a slow drumbeat of anger. He was not going to quit easily, he knew that.

The old Ambassador treated it as a social call, pumped his hand, had his mechanical bartender rolled in, and would not allow any discussion of business over the first two drinks. Junz used the opportunity for worthwhile small talk, asked about the Florinian Civil Service and received the exposition on the practical genetics of Sark. His sense of anger deepened.

Junz always remembered Abel as he had been that day. Deep-set eyes half closed under startling white eyebrows, beaky nose hovering intermittently over his goblet of wine, insunken cheeks accentuating the thinness of his face and body, and a gnarled finger slowly keeping time to some unheard music. Junz began his story, telling it with stolid economy. Abel listened carefully and without interruption.

When Junz was finished, he dabbed delicately at his lips and said, "Look now, do you know this man who has disappeared?"

"No."

"Nor met him?"

"Our field analysts are hard men to meet."

"Has he had delusions before this?"

"This is his first, according to the records at central I.S.B. offices, if it is a delusion."

"If?" The Ambassador did not follow that up. He said, "And why have you come to me?"

"For help."

"Obviously. But in what way? What can I do?"

"Let me explain. The Sarkite Bureau of Extra-Planetary Transportation has checked near space for the energy pattern of the motors of our man's ship, and there is no sign of it. They wouldn't be lying about that. I do not say that the Sarkites are above lying, but they are certainly above useless lying, and they must know that I can have the matter checked in the space of two or three hours."

"True. What then?"

"There are two times when an energy-pattern trace will fail. One, when the ship is not in near space, because it has jumped through hyperspace and is in another region of the Galaxy, and two, when it is not in space at all because it has landed on a planet. I cannot believe our man has jumped. If his statements about peril to Florina and Galactic importance are megalomanic delusions, nothing would stop him from coming to Sark to report on them. He would *not* have changed his mind and left. I've had fifteen years experience with such things. If, by any chance, his statements were sane and real, then certainly the matter would be too serious to allow him to change his mind and leave near space."

The old Trantorian lifted a finger and waved it gently. "Your conclusion then is that he is on Sark."

"Exactly. Again, there are two alternatives. First, if he *is* in the grip of a psychosis, he may have landed anywhere on the planet other than at a recognized spaceport. He may be wandering about, sick and semi-amnesiac. These things are very unusual, even for field men, but they have happened. Usually, in such a case, the fits are temporary. As they pass, the victim finds the details of his job returning first, before any personal memories at all. After all, the Spatio-analyst's job is his life. Very often the amnesiac is picked up because he wanders into a public library to look up references on Spatio-analysis."

"I see. Then you want to have me help you arrange with the Board of Librarians to have such a situation reported to you."

"No, because I don't anticipate any trouble there. I will ask that certain standard works on Spatio-analysis be placed on reserve and that any man asking for them, other than those who can prove they are native Sarkians, be held for questioning. They will agree to that because they will know, or certain of their superiors will know, that such a plan will come to nothing."

"Why not?"

"Because," and Junz was speaking rapidly now, caught up in a trembling cloud of fury, "I am certain that our man landed at Sark City spaceport exactly as he planned and, sane or psychotic, was then possibly imprisoned but probably killed by the Sarkite authorities."

Abel put down his nearly empty glass. "Are you joking?"

"Do I look as if I were? What did you tell me just half an hour ago about Sark? Their lives, prosperity and power depend upon their control of Florina. What has all my own reading in this past twenty-four hours shown me? That the kyrt fields of Florina are the wealth of Sark. And here comes a man, sane or psychotic, it doesn't matter, who claims that something of Galactic importance has put the life of every man and woman on Florina in danger. Look at this transcript of our man's last known conversation."

Abel picked up the sliver of film that had been dashed upon his lap by Junz and accepted the reader held out to him. He ran it through slowly, his faded eyes blinking and peering at the eyepiece.

"It's not very informative."

"Of course not. It says there is a danger. It says there is horrible urgency. That's all. But it should never have been sent to the Sarkites. Even if the man were wrong, could the Sarkite government allow him to broadcast whatever madness, granting it be madness, he has in his mind and fill the Galaxy with it? Leaving out of consideration the panic it might give rise to on Florina, the interference with the production of kyrt thread, it remains a fact that the whole dirty mess of Sark-Florina political relationships would be exposed to the view of the Galaxy as a whole. Consider that they need do away with only one man to prevent all that, since I can't take action on this transcript alone and they know it. Would Sark hesitate to stop at murder in such a case? The world of such genetic experimenters as you describe would not hesitate."

"And what would you have me do? I am still, I must say, not certain." Abel seemed unmoved.

"Find out if they have killed him," said Junz grimly. "You must have an organization for espionage here. Oh, let's not quibble. I have been knocking about the Galaxy long enough to have passed my political adolescence. Get to the bottom of this while I distract their attention with my library negotiations. And when you find them out for the murderers they are, I want Trantor to see to it that no government anywhere in the Galaxy ever again has the notion it can kill an I.S.B. man and get away with it."

And there his first interview with Abel had ended.

Junz was right in one thing. The Sarkite officials were co-operative and even sympathetic as far as making library arrangements were concerned.

But he seemed right in nothing else. Months passed, and Abel's agents could find no trace of the missing field man anywhere on Sark, alive or dead.

For over eleven months that held true. Almost, Junz began to feel ready to quit. Almost, he decided to wait for the twelfth month to be done and then no more. And then the break had come and it was not from Abel at all, but from the nearly forgotten straw man he had himself set up. A report came from Sark's Public Library and Junz found himself sitting across the desk from a Florinian civil servant in the Bureau of Florinian Affairs.

The Clerk completed his mental arrangement of the case. He had turned the last sheet.

He looked up. "Now what can I do for you?"

Junz spoke with precision. "Yesterday, at 4:22 P.M., I was informed that the Florinian branch of the Public Library of Sark was holding a man for me who had attempted to consult two standard texts on Spatio-analysis and who was not a native Sarkite. I have not heard from the library since."

He continued, raising his voice to override some comment begun by the Clerk. He said, "A tele-news bulletin received over a public instrument owned by the hotel at which I maintain residence, and timed 5:05 P.M. yesterday, claimed that a member of the Florinian Patrol had been knocked unconscious in the Florinian branch of the Public Library of Sark and that three native Florinians believed responsible for the outrage were being pursued. That bulletin was not repeated in later news-broadcast summaries.

"Now I have no doubt that the two pieces of information are connected. I have no doubt that the man I want is in the custody of the Patrol. I have asked for permission to travel to Florina and been refused. I have subethered Florina to send the man in question to Sark and have received no answer. I come to the Bureau of Florinian Affairs to demand action in this respect. Either I go there or he comes here."

The Clerk's lifeless voice said, "The government of Sark cannot accept ultimata from officers of the I.S.B. I have been warned by my superiors that you would probably be questioning me in these matters and I have been instructed as to the facts I am to make known to you. The man who was reported to be consulting the reserved texts, along with two companions, a Townman and a Florinian female, did indeed commit the assault you referred to, and they were pursued by the Patrol. They were not, however, apprehended."

A bitter disappointment swept over Junz. He did not bother to try to hide it. "They have escaped?"

"Not exactly. They were traced to the bakery shop of one Matt Khorov."

Junz stared. "And allowed to remain there?"

"Have you been in conference with His Excellency, Ludigan Abel, lately?"

"What has that to do with——"

"We are informed that you have been frequently seen at the Trantorian Embassy."

"I have not seen the Ambassador in a week."

"Then I suggest you see him. We allowed the criminals to remain unharmed at Khorov's shop out of respect for our delicate interstellar relationships with Trantor. I have been instructed to tell you, if it seemed necessary, that Khorov, as you probably will not be surprised to hear," and here the white face took on something uncommonly like a sneer, "is well known to our Department of Security as an agent of Trantor."

Six: *THE AMBASSADOR*

It was ten hours before Junz had his interview with the Clerk that Terens left Khorov's bakery.

Terens kept a hand on the rough surfaces of the workers' hovels he passed, as he stepped gingerly along the alleys of the City. Except for the pale light that washed down in a periodic glimmer from the Upper City, he was in total darkness. What light might exist in Lower City would be the pearly flashes of the patrollers, marching in twos and threes.

Lower City lay like a slumbering noxious monster, its greasy coils hidden by the glittering cover of Upper City. Parts of it probably maintained a shadowy life as produce was brought in and stored for the coming day, but that was not here, not in the slums.

Terens shrank into a dusty alley (even the nightly showers of Florina could scarcely penetrate into the shadowy regions beneath the cementalloy) as the distant clank of footsteps reached him. Lights appeared, passed, and disappeared a hundred yards away.

All night long the patrollers marched back and forth. They needed only to march. The fear they inspired was strong enough to maintain order with scarcely any display of force. With no City lights, the darkness might well be cover for innumerable crawling humans, but even without patrollers as a distant threat, that danger could have been discounted. The food stores and workshops were well guarded; the luxury of Upper City was unattainable; and to steal from one another, to parasitize on one another's misery, was obviously futile.

What would be considered crime on other worlds was virtually nonexistent here in the dark. The poor were at hand but had been picked clean, and the rich were strictly out of reach.

Terens flitted on, his face gleaming white when he passed under one of the openings in the cementalloy above, and he could not help but look up.

Out of reach!

Were they indeed out of reach? How many changes in attitude toward the Squires of Sark had he endured in his life? As a child, he had been but a child. Patrollers were monsters in black and silver, from whom one fled as a matter of course, whether one had done wrong or not. The Squires were misty and mystical supermen, enormously good, who lived in a paradise known as Sark and brooded watchfully and patiently over the welfare of the foolish men and women of Florina.

He would repeat every day in school: May the Spirit of the Galaxy watch over the Squires as they watch over us.

Yes, he thought now, exactly. Exactly! Let the Spirit be to them as they to us. No more and no less. His fists clenched and burned in the shadows.

When he was ten, he had written an essay for school about what he imagined life to be like on Sark. It had been a work of purely creative imagination, designed to show off his penmanship. He remembered very little, only one passage in fact. In that, he described the Squires, gathering every morning in a great hall with colors like those of the kyrt blossoms and standing about gravely in twenty-foot-high splendor, debating on the sins of the Florinians and sorrowfully somber over the necessities of winning them back to virtue.

The teacher had been very pleased, and at the end of the year, when the other boys and girls proceeded with their short sessions on reading, writing and morality, he had been promoted to a special class where he learned arithmetic, galactography, and Sarkite history. At the age of sixteen he had been taken to Sark.

He could still remember the greatness of that day, and he shuddered away from the memory. The thought of it shamed him.

Terens was approaching the outskirts of the city now. An occasional breeze brought him the heavy night odor of the kyrt blossoms. A few minutes now and he would be out in the relative safety of the open fields where there were no regular patroller beats and where, through the ragged night clouds, he would see the stars again. Even the hard, bright yellow star that was Sark's sun.

It had been *his* sun for half his life. When he first saw it through a spaceship's porthole as more than a star, as an unbearably bright little marble, he wanted to get on his knees. The thought that he was approaching paradise removed even the paralyzing fright of his first space flight.

He had landed on his paradise, and been delivered to an old Florinian who saw to it that he was bathed and clothed becomingly. He was brought to a large building, and on the way there his elderly guide had bowed low to a figure that passed.

"Bow!" the old one muttered angrily to the young Terens.

Terens did so and was confused. "Who was that?"

"A Squire, you ignorant farm hand."

"He! A Squire?"

He stopped dead in his tracks and had to be urged forward. It was his first sight of a Squire. Not twenty feet tall at all, but a man like men. Other Florinian youths might have recovered from the shock of such a disillusion, but not Terens. Something changed inside him, changed permanently.

In all the training he received, through all the studies in which he did so well, he never forgot that Squires were men.

For ten years he studied, and when he neither studied nor ate nor slept, he was taught to make himself useful in many small ways. He was taught to run messages and empty wastebaskets, to bow low when a Squire passed and to turn his face respectfully to the wall when a Squire's Lady passed.

For five more years he worked in the Civil Service, shifted as usual from post to post in order that his capacities might best be tested under a variety of conditions.

A plump, soft Florinian visited him once, smiling his friendship, pinching his shoulder gently, and asked what he thought of the Squires.

Terens repressed a desire to turn away and run. He wondered if his thoughts could have imprinted themselves in some obscure code upon the lines of his face. He shook his head, murmured a string of banalities on the goodness of the Squires.

But the plump one stretched his lips and said, "You don't mean that. Come to this place tonight." He gave him a small card, that crumbled and charred in a few minutes.

Terens went. He was afraid, but very curious. There he met friends of his, who looked at him with secrecy in their eyes and who met him at work later with bland glances of indifference. He listened to what they said and found that many seemed to believe what he had been hoarding in his own mind and honestly had thought to be his own creation and no one else's.

He learned that at least some Florinians thought the Squires to be vile brutes who milked Florina of its riches for their own useless good while they left the hard-working natives to wallow in ignorance and poverty. He learned that the time was coming when there would be a giant uprising against Sark and all the luxury and wealth of Florina would be appropriated by their rightful owners.

How? Terens asked. He asked it over and over again. After all, the Squires and the patrollers had the weapons.

And they told him of Trantor, of the gigantic empire that had swollen in the last few centuries until half the inhabited worlds of the Galaxy were part of it. Trantor, they said, would destroy Sark with the help of the Florinians.

But, said Terens, first to himself, then to others, if Trantor was so large and Florina so small, would not Trantor simply replace Sark as a still larger and more tyrannical master? If that were the only escape, Sark was to be endured in preference. Better the master they knew than the master they knew not.

He was derided and ejected, with threats against his life if he ever talked of what he had heard.

But some time afterward, he noted that one by one those of the conspiracy disappeared, until only thc original plump one was left.

Occasionally he saw that one whisper to some newcomer here and there, but it would not have been safe to warn the young victim that he was being presented with a temptation and a test. He would have to find his own way, as had Terens.

Terens even spent some time in the Department of Security, which only a few Florinians could ever expect to accomplish. It was a short stay, for the power attached to an official in Security was such that the time spent there by any individual was even shorter than elsewhere.

But here Terens found, somewhat to his surprise, that there were real conspiracies to be countered. Somehow men and women met on Florina and plotted rebellion. Usually these were surreptitiously supported by Trantorian money. Sometimes the would-be rebels actually thought Florina could succeed unaided.

Terens meditated on the matter. His words were few, his bearing correct, but his thoughts ranged unchecked. The Squires he hated, partly because they were not twenty feet tall, partly because he might not look at their women, and partly because he had served a few, with bowed head, and had found that for all their arrogance they were foolish creatures no better educated than himself and usually far less intelligent.

Yet what alternative to this personal slavery was there? To exchange the stupid Sarkite Squire for the stupid Trantorian Imperial was useless. To expect the Florinian peasants to do something on their own was fantastically foolish. So there was no way out.

It was the problem that had been in his mind for years, as student, as petty official, and as Townman.

And then there had arisen the peculiar set of circumstances that put an undreamed-of answer in his hands in the person of this insignificant-looking man who had once been a Spatio-analyst and who now babbled of something that put the life of every man and woman on Florina in danger.

Terens was out in the fields now, where the night rain was ending and the stars gleamed wetly among the clouds. He breathed deeply of the kyrt that was Florina's treasure and her curse.

He was under no illusions. He was no longer a Townman. He was not even a free Florinian peasant. He was a criminal on the run, a fugitive who must hide.

Yet there was a burning in his mind. For the last twenty-four hours he had had in his hands the greatest weapon against Sark anyone could have dreamed of. There was no question about it. He *knew* that Rik remembered correctly, that he *had* been a Spatio-analyst once, that he *had* been psycho-probed into near brainlessness; and that what he remembered was something true and horrible and —powerful.

He was sure of it.

And now this Rik was in the thick hands of a man who pretended to be a Florinian patriot but was actually a Trantorian agent.

Terens felt the bitterness of his anger in the back of his throat. Of course this Baker was a Trantorian agent. He had had no doubt about that from the first moment. Who else among dwellers in the Lower City would have the capital to build dummy radar ovens?

He could not allow Rik to fall into the hands of Trantor. He *would not* allow Rik to fall into the hands of Trantor. There was no limit to the risks he was prepared to run. What matter the risks? He had incurred the death penalty already.

There was a dim gleam in the corner of the sky. He would wait for dawn. The various patroller stations would have his description, of course, but it might take several minutes for his appearance to register.

And during those several minutes he would be a Townman. It would give him time to do something that even now, even now, he did not dare let his mind dwell upon.

It was ten hours after Junz had had his interview with the Clerk that he met Ludigan Abel again.

The Ambassador greeted Junz with his usual surface cordiality, yet with a definite and disturbing sensation of guilt. At their first meeting (it had been a long time ago; nearly a Standard Year had passed) he had paid no attention to the man's story *per se*. His only thought had been: Will this, or can this, help Trantor?

Trantor! It was always first in his thought, yet he was not the kind of fool who would worship a cluster of stars or the yellow emblem of Spaceship-and-Sun that the Trantorian armed forces wore. In short, he was not a patriot in the ordinary meaning of the word and Trantor as Trantor meant nothing to him.

But he did worship peace; all the more so because he was growing old and enjoyed his glass of wine, his atmosphere saturated with mild music and perfume, his afternoon nap, and his quiet wait for death. It was how he imagined all men must feel; yet all men suffered war and destruction. They died frozen in the vacuum of space, vaporized in the blast of exploding atoms, famished on a besieged and bombarded planet.

How then to enforce peace? Not by reason, certainly, nor by education. If a man could not look at the fact of peace and the fact of war and choose the former in preference to the latter, what additional argument could persuade him? What could be more eloquent as a condemnation of war than war itself? What tremendous feat of dialectic could carry with it a tenth the power of a single gutted ship with its ghastly cargo?

So then, to end the misuse of force, only one solution was left, force itself.

Abel had a map of Trantor in his study, so designed as to show the application of that force. It was a clear crystalline ovoid in which the Galactic lens was three-dimensionally laid out. Its stars were specks of white diamond dust, its nebulae, patches of light or dark fog, and in its central depths there were the few red specks that had been the Trantorian Republic.

Not "were" but "had been." The Trantorian Republic had been a mere five worlds, five hundred years earlier.

But it was a historical map, and showed the Republic at that stage only when the dial was set at zero. Advance the dial one notch and the pictured Galaxy would be as it was fifty years later and a sheaf of stars would redden about Trantor's rim.

In ten stages, half a millennium would pass and the crimson would spread like a widening bloodstain until more than half the Galaxy had fallen into the red puddle.

That red was the red of blood in more than a fanciful way. As the Trantorian Republic became the Trantorian Confederation and then the Trantorian Empire, its advance had lain through a tangled forest of gutted men, gutted ships, and gutted worlds. Yet through it all Trantor had become strong and within the red there was peace.

Now Trantor trembled at the brink of a new conversion: from Trantorian Empire to Galactic Empire and then the red would engulf all the stars and there would be universal peace—*pax Trantorica.*

Abel wanted that. Five hundred years ago, four hundred years ago, even two hundred years ago, he would have opposed Trantor as an unpleasant nest of nasty, materialistic and aggressive people, careless of the rights of others, imperfectly democratic at home though quick to see the minor slaveries of others, and greedy without end. But the time had passed for all that.

He was not for Trantor, but for the all-embracing end that Trantor represented. So the question: How will this help Galactic peace? naturally became: How will this help Trantor?

The trouble was that in this particular instance he could not be certain. To Junz the solution was obviously a straightforward one. Trantor must uphold the I.S.B. and punish Sark.

Possibly this would be a good thing, if something could definitely be proven against Sark. Possibly not, even then. Certainly not, if nothing could be proven. But in any case Trantor could not move rashly. All the Galaxy could see that Trantor stood at the edge of Galactic dominion and there was still a chance that what yet remained of the non-Trantorian planets might unite against that. Trantor could win even such a war, but perhaps not without paying a price that would make victory only a pleasanter name for defeat.

So Trantor must never make an incautious move in this final stage of the game. Abel had therefore proceeded slowly, casting his gentle web across the labyrinth of the Civil Service and the glitter of the Sarkite Squiredom, probing with a smile and questioning without seeming to. Nor did he forget to keep the fingers of the Trantorian secret service upon Junz himself lest the angry Libairian do in a moment damage that Abel could not repair in a year.

Abel was astonished at the Libairian's persistent anger. He had asked him once, "Why does one agent concern you so?"

He half expected a speech on the integrity of the I.S.B. and the duty of all to uphold the Bureau as an instrument not of this world or that, but of all humanity. He did not get it.

Instead Junz frowned and said, "Because at the bottom of all this lies the relationship between Sark and Florina. I want to expose that relationship and destroy it."

Abel felt nothing less than nausea. Always, everywhere, there was this preoccupation with single worlds that prevented, over and over again, any intelligent concentration upon the problem of Galactic unity. Certainly social injustices existed here and there. Certainly they seemed sometimes impossible to stomach. But who could imagine that such injustice could be solved on any scale less than Galactic? First, there must be an end to war and national rivalry and only then could one turn to the internal miseries that, after all, had external conflict as their chief cause.

And Junz was not even of Florina. He had not even that cause for emotionalized shortsightedness.

Abel said, "What is Florina to you?"

Junz hesitated. He said, "I feel a kinship."

"But you are a Libairian. Or at least that is my impression."

"I am, but there lies the kinship. We are both extremes in a Galaxy of the average."

"Extremes? I don't understand."

Junz said, "In skin pigmentation. They are unusually pale. We are unusually dark. It means something. It binds us together. It gives us something in common. It seems to me our ancestors must have had long histories of being different, even of being excluded from the social majority. We are unfortunate whites and darks, brothers in being different."

By that time, under Abel's astonished gaze, Junz stumbled to a halt. The subject had never been sounded again.

And now, after a year, without warning, without any previous intimations, just at the point where, perhaps, a quiet trailing end might be expected of the whole wretched matter and where even Junz showed signs of flagging zeal, it all exploded.

He faced a different Junz now, one whose anger was not reserved for Sark, but spilled and overflowed onto Abel as well.

"It is not," the Libairian said in part, "that I resent the fact that your agents have been set upon my heels. Presumably you are cautious and must rely on nothing and nobody. Good, as far as that goes. But why was I not informed as soon as our man was located?"

Abel's hand smoothed the warm fabric of the arm of his chair. "Matters are complicated. Always complicated. I had arranged that any report on an unauthorized seeker after Spatio-analytic data be reported to certain of my own agents as well as to you. I even thought you might need protection. But on Florina——"

Junz said bitterly, "Yes. We were fools not to have considered that. We spent nearly a year proving we could find him nowhere on Sark. He *had* to be on Florina and we were blind to that. In any case, we have him now. Or you have, and presumably it will be arranged to have me see him?"

Abel did not answer directly. He said, "You say they told you this man Khorov was a Trantorian agent?"

"Isn't he? Why should they lie? Or are they misinformed?"

"They neither lie nor are they misinformed. He has been an agent of ours for a decade, and it is disturbing to me that they were aware of it. It makes me wonder what more they know of us and how shaky our structure may be altogether. But doesn't it make you wonder why they told you baldly that he was one of our men?"

"Because it was the truth, I imagine, and to keep me, once and for all, from embarrassing them by further demands that could only cause trouble between themselves and Trantor."

"Truth is a discredited commodity among diplomats and what greater trouble can they cause for themselves than to let us know the extent of their knowledge about us: to give us the opportunity, before it is too late, to draw in our damaged net, mend it and put it out whole again?"

"Then answer your own question."

"I say they told you of their knowledge of Khorov's true identity as a gesture of triumph. They knew that the fact of their knowledge could no longer either help or harm them since I have known for twelve hours that they knew Khorov was one of our men."

"But how?"

"By the most unmistakable hint possible. Listen! Twelve hours ago Matt Khorov, agent for Trantor, was killed by a member of the Florinian Patrol. The two Florinians he held at the time, a woman and the man who, in all probability, is the field man you have been seeking, are gone, vanished. Presumably they are in the hands of the Squires."

Junz cried out and half rose from his seat.

Abel lifted a glass of wine to his lips calmly and said, "There is nothing I can do officially. The dead man was a Florinian and those who have vanished, for all we can prove to the contrary, are likewise Florinians. So, you see, we have been badly outplayed, and are now being mocked in addition."

Seven: *THE PATROLLER*

Rik saw the Baker killed. He saw him crumple without a sound, his chest driven in and charred into smoking ruins under the silent push of the blaster. It was a sight that drowned out for him most of what had preceded and almost all that had followed.

There was the dim memory of the patroller's first approach, of the quiet but terribly intent manner in which he had drawn his weapon. The Baker had looked up and shaped his lips for one last word that he had no time to utter. When the deed was done, there was the rushing of blood in Rik's ears and the wild screaming scramble of the mob swirling in all directions, like a river in flood.

For a moment it negated the improvement Rik's mind had made in those last few hours of sleep. The patroller had plunged toward him, throwing himself forward upon yelling men and women as though they were a viscous sea of mud he would have to slog through. Rik and Lona turned with the current and were carried away. There were eddies and subcurrents, turning and quivering as the flying patrollers' cars began to hover overhead. Valona urged Rik forward, ever outward to the outskirts of the City. For a while he was the frightened child of yesterday, not the almost adult of that morning.

He had awakened that morning in the grayness of a dawn he could not see in the windowless room he slept in. For long minutes he lay there, inspecting his mind. Something had healed during the night; something had knit together and become whole. It had been getting ready to happen ever since the moment, two days before, when he had begun to "remember." The process had been proceeding all through yesterday. The trip to the Upper City and the library, the attack upon the patroller and the flight that followed, the encounter with the Baker—it had all acted upon him like a ferment. The shriveled fibers of his mind, so long dormant, had been seized and stretched, forced into an aching activity, and now, after a sleep, there was a feeble pulsing about them.

He thought of space and the stars, of long, long, lonely stretches, and great silences.

Finally he turned his head to one side and said, "Lona."

She snapped awake, lifting herself to an elbow, peering in his direction.

"Rik?"

"Here I am, Lona."

"Are you all right?"

"Sure." He couldn't hold down his excitement. "I feel fine, Lona. Listen! I remember more. I was in a ship and I know exactly——"

But she wasn't listening to him. She slipped into her dress and with her back to him smoothed the seam shut down the front and then fumbled nervously with her belt.

She tiptoed toward him. "I didn't mean to sleep, Rik. I tried to stay awake."

Rik felt the infection of her nervousness. He said, "Is something wrong?"

"Sh, don't speak so loudly. It's all right."

"Where's the Townman?"

"He's not here. He—he had to leave. Why don't you go back to sleep, Rik?"

He pushed her consoling arm aside. "I'm all right. I don't want to sleep. I wanted to tell the Townman about my ship."

But the Townman wasn't there and Valona would not listen. Rik subsided and for the first time felt actively annoyed with Valona. She treated him as though he were a child and he was beginning to feel like a man.

A light entered the room and the broad figure of the Baker entered with it. Rik blinked at him and was, for a moment, daunted. He did not entirely object when Valona's comforting arm stole about his shoulder.

The Baker's thick lips stretched in a smile. "You're early awake."

Neither answered.

The Baker said, "It's just as well. You'll be moving today."

Valona's mouth was dry. She said, "You'll not be giving us to the patrollers?"

She remembered the way he had looked at Rik after the Townman had left. He was still looking at Rik; only at Rik.

"Not to the patrollers," he said. "The proper people have been informed and you'll be safe enough."

He left, and when he returned shortly thereafter he brought food, clothes and two basins of water. The clothes were new and looked completely strange.

He watched them as they ate, saying, "I'm going to give you new names and new histories. You're to listen, and I don't want you to forget. You're not Florinians, do you understand? You're brother and sister from the planet Wotex. You've been visiting Florina——"

He went on, supplying details, asking questions, listening to their answers.

Rik was pleased to be able to demonstrate the workings of his memory, his easy ability to learn, but Valona's eyes were dark with worry.

The Baker was not blind to that. He said to the girl, "If you give me the least trouble I'll send him on alone and leave you behind."

Valona's strong hands clenched spasmodically. "I will give you no trouble."

It was well into the morning when the Baker rose to his feet and said, "Let's go!"

His last action was to place little black sheets of limp leatherette in their breast pockets.

Once outside, Rik looked with astonishment at what he could see of himself. He did not know clothing could be so complicated. The Baker had helped him get it on, but who would help him take it off? Valona didn't look like a farm girl at all. Even her legs were covered with thin material, and her shoes were raised at the heels so that she had to balance carefully when she walked.

Passers-by gathered, staring and gawking, calling to one another. Mostly they were children, marketing women, and skulking, ragged idlers. The Baker seemed oblivious to them. He carried a thick stick which found itself occasionally, as though by accident, between the legs of any who pressed too closely.

And then, when they were still only a hundred yards from the bakery and had made but one turning, the outer reaches of the surrounding crowd swirled excitedly and Rik made out the black and silver of a patroller.

That was when it happened. The weapon, the blast, and again a wild flight. Was there ever a time when fear had not been with him, when the shadow of the patroller had not been behind him?

They found themselves in the squalor of one of the outlying districts of the City. Valona was panting harshly; her new dress bore the wet stains of perspiration.

Rik gasped, "I can't run any more."

"We've got to."

"Not like this. Listen." He pulled back firmly against the pressure of the girl's grip. "Listen to me."

The fright and panic were leaving him.

He said, "Why don't we go on and do what the Baker wanted us to do?"

She said, "How do you know what he wanted us to do?" She was anxious. She wanted to keep moving.

He said, "We were to pretend we were from another world and he gave us these." Rik was excited. He pulled the little rectangle out of his pocket, staring at both sides and trying to open it as though it were a booklet.

He couldn't. It was a single sheet. He felt about the edges and as his fingers closed at one corner he heard, or rather felt, something give, and the side toward him turned a startling milky white. The close wording on the new surface was difficult to understand though he began carefully making out the syllables.

Finally he said, "It's a passport."

"What's that?"

"Something to get us away." He was sure of it. It had popped into his head. A single word, "passport," like that. "Don't you see? He was going to have us leave Florina. On a ship. Let's go through with that."

She said, "No. They stopped him. They killed him. We couldn't, Rik, we couldn't."

He was urgent about it. He was nearly babbling. "But it would be the best thing to do. They wouldn't be expecting us to do that. And we wouldn't go on the ship he wanted us to go on. They'd be watching that. We'd go on another ship. Any other ship."

A ship. Any ship. The words rang in his ears. Whether his idea was a good one or not, he didn't care. He wanted to be on a ship. He wanted to be in space.

"*Please*, Lona!"

She said, "All right. If you really think so. I know where the spaceport is. When I was a little girl we used to go there on idle-days sometimes and watch from far away to see the ships shoot upward."

They were on their way again, and only a slight uneasiness scratched vainly at the gateway of Rik's consciousness. Some memory not of the far past but of the very near past; something he should remember and could not; could just barely not. Something.

He drowned it in the thought of the ship that waited for them.

The Florinian at the entry gate was having his fill of excitement that day, but it was excitement at long distance. There had been the wild stories of the previous evening, telling of patrollers attacked and of daring escapes. By this morning the stories had expanded and there were whispers of patrollers killed.

He dared not leave his post, but he craned his neck and watched the air-cars pass, and the grim-faced patrollers leave, as the spaceport contingent was cut and cut till it was almost nothing.

They were filling the City with patrollers, he thought, and was at once frightened and drunkenly uplifted. Why should it make him happy to think of patrollers being killed? They never bothered him. At least not much. He had a good job. It wasn't as though he were a stupid peasant.

But he was happy.

He scarcely had time for the couple before him, uncomfortable and perspiring in the outlandish clothing that marked them at once as foreigners. The woman was holding a passport through the slot.

A glance at her, a glance at the passport, a glance at the list of reservations. He pressed the appropriate button and two translucent ribbons of film sprang out at them.

"Go on," he said impatiently. "Get them on your wrists and move on."

"Which ship is ours?" asked the woman in a polite whisper.

That pleased him. Foreigners were infrequent at the Florinian spaceport. In recent years they had grown more and more infrequent. But when they did come they were neither patrollers nor Squires. They didn't seem to realize you were only a Florinian yourself and they spoke to you politely.

It made him feel two inches taller. He said, "You'll find it in Berth 17, madam. I wish you a pleasant trip to Wotex." He said it in the grand manner.

He then returned to his task of putting in surreptitious calls to friends in the City for more information and of trying, even more unobtrusively, to tap private power-beam conversations in Upper City.

It was hours before he found out that he had made a horrible mistake.

Rik said, "Lona!"

He tugged at her elbow, pointed quickly and whispered, "That one!"

Valona looked at the indicated ship doubtfully. It was much smaller than the ship in Berth 17, for which their tickets held good. It looked more burnished. Four air locks yawned open and the main port gaped, with a ramp leading from it like an out-stretched tongue reaching to ground level.

Rik said, "They're airing it. They usually air passenger ships before flight to get rid of the accumulated odor of canned oxygen, used and reused."

Valona stared at him. "How do you know?"

Rik felt a sprig of vanity grow within himself. "I just know. You see, there wouldn't be anyone in it now. It isn't comfortable, with the draft on."

He looked about uneasily. "I don't know why there aren't more people about, though. Was it like this when you used to watch it?"

Valona thought not, but she could scarcely remember. Childhood memories were far away.

There was not a patroller in sight as they walked up the ramp on quivering legs. What figures they could see were civilian employees, intent on their own jobs, and small in the distance.

Moving air cut through them as they stepped into the hold and Valona's dress bellied so that she had to bring her hands down to keep the hemline within bounds.

"Is it always like this?" she asked. She had never been on a spaceship before; never dreamed of being on one. Her lips stuck together and her heart pounded.

Rik said, "No. Just during aeration."

He walked joyfully over the hard metallite passageways, inspecting the empty rooms eagerly.

"Here," he said. It was the galley.

He spoke rapidly. "It isn't food so much. We can get along without food for quite a while. It's water."

He rummaged through the neat and compact nestings of utensils and came up with a large, capped container. He looked about for the water tap, muttered a breathless hope that they had not neglected to fill the water tanks, then grinned his relief when the soft sound of pumps came, and the steady gush of liquid.

"Now just take some of the cans. Not too many. We don't want them to take notice."

Rik tried desperately to think of ways of countering discovery. Again he groped for something he could not quite remember. Occasionally he still ran into those gaps in his thought and, cowardlike, he avoided them, denied their existence.

He found a small room devoted to fire-fighting equipment, emergency medical and surgical supplies, and welding equipment.

He said with a certain lack of confidence, "They won't be in here, except in emergencies. Are you afraid, Lona?"

"I won't be afraid with you, Rik," she said humbly. Two days before, no, twelve hours before, it had been the other way around. But on board ship, by some transmutation of personality she did not question, it was Rik who was the adult, she who was the child.

He said, "We won't be able to use lights because they would notice the power drain, and to use the toilets, we'll have to wait for rest periods and try to get out past any of the night crew."

The draft cut off suddenly. Its cold touch on their faces was no longer there and the soft, steady humming sound, that had distantly accompanied it, stopped and left a large silence to fill its place.

Rik said, "They'll be boarding soon, and then we'll be out in space."

Valona had never seen such joy in Rik's face. He was a lover going to meet his love.

If Rik had felt a man on awaking that dawn, he was a giant now, his arms stretching the length of the Galaxy. The stars were his marbles, and the nebulae were cobwebs to brush away.

He was on a ship! Memories rushed back continuously in a long flood and others left to make room. He was forgetting the kyrt fields and the mill and Valona crooning to him in the dark. They were only momentary breaks in a pattern that was now returning with its raveled ends slowly knitting.

It was the ship!

If they had put him on a ship long ago, he wouldn't have had to wait so long for his burnt-out brain cells to heal themselves.

He spoke softly to Valona in the darkness. "Now don't worry. You'll feel a vibration and hear a noise but that will be just the motors. There'll be a heavy weight on you. That's acceleration."

There was no common Florinian word for the concept and he used another word for it, one that came easily to mind. Valona did not understand.

She said, "Will it hurt?"

He said, "It will be very uncomfortable, because we don't have anti-acceleration gear to take up the pressure, but it won't last. Just stand against this wall, and when you feel yourself being pushed against it, relax. See, it's beginning."

He had picked the right wall, and as the thrumming of the thrusting hyperatomics swelled, the apparent gravity shifted, and what had been vertical wall seemed to grow more and more diagonal.

Valona whimpered once, then lapsed into a hard-breathing silence. Their throats rasped as their chest walls, unprotected by straps and hydraulic absorbers, labored to free their lungs sufficiently for just a little air intake.

Rik managed to pant out words, any words that might let Valona know he was there and ease the terrible fear of the unknown that he knew must be filling her. It was only a ship, only a wonderful ship; but she had never been on a ship before.

He said, "There's the jump, of course, when we go through hyperspace and cut across most of the distance between the stars all at once. That won't bother you at all. You won't even know it happened. It's nothing compared to this. Just a little twitch in your insides and it's over." He got the words out syllable by grunted syllable. It took a long time.

Slowly, the weight on their chests lifted and the invisible chain holding them to the wall stretched and dropped off. They fell, panting, to the floor.

Finally Valona said, "Are you hurt, Rik?"

"I, hurt?" He managed a laugh. He had not caught his breath yet, but he laughed at the thought that he could be hurt on a ship.

He said, "I lived on a ship for years once. I didn't land on a planet for months at a time."

"Why?" she asked. She had crawled closer and put a hand to his cheek, making sure he was there.

He put his arm about her shoulder, and she rested within it quietly, accepting the reversal.

"Why?" she asked.

Rik could not remember why. He had done it; he had hated to land on a planet. For some reason it had been necessary to stay in space, but he could not remember why. Again he dodged the gap.

He said, "I had a job."

"Yes," she said. "You analyzed Nothing."

"That's right." He was pleased. "That's exactly what I did. Do you know what that means?"

"No."

He didn't expect her to understand, but he had to talk. He had to revel in memory, to delight drunkenly in the fact that he could call up past facts at the flick of a mental finger.

He said, "You see, all the material in the universe is made up of a hundred different kinds of substances. We call those substances elements. Iron and copper are elements."

"I thought they were metals."

"So they are, and elements too. Also oxygen, and nitrogen, carbon and palladium. Most important of all, hydrogen and helium. They're the simplest and most common."

"I never heard of those," Valona said wistfully.

"Ninety-five per cent of the universe is hydrogen and most of the rest is helium. Even space."

"I was once told," said Valona, "that space was a vacuum. They said that meant there was nothing there. Was that wrong?"

"Not quite. There's *almost* nothing there. But you see, I was a Spatio-analyst, which meant that I went about through space collecting the extremely small amounts of elements there and analyzing them. That is, I decided how much was hydrogen, how much helium and how much other elements."

"Why?"

"Well, that's complicated. You see, the arrangement of elements isn't the same everywhere in space. In some regions there is a little more helium than normal; in other places, more sodium than normal; and so on. These regions of special analytic make-up wind through space like currents. That's what they call them. They're the currents of space. It's important to know how these currents are arranged because that might explain how the universe was created and how it developed."

"How would it explain that?"

Rik hesitated. "Nobody knows exactly."

He hurried on, embarrassed that this immense store of knowledge in which his mind was thankfully wallowing could come so easily to an end marked "unknown" under the questioning of . . . of . . . It suddenly occurred to him that Valona, after all, was nothing but a Florinian peasant girl.

He said, "Then, again, we find out the density, you know, the thickness, of this space gas in all regions of the Galaxy. It's different in different places and we have to know exactly what it is in order to allow ships to calculate exactly how to jump through hyperspace. It's like . . ." His voice died away.

Valona stiffened and waited uneasily for him to continue, but only silence followed. Her voice sounded hoarsely in the complete darkness.

"Rik? What's wrong, Rik?"

Still silence. Her hands groped to his shoulders, shaking him. "Rik! Rik!"

And it was the voice of the old Rik, somehow, that answered. It was weak, frightened, its joy and confidence vanished.

"Lona. We did something wrong."

"What's the matter? We did what wrong?"

The memory of the scene in which the patroller had shot down the Baker was in his mind, etched hard and clear, as though called back by his exact memory of so many other things.

He said, "We shouldn't have run away. We shouldn't be here on this ship."

He was shivering uncontrollably, and Valona tried futilely to wipe the moisture from his forehead with her hand.

"Why?" she demanded. "Why?"

"Because we should have known that if the Baker were willing to take us out in daylight he expected no trouble from patrollers. Do you remember the patroller? The one who shot the Baker?"

"Yes."

"Do you remember his face?"

"I didn't dare look."

"I did, and there was something queer, but I didn't think. I didn't think. Lona, that *wasn't* a patroller. It was the Townman, Lona. It was the Townman dressed like a patroller."

Eight: *THE LADY*

Samia of Fife was five feet tall, exactly, and all sixty inches of her were in a state of quivering exasperation. She weighed one and a half pound per inch and, at the moment, each of her ninety pounds represented sixteen ounces of solid anger.

She stepped quickly from end to end of the room, her dark hair piled in high masses, her spiked heels lending a spurious height and her narrow chin, with its pronounced cleft, trembling.

She said, "Oh no. He wouldn't do it to me. He *couldn't* do it to me. Captain!"

Her voice was sharp and carried the weight of authority. Captain Racety bowed with the storm. "My Lady?"

To any Florinian, of course, Captain Racety would have been a "Squire." Simply that. To any Florinian, all Sarkites were Squires. But to the Sarkites there were Squires and *real* Squires. The Captain was simply a Squire. Samia of Fife was a *real* Squire; or the feminine equivalent of one, which amounted to the same thing.

"My Lady?" he asked.

She said, "I am not to be ordered about. I am of age. I am my own mistress. I choose to remain here."

The Captain said carefully, "Please to understand, my Lady, that no orders of mine are involved. My advice was not asked. I have been told plainly and flatly what I am to do."

He fumbled for the copy of his orders halfheartedly. He had tried to present her with the evidence twice before and she had refused to consider it, as though by not looking she could continue, with a clear conscience, to deny where his duty lay.

She said once again, exactly as before, "I am not interested in your orders."

She turned away with a ringing of her heels and moved rapidly away from him.

He followed and said softly, "The orders include directions to the effect that, if you are not willing to come, I am, if you will excuse my saying so, to have you carried to the ship."

She whirled. "You wouldn't dare do such a thing."

"When I consider," said the Captain, "who it is who has ordered me to do it, I would dare anything."

She tried cajolery. "Surely, Captain, there is no real danger. This is quite ridiculous, entirely mad. The City is peaceful. All that has happened is that one patroller was knocked down yesterday afternoon in the library. Really!"

"Another patroller was killed this dawn, again by Florinian attack."

That rocked her, but her olive skin grew dusky and her black eyes flashed. "What has that to do with me? I am not a patroller."

"My Lady, the ship is being prepared right now. It will leave shortly. You will have to be on it."

"And my work? My research? Do you realize—— No, you wouldn't realize."

The Captain said nothing. She had turned from him. Her gleaming dress of copper kyrt, with its strands of milky silver, set off the extraordinary warm smoothness of her shoulders and upper arms. Captain Racety looked at her with something more than the bald courtesy and humble objectivity a mere Sarkite owed such a great Lady. He wondered why such an entirely desirable bite-size morsel should choose to spend her time in mimicking the scholarly pursuits of a university don.

Samia knew well that her earnest scholarship made her an object of mild derision to people who were accustomed to thinking of the aristocratic Ladies of Sark as devoted entirely to the glitter of polite society and, eventually, acting as incubators for at least, but not more than, two future Squires of Sark. She didn't care.

They would come to her and say, "Are you really writing a book, Samia?" and ask to see it, and giggle.

Those were the women. The men were even worse, with their gentle condescension and obvious conviction that it would only take a glance from themselves or a man's arm about her waist to cure her of her nonsense and turn her mind to things of real importance.

It had begun as far back, almost, as she could remember, because she had always been in love with kyrt, whereas most people took it for granted. Kyrt! The king, emperor, *god* of fabrics. There was no metaphor strong enough.

Chemically, it was nothing more than a variety of cellulose. The chemists swore to that. Yet with all their instruments and theories they had never yet explained why on Florina, and only on Florina in all the Galaxy, cellulose became kyrt. It was a matter of the physical state; that's what they said. But ask them exactly in what way the physical state varied from that of ordinary cellulose and they were mute.

She had learned ignorance originally from her nurse.

"Why does it shine, Nanny?"

"Because it's kyrt, Miakins."

"Why don't other things shine so, Nanny?"

"Other things aren't kyrt, Miakins."

There you had it. A two-volume monograph on the subject had been written only three years before. She had read it carefully and it could all have been boiled down to her Nanny's explanation. Kyrt was kyrt because it was kyrt. Things that weren't kyrt, weren't kyrt because they weren't kyrt.

Of course kyrt didn't really shine of itself but, properly spun, it would gleam metallically in the sun in a variety of colors or in all colors at once. Another form of treatment could impart a diamond sparkle to the thread. It could be made, with little effort, completely impervious to heat up to 600 degrees Centigrade, and quite inert to almost all chemicals. Its fibers could be spun finer than the most delicate synthetics and those same fibers had a tensile strength no steel alloy known could duplicate.

It had more uses, more versatility than any substance known to man. If it were not so expensive it could be used to replace glass, metal, or plastic in any of infinite industrial applications. As it was, it was the only material used for cross hairs on optical equipment, as molds in the casting of hydrochrons used in hyperatomic motors, and as lightweight, long-lived webbing where metal was too brittle or too heavy or both.

But this was, as said, small-scale use, since use in quantity was prohibitive. Actually the kyrt harvest of Florina went into the manufacture of cloth that was used for the most fabulous garments in Galactic history. Florina clothed the aristocracy of a million worlds, and the kyrt harvest of the one world, Florina, had to be spread thin for that. Twenty women on a world might have outfits in kyrt; two thousand more might have a holiday jacket of the material, or perhaps a pair of gloves. Twenty million more watched from a distance and wished.

The million worlds of the Galaxy shared a slang expression for the snob. It was the only idiom in the language that was easily and exactly understood everywhere. It went: "You'd think she blew her nose in kyrt!"

When Samia was older she went to her father.

"What is kyrt, Daddy?"

"It's your bread and butter, Mia."

"Mine?"

"Not just yours, Mia. It's Sark's bread and butter."

Of course! She learned the reason for that easily enough. Not a world in the Galaxy but had tried to grow kyrt on its own soil. At first Sark had applied the death penalty to anyone, native or foreign, caught smuggling kyrt seed out of the planet. That had not prevented successful smuggling, and as the centuries passed, and the truth dawned on Sark, that law had been abolished. Men from anywhere were welcome to kyrt seed at the price, of course (weight for weight), of finished kyrt cloth.

They might have it, because it turned out that kyrt grown anywhere in the Galaxy but on Florina was simply cellulose. White, flat, weak and useless. Not even honest cotton.

Was it something in the soil? Something in the characteristics of the radiation of Florina's sun? Something about the bacterial makeup of Florinian life? It had all been tried. Samples of Florinian soil had been taken. Artificial arc lights duplicating the known spectrum of Florina's sun had been constructed. Foreign soil had been infected with Florinian bacteria. And always the kyrt grew white, flat, weak and useless.

There was so much to be said about kyrt that had never been said. Material other than that contained in technical reports or in research papers or even in travel books. For five years Samia had been dreaming of writing a real book about the story of kyrt; of the land it grew on and of the people who grew it.

It was a dream surrounded by mocking laughter, but she held to it. She had insisted on traveling to Florina. She was going to spend a season in the fields and a few months in the mills. She was going to—

But what did it matter what she was going to do? She was being ordered back.

With the sudden impulsiveness that marked her every act she made her decision. She would be able to fight this on Sark. Grimly she promised herself she would be back on Florina in a week.

She turned to the Captain and said coolly, "When do we leave, sir?"

Samia remained at the observation port for as long as Florina was a visible globe. It was a green, springlike world, much pleasanter than Sark in climate. She had looked forward to studying the natives. She didn't like the Florinians on Sark, sapless men who dared not look at her but turned away when she passed, in accordance with the law. On their own world, however, the natives, by universal report, were happy and carefree. Irresponsible, of course, and like children, but they had charm.

Captain Racety interrupted her thoughts. He said, "My lady, would you retire to your room?"

She looked up, a tiny vertical crease between her eyes. "What new orders have you received, Captain? Am I a prisoner?"

"Of course not. Merely a precaution. The space field was unusually empty before the take-off. It seems that another killing had taken place, again by a Florinian, and the field's patroller contingent had joined the rest on a man hunt through the City."

"And the connection of that with myself?"

"It is only that under the circumstances, which I ought to have reacted to by placing a guard of my own (I do not minimize my own offense), unauthorized persons may have boarded the ship."

"For what reason?"

"I could not say, but scarcely to do our pleasure."

"You are romancing, Captain."

"I am afraid not, my Lady. Our energometrics were, of course, useless within planetary distance of Florina's sun, but that is not the case now and I am afraid there is definite excess heat radiation from Emergency Stores."

"Are you serious?"

The Captain's lean, expressionless face regarded her aloofly for a moment. He said, "The radiation is equivalent to that which would be given off by two ordinary people."

"Or a heating unit someone forgot to turn off."

"There is no drain on our power supply, my Lady. We are ready to investigate, my Lady, and ask only that you first retire to your room."

She nodded silently and left the room. Two minutes later his calm voice spoke unhurriedly into the communi-tube. "Break into Emergency Stores."

Myrlyn Terens, had he released his taut nerves the slightest, might easily, and even thankfully, have gone into hysteria. He had been a trifle too late in returning to the bakery. They had already left it and it was only by good fortune that he met them in the street. His next action had been dictated; it was in no way a matter of free choice; and the Baker lay quite horribly dead before him.

Afterward, with the crowd swirling, Rik and Valona melting into the crowd, and the air-cars of the patrollers, the *real* patrollers, beginning to put in their vulture appearance, what could he do?

His first impulse to race after Rik he quickly fought down. It would do no good. He would never find them, and there was too great a chance that the patrollers would not miss him. He scurried in another direction, toward the bakery.

His only chance lay in the patroller organization itself. There had been generations of a quiet life. At least there had been no Florinian revolts to speak of in two centuries. The institution of the Townman (he grinned savagely at the thought) had worked wonders and the patrollers had only perfunctory police duties since. They lacked the fine-pointed teamwork that would have developed under more strenuous conditions.

It had been possible for him to walk into a patroller station at dawn, where his description must have already been sent, though obviously it had not been much regarded. The lone patroller on duty was a mixture of indifference and sulkiness. Terens had been asked to state his business, but his business included a plastic two-by-four he had wrenched from the side of a crazy hovel at the outskirts of town.

He had brought it down upon the patroller's skull, changed clothing and weapons. The list of his crimes was already so formidable that it did not bother him in the least to discover that the patroller had been killed, not stunned.

Yet he was still at large and the rusty machinery of patroller justice had so far creaked after him in vain.

He was at the bakery. The Baker's elderly helper, standing in the doorway in a vain attempt to peer knowledge of the disturbance into himself, squeaked thinly at the sight of the dread black and silver of patrollerhood and oozed back into his shop.

The Townman lunged after him, crumpling the man's loose, floury collar into his pudgy fist and twisting. "Where was the Baker going?"

The old man's lips yawned open, but no sound came.

The Townman said, "I killed a man two minutes ago. I don't care if I kill another."

"Please. Please. I do not know, sir."

"You will die for not knowing."

"But he did not tell me. He made some sort of reservations."

"You have overheard so much, have you? What else did you overhear?"

"He mentioned Wotex once. I think the reservations were on a spaceship."

Terens thrust him away.

He would have to wait. He would have to let the worst of the excitement outside die. He would have to risk the arrival of real patrollers at the bakery.

But not for long. Not for long. He could guess what his erstwhile companions would do. Rik was unpredictable, of course, but Valona was an intelligent girl. From the way they ran, they must have taken him for a patroller indeed and Valona was sure to decide that their only safety lay in continuing the flight that the Baker had begun for them.

The Baker had made reservations for them. A spaceship would be waiting. They would be there.

And he would have to be there first.

There was this about the desperation of the situation. Nothing more mattered. If he lost Rik, if he lost that potential weapon against the tyrants of Sark, his life was a small additional loss.

So when he left, it was without a qualm, though it was broad daylight, though the patrollers must know by now it was a man in patroller uniform they sought, and though two air-cars were in easy sight.

Terens knew the spaceport that would be involved. There was only one of its type on the planet. There were a dozen tiny ones in Upper City for the private use of space-yachts and there were hundreds all over the planet for the exclusive use of the ungainly freighters that carried gigantic bolts of kyrt cloth to Sark, and machinery and simple consumer goods back. But among all those there was only one spaceport for the use of ordinary travelers, for the poorer Sarkites, Florinian civil servants and the few foreigners who managed to obtain permission to visit Florina.

The Florinian at the port's entry gate observed Terens' approach with every symptom of lively interest. The vacuum that surrounded him had grown insupportable.

"Greetings, sir," he said. There was a slyly eager tone in his voice.

After all, patrollers were being killed. "Considerable excitement in the City, isn't there?"

Terens did not rise to the bait. He had drawn the arced visor of his hat low and buttoned the uppermost button of the tunic.

Gruffly he snapped, "Did two persons, a man and a woman, enter the port recently en route to Wotex?"

The gatekeeper looked startled. For a moment he gulped and then, in a considerably subdued tone, said, "Yes, Officer. About half an hour ago. Maybe less." He reddened suddenly. "Is there any connection between them and—— Officer, they had reservations which were entirely in order. I wouldn't let foreigners through without proper authority."

Terens ignored that. Proper authority! The Baker had managed to establish that in the course of a night. Galaxy, he wondered, how deeply into the Sarkite administration did the Trantorian espionage organization go?

"What names did they give?"

"Gareth and Hansa Barne."

"Has their ship left? Quickly!"

"N-no, sir."

"What berth?"

"Seventeen."

Terens forced himself to refrain from running, but his walk was little short of that. Had there been a real patroller in sight that rapid, undignified half run of his would have been his last trip in freedom.

A spaceman in officer's uniform stood at the ship's main air lock.

Terens panted a little. He said, "Have Gareth and Hansa Barne boarded ship?"

"No, they haven't," said the spaceman phlegmatically. He was a Sarkite and a patroller was only another man in uniform to him. "Do you have a message for them?"

With cracking patience Terens said, "They *haven't* boarded!"

"That's what I've said. And we're not waiting for them. We leave on schedule, with or without them."

Terens turned away.

He was at the gatekeeper's booth again. "Have they left?"

"Left? Who, sir?"

"The Barnes. The ones for Wotex. They're not on board ship. Did they leave?"

"No, sir. Not to my knowledge."

"What about the other gates?"

"They're not exits, sir. This is the only exit."

"Check them, you miserable idiot."

The gatekeeper lifted the communi-tube in a state of panic. No patroller had ever spoken to him so in anger and he dreaded the results. In two minutes he put it down.

He said, "No one has left, sir."

Terens stared at him. Under his black hat his sandy hair was damping against his skull and down each cheek there was the gleaming mark of perspiration.

He said, "Has any ship left the port since they entered?"

The gatekeeper consulted the schedule. "One," he said, "the liner *Endeavor*."

Volubly he went on, eager to gain favor with the angry patroller by volunteering information. "The *Endeavor* is making a special trip to Sark to carry the Lady Samia of Fife back from Florina."

He did not bother to describe exactly by what refined manner of eavesdropping he had managed to acquaint himself with the "confidential report."

But to Terens now, nothing mattered.

He backed slowly away. Eliminate the impossible and whatever remained, however improbable, was the truth. Rik and Valona had entered the spaceport. They had not been captured or the gatekeeper would certainly have known about it. They were not simply wandering about the port, or they would by now have been captured. They were not on the ship for which they had tickets. They had not left the field. The only object that had left the field was the *Endeavor*. Therefore, on it, possibly as captives, possibly as stowaways, were Rik and Valona.

And the two were equivalent. If they were stowaways they would soon be captives. Only a Florinian peasant girl and a mind-wrecked creature would fail to realize that one could not stow away on a modern spaceship.

And of all spaceships to choose, they chose that which carried the daughter of the Squire of Fife.

The Squire of Fife!

Nine: *THE SQUIRE*

The Squire of Fife was the most important individual on Sark and for that reason did not like to be seen standing. Like his daughter, he was short, but unlike her, he was not perfectly proportioned, since most of the shortness lay in his legs. His torso was even beefy, and his head was undoubtedly majestic, but his body was fixed upon stubby legs that were forced into a ponderous waddle to carry their load.

So he sat behind a desk and except for his daughter and personal servants and, when she had been alive, his wife, none saw him in any other position.

There he looked the man he was. His large head, with its wide, nearly lipless mouth, broad, large-nostriled nose, and pointed, cleft chin, could look benign and inflexible in turn, with equal ease. His hair, brushed rigidly back and, in careless disregard for fashion, falling nearly to his shoulders, was blue-black, untouched by gray. A shadowy blue marked the regions of his cheeks, lips and chin where his Florinian barber twice daily battled the stubborn growth of facial hair.

The Squire was posing and he knew it. He had schooled expression out of his face and allowed his hands, broad, strong and short-fingered, to remain loosely clasped on a desk whose smooth, polished surface was completely bare. There wasn't a paper on it, no communi-tube, no ornament. By its very simplicity the Squire's own presence was emphasized.

He spoke to his pale, fish-white secretary with the special lifeless tone he reserved for mechanical appliances and Florinian civil servants. "I presume all have accepted?"

He had no real doubt as to the answer.

His secretary replied in a tone as lifeless, "The Squire of Bort stated that the press of previous business arrangements prevented his attending earlier than three."

"And you told him?"

"I stated that the nature of the present business made any delay inadvisable."

"The result?"

"He will be here, sir. The rest have agreed without reservation."

Fife smiled. Half an hour this way or that would have made no difference. There was a new principle involved, that was all. The Great Squires were too touchy with regard to their own independence, and such touchiness would have to go.

He was waiting, now. The room was large, the places for the others were prepared. The large chronometer, whose tiny powering spark of radioactivity had not failed or faltered in a thousand years, said two twenty-one.

What an explosion in the last two days! The old chronometer might yet witness events equal to any in the past.

Yet that chronometer had seen many in its millennium. When it counted its first minutes Sark had been a new world of hand-hewn cities with doubtful contacts among the other, older worlds. The timepiece had been in the wall of an old brick building then, the very bricks of which had since become dust. It had counted its even tenor through three short-lived Sarkite "empires" when the undisciplined soldiers of Sark managed to govern, for a longer or shorter interval, some half a dozen surrounding worlds. Its radioactive atoms had exploded in strict statistical sequence through two periods when the fleets of neighboring worlds dictated policy on Sark.

Five hundred years ago it had marked cool time as Sark discovered that the world nearest to it, Florina, had a treasure in its soil past counting. It had moved evenly through two victorious wars and recorded solemnly the establishment of a conqueror's peace. Sark had abandoned its empires, absorbed Florina tightly, and become powerful in a way that Trantor itself could not duplicate.

Trantor wanted Florina and other powers had wanted it. The centuries had marked Florina as a world for which hands stretched out through space, groping and reaching eagerly. But it was Sark whose hand clasped it and Sark, sooner than release that grasp, would allow Galactic war.

Trantor knew that! Trantor knew that!

It was as though the silent rhythm of the chronometer set up the little singsong in the Squire's brain.

It was two twenty-three.

Nearly a year before, the five Great Squires of Sark had met. Then, as now, it had been here, in his own hall. Then, as now, the

Squires, scattered over the face of the planet, each on his own continent, had met in trimensic personification.

In a bald sense, it amounted to three-dimensional television in life size with sound and color. The duplicate could be found in any moderately well-to-do private home on Sark. Where it went beyond the ordinary was in the lack of any visible receiver. Except for Fife, the Squires present were present in every possible way but reality. The wall could not be seen behind them, they did not shimmer, yet a hand could have been passed through their bodies.

The true body of the Squire of Rune was sitting in the antipodes, his continent the only one upon which, at the moment, night prevailed. The cubic area immediately surrounding his image in Fife's office had the cold, white gleam of artificial light, dimmed by the brighter daylight about it.

Gathered in the one room, in body or in image, was Sark itself. It was a queer and not altogether heroic personification of the planet. Rune was bald and pinkly fat, while Balle was gray and dryly wrinkled. Steen was powdered and rouged, wearing the desperate smile of a worn-out man pretending to a life force he no longer had, and Bort carried indifference to creature comforts to the unpleasant point of a two-day growth of beard and dirty fingernails.

Yet they were the five Great Squires.

They were the topmost of the three rungs of ruling powers on Sark. The lowest rung was, of course, the Florinian Civil Service, which remained steady through all the vicissitudes that marked the rise and fall of the individual noble houses of Sark. It was they who actually greased the axles and turned the wheels of government. Above them were the ministers and department heads appointed by the hereditary (and harmless) Chief of State. Their names and that of the Chief himself were needed on state papers to make them legally binding, but their only duties consisted of signing their names.

The highest rung was occupied by these five, each tacitly allowed a continent by the remaining four. They were the heads of the families that controlled the major volume of the kyrt trade, and the revenues therefrom derived. It was money that gave power and eventually dictated policy on Sark, and these had it. And of the five, it was Fife who had the most.

The Squire of Fife had faced them that day, nearly a year ago, and said to the other masters of the Galaxy's second richest single planet (second richest after Trantor, which, after all, had half a million worlds to draw upon, rather than two):

"I have received a curious message."

They said nothing. They waited.

Fife handed a slip of metallite film to his secretary, who stepped from one seated figure to another, holding it well up for each to see, lingering just long enough for each to read.

To each of the four who attended the conference in Fife's office, he, himself, was real, and the others, including Fife, only shadows. The metallite film was a shadow as well. They could only sit and observe the light rays that focused across vast world sectors from the Continent of Fife to those of Balle, Bort, Steen and the island Continent of Rune. The words they read were shadows on shadow.

Only Bort, direct and ungiven to subtleties, forgot that fact and reached for the message.

His hand extended to the edge of the rectangular image-receptor and was cut off. His arm ended in a featureless stump. In his own chambers, Fife knew, Bort's arm had succeeded merely in closing upon nothingness and passing through the filmed message. He smiled, and so did the others. Steen giggled.

Bort reddened. He drew back his arm and his hand reappeared.

Fife said, "Well, you have each seen it. If you don't mind, I will now read it aloud so that you may consider its significance."

He reached upward, and his secretary, by hastening his steps, managed to hold the film in the proper position for Fife's grasp to close upon it without an instant's groping.

Fife read mellowly, imparting drama to the words as though the message were his own and he enjoyed delivering it.

He said, "This is the message: 'You are a Great Squire of Sark and there is none to compete with you in power and wealth. Yet that power and wealth rest on a slender foundation. You may think that a planetary supply of kyrt, such as exists on Florina, is by no means a slender foundation, but ask yourself, how long will Florina exist? Forever?

"'No! Florina may be destroyed tomorrow. It may exist for a thousand years. Of the two, it is more likely to be destroyed tomorrow. Not by myself, to be sure, but in a way you cannot predict or foresee. Consider that destruction. Consider, too, that your power and wealth are already gone, for I demand the greater part of them. You will have time to consider, but not too much time.

"'Attempt to take too much time and I shall announce to all the Galaxy and particularly to Florina the truth about the waiting destruction. After that there will be no more kyrt, no more wealth, no more power. None for me, but then I am used to that. None for you, and that would be extremely serious, since you were born to great wealth.

"'Turn over most of your estates to myself in the amount and in the manner which I shall dictate in the near future and you will remain in secure possession of what remains. Not a great deal will be left you by your present standards, to be sure, but it will be more than the nothing that will otherwise be left you. Do not sneer at the fragment you will retain, either. Florina *may* last your lifetime and you will live, if not lavishly, at least comfortably.'"

Fife had finished. He turned the film over and over in his hand, then folded it gently into a silvery translucent cylinder through which the stenciled letters merged into a reddish blur.

He said in his natural voice, "It is an amusing letter. There is no signature and the tone of the letter, as you heard, is stilted and pompous. What do you think of it, Squires?"

Rune's ruddy face was set in displeasure. He said, "It's obviously the work of a man not far removed from the psychotic. He writes like a historical novel. Frankly, Fife, I don't see that such rubbish is a decent excuse to disrupt our traditions of continental autonomy by calling us together. And I don't like all this going on in the presence of your secretary."

"My secretary? Because he is a Florinian? Are you afraid his mind will be unsettled by such things as this letter? Nonsense." His tone shifted from one of mild amusement to the unmodulated syllables of command. "Turn to the Squire of Rune."

The secretary did so. His eyes were discreetly lowered and his white face was uncreased by lines and unmarred by expression. It almost seemed untouched by life.

"This Florinian," said Fife, careless of the man's presence, "is my personal servant. He is never away from me, never with others of his kind. But it is not for that reason that he is absolutely trustworthy. Look at him. Look at his eyes. Isn't it obvious to you that he has been under the psychic probe? He is incapable of any thought which is disloyal to myself in the slightest degree. With no offense intended, I can say that I would sooner trust him than any of you."

Bort chuckled. "I don't blame you. None of us owes you the loyalty of a probed Florinian servant."

Steen giggled again and writhed in his seat as though it were growing gently warm.

Not one of them made any comment on Fife's use of a psychic probe for personal servants. Fife would have been tremendously astonished had they done so. The use of the psychic probe for any reason other than the correction of mental disorders or the removal of criminal impulses was forbidden. Strictly speaking, it was forbidden even to the Great Squires.

Yet Fife probed whenever he felt it necessary, particularly when the subject was a Florinian. The probing of a Sarkite was a much more delicate matter. The Squire of Steen, whose writhings at the mention of the probing Fife did not miss, was well reputed to make use of probed Florinians of both sexes for purposes far removed from the secretarial.

"Now." Fife put his blunt fingers together. "I did not bring you all together for the reading of a crackpot letter. That, I hope, is understood. Actually I am afraid we have an important problem on our hands. First of all, I ask myself, why bother only with me? To be sure, I am the wealthiest of the Squires, but alone, I control only a third of the kyrt trade. Together the five of us control it all. It is easy to make five cello-copies of a letter, as easy as it is to make one."

"You use too many words," muttered Bort. "What do you want?"

Balle's withered and colorless lips moved in a dully gray face. "He wants to know, my Lord of Bort, if we have received copies of this letter."

"Then let him say so."

"I thought I was saying so," said Fife evenly. "Well?"

They looked at one another, doubtfully or defiantly, as the personality of each dictated.

Rune spoke first. His pink forehead was moist with discrete drops of perspiration and he lifted a soft square of kyrt to mop the dampness out of the creases between the folds of fat that ran semicircles from ear to ear.

He said, "I wouldn't know, Fife. I can ask my secretaries, who are all Sarkites, by the way. After all, even if such a letter had reached my office, it would have been considered a—what is it we say?—a crank letter. It would never have come to me. That's certain. It's only your own peculiar secretarial system that kept you from being spared this trash yourself."

He looked about and smiled, his gums gleaming wetly between his lips above and below artificial teeth of chrome-steel. Each individual tooth was buried deeply, knit to the jawbone, and stronger than any tooth of mere enamel could ever be. His smile was more frightening than his frown could possibly be.

Balle shrugged. "I imagine that what Rune has just said can hold for all of us."

Steen tittered. "I never read mail. Really, I never do. It's such a bore, and such loads come in that I just wouldn't have any *time*." He looked about him earnestly, as though it were really necessary to convince the company of this important fact.

Bort said, "Nuts. What's wrong with you all? Afraid of Fife? Look here, Fife, I don't keep any secretary because I don't need anyone between myself and my business. I got a copy of that letter and I'm sure these three did too. Want to know what I did with mine? I threw it into the disposal chute. I'd advise you to do the same with yours. Let's stop this. I'm tired."

His hand reached upward for the toggle switch that would cut contact and release his image from its presence in Fife.

"Wait, Bort." Fife's voice rang out harshly. "Don't do that. I'm not done. You wouldn't want us to take measures and come to decisions in your absence. Surely you wouldn't."

"Let us linger, Squire Bort," urged Rune in his softer tones, though his little fat-buried eyes were not particularly amiable. "I wonder why Squire Fife seems to worry so about a trifle."

"Well," said Balle, his dry voice scratching at their ears, "perhaps Fife thinks our letter-writing friend has information about a Trantorian attack on Florina."

"Pooh," said Fife with scorn. "How would he know, whoever he is? Our secret service is adequate, I assure you. And how would he stop the attack if he received our properties as bribe? No, no. He speaks of the destruction of Florina as though he meant physical destruction and not political destruction."

"It's just too *insane*," said Steen.

"Yes?" said Fife. "Then you don't see the significance of the events of the last two weeks?"

"Which particular events?" asked Bort.

"It seems a Spatio-analyst has disappeared. Surely you've heard of that."

Bort looked annoyed and in no way soothed. "I've heard from Abel of Trantor about it. What of it? I know nothing of Spatio-analysts."

"At least you've read a copy of the last message to his base on Sark before he turned up missing."

"Abel showed it to me. I paid no attention to it."

"What about the rest of you?" Fife's eyes challenged them one by one. "Your memory goes back a week?"

"I read it," said Rune. "I remember it too. Of course! It spoke of destruction also. Is that what you're getting at?"

"Look here," Steen said shrilly, "it was full of nasty hints that made no sense. Really, I do hope we're not going to discuss it now. I could scarcely get rid of Abel, and it was just before dinner, too. Most distressing. Really."

"There's no help for it, Steen," said Fife with more than a trace of impatience. (What could one do with a thing like Steen?) "We must speak of it again. The Spatio-analyst spoke of the destruction of Florina. Coincident with his disappearance, we receive messages also threatening the destruction of Florina. *Is* that coincidence?"

"You are saying that the Spatio-analyst sent the blackmailing message?" whispered old Balle.

"Not likely. Why say it first in his own name, then anonymously?"

"When he spoke of it at first," said Balle, "he was communicating with his district office, not with us."

"Even so. A blackmailer deals with no one but his victim if he can help it."

"Well then?"

"He has disappeared. Call the Spatio-analyst honest. But he broadcast dangerous information. He is now in the hands of others who are *not* honest and they are blackmailers."

"What others?"

Fife sat grimly back in his chair, his lips scarcely moving. "You ask me seriously? Trantor."

Steen shivered. "Trantor!" His high-pitched voice broke.

"Why not? What better way to gain control of Florina? It's one of the prime aims of their foreign policy. And if they can do it without war, so much the better for them. Look here, if we accede to this impossible ultimatum, Florina is theirs. They offer us a little"—he brought two fingers close together before his face—"but how long shall we keep even that?

"On the other hand, suppose we ignore this, and, really, we have no choice. What would Trantor do then? Why, they will spread rumors of an imminent end of the world to the Florinian peasants. As their rumors spread the peasants will panic, and what can follow but disaster? What force can make a man work if he thinks the end of the world will come tomorrow? The harvest will rot. The warehouses will empty."

Steen lifted a finger to smooth the coloring on one cheek, as he glanced at a mirror in his own apartments, out of range of the receptor-cube.

He said, "I don't think that would harm us much. If the supply goes down, wouldn't the price go up? Then after a while it would turn out that Florina was still there and the peasants would go back to work. Besides, we could always threaten to clamp down on exports. Really, I don't see how any cultured world could be expected to live without kyrt. Oh, it's King Kyrt all right. I think this is a fuss about nothing."

He threw himself into an attitude of boredom, one finger placed delicately upon his cheek.

Balle's old eyes had been closed through all of this last. He said, "There can be no price increases now. We've got them at absolute ceiling height."

"Exactly," said Fife. "It won't come to serious disruption anyway. Trantor waits for any sign of disorder on Florina. If they could present the Galaxy with the prospect of a Sark that was unable to guarantee kyrt shipments, it would be the most natural thing in the universe for them to move in to maintain what they call order and to keep the kyrt coming. And the danger would be that the free worlds of the Galaxy would probably play along with them for the sake of the kyrt. Especially if Trantor agreed to break the monopoly, increase production and lower prices. Afterward it would be another story, but meanwhile, they would get their support.

"It's the only logical way that Trantor could possibly grip Florina.

If it were simple force, the free Galaxy outside the Trantorian sphere of influence would join us in sheer self-protection."

Rune said, "How does the Spatio-analyst fit in this? Is he necessary? If your theory is adequate it should explain that."

"I think it does. These Spatio-analysts are unbalanced for the most part, and this one has developed some"—Fife's fingers moved, as though building a vague structure—"some crazy theory. It doesn't matter what. Trantor can't let it come out, or the Spatio-analytic Bureau would quash it. To seize the man and learn the details would, however, give them something that would probably possess a surface validity to non-specialists. They could use it, make it sound real. The Bureau is a Trantorian puppet, and their denials, once the story is spread by way of scientific rumormongering, would never be forceful enough to overtake the lie."

"It sounds too complicated," said Bort. "Nuts. They can't let it come out, but then again they will let it come out."

"They can't let it come out as a serious scientific announcement, or even reach the Bureau as such," said Fife patiently. "They can let it leak out as a rumor. Don't you see that?"

"What's old Abel doing wasting his time looking for the Spatio-analyst then?"

"You expect him to advertise the fact that he's got him? What Abel does and what Abel seems to be doing are two different things."

"Well," said Rune, "if you're right, what are we to do?"

Fife said, "We have learned the danger, and that is the important thing. We'll find the Spatio-analyst if we can. We must keep all known agents of Trantor under strict scrutiny without really interfering with them. From their actions we may learn the course of coming events. We must suppress thoroughly any propaganda on Florina to the effect of the planet's destruction. The first faint whisper must meet with instant counteraction of the most violent sort.

"Most of all, we must remain united. That is the whole purpose of this meeting, in my eyes; the forming of a common front. We all know about continental autonomy and I'm sure there is no one more insistent upon it than I am. That is, under ordinary circumstances. These are not ordinary circumstances. You see that?"

More or less reluctantly, for continental autonomy was not a thing to be abandoned lightly, they saw that.

"Then," said Fife, "we will wait for the second move."

That had been a year ago. They had left and there had followed the strangest and most complete fiasco ever to have fallen to the lot of the Squire of Fife in a moderately long and a more than moderately audacious career.

No second move followed. There were no further letters to any of them. The Spatio-analyst remained unfound, while Trantor maintained a desultory search. There was no trace of apocalyptic rumors on Florina, and the harvesting and processing of kyrt continued its smooth pace.

The Squire of Rune took to calling Fife at weekly intervals.

"Fife," he would call. "Anything new?" His fatness would quiver with delight and thick chuckles would force their way out of his gullet.

Fife took it bleakly and stolidly. What could he do? Over and over again he sifted the facts. It was no use. Something was missing. Some vital factor was missing.

And then it all began exploding at once, and he had the answer. He *knew* he had the answer and it was what he had *not* expected.

He had called a meeting once again. The chronometer now said two twenty-nine.

They were beginning to appear now. Bort first, lips compressed and a rough hangnailed finger rasping against the grain of his grizzly-stubbled cheek. Then Steen, his face freshly washed clear of its paint and presenting a pallid, unhealthy appearance. Balle, indifferent and tired, his cheeks sunken, his armchair well cushioned, a glass of warm milk at his side. Lastly Rune, two minutes late, wet-lipped and sulky, sitting in the night once again. This time his lights were dimmed to the point where he was a hazy bulk sitting in a cube of shadow which Fife's lights could not have illuminated though they had had the power of Sark's sun.

Fife began. "Squires! Last year I speculated on a distant and complicated danger. In so doing I fell into a trap. The danger exists, but it is not distant. It is near us, very near. One of you already knows what I mean. The others will find out shortly."

"What *do* you mean?" asked Bort shortly.

"High treason!" shot back Fife.

Ten: *THE FUGITIVE*

Myrlyn Terens was not a man of action. He told himself that as an excuse, since now, leaving the spaceport, he found his mind paralyzed.

He had to pick his pace carefully. Not too slowly, or he would seem to be dawdling. Not too quickly, or he would seem to be running. Just briskly, as a patroller would walk, a patroller who was about his business and ready to enter his ground-car.

If only he could enter a ground-car! Driving one, unfortunately, did not come within the education of a Florinian, not even a Florinian Townman, so he tried to think as he walked and could not. He needed silence and leisure.

And he felt almost too weak to walk. He might not be a man of action but he *had* acted quickly now for a day and a night and part of another day. It had used up his lifetime's supply of nerve.

Yet he dared not stop.

If it were night he might have had a few hours to think. But it was early afternoon.

If he could drive a ground-car he could put the miles between himself and the City. Just long enough to think a bit before deciding on the next step. But he had only his legs.

If he could think. That was it. If he could think. If he could suspend all motion, all action. If he could catch the universe between instants of time, order it to halt, while he thought things through. There must be some way.

He plunged into the welcome shade of Lower City. He walked stiffly, as he had seen the patrollers walk. He swung his shock stick in a firm grip. The streets were bare. The natives were huddling in their shacks. So much the better.

The Townman chose his house carefully. It would be best to choose one of the better ones, one with patches of colored plastic briquets and polarized glass in the windows. The lower orders were sullen. They had less to lose. An "upper man" would be falling over himself to help.

He walked up a short path to such a house. It was set back from the street, another sign of affluence. He knew he would have no need of pounding the door or breaking it in. There had been a noticeable movement at one window as he walked up the ramp. (How generations of necessity enabled a Florinian to smell the approach of a patroller.) The door would open.

It did open.

A young girl opened it, her eyes white-rimmed circles. She was gawky in a dress whose frills showed a determined effort on the part of her parents to uphold their status as something more than the ordinary run of "Florinian trash." She stood aside to let him pass, her breath coming quickly between parted lips.

The Townman motioned to her to shut the door. "Is your father here, girl?"

She screamed, "Pa!" then gasped, "Yes, sir!"

"Pa" was moving in apologetically from another room. He came slowly. It was no news to him that a patroller was at the door. It was simply safer to let a young girl admit him. She was less apt to be knocked down out of hand than he himself was, if the patroller happened to be angry.

"Your name?" asked the Townman.

"Jacof, if it please you, sir."

The Townman's uniform had a thin-sheeted notebook in one of its pockets. The Townman opened it, studied it briefly, made a crisp check mark and said, "Jacof! Yes! I want to see every member of the household. Quickly!"

If he could have found room for any emotion but one of hopeless oppression, Terens would almost have enjoyed himself. He was not immune to the seductive pleasures of authority.

They filed in. A thin woman, worried, a child of about two years wriggling in her arms. Then the girl who had admitted him and a younger brother.

"That's all?"

"Everyone, sir," said Jacof humbly.

"Can I tend the baby?" asked the woman anxiously. "It's her nap time. I was putting her to bed." She held the young child out as though the sight of young innocence might melt a patroller's heart.

The Townman did not look at her. A patroller, he imagined, would not have, and he was a patroller. He said, "Put it down and give it a sugar sucker to keep it quiet. Now, you! Jacof!"

"Yes, sir."

"You're a responsible boy, aren't you?" A native of whatever age was, of course, a "boy."

"Yes, sir." Jacof's eyes brightened and his shoulders lifted a trifle. "I'm a clerk in the food-processing center. I've had mathematics, long division. I can do logarithms."

Yes, the Townman thought, they've shown you how to use a table of logarithms and taught you how to pronounce the word.

He knew the type. The man would be prouder of his logarithms than a Squireling of his yacht. The polaroid in his windows was the consequence of his logarithms and the tinted briquets advertised his long division. His contempt for the uneducated native would be equal to that of the average Squire for all natives and his hatred would be more intense since he had to live among them and was taken for one of them by his betters.

"You believe in the law, don't you, boy, and in the good Squires?" The Townman maintained the impressive fiction of consulting his notebook.

"My husband is a good man," burst in the woman volubly. "He hasn't ever been in trouble. He doesn't associate with trash. And I don't. No more do the children. We always——"

Terens waved her down. "Yes. Yes. Now look, boy, I want you to sit right here and do what I say. I want a list of everyone you know about on this block. Names, addresses, what they do, and what kind of boys they are. Especially the last. If there's one of these trouble-makers, I want to know. We're going to clean up. Understand?"

"Yes, sir. Yes, sir. There's Husting first of all. He's down the block a way. He——"

"Not like that, boy. Get him a piece of paper, you. Now you sit there and write it all down. Every bit. Write it slowly because I can't read native chicken tracks."

"I have a trained writing hand, sir."

"Let's see it, then."

Jacof bent to his task, hand moving slowly. His wife looked over his shoulder.

Terens spoke to the girl who had let him in. "Go to the window and let me know if any other patrollers come this way. I'll want to speak to them. Don't *you* call them. Just tell me."

And then, finally, he could relax. He had made a momentarily secure niche for himself in the midst of danger.

Except for the noisy sucking of the baby in the corner, there was reasonable silence. He would be warned of the enemy's approach in time for a fighting chance to escape.

Now he could think.

In the first place, his role as patroller was about over. There were undoubtedly road blocks at all possible exits from the town, and they knew he could use no means of transportation more complicated than a diamagnetic scooter. It would not be long before it would dawn on the search-rusty patrollers that only by a systematic quartering of the town, block by block and house by house, could they be sure of their man.

When they finally decided that, they would undoubtedly start at the outskirts and work inward. If so, this house would be among the first to be entered, so his time was particularly limited.

Until now, despite its black and silver conspicuousness, the patroller uniform had been useful. The natives themselves had not questioned it. They had not stopped to see his pale Florinian face; they had not studied his appearance. The uniform had been enough.

Before long the pursuing hounds would find that fact dawning upon them. It would occur to them to broadcast instructions to all natives to hold any patroller unable to show proper identification, particularly one with a white skin and sandy hair. Temporary identifications would be passed out to all legitimate patrollers. Rewards would be offered. Perhaps only one native in a hundred would be courageous enough to tackle the uniform no matter how patently false the occupant was. One in a hundred would be enough.

So he would have to stop being a patroller.

That was one thing. Now another. He would be safe nowhere on Florina from now on. Killing a patroller was the ultimate crime and in fifty years, if he could elude capture so long, the chase would remain hot. So he would have to leave Florina.

How?

Well, he gave himself one more day of life. This was a generous estimate. It assumed the patrollers to be at maximum stupidity and himself in a state of maximum luck.

In one way this was an advantage. A mere twenty-four hours of life was not much to risk. It meant he could take chances no sane man could possibly take.

He stood up.

Jacof looked up from his paper. "I'm not quite done, sir. I'm writing very carefully."

"Let me see what you have written."

He looked at the paper handed him and said, "It is enough. If other patrollers should come, don't waste their time saying that you have already made a list. They are in a hurry and may have other tasks for you. Just do as they say. Are there any coming now?"

The girl at the window said, "No, sir. Shall I go out in the street and look?"

"It's not necessary. Let's see now. Where is the nearest elevator?"

"It's about a quarter of a mile to the left, sir, as you leave the house. You can——"

"Yes, yes. Let me out."

A squad of patrollers turned into the street just as the door of the elevator ground into place behind the Townman. He could feel his heart pound. The systematic search was probably starting, and they were at his heels.

A minute later, heartbeat still drumming, he stepped out of the elevator into Upper City. There would be no cover here. No pillars. No cementalloy hiding him from above.

He felt like a moving black dot among the glare of the garish buildings. He felt visible for two miles on every side and for five miles up in the sky. There seemed to be large arrows pointing to him.

There were no patrollers in view. The Squires who passed looked through him. If a patroller was an object of fear to a Florinian, he was an object of nothing-at-all to a Squire. If anything would save him, that would.

He had a vague notion of the geography of Upper City. Somewhere in this section was City Park. The most logical step would have been to ask directions, the next most logical to enter any moderately tall building and look out from several of the upper-story terraces. The first alternative was impossible. No patroller could possibly need directions. The second was too risky. Inside a building, a patroller would be more conspicuous. Too conspicuous.

He simply struck out in the direction indicated by his memory of the maps of Upper City he had seen on occasion. It served well enough. It was unmistakably City Park that he came across in five minutes' time.

City Park was an artificial patch of greenery about one hundred acres in area. On Sark itself, City Park had an exaggerated reputation for many things from bucolic peace to nightly orgies. On Florina, those who had vaguely heard of it imagined it ten to a hundred times its actual size and a hundred to a thousand times its actual luxuriance.

The reality was pleasant enough. In Florina's mild climate it was green all year round. It had its patches of lawn, wooded areas and stony grottoes. It had a little pool with decorative fish in it and a larger pool for children to paddle in. At night it was aflame with colored illumination till the light rain started. It was between twilight and the rain that it was most alive. There was dancing, trimensional shows, and couples losing themselves along the winding walks.

Terens had never actually been inside it. He found its artificiality repellent when he entered the Park. He knew that the soil and rocks he stepped on, the water and trees around him, all rested on a dead-flat cementalloy bottom and it annoyed him. He thought of the kyrt fields, long and level, and the mountain ranges of the south. He despised the aliens who had to build toys for themselves in the midst of magnificence.

For half an hour Terens tramped the walks aimlessly. What he had to do would have to be done in City Park. Even here it might be impossible. Elsewhere it *was* impossible.

No one saw him. No one was conscious of him. He was sure of that. Let them ask the Squires and Squirettes who passed him, "Did you see a patroller in the Park yesterday?"

They could only stare. They might as well be asked whether they had seen a tree midge skitter across the path.

The Park was *too* tame. He felt panic begin to grow. He made his way up a staircase between boulders and began descending into the cuplike hollow circled by small caves designed to shelter couples caught in the nightly rainfall. (More were caught than could be accounted for by chance alone.)

And then he saw what he was looking for.

A man! A Squire, rather. Stepping back and forth quickly. Smoking the stub of a cigarette with sharp drags, cramming it into an ash recess, where it lay quietly for a moment, then vanished with a quick flash. Consulting a pendant watch.

There was no one else in the hollow. It was a place made for the evening and night.

The Squire was waiting for someone. So much was obvious. Terens looked about him. No one was following him up the stairs.

There might be other stairs. There were sure to be. No matter. He could not let the chance go.

He stepped down toward the Squire. The Squire did not see him, of course, until Terens said, "If you'll pardon me?"

It was respectful enough, but a Squire is not accustomed to having a patroller touch the crook of his elbow in however respectful a fashion.

"What the hell?" he said.

Terens abandoned neither the respect nor the urgency in his tone. (Keep him talking. Keep his eyes on yours for just half a minute!) He said, "This way, sir. It is in connection with the City-wide search for the native murderer."

"What are you talking about?"

"It will take just a moment."

Unobtrusively Terens had drawn his neuronic whip. The Squire never saw it. It buzzed a little and the Squire strained into rigor and toppled.

The Townman had never raised a hand against a Squire before. He was surprised at how sick and guilty he felt.

There was still no one in sight. He dragged the wooden body, with its glazed and staring eyes, into the nearest cave. He dragged it to the cave's shallow end.

He stripped the Squire, yanking clothing off the stiffened arms and legs with difficulty. He stepped out of his own dusty, sweat-stained patroller uniform and climbed into the Squire's underclothing. For the first time he felt kyrt fabric with some part of himself beside his fingers.

Then the rest of the clothing, and the Squire's skullcap. The last was necessary. Skullcaps were not entirely fashionable among the younger set but some wore them, this Squire luckily among them. To Terens it was a necessity as otherwise his light hair would make the masquerade impossible. He pulled the cap down tightly, covering his ears.

Then he did what had to be done. The killing of a patroller was, he suddenly realized, not the ultimate crime after all.

He adjusted his blaster to maximum dispersion and turned it on the unconscious Squire. In ten seconds only a charred mass was left. It would delay identification, confuse the pursuers.

He reduced the patroller's uniform to a powdery white ash with the blaster and clawed out of the heap blackened silver buttons and buckles. That, too, would make the chase harder. Perhaps he was buying only an additional hour, but that, too, was worth it.

And now he would have to leave without delay. He paused a moment just outside the mouth of the cave to sniff. The blaster worked cleanly. There was only the slightest odor of burned flesh and the light breeze would clear it in a few moments.

He was walking down the steps when a young girl passed him on the way up. For a moment he dropped his eyes out of habit. She was a Lady. He lifted them in time to see that she was young and quite good-looking, and in a hurry.

His jaws set. She wouldn't find him, of course. But she was late, or he wouldn't have been staring at his watch so. She might think he had grown tired of waiting and had left. He walked a trifle faster. He didn't want her returning, pursuing him breathlessly, asking if he had seen a young man.

He left the Park, walking aimlessly. Another half hour passed.

What now? He was no longer a patroller, he was a Squire.

But what now?

He stopped at a small square in which a fountain was centered in a plot of lawn. To the water a small quantity of detergent had been added so that it frothed and foamed in gaudy iridescence.

He leaned against the railing, back to the western sun, and, bit by bit, slowly, he dropped blackened silver into the fountain.

He thought of the girl who had passed him on the steps as he did so. She had been very young. Then he thought of Lower City and the momentary spasm of remorse left him.

The silver remnants were gone and his hands were empty. Slowly he began searching his pockets, doing his best to make it seem casual.

The contents of the pockets were not particularly unusual. A booklet of key slivers, a few coins, an identification card. (Holy Sark! Even the Squires carried them. But then, they didn't have to produce them for every patroller that came along.)

His new name, apparently, was Alstare Deamone. He hoped he

wouldn't have to use it. There were only ten thousand men, women and children in Upper City. The chance of his meeting one among them who knew Deamone personally was not large, but it wasn't insignificant either.

He was twenty-nine. Again he felt a rising nausea as he thought of what he had left in the cave, and fought it. A Squire was a Squire. How many twenty-nine-year-old Florinians had been done to death at their hands or by their directions? How many nine-year-old Florinians?

He had an address, too, but it meant nothing to him. His knowledge of Upper City geography was rudimentary.

Say!

A color portrait of a young boy, perhaps three, in pseudo-trimension. The colors flashed as he drew it out of its container, faded progressively as he returned it. A young son? A nephew? There had been the girl in the Park so it couldn't be a son, could it?

Or was he married? Was the meeting one of those they called "clandestine"? Would such meeting take place in daylight? Why not, under certain circumstances?

Terens hoped so. If the girl were meeting a married man she would not quickly report his absence. She would assume he had not been able to evade his wife. That would give him time.

No, it wouldn't. Instant depression seized him. Children playing hide-and-seek would stumble on the remains and run screaming. It was bound to happen within twenty-four hours.

He turned to the pocket's contents once more. A pocket-copy license as yacht pilot. He passed it by. All the richer Sarkites owned yachts and piloted them. It was this century's fad. Finally, a few strips of Sarkite credit vouchers. Now those might be temporarily useful.

It occurred to him that he hadn't eaten since the night before at the Baker's place. How quickly one could grow conscious of hunger.

Suddenly he turned back to the yacht license. Wait, now, the yacht wasn't in use now, not with the owner dead. And it was *his* yacht. Its hangar number was 26, at Port 9. Well . . .

Where was Port 9? He hadn't the slightest notion.

He leaned his forehead against the coolness of the smooth railing around the fountain. What now? What now?

The voice startled him.

"Hello," it said. "Not sick?"

Terens looked up. It was an older Squire. He was smoking a long cigarette containing some aromatic leaf while a green stone of some sort hung suspended from a gold wristband. His expression was one of kindly interest that astonished Terens into a moment of speechlessness, until he remembered. He was one of the clan himself now. Among themselves, Squires might well be decent human beings.

The Townman said, "Just resting. Decided to take a walk and lost track of time. I'm afraid I'm late for an appointment now."

He waved his hand in a wry gesture. He could imitate the Sarkite accent fairly well from long association but he didn't make the mistake of trying to exaggerate it. Exaggeration was easier to detect than insufficiency.

The other said, "Stuck without a skeeter, hey?" He was the older man, amused by the folly of youth.

"No skeeter," admitted Terens.

"Use mine," came the instant offer. "It's parked right outside. You can set the controls and send it back here when you're through. I won't be needing it for the next hour or so."

To Terens, that was almost ideal. The skeeters were fast and skittery as chain lightning, could outspeed and outmaneuver any patroller ground-car. It fell short of ideal only in that Terens could no more drive the skeeter than he could fly without it.

"From here to Sark," he said. He knew that piece of Squire slang for "thanks," and threw it in. "I think I'll walk. It isn't far to Port 9."

"No, it isn't far," agreed the other.

That left Terens no better off than before. He tried again. "Of course, I wish I were closer. The walk to Kyrt Highway is healthy enough by itself."

"Kyrt Highway? What's that got to do with it?"

Was he looking queerly at Terens? It occurred to the Townman, suddenly, that his clothing probably lacked the proper fitting. He said quickly, "Wait! I'm twisted at that. I've got myself crossed up walking. Let's see now." He looked about vaguely.

"Look. You're on Recket Road. All you have to do is go down to Triffis and turn left, then follow it into the port." He had pointed automatically.

Terens smiled. "You're right. I'm going to have to stop dreaming and start thinking. From here to Sark, sir."

"You can still use my skeeter."

"Kind of you, but . . ."

Terens was walking away, a bit too quickly, waving his hand. The Squire stared after him.

Perhaps tomorrow, when they found the corpse in the rocks and began searching, the Squire might think of this interview again. He would probably say, "There was something queer about him, if you know what I mean. He had an odd turn of phrase and didn't seem to know where he was. I'll swear he'd never heard of Triffis Avenue."

But that would be tomorrow.

He walked in the direction that the Squire had pointed out. He came to the glittering sign "Triffis Avenue," almost drab against the iridescent orange structure that was its background. He turned left.

Port 9 was alive with youth in yachting costume, which seemed to feature high-peaked hats and hip-bellying breeches. Terens felt conspicuous but no one paid attention to him. The air was full of conversation spiced with terms he did not understand.

He found Booth 26 but waited for minutes before approaching it. He wanted no Squire remaining persistently in its vicinity, no Squire who happened to own a yacht in a nearby booth who would know the real Alstare Deamone by sight and would wonder what a stranger was doing about his ship.

Finally, with the booth's neighborhood apparently safe, he walked over. The yacht's snout peered out from its hangar into the open field about which the booths were placed. He craned his neck to stare at it.

Now what?

He had killed three men in the last twelve hours. He had risen from Florinian Townman to patroller, from patroller to Squire. He had come from Lower City to Upper City and from Upper City to a spaceport. To all intents and purposes he owned a yacht, a vessel sufficiently spaceworthy to take him to safety on any inhabited world in this sector of the Galaxy.

There was only one catch.

He could not pilot a yacht.

He was tired to the bone, and hungry to boot. He had come this far, and now he could go no further. He was on the edge of space but there was no way of crossing the edge.

By now the patrollers must have decided he was nowhere in Lower City. They would turn the search to Upper City as soon as they could get it through their thick skulls that a Florinian would *dare*. Then the body would be found and a new direction would be taken. They would look for an impostor Squire.

And here he was. He had climbed to the farthest niche of the blind alley and with his back to the closed end he could only wait for the faint sounds of pursuit to grow louder and louder until eventually the bloodhounds would be on him.

Thirty-six hours ago the greatest opportunity of his life had been in his hands. Now the opportunity was gone and his life would soon follow.

Eleven: *THE CAPTAIN*

It was the first time, really, that Captain Racety had found himself unable to impose his will upon a passenger. Had that passenger been one of the Great Squires themselves, he might still have counted on co-operation. A Great Squire might be all-powerful on his own continent, but on a ship he would recognize that there could be only one master, the Captain.

A woman was different. Any woman. And a woman who was daughter of a Great Squire was completely impossible.

He said, "My Lady, how can I allow you to interview them in private?"

Samia of Fife, her dark eyes snapping, said, "Why not? Are they armed, Captain?"

"Of course not. That's not the point."

"Anyone can see they're only a pair of very frightened creatures. They're half scared to death."

"Frightened people can be very dangerous, my Lady. They can't be counted on to act sensibly."

"Then why do you keep them frightened?" She had the tiniest stammer when she was angry. "You've got three tremendous sailors standing over them with blasters, poor things. Captain, I'll not forget this."

No, she wouldn't, the Captain thought. He could feel himself beginning to give way.

"If Your Ladyship pleases, will you tell me exactly what it is that you want?"

"It's simple. I've told you. I want to speak to them. If they're Florinians, as you say they are, I can get tremendously valuable information from them for my book. I can't do that, though, if they're too frightened to speak. If I could be with them alone it would be fine. Alone, Captain! Can you understand a simple word? *Alone!*"

"And what would I say to your father, my Lady, if he discovers that I allowed you to remain unguarded in the presence of two desperate criminals?"

"Desperate criminals! Oh, Great Space! Two poor fools that tried to escape their planet and had no more sense than to board a ship going to Sark! Besides, how would my father know?"

"If they hurt you he would know."

"Why should they hurt me?" Her small fist lifted and vibrated, while she put every atom of force she could find into her voice. "I *demand* it, Captain."

Captain Racety said, "How about this then, my Lady? I will be present. I shall not be three sailors with blasters. I shall be one man with no blaster in view. Otherwise"—and in his turn he put all his resolution into his voice—"I must refuse your demand."

"Very well, then." She was breathless. "Very well. But if I can't get them to speak because of you I will personally see to it that you captain no more ships."

Valona put her hand hastily over Rik's eyes as Samia entered the brig.

"What's the matter, girl?" asked Samia sharply, before she could remember that she was going to speak to them comfortingly.

Valona spoke with difficulty. She said, "He is not bright, Lady. He wouldn't know you were a Lady. He might have looked at you. I mean without intending any harm, Lady."

"Oh, goodness," said Samia. "Let him look." She went on, "Must they stay here, Captain?"

"Would you prefer a stateroom, my Lady?"

Samia said, "Surely you could manage a cell not quite so grim."

"It is grim to you, my Lady. To them, I am sure this is luxury. There is running water here. Ask them if there was any in their hut on Florina."

"Well, tell those men to leave."

The Captain motioned to them. They turned, stepping out nimbly.

The Captain set down the light aluminum folding chair he had brought with him. Samia took it.

He said brusquely to Rik and Valona, "Stand up."

Samia broke in instantly. "No! Let them sit. You're not to interfere, Captain."

She turned to them. "So you are a Florinian, girl."

Valona shook her head. "We're from Wotex."

"You needn't be frightened. It docsn't matter that you're from Florina. No one will hurt you."

"We're from Wotex."

"But don't you see that you've practically admitted you're from Florina, girl? Why did you cover the boy's eyes?

"He's not allowed to look at a Lady."

"Even if he's from Wotex?"

Valona was silent.

Samia let her think about it. She tried to smile in a friendly way. Then she said, "Only Florinians aren't allowed to look at Ladies. So you see you've admitted that you're a Florinian."

Valona burst out, "*He's* not."

"Are *you?*"

"Yes, I am. But he's not. Don't do anything to him. He *really* isn't a Florinian. He was just found one day. I don't know where he comes from, but it's not Florina." Suddenly she was almost voluble.

Samia looked at her with some surprise. "Well, I'll speak to him. What's your name, boy?"

Rik was staring. Was that how women Squires looked? So small, and friendly-looking. And she smelled so nice. He was very glad she had let him look at her.

Samia said again, "What's your name, boy?"

Rik came to life but stumbled badly in the attempt to shape a monosyllable.

"Rik," he said. Then he thought, Why, that's not my name. He said, "I think it's Rik."

"Don't you know?"

Valona, looking woebegone, tried to speak, but Samia held up a sharply restraining hand.

Rik shook his head. "I don't know."

"Are you a Florinian?"

Rik was positive here. "No. I was on a ship. I came here from somewhere else." He could not bear to look away from Samia but he seemed to see the ship co-existing with her. A small and very friendly and homelike ship.

He said, "It was on a ship that I came to Florina and before that I lived on a planet."

"What planet?"

It was as though the thought were forcing its way painfully through mental channels too small for it. Then Rik remembered and was delighted at the sound his voice made, a sound so long forgotten.

"Earth! I came from Earth!"

"Earth?"

Rik nodded.

Samia turned to the Captain. "Where is this planet Earth?"

Captain Racety smiled briefly. "I never heard of it. Don't take the boy seriously, my Lady. A native lies the way he breathes. It comes naturally to him. He says whatever comes first into his mind."

"He doesn't *talk* like a native." She turned to Rik again. "Where is Earth, Rik?"

"I——" He put a shaking hand to his forehead. Then he said, "It's in the Sirius Sector." The intonation of the statement made it half a question.

Samia said to the Captain, "There is a Sirius Sector, isn't there?"

"Yes, there is. I'm amazed he had that right. Still, that doesn't make Earth any more real."

Rik said vehemently, "But it is. I remember, I tell you. It's been so long since I remembered. I can't be wrong now. I can't."

He turned, gripping Valona's elbows and clawing at her sleeve. "Lona, tell them I come from Earth. I do. I do."

Valona's eyes were wide with anxiety. "We found him one day, Lady, and he had no mind at all. He couldn't dress himself or talk or walk. He was nothing. Ever since then he's been remembering little by little. So far everything he's remembered has been so." She cast a quick, fearful glance at the bored face of the Captain. "He may really have come from Earth, Squire. No contradiction intended."

The last was a long-established conventional phrase that went with any statement that seemed in contradiction to a previous statement by a superior.

Captain Racety grunted. "He may have come from the center of Sark for all that story proves, my Lady."

"Maybe, but there's something queer about all this," insisted Samia, making up her mind flatly, woman-wise, on the side of romance. "I'm sure of it. . . . What made him so helpless when you found him, girl? Had he been hurt?"

Valona said nothing at first. Her eyes darted helplessly back and forth. First to Rik, whose fingers clutched at his hair, then to the Captain, who was smiling without humor, finally to Samia, who waited.

"Answer me, girl," said Samia.

It was a hard decision for Valona to make, but no conceivable lie could substitute for the truth in this place and at this time. She said, "A doctor once looked at him. He said m—my Rik was psycho-probed."

"Psycho-probed!" Samia felt a slight wash of repulsion well over her. She pushed her chair away. It squeaked against the metal floor. "You mean he was psychotic?"

"I don't know what that means, Lady," said Valona humbly.

"Not in the sense you're thinking of, my Lady," said the Captain almost simultaneously. "Natives aren't psychotic. Their needs and desires are too simple. I've never heard of a psychotic native in my life."

"But then——"

"It's simple, my Lady. If we accept this fantastic story the girl tells, we can only conclude that the boy had been a criminal, which is a way of being psychotic, I suppose. If so, he must have been treated by one of those quacks who practice among the natives, been nearly killed and was then dumped in a deserted section to avoid detection and prosecution."

"But it would have to be someone with a psycho-probe," protested

Samia. "Surely you wouldn't expect natives to be able to use them."

"Perhaps not. But then you wouldn't expect an authorized medical man to use one so inexpertly. The fact that we arrive at a contradiction proves the story to be a lie throughout. If you will accept my suggestion, my Lady, you will leave these creatures to our handling. You see that it's useless to expect anything out of them."

Samia hesitated. "Perhaps you're right."

She rose and looked uncertainly at Rik. The Captain stepped behind her, lifted the little chair and folded it with a snap.

Rik jumped to his feet. "Wait!"

"If you please, my Lady," said the Captain, holding the door open for her. "My men will quiet him."

Samia stopped at the threshold. "They won't hurt him?"

"I doubt if he'll make us go to extremes. He will be easy handling."

"Lady! Lady!" Rik called. "I can prove it. I'm from Earth."

Samia stood irresolute for a moment. "Let's hear what he has to say."

The Captain said coldly, "As you wish, my Lady."

She returned, but not very far. She remained a step from the door.

Rik was flushed. With the effort of remembering, his lips drew back into the caricature of a smile. He said, "I remember Earth. It was radioactive. I remember the Forbidden Areas and the blue horizon at night. The soil glowed and nothing would grow in it. There were just a few spots men could live on. That's why I was a Spatioanalyst. That's why I didn't mind staying in space. My world was a dead world."

Samia shrugged. "Come along, Captain. He's simply raving."

But this time it was Captain Racety who stood there, openmouthed. He muttered, "A radioactive world!"

She said, "You mean there *is* such a thing?"

"Yes." He turned wondering eyes on her. "Now where could he have picked *that* up?"

"How could a world be radioactive and inhabited?"

"But there *is* one. And it *is* in the Sirius Sector. I don't remember its name. It might even be Earth."

"It *is* Earth," said Rik, proudly and with confidence. "It is the oldest planet of the Galaxy. It is the planet on which the whole human race originated."

The Captain said softly, "That's so!"

Samia said, mind whirling, "You mean the human race originated on this Earth?"

"No, no," said the Captain abstractedly. "That's superstition. It's just that that's how I came to hear about the radioactive planet. It claims to be Man's home planet."

"I didn't know we were supposed to have a home planet."

"I suppose we started somewhere, my Lady, but I doubt that anyone can possibly know on what planet it happened."

With sudden decision he walked toward Rik. "What else do you remember?"

He almost added "boy," but held it back.

"The ship mostly," said Rik, "and Spatio-analysis."

Samia joined the Captain. They stood there, directly before Rik, and Samia felt the excitement returning. "Then it's all true? But then how did he come to be psycho-probed?"

"Psycho-probed!" said Captain Racety thoughtfully. "Suppose we ask him. Here, you, native or outworlder or whatever you are. How did you come to be psycho-probed?"

Rik looked doubtful. "You all say that. Even Lona. But I don't know what the word means."

"When did you stop remembering, then?"

"I'm not sure." He began again, desperately. "I was on a ship."

"We know that. Go on."

Samia said, "It's no use barking, Captain. You'll drive out what few wits are left him."

Rik was entirely absorbed in wrenching at the dimness within his mind. The effort left no room for any emotion. It was to his own astonishment that he said, "I'm not afraid of him, Lady. I'm trying to remember. There was danger. I'm sure of that. Great danger to Florina, but I can't remember the details about it."

"Danger to the whole planet?" Samia cast a swift glance at the Captain.

"Yes. It was in the currents."

"What currents?" asked the Captain.

"The currents of space."

The Captain spread his hands and let them drop. "This is madness."

"No, no. Let him go on." The tide of belief had shifted to Samia again. Her lips were parted, her dark eyes gleamed and little dimples between cheek and chin made their appearance as she smiled. "What are the currents of space?"

"The different elements," said Rik vaguely. He had explained that before. He didn't want to go through that again.

He went on rapidly, nearly incoherently, speaking as the thoughts came to him, driven by them. "I sent a message to the local office on Sark. I remember that very clearly. I had to be careful. It was a danger that went beyond Florina. Yes. Beyond Florina. It was as wide as the Milky Way. It had to be handled carefully."

He seemed to have lost all real contact with those who listened to him, to be living in a world of the past before which a curtain was tearing away in places. Valona placed a soothing hand upon his shoulder and said, "Don't!" but he was unresponsive even to that.

"Somehow," he went on breathlessly, "my message was intercepted by some official on Sark. It was a mistake. I don't know how it happened."

He frowned. "I'm sure I sent it to the local office on the Bureau's own wave length. Do you suppose the sub-ether could have been tapped?" He did not even wonder that the word "sub-ether" came so easily to him.

He might have been waiting for an answer, but his eyes were still unseeing. "Anyway, when I landed on Sark they were waiting for me."

Again a pause, this time long and meditative. The Captain did nothing to break it; he seemed to be meditating himself.

Samia, however, said, "Who was waiting for you? Who?"

Rik said, "I—I don't know. I can't remember. It wasn't the office. It was someone of Sark. I remember speaking to him. He knew about the danger. He spoke of it. I'm sure he spoke of it. We sat at a table together. I remember the table. He sat opposite me. It's as clear as space. We spoke for quite a while. It seems to me I wasn't anxious to give details. I'm sure of that. I would have had to speak to the office first. And then he . . ."

"Yes?" prompted Samia.

"He did something. He—— No, nothing more will come. *Nothing will come!*"

He screamed the words and then there was silence, a silence that was anticlimactically broken by the prosaic buzz of the Captain's wrist communo.

He said, "What is it?"

The answering voice was reedy and precisely respectful. "A message to the Captain from Sark. It is requested that he accept it personally."

"Very well. I will be at the sub-etherics presently."

He turned to Samia. "My Lady, may I suggest that it is, in any case, dinnertime."

He saw that the girl was about to protest her lack of appetite, to urge him to leave and not to bother about her. He continued, more diplomatically, "It is also time to feed these creatures. They are probably tired and hungry."

Samia could say nothing against that. "I must see them again, Captain."

The Captain bowed silently. It might have been acquiescence. It might not.

Samia of Fife was thrilled. Her studies of Florina satisfied a certain aspiration to intellect within her, but the Mysterious Case of the Psycho-probed Earthman (she thought of the matter in capitals) appealed to something much more primitive and much more demanding. It roused the sheer animal curiosity in her.

It was a mystery!

There were three points that fascinated her. Among these was not the perhaps reasonable question (under the circumstances) of whether the man's story was a delusion or a deliberate lie, rather than the truth. To believe it anything other than truth would spoil the mystery and Samia could not allow that.

The three points were therefore these. (1) What was the danger that threatened Florina, or, rather, the entire Galaxy? (2) Who was the person who had psycho-probed the Earthman? (3) Why had the person used the psycho-probe?

She was determined to sift the matter to her own thorough satisfaction. No one is so modest as not to believe himself a competent amateur sleuth, and Samia was far from modest.

As soon after dinner as she could politely manage, she hurried down to the brig.

She said to the guard, "Open the door!"

The sailor remained perfectly erect, staring blankly and respectfully ahead. He said, "If Your Ladyship pleases, the door is not to be opened."

Samia gasped. "How dare you say so? If you do not open the door instantly, the Captain shall be informed."

"If Your Ladyship pleases, the door is not to be opened. That is by the strict order of the Captain."

She stormed up the levels once more, bursting into the Captain's stateroom like a tornado compressed into sixty inches.

"Captain!"

"My Lady?"

"Have you ordered the Earthman and the native woman to be kept from me?"

"I believe, my Lady, it was agreed that you were to interview them only in my presence."

"Before dinner, yes. But you saw they were harmless?"

"I say that they *seemed* harmless."

Samia simmered. "In that case I order you to come with me now."

"I cannot, my Lady. The situation has changed."

"In what way?"

"They must be questioned by the proper authorities on Sark and until then I think they should be left alone."

Samia's lower jaw dropped, but she rescued it from its undignified position almost immediately. "Surely you are not going to deliver them to the Bureau of Florinian Affairs."

"Well," temporized the Captain, "that was certainly the original intention. They have left their village without permission. In fact they have left their planet without permission. In addition, they have taken secret passage on a Sarkite vessel."

"The last was a mistake."

"Was it?"

"In any case, you knew all their crimes before our last interview."

"But it was only at the interview that I heard what the so-called Earthman had to say."

"So-called. You said yourself that the planet Earth existed."

"I said it might exist. But, my Lady, may I be so bold as to ask what you would like to see done with these people?"

"I think the Earthman's story should be investigated. He speaks of a danger to Florina and of someone on Sark who has deliberately attempted to keep knowledge of that danger from the proper authorities. I think it is even a case for my father. In fact I would take him to my father, when the proper time came."

The Captain said, "The cleverness of it all!"

"Are you being sarcastic, Captain?"

The Captain flushed. "Your pardon, my Lady. I was referring to our prisoners. May I be allowed to speak at some length?"

"I don't know what you mean by 'some length,'" she retorted angrily, "but I suppose you may begin."

"Thank you. In the first place, my Lady, I hope you will not minimize the importance of the disturbances on Florina."

"What disturbances?"

"You cannot have forgotten the incident in the library."

"A patroller killed! Really, Captain!"

"And a second patroller killed this morning, my Lady, and a native as well. It is not very usual for natives to kill patrollers and here is one who has done it twice, and yet remains uncaught. Is he a lone hand? Is it an accident? Or is it all part of a carefully laid scheme?"

"Apparently you believe the last."

"Yes, I do. The murdering native had two accomplices. Their description is rather like that of our two stowaways."

"You never said so!"

"I did not wish to alarm Your Ladyship. You'll remember, however, that I told you repeatedly that they could be dangerous."

"Very well. What follows from all this?"

"What if the murders on Florina were simply side shows intended to distract the attention of the patroller squadrons while these two sneaked aboard our ship?"

"That sounds so silly."

"Does it? Why are they running away from Florina? We haven't asked them. Let us suppose they are running away from the patrollers since that is certainly the most reasonable assumption. Would they be running to Sark of all places? And on a ship that carries Your Ladyship? And then he claims to be a Spatio-analyst."

Samia frowned. "What of that?"

"A year ago a Spatio-analyst was reported missing. The story was never given wide publicity. I knew, of course, because my ship was one of those that searched near space for signs of his ship. Whoever is backing these Florinian disorders has undoubtedly seized on that fact, and just knowing that the matter of the missing Spatio-analyst is known to them shows what a tight and unexpectedly efficient organization they have."

"It might be that the Earthman and the missing Spatio-analyst have no connection."

"No real connection, my Lady, undoubtedly. But to expect no connection at all is to expect too much of coincidence. It is an impostor we are dealing with. That is why he claims to have been psycho-probed."

"Oh?"

"How can we prove he *isn't* a Spatio-analyst? He knows no details of the planet Earth beyond the bare fact that it is radioactive. He cannot pilot a ship. He knows nothing of Spatio-analysis. And he covers up by insisting he was psycho-probed. Do you see, my Lady?"

Samia could make no direct answer. "But to what purpose?" she demanded.

"So that you might do exactly what you said you intended to do, my Lady."

"Investigate the mystery?"

"No, my Lady. Take the man to your father."

"I still see no point."

"There are several possibilities. At the best, he could be a spy upon your father, either for Florina or possibly for Trantor. I imagine old Abel of Trantor would certainly come forward to identify him as an Earthman, if for no other reason than to embarrass Sark by demanding the truth concerning this fictitious psycho-probing. At the worst, he will be your father's assassin."

"Captain!"

"My Lady?"

"This is ridiculous!"

"Perhaps, my Lady. But if so, the Department of Security is also ridiculous. You will recall that just before dinner I was called away to receive a message from Sark."

"Yes."

"This is it."

Samia received the thin translucent foil with its red lettering. It said: "Two Florinians are reported to have taken secret, illegal passage on your ship. Secure them immediately. One of them may claim to be a Spatio-analyst and not a Florinian native. You are to take no action in this matter. You will be held strictly responsible for the safety of these people. They are to be held for delivery to Depsec. Extreme secrecy. Extreme urgency."

Samia felt stunned. "Depsec," she said. "The Department of Security."

"Extreme secrecy," said the Captain. "I stretch a point to tell you this, but you have left me no choice, my Lady."

She said, "What will they do to him?"

"I cannot say for certain," said the Captain. "Certainly a suspected spy and assassin cannot expect gentle treatment. Probably his pretense will become partly a reality and he will learn what a psycho-probe is really like."

Twelve: *THE DETECTIVE*

The Four Great Squires regarded the Squire of Fife each in his own way. Bort was angry, Rune was amused, Balle was annoyed, and Steen was frightened.

Rune spoke first. He said, "High treason? Are you trying to frighten us with a phrase? What does it mean? Treason against you? Against Bort? Against myself? By whom and how? And for Sark's sake, Fife, these conferences interfere with my normal sleeping hours."

"The results," said Fife, "may interfere with many sets of sleeping hours. I don't refer to treason against any of us, Rune. I mean treason against Sark."

Bort said, "Sark? What's that, anyway, if not us?"

"Call it a myth. Call it something ordinary Sarkites believe in."

"I don't understand," moaned Steen. "You men always seem so interested in talking each other down. Really! I wish you'd get all this over with."

Balle said, "I agree with Steen." Steen looked gratified.

Fife said, "I'm perfectly willing to explain immediately. You have heard, I suppose, of the recent disturbances on Florina."

Rune said, "The Depsec dispatches speak of several patrollers killed. Is that what you mean?"

Bort broke in angrily. "By Sark, if we must have a conference, let's talk about that. Patrollers killed! They deserve to be killed! Do you mean to say a native can simply come up to a patroller and bash his head in with a two-by-four? Why should any patroller let any native with a two-by-four in his hand come close enough to use it? Why wasn't the native burned down at twenty paces?

"By Sark, I'd rattle the Patrol Corps from captain to recruit and send every dunderhead out on ship duty. The entire Corps is just an accumulation of fat. It's too easy a life for them down there. I say that every five years we should put Florina under martial law and scrape out the troublemakers. It would keep the natives quiet and our own men on their toes."

"Are you through?" asked Fife.

"For now, yes. But I'll take it up again. It's my investment down there, too, you know. It may not be as big as yours, Fife, but it's big enough for me to worry about."

Fife shrugged. He turned suddenly to Steen. "And have *you* heard of the disturbances?"

Steen jumped. "I have. I mean, I've heard you just saying——"

"You haven't read the Depsec announcements?"

"Well, really!" Steen became intensely interested in his long, pointed fingernails with their exquisitely applied coppery coating. "I don't always have time to read *all* the announcements. I didn't know it was required of me. In fact," and he gathered his courage in both hands and looked full at Fife, "I didn't know you were making rules for me. Really!"

"I haven't," said Fife. "Just the same since you, at least, know none of the details, let me summarize it for you. The rest may find it interesting as well."

It was surprising into how few words the events of forty-eight hours could be put and how flat they could sound. First, there had been an unexpected reference to Spatio-analysis texts. Then a blow on the head of a superannuated patroller who died of a fractured skull two hours later. Then a pursuit that ended with untouchability in the lair of a Trantorian agent. Then a second patroller dead at dawn with the murderer tricked out in the patroller's uniform and the Trantorian agent dead in his turn some hours later.

"If you wish the very latest nugget of news," Fife concluded, "you might add this to the catalog of apparent trivia. Some hours ago a body, or, rather, the bony remnants of one, was found in City Park on Florina."

"Whose body?" asked Rune.

"Just a moment, please. Lying next to it was a pile of ash that seemed to be the charred remnants of clothing. Anything of metal had been carefully removed from it, but the ash analysis proved it to be what was left of a patroller uniform."

"Our impostoring friend?" asked Balle.

"Not likely," said Fife. "Who would kill him in secret?"

"Suicide," said Bort viciously. "How long did the bloody bastard expect to keep out of our hands? I imagine he had a better death this way. Personally, I'd find out who in the Corps were responsible for letting him reach the suicide stage and put a one-charge blaster in *their* hands."

"Not likely," said Fife again. "If the man committed suicide he either killed himself first, then took off his uniform, blasted it to ash, removed the buckles and braid, and then got rid of them. Or else he first removed his uniform, ashed it, removed the buckles and braid, left the cave naked, or perhaps in his underwear, discarded them, came back and killed himself."

"The body was in a cave?" asked Bort.

"In one of the ornamental caves of the Park. Yes."

"Then he had plenty of time and plenty of privacy," said Bort belligerently. He hated to give up a theory. "He could have taken off the buckles and braid first, then——"

"Ever try to remove braid from a patroller uniform that hasn't been ashed first?" asked Fife sarcastically. "And can you suggest a motive, if the body were that of the impostor after suicide? Besides, I have a report from the medical examiners who studied the bone structure. The skeleton is that of neither a patroller nor a Florinian. It is of a Sarkite."

Steen cried, "Really!"; Balle's old eyes opened wide; Rune's metal teeth, which, by catching a gleam of light now and then, added a bit of life to the cube of dusk in which he sat, vanished as he closed his mouth. Even Bort was dumfounded.

"Do you follow?" asked Fife. "Now you see why the metal was removed from the uniform. Whoever killed the Sarkite wanted the ash to be taken for that of the Sarkite's own clothing, removed and ashed before the killing, which we might then take for suicide or for the result of a private feud in no way connected with our patroller-impostor friend. What he did not know was that ash analysis could distinguish between the kyrt of Sarkite clothing and the cellulite of a patroller uniform even with the buckles and braid removed.

"Now given a dead Sarkite and the ash of a patroller uniform, we can only assume that somewhere in Upper City there is a live Townman in Sarkite clothing. Our Florinian, having posed as a patroller long enough, and finding the danger too great and growing greater, decided to become a Squire. And he did that in the only way he could."

"Has he been caught?" inquired Bort thickly.

"No, he hasn't."

"Why not? By Sark, why not?"

"He will be caught," said Fife indifferently. "At the moment we have more important things to wonder about. This last atrocity is a trifle in comparison."

"Get to the point!" demanded Rune instantly.

"Patience! First, let me ask you if you remember the missing Spatio-analyst of last year."

Steen giggled.

Bort said with infinite contempt, "That again?"

Steen asked, "Is there a connection? Or are we just going to talk about that horrible affair of last year all over again? I'm tired."

Fife was unmoved. He said, "This explosion of yesterday and day before yesterday began with a request at the Florinian library for reference books on Spatio-analysis. That is connection enough for me. Let's see if I can't make it connection for the rest of you as well. I will begin by describing the three people involved in the library incident, and please, let me have no interruptions for a few moments.

"First, there is a Townman. He is the dangerous one of the three. On Sark he had an excellent record as an intelligent and faithful piece of material. Unfortunately he has now turned his abilities against us. He is undoubtedly the one responsible for four killings now. Quite a record for anyone. Considering that the four include two patrollers and a Sarkite, it is unbelievably remarkable for a native. And he is still uncaught.

"The second person involved is a native woman. She is uneducated and completely insignificant. However, the last couple of days have seen an extensive search into every facet of this affair and we know her history. Her parents were members of the 'Soul of Kyrt' if any of you remember that rather ridiculous peasant conspiracy that was wiped out without trouble some twenty years ago.

"This brings us to the third person, the most unusual one of the three. This third person was a common mill hand and an idiot."

There was an expulsion of breath from Bort and another high-pitched giggle from Steen. Balle's eyes remained closed and Rune was motionless in the dark.

Fife said, "The word 'idiot' is not used figuratively. Depsec has driven itself mercilessly but his history could not be traced back more than ten and a half months. At that time he was found in a village just outside Florina's main metropolis in a state of complete mindlessness. He could neither walk nor talk. He could not even feed himself.

"Now note that he made this first appearance some few weeks after the disappearance of the Spatio-analyst. Note in addition that, in a matter of months, he learned how to talk and even how to fill a job at a kyrt mill. What kind of an idiot could learn so quickly?"

Steen began, almost eagerly. "Oh, really, if he were psycho-probed properly, it could be arranged so . . ." His voice trailed off.

Fife said sardonically, "I can think of no greater authority on the subject. Even without Steen's expert opinion, however, the same thought occurred to me. It was the only possible explanation.

"Now the psycho-probing could have taken place only on Sark or in Upper City of Florina. As a matter of simple thoroughness, doctors' offices in Upper City were checked. There was no trace of any unauthorized psycho-probing. It was then the notion of one of our agents to check the records of doctors who had died since the idiot first made his appearance. I shall see to it that he is promoted for that idea.

"We found a record of our idiot in just one of those offices. He had been brought in for a physical checkup about six months ago by the peasant woman who is the second of our trio. Apparently this was done secretly since she was absent that day from her job on quite another pretext. The doctor examined the idiot and recorded definite evidence of psycho-probic tampering.

"Now here is the interesting point. The doctor was one of those who kept double-deck offices in Upper City and Lower City. He was one of these idealists who thought the natives deserved first-rate medical care. He was a methodical man and kept duplicate records in full in both his offices to avoid unnecessary elevator travel. Also it pleased his idealism, I imagine, to practice no segregation between Sarkite and Florinian in his files. But the record of the idiot in question was not duplicated, and it was the *only* record not duplicated.

"Why should that be? If, for some reason, he had decided of his own accord not to duplicate that particular record, why should it have appeared only in the Upper City records, which is where it did appear? Why not only in the Lower City records, which is where it did not appear? After all, the man was a Florinian. He had been brought in by a Florinian. He had been examined in the Lower City office. All that was plainly recorded in the copy we found.

"There is only one answer to that particular puzzle. The record *was* duly entered in both files, but it was destroyed in the Lower City files by somebody who did not realize there would remain another record in the Upper office. Now let's pass on.

"Included with the idiot's examination record was the definite notation to include the findings of this case with the doctor's next routine report to Depsec. That was entirely proper. Any case of psychoprobing could involve a criminal or even a subversive. But no such report was ever made. Within the week he was dead in a traffic accident.

"The coincidences pile up past endurance, don't they?"

Balle opened his eyes. He said, "This is a detective thriller you are telling us."

"Yes," cried Fife with satisfaction, "a detective thriller. And for the moment I am the detective."

"And who are the accused?" asked Balle in a tired whisper.

"Not yet. Let me play the detective for a moment longer."

In the middle of what Fife considered to be the most dangerous crisis that had ever confronted Sark, he suddenly found that he was enjoying himself hugely.

He said, "Let's approach the story from the other end. We will, for the moment, forget the idiot and remember the Spatio-analyst.

The first we hear of him is the notification to the Bureau of Transportation that his ship will soon land. A message received from him earlier accompanies the notification.

"The Spatio-analyst never arrives. He is located nowhere in near space. Furthermore, the message sent by the Spatio-analyst, which had been forwarded to BuTrans, disappeared. The I.S.B. claimed that we were deliberately concealing the message. Depsec believed that they were inventing a fictitious message for propaganda purposes. It now occurs to me that we were both wrong. The message *had* been delivered but it had *not* been concealed by the government of Sark.

"Let us invent someone and, for the moment, call him X. X has access to the records of BuTrans. He learns of this Spatio-analyst and his message and has the brains and ability to act quickly. He arranges that a secret sub-ethergram be sent out to the Spatio-analyst's ship, directing the man's landing on some small, private field. The Spatio-analyst does so and X meets him there.

"X has taken the Spatio-analyst's message of doom with him. There may be two reasons for that. First, it would confuse possible attempts at detection by eliminating a piece of evidence. Second, it would serve, perhaps, to win the confidence of the mad Spatio-analyst. If the Spatio-analyst felt he could talk only to his own superiors, and he might well feel that, X might persuade him to grow confidential by proving that he was already in possession of the essentials of the story.

"Undoubtedly the Spatio-analyst talked. However incoherent, mad, and generally impossible that talk might have been, X recognized it as an excellent handle for propaganda. He sent out his blackmailing letter to the Great Squires, to us. His procedure, as then planned, was probably precisely that which I attributed to Trantor at the time. If we didn't come to terms with him, he intended to disrupt Florinian production by rumors of destruction until he forced surrender.

"But then came his first miscalculation. Something frightened him. We'll consider exactly what that was later. In any case, he decided he would have to wait before continuing. Waiting, however, involved one complication. X didn't believe the Spatio-analyst's story, but there is no question that the Spatio-analyst himself was madly sincere. X would have to arrange affairs so that the Spatio-analyst would be willing to allow his 'doom' to wait.

"The Spatio-analyst could not do that unless his warped mind was put out of action. X might have killed him, but I am of the opinion that the Spatio-analyst was necessary to him as a source of further information (after all, he knew nothing of Spatio-analysis himself and he couldn't conduct successful blackmail on total bluff) and, perhaps, as ransom in case of ultimate failure. In any case, he used a psycho-probe. After treatment, he had on his hands, not a Spatio-analyst, but a mindless idiot who would, for a time, cause him no trouble. And after a time his senses would be recovered.

"The next step? That was to make certain that during the year's wait the Spatio-analyst would not be located, that no one of importance would see him even in his role as idiot. So he proceeded with a masterly simplicity. He carried his man to Florina and for nearly a year the Spatio-analyst was simply a half-wit native, working in the kyrt mills.

"I imagine that during that year he, or some trusted subordinate, visited the town where he had 'planted' the creature, to see that he was safe and in reasonable health. On one of these visits he learned, somehow, that the creature had been taken to a doctor who knew a psycho-probing when he saw one. The doctor died and his report disappeared, at least from his Lower City office. That was X's first miscalculation. He never thought a duplicate might be in the office above.

"And then came his second miscalculation. The idiot began regaining his senses a little too quickly and the village Townman had brains enough to see that there was something more to it than simple raving. Perhaps the girl who took care of the idiot told the Townman about the psycho-probing. That's a guess.

"There you have the story."

Fife clasped his strong hands and waited for the reaction.

Rune supplied it first. The light had turned on in his cubicle some moments earlier and he sat there, blinking and smiling. He said, "And a moderately dull story it was, Fife. Another moment in the dark and I would have been asleep."

"As nearly as I can see," said Balle slowly, "you have created a structure as insubstantial as the one of last year. It is nine tenths guesswork."

"Hogwash!" said Bort.

"Who is X, anyway?" asked Steen. "If you don't know who X is, it just doesn't make any sense." And he yawned delicately, covering his small white teeth with a bent forefinger.

Fife said, "At least one of you sees the essential point. The identity of X is the nub of the affair. Consider the characteristics that X must possess if my analysis is accurate.

"In the first place, X is a man with contacts in the Civil Service. He is a man who can order a psycho-probing. He is a man who thinks he can arrange a powerful blackmailing campaign. He is a man who can take the Spatio-analyst from Sark to Florina without trouble. He is a man who can arrange the death of a doctor on Florina. He isn't a nobody, certainly.

"In fact he is a very definite somebody. He must be a Great Squire. Wouldn't you say so?"

Bort rose from his seat. His head disappeared and he sat down again. Steen burst into high, hysterical laughter. Rune's eyes, half buried in the pulpy fat that surrounded them, glittered feverishly. Balle slowly shook his head.

Bort yelled, "Who in Space is being accused, Fife?"

"No one yet." Fife remained even-tempered. "No one specifically. Look at it this way. There are five of us. Not another man on Sark could have done what X did. Only we five. That can be taken as settled. Now which of the five is it? To begin with, it isn't myself."

"We can take your word for it, can we?" sneered Rune.

"You don't have to take my word for it," retorted Fife. "I'm the only one here without a motive. X's motive is to gain control of the kyrt industry. I *have* control of it. I own a third of Florina's land outright. My mills, machine plants and shipping fleets are sufficiently predominant to force any or all of you out of business if I wish. I wouldn't have to resort to complicated blackmail."

He was shouting over their united voices. "Listen to me! The rest of you have every motive. Rune has the smallest continent and the smallest holdings. I know he doesn't like that. He can't pretend he likes it. Balle has the oldest lineage. There was a time when his family ruled all of Sark. He probably hasn't forgotten that. Bort resents the fact that he is always outvoted in council and cannot therefore conduct business in his territories in quite the whip-and-blaster fashion he would like. Steen has expensive tastes and his finances are in a bad way. The necessity of recouping is a hard-driving one. We have it there. All the possible motives. Envy. Greed for power. Greed for money. Questions of prestige. Now which of you is it?"

There was a gleam of sudden malice in Balle's old eyes. "You don't know?"

"It doesn't matter. Now hear this. I said that something frightened X (let's still call him X) after his first letters to us. Do you know what it was? It was our first conference when I preached the necessity of united action. X was here. X was, and is, one of us. He knew united action meant failure. He had counted on winning over us because he knew that our rigid ideal of continental autonomy would keep us at odds to the last moment and beyond. He saw that he was wrong and he decided to wait until the sense of urgency vanished and he could proceed again.

"But he is still wrong. We will still take united action and there is only one way we can do it safely, considering that X is one of us. Continental autonomy is at an end. It is a luxury we can no longer afford, for X's schemes will end only with the economic defeat of the rest of us or the intervention of Trantor. I, myself, am the only one I can trust, so from now on I head a united Sark. Are you with me?"

They were out of their seats, shouting. Bort was waving his fist. There was a light froth at the corner of his lips.

Physically, there was nothing they could do. Fife smiled. Each was a continent away. He could sit behind his desk and watch them foam.

He said, "You have no choice. In the year since our first conference, I, too, have made my preparations. While you four have been quietly in conference, listening to me, officers loyal to myself have taken charge of the Navy."

"Treason!" they howled.

"Treason to continental autonomy," retorted Fife. "Loyalty to Sark."

Steen's fingers intertwined nervously, their ruddy, copper tips the only splash of color upon his skin. "But it's X. Even if X is one of us, there are three innocent. I'm not X." He cast a poisonous glance about him. "It's one of the others."

"Those of you who are innocent will form part of my government if they wish. They have nothing to lose."

"But you won't say who is innocent," bawled Bort. "You will keep us all out on the story of X, on the—on the——" Breathlessness brought him to a halt.

"I will not. In twenty-four hours I will know who X is. I have not told you. The Spatio-analyst we have all been discussing is now in my hands."

They fell silent. They looked at one another with reserve and suspicion.

Fife chuckled. "You are wondering which of you can be X. One of you knows, be sure of that. And in twenty-four hours we shall all know. Now keep in mind, gentlemen, that you are all quite helpless. The ships of war are mine. Good day!"

His gesture was one of dismissal.

One by one they went out, like stars in the depths of the vacuum being blotted out on the visiplate by the passing and unseen bulk of a wrecked spaceship.

Steen was the last to leave. "Fife," he said tremulously.

Fife looked up. "Yes? You wish to confess now that we two are alone? You are X?"

Steen's face twisted in wild alarm. "No, no. Really. I just wanted to ask if you're really serious. I mean, continental autonomy and all that. Really?"

Fife stared at the old chronometer in the wall. "Good day."

Steen whimpered. His hand went up to the contact switch and he, too, disappeared.

Fife sat there, stony and unmoving. With the conference over, the heat of the crisis gone, depression seized him. His lipless mouth was a severe gash in his large face.

All calculations began with this fact: that the Spatio-analyst was mad, there was no doom. But over a madman, so much had taken place. Would Junz of the I.S.B. have spent a year searching for a madman? Would he be so unyielding in his chase after fairy stories?

Fife had told no one this. He scarcely dared share it with his own soul. What if the Spatio-analyst had never been mad? What if destruction dangled over the world of kyrt?

The Florinian secretary glided before the Great Squire, his voice pallid and dry.

"Sir!"

"What is it?"

"The ship with your daughter has landed."

"The Spatio-analyst and the native woman are safe?"

"Yes, sir."

"Let there be no questioning in my absence. They are to be held incommunicado until I arrive. . . . Is there news from Florina?"

"Yes, sir. The Townman is in custody and is being brought to Sark."

Thirteen: *THE YACHTSMAN*

The port's lights brightened evenly as the twilight deepened. At no time did the over-all illumination vary from that to be expected of a somewhat subdued late afternoon. At Port 9, as at the other yacht ports of Upper City, it was daylight throughout Florina's rotation. The brightness might grow unusually pronounced under the midday sun, but that was the only deviation.

Markis Genro could tell that the day proper had passed only because, in passing into the port, he had left the colored night lights of the City behind him. Those were bright against the blackening sky but they made no pretense of substituting for day.

Genro paused just inside the main entrance and seemed in no way impressed by the gigantic horseshoe with its three dozen hangars and five take-off pits. It was part of him, as it was part of any experienced yachtsman.

He took a long cigarette, violet in color and tipped with the filmiest touch of silvery kyrt, and put it to his lips. He cupped his palms about the exposed tip and watched it glow to greenish life as he inhaled. It burned slowly and left no ash. An emerald smoke filtered out his nostrils.

He murmured, "Business as usual!"

A member of the yacht committee, in yachting costume, with only a discreet and tasteful lettering above one tunic button to indicate that he was a member of the committee, had moved up quickly to meet Genro, carefully avoiding any appearance of hurry.

"Ah, Genro! And why not business as usual?"

"Hello, Doty. I only thought that with all this fume and fuss going on it might occur to some bright boy to close the ports. Thank Sark it hasn't."

The committeeman sobered. "You know, it may come to that. Have you heard the latest?"

Genro grinned. "How can you tell the latest from the next-to-the-latest?"

"Well, have you heard that it's definite now about the native? The killer?"

"You mean they've caught him? I hadn't heard that."

"No, they haven't caught him. But they know he's not in Lower City!"

"No? Where is he then?"

"Why, in Upper City. Here."

"Go on." Genro's eyes widened, then narrowed in disbelief.

"No, really," said the committeeman, a little hurt, "I have it for a fact. The patrollers are swooping up and down Kyrt Highway. They've got City Park surrounded and they're using Central Arena as a co-ordination point. This is all authentic."

"Well, maybe." Genro's eyes roved carelessly over the hangared ships. "I haven't been at 9 for two months, I think. Are there any new ships in the place?"

"No. Well, yes, there's Hjordesse's *Flame Arrow*."

Genro shook his head. "I've seen that. It's all chromium and nothing else. I hate to think I'll have to end by designing my own."

"Are you selling *Comet V?*"

"Selling it or junking it. I'm tired of these late models. They're too automatic. With their automatic relays and trajectory computers, they're killing the sport."

"You know, I've heard others say the same thing," agreed the committeeman. "Tell you what. If I hear of an old model in good condition on the market, I'll let you know."

"Thanks. Mind if I wander about the place?"

"Of course not. Go ahead." The committeeman grinned, waved, trotted away.

Genro made his slow rounds, his cigarette, half gone, drooping from one side of his mouth. He stopped at each occupied hangar, appraising its contents shrewdly.

At Hangar 26 he displayed a heightened interest. He looked over the low barrier and said, "Squire?"

The call was one of polite inquiry, but after a pause of several moments he had to call again, a little more peremptorily, a little less politely.

The Squire who emerged to view was not an impressive sight. For one thing, he was not in yachting costume. Secondly, he needed a shave, and his rather repellent-looking skullcap was yanked down in a most unfashionable manner. It seemed to cover half his face. Lastly, his attitude was one of peculiarly suspicious overcaution.

Genro said, "I'm Markis Genro. Is this your craft, sir?"

"Yes, it is." The words were slow and tense.

Genro disregarded that. He tilted his head back and looked over the yacht's lines carefully. He removed what was left of his cigarette from between his lips and flicked it high in the air. It had not yet reached the high point of its arc when, with a little flash, it vanished.

Genro said, "I wonder if you'd mind my coming in?" The other hesitated, then stepped aside. Genro entered.

He said, "What kind of motor does the craft carry, sir?"

"Why do you ask?"

Genro was tall, skin and eyes were dark, hair crisp and cut short. He topped the other by half a head, and his smile showed white, evenly spaced teeth. He said, "To be very frank, I'm in the market for a new ship."

"You mean you're interested in this one?"

"I don't know. Something like it, maybe, if the price is right. But anyway, I wonder if you'd mind my looking at the controls and engines?"

The Squire stood there silently.

Genro's voice grew a trifle colder. "As you please, of course." He turned away.

The Squire said, "I might sell." He fumbled in his pockets. "Here's the license!"

Genro looked at each side with a quick, experienced glance. He handed it back. "You're Deamone?"

The Squire nodded. "You can come in if you wish."

Genro looked briefly at the large port-chronometer, the luminescent hands, sparking brightly even in the daylight illumination, indicating the beginning of the second hour after sunset.

"Thank you. Won't you lead the way?"

The Squire rummaged his pockets again and held out a booklet of key slivers. "After you, sir."

Genro took the booklet. He leafed through the slivers, looking at the small code marks for the "ship stamp." The other man made no attempt to help him.

Finally he said, "This one, I suppose?"

He walked up the short ramp to the air-lock balcony and considered the fine seam at the right of the lock carefully. "I don't see—— Oh, here it is," and he stepped to the other side of the lock.

Slowly, noiselessly, the lock yawned and Genro moved into the blackness. The red air-lock light went on automatically as the door closed behind them. The inner door opened and as they stepped into the ship proper white lights flickered on over all the length of the ship.

Myrlyn Terens had no choice. He no longer remembered the time, long since, when such a thing as "choice" had existed. For three long, wretched hours, now, he had remained near Deamone's ship, waiting and helpless to do anything else. It had led to nothing till now. He did not see that it could lead to anything but capture.

And then this fellow had come with an eye to the ship. To deal with him at all was madness. He could not possibly maintain his imposture at such close quarters. But then he could not possibly remain where he was, either.

At least within the ship there might be food. Strange that that had not occurred to him before.

There was.

Terens said, "It's close to dinnertime. Would you like to have something?"

The other had scarcely looked over his shoulder. "Why, later, perhaps. Thank you."

Terens did not urge him. He let him roam the ship and applied himself thankfully to the potted meat and cellulite-wrapped fruit. He drank thirstily. There was a shower across the corridor from the kitchen. He locked its door and bathed. It was a pleasure to be able to remove the tight skullcap, at least temporarily. He even found a shallow closet from which he could choose a change of clothing.

He was far more master of himself when Genro returned.

Genro said, "Say, would you mind if I tried to fly this ship?"

"I have no objection. Can you handle this model?" asked Terens with an excellent imitation of nonchalance.

"I think so," said the other with a little smile. "I flatter myself I can handle any of the regular models. Anyway, I've taken the liberty of calling the control tower and there's a take-off pit available. Here's my yachtsman's license if you'd like to see it before I take over."

Terens gave it as cursory a glance as Genro had given his. "The controls are yours," he said.

The ship rolled out of the hangar like an air-borne whale, moving slowly, its diamagnetized hull clearing the smooth-packed clay of the field by three inches.

Terens watched Genro handling the controls with finger-tip precision. The ship was a live thing under his touch. The small replica of the field that was upon the visiplate shifted and changed with every tiny motion of every contact.

The ship came to a halt, pinpointed at the lip of a take-off pit. The diamagnetic field strengthened progressively towards the ship's prow and it began tipping upward. Terens was mercifully unaware of this as the pilot room turned on its universal gimbals to meet the shifting gravity. Majestically, the ship's rear flanges fitted into the appropriate grooves of the pit. It stood upright, pointing to the sky.

The duralite cover of the take-off pit slipped into its recess, revealing the neutrized lining, a hundred yards deep, that received the first energy thrusts of the hyperatomic motors.

Genro kept up a cryptic exchange of information with the control tower. Finally, "Ten seconds to take-off," he said.

A rising red thread in a quartz tube marked off the disappearing seconds. It made contact and the first surge of power tore backward.

Terens grew heavier, felt himself pressing against the seat. Panic tore at him.

He grunted, "How does it handle?"

Genro seemed impervious to acceleration. His voice had almost its natural timbre as he said, "Moderately well."

Terens leaned back in his chair, trying to relax with the pressure, watching the stars in the visiplate turn hard and bright as the atmosphere vanished from between himself and them. The kyrt next to his skin felt cold and damp.

They were out in space now. Genro was putting the ship through its paces. Terens had no way of telling that first hand but he could see the stars march steadily across the visiplate as the yachtsman's long, slim fingers played with the controls as though they were the keys of a musical instrument. Finally a bulky orange segment of a globe filled the visiplate's clear surface.

"Not bad," said Genro. "You keep your craft in good condition, Deamone. It's small but it has its points."

Terens said carefully, "I suppose you'd like to test its speed and its jumping capacity. You may, if you like. I have no objection."

Genro nodded. "Very well. Where do you suggest we take ourselves? What about——" He hesitated, then went on, "Well, why not to Sark?"

Terens breathed a little more quickly. He had expected that. He was on the point of believing himself to be living in a world of magic. How things forced his moves, even without his connivance. It would not have been difficult to convince him that it was not "things" but design that prompted the moves. His childhood had been steeped in the superstitions that the Squires fostered among the natives and such things are hard to outgrow. On Sark was Rik with his returning memories. The game was not over.

He said wildly, "Why not, Genro?"

Genro said, "Sark it is then."

With gathering speed, the globe of Florina slanted out beyond the visiplate's view and the stars returned.

"What's your best time on the Sark–Florina run?" asked Genro.

"Nothing record-breaking," said Terens. "About average."

"Then you've done it in better than six hours, I suppose?"

"On occasion, yes."

"Do you object to my trying to shave five?"

"Not at all," said Terens.

It took hours to reach a point far enough from star-mass distortion of the space fabric to make a jump possible.

Terens found wakefulness a torture. This was his third night with little or no sleep and the tensions of the days had exaggerated that lack.

Genro looked at him askance. "Why don't you turn in?"

Terens forced an expression of liveliness onto his sagging facial muscles. He said, "It's nothing. Nothing."

He yawned prodigiously and smiled in apology. The yachtsman turned back to his instruments and Terens' eyes glazed over once again.

Seats in a space-yacht are comfortable by very necessity. They must cushion the person against accelerations. A man not particularly tired can easily and sweetly fall asleep upon them. Terens, who could, at the moment, have slept on broken glass, never knew when he passed the border line.

He slept for hours; he slept as deeply and as dreamlessly as ever in his life.

He did not stir; he showed no single life other than his even breathing when the skullcap was removed from his head.

Terens woke blearily, slowly. For long minutes he had not the slightest notion of his whereabouts. He thought he was back in his Townman's cottage. The true state of affairs seeped back in stages. Eventually he could smile at Genro, who was still at the controls, and say, "I guess I fell asleep."

"I guess you did. There's Sark." Genro nodded toward the large white crescent in the visiplate.

"When do we land?"

"About an hour."

Terens was awake enough now to sense a subtle change in the other's attitude. It was an icy shock to him that the steel-gray object in Genro's hand turned out to be the graceful barrel of a needle-gun.

"What in Space——" began Terens, rising to his feet.

"Sit down," said Genro carefully. There was a skullcap in his other hand.

Terens raised a hand to his head and his fingers found themselves clutching sandy hair.

"Yes," said Genro, "it's quite obvious. You're a native."

Terens stared and said nothing.

Genro said, "I knew you were a native before I ever got on poor Deamone's ship."

Terens' mouth was cotton-dry and his eyes burned. He watched the tiny, deadly muzzle of the gun and waited for a sudden, noiseless flash. He had carried it so far, so far, and had lost the gamble after all.

Genro seemed in no hurry. He held the needle-gun steady and his words were even and slow.

"Your basic mistake, Townman, was the thought that you could really outwit an organized police force indefinitely. Even so, you would have done better if you hadn't made the unfortunate choice of Deamone as your victim."

"I didn't choose him," croaked Terens.

"Then call it luck. Alstare Deamone, some twelve hours ago, was standing in City Park, waiting for his wife. There was no reason, other than sentiment, for him to meet her there of all places. They had met in that very spot originally, and they met there again on every anniversary of that meeting. There's nothing particularly original about that sort of ceremony between young husbands and wives, but it seems important to them. Of course Deamone did not realize that the comparative isolation of the spot made him an appropriate victim for a murderer. Who would have thought that in Upper City?

"In the ordinary course of events the murder might not have been discovered for days. Deamone's wife, however, was on the scene within half an hour of the crime. The fact that her husband was not there astonished her. He was not the type, she explained, to leave in a fury because she herself was a trifle late. She was often late. He would more or less have expected that. It occurred to her that her husband might be waiting for her inside 'their' cave.

"Deamone had been waiting outside 'their' cave, naturally. It was the nearest one to the scene of the assault, consequently, and the one into which he was dragged. His wife entered that cave and found—well, you know what she found. She managed to relay the news to the Patrol Corps through our own Depsec offices, although she was almost incoherent with shock and hysteria.

"How does it feel, Townman, to kill a man in cold blood, leaving him to be found by his wife at the one spot most steeped with happy memories for them both?"

Terens was choking. He gasped out, through a red mist of anger and frustration, "You Sarkites have killed millions of Florinians. Women. Children. You've grown rich out of us. This yacht——" It was all he could manage.

"Deamone wasn't responsible for the state of affairs he found at birth," said Genro. "If you had been born a Sarkite, what would you have done? Resigned your estates, if any, and gone to work in the kyrt fields?"

"Well then, shoot," cried Terens, writhing. "What are you waiting for?"

"There's no hurry. There is plenty of time to finish my story. We weren't certain as to the identity of either the corpse or the murderer, but it was a very good guess that they were Deamone and yourself respectively. It seemed obvious to us from the fact that the ashes next to the body were of a patroller uniform that you were masquerading as a Sarkite. It seemed further probable that you would make for Deamone's yacht. Don't overestimate our stupidity, Townman.

"Matters were still rather complex. You were a desperate man. It was insufficient to track you down. You were armed and would undoubtedly commit suicide if trapped. Suicide was something we did not wish. They wanted you on Sark and they wanted you in working order.

"It was a particularly delicate affair for myself and it was quite necessary to convince Depsec that I could handle it alone, that I could get you to Sark without noise or difficulty. You'll have to admit that is just what I'm doing.

"To tell you the truth, I wondered at first if you were really our man. You were dressed in ordinary business costume on the yachtport grounds. It was in incredibly bad taste. No one, it seemed to me, would dream of impersonating a yachtsman without the proper costume. I thought you were being deliberately sent in as a decoy, that you were *trying* to be arrested while the man we wanted escaped in another direction.

"I hesitated and tested you in other ways. I fumbled with the ship's key in the wrong place. No ship ever invented opened at the right side of the air lock. It opens always and invariably at the left side. You never showed any surprise at my mistake. None at all. Then I asked you if your ship had ever made the Sark–Florina run in less than six hours. You said you had—occasionally. That is quite remarkable. The record time for the run is over 9 hours.

"I decided you couldn't be a decoy. The ignorance was too supreme. You had to be naturally ignorant and probably the right man. It was only a question of your falling asleep (and it was obvious from your face that you needed sleep desperately), disarming you and covering you quietly with an adequate weapon. I removed your hat more out of curiosity than anything else. I wanted to see what a Sarkite costume looked like with a red-haired head sticking out of it."

Terens kept his eyes on the whip. Perhaps Genro saw his jaw muscles bunch. Perhaps he simply guessed at what Terens was thinking.

He said, "Of course I must not kill you, even if you jump me. I can't kill you even in self-defense. Don't think that gives you an advantage. Begin to move and I'll shoot your leg off."

The fight went out of Terens. He put the heels of his palms to his forehead and sat rigid.

Genro said softly, "Do you know why I tell you all this?"

Terens did not answer.

"First," said Genro, "I rather enjoy seeing you suffer. I don't like murderers and I particularly don't like natives who kill Sarkites. I've been ordered to deliver you alive but nothing in my orders says I have to make the trip pleasant for you. Secondly, it is necessary for you to be fully aware of the situation since, after we land on Sark, the next steps will be up to you."

Terens looked up. "What!"

"Depsec knows you're coming in. The Florinian regional office sent the word as soon as this craft cleared Florina's atmosphere. You can be sure of that. But I said it was quite necessary for me to convince Depsec that I could handle this alone and the fact that I have makes all the difference."

"I don't understand you," said Terens desperately.

With composure, Genro answered, "I said 'they' wanted you on Sark, 'they' wanted you in working order. By 'they' I don't mean Depsec, I mean Trantor!"

Fourteen: *THE RENEGADE*

Selim Junz had never been the phlegmatic type. A year of frustration had done nothing to improve that. He could not sip wine carefully while his mental orientation sat upon suddenly trembling foundations. In short, he was not Ludigan Abel.

And when Junz had done with his angry shouting that on no account was Sark to be allowed freedom to kidnap and imprison a member of the I.S.B. regardless of the condition of Trantor's espionage network, Abel merely said, "I think you had better spend the night here, Doctor."

Junz said freezingly, "I have better things to do."

Abel said, "No doubt, man, no doubt. Just the same, if my men are being blasted to death, Sark must be bold indeed. There is a great possibility that some accident may happen to you before the night is over. Let us wait a night then and see what comes of a new day."

Junz's protests against inaction came to nothing. Abel, without ever losing his cool, almost negligent air of indifference, was suddenly hard of hearing. Junz was escorted with firm courtesy to a chamber.

In bed, he stared at the faintly luminous, frescoed ceiling (on which glowed a moderately skillful copy of Lenhaden's "Battle of the Arcturian Moons") and knew he would not sleep. Then he caught one whiff, a faint one, of the gas, somnin, and was asleep before he could catch another. Five minutes later, when a forced draft swept the room clean of the anesthetic, enough had been administered to assure a healthful eight hours.

He was awakened in the cold half-light of dawn. He blinked up at Abel.

"What time is it?" he asked.

"Six."

"Great Space." He looked about and thrust his bony legs out from under the sheet. "You're up early."

"I haven't slept."

"What?"

"I feel the lack, believe me. I don't respond to anti-somnin as I did when I was younger."

Junz murmured, "If you will allow me a moment."

This once his morning preparations for the day took scarcely more than that. He re-entered the room, drawing the belt about his tunic and adjusting the magneto-seam.

"Well?" he asked. "Surely you don't wake through the night and rouse me at six unless you have something to tell me."

"You're right. You're right." Abel sat down on the bed vacated by Junz and threw his head back in a laugh. It was high-pitched and rather subdued. His teeth showed, their strong, faintly yellow plastic incongruous against his shrunken gums.

"I beg your pardon, Junz," he said. "I am not quite myself. This drugged wakefulness has me a little lightheaded. I almost think I will advise Trantor to replace me with a younger man."

Junz said, with a flavor of sarcasm not entirely unmixed with sudden hope, "You find they haven't got the Spatio-analyst after all?"

"No, they do. I'm sorry but they do. I'm afraid that my amusement is due entirely to the fact that our nets are intact."

Junz would have liked to say, "Damn your nets," but refrained.

Abel went on, "There is no doubt they knew Khorov was one of our agents. They may know of others on Florina. Those are small fry. The Sarkites knew that and never felt it worth while to do more than hold them under observation."

"They killed one," Junz pointed out.

"They did not," retorted Abel. "It was one of the Spatio-analyst's own companions in a patroller disguise who used the blaster."

Junz stared. "I don't understand."

"It's a rather complicated story. Won't you join me at breakfast? I need food badly."

Over the coffee, Abel told the story of the last thirty-six hours.

Junz was stunned. He put down his own coffee cup, half full, and returned to it no more. "Even allowing them to have stowed away on that ship of all ships, the fact still remains they might not have been detected. If you send men to meet that ship as it lands——"

"Bah. You know better than that. No modern ship could fail to detect the presence of excess body heat."

"It might have been overlooked. Instruments may be infallible but men are not."

"Wishful thinking. Look here. At the very time that the ship with the Spatio-analyst aboard is approaching Sark, there are reports of excellent reliability that the Squire of Fife is in conference with the other Great Squires. These intercontinental conferences are spaced as widely as the stars of the Galaxy. Coincidence?"

"An intercontinental conference over a Spatio-analyst?"

"An unimportant subject in itself, yes. But we have made it important. The I.S.B. has been searching for him for nearly a year with remarkable pertinacity."

"Not the I.S.B.," insisted Junz. "Myself. I've been working in almost an unofficial manner."

"The Squires don't know that and wouldn't believe it if you told them. Then, too, Trantor has been interested."

"At my request."

"Again they don't know that and wouldn't believe it."

Junz stood up and his chair moved automatically away from the table. Hands firmly interlocked behind his back, he strode the carpet. Up and back. Up and back. At intervals he glanced harshly at Abel.

Abel turned unemotionally to a second cup of coffee.

Junz said, "How do you know all this?"

"All what?"

"Everything. How and when the Spatio-analyst stowed away. How and in what manner the Townman has been eluding capture. Is it your purpose to deceive me?"

"My dear Dr. Junz."

"You admitted you had your men watching for the Spatio-analyst independently of myself. You saw to it that I was safely out of the way last night, leaving nothing to chance." Junz remembered, suddenly, that whiff of somnin.

"I spent a night, Doctor, in constant communication with certain of my agents. What I did and what I learned comes under the heading of, shall we say, classified material. You had to be out of the way, and yet safe. What I have told you just now I learned from my agents last night."

"To learn what you did you would need spies in the Sarkite government itself."

"Well, naturally."

Junz whirled on the ambassador. "Come, now."

"You find that surprising? To be sure, Sark is proverbial for the stability of its government and the loyalty of its people. The reason is simple enough since even the poorest Sarkite is an aristocrat in comparison with Florinians and can consider himself, however fallaciously, to be a member of a ruling class.

"Consider, though, that Sark is not the world of billionaires most of the Galaxy thinks it is. A year's residence must have well convinced you of that. Eighty per cent of its population has its living standard at a par with that of other worlds and not much higher than the standard of Florina itself. There will always be a certain number of Sarkites who, in their hunger, will be sufficiently annoyed with the small fraction of the population obviously drenched in luxury to lend themselves to my uses.

"It is the great weakness of the Sarkite government that for centuries they have associated rebellion only with Florina. They have forgotten to watch over themselves."

Junz said, "These small Sarkites, assuming they exist, can't do you much good."

"Individually, no. Collectively, they form useful tools for our more important men. There are members even of the real ruling class who have taken the lessons of the last two centuries to heart. They are convinced that in the end Trantor will have established its rule over all the Galaxy, and, I believe, rightly convinced. They even suspect that the final dominion may take place within their lifetimes, and they prefer to establish themselves, in advance, on the winning side."

Junz grimaced. "You make interstellar politics sound a very dirty game."

"It is, but disapproving of dirt doesn't remove it. Nor are all its facets unrelieved dirt. Consider the idealist. Consider the few men in Sark's government who serve Trantor neither for money nor for promises of power but only because they honestly believe that a unified Galactic government is best for humanity and that only Trantor can bring such a government about. I have one such man, my best one, in Sark's Department of Security, and at this moment he is bringing in the Townman."

Junz said, "You said he had been captured."

"By Depsec, yes. But my man is Depsec *and my man*." For a moment Abel frowned and turned pettish. "His usefulness will be sharply reduced after this. Once he lets the Townman get away, it will mean demotion at the best and imprisonment at the worst. Oh well!"

"What are you planning now?"

"I scarcely know. First, we must have our Townman. I am sure of him only to the point of arrival at the spaceport. What happens thereafter . . ." Abel shrugged, and his old, yellowish skin stretched parchmentlike over his cheekbones.

Then he added, "The Squires will be waiting for the Townman as well. They are under the impression they have him, and until one or the other of us has him in our fists, nothing more can happen."

But that statement was wrong.

Strictly speaking, all foreign embassies throughout the Galaxy maintained extraterritorial rights over the immediate areas of their location. Generally this amounted to nothing more than a pious wish, except where the strength of the home planet enforced respect. In actual practice it meant that only Trantor could truly maintain the independence of its envoys.

The grounds of the Trantorian Embassy covered nearly a square mile and within it armed men in Trantorian costume and insignia maintained patrol. No Sarkite might enter but on invitation, and no armed Sarkite on any account. To be sure, the sum of Trantorian men and arms could withstand the determined attack of a single Sarkite armored regiment for not more than two or three hours, but behind the small band was the power of reprisal from the organized might of a million worlds.

It remained inviolate.

It could even maintain direct material communication with Trantor, without the need of passing through Sarkite ports of entry or debarkation. From the hold of a Trantorian mothership, hovering just outside the hundred-mile limit that marked off the boundary between "planetary space" and "free space," small gyro-ships, vane-equipped for atmospheric travel with minimum power expenditure, might emerge and needle down (half coasting, half driven) to the small port maintained within the embassy grounds.

The gyro-ship which now appeared over the embassy port, however, was neither scheduled nor Trantorian. The mosquito-might of the embassy was brought quickly and truculently into play. A needle-cannon lifted its puckered muzzle into the air. Force screens went up.

Radioed messages whipped back and forth. Stubborn words rode the impulses upward, agitated ones slipped down.

Lieutenant Camrum turned away from the instrument and said, "I don't know. He claims he'll be shot out of the sky in two minutes if we don't let him down. He claims sanctuary."

Captain Elyut had just entered. He said, "Sure. Then Sark will claim we're interfering in politics and if Trantor decides to let things ride, you and I are broken as a gesture. Who is he?"

"Won't say," said the lieutenant with more than a little exasperation. "Says he must speak to the Ambassador. Suppose you tell me what to do, Captain."

The short-wave receiver sputtered and a voice, half hysterical, said, "Is anyone *there?* I'm just coming down, that's all. Really! I can't wait another moment, I tell you." It ended in a squeak.

The Captain said, "Great Space, I know that voice. Let him down! My responsibility!"

The orders went out. The gyro-ship sank vertically, more quickly than it should have, the result of a hand at the controls that was both inexperienced and panicky. The needle-cannon maintained focus.

The Captain established a through line to Abel and the embassy was thrown into full emergency. The flight of Sarkite ships that hovered overhead not ten minutes after the first vessel had landed maintained a threatening vigil for two hours, then departed.

They sat at dinner, Abel, Junz and the newcomer. With admirable aplomb, considering the circumstances, Abel had acted the unconcerned host. For hours he had refrained from asking why a Great Squire needed sanctuary.

Junz was far less patient. He hissed at Abel, "Space! What are you going to do with him?"

And Abel smiled back. "Nothing. At least until I find out whether I have my Townman or not. I like to know what my hand is before tossing chips onto the table. And since he's come to me, waiting will rattle him more than it will us."

He was right. Twice the Squire launched into rapid monolog and twice Abel said, "My dear Squire! Surely serious conversation is unpleasant on an empty stomach." He smiled gently and ordered dinner.

Over the wine, the Squire tried again. He said, "You'll want to know why I have left Steen Continent."

"I cannot conceive of any reason," admitted Abel, "for the Squire of Steen ever to have run from Sarkite vessels."

Steen watched them carefully. His slight figure and thin, pale face were tense with calculation. His long hair was bound into carefully arranged tufts held by tiny clips that rubbed against one another with a rustling sound whenever he moved his head, as though to call attention to his disregard for the current Sarkite clipped-hair fashion. A faint fragrance came from his skin and clothing.

Abel, who did not miss the slight tightening of Junz's lips and the quick way in which the Spatio-analyst patted his own short, woolly hair, thought how amusing Junz's reaction might have been if Steen had appeared more typically, with rouged cheeks and coppered fingernails.

Steen said, "There was an intercontinental conference today."

"Really?" said Abel.

Abel listened to the tale of the conference without a quiver of countenance.

"And we have twenty-four hours," Steen said indignantly. "It's sixteen hours now. Really!"

"And you're X," cried Junz, who had been growing increasingly restless during the recitation. "You're X. You've come here because he's caught you. Well now, that's fine. Abel, here's our proof as to the identity of the Spatio-analyst. We can use him to force a surrender of the man."

Steen's thin voice had difficulty making itself heard over Junz's staunch baritone.

"Now really. I say, now really. You're mad. Stop it! Let me speak, I tell you. . . . Your Excellency, I can't remember this man's name."

"Dr. Selim Junz, Squire."

"Well then, Dr. Selim Junz, I have never in my life seen this idiot or Spatio-analyst or whatever in the world he may be. Really! I never heard such nonsense. I am certainly not X. Really! I'll thank you not even to use the silly letter. Imagine believing Fife's ridiculous melodrama! Really!"

Junz clung to his notion. "Why did you run then?"

"Good Sark, isn't it clear? Oh, I could choke. Really! Look here, don't you see what Fife was doing?"

Abel interrupted quietly. "If you'll explain, Squire, there will be no interruptions."

"Well, thank *you* at least." He continued, with an air of wounded dignity. "The others don't think much of me because I don't see the point of bothering with documents and statistics and all those boring details. But, really, what is the Civil Service for, I'd like to know? If a Great Squire can't *be* a Great Squire?

"Still that doesn't mean I'm a ninny, you know, just because I like my comfort. Really! Maybe the others are blind, but I can see that Fife doesn't give a darn for the Spatio-analyst. I don't even think he exists. Fife just got the idea a year ago and he's been manipulating it ever since.

"He's been playing us for fools and idiots. Really! And so the others are. Disgusting fools! He's *arranged* all this perfectly awful nonsense about idiots and Spatio-analysis. I wouldn't be surprised if the native who's supposed to be killing patrollers by the dozen isn't just one of Fife's spies in a red wig. Or if he's a real native, I suppose Fife has hired him.

"I wouldn't put it past Fife. Really! He would use natives against his own kind. That's how low he is.

"Anyway, it's obvious that he's using it just as an excuse to ruin the rest of us and to make himself dictator of Sark. Isn't it obvious to you?

"There isn't any X at all, but tomorrow, unless he's stopped, he'll spread the sub-etherics full of conspiracies and declarations of emergencies and he'll have himself declared Leader. We haven't had a Leader on Sark in five hundred years but that won't stop Fife. He'd just let the constitution go hang. Really!

"Only I mean to stop him. That's why I had to leave. If I were still in Steen, I'd be under house arrest.

"As soon as the conference was over I had my own personal port checked, and, you know, his men had taken over. It was in clear disregard of continental autonomy. It was the act of a cad. Really! But nasty as he is, he isn't so bright. He thought some of us might try to leave the planet so he had the spaceports watched, but"—here he smiled in vulpine fashion and emitted the ghost of a giggle—"it didn't occur to him to watch the gyro-ports.

"Probably he thought there wasn't a place on the planet that would be safe for us. But I thought of the Trantorian Embassy. It's more than the others did. They make me tired. Especially Bort. Do you know Bort? He's terribly uncouth. Actually *dirty*. Talks at me as though there were something wrong with being clean and smelling pleasant."

He put his finger tips to his nose and inhaled gently.

Abel put a light hand on Junz's wrist as the latter moved restlessly in his seat. Abel said, "You have left a family behind. Have you thought that Fife can still hold a weapon over you?"

"I couldn't very well pile all my pretty ones in my gyro-plane." He reddened a trifle. "Fife wouldn't dare touch them. Besides, I'll be back in Steen tomorrow."

"How?" asked Abel.

Steen looked at him in astonishment. His thin lips parted. "I'm offering alliance, Your Excellency. You can't pretend Trantor isn't *interested* in Sark. Surely you'll tell Fife that any attempt to change Sark's constitution would necessitate Trantor's intervention."

"I scarcely see how that can be done, even if I felt my government would back me," said Abel.

"How can it *not* be done?" asked Steen indignantly. "If he controls the entire kyrt trade he'll raise the price, ask concessions for rapid delivery and all sorts of things."

"Don't the five of you control the price as is?"

Steen threw himself back in the seat. "Well, really! I don't know all the details. Next you'll be asking me for figures. Goodness, you're as bad as Bort." Then he recovered and giggled. "I'm just teasing, of course. What I mean is that, with Fife out of the way, Trantor *might* make an arrangement with the rest of us. In return for your help, it would only be right that Trantor get preferential treatment, or even maybe a small interest in the trade."

"And how would we keep intervention from developing into a Galaxy-wide war?"

"Oh, but really, don't you see? It's plain as day. You wouldn't be *aggressors*. You would just be preventing civil war to keep the kyrt trade from disruption. I'd announce that I'd appealed to you for help. It would be worlds removed from aggression. The whole Galaxy would be on your side. Of course, if Trantor benefits from it afterward, why, that's nobody's business at all. Really!"

Abel put his gnarled fingers together and regarded them. "I can't believe you really mean to join forces with Trantor."

An intense look of hatred passed momentarily over Steen's weakly smiling face. He said, "Rather Trantor than Fife."

Abel said, "I don't like threatening force. Can't we wait and let matters develop a bit——"

"No, no," cried Steen. "Not a day. Really! If you're not firm now, right now, it will be too late. Once the deadline is past, he'll have gone too far to retreat without losing face. If you'll help me now, the people of Steen will back me, the other Great Squires will join me. If you wait even a day, Fife's propaganda mill will begin to grind. I'll be smeared as a renegade. Really! I! *I!* A renegade! He'll use all the anti-Trantor prejudice he can whip up and you know, meaning no offense, that's quite a bit."

"Suppose we ask him to allow us to interview the Spatio-analyst?"

"What good will that do? He'll play both ends. He'll tell us the Florinian idiot is a Spatio-analyst, but he'll tell you the Spatio-analyst is a Florinian idiot. You don't know the man. He's *awful!*"

Abel considered that. He hummed to himself, his forefinger keeping gentle time. Then he said, "We have the Townman, you know."

"What Townman?"

"The one who killed the patrollers and the Sarkite."

"Oh! Well, really! Do you suppose Fife will care about that if it's a question of taking all Sark?"

"I think so. You see, it isn't that we have the Townman. It's the circumstances of his capture. I think, Squire, that Fife will listen to me and listen very humbly, too."

For the first time in his acquaintance with Abel, Junz sensed a lessening of coolness in the old man's voice, a substitution for it of satisfaction, almost of triumph.

Fifteen: *THE CAPTIVE*

It was not very usual for the Lady Samia of Fife to feel frustrated. It was unprecedented, even inconceivable, that she had felt frustrated for hours now.

The commander of the spaceport was Captain Racety all over again. He was polite, almost obsequious, looked unhappy, expressed his regrets, denied the least willingness to contradict her, and stood like iron against her plainly stated wishes.

She was finally forced from stating her desires to demanding her rights as though she were a common Sarkite. She said, "I suppose that as a citizen I have the right to meet any incoming vessel if I wish."

She was poisonous about it.

The commander cleared his throat and the expression of pain on his lined face grew, if anything, clearer and more definite. Finally he said, "As a matter of fact, my Lady, we have no wish at all to exclude you. It is only that we have received specific orders from the Squire, your father, to forbid your meeting the ship."

Samia said frozenly, "Are you ordering me to leave the port, then?"

"No, my Lady." The commander was glad to compromise. "We were not ordered to exclude you from the port. If you wish to remain here you may do so. But, with all due respect, we will have to stop you from approaching closer to the pits."

He was gone and Samia sat in the futile luxury of her private ground-car, a hundred feet inside the outermost entrance of the port. They had been waiting and watching for her. They would probably keep on watching her. If she as much as rolled a wheel onward, she thought indignantly, they would probably cut her power-drive.

She gritted her teeth. It was unfair of her father to do this. It was all of a piece. They always treated her as though she understood nothing. Yet she had thought he understood.

He had risen from his seat to greet her, a thing he never did for anyone else now that Mother was dead. He had clasped her, squeezed her tightly, abandoned all his work for her. He had even sent his secretary out of the room because he knew she was repelled by the native's still, white countenance.

It was almost like the old days before Grandfather died when Father had not yet become Great Squire.

He said, "Mia, child, I've counted the hours. I never knew it was such a long way from Florina. When I heard that those natives had hidden on your ship, the one I had sent just to insure your safety, I was nearly wild."

"Daddy! There was nothing to worry about."

"Wasn't there? I almost sent out the entire fleet to take you off and bring you in with full military security."

They laughed together at the thought. Minutes passed before Samia could bring the conversation back to the subject that filled her.

She said casually, "What are you going to do with the stowaways, Dad?"

"Why do you want to know, Mia?"

"You don't think they've plans to assassinate you, or anything like that?"

Fife smiled. "You shouldn't think morbid thoughts."

"You don't think so, do you?" she insisted.

"Of course not."

"Good! Because I've talked to them, Dad, and I just don't believe they're anything more than poor harmless people. I don't care what Captain Racety says."

"They've broken a considerable number of laws for 'poor harmless people,' Mia."

"You can't treat them as common criminals, Dad." Her voice rose in alarm.

"How else?"

"The man isn't a native. He's from a planet called Earth and he's been psycho-probed and he's not responsible."

"Well then, dear, Depsec will realize that. Suppose you leave it to them."

"No, it's too important to just leave to them. They won't understand. Nobody understands. Except me!"

"Only you in the whole world, Mia?" he asked indulgently, and put out a finger to stroke a lock of hair that had fallen over her forehead.

Samia said with energy, "Only I! Only I! Everyone else is going to think he's crazy, but I'm *sure* he isn't. He says there is some great danger to Florina and to all the Galaxy. He's a Spatio-analyst and you know they specialize in cosmogony. He would *know!*"

"How do you know he's a Spatio-analyst, Mia?"

"He says so."

"And what are the details of the danger?"

"He doesn't know. He's been psycho-probed. Don't you see that that's the best evidence of all? He knew too much. Someone was interested in keeping it dark." Her voice instinctively fell and grew huskily confidential. She restrained an impulse to look over her shoulder. She said, "If his theories were false, don't you see, there wouldn't have been any need to psycho-probe him."

"Why didn't they kill him, if that's the case?" asked Fife and instantly regretted the question. There was no use in teasing the girl.

Samia thought awhile, fruitlessly, then said, "If you'll order Depsec to let me speak to him, I'll find out. He trusts me. I know he does. I'll get more out of him than Depsec can. Please tell Depsec to let me see him, Dad. It's *very* important."

Fife squeezed her clenched fists gently and smiled at her. "Not yet, Mia. Not yet. In a few hours we'll have the third person in our hands. After that, perhaps."

"The third person? The native who did all the killings?"

"Exactly. The ship carrying him will land in about an hour."

"And you won't do anything with the native girl and the Spatio-analyst till then?"

"Not a thing."

"Good! I'll meet the ship." She rose.

"Where are you going, Mia?"

"To the port, Father. I have a great deal to ask of this other native." She laughed. "I'll show you that your daughter can be quite a detective."

But Fife did not respond to her laughter. He said, "I'd rather you didn't."

"Why not?"

"It's essential that there be nothing out of the way about this man's arrival. You'd be too conspicuous at the port."

"What of it?"

"I can't explain statecraft to you, Mia."

"Statecraft, pooh." She leaned toward him, pecked a quick kiss at the center of his forehead and was gone.

Now she sat helplessly car-bound in the port while far overhead there was a growing speck in the sky, dark against the brightness of the late afternoon.

She pressed the button that opened the utility compartment and took out her polo-glasses. Ordinarily they were used to follow the gyrating antics of the one-man speedsters which took part in stratospheric polo. They could be put to more serious use too. She put them to her eyes and the descending dot became a ship in miniature, the ruddy glow of its stern drive plainly visible.

She would at least see the men as they left, learn as much as she could by the one sense of sight, arrange an interview somehow, *somehow* thereafter.

Sark filled the visiplate. A continent and half an ocean, obscured in part by the dead cotton-white of clouds, lay below.

Genro said, his words a trifle uneven as the only indication that the better part of his mind was perforce on the controls before him, "The spaceport will not be heavily guarded. That was at my suggestion too. I said that any unusual treatment of the arrival of the ship might warn Trantor that something was up. I said that success depended upon Trantor being at no time aware of the true state of affairs until it was too late. Well, never mind that."

Terens shrugged his shoulders glumly. "What's the difference?"

"Plenty, to you. I will use the landing pit nearest the East Gate. You will get out the safety exit in the rear as soon as I land. Walk quickly but not too quickly toward that gate. I have some papers that may get you through without trouble and may not. I'll leave it to you to take necessary action if there is trouble. From past history, I judge I can trust you that far. Outside the gate there will be a car waiting to take you to the embassy. That's all."

"What about you?"

Slowly Sark was changing from a huge featureless sphere of blinding browns and greens and blues and cloud-white into something more alive, into a surface broken by rivers and wrinkled by mountains.

Genro's smile was cool and humorless. "Your worries may end with yourself. When they find you gone, I may be shot as a traitor. If they find me completely helpless and physically unable to stop you, they may merely demote me as a fool. The latter, I suppose, is preferable, so I will ask you, before you leave, to use a neuronic whip on me."

The Townman said, "Do you know what a neuronic whip is like?"

"Quite." There were small drops of perspiration at his temples.

"How do you know I won't kill you afterward? I'm a Squire-killer, you know."

"I know. But killing me won't help you. It will just waste your time. I've taken worse chances."

The surface of Sark as viewed in the visiplate was expanding, its edges rushed out past the border of visibility, its center grew and the new edges rushed out in turn. Something like the rainbow of a Sarkite city could be made out.

"I hope," said Genro, "you have no ideas of striking out on your own. Sark is no place for that. It's either Trantor or the Squires. Remember."

The view was definitely that of a city now and a green-brown patch on its outskirts expanded and became a spaceport below them. It floated up toward them at a slowing pace.

Genro said, "If Trantor doesn't have you in the next hour the Squires will have you before the day is out. I don't guarantee what Trantor will do to you, but I can guarantee what Sark will do to you."

Terens had been in the Civil Service. He knew what Sark would do with a Squire-killer.

The port held steady in the visiplate, but Genro no longer regarded it. He was switching to instruments, riding the pulse-beam downward. The ship turned slowly in air, a mile high, and settled, tail down.

A hundred yards above the pit, the engines thundered high. Over the hydraulic springs, Terens could feel their shuddering. He grew giddy in his seat.

Genro said, "Take the whip. Quickly now. Every second is important. The emergency lock will close behind you. It will take them five minutes to wonder why I don't open the main lock, another five minutes to break in, another five minutes to find you. You have fifteen minutes to get out of the port and into the car."

The shuddering ceased and in the thick silence Terens knew they had made contact with Sark.

The shifting diamagnetic fields took over. The yacht tipped majestically and slowly moved down upon its side.

Genro said, "Now!" His uniform was wet with perspiration.

Terens, with swimming head, and eyes that all but refused to focus, raised his neuronic whip. . . .

Terens felt the nip of a Sarkite autumn. He had spent years in its harsh seasons until he had almost forgotten the soft eternal June of Florina. Now his days in Civil Service rushed back upon him as though he had never left this world of Squires.

Except that now he was a fugitive and branded upon him was the ultimate crime, the murder of a Squire.

He was walking in time to the pounding of his heart. Behind him was the ship and in it was Genro, frozen in the agony of the whip. The lock had closed softly behind him, and he was walking down a broad, paved path. There were workmen and mechanics in plenty about him. Each had his own job and his own troubles. They didn't stop to stare a man in the face. They had no reason to.

Had anyone actually seen him emerge from the ship?

He told himself no one had, or by now there would have been the clamor of pursuit.

He touched his hat briefly. It was still down over his ears, and the little medallion it now carried was smooth to the touch. Genro had said that it would act as identification. The men from Trantor would be watching for just that medallion, glinting in the sun.

He could remove it, wander away on his own, find his way to another ship—somehow. He would get away from Sark—somehow. He would escape—somehow.

Too many somehows! In his heart he knew he had come to the final end, and as Genro had said, it was either Trantor or Sark. He hated and feared Trantor, but he knew that in any choice it could not and must not be Sark.

"You! You there!"

Terens froze. He looked up in cold panic. The gate was a hundred feet away. If he ran . . . But they wouldn't allow a running man to get out. It was a thing he dared not do. He must not run.

The young woman was looking out the open window of a car such as Terens had never seen, not even during fifteen years on Sark. It gleamed with metal and sparkled with translucent gemmite.

She said, "Come here."

Terens' legs carried him slowly to the car. Genro had said Trantor's car would be waiting outside the port. Or had he? And would they send a woman on such an errand? A girl, in fact. A girl with a dark, beautiful face.

She said, "You arrived on the ship that just landed, didn't you?"

He was silent.

She became impatient. "Come, I saw you leave the ship!" She tapped her polo-glasses. He had seen such glasses before.

Terens mumbled, "Yes. Yes."

"Get in then."

She held the door open for him. The car was even more luxurious inside. The seat was soft and it all smelled new and fragrant and the girl was beautiful.

She said, "Are you a member of the crew?"

She was testing him, Terens imagined. He said, "You know who I am." He raised his fingers momentarily to the medallion.

Without any sound of motive power the car backed and turned.

At the gate Terens shrank back into the soft, cool, kyrt-covered upholstery, but there was no need for caution. The girl spoke peremptorily and they passed through.

She said, "This man is with me. I am Samia of Fife."

It took seconds for the tired Terens to hear and understand that. When he lurched tensely forward in his seat the car was traveling along the express lanes at a hundred per.

A laborer within the port looked up from where he stood and muttered briefly into his lapel. He entered the building then and returned to his work. His superintendent frowned and made a mental note to talk to Tip about this habit of lingering outside to smoke cigarettes for half an hour at a time.

Outside the port one of two men in a ground-car said with annoyance, "Got into a car with a girl? What car? What girl?" For all his Sarkite costume, his accent belonged definitely to the Arcturian worlds of the Trantorian Empire.

His companion was a Sarkite, well versed in the visicast news releases. When the car in question rolled through the gate and picked up speed as it began to veer off and upward to the express level, he half rose in his seat and cried, "It's the Lady Samia's car. There isn't another like it. Good Galaxy, what do we do?"

"Follow," said the other briefly.

"But the Lady Samia——"

"She's nothing to me. She shouldn't be anything to you either. Or what are you doing here?"

Their own car was making the turn, climbing upward onto the broad, nearly empty stretches on which only the speediest of ground travel was permitted.

The Sarkite groaned, "We can't catch that car. As soon as she spots us she'll kick out resistance. That car can make two-fifty."

"She's staying at a hundred so far," said the Arcturian.

After a while he said, "She's not going to Depsec. That's for sure."

And after another while he said, "She's not going to the Palace of Fife."

Still another interval and he said, "I'll be spun in space if I know *where* she's going. She'll be leaving the city again."

The Sarkite said, "How do we know it's the Squire-killer that's in there? Suppose it's a game to get us away from the post. She's not trying to shake us and she wouldn't use a car like that if she didn't *want* to be followed. You can't miss it at two miles."

"I know, but Fife wouldn't send his girl to get us out of the way. A squad of patrollers would have done the job better."

"Maybe it isn't really the Lady in it."

"We're going to find out, man. She's slowing. Flash past and stop around a curve!"

"I want to speak to you," said the girl.

Terens decided it was not the ordinary kind of trap he had first considered it. She *was* the Lady of Fife. She must be. It did not seem to occur to her that anyone could or ought to interfere with her.

She had never looked back to see if she were followed. Three times as they turned he had noted the same car to the rear, keeping its distance, neither closing the gap nor falling behind.

It was not just a car. That was certain. It might be Trantor, which would be well. It might be Sark, in which case the Lady would be a decent sort of hostage.

He said, "I'm ready to speak."

She said, "You were on the ship that brought the native from Florina? The one wanted for all those killings?"

"I said I was."

"Very well. Now I've brought you out here so that there'll be no interference. Was the native questioned during the trip to Sark?"

Such naïveté, Terens thought, could not be assumed. She really did not know who he was. He said guardedly, "Yes."

"Were you present at the questioning?"

"Yes."

"Good. I thought so. Why did you leave the ship, by the way?"

That, thought Terens, was the question she should have asked first of all.

He said, "I was to bring a special report to——" He hesitated.

She seized on the hesitation eagerly. "To my father? Don't worry about that. I'll protect you completely. I'll say you came with me at my orders."

He said, "Very well, my Lady."

The words "my Lady" struck deeply into his own consciousness. She was a Lady, the greatest in the land, and he was a Florinian. A man who could kill patrollers could learn easily how to kill Squires, and a Squire-killer might, by the same token, look a Lady in the face.

He looked at her, his eyes hard and searching. He lifted his head and stared down at her.

She was very beautiful.

And because she was the greatest Lady in the land, she was unconscious of his regard. She said, "I want you to tell me everything that you heard at the questioning. I want to know all that was told you by the native. It's very important."

"May I ask why you are interested in the native, my Lady?"

"You may not," she said flatly.

"As you wish, my Lady."

He didn't know what he was going to say. With half his consciousness he was waiting for the pursuing car to catch up. With the other half he was growing more aware of the face and body of the beautiful girl sitting near him.

Florinians in the Civil Service and those acting as Townmen were theoretically, celibates. In actual practice, most evaded that restriction when they could. Terens had done what he dared and what was expedient in that direction. At best, his experiences had never been satisfactory.

So it was all the more important that he had never been so near a beautiful girl in a car of such luxuriance under conditions of such isolation.

She was waiting for him to speak, dark eyes (such dark eyes) aflame with interest, full red lips parted in anticipation, a figure more beautiful for being set off in beautiful kyrt. She was completely unaware that anyone, *anyone*, could possibly dare harbor dangerous thought with regard to the Lady of Fife.

The half of his consciousness that waited for the pursuers faded out.

He suddenly knew that the killing of a Squire was not the ultimate crime after all.

He wasn't quite aware that he moved. He knew only that her

small body was in his arms, that it stiffened, that for an instant she cried out, and then he smothered the cry with his lips. . . .

There were hands on his shoulder and the drift of cool air on his back through the opened door of the car. His fingers groped for his weapon, too late. It was ripped from his hand.

Samia gasped wordlessly.

The Sarkite said with horror, "Did you see what he did?"

The Arcturian said, "Never mind!"

He put a small black object into his pocket and smoothed the seam shut. "Get him," he said.

The Sarkite dragged Terens out of the car with the energy of fury. "And she let him," he muttered. "She let him."

"Who *are* you?" cried Samia with sudden energy. "Did my father send you?"

The Arcturian said, "No questions, please."

"You're a foreigner," said Samia angrily.

The Sarkite said, "By Sark, I ought to bust his head in." He cocked his fist.

"Stop it!" said the Arcturian. He seized the Sarkite's wrist and forced it back.

The Sarkite growled sullenly, "There are limits. I can take the Squire-killing. I'd like to kill a few myself, but standing by and watching a native do what he did is just about too much for me."

Samia said in an unnaturally high-pitched voice, "Native?"

The Sarkite leaned forward, snatched viciously at Terens' cap. The Townman paled but did not move. He kept his gaze steadily upon the girl and his sandy hair moved slightly in the breeze.

Samia moved helplessly back along the car seat as far as she could and then, with a quick movement, she covered her face with both hands, her skin turning white under the pressure of her fingers.

The Sarkite said, "What are we going to do with her?"

"Nothing."

"She saw us. She'll have the whole planet after us before we've gone a mile."

"Are you going to kill the Lady of Fife?" asked the Arcturian sarcastically.

"Well, no. But we can wreck her car. By the time she gets to a radiophone, we'll be all right."

"Not necessary." The Arcturian leaned into the car. "My Lady, I have only a moment. Can you hear me?"

She did not move.

The Arcturian said, "You had better hear me. I am sorry I interrupted you at a tender moment but luckily I have put that moment to use. I acted quickly and was able to record the scene by tri-camera. This is no bluff. I will transmit the negative to a safe place minutes after I leave you and thereafter any interference on your part will force me to be rather nasty. I'm sure you understand me."

He turned away. "She won't say anything about this. Not a thing. Come along with me, Townman."

Terens followed. He could not look back at the white, pinched face in the car.

Whatever might now follow, he had accomplished a miracle. For one moment he had kissed the proudest Lady on Sark, had felt the fleeting touch of her soft, fragrant lips.

Sixteen: *THE ACCUSED*

Diplomacy has a language and a set of attitudes all its own. Relationships between the representatives of sovereign states, if conducted strictly according to protocol, are stylized and stultifying. The phrase "unpleasant consequences" becomes synonymous with war and "suitable adjustment" with surrender.

When on his own, Abel preferred to abandon diplomatic double-talk. With a tight personal beam connecting himself and Fife, he might merely have been an elderly man talking amiably over a glass of wine.

He said, "You have been hard to reach, Fife."

Fife smiled. He seemed at ease and undisturbed. "A busy day, Abel."

"Yes. I've heard a bit about it."

"Steen?" Fife was casual.

"Partly. Steen's been with us about seven hours."

"I know. My own fault, too. Are you considering turning him over to us?"

"I'm afraid not."

"He's a criminal."

Abel chuckled and turned the goblet in his hand, watching the lazy bubbles. "I think we can make out a case for his being a political refugee. Interstellar law will protect him on Trantorian territory."

"Will your government back you?"

"I think it will, Fife. I haven't been in the foreign service for thirty-seven years without knowing what Trantor will back and what it won't."

"I can have Sark ask for your recall."

"What good would that do? I'm a peaceable man with whom you are well acquainted. My successor might be anybody."

There was a pause. Fife's leonine countenance puckered. "I think you have a suggestion."

"I do. You have a man of ours."

"What man of yours?"

"A Spatio-analyst. A native of the planet Earth, which by the way, is part of the Trantorian domain."

"Steen told you this?"

"Among other things."

"Has he seen this Earthman?"

"He hasn't said he has."

"Well, he hasn't. Under the circumstances, I doubt that you can have faith in his word."

Abel put down his glass. He clasped his hands loosely in his lap and said, "Just the same, I'm sure the Earthman exists. I tell you, Fife, we should get together on this. I have Steen and you have the Earthman. In a sense we're even. Before you go on with your current plans, before your ultimatum expires and your *coup d'état* takes place, why not a conference on the kyrt situation generally?"

"I don't see the necessity. What is happening on Sark now is an internal matter entirely. I'm quite willing to guarantee personally that there will be no interference with the kyrt trade regardless of political events here. I think that should end Trantor's legitimate interests."

Abel sipped at his wine, seemed to consider. He said, "It seems we have a second political refugee. A curious case. One of your Florinian subjects, by the way. A Townman. Myrlyn Terens, he calls himself."

Fife's eyes blazed suddenly. "We half suspected that. By Sark,

Abel, there's a limit to the open interference of Trantor on this planet. The man you have kidnaped is a murderer. You can't make a political refugee out of him."

"Well, now, do you want the man?"

"You have a deal in mind? Is that it?"

"The conference I spoke of."

"For one Florinian murderer. Of course not."

"But the manner in which the Townman managed to escape to us is rather curious. You may be interested . . ."

Junz paced the floor, shaking his head. The night was already well advanced. He would like to be able to sleep but he knew he would require somnin once again.

Abel said, "I might have had to threaten force, as Steen suggested. That would have been bad. The risks would have been awful, the results uncertain. Yet until the Townman was brought to us I saw no alternative, except of course, a policy of do-nothing."

Junz shook his head violently. "No. Something had to be done. Yet it amounted to blackmail."

"Technically, I suppose so. What would you have had me do?"

"Exactly what you did. I'm not a hypocrite, Abel. Or I try not to be. I won't condemn your methods when I intend to make full use of the results. Still, what about the girl?"

"She won't be hurt as long as Fife keeps his bargain."

"I'm sorry for her. I've grown to dislike the Sarkite aristocrats for what they've done to Florina, but I can't help feeling sorry for her."

"As an individual, yes. But the true responsibility lies with Sark itself. Look here, old man, did you ever kiss a girl in a ground-car?"

The tip of a smile quivered at the corners of Junz's mouth. "Yes."

"So have I, though I have to call upon longer memories than you do, I imagine. My eldest granddaughter is probably engaged in the practice at this moment, I shouldn't wonder. What is a stolen kiss in a ground-car, anyway, except the expression of the most natural emotion in the Galaxy?

"Look here, man. We have a girl, admittedly of high social standing, who, through mistake, finds herself in the same car with, let us say, a criminal. He seizes the opportunity to kiss her. It's on impulse and without her consent. How ought she to feel? How ought her father to feel? Chagrined? Perhaps. Annoyed? Certainly. Angry?

Offended? Insulted? All that, yes. But disgraced? No! Disgraced enough to be willing to endanger important affairs of state to avoid exposure? Nonsense.

"But that's exactly the situation and it could happen only on Sark. The Lady Samia is guilty of nothing but willfulness and a certain naïveté. She has, I am sure, been kissed before. If she kissed again, if she kissed innumerable times, anyone but a Florinian, nothing would be said. But she *did* kiss a Florinian.

"It doesn't matter that she did not know he was a Florinian. It doesn't matter that he forced the kiss upon her. To make public the photograph we have of the Lady Samia in the arms of the Florinian would make life unbearable for her and for her father. I saw Fife's face when he stared at the reproduction. There was no way of telling for certain that the Townman was a Florinian. He was in Sarkite costume with a cap that covered his hair well. He was light-skinned, but that was inconclusive. Still, Fife knew that the rumor would be gladly believed by many who were interested in scandal and sensation and that the picture would be considered incontrovertible proof. And he knew that his political enemies would make the greatest possible capital out of it. You may call it blackmail, Junz, and maybe it is, but it's a blackmail that would not work on any other planet in the Galaxy. Their own sick social system gave us this weapon and I have no compunction about using it."

Junz sighed. "What's the final arrangement?"

"We'll meet at noon tomorrow."

"His ultimatum has been postponed then?"

"Indefinitely. I will be at his office in person."

"Is that a necessary risk?"

"It's not much of one. There will be witnesses. And I am anxious to be in the material presence of this Spatio-analyst you have been searching for so long."

"I'll attend?" asked Junz anxiously.

"Oh yes. The Townman as well. We'll need him to identify the Spatio-analyst. And Steen, of course. All of you will be present by trimensic personification."

"Thank you."

The Trantorian Ambassador smothered a yawn and blinked at Junz through watering eyes. "Now, if you don't mind, I've been awake for two days and a night and I'm afraid my old body can take no more antisomnin. I must sleep."

With trimensic personification perfected, important conferences were rarely held face to face. Fife felt strongly an element of actual indecency in the material presence of the old Ambassador. His olive complexion could not be said to have darkened, but its lines were set in silent anger.

It had to be silent. He could say nothing. He could only stare sullenly at the men who faced him.

Abel! An old dotard in shabby clothes with a million worlds behind him.

Junz! A dark-skinned, woolly-haired interferer whose perseverance had precipitated the crisis.

Steen! The traitor! Afraid to meet his eyes!

The Townman! To look at him was most difficult of all. He was the native who had dishonored his daughter with his touch yet who could remain safe and untouchable behind the walls of the Trantorian Embassy. He would have been glad to grind his teeth and pound his desk if he had been alone. As it was, not a muscle of his face must move though it tore beneath the strain.

If Samia had not . . . He dropped that. His own negligence had cultivated her willfulness and he could not blame her for it now. She had not tried to excuse herself or soften her own guilt. She had told him all the truth of her private attempts to play the interstellar spy and how horribly it had ended. She had relied completely, in her shame and bitterness, on his understanding, and she would have that much. She would have that much, if it meant the ruin of the structure he had been building.

He said, "This conference has been forced upon me. I see no point in saying anything. I'm here to listen."

Abel said, "I believe Steen would like to have his say first."

Fife's eyes filled with contempt that stung Steen.

Steen yelled his answer. "You made me turn to Trantor, Fife. You violated the principle of autonomy. You couldn't expect me to stand for that. Really."

Fife said nothing and Abel said, not without a little contempt of his own, "Get to your point, Steen. You said you had something to say. Say it."

Steen's sallow cheekbones reddened without benefit of rouge. "I will, and right now. Of course I don't claim to be the detective that the Squire of Fife represents himself to be, but I can think. Really! And I've *been* thinking. Fife had a story to tell yesterday, all about a mysterious traitor he called X. I could see it was just a lot of talk so that he could declare an emergency. I wasn't fooled a minute."

"There's no X?" asked Fife quietly. "Then why did *you* run? A man who runs needs no other accusation."

"Is that so? Really?" cried Steen. "Well, I would run out of a burning building even if I had not set the fire myself."

"Go on, Steen," said Abel.

Steen licked his lips and turned to a minute consideration of his fingernails. He smoothed them gently as he spoke. "But then I thought, why make up that particular story with all its complications and things? It's not his way. Really! It's not Fife's way. I know him. We all know him. He has no imagination at all, Your Excellency. A brute of a man! Almost as bad as Bort."

Fife scowled. "Is he saying something, Abel, or is he babbling?"

"Go on, Steen," said Abel.

"I will, if you'll let me talk. My goodness! Whose side are you on? I said to myself (this was after dinner), I said, Why would a man like Fife make up a story like that? There was only one answer. He couldn't make it up. Not with *his* mind. So it was true. It must be true. And, of course, patrollers *had* been killed, though Fife is quite capable of arranging to have that happen."

Fife shrugged his shoulders.

Steen drove on. "Only who is X? It isn't I. Really! I know it isn't I! And I'll admit it could only have been a Great Squire. But what Great Squire knew most about it, anyway? What Great Squire has been trying to use the story of the Spatio-analyst for a year now to frighten the others into some sort of what he calls 'united effort' and what I call surrender to a Fife dictatorship?

"I'll tell you who X is." Steen stood up, the top of his head brushing the edge of the receptor-cube and flattening as the uppermost inch sliced off into nothingness. He pointed a trembling finger. "*He's* X. The Squire of Fife. He found this Spatio-analyst. He put him out of the way, when he saw the rest of us weren't impressed with his silly remarks at our first conference, and then he brought him out again after he had already arranged a military coup."

Fife turned wearily to Abel. "Is he through? If so, remove him. He is an unbearable offense to any decent man."

Abel said, "Have you any comment to make on what he says?"

"Of course not. It isn't worth comment. The man is desperate. He'll say anything."

"You can't just brush it off, Fife," called Steen. He looked about at the rest. His eyes narrowed and the skin at his nostrils was white with tension. He remained standing. "Listen. He said his investigators found records in a doctor's office. He said the doctor had died by accident after diagnosing the Spatio-analyst as the victim of psycho-probing. He said it was murder by X to keep the identity of the Spatio-analyst secret. That's what he said. Ask him. Ask him if that isn't what he said."

"And if I did?" asked Fife.

"Then ask him how he could get the records from the office of a doctor who was dead and buried for months unless he had them all along. Really!"

Fife said, "This is foolish. We can waste time indefinitely this way. Another doctor took over the dead man's practice and his records as well. Do any of you think medical records are destroyed along with a physician?"

Abel said, "No, of course not."

Steen stuttered, then sat down.

Fife said, "What's next? Have any of you more to say? More accusations? More anything?" His voice was low. Bitterness showed through.

Abel said, "Why, that was Steen's say, and we'll let it pass. Now Junz and I, we're here on another kind of business. We would like to see the Spatio-analyst."

Fife's hands had been resting upon the desk top. They lifted now and came down to clutch the edge of the desk. His black eyebrows drew together.

He said, "We have in custody a man of subnormal mentality who claims to be a Spatio-analyst. I'll have him brought in!"

Valona March had never, never in her life dreamed such impossibilities could exist. For over a day now, ever since she had landed on this planet of Sark, there had been a touch of wonder about everything. Even the prison cells in which she and Rik had been separately placed seemed to have an unreal quality of magnificence about them. Water came out of a hole in a pipe when you pressed a button. Heat came out of the wall, although the air outside had been colder than she had thought air could possibly get. And everyone who spoke to her wore such beautiful clothes.

She had been in rooms in which were all sorts of things she had never seen before. This one now was larger than any yet but it was almost bare. It had more people in it, though. There was a stern-looking man behind a desk, and a much older, very wrinkled man in a chair, and three others . . .

One was the Townman!

She jumped up and ran to him. "Townman! Townman!"

But he wasn't there!

He had gotten up and waved at her. "Stay back, Lona. Stay back!"

And she passed right through him. She had reached out to seize his sleeve, he moved it away. She lunged, half stumbling, and passed right through him. For a moment the breath went out of her body. The Townman had turned, was facing her again, but she could only stare down at her legs.

Both of them were thrusting through the heavy arm of the chair in which the Townman had been sitting. She could see it plainly, in all its color and solidity. It encircled her legs but she did not feel it. She put out a trembling hand and her fingers sank an inch deep into upholstery they could not feel either. Her fingers remained visible.

She shrieked and fell, her last sensation being that of the Townman's arms reaching automatically for her and herself falling through their circle as though they were pieces of flesh-tinted air.

She was in a chair again, Rik holding one hand tightly and the old, wrinkled man leaning over her.

He was saying, "Don't be frightened, my dear. It's just a picture. A photograph, you know."

Valona looked about. The Townman was still sitting there. He wasn't looking at her.

She pointed a finger, "Isn't he there?"

Rik said suddenly, "It's a trimensic personification, Lona. He's somewhere else, but we can see him from here."

Valona shook her head. If Rik said so, it was all right. But she lowered her eyes. She dared not look at people who were there and not there at the same time.

Abel said to Rik, "So you know what trimensic personification is, young man?"

"Yes, sir." It had been a tremendous day for Rik, too, but where Valona was increasingly dazzled, he had found things increasingly familiar and comprehensible.

"Where did you learn that?"

"I don't know. I knew it before—before I forgot."

Fife had not moved from his seat behind the desk during the wild plunge of Valona March toward the Townman.

He said acidly, "I am sorry to have to disturb this meeting by bringing in a hysterical native woman. The so-called Spatio-analyst required her presence."

"It's all right," said Abel. "But I notice that your Florinian of subnormal mentality seems to be acquainted with trimensic personification."

"He has been well drilled, I imagine," said Fife.

Abel said, "Has he been questioned since arriving on Sark?"

"He certainly has."

"With what result?"

"No new information."

Abel turned to Rik. "What's your name?"

"Rik is the only name I remember," said Rik calmly.

"Do you know anyone here?"

Rik looked from face to face, without fear. He said, "Only the Townman. And Lona, of course."

"This," said Abel, gesturing toward Fife, "is the greatest Squire that ever lived. He owns the whole world. What do you think of him?"

Rik said boldly, "I'm an Earthman. He doesn't own *me*."

Abel said in an aside to Fife, "I don't think an adult native Florinian could be trained into that sort of defiance."

"Even with a psycho-probe?" returned Fife scornfully.

"Do you know this gentleman?" asked Abel, returning to Rik.

"No, sir."

"This is Dr. Selim Junz. He's an important official at the Interstellar Spatio-analytic Bureau."

Rik looked at him intently. "Then he'd be one of my chiefs. But," with disappointment, "I don't know him. Or maybe I just don't remember."

Junz shook his head gloomily. "I've never seen him, Abel."

"That's something for the record," muttered Fife.

"Now listen, Rik," said Abel. "I'm going to tell you a story. I want you to listen with all your mind and think. Think and think! Do you understand me?"

Rik nodded.

Abel talked slowly. His voice was the only sound in the room for long minutes. As he went on, Rik's eyelids closed and screwed themselves tight shut. His lips drew back, his fists moved up to his chest, and his head bent forward. He had the look of a man in agony.

Abel talked on, passing back and forth across the reconstruction of events as they had originally been presented by the Squire of Fife. He talked of the original message of disaster, of its interception, of the meeting between Rik and X, of the psycho-probing, of how Rik had been found and brought up on Florina, of the doctor who diagnosed him and then died, of his returning memory.

He said, "That's the whole story, Rik. I've told you all of it. Does anything sound familiar to you?"

Slowly, painfully, Rik said, "I remember the last parts. You know, the last few days. I remember something further back, too. Maybe it was the doctor, when I first started talking. It's very dim. . . . But that's all."

Abel said, "But you *do* remember further back. You remember danger to Florina."

"Yes. Yes. That was the first thing I remembered."

"Then can't you remember after that? You landed on Sark and met a man."

Rik moaned, "I can't. I can't remember."

"Try! Try!"

Rik looked up. His white face was wet with perspiration. "I remember a word."

"What word, Rik?"

"It doesn't make sense."

"Tell us anyway."

"It goes along with a table. Long, long ago. Very dim. I was sitting. I think, maybe, someone else was sitting. Then he was standing, looking down at me. And there's a word."

Abel was patient. "What word?"

Rik clenched his fists and whispered, "Fife!"

Every man but Fife rose to his feet. Steen shrieked, "I told you," and burst into a high-pitched bubbling cackle.

Seventeen: *THE ACCUSER*

Fife said with tightly controlled passion, "Let us end this farce."

He had waited before speaking, his eyes hard and his face expressionless, until in sheer anticlimax the rest were forced to take their seats again. Rik had bent his head, eyes screwed painfully shut, probing his own aching mind. Valona pulled him toward herself, trying hard to cradle his head on her shoulder, stroking his cheek softly.

Abel said shakily, "Why do you say this is a farce?"

Fife said, "Isn't it? I agreed to this meeting in the first place only because of a particular threat you held over me. I would have refused even so if I had known the conference was intended to be a trial of myself with renegades and murderers acting as both prosecutors and jury."

Abel frowned and said with chilling formality, "This is not a trial, Squire. Dr. Junz is here in order to recover the person of a member of the I.S.B., as is his right and duty. I am here to protect the interests of Trantor in a troubled time. There is no doubt in my mind that this man, Rik, is the missing Spatio-analyst. We can end this part of the conference immediately if you will agree to turn over the man to Dr. Junz for further examination, including a check of physical characteristics. We would naturally require your further help in finding the guilty psycho-prober and in setting up safeguards against a future repetition of such acts against what is, after all, an interstellar agency which has consistently held itself above regional politics."

Fife said, "Quite a speech! But the obvious remains obvious and your plans are quite transparent. What would happen if I gave up this man? I rather think that the I.S.B. will manage to find out exactly what it wants to find out. It claims to be an interstellar agency with no regional ties, but it's a fact, isn't it, that Trantor contributes two thirds of its annual budget? I doubt that any reasonable observer would consider it really neutral in the Galaxy of today. Its findings with regard to this man will surely suit Trantor's imperial interests.

"And what will these findings be? That's obvious too. The man's memory will slowly come back. The I.S.B. will issue daily bulletins. Bit by bit he will remember more and more of the necessary details. First my name. Then my appearance. Then my exact words. I will be solemnly declared guilty. Reparations will be required and Trantor will be forced to occupy Sark temporarily, an occupation which will somehow become permanent.

"There are limits beyond which any blackmail breaks down. Yours, Mr. Ambassador, ends here. If you want this man, have Trantor send a fleet after him."

"There is no question of force," said Abel. "Yet I notice that you have carefully avoided denying the implication in what the Spatio-analyst has last said."

"There isn't any implication that I need dignify by a denial. He remembers a word, or says he does. What of it?"

"Doesn't it mean anything that he does?"

"Nothing at all. The name Fife is a great one on Sark. Even if we assume the so-called Spatio-analyst is sincere, he had a year's opportunity to hear the name on Florina. He came to Sark on a ship that carried my daughter, a still better opportunity to have heard the name of Fife. What is more natural than that the name became involved with his trace memories? Of course, he may not be sincere. This man's bit-by-bit disclosures may be well rehearsed."

Abel thought of nothing to say. He looked at the others. Junz was frowning darkly, the fingers of his right hand slowly kneading his chin. Steen was simpering foolishly and muttering to himself. The Florinian Townman stared blankly at his knees.

It was Rik who spoke, forcing himself from Valona's grasp and standing up.

"Listen," he said. His pale face was twisted. His eyes mirrored pain.

Fife said, "Another disclosure, I suppose."

Rik said, "Listen! We were sitting at a table. The tea was drugged. We had been quarreling. I don't remember why. Then I couldn't move. I could only sit there. I couldn't talk. I could only think, Great Space, I've been drugged. I wanted to shout and scream and run, but I couldn't. Then the other one, Fife, came. He had been shouting at me. Only now he wasn't shouting. He didn't have to. He came around the table. He stood there, towering over me. I couldn't say anything. I couldn't do anything. I could only try to turn my eyeballs up toward him."

Rik remained standing, silent.

Selim Junz said, "This other man was Fife?"

"I remember his name was Fife."

"Well, was he that man?"

Rik did not turn to look. He said, "I can't remember what he looked like."

"Are you sure?"

"I've been trying." He burst out, "You don't know how hard it is. It hurts! It's like a red-hot needle. Deep! In here!" He put his hands to his head.

Junz said softly, "I know it's hard. But you must try. Don't you see, you must keep on trying. Look at that man! Turn and look at him!"

Rik twisted toward the Squire of Fife. For a moment he stared, then turned away.

Junz said, "Can you remember now?"

"No! No!"

Fife smiled grimly. "Has your man forgotten his lines, or will the story seem more believable if he remembers my face the next time around?"

Junz said hotly, "I have never seen this man before, and I have never spoken to him. There has been no arrangement to frame you and I am tired of your accusations in that direction. I am after the truth only."

"Then may I ask him a few questions?"

"Go ahead."

"Thank you, I'm sure, for your kindness. Now you—Rik, or whatever your real name is—"

He was a Squire, addressing a Florinian.

Rik looked up. "Yes, sir."

"You remember a man approaching you from the other side of the table as you sat there, drugged and helpless."

"Yes, sir."

"The last thing you remember is this man staring down at you."

"Yes, sir."

"You stared up at him, or tried to."

"Yes, sir."

"Sit down."

Rik did so.

For a moment Fife did nothing. His lipless mouth might have grown tighter, the jaw muscles under the blue-black sheen of the stubble on his cheeks and chin bunched a bit. Then he slid down from his chair.

Slid *down!* It was as though he had gotten down on his knees there behind the desk.

But he moved from behind it and was seen plainly to be standing.

Junz's head swam. The man, so statuesque and formidable in his seat, had been converted without warning into a pitiful midget.

Fife's deformed legs moved under him with an effort, carrying the ungainly mass of torso and head forward. His face flushed but his eyes kept their look of arrogance intact. Steen broke into a wild giggle and choked it off when those eyes turned on him. The rest sat in fascinated silence.

Rik, wide-eyed, watched him approach.

Fife said, "Was I the man who approached you around the table?"

"I can't remember his face, sir."

"I don't ask you to remember his face. Can you have forgotten this?" His two arms went wide, framing his body. "Can you have forgotten my appearance, my walk?"

Rik said miserably, "It seems I shouldn't, sir, but I don't know."

"But you were sitting, he was standing, and you were looking up at him."

"Yes, sir."

"He was looking down at you, 'towering' over you, in fact."

"Yes, sir."

"You remember that at least? You're certain of that?"

"Yes, sir."

The two were now face to face.

"Am I looking down at you?"

Rik said, "No, sir."

"Are you looking up at me?"

Rik, sitting, and Fife, standing, stared levelly at one another, eye to eye.

"No, sir."

"Could I have been the man?"

"No, sir."

"Are you certain?"

"Yes, sir."

"You still say the name you remember is Fife?"

"I remember that name," insisted Rik stubbornly.

"Whoever it was, then, used my name as a disguise?"

"He—he must have."

Fife turned and with slow dignity struggled back to his desk and climbed into his seat.

He said, "I have never allowed any man to see me standing before this in all my adult life. Is there any reason why this conference should continue?"

Abel was at once embarrassed and annoyed. So far the conference had backfired badly. At every step Fife had managed to put himself in the right, the others in the wrong. Fife had successfully presented himself as a martyr. He had been forced into conference by Trantorian blackmail, and made the subject of false accusations that had broken down at once.

Fife would see to it that his version of the conference flooded the Galaxy and he would not have to depart very far from the truth to make it excellent anti-Trantorian propaganda.

Abel would have liked to cut his losses. The psycho-probed Spatio-analyst would be of no use to Trantor now. Any "memory" he might have thereafter would be laughed down, made ridiculous, however true it might be. He would be accepted as an instrument of Trantorian imperialism, and a broken instrument at that.

But he hesitated, and it was Junz who spoke.

Junz said, "It seems to me there's a very good reason for not ending the conference just yet. We have not yet determined exactly who is responsible for the psycho-probing. You have accused the Squire of Steen, and Steen has accused you. Granting that both of you are mistaken and that both are innocent, it still remains true that you each believe one of the Great Squires is guilty. Which one, then?"

"Does it matter?" asked Fife. "As far as you're concerned, I'm sure it doesn't. That matter would have been solved by now except for the interference of Trantor and the I.S.B. Eventually I will find the traitor. Remember that the psycho-prober, whoever he is, had the original intention of forcing a monopoly of the kyrt trade into his own hands, so I am not likely to let him escape. Once the psycho-prober is identified and dealt with, your man here will be returned unharmed to you. That is the only offer I can make and it is a very reasonable one."

"What will you do with the psycho-prober?"

"That is a purely internal matter that does not concern you."

"But it does," Junz said energetically. "This is not just a question of the Spatio-analyst. There's something of greater importance involved and I'm surprised that it hasn't been mentioned yet. This man Rik wasn't psycho-probed just because he was a Spatio-analyst."

Abel was not sure what Junz's intentions were, but he threw his weight into the scales. He said blandly, "Dr. Junz is referring, of course, to the Spatio-analyst's original message of danger."

Fife shrugged. "As far as I know, no one has yet attached any importance to that, including Dr. Junz over the past year. However, your man is here, Doctor. Ask him what it's all about."

"Naturally, he won't remember," Junz retorted angrily. "The psycho-probe is most effective upon the more intellectual chains of reasoning stored in the mind. The man may never recover the quantitative aspects of his lifework."

"Then it's gone," said Fife. "What can be done about that?"

"Something very definite. That's the point. There's someone else who knows, and that's the psycho-prober. He may not have been a Spatio-analyst himself; he may not know the precise details. However, he spoke to the man in a state of untouched mind. He will have learned enough to put us far on the right track. Without having learned enough he would not have dared to destroy the source of his information. Still, for the record, *do* you remember, Rik?"

"Only that there was danger and that it involved the currents of space," muttered Rik.

Fife said, "Even if you find out, what will you have? How reliable are any of the startling theories that sick Spatio-analysts are forever coming up with? Many of them think they know the secrets of the universe when they're so sick they can barely read their instruments."

"It may be that you are right. Are you afraid to let me find out?"

"I am against starting any morbid rumors that might, whether true or false, affect the kyrt trade. Don't you agree with me, Abel?"

Abel squirmed inwardly. Fife was maneuvering himself into the position where any break in kyrt deliveries resulting from his own *coup* could be blamed on Trantorian maneuvers. But Abel was a good gambler. He raised the stakes calmly and unemotionally.

He said, "I don't. I suggest you listen to Dr. Junz."

"Thanks," said Junz. "Now you have said, Squire Fife, that whoever the psycho-prober was, he must have killed the doctor who examined this man Rik. That implies that the psycho-prober had kept some sort of watch over Rik during his stay on Florina."

"Well?"

"There must be traces of that kind of watching."

"You mean you think these natives would know who was watching them."

"Why not?"

Fife said, "You are not a Sarkite and so you make mistakes. I assure you that natives keep their places. They don't approach Squires and if Squires approach them they know enough to keep their eyes on their toes. They would know nothing of being watched."

Junz quivered visibly with indignation. The Squires had their despotism so ingrained that they saw nothing wrong or shameful in speaking of it openly.

He said, "Ordinary natives perhaps. But we have a man here who is not an ordinary native. I think he has shown us rather thoroughly that he is not a properly respectful Florinian. So far he has contributed nothing to the discussion and it is time to ask him a few questions."

Fife said, "That native's evidence is worthless. In fact, I take the opportunity once more to demand that Trantor surrender him to proper trial by the courts of Sark."

"Let me speak to him first."

Abel put in mildly, "I think it will do no harm to ask him a few questions, Fife. If he proves unco-operative or unreliable, we may consider your request for extradition."

Terens, who, till now, had stolidly concentrated on the fingers of his clasped hands, looked up briefly.

Junz turned to Terens. He said, "Rik has been in your town since he was first found on Florina, hasn't he?"

"Yes."

"And you were in town all that time? I mean you weren't on any extended business trips, were you?"

"Townmen don't make business trips. Their business is in their town."

"All right. Now relax and don't get touchy. It would be part of your business to know about any Squire that might come to town, I imagine."

"Sure. When they come."

"Did they come?"

Terens shrugged. "Once or twice. Pure routine, I assure you. Squires don't dirty their hands with kyrt. Unprocessed kyrt, that is."

"Be respectful!" roared Fife.

Terens looked at him and said, "Can you make me?"

Abel interrupted smoothly, "Let's keep this between the man and Dr. Junz, Fife. You and I are spectators."

Junz felt a glow of pleasure at the Townman's insolence, but he said, "Answer my questions without side comments please, Townman. Now who exactly were the Squires who visited your town this past year?"

Terens said fiercely, "How can I know? I can't answer that question. Squires are Squires and natives are natives. I may be a Townman but I'm still a native to them. I don't greet them at the town gatcs and ask their names.

"I get a message, that's all. It's addressed 'Townman.' It says there'll be a Squire's Inspection on such-and-such a day and I'm to make the necessary arrangements. I must then see to it that the millworkers have on their best clothes, that the mill is cleaned up and working properly, that the kyrt supply is ample, that everyone looks contented and pleased, that the houses have been cleaned and the streets policed, that some dancers are on hand in case the Squires would care to view some amusing native dance, that maybe a few pretty g——"

"Never mind that, Townman," said Junz.

"*You* never mind that. I do."

After his experiences with the Florinians of the Civil Service, Junz found the Townman as refreshing as a drink of cold water. He made up his mind that what influence the I.S.B. could bring to bear would be used to prevent any surrender of the Townman to the Squires.

Terens went on, in calmer tones, "Anyway, that's my part. When they come, I line up with the rest. I don't know who they are. I don't speak to them."

"Was there any such inspection the week before the City Doctor was killed? I suppose you know what week that happened."

"I think I heard about it in the newscasts. I don't think there was any Squire's Inspection at that time. I can't swear to it."

"Whom does your land belong to?"

Terens pulled the corners of his mouth back. "To the Squire of Fife."

Steen spoke up, breaking into the give-and-take with rather surprising suddenness. "Oh, look here. Really! You're playing into Fife's hands with this kind of questioning, Dr. Junz. Don't you see you won't get anywhere? Really! Do you suppose if Fife were interested in keeping tabs on that creature there that he would go to all the trouble of making trips to Florina to look at him? What are patrollers for? Really!"

Junz looked flustered. "In a case like this, with a world's economy and maybe its physical safety resting on the contents of one man's mind, it's natural that the psycho-prober would not care to leave the guardianship to patrollers."

Fife intervened. "Even after he had wiped out that mind, to all intents?"

Abel pushed out his lower lip and frowned. He saw his latest gamble sliding into Fife's hands with all the rest.

Junz tried again, hesitantly. "Was there any particular patroller or group of patrollers that was always underfoot?"

"I'd never know. They're just uniforms to me."

Junz turned to Valona with the effect of a sudden pounce. A moment before she had gone a sickly white and her eyes had become wide and stary. Junz had not missed that.

He said, "What about you, girl?"

But she only shook her head, wordlessly.

Abel thought heavily, There's nothing more to do. It's all over.

But Valona was on her feet, trembling. She said in a husky whisper, "I want to say something."

Junz said, "Go ahead, girl. What is it?"

Valona talked breathlessly and with fright obvious in every line of her countenance and every nervous twitch of her fingers. She said, "I'm just a country girl. Please don't be angry with me. It's just that it seems that things can only be one way. Was my Rik so very important? I mean, the way you said?"

Junz said gently, "I think he was very, very important. I think he still is."

"Then it must be like you said. Whoever it was who had put him on Florina wouldn't have dared take his eye away for even a minute hardly. Would he? I mean, suppose Rik was beaten by the mill superintendent or was stoned by the children or got sick and died. He wouldn't be left helpless in the fields, would he, where he might die before anyone found him? They wouldn't suppose that it would just be *luck* that would keep him safe." She was speaking with an intense fluency now.

"Go on," said Junz, watching her.

"Because there was one person who did watch Rik from the start. He found him in the fields, fixed it so I would take care of him, kept him out of trouble and knew about him every day. He even knew all about the doctor, because I told him. It was he! It was he!"

With her voice at screaming intensity, her finger pointed rigidly at Myrlyn Terens, Townman.

And this time even Fife's superhuman calm broke and his arms stiffened on his desk, lifting his massive body a full inch off his seat, as his head swiveled quickly toward the Townman.

Eighteen: *THE VICTORS*

It was as though a vocal paralysis had gripped them all. Even Rik, with disbelief in his eyes, could only stare woodenly, first at Valona, then at Terens.

Then came Steen's high-pitched laugh and the silence was broken.

Steen said, "I believe it. Really! I said so all along. I said the native was in Fife's pay. That shows you the kind of man Fife is. He'd pay a native to——"

"That's an infernal lie."

It wasn't Fife who spoke, but the Townman. He was on his feet, eyes glistening with passion.

Abel, who of them all seemed the least moved, said, "What is?"

Terens stared at him a moment, not comprehending, then said chokingly, "What the Squire said. I am in the pay of no Sarkite."

"And what the girl said? Is that a lie too?"

Terens wet his dry lips with the tip of his tongue. "No, that's true. I am the psycho-prober." He hurried on. "Don't look at me like that, Lona. I didn't mean to hurt him. I didn't intend any of what happened." He sat down again.

Fife said, "This is a sort of device. I don't know exactly what you're planning, Abel, but it's impossible on the face of it that this criminal could have included this particular crime in his repertoire. It's definite that only a Great Squire could have had the necessary knowledge and facilities. Or are you anxious to take your man Steen off the hook by arranging for a false confession?"

Terens, hands tightly clasped, leaned forward in his seat. "I don't take Trantorian money, either."

Fife ignored him.

Junz was the last to come to himself. For minutes, he could not adjust to the fact that the Townman was not really in the same room with him, that he was somewhere else on the embassy grounds, that he could see him only in image form, no more real actually than was Fife, who was twenty miles away. He wanted to go to the Townman, grip him by the shoulder, speak to him alone, but he couldn't. He said, "There's no point in arguing before we hear the man. Let's have the details. If he *is* the psycho-prober, we need the details badly. If he isn't, the details he'll try to give us will prove it."

"If you want to know what happened," cried Terens, "I'll tell you. Holding it back won't do me any good any longer. It's Sark or Trantor after all, so to Space with it. This will at least give me a chance to get one or two things into the open."

He pointed at Fife in scorn. "There's a Great Squire. Only a Great Squire, says this Great Squire, can have the knowledge or the facilities to do what the psycho-prober did. He believes it, too. But what does he know? What do any of the Sarkites know?

"They don't run the government. Florinians do! The Florinian Civil Service does. They get the papers, they make the papers, they file the papers. And it's the papers that run Sark. Sure, most of us are too beaten even to whimper, but do you know what we could do if we wanted to, even under the noses of our damned Squires? Well, you see what I've done.

"I was temporarily traffic manager at the spaceport a year ago. Part of my training. It's in the records. You'll have to dig a little to find it because the listed traffic manager is a Sarkite. He had the title but I did the actual work. My name would be found in the special section headed Native Personnel. No Sarkite would have dirtied his eyes looking there.

"When the local I.S.B. sent the Spatio-analyst's message to the port with a suggestion that we meet the ship with an ambulance, *I* got the message. I passed on what was safe. This matter of the destruction of Florina was not passed on.

"I arranged to meet the Spatio-analyst at a small suburban port. I could do that easily. All the wires and strings that ran Sark were at my finger tips. I was in the Civil Service, remember. A Great Squire who wanted to do what I did, couldn't, unless he ordered some Florinian to do it for him. I could do it without anyone's help. So much for knowledge and facility.

"I met the Spatio-analyst, kept him away from both Sark and the I.S.B. I squeezed as much information out of him as I could and set about using that information for Florina and against Sark."

Words were forced out of Fife. "You sent those first letters?"

"I sent those first letters, Great Squire," said Terens calmly. "I thought I could force control of enough of the kyrt lands into my own hands to make a deal with Trantor on my terms and drive you off the planet."

"You were mad."

"Maybe. Anyway, it didn't work. I had told the Spatio-analyst I was the Squire of Fife. I had to, because he knew that Fife was the biggest man on the planet, and as long as he thought I was Fife, he was willing to talk openly. It made me laugh to realize that he thought Fife was anxious to do whatever was best for Florina.

"Unfortunately, he was more impatient than I was. He insisted that every day lost was a calamity, while I knew that my dealings with Sark needed time more than anything else. I found it difficult to control him and eventually had to use a psychic probe. I could get one. I had seen it used in hospitals. I knew something about it. Unfortunately, not enough.

"I set the probe to wipe out the anxiety from the surface layers of his mind. That's a simple operation. I still don't know what happened. I think the anxiety must have run deeper, very deep, and the probe automatically followed it, digging out most of the conscious mind along with it. I was left with a mindless thing on my hands. . . . I'm sorry, Rik."

Rik, who had been listening intently, said sadly, "You shouldn't have interfered with me, Townman, but I know how you must have felt."

"Yes," said Terens, "you've lived on the planet. You know about patrollers and Squires and the difference between Lower City and Upper City."

He took up the current of his story again. "So there I was with the Spatio-analyst completely helpless. I couldn't let him be found by anyone who might trace his identity. I couldn't kill him. I felt sure his memory would return and I would still need his knowledge, to say nothing of the fact that killing him would forfeit the good will of Trantor and the I.S.B., which I would eventually need. Besides, in those days, I was incapable of killing.

"I arranged to be transferred to Florina as Townman and I took the Spatio-analyst with me on forged papers. I arranged to have him found, I picked Valona to take care of him. There was no danger thereafter except for that one time with the doctor. Then I had to enter the power plants of Upper City. That was not impossible. The engineers were Sarkites but the janitors were Florinian. On Sark I learned enough about power mechanics to know how to short a power line. It took me three days to find the proper time for it. After that, I could murder easily. I never knew, though, that the doctor kept duplicate records in both halves of his office. I wish I had."

Terens could see Fife's chronometer from where he sat. "Then, one hundred hours ago—it seems like a hundred years—Rik began remembering again. Now you have the whole story."

"No," said Junz, "we have not. What are the details of the Spatio-analyst's story of planetary destruction?"

"Do you think I understood the details of what he had to say? It was some sort of—pardon me, Rik—madness."

"It wasn't," blazed Rik. "It couldn't have been."

"The Spatio-analyst had a ship," said Junz. "Where is it?"

"On the scrap heap long ago," said Terens. "An order scrapping it was sent out. My superior signed it. A Sarkite never reads papers, of course. It was scrapped without question."

"And Rik's papers? You said he showed you papers!"

"Surrender that man to us," said Fife suddenly, "and we'll find out what he knows."

"No," said Junz. "His first crime was against the I.S.B. He kidnaped and damaged the mind of a Spatio-analyst. He belongs to us."

Abel said, "Junz is correct."

Terens said, "Now look here. I don't say a word without safeguards. I know where Rik's papers are. They're where no Sarkite or Trantorian will ever find them. If you want them you'll have to agree that I'm a political refugee. Whatever I did was out of patriotism, out of a regard for the needs of my planet. A Sarkite or a Trantorian may claim to be patriotic; why not a Florinian as well?"

"The Ambassador," said Junz, "has said you will be given over to the I.S.B. I assure you that you will not be turned over to Sark. For your treatment of the Spatio-analyst, you will be tried. I cannot guarantee the result, but if you co-operate with us now, it will count in your favor."

Terens looked searchingly at Junz. Then he said, "I'll take my chance with you, Doctor. . . . According to the Spatio-analyst, Florina's sun is in the pre-nova stage."

"What!" The exclamation or its equivalent came from all but Valona.

"It's about to explode and go boom," said Terens sardonically. "And when that happens all of Florina will go poof, like a mouthful of tobacco smoke."

Abel said, "I'm no Spatio-analyst, but I have heard that there is no way of predicting when a star will explode."

"That's true. Until now, anyway. Did Rik explain what made him think so?" asked Junz.

"I suppose his papers will show that. All I can remember is about the carbon current."

"What?"

"He kept saying, 'The carbon current of space. The carbon current of space.' That, and the words 'catalytic effect.' There it is."

Steen giggled. Fife frowned. Junz stared.

Then Junz muttered, "Pardon me. I'll be right back." He stepped out of the limits of the receptor cube and vanished.

He was back in fifteen minutes.

Junz looked about in bewilderment when he returned. Only Abel and Fife were present.

He said, "Where——"

Abel broke in instantly. "We have been waiting for you, Dr. Junz.

The Spatio-analyst and the girl are on their way to the Embassy. The conference is ended."

"Ended! Great Galaxy, we have only begun. I've got to explain the possibilities of nova formation."

Abel shifted uneasily in his seat. "It is not necessary to do that, Doctor."

"It is very necessary. It is essential. Give me five minutes."

"Let him speak," said Fife. He was smiling.

Junz said, "Take it from the beginning. In the earliest recorded scientific writings of Galactic civilization it was already known that stars obtained their energy from nuclear transformations in their interiors. It was also known that, given what we know about conditions in stellar interiors, two types, and only two types, of nuclear transformations can possibly yield the necessary energy. Both involve the conversion of hydrogen to helium. The first transformation is direct: two hydrogens and two neutrons combine to form one helium nucleus. The second is indirect, with several steps. It ends up with hydrogen becoming helium, but in the intermediate steps, carbon nuclei take part. These carbon nuclei are not used up but are re-formed as the reactions proceed, so that a trifling amount of carbon can be used over and over again, serving to convert a great deal of hydrogen to helium. The carbon acts as a catalyst, in other words. All this has been known back to the days of prehistory, back to the time when the human race was restricted to a single planet, if there ever was such a time."

"If we all know it," said Fife, "I would suggest that you are contributing nothing but a waste of time."

"But this is *all* we know. Whether stars use one or the other, or both, nuclear processes has never been determined. There have always been schools of thought in favor of each of the alternatives. Usually the weight of opinion has been in favor of the direct hydrogen-helium conversion as being the simpler of the two.

"Now Rik's theory must be this. The hydrogen-helium direct conversion is the *normal* source of stellar energy, but under certain conditions the carbon catalysis adds its weight, hastening the process, speeding it up, heating up the star.

"There are currents in space. You all know that well. Some of these are carbon currents. Stars passing through the currents pick up innumerable atoms. The total mass of atoms attracted, however, is incredibly microscopic in comparison to the star's weight and does not affect it in any way. *Except for carbon!* A star that passes through a current containing unusual concentrations of carbon becomes unstable. I don't know how many years or centuries or millions of years it takes for the carbon atoms to diffuse into the star's interior, but it probably takes a long time. That means that a carbon current must be wide and a star must intersect it at a small angle. In any case, once the quantity of carbon percolating into the star's interior passes a certain critical amount, the star's radiation is suddenly boosted tremendously. The outer layers give way under an unimaginable explosion and you have a nova.

"Do you see?"

Junz waited.

Fife said, "Have you figured all this out in two minutes as a result of some vague phrase the Townman remembered the Spatio-analyst to have said a year ago?"

"Yes. Yes. There's nothing surprising in that. Spatio-analysis is ready for that theory. If Rik had not come up with it, someone else would have shortly. In fact, similar theories have been advanced before, but they were never taken seriously. They were put forward before the techniques of Spatio-analysis were developed and no one was ever able to account for the sudden acquisition of excess carbon by the star in question.

"But now we know there *are* carbon currents. We can plot their courses, find out what stars intersected those courses in the past ten thousand years, check that against our records for nova formation and radiation variations. That's what Rik must have done. Those must have been the calculations and observations he tried to show the Townman. But that's all beside the immediate point.

"What must be arranged for now is the immediate beginning of an evacuation of Florina."

"I thought it would come to that," said Fife composedly.

"I'm sorry, Junz," said Abel, "but that's quite impossible."

"Why impossible?"

"*When* will Florina's sun explode?"

"I don't know. From Rik's anxiety a year ago, I'd say we had little time."

"But you can't set a date?"

"Of course not."

"When will you be able to set a date?"

"There's no way of telling. Even if we get Rik's calculations, it would all have to be rechecked."

"Can you guarantee that the Spatio-analyst's theory will prove to be correct?"

Junz frowned. "I am personally certain of it, but no scientist can guarantee any theory in advance."

"Then it turns out that you want Florina evacuated on mere speculation."

"I think the chance of killing the population of a planet is not one that can be taken."

"If Florina were an ordinary planet I would agree with you. But Florina bears the Galactic supply of kyrt. It can't be done."

Junz said angrily, "Is that the agreement you came to with Fife while I was gone?"

Fife intervened. He said, "Let me explain, Dr. Junz. The government of Sark would never consent to evacuate Florina, even if the I.S.B. claimed it had proof of this nova theory of yours. Trantor cannot force us because while the Galaxy might support a war against Sark for the purpose of maintaining the kyrt trade, it will never support one for the purpose of ending it."

"Exactly," said Abel. "I am afraid our own people would not support us in such a war."

Junz found revulsion growing strong within him. A planet full of people meant nothing against the dictates of economic necessity!

He said, "Listen to me. This is not a matter of one planet, but of a whole Galaxy. There are now twenty full novae originating within the Galaxy every year. In addition, some two thousand stars among the Galaxy's hundred billion shift their radiation characteristics sufficiently to render uninhabitable any habitable planets they may have. Human beings occupy one million stellar systems in the Galaxy. That means that on an average of once every fifty years some inhabited planet somewhere becomes too hot for life. Such cases are a matter of historical record. Every five thousand years some inhabited planet has a fifty-fifty chance of being puffed to gas by a nova.

"If Trantor does nothing about Florina, if it allows it to vaporize with its people on it, that will serve notice to all the people of the Galaxy that when their own turn comes they may expect no help, if such help is in the way of the economic convenience of a few powerful men. Can you risk that, Abel?

"On the other hand, help Florina and you will have shown that Trantor puts its responsibility to the people of the Galaxy above the maintenance of mere property rights. Trantor will win good will that it could never win by force."

Abel bowed his head. Then he shook it wearily. "No, Junz. What you say appeals to me, but it is not practical. I can't count on emotions as against the assured political effect of any attempt to end the kyrt trade. In fact, I think it would be wise to avoid investigating the theory. The thought that it might be true would do too much harm."

"But what if it *is* true?"

"We must work on the assumption that it is not. I take it that when you were gone a few moments ago it was to contact the I.S.B."

"Yes."

"No matter. Trantor, I think, will have enough influence to stop their investigations."

"I'm afraid not. Not these investigations. Gentlemen, we will soon have the secret of cheap kyrt. There will be no kyrt monopoly within a year, whether or not there is a nova."

"What do you mean?"

"The conference is reaching the essential point now, Fife. Kyrt grows only on Florina of all inhabited planets. Its seeds produce ordinary cellulose elsewhere. Florina is probably the only inhabited planet, on a chance basis, that is currently pre-nova, and it has probably been pre-nova since it first entered the carbon current, perhaps thousands of years ago, if the angle of intersection was small. It seems quite probable, then, that kyrt and the pre-nova stage go together."

"Nonsense," said Fife.

"Is it? There must be a reason why kyrt is kyrt on Florina and cotton elsewhere. Scientists have tried many ways of artificially producing kyrt elsewhere, but they tried blindly, so they've always failed. Now they will know it is due to factors induced in a pre-nova stellar system."

Fife said scornfully, "They've tried duplicating the radiation qualities of Florina's sun."

"With appropriate arc lights, yes, that duplicated the visible and ultraviolet spectrum only. What about radiation in the infrared and beyond? What about magnetic fields? What about electron emission? What about cosmic-ray effects? I'm not a physical biochemist so there may be factors I know nothing about. But people who are physical biochemists will be looking now, a whole Galaxy of them. Within the year, I assure you, the solution will be found.

"Economics is on the side of humanity now. The Galaxy wants cheap kyrt, and if they find it or even if they imagine they will shortly find it, they will want Florina evacuated, not only out of humanity, but out of a desire to turn the tables, at long last, on the kyrt-gouging Sarkites."

"Bluff!" growled Fife.

"Do you think so, Abel?" demanded Junz. "If you help the Squires, Trantor will be looked on not as the saviors of the kyrt trade but of the kyrt monopoly. Can you chance that?"

"Can Trantor chance a war?" demanded Fife.

"War? Nonsense! Squire, in one year your holdings on Florina will be worthless, nova or not. Sell out. Sell out all Florina. Trantor can pay for it."

"Buy a planet?" said Abel in dismay.

"Why not? Trantor has the funds, and its gain in good will among the people of the universe will pay it back a thousandfold. If telling them that you are saving hundreds of millions of lives is not enough, tell them that you will bring them cheap kyrt. That will do it."

"I'll think about it," said Abel.

Abel looked at the Squire. Fife's eyes fell.

After a long pause he too said, "I'll think about it."

Junz laughed harshly. "Don't think too long. The kyrt story will break quickly enough. Nothing can stop it. After that, neither one of you will have freedom of action. You can each strike a better bargain now."

The Townman seemed beaten. "It's really true?" he kept repeating. "Really true? No more Florina?"

"It's true," said Junz.

Terens spread his arms, let them fall against his side. "If you want the papers I got from Rik, they're filed among vital statistic files in my home town. I picked the dead files, records a century back and more. No one would ever look there for any reason."

"Look," said Junz, "I'm sure we can make an agreement with the I.S.B. We'll need a man on Florina, one who knows the Florinian people, who can tell us how to explain the facts to them, how best to organize the evacuation, how to pick the most suitable planets of refuge. Will you help us?"

"And beat the game that way, you mean? Get away with murder? Why not?" There were sudden tears in the Townman's eyes. "But I lose anyway. I will have no world, no home. We all lose. The Florinians lose their world, the Sarkites lose their wealth, the Trantorians their chance to get that wealth. There are no winners at all."

"Unless," said Junz gently, "you realize that in the new Galaxy—a Galaxy safe from the threat of stellar instability, a Galaxy with kyrt available to all, and a Galaxy in which political unification will be so much closer—there will be winners after all. One quadrillion winners. The people of the Galaxy, *they* are the victors."

Epilog: *A YEAR AFTER*

"Rik! Rik!" Selim Junz hurried across the port grounds toward the ship, hands outstretched. "And Lona! I'd never have recognized either of you. How are you? How are you?"

"As well as we could wish. Our letter reached you, I see," said Rik.

"Of course. Tell me, what do you think of it all?" They were walking back together, toward Junz's offices.

Valona said sadly, "We visited our old town this morning. The fields are so empty." Her clothing was now that of a woman of the Empire, rather than that of a peasant of Florina.

"Yes, it must be dreary for a person who has lived here. It grows dreary even for me, but I will stay as long as I can. The radiation recordings of Florina's sun are of tremendous theoretical interest."

"So much evacuation in less than a year! It speaks for excellent organization."

"We're doing our best, Rik. Oh, I think I should be calling you by your real name."

"Please don't. I'll never be used to it. I'm Rik. That's still the only name I remember."

Junz said, "Have you decided whether you're going to return to Spatio-analysis?"

Rik shook his head. "I've decided, but the decision is, no. I'll never remember enough. That part's gone forever. It doesn't bother me, though. I'll be returning to Earth. . . . By the way, I rather hoped I'd see the Townman."

"I think not. He decided to go off today. I think he'd rather not see you. He feels guilty, I think. You have no grudge against him?"

Rik said, "No. He meant well, and he changed my life in many ways for the better. For one thing, I met Lona." His arm went about her shoulder.

Valona looked at him and smiled.

"Besides," Rik went on, "he cured me of something. I've found out why I was a Spatio-analyst. I know why nearly a third of all Spatio-analysts are recruited from the one planet, Earth. Anyone living on a radioactive world is bound to grow up in fear and insecurity. A misstep can mean death and our planet's own surface is the greatest enemy we have.

"That makes for a sort of anxiety bred into us, Dr. Junz, a fear of planets. We're only happy in space; that's the only place we can feel safe."

"And you don't feel that way any longer, Rik?"

"I certainly don't. I don't even remember feeling that way. That's it, you see. The Townman had set his psychic probe to remove feelings of anxiety and he hadn't bothered to set the intensity controls. He thought he had a recent, superficial trouble to deal with. Instead there was this deep, ingrained anxiety he knew nothing of. He got rid of all of it. In a sense, it was worth getting rid of it even though so much else went with it. I don't have to stay in space now. I can go back to Earth. I can work there and Earth needs men. It always will."

"You know," Junz said, "why can't we do for Earth what we're doing for Florina? There's no need to bring up Earthmen in such fear and insecurity. The Galaxy is big."

"No," said Rik vehemently. "It's a different case. Earth has its past, Dr. Junz. Many people may not believe it, but we of Earth know that Earth was the original planet of the human race."

"Well, perhaps. I can't say, one way or the other."

"It *was.* It's a planet that can't be abandoned; it *mustn't* be abandoned. Someday we'll change it, change its surface back to what it once must have been. Till then—we're staying."

Valona said softly, "And I'm an Earthwoman now."

Rik was looking out at the horizon. Upper City was as garish as ever, but the people were gone.

He said, "How many are left on Florina?"

"About twenty million," said Junz. "We work slower as we go along. We have to keep our withdrawals balanced. The people that are left must always maintain themselves as an economic unit in the months that are left. Of course, resettlement is in its earliest stages. Most of the evacuees are still in temporary camps on neighboring worlds. There is unavoidable hardship."

"When will the last person leave?"

"Never, really."

"I don't understand."

"The Townman has applied unofficially for permission to remain. It's been granted, also unofficially. It won't be a matter of public record."

"Remain?" Rik was shocked. "But for the sake of all the Galaxy, why?"

"I didn't know," said Junz, "but I think you explained it when you talked of Earth. He feels as you do. He says he can't bear the thought of leaving Florina to die alone."